ALL THAT LIVES MUST DIE

OTHER BOOKS BY ERIC NYLUND

Pawn's Dream
A Game of Universe
Dry Water
Signal to Noise
A Signal Shattered

Halo® Novels
Halo®: The Fall of Reach
Halo®: First Strike
Halo®: Ghosts of Onyx

Mortal Coils Series
Mortal Coils

ALL THAT LIVES MUST DIE

ERIC NYLUND

BOOK TWO IN THE MORTAL COILS SERIES

A TOM DOHERTY ASSOCIATES BOOK
NEW YORK

ALL THAT LIVES MUST DIE

Copyright © 2010 by Eric Nylund

Reader's Guide copyright © 2010 by Eric Nylund

A Tor Book
Published by Tom Doherty Associates, LLC
175 Fifth Avenue
New York, NY 10010

www.tor-forge.com

Tor® is a registered trademark of Tom Doherty Associates, LLC.

ISBN 978-0-7653-2304-0

First Edition: July 2010

Printed in the United States of America

0 9 8 7 6 5 4 3 2 1

For Syne, the passion of my life and the one woman
I'd go to Hell and battle the Legions of the Damned for
&
For Kai, your father promises he will never make you
go to the Paxington Institute (unless you want to)

ACKNOWLEDGMENTS

My gratitude to the following people for their help, confidence, and being some of the best friends a writer could have: Richard Curtis, Tom Doherty, Alexis Ortega, Eric Raab, and John Sutherland.

EDITOR'S NOTE

We at Tor have received numerous requests to publish the many-volume set of *Gods of the First and Twenty-first Century*, as well as the notorious *Golden's Guide to Extraordinary Books* and, of course, the apocalyptically difficult to obtain and decipher *Mythica Improbiba*. At this time, however, the rights for these rare books (and others within *All That Lives Must Die*) reside with academic institutes, religious organizations, and private collectors. While excerpts have been graciously provided for Mr. Nylund's footnotes, the remaining bodies of these works are fated to remain in obscurity (and please, please stop sending me e-mail and letters about this).

ERIC RAAB
Editor, Tor Books
New York

QUEEN GERTRUDE
Do not for ever with thy vailed lids
Seek for thy noble father in the dust:
Thou know'st 'tis common; all that lives must die,
Passing through nature to eternity.

HAMLET
Ay, madam, it is common.

QUEEN GERTRUDE
If it be,
Why seems it so particular with thee?

WILLIAM SHAKESPEARE
Hamlet (ACT 1, SCENE 2)

ALL THAT LIVES MUST DIE

Prologue

WHAT I DID OVER MY SUMMER VACATION
by Fiona Paige Post

This summer, my brother and I joined the League of Immortals. One minute, I'm a homeschooled hermit; the next, I'm a fledgling goddess-in-training and the newest member of the Order of the Celestial Rose.

You'd think, being an actual goddess, I'd end up with killer Botticelli hair. No luck there, I'm afraid.

Let me start at the beginning.

Gods and fallen angels exist.

And they don't get along.

Despite this, sixteen years ago—Atropos, the Eldest Fate, and Lucifer, Prince of Darkness, fell in love.

They're my mother and father.

When my twin brother and I were born, my mother didn't want either side of the family finding us. Neither the gods nor fallen angels treat their nieces and nephews well: turning them into animals, trees, weeping stones, or casting them into pits of eternal torture. Nice, huh?

So for fifteen years, my brother, Eliot, and I were hidden from our relatives and raised to think we were nerdy and normal.

The Immortals found us, however, and to decide which family we belong to—diabolical or divine—they subjected us to three life-or-death tests (what they prosaically called heroic trials).

Long story short: We passed their tests and came out divine.

It wasn't all happy endings, though. My father's side of the family still wanted us. The Infernal Lord of All That Flies, Beelzebub, almost killed us and dragged our souls to Hell. That ended in a huge fight in Del Sombra (where we used to live); I killed Beelzebub, and the entire town burned to the ground.

Our father said he still wants to get to know us, but I don't think Mother is going to let him.

I agree. I don't trust him.

After all this, my brother, mother, great-grandmother, and I went to San Francisco, and we've barely moved into a new place in time for school.

It has been a tumultuous summer. I just want to settle down and begin at the Paxington Institute so I can figure out how I fit into this new world where legends are real.

September 22, San Francisco

WHAT I DID OVER MY SUMMER VACATION
by Eliot Zachariah Post

This summer, I found out that my father and mother are alive. My sister and I spent our entire lives thinking they were dead, told that they were drowned in a boat accident.

One more thing: Our mother is the goddess Atropos, and our father is Lucifer, Prince of Darkness.

Mother's side of the family are gods and goddesses in the League of Immortals. They smile at you, but you can see them thinking behind those smiles, wondering how you fit in their orderly view of the world.

And Dad's side of the family? Not so wonderful, either. They tried to kill me and my sister, Fiona. They also managed to poison Fiona with a box of magical chocolates.

Besides our parents, we discovered another important thing this summer: We inherited special powers from our families.

Fiona can cut with a thread stretched between her fingers, kind of like a wire cheese slicer. When I say "cut," I mean she can cut through anything when she puts her mind to it: cinder block walls, a solid steel vault door, even a person. I'm not sure how she keeps the thread from cutting off her fingers. She doesn't talk much about it.

I think it scares her. I know it scares me.

I learned how to use the violin. My father showed me the basics, but I play like I've been practicing all my life . . . and my music makes things happen. Magical things, like conjuring a fog filled with ghosts or charming a million hungry sewer rats so they wouldn't eat me.

Then, once, I got a glimpse of the end of the world. I played a song about the end of things, which I call "The Symphony of Existence." If that sounds dangerous, it was, but I had to, believe me, because I was facing the Infernal Beelzebub, Lord of All That Flies, who was trying to part my right side from the left with a gigantic obsidian knife.

When I played that song, I felt the world come apart around me, and I heard the death rattle of the universe as protons and neutrons and electrons tore into smaller subatomic bits . . . and then into void.

I still hear it in my dreams. It worries me sometimes.

I've learned a lot this summer, but I'm ready to learn more at Paxington and find out what I'm supposed to be doing with these amazing and dangerous gifts.

September 22, San Francisco

Eliot watched and worried as his sister read his essay.

Her brows furrowed.

Eliot knew people liked his writing style better, but Fiona was good at putting facts together and impressing people with her logic. Besides, her essay pretty much told the entire story of what had happened to them this summer. He hoped the teachers at Paxington read his paper first.

"Well?" he asked her. "What do you think?"

"Just a second." She held up a hand, rereading from the top of the page.

Eliot paced. Sunlight filtered into his new bedroom from the garden. Outside were rows of pink and yellow daisies, and beyond, he could make out misty San Francisco Bay—a spectacular view.

Inside their new house, however, especially in his bedroom, the view was not so spectacular—crowded with mountains and mazes of cardboard U-Haul boxes, each one filled with a hundred pounds of books. If there was the slightest shudder from the San Andreas Fault, Eliot knew he'd be buried under an avalanche of Chaucer, Twain, and Shakespeare.

Fiona looked up from his essay and brushed her long, dark hair from her face. "You don't have *all* the facts," she said. "You should have added something about your *girlfriend*."

"She wasn't my girlfriend," Eliot replied.

Fiona meant Julie Marks, the girl he had met this summer, the girl he had liked an awful lot. She'd even kissed him . . . but then ended up leaving. Every time he thought about her, he felt that he had done something to drive her away. Fiona had never liked Julie, for some reason.

He glared at his sister, suddenly irritated.

Then he understood: Fiona wasn't trying to be mean on purpose. She couldn't help it. Anyone would be a little nasty if they looked the way she did this morning.

Normally, he and his sister had to wear their great-grandmother's handmade clothing—bad enough because it looked like something out of the "wrong clothes that didn't fit" catalog.

Today was worse. They had on their new Paxington school uniforms.

The new clothes looked fine when Eliot and Fiona had first gotten them: khaki slacks for him, pleated tartan skirt for his sister, white button-down linen shirts and navy blue blazers for them both. No ties, thank goodness—they probably would have strangled themselves. Fiona had stockings and flats. He had leather loafers with no heels that made him look (if possible) shorter than usual.

All well and good, Eliot supposed . . . if you actually knew how to wear such things.

But Fiona had never owned, let alone worn, a pair of stockings. Her skinny legs looked like crumpled caterpillars that had cocooned themselves and died there. Add to this that no one in the Post family knew how to use an iron (or at least, no one was willing to let the doddering 104-year-old Cecilia near an iron), and they both ended up looking like they had slept in their new uniforms.

Eliot shifted underneath his blazer—one size too big for him—and felt just as uncomfortable and annoyed as his sister must. He exhaled a great sigh, smelling something off. Maybe his clothes should have been washed first.

This was just what they needed today. He ran a hand through his hair, whose cowlicks, as usual, resisted any attempts at grooming. Not only would they have to deal with dozens of strange new students on their first day at school, but they also looked like dorks.

Eliot tapped Fiona's essay and told her, "I see you didn't mention Robert, either."

"What's to mention?" Fiona said. "We haven't seen him in two months."

Robert Farmington was the boy Fiona had met this summer. They weren't exactly boyfriend and girlfriend, but there had been *something* between them. He had been a Driver for their uncle Henry in the League of Immortals . . . before Robert got fired.

Fiona had a far-off look in her eyes—which sharpened to a glare that she aimed directly at Eliot. "Cupulate temporal cranium?" she asked.

This was the game they played to get back at each other: vocabulary insult.

Eliot ran over the line in his head, trying to figure out what she had meant. Brain . . . cranium . . . something about his head.

Temporal? Did that mean "time"? No, the bone on the side of the head was the "temporal" part of the skull.

But *cupulate?* He didn't have a clue . . . unless she was making it simple in order to throw him. *Cupulate* could just mean "cup shaped."

She meant his ears.

They stuck out, and she knew how sensitive Eliot was about them.

"At least I need a cup, handles or not," Eliot replied, "to hold *my* brain."

That was a weak comeback, so he added: "Countenance of verruciform," and then with a sweeping gesture down to her toes, "vermiform locomotion borne."[1, 2]

Fiona puzzled over that a moment, and then her face reddened.

Good. It was pretty easy to figure out. Eliot had wanted her to get it.

"No fair," she said. "That's two vocabulary words at once."

She said this, despite having just used two herself.

"Breakfast!" Cee called from the kitchen.

Eliot sniffed the air and realized that the "off" smell he'd detected before was stronger, and now recognizable—half-cooked oatmeal and carbonized bacon.

Fiona spotted Eliot's rusty alarm clock in the corner. Her eyes widened. "We're going to be late!" She rushed out, bumping a tower of boxes, almost knocking them over.

Of course they were going to be late for their first day of school. That would be the perfect start to this morning. Eliot scrambled after her. There was no way she was getting to the kitchen first to pick out the few edible bits from Cee's cooking.

1. Verruciform: having the shape of a wart. —Editor.

2. Vermiform: worm shaped. —Editor.

THE FIRST DAY OF SCHOOL

1

NEW RULES

Fiona scrambled over the cool terra-cotta tiles and skidded to a halt in their new dining room. Bookshelves and half-built china cabinets were constructed along the walls. Unlike their old apartment in Del Sombra, this room had enough space for shelves *without* crowding the glorious picture window and its built-in seats.

The window framed the Golden Gate Bridge in the distance. Early-morning light spilled through and made the plaster cornices of the room glow gold.

Cee carried in two trays from the kitchen. Their 104-year-old great-grandmother wore a brown dress with lace ruffles and looked like she belonged in a nineteenth-century tin daguerreotype with her hair pulled up tight and pinned in place. Some things would never change. That was okay. Cee, shaking and smiling, was always there for them.

"Let me help," Fiona offered.

"No, no, my darlings," Cecilia replied. "Just sit and eat. You have a momentous day ahead of you."

With trembling arms, she set a platter of smoking black bacon on the table, and another platter with bowls of lumpy half-cooked oatmeal.

"Don't you two look splendid in your uniforms?" Cee kissed Eliot on the cheek and then Fiona. It felt like the brush of dry leaves. She then went back into the kitchen.

"Thanks, Cee," Fiona said, and tugged on her stockings. How could something so tight fit so poorly?

"Thanks," Eliot murmured. He sat and dragged a bowl closer, grimacing.

Fiona shot him a look. Cee *did* try. It wasn't her fault she no longer had a sense of smell or taste.

Eliot stirred the mixture in front of him in an attempt to make it palatable.

She pulled a bowl closer as well and segregated the inedible bits from the stuff that looked like it could be choked down.

Sometimes having a severed and only partially repaired appetite had its advantages.

Fiona spooned the lumps into her mouth. It tasted like sawdust . . . but then almost everything did these days. She knew she had to force herself to eat, or she'd faint from malnutrition.

So she chewed until the oatmeal could be swallowed without gagging.

In fact, if she didn't force herself to feel something, she didn't feel much of anything. That was because when she'd cut her appetite to save herself from those addictive Infernal chocolates . . . she cut deeper . . . cut part of the connection to her emotions. Like what she felt for Robert. It was so unclear. Did she really miss him? Or had it been some crush brought on by their shared adventures this summer?

No, there *was* something there.

It was complicated, because she was now part of the League of Immortals, and Robert had just been fired by the League. *Fired* meaning that some Immortals had a grudge against him, and if they ever saw him, it might be the end of his life.

How could she be with someone who was endangered by her very presence?

She watched Eliot struggle with his oatmeal, his face contorting through various shades of discomfort and strangulation as he swallowed. She *did* feel some tiny punitive pleasure from that.

Vermiform locomotion borne, huh? She tried to smooth her stockings again, but it was hopeless. Her legs *did* look like two wrinkled worms.

Outside, fog covered the sun. The golden light tinged iron gray, and the temperature in the room dropped.

Audrey descended the spiral staircase that led to her office. She joined them at the table.

She wore faded jeans, chamois soft boots, and a deep blue silk blouse that matched the color of San Francisco Bay. Diamond studs adorned her earlobes and flashed cold rainbows upon her throat and slicked-back silver hair. She carried a slender briefcase. She was the picture of grace and understated elegance, and looked perfectly at ease in their new surroundings.

But it wasn't only the new clothes that made Audrey look different today.

When Fiona came back from her summer vacation, this woman was no longer the "grandmother" she had known for the last fifteen years. That masquerade was over. She was her mother now and the goddess Atropos, and *both* titles seems equally perplexing to Fiona.

"Good morning, Audrey," Fiona said. She couldn't call her Grandmother anymore, and the word *Mother* caught in her throat, so Fiona had settled on Audrey.

"Good morning," Eliot echoed.

"Good morning, children," Audrey replied. She poked carbonized bacon with a fork and then decided to pour herself a glass of juice. "I've ordered the books you'll need for Paxington . . . assuming you do well enough on the entrance examinations today. I have every confidence that you will."

If she had every confidence, then why even mention it?

Those books—which would join the thousands and thousands already here—had to be ordered because many of their books had pages crossed out to the point of unreadability. Those were the books on mythologies, legends and folklores, ghost stories, tales of demons and gods—all omitted because their mother had the notion that she could hide Fiona and Eliot from the truth . . . and hide the truth from them.

"I guess . . . ," Eliot started, but his voice died. He swallowed and tried again. "I guess that means Rule Fifty-five doesn't apply anymore?"

Rule 55 was one of the 106 household rules that governed every aspect of Fiona's and her brother's lives. It was the "nothing made up" rule.

RULE 55: No books, comics, films, or other media of the science fiction, fantasy, or horror genres—especially, but not limited to, the occult or pseudosciences (alchemy, spirituality, numerology, etc.) or any ancient or urban mythology.

Audrey looked at Eliot as if he spoke a language she didn't understand.

How typical. Audrey was very good at telling them what to do—not so good at listening to anything they had to say.

"That's why you're sending us to Paxington, right?" Fiona asked. She worked very hard to keep anger from creeping into her voice. She made herself sound polite, quizzical—keeping this discussion on an intellectual level. "I mean, you're sending us there to learn about our family, their history, and how we're supposed to fit into this world."

Audrey blinked. "Yes, Rule Fifty-five is naturally abolished. You must learn everything that has been omitted from your education as quickly as possible."

Fiona nodded and kept her face an impassive mask, hiding her glee.

Audrey had never *lifted* a rule. The only changes to the rules for as long as Fiona had lived were *additions*.

She and Eliot would have to be careful. They couldn't push. Audrey tended to push back ten times harder when confronted with the slightest force.

As if sensing the precise *wrong* thing to say, Eliot leaned forward and asked, "So, what about all the other rules?"

Fiona could have killed him.

"We will revisit them on a case-by-case basis." Audrey took a sip of orange juice. "*If* necessary."

"So then, what about Rule Thirty-four?" Eliot said. Both his hands gripped the edge of the dining table.

Fiona gave him a kick—hard.

Eliot flinched, but he didn't look away from Audrey.

Rule 34 was the "no music" rule.

> **RULE 34:** No music, including the playing of any instruments (actual or improvised), singing, humming, electronically or by any means producing or reproducing a rhythmic melodic form.

Eliot had this stupid fascination with music—and an even greater fascination with the violin their father had given him.

In truth, though, Eliot and his music had done some amazing things. Magical things. Terrible things. But it was unpredictable, and that scared Fiona.

"Your music . . . ," Audrey said.

She opened her mouth to say more, but for some reason Audrey hesitated, as if she was actually weighing the issues. Fiona had never seen her perseverate over anything in her life. Audrey always knew her mind—and she never changed it once made.

"We shall lift this rule as well," Audrey finally said. "Play you must. I sense it is in your blood. But go slowly, Eliot, for you play with fire."

"Yes, Mother." Eliot eased back into his seat. "Thank you."

So he was calling her Mother now? How annoying.

But maybe it was okay as long as he kept his mouth shut about the other rules. Even Eliot had to know better than to push their luck further. Two rules lifted in one day was real progress.

"Ah!" Audrey brightened. "I'd almost forgotten." She opened her briefcase and retrieved a sheaf of legal-sized pages.

She set the inch-thick stack on the table and pushed it toward Fiona and Eliot.

Fiona grabbed it and pulled it away from her brother.

"The Council sent it this morning," Audrey told them. "Turn to page six. That is the only relevant piece you need concern yourself with."

Fiona flipped ahead.

She and Eliot read:

EDICTS GOVERNING NEW LEAGUE MEMBERS

1. New members must not under any circumstance, or by any means, convey, imply, or by means of not providing answers reveal the existence of the League of Immortals to non–League members.
2. With identical limitations as per Provision One, new members must not reveal their nonmortal status to mortals.
3. New members must not discuss the subjects of Provisions One and Two in public, where third parties may clandestinely eavesdrop, lip-read, or record conversations.
4. New members are accountable to these provisions/edicts and subject to penalties provided in Appendix D as sent forth by the Punishment and Enforcement Bureau circa 1878.
   (continued on the next page . . .)

"I hope," Audrey said, "you two realized how seriously the League takes these matters." She retrieved the pages, straightened them, and returned them to her briefcase.

"Wait . . . ," Fiona said. The words she had read felt like concrete poured around her . . . slowly but inexorably solidifying. "So we're in the League of Immortals, and for the first time special and different—but we can't tell anyone who we are?"

"Of course you can tell people who you are," Audrey said. The warmth she had had in her voice earlier evaporated. "You will, naturally, say that you are Fiona and Eliot Post. That should be enough for anyone—including yourselves."

A spark of resentment fanned to life in Fiona. More lies? That's what the League was expecting from them?

"Fine," Fiona muttered. "Whatever." She stood and turned to her brother. "Come on. We better go."

Although Fiona now stood while her mother remained sitting, Audrey still managed to make it feel like she was looking down at her.

Fiona hated that imperial look.

So she had finally called her Mother . . . at least, in her mind.

But Audrey would never be the kind of mother who showed her how to put makeup on, or helped her pick out clothes, or had that heartfelt talk about the pleasures and perils of boys.

No. Fiona knew *exactly* what kind of mother Audrey was: the kind she read about in Shakespeare's plays—mothers who plotted and schemed and murdered and then compulsively washed their hands.

"Sit, young lady," Audrey told her. "We are not done."

The spark of resentment in Fiona chilled. She obediently sank into her seat.

"You are correct," Audrey told them. "There is a need to start school with all due haste, but you also need these materials if you are to have any chance of success . . . success, I might add, which the League considers *mandatory*."

Fiona shot Eliot a look. He shrugged, and his forehead wrinkled at this new development.

If they didn't do well at school, the Immortals would do what? Kick them out of the League? Something worse? Maybe. The League considered passing and failing tests a life-or-death matter. If they'd failed its three heroic trials, the League would have killed her and Eliot.

But come on—they were *in* the League now, considered an official part of the family. They didn't have to constantly prove themselves. Did they?

Audrey withdrew a blue envelope from her briefcase and slid it to them.

The envelope had a bar code sticker and a bewildering collection of stamps from Greece, Italy, Russia, places Fiona did not recognize, and finally the United States. It was addressed to "Master Eliot Zachariah Post and the Lady Fiona Paige Post" at their new San Francisco address.

And it had been opened.

As if her mother anticipated Fiona's objections, she said, "I filled out all the forms to save time. There is a list of rules and regulations, which you may read after the entrance and placement exams today." Audrey pinned the envelope with a stare. "Most important, however, there is a map—which you require immediately."

Fiona pulled out the first page.

The impressive Paxington Institute crest—a heraldic device with shield, helmet, and sword; a sleeping dragon; snarling wolf head; winged chevron; and gold scarab—dominated the scrollwork of a letterhead. Fiona's eyes gravitated to the boldface portion of the letter:

> *All students must be at Bristlecone Hall before 10:00 A.M., September 22, for placement examinations or their enrollment at Paxington will be FORFEITED.*

Fiona and Eliot wheeled around. Their grandfather clock sat in the corner. It read a quarter until nine.

"Where is Paxington?" Eliot asked, sounding embarrassed he didn't know.

Fiona riffled through the envelope, found the map, and pulled it out. She unfolded heavy cotton paper and saw exacting details of streets and landmarks like Presidio Park, Chinatown, and Fisherman's Wharf. The edges of the map were yellowed with age.

She found the Paxington Institute address as well as these helpful directions:

> *The main entrance to the San Francisco Paxington campus is conveniently located at the intersection of Chestnut and Lombard Streets.*

They glanced back at the map. Chestnut and Lombard were only a few blocks away.

"Only a fifteen-minute walk," Eliot said.

"I can see that," Fiona replied.

Something was wrong about this. She ran her fingertips over the map. The rough cotton fibers had a texture that felt like woven canvas. It made her skin itch.

Of course there was something wrong. You'd have thought they might for once treat her and Eliot like adults. Instead of outgrowing their house-hold rules, though, they still had 104 old rules *plus* new League edicts to follow (along with some veiled threats if they failed) *and* a bunch of Pax-ington regulations to worry about.

Audrey stood and told them, "You must be on your way. Now. You will require every minute." Her face was unreadable.

Cecilia then emerged from the kitchen, a paper lunch sack in either hand. To Fiona's utter embarrassment, their names had been written on the outside as if they were little kids.

Cee shook the bags. "Special lunches today," she said, and smiled, "for my special darlings." She gave one to Fiona and then Eliot, and hugged them both. "You'll do fine today." Her face darkened, and she whispered, "Remember to work *with* each other. You're far stronger together." Cecilia stood back and beamed at them. "Their first day of—"

"Which will be their last," Audrey told her, "if they delay."

"Oh, yes, silly me." Cecilia backed away.

"Thanks, Cee," Fiona said.

"Thanks," Eliot said.

She and Eliot moved to Audrey and gave her a kiss on the cheek. To Fiona, this felt like one of her morning chores, like brushing her teeth or taking out the trash.

Eliot ran down the hall.

Fiona sprinted after him and got ahead, tramping down the spiral stair-case first, and halted at the front door. "Too slow again," she told him.

The front door was redwood and had four stained glass windows depicting a rose-hedge maze, a meander of river, a field of grapevines and harvesters, and a coastline with churning waves. A million colors sparkled on the tiled floor.[3]

Fiona loved this door and paused to admire it.

"We'd better go," Eliot whispered. "There's something weird about this Paxington map deal."

---

3. The Door of Four Paths and the Post residence were some of the few structures to miracu-lously survive the devastation that flattened the San Francisco peninsula in the War of Last Judgment. The four windows depict (or some claim are) doorways to the Middle Realms. This artifact from the Fifth Celestial Age continues to undergo intense and cautious study. For hu-manity, these windows remain symbols of mystery, wonder, and hope. *Gods of the First and Twenty-first Century, Volume 11, The Post Family Mythology.* Zypheron Press Ltd., Eighth Edition.

"I know," Fiona said. "I feel it, too."

She glanced back up the stairwell, hoping to see Audrey looking down, maybe with the tiniest farewell wave.

But her mother wasn't there . . . only shadows.

2

CIRCLES OF POWER AND REGRET

Audrey watched from the second-story window as the children walked down the street. They paused at the intersection and looked both ways before crossing. She reached up and touched the glass.

Always so careful. Good for them. The world was a dangerous place, and it was wise to look before one leaped. But sometimes being cautious was bad. Wait too long to cross the road, and one might be hit from behind by a bus careening out of control down the sidewalk.

She withdrew her hand, returned to the dining table, and sat.

"We must talk," Cecilia whispered to her. "The children—"

Audrey held up one finger. "Tea first, Cecilia. And bring the Towers game. I fear the time will crawl today without some distraction."

Cecilia obediently nodded and backed into the kitchen.

Boiling water for tea. The old woman hopefully could manage that.

Audrey nibbled on a piece of curled burnt bacon and reminded herself to make a list of all the restaurants nearby that delivered breakfast, lunch, and dinner. There was no need anymore to pretend they did not have the money for such "luxuries" as edible food.

Cecilia returned with a tea service tray and a rolled-up piece of leather.

Indeed, there was no need anymore to pretend *many* things.

Cecilia smiled nervously. "You have that look on your face"—she poured hot water into a teapot with spiderweb patterns etched into its white glaze—"the look where people go missing."

Odors of chamomile, mint, and mandrake wafted across the table.

"I was just thinking that there are advantages to having some things cut." Audrey sighed. "Set up the game and ask no more foolish questions."

Cecilia paled. She unrolled the leather mat upon the table and then removed the game cubes from their pouch.

Long ago, Audrey had had to sever herself from a collection of feelings and instincts that some might call motherhood. She'd left only one connection: the instinct to protect.

Did she still love her children? Was there some vestige of a desire to give them the best of everything? Where was the urge to hold them and soothe away their fears when they had nightmares? Or were these things forever lost to her?

It had to be that way, though. Otherwise, she would not have had the strength to do what was best for them all.

Audrey shifted her focus to the game. It was a study on the forms of combat, on strategies and death, a metaphor on the families and their never-ending politics. They called the game Towers.[4]

Audrey smoothed the rumpled leather mat and ran her fingers over the lines that radiated from the center, around the circles that divided the space into four tiers. Slaves (or their modern equivalent, Pawns) sat on the outer edge. Warriors took the second tier. Princes collected near the nexus of power on the third tier. The Master sat in the center space. Rings about rings. Rings of power and love and deception and regret.

She and Cecilia divided the stone cubes and took alternating turns, selecting their starting positions along their respective inner areas.

Much of the game was decided by this deceptively simple planning stage. Good players could tell how their game would end from such opening moves. One could set up near an opponent's boundary, preparing for

---

4. Fragments of one Towers set were found in the Neolithic hunter-gatherer settlement, Göbekli Tepe (southeast Turkey c. 9000 B.C.E.). This makes Towers the oldest (nontrivial) game, predating Chinese Go and Egyptian Senet by more than four thousand years. A Towers board is circular. Lines radiate outward to make thirty-two spaces of alternating color on the circumference, a second tier closer of sixteen spaces, a third tier with eight spaces, and a single circular space in the center. Placed on the board are sixteen white cubes and sixteen black. A simple checkers mechanism was assumed, but in 1753, a set was discovered in Pompeii preserved *in the middle* of a game. Cubes were stacked into towers (of increasing size) on the inner circles, while others remained as single stones, indicating a complexity of rules that experts agree no Neolithic hunter-gathers could have developed. *Gods of the First and Twenty-first Century, Volume 1, Earliest Myths.*

an aggressive rush. Or they could set up in the back regions and strategize to take the center—a longer game of dominance and subtlety.

Like the twins. How things went today at school would very much affect their endgame.

Cecilia set up on Audrey's boundary. In response, Audrey placed only a few weak defenders to counter her and concentrated her efforts on the longer back-region game.

Cee immediately took one of Audrey's border guards. "I am worried about their father," she said, a smug smile appearing on her face as she removed Audrey's piece.

"There has been no word from him," Audrey replied.

"Exactly!" Cee said. "It can mean only one thing: He's plotting something."

Audrey's answer to this obvious statement was silence.

She countered Cecilia's move by advancing a stone from her first circle to the second, blocking Cee's clumsy advance.

"We should tell the children," Cecilia said. "Tell them everything." She poured Audrey and herself cups of tea. Steam curled around the old woman like living tendrils. "We should prepare them for the coming violence."

"No."

"But this is not like the last time, when their ignorance protected them."

"Their ignorance serves a purpose still," Audrey told her. "They have lessons to learn. The entire truth would only distract them."

"But they are so smart." Cecilia moved another piece along her opposite border, poised to attack.

Audrey moved another cube onto her second tier, stacking it with the first to make a low Tower.

Cecilia frowned at this, realizing her error. She moved one of her own cubes to the second tier. Too late, however, to be an effective counter.

"'Smart' will help them only so much," Audrey said. "Better they learn how to be *ruthless*. They must be pushed to the brink, broken, and then remolded. It is the only way they have a chance of surviving."

"And the place for this is Paxington? That so-called Headmistress, Miss Westin. We will be lucky if she does not kill them first."

"Westin is not the threat she once was to children," Audrey told her. She toppled her fledgling Tower, casting its pieces into Cecilia's territory, capturing two of her cubes. "Besides, I have spoken with her. All is arranged."

"Oh, I see," Cecilia said, now ignoring the game. "Miss Westin and

Paxington are vastly reformed since the old days, eh? Did you know that seventeen children were so severely injured last year that they could not continue? That there were five fatalities?"

"Of course," Audrey replied. "I believe that's the point."

Cecilia sipped her tea. "That is not the only danger. The students, they are from the families, ours, theirs, all the other great ones, mortal and immortal—the social elite and privileged few." She huffed. "Do you know what they will do to our poor little lambs?"

"They will devour them," Audrey told her, "if Eliot and Fiona fail to grow."

Cecilia glowered at Audrey. Without looking at the board, she moved another cube onto the second tier.

Audrey raised an eyebrow. Interesting. In three moves, Cecilia would capture the entire second ring. The old witch apparently had some spark left to her.

"You think me a monster," Audrey replied. "But you've forgotten the real monsters in our world: horrors with bat wings and serpent tongues, nightmares made real." She cocked her head, hearing the heartbeat and breath she'd been waiting for all morning. "Especially the monsters with sharp smiles and large ears 'the better to hear with.'"

Audrey turned to face the stairwell. "Come in, Old Wolf. The door is open to you."

Beneath them came the sound of the door's locks clicking open, the knob turning, and whisper-silent footfalls.

Faint gray shadows crisscrossed the spiral of stairs as a figure came up.

His smile was the first thing she saw, like some hybrid Cheshire cat and great white shark making a grand entrance. Henry Mimes gave her a short bow and then gave one to Cecilia as well. He was dressed for walking today: gray slacks, sensible sneakers, a black turtleneck, and a baseball cap that framed his silver hair.

Dangerously handsome and dangerously deceptive.

And yet . . . Audrey could not help but smile back at the fool, if only a little.

"What do you want, Henry?" Audrey said. "Your visits are never merely to exchange pleasantries."

"It could be that way . . . if you desired, my Queen of Swords." Henry looked about the room. "How quaint. I see you still have my grandfather clock in good repair." His gaze caught the picture window and its view of the bay and the Golden Gate Bridge. "A lovely location. I approve."

Cecilia, stone-faced, poured a cup of tea for Henry and offered it to him.

He smiled, accepted her gift . . . but paused as the vapors reached his nose. "Thank you, dear witch of the Isle Eea." He set the cup back on the table. "I think we'll pass on your poison this morning."

Cecilia wisely said nothing.

"You're in an unusually good mood," Audrey said.

"Am I not always?" His attention drifted to the game of Towers. "But you're right, today is special: my favorite nephew and niece's first day of high school. So many plots and devices afoot. It makes for a delectable mix."

"So many words," Cecilia hissed, "and yet he says so little."

Henry's smile cooled a few degrees, but his gaze did not lift from the board. "You know, old woman, that you can win in six turns? Here." He reached over and slid two cubes at once to flank Audrey's collapsed tower.

"That's not a legitimate move," Cecilia told him.

"It is," Henry said. "Just one that you, in your too-long years, have failed to learn. Or perhaps senility has settled upon your once-keen mind?"

Audrey saw that her captured pieces could be used to build additional Towers on Cecilia's side in three moves—and her own border defenses after that would be insufficient. While she could still get to the center, Henry's new strategy had her losing her entire backcourt . . . and then the game.

She locked eyes with him. There was no more emotion or additional truths, however, behind his sparkling empty eyes.

"One must practice to keep one's defenses sharpened, no?" he asked.

"The Council?"

"Meeting today," Henry replied. "They require our presence. I thought that I would offer you a ride."

"Always and never the gentleman," Audrey said, and stood. "I accept your offer."

"Splendid," Henry cooed. He turned to Cecilia, and his slender hand reached out to caress her face. Cecilia recoiled before this gesture. "Ah, I would bring you as well, my lovely," he said, "but there are some on the Council who would love to part your head from your shoulders should you cross their path."

Cecilia gripped a butter knife.

Henry spared a glance at its edge. "Perhaps another time you and I will dance." He moved to the stairs. "Today, regrettably, we have business to attend to: The Council wishes to discuss its newest members, and provided they are allowed to live . . . we shall discuss how to avert the end of the world."

Audrey gathered her courage and followed. "I expected no less."

3

ENTRANCE EXAM

Eliot had this creepy feeling he and Fiona were being watched. Fog and shafts of sunlight swirled around them on the sidewalk. He glanced up at their new house.

He liked it. It wasn't "home." That had been their apartment in Del Sombra. This place, though, made up for it by at least having more than one bathroom.

It was a modern Victorian squished on all sides so it towered three stories tall on their lot. The trim was green and gold geometric art deco lines. Three scalloped balconies cupped the sides of the house like bracket mushrooms. A gold solar system weather vane topped the highest spire. It was an odd melding of styles . . . but it somehow worked, like something a mad genius architect might have sketched.

Every building was tall and quirky on their street—stacked at least three stories tall. Most had been built with so little room, they actually touched their neighbors. Cee said it was the high cost of real estate that made every home tiny and built this way.

That feeling of being watched, however, was still there. Eliot squinted, but the windows of his house were solid reflections of sky.

Fiona glanced around, too, perhaps sensing the same unease he felt.

"Are you ready?" she asked.

"Hang on a sec." Eliot tightened the strap of his canvas backpack. Inside were pencils, notebooks, Cee's lunch, and a battered violin case (sticking slightly out of the top of the pack), which contained his most prized possession: the violin Lady Dawn. He shifted his shoulders inside his too-big

Paxington jacket. No luck there—it still looked all wrong. "Okay," he told her. "Let's go."

Fiona unfolded their map, got oriented, and then pointed. "That way to Lombard Street." She marched ahead and Eliot followed. She was in her figure-it-out mode, and nothing got in Fiona's way when she was like that.

For several blocks they tromped in silence and then turned onto Lombard.

A nonstop stream of cars and trucks rolled by. Eliot and Fiona took a step back. The scents of coffee and freshly baked bread drifted with the odors of exhaust. People queued in line for coffee from latte carts.

"All we have to do is follow this street west," she told him. "That'll get us there." She scrutinized the map but looked unconvinced.

"What's the matter?" he asked.

"Nothing."

Eliot knew it was *something,* but before he could get it out of his sister, she started walking.

Why did she always do that? Leave him behind, thinking she got to lead. Eliot had half a mind to go his own way . . . but then, Fiona might get lost and never find the place by herself.

So he followed. For her sake.

One day, though, she was going to find out just how much she needed him.

They passed shoe stores and a Taco Bell and one store that sold nothing but globes and maps. Fiona paused to admire a massive world that levitated magnetically on its pedestal. She checked the building's street number and then compared it to the address on their welcome letter.

"This is the right direction," she said. "We should almost be there."

Lombard veered southwest. The street narrowed and filled with houses and apartments. Eliot didn't see anything that looked like a school.

They walked another entire block—passing the address where Paxington should have been—the last two digits of the closest number jumped from 16 to 22.

"You're reading that map wrong," Eliot told her.

"I'm not," she replied.

Eliot then did the one thing he had vowed he wouldn't do this morning. He dug into his pack, found a slender case, and pulled it out. Inside were his new glasses. The silver wire rims made him look like an ultra-dork when he wore them.

"Let me try," he said.

Fiona glanced back down the street, confused. "Fine." She handed him the map and letter.

He donned his glasses, cringing as he did so, but the pages came into focus. He checked the Paxington address, and then their map.

"Look," he told Fiona, "it says it's at the intersection of Lombard and Chestnut Streets. We've checked Lombard. We should go down Chestnut instead."

Fiona examined the map. "It's only one block north of here." She almost looked impressed with this idea, but then added: "Not bad . . . for an *Architeuthis dux*."

Eliot ground his teeth at this simultaneous compliment and insult. *Architeuthis dux* was the scientific name for the giant squid. Its eye was one of the largest in the animal kingdom—the size of a volleyball—and could spot prey in the murkiest ocean depths. Her commentary on his new glasses.

As he mulled over the appropriate counterinsult, Fiona grabbed the map and letter and flounced down a side street. "Come on," she called back. "Don't sulk . . . it was a good idea."

Eliot removed his glasses, placed them back in their case, and dashed after her.

They emerged on Chestnut Street with its quaint pastel and stucco houses and apartments jam-packed together, every parking spot filled, and even more people on the sidewalks—all of whom seem to be very much in a hurry to get to work, or jogging as fast as they could, or delivering very important-looking packages.

. . . or like them, just trying to get school.

Eliot spotted a navy blue wool jacket, khaki slacks, and a flash of gold threads shimmering from an embroidered Paxington crest.

Another student.

Eliot pointed to this boy on the opposite side of the street. "Let's follow him."

Fiona nodded, and they raced alongside, shadowing the other student until they came to a crosswalk. The light was red. The other boy crossed; they had to wait.

Eliot watched the traffic. There was a break coming. They could sprint across the street, but technically, that was against the law—jaywalking—and something Audrey would definitely have disapproved of.

He thought, however, she'd disapprove *more* of them being late for their first day of school.

Eliot started to cross.

"You can't do that!" Fiona shouted after him—but nonetheless she followed.

A truck pulled out of a driveway and accelerated toward them.

Eliot and Fiona sprinted.

The truck blared its horn.

They jumped together onto the sidewalk. A whirlwind of dust and fumes and papers swirled around them.

"That was stupid," she hissed.

"There he is!" Eliot said, ignoring her, and ran after the boy from Paxington.

The student must have heard him, because he turned. The boy was older, eighteen maybe, two heads taller than Eliot, and he had a faint mustache. His dark hair was long and wavy and combed back. He was deeply tanned and muscular. He smiled at them.

Eliot found himself smiling back. A friendly face was the last thing he expected today, but he was glad to find one.

The boy held out his hand for Eliot to shake and asked, "Paxington? Transfer students?" His voice was embroidered with a rich Italian accent.

"Yes," Eliot replied. "And no."

Up close, Eliot noticed the boy's uniform was different from theirs. The fabric was smoother and of a more luxuriant texture. It looked like it had been custom tailored.

Fiona and Eliot shifted uncomfortably in their too-baggy and too-tight uniforms.

The boy gave Fiona a slight bow. "You look like you might need some help. Allow me to introduce myself. I am from the family Scalagari. My given name is Dante."

"It's great to meet you. I'm Eliot. Eliot Post. And this is my sister—"

"Fiona." She tried to smile, but it wavered and failed. "We were beginning to worry that we had the wrong street."

"Can you help us find the school?" Eliot asked.

Dante Scalagari's smile faded. "Ah, I see. You must forgive me. I did not know you were freshmen. You both look . . . well, take no offense, but you look like you've seen more of the world than our typical freshman."

"Yeah, I guess so," Eliot said.

Fiona cleared her throat and glanced at the sidewalk. "If you don't mind very much . . . we have to get to the placement exams before the time runs out."

Dante held out his hands in an apologetic gesture. "Believe me," he said, "I've nothing against you. In fact, you have my deepest sympathies. But, alas, I cannot show you the way."

"What?" Eliot said. "Why!"

Dante's hands clasped and his fingers interlaced. "Tradition," he said. "Rules. And because I'm late for school myself. Perhaps I will see you again on campus."

"If you just point us in the right direction," Fiona said, and started to unfold their map.

Eliot leaned closer and traced their route, explaining, "We tried following Lombard, but that didn't . . ."

He glanced up.

Eliot looked back and forth along the sidewalk. There was no trace of Dante Scalagari.

"Impossible," Fiona breathed. Her head snapped sideways. "Wait, there's another student."

Eliot saw them as well. A girl this time; he caught just a glimpse of platinum curls over the Paxington navy blue blazer—as she turned a corner, entered the shadows, and disappeared from view.

Fiona sighed. She looked over the map again. "Well, with two students so close, the school has to be nearby. Let's go this way."

They followed the street numbers as they increased, and once more passed where Paxington *should have* been—but clearly wasn't.

Fiona clutched the map, crinkling its edges. "What are we doing wrong?"

Eliot leaned closer and examined the map. "The directions said it was at the intersection of Lombard and Chestnut?" He followed those two roads with his fingers. "That can't be right. They must mean Richardson Avenue. That cuts across both."

"Not Richardson," Fiona told him. "It specifically said the intersection of Lombard and Chestnut."

"I remember what it said," Eliot answered, anger creeping into his voice. "I'm not an idiot. I'm saying that's impossible because they run parallel. They *never* cross."

Fiona checked, and then double-checked this.

"Give me the map." Eliot gently took hold of one corner. "I'll puzzle it out."

Fiona refused to release her grip. She pulled away. "They *have* to cross somewhere."

Eliot didn't let go either. The map snapped taut between them. He pulled hard.

Fiona yanked the map, too.

The yellowed parchment tore down the middle . . . almost all the way through.

Eliot stared at the ruined map, remembering how Cee had told them to work together. And here they were: they hadn't found Paxington, let alone faced the placement exams, and were already fighting each other.

He glared at his sister.

She glared back at him. "Great," she said. "Like we don't have enough trouble already."

"Thanks to you," Eliot said. "Just because you're a 'goddess' now doesn't mean you know everything . . . or even anything."

Fiona tilted her chin up and tried to look "down" at him the way Audrey could. It didn't work.

"At least *now* you know how to make two parallel lines meet," Eliot told her.

"What do you mean?"

Eliot snorted. "It's easy, but useless, really." He crossed one of the map's torn flaps so Lombard and Chestnut Streets, once parallel, angled toward each other.

Static electricity raced up his fingertips, growing stronger as he brought the pieces of the map together.

Fiona guided the other part of the map toward his. "I've felt something like this before," she whispered.

The two portions of the map wavered as if magnetically attracted and then repulsed . . . and then the two sides snapped together.

Lombard and Chestnut crossed—at least on paper.

Fiona ran her fingers over the parchment. "This feels like that spot in the Valley of the New Year where there was a hidden exit. A spot where space *folded.*"

"Like there's an extra space or a doorway"—Eliot pointed to the spot where the two streets intersected—"here?"

"We passed that spot and didn't see anything," she said.

"But did we *really* look?"

They stared at the map. The "intersection" was a block and a half away.

Fiona crumpled the outer edges of the map, and they both ran.

They dodged people on the sidewalk; Eliot careened off a trash can, stumbled, but kept going. He caught glimpses of other Paxington students, but didn't bother to ask for help. There was no time left.

They sprinted toward the address where Paxington was supposed to be, where the lines crossed on the map.

It looked like the same place they had walked by earlier . . . but it *felt* different.

That static electricity sensation was here.

He slowed and stopped.

So did Fiona.

They looked for something out of the ordinary. There was only a wall made of roughened granite blocks.

Eliot ran his hand over the surface.

It was just rock . . . but there *was* something else, faint at first, and then stronger. Deep inside the stone there was a vibration, almost like he was touching the strings of his violin.

Fiona felt the wall with both her hands. "It's like threads," she whispered.

"Like music," he said.

He spied a minuscule crack in the stone, and as he touched its edges, there was a pause in the music.

Fiona found the spot as well.

Eliot stared at the crack and found that when he looked at it from a particular angle—*an angle that hadn't been there before*—the crack tilted and expanded and was really a *four*-dimensional corner.

Disorientation washed over him as this new space revealed itself. The sensation was like staring at one of those crazy M. C. Escher drawings: Everything appeared normal, until suddenly you saw an extra dimension tilting sideways.

Eliot and Fiona stepped around this new corner and found themselves—

—on a cobblestone boulevard running *perpendicular* to the main street.

It wasn't as if this new passage were hidden. It opened quite plainly onto the main street behind them.

Eliot waved to a man as he rushed past on the sidewalk. "Hey, mister," he called.

The man ignored him.

Apparently no one on the outside could sense this place, unless they knew exactly what they were looking for.[5]

There were a dozen stores on this in-between street: antique and curio shops, a few high-end fashion boutiques, a Chinese noodle house, and a café on the corner, where older Paxington students sat at canopy-covered tables. Farther down the boulevard, brick walls rose along the sides, weathered and ivy-covered, which ended a half block away at an intricate wrought iron gate.

Beyond those gates were majestic cathedral-like buildings stained black with age, structures with Greek columns that rose like a forest of marble, and wavering in and out of the ever-present Bay Area fog lorded a clock tower glinting with hints of gold filigree.

"It's amazing," Eliot said.

"Yeah. . . ." Fiona immediately sobered. "But the time!" She grabbed his hand and pulled him along.

Eliot shook off his wonderment and ran with her.

As they neared the gate, Eliot saw that it was shut. Had they let everyone inside already and locked the place up?

A man with a stern look on his face stepped out of the gatehouse. He wore a navy blue suit with an embroidered Paxington crest. His blond hair was buzz-cut, and his beard was trimmed square, save the two braids that dangled from his chin.

He towered over Eliot and Fiona, but more impressive than his height was his girth. It would've taken three muscular men standing side by side to occupy the same space where he stood. His biceps flexed and stretched taut the fabric of his jacket.

He raised a clipboard and made two checks. "Master Eliot Post," he muttered, "and the Lady Fiona Post. Good morning."

---

5. In the late twentieth and early twenty-first centuries, inspectors from the State, Fire, and School Accreditation Boards easily found the Main Gate entrance of the Paxington Institute, but when reporters or tourists attempted to locate the entrance, they failed. This might simply be the nature of San Francisco's convoluted street geometry. In old satellite images, the original Paxington campus does appear exactly where school officials claim (adjacent Presidio Park). Similar modern accounts, however, of the school's "selectively appearing entrance" have been claimed of the new Paxington Institute on the San Francisco Archipelago. Inquiries made to the Institute result in a detailed set of directions . . . which ultimately prove useless. *Gods of the First and Twenty-first Century, Volume 6, Modern Myths*. Zypheron Press Ltd., Eighth Edition.

"Yes, sir." Eliot panted. "Good morning. Sorry." He gave this man a short bow, unsure what the protocol was, but very sure that he deserved respect.

Fiona curtsied.

"Congratulations on passing the entrance exam," the man said.

"Entrance exam?" Eliot echoed.

"A test to see if you have a spark. You'd be surprised how many potential freshmen wander just outside this street, sometimes for days, never giving up, but never having what it takes to get inside, either. So sad."

The man's iron stance relaxed a notch. "I am Harlan Dells," he said. "Head of security at Paxington. Mind you two break no rules while on school grounds or you will answer to me."

Eliot swallowed.

Harlan Dells glared at Eliot's backpack.

Eliot felt his violin case shift inside. His hand tingled where Lady Dawn's snapped string had cut and infected him . . . apparently not so healed as he had thought.

Harlan Dells turned and opened the gate.

Something about the man was familiar. It was like when they had met Uncle Henry; Eliot felt an instinctual fear and some déjà vu. He sensed that Mr. Dells was related in *some* way. He was an Immortal.

Mr. Dells faced them. "I can hear the grass grow on the other side of the world. I can see the farthest shore, the most distant star . . . and I can be in more than one place at a time, so I can easily spot and catch two trouble-makers. Understand?"

"Yes, sir," Eliot and Fiona said together.

"Good." Mr. Dells pointed past the gates—over manicured lawns and marble fountains, across the courtyard to the clock tower and a domed building next to it. "Bristlecone Hall," he told them. "That's where your placement exams are this morning."

The minute hand of the tower clock ticked into the straight-up position, and bells tolled.

"I suggest," Mr. Dells said, "that you run for it."

They did.

4

WHAT WE DO BEST

Louis Piper, often called the Prince of Darkness, Lucifer, or the Morning Star, mused on the nature of time . . . how when one doted upon a beautiful woman, a moment stretched into days . . . or like now, when one waited for his cousins to deliberate on their endless scheming—it took an eternity.

Louis shifted on the vinyl couch.

This waiting room was devoid of comfort. Windowless, the only ornamentation on the water-stained walls was a USA AS SEEN FROM LAS VEGAS poster. The odor of urinal cake wafted from the adjacent restroom.

Aside from the door marked EXIT, the only other egress was the door leading to the recently relocated Las Vegas Boardroom.

"They should've called me in already," he told Amberflaxus. "Something is wrong."

Next to him on the couch, his cat ceased licking its iridescent black fur and blinked.

"Yes, yes, I know," Louis replied. "One cannot go from King of the Panhandlers to Chairman of the Board in a single season, can one?"

Louis reached to stroke Amberflaxus.

The cat, lightning quick, batted his hand away and gave a look of offense.

"No? You're saying what right do I have to make such claims? I, who have wandered homeless and clueless as a mortal for sixteen years, his power severed and heart ripped asunder by the woman he loved?"

Had he really loved? Louis had forgotten. Perhaps it was just a bad dream.

His cat returned to licking himself.

Louis leaned closer. "You make perfect sense. Consider, though, my friend, that in the span of a few days, I have regained my Infernal status, killed our loathsome cousin Beelzebub, and absorbed his power. What stops me from marching in there and *demanding* a seat on the Board?"

Amberflaxus tore into the vinyl couch—shredding wildly as if the plastic were alive.

His sentiments were obvious: Louis was a fool.

Any of Louis's relations had the power to slay hero or demon. But without land, Louis was a pale imitation of a *real* Infernal. Land made them what they were.

The door to the Boardroom eased open.

No one emerged to invite Louis in, a sign of his lower-than-dirt status. So be it.

He stood, brushed cat hair from his charcoal gray suit, and straightened his bloodred tie.

Amberflaxus bit into the couch's stuffing, shaking nubs of fluff.

"Wait here," he told the animal.

Louis turned, donned his armored smile, and entered.

The Boardroom had been a private gambling den during Prohibition. Six billiard lamps hung from the rafters, making cones of dust-filled light. On the far wall hung a gigantic computer screen showing the local news coverage of the Babylon Garden Hotel and Casino as preparations were made to demolish the place in one well-engineered implosion. That was Beelzebub's nightclub, the last of his old bones being scattered in a final act of well-deserved degradation.

In the center of the room was a craps table padded with green felt, its lines and numbers worn smooth with age where bets were placed with chips, gold coins, or souls.

About the table stood the Infernal Board of Directors.

Louis bowed without taking his eyes off any of them.

Sealiah turned to face Louis. She stood at the foot of the table. She wore an evening gown of opal-flecked orchids and clinging copper vines that wrapped her sinuous curves for a predictable effect upon his libido. Her hair flashed red gold, her sharp smile, pure white, and her eyes, slits of emerald.

"We welcome the glorious Morning Star," Sealiah told him (although from her icy tone, Louis was sure *welcome* was the last thing she meant).

"Greetings to you, Cousin, Queen of Poppies and Mistress of the Many-Colored Jungles."

Louis stared past her to the head of the table at the Board's new Chairman, Ashmed, the Master Architect of Evil.

Ashmed was the most careful among their kind. His friends remained loyal . . . and those who did not lived short lives. The Chairman was all business—crew-cut hair, clean shaved, and in a black business suit.

"Welcome, Louis." Ashmed puffed on a Sancho Panza Belicoso cigar and blew a trail of serpentine smoke. "Kind of you to appear on short notice."

"Anything for the Board," Louis replied.

Lev, called Leviathan by some, the Master of the Endless Abyssal Seas, stood on Ashmed's right. A hundred strands of Mardi Gras beads coiled about his throat, which almost covered his straining-to-the-bursting-point wife-beater tank top. His corpulence matched his endless strength.

"Really?" Lev asked, and his beady eyes widened. "If you'd do 'anything'—then cut off your right arm. You owe me for that business in Mozambique."

Lev was too powerful to insult directly, but thankfully his intellect was as dull as his doughy features.

"Almost anything for you, Cousin, would I not do," Louis told him.

Lev's fat forehead crinkled as he puzzled this grammatical knot.

The doors behind Louis shut . . . which was not a good sign.

"Please, Lev," a girl whispered, "do not play with your food."

Louis spied a slender form standing between Sealiah and Leviathan.

"Abigail," Louis cooed. "I did not see you." He bowed to her. "A thousand apologies. Destroy everything you touch."

"Lies and salutations to you, dear Cousin," Abby replied.

She was so quiet, so lithe—her delicate childlike features artfully covered in translucent gauze and seed pearls—so enticing that Louis could *almost* forget she was the Destroyer, Handmaiden of Armageddon, and Mistress of the Palace of Abomination.

However, those who underestimated Abby found their guts trailing from their torsos.

Abby held a locust in the palm of her white hand. It shivered and made the most unpleasant buzzing sound imaginable. She stroked the insect and it calmed. "Did you hear? Oz has retired, poor thing. Allow me to introduce our newest Board member." She tilted her chin to the other side of the table.

Oz had crossed Lev and Abby earlier this year. He was lucky to have escaped with most of his skin intact, a tribute to his eel slipperiness.

Louis peered into the shadows and saw a silhouette on the other side of the table, one he had failed to detect earlier . . . which, when you considered that all Infernals lived, breathed, and were part darkness themselves, made this a masterwork of deception indeed.

"Mephistopheles," Louis said.

Naturally, Louis was disappointed. He had hoped the Board brought him here to offer *him* a seat.

But why should they? He was dirt, worthless and landless, having the barest scraps of power to his name. Only his reputation for being the Great Liar enabled him to hold his head high among them.

Yet why Mephistopheles? Irritation prickled Louis. After his scandalous behavior at the end of the Dark Ages with that fop Dr. Faustus—and then the operas—all the fame and the paparazzi. This sparked a hundred imitators trying to summon "the Devil" to sell their souls for trinkets. It had been a public relations nightmare.

Mephistopheles had retired, eschewing his family, claiming he had to strengthen his lands and borders.

Sulking, Louis called it.

Or could the rumors have been true? That he actually enjoyed the company of mortals . . . perhaps enjoyed them too much? Louis's smile faltered a split second. If that were the case, if he had fallen in love, had his heart broken as Louis had, he deserved pity.

"So good to . . . well . . . not see you, Lord of the House of Umbra, Ruler of the Hysterical Kingdom, and Prince of the Mirrored City," Louis told the darkness.

"Toy not with me, Louis," Mephistopheles rumbled. A taloned hand extended from the shadows and rested upon the table's railing, claws dimpling the green felt.

Sealiah cleared her throat. "Gentlemen, let us avoid tearing Louis into bits before we're done with him, as tempting as that may be. We have business."

"Yes," Ashmed said, setting down his cigar. "The business of the twins. We have called you among us to serve as consultant. You're close to the boy?"

"And the girl," Louis added. "I am, after all, their father."

He put on a brave face, but inside, Louis was wounded. They had summoned him here for the children's sake? Yes, yes, *they* were important: the key to unraveling the neutrality treaty with the League of Immortals.

But could someone, just once, want him for his own sparkling self?

This was the problem with being a narcissist: No one appreciated you as much as you knew you deserved.

"How can I be of service today?" Louis asked.

"This Board's previous efforts position the children on a knife's edge," Mephistopheles said from his shadows, and his hand chopped down onto the table for emphasis. "Half Immortal, half Infernal. We must bring them into our jurisdiction."

"Temptations backfired on us," Lev said. "Those chocolates, the Valley of the New Year. Who knew the kids could use them to their advantage so quickly?"

"I believe," Abby interrupted, "that Sealiah's seductress—this new Jezebel—had *some* success?"

Sealiah betrayed no emotion on her beautiful features. A sign of deception, to be certain.

"Jezebel's real influence has yet to be seen," she said.

"And Beelzebub's attempt to *force* a solution," Ashmed continued, "proved disastrous."

Indeed. Louis had been there when his darling Fiona had parted the head of the Lord of All That Flies from his body.

"We need a new deception to bring them into the family," Abby said. "And since your blood runs through their veins, Louis, we had hoped you had a suggestion."

There it was, the one shred of truth in this maneuvering: They *needed* him.

The universe spun around Louis. He, who was a second ago more common than dirt, was suddenly the golden key to the ambitions of the Infernal clans. This was his chance, but to do what? Place his only two children in danger to gain advantage and power? And land . . . one could not forget the land to be gained.

But Eliot was so talented, playing his Lady Dawn.

And Fiona was so beautiful and so strong, and she didn't even know it.

Poisonous fatherly concern coursed through his veins and muddled his thinking.

This weakness—the vestiges of Louis's human form, no doubt—would destroy him if he allowed such a cancerous influence to run its full course.

Thankfully, rational thinking prevailed.

Louis was many things, perhaps even a father to his children, but he had *never* been a fool in the face of opportunity.

"Yes," Louis replied to the Board, "I know how this might be accomplished."

The shadow form of Mephistopheles chuckled, and the subsonic noise made Louis's teeth rattle.

"Doubt if you will," Louis said, "but I know their weakness: They have been brought up to be 'good' children."

They stared at him, rapt. Louis had them now.

"A good little boy and girl, with all the ingredients that lead to moral downfall, including the most important: *good intentions*."

Ashmed nodded, picked up his cigar, and puffed, greatly pleased with this.

"Go on," Abby said, her eyes sparkling.

"We require a theater of Shakespearean proportions to draw the twins closer . . . as they have proved themselves highly susceptible to familial drama."

"Shakes-whos-its?" Lev asked. "You lost me."

"Shakespeare: the basis for all those Mexican soap operas you so love, Cousin," Louis explained.

"How, specifically, would one engineer this 'drama'?" Sealiah asked.

"We shall do what we do best," Louis said, and spread his arms wide. He congratulated himself on a smooth transition to using *we* to refer to himself and the Board as partners on this venture. "We shall do it by fighting amongst ourselves. A war, just a little one, should do the trick."

Of course, he was telling them all this because wars had their winners and losers . . . and where there were losers, there would be pieces of land and power for Louis to scavenge.

Ashmed's dark gaze was light-years distant. "A sanctioned Civil War could destroy many clans," he said. "Are these two children worth that?"

"It need not be a full Civil War," Sealiah said. "Two clans would suffice. Something intimate. With only two involved, the loss to us would be trivial—negligible after we reabsorb the power base of the loser. Naturally, the specifics of how to draw Eliot and Fiona into the conflict would be left up to the individuals with the most at stake."

Despite this coming from Sealiah, Louis liked the addendum to his plan. With only two factions involved, he would not have to personally risk doing any of the dirty work.

"The destruction, however, of even a single clan," Ashmed reminded them, "is still a considerable tactical liability, since we are on the eve of war with the Immortals."

Lev laughed. "Terrible for the loser. Which *wouldn't* be me. Sign me up."

"I, too, want the chance to play," Abby whispered. "It has been too long since we had such sport. I volunteer my clan to go to war." Her hand clutched her pet locust, and it squealed.

"As do I," Sealiah stated.

Mephistopheles hammered a fist upon the railing, and the entire table jumped. "Fools—we all want blood on our hands. I propose we dispense with the usual discussion and move directly either to violence or dice to settle this."

"Excellent motion," Ashmed said. "Do we have a second?"

Louis took a step back from the table, feeling gravity condense about the Board members. He weighed who would fight whom . . . and who would survive. Lev was powerful but slow. Abby was unstoppable but gullible. Sealiah was ever full of tricks. Ashmed, he had never seen fight. And Mephistopheles? Perhaps the most dangerous here, with his pitchfork of shadow smoke.

With one wrong twitch, Louis could be caught in the middle of the mayhem.

"I will second the motion," Sealiah breathed, "for dice."

Louis exhaled.

Sealiah rubbed her palms, and a die appeared: a Naga of Dharma.

The last few times Louis had seen one of the legendary dice, they had decided Charlemagne would become Emperor, that they'd test-fire Mount Krakatoa in the fifth, sixth, and seventeenth centuries, and that some utterly forgettable film would win the Academy Award.

It was a cube of scrimshawed ivory carved from the spine of the world serpent. Only five such dice existed. On the faces were etched six crows, five hands (each making its own rude gesture), four stars, three crossed swords, two prancing dogs, and a single head-eating-tail asp.

Ashmed called for a vote.

Ashmed raised his hand—as did Sealiah and, curiously, even Mephistopheles. Abby and Lev did not.

This shocked Louis. Usually there was at least a minor brawl and a few broken bones on the Board to settle even trivial matters. The civilized approach left him with an uneasy feeling.

"Dice it is," Ashmed announced. "For such a weighty decision, I will require a broader probability distribution."

From his pocket, he produced a second of the remarkable Nagas. Sealiah graciously let him borrow her die.

"Highest and lowest numbers shall have sanction to wage open war," Ashmed explained. "The victor shall have all the usual rights of spoils."

"Fine," Lev grumbled. "Just let me roll those bones."

Ashmed raised an eyebrow at his impudence. The Chairman rolled first, the dice tumbling onto the table. They came to rest neatly on the pass line. A five and a four—hands touching stars—nine total.

Lev scooped up the dice, scowled, shook them violently, and threw.

The dice cracked together like a billiard break—bounced against the far bumpers, and rolled back in front of him. Four and three—seven: dead center in the probability distribution. The worst possible roll.

Lev's giant hands clenched about the table's railing and crushed it. He swallowed his rage, muttering.

Infernals heeded no rules . . . save one: No one ever went back on an agreement once dice were on the table.

Abby set her pet locust down, and it skittered out under the door. She stood on her tiptoes to reach the dice and rolled next.

A pair of the dancing dogs. Four. The lowest result yet.

She turned to Sealiah, challenge glimmering in her red eyes.

Sealiah toyed with the dice on the table, as if she could commune with their delectable randomness. She snatched them up and, with one graceful toss, sent them flying across the table, bouncing off the far end—impacting each other and coming to rest in the center. Two sixes, twelve crows on the wing—a *murder,* so called, or more commonly among mortals, *boxcars,* as they resembled a pair of freight cars on a train.

"Congratulations," Ashmed said. "We have one side." He looked between Sealiah and Abby. "Perhaps a matchup?" The Chairman's face was unreadable.

"Perhaps . . ." Sealiah plucked up the dice. To Louis's astonishment, she offered them to him.

Louis held up both hands. "I'm no Board member. I have no place in this."

In truth, he had no place because he was not a tenth as powerful as his cousins. Engaging in a war with a landed Infernal Lord was guaranteed suicide.

"You were present when we voted," Ashmed said. "I do not remember specifically excluding you." He pointed his smoldering cigar at Louis. "Your children should care for you more than for any of us. So your involvement would guarantee them running to your aid."

Sealiah smiled. "The way I hear it, they might run to aid his destruction." Her hand remained outstretched, offering him the dice.

"Stop squirming," Lev told him. "Roll." He took a step closer, one meaty hand curling into a titanic fist.

"Well . . ." Louis's smile never wavered as he reached for the dice. "Since you insist. I am honored."

He grabbed the cubes without touching Sealiah.

Louis tilted his palm . . . and with the most undramatic of gestures let the dice fall.

The cubes bounced onto the table once and stopped: a one and a two. A total of three.

His heart skipped a beat.

Abby growled and stamped her foot.

"It seems, Louis, we are fated to dance once more," Sealiah said.

"Not so fast, peddler of poppies," Mephistopheles said.

Talons raked the Nagas of Dharma across the green felt. Mephistopheles grabbed them, shook, and tossed. They came to rest directly in front of Sealiah: a pair of the self-consuming ouroboros serpents.

She flinched. "Snake eyes," Sealiah said. "How appropriate."

Louis almost fell over with relief.

Mephistopheles vanished. Only shadows remained where he had once stood.

"So be it," Ashmed declared. "The Board sanctions Civil War between Sealiah, Queen of Poppies, and Mephistopheles, Lord of the House of Umbra." He glanced at Louis with disdain. "You are dismissed."

The door behind him squeaked open.

"Happy to have been of assistance." Louis bowed and scraped and stepped backwards and bowed once more—as the door slammed shut in his face.

"Too close," he breathed.

Louis turned in time to see Amberflaxus tearing the head off Abigail's locust, munching and crunching its fat body.

"Come, my friend," Louis whispered. "There's much to prepare. Chaos and opportunity abound today!"

He paused, however, wondering if placing his children in the greatest of dangers had been the best possible outcome.

For him—yes.

But what of them?

There was a faint, annoying whisper of doubt, a remnant of his mortal being. . . . Perhaps in time, it would go away like a blister healed after being popped.

No matter. He had plans and schemes and double-crosses to orchestrate.

5

PLACEMENT AND DISPLACEMENT

The clock tower chimed its ninth bell as Fiona and Eliot trampled up the worn marble steps of Bristlecone Hall.

There was a central yard dominated by a large silver tree, and classrooms extended to either side. Four doors down on the right was a sign: PLACEMENT EXAMS.

They sprinted for it, crossing the threshold of the classroom as the tenth and last bell sounded.

Panting, ready to fall over, Fiona saw one wall was floor-to-ceiling panes of glass—panes as small as a postage stamp on up to bedsheet-sized, and each slightly tilted or out of focus, magnifying or inverting the image of the old tree in the yard.

Her eyes adjusted to the darker room and she saw twelve rows of desks, twelve deep. They had rolled tops, ancient inkwells, attached stools that swung out, and wrought-iron footrests. At the front of this room was a massive blackboard, and along the walls were gaslight globes of opal glass.

As the last bit of her vision cleared, Fiona saw students at all the desks save two—and *all the students* turned to stare at Eliot and her.

"S-s-sorry," she said, and flushed.

"Apologize only if there is reason to," said a woman with a slight British accent.

This woman was the only person standing in the classroom besides Fiona and Eliot. She might have been thirty years old, and wore a long black skirt and a high-necked linen shirt with black pearl buttons. Her dark hair was up, and she wore octagonal spectacles that magnified her eyes.

She wasn't human.

The woman's skin and features were too perfect, too pale, more alabaster than organic, like a Greek statue.

Or perhaps an Immortal.

There was something else, too, in her brown-eyed stare. Fiona felt herself fall into that gaze until the world was swallowed. Fiona had felt this before, staring down the endless maw of Sobek, the crocodile eater of souls.

It was death. It was oblivion.

Fiona blinked, came out of the trace, and shuddered.

The woman opened a tiny leather book and consulted it. "Miss Fiona and Master Eliot Post." She made marks with a fountain pen. "On time." She spared them a glance. "By the skin of your teeth. Sit."

Fiona and Eliot obeyed, taking the only two unoccupied desks halfway to the front, on opposite sides of the center aisle.

The woman walked to the lectern. "I am Miss Westin, the Headmistress of the Paxington Institute," she said. "I wield absolute authority here."

No one spoke or shifted in their seats.

"You will find today's placement exam in your desks," Miss Westin continued, "along with three pencils and an eraser. See that you have these materials now. Do *not* break the seal on the examination."

Every student opened a rolltop desk.

In hers, Fiona found a stack of twenty pages secured with a cardboard band. All three pencils had been sharpened to a deadly point.

Miss Westin waited as the students settled down, keenly observing all. "I am delighted that you can follow instructions."

Fiona swallowed and heard the collective inhalation of the other students.

"You will find," Miss Westin said, "that at Paxington, we take our rules seriously. Last year, two students prematurely opened their examinations and were expelled."

Fiona felt like she was going to faint or throw up. Had Miss Westin briefed everyone on other rules before she and Eliot got here? What if they made a mistake?

She caught a motion in the corner of her eye.

The boy on her left waved to her. He was cute, with brown curly hair to his shoulders, and expressive eyes. He flashed a smile, nodded reassuringly, and then turned his attention back to Miss Westin.

Those simple gestures eased her fear. Fiona wanted to thank the boy, but thought better of doing so while Miss Westin spoke.

Miss Westin produced a silver pocket watch and flipped it open. "We shall begin the examination in sixty-four seconds. You will have one hour twenty minutes—which is four minutes per page—to finish. Budget your time accordingly."

One boy near the windows raised his hand. "If I break one of these marvelous writing implements?" he asked, brandishing a pencil.

Fiona recognized the Scottish accent. She squinted against the glare. Yes . . . it took a second for her to be sure . . . the blond hair, the roguish grin: it *was* Jeremy Covington, the boy she and Robert had found in the Valley of the New Year. He had escaped with them.

But the Valley was part of Purgatory. That meant Jeremy had been dead, didn't it?

"You have two spares, Mr. Covington," Miss Westin told him. "I suggest you break no more than three."

"And if I need the little boys' room, ma'am?" There was an undertone of smarm to his question.

Miss Westin stared him down. "Then I shall escort you myself to the urinal."

Jeremy's head dropped, and Fiona saw his ears redden.

"Hey," Eliot whispered. "Good luck!"

You, too, she mouthed back.

Four other older students entered the room.

Miss Westin nodded to them as they took positions in the corners. Miss Westin then glanced at her watch. "Begin . . . *now.*"

A hundred-some cardboard bands ripped, and a multitude of pages turned, sounding like a flock of birds taking wing.

The first section was on history. That should be a breeze. Fiona and Eliot had studied all of history from Earth's formation to global warming.

There were questions on Egyptian pharaohs, the reasons for the American Civil War, and influences on the Industrial Revolution.

She answered them all—could have done it in her sleep.

She turned to the next page, and there was a list of events to be chronologically ordered: Sargon and the formation of the Akkadian Empire . . . the discovery of the Americas . . . the founding of Rome by Romulus and Remus . . .

But Fiona froze when she got to, *King Arthur dies/departs for Avalon.*

The tales of King Arthur had been banned by Audrey. *"Too many fairy tales and lies,"* she had told them.

Fiona scrunched her lips in irritation. She marked this with a question mark and moved on. She'd have to come back later and figure it out.

The next section was on mathematics.

She blasted through geometry and algebra problems, and slowed only a little on the trigonometry.

Fiona thought this was going well, but she wished she had a watch.

She looked around but spotted no clock. She did see, however, that Miss Westin walked the aisles, and the four older student proctors watched everyone with hawklike intensity.

Fiona noticed that Eliot (now wearing his spectacles) was ahead on his test, scribbling away on some essay.

She was about to get back to her test when she saw a girl three rows over staring at her. The girl had acne and long brown hair that fell into her face. Fiona knew her . . . but couldn't quite recall from where or when.

She turned back to her test; Fiona didn't want anyone to think she was cheating.

She focused on the next section: English.

Fiona knew all the great authors, their themes, styles, and techniques. In her comparative essay, she quoted Shakespeare and Shelley and Shaw from memory. She paused to admire her dramatic cursive handwriting before she flipped to the next section.

All her confidence drained as she read the heading: *Magic—Theory, Engineering, and History.*

Magic, legends, fairy tales, fantasy, and science fiction—all the things specifically forbidden in their household for the last fifteen years.

She took a deep breath, willed herself to stay calm.

The first question was, *Name the four classical elements, and discuss Plato's and Aristotle's inclusion of the fifth element.*

Five elements? There were more than *one hundred* elements: hydrogen, helium, carbon, nitrogen . . . Were they talking about something else?

She wouldn't panic. Not yet.

She skipped ahead to see if there were easier ones.

The next question was, *Name seven mortal magical families. Compare and contrast. Bonus: Name three extinct families.*

Mortal magical families? She knew there were Immortals, fallen angels . . . but there were *more* collections of magical people?

The back of Fiona's throat burned. She paged ahead.

There were questions on alchemy, divination, and necromancy.

How was she ever going to figure any of this out?

Next to her she heard pages rustle. She saw Eliot flip back and forth through this section as well —but then he stopped, and started scribbling.

He was guessing. Had to be.

It was just like Eliot to try something reckless when he didn't know the answer.

But why not? Miss Westin hadn't said it was forbidden.

Fiona set the tip of her pencil on the page, but couldn't force herself to write. It felt like a lie.

Across the classroom, she heard whispers. She ignored these voices and flipped back to the history section and King Arthur. If she had to make a guess, she'd make an *educated* one.

The whispers, however, got louder. There was a tiny laugh.

She looked up and saw Jeremy Covington, eyes sparkling, talking to a redheaded girl next to him—both had their test booklets closed, pencils set neatly on top. They were done already!

Jeremy had been just as rude in Purgatory: trying to kiss Fiona when he hadn't been invited to. She had a feeling he was going to be three times the trouble alive that he had been dead.

She couldn't waste energy thinking about him. She had to—

"Time!" Miss Westin announced, and snapped her pocket watch shut. "Pencils up."

Every student instantly complied.

Fiona was furious. She'd never *not* finished a test before.

She looked over to Eliot. He gave a little apologetic shrug, as if to say, *What can you do?*

There had to be something. She could claim extenuating circumstances—explain to Miss Westin about their weird mother and how they were brought up.

Miss Westin and the proctors moved to the head of each row. They picked up the test and graded them right in front of everyone—marking wrong answers with a red pen.

Miss Westin finished grading first and scrawled a large *D* on the front.

"Insufficient," Miss Westin told the crestfallen boy. "We allow only those with the potential for excellence into Paxington, young man. You may leave."

The boy hung his head and skulked from the room.

This was so cruel. A trickle of molten iron anger flared within Fiona. She gripped the edge of her desk. Her nails dug into the wood, splitting the grain.

Ever since Fiona severed her appetite, she'd been unable to easily feel anything—except this sudden anger.

She imagined grabbing the desk and throwing it across the classroom and through the window. Destroying everything.

The shadow of Miss Westin crossed her gaze. "Test, Miss Post?"

Fiona's anger instantly quenched, as if it'd been plunged into liquid nitrogen. Chill bumps crawled over her arms.

"Yes, ma'am." She handed her the pages and noticed the Headmistress's hands were slender and bony.

Miss Westin flipped through the pages, barely making a mark until she got to the section on magic—and then she made a flurry of Xs.

It felt like the blood was draining out of her. Fiona wondered if she'd have the courage to stand and walk out of the classroom if she failed. What would she tell Audrey? Or the League?

Miss Westin turned to the cover, scribbled on it, and handed it back.

A fat red C stared at Fiona . . . which looked like it was laughing at her.

"Welcome to Paxington," Miss Westin said, and moved on.

Fiona stared at the grade. A C was barely passing, and failure by Audrey's standards. On the other hand—she exhaled—it was apparently sufficient to get her into Paxington.

She turned to Eliot for reassurance, but Miss Westin was grading his test, too.

She finished, leaving Eliot looking confused and worried . . . but also relieved. On the cover of his examination was a C+.

Fiona flashed him her test. "How did you do better?" she asked.

She *was* happy that he'd passed—Fiona couldn't even imagine what it would have been like if only one of them had gotten into Paxington—but how had he scored better?

Fiona watched as a girl behind her failed the test, and then two more students, who quickly picked up their bags and shuffled out of the room. Miss Westin was ruthless in her pronunciations to them: "failed . . . ," "insufficient . . . ," and ". . . you must now leave."

By the time she and the student proctors finished, one in ten had been dismissed.

Some students murmured: *"I heard one girl killed herself last year after she flunked out . . . ,"* and *"it's supposed to get* really *hard now,"* and *"fewer losers around here—good."*

That last cruel remark had come from the redheaded girl next to Jeremy. She looked inordinately pleased with her test, which she held up so everyone could see her A–.

Miss Westin returned to the lectern.

Everyone fell silent.

"Welcome, freshman class, to the Paxington Institute," Miss Westin told them. Sunlight reflected off her glasses and made her eyes appear luminous and preternaturally large. "We will now cover some basics."

She pushed on the blackboard, revealing another blackboard behind it covered with pie charts and handwriting so perfect it made Fiona's look like epileptic scratches. Miss Westin indicated the title: *Mandatory Courses for First-Semester Freshmen.*

"All freshmen have two classes their first semester," she explained. "Mythology 101, in which I shall be your instructor, and gym class, taught by Mr. Ma."

Mythology? Was that the equivalent of their family history? She and Eliot might actually learn something practical about their world.

But gym class? Calisthenics, running, and softball? The thought of wearing skimpy shorts and a T-shirt and competing with other girls gave Fiona pause. And what about Eliot?

She glanced at him. His glasses had come off, and he looked more pale than normal. He hated sports. He'd always been smaller than boys his age. Cee said he would grow quick once puberty hit, and one day be tall and strong.

Fiona doubted that. Eliot would always be her "little brother," no matter what.

The redhead next to Jeremy Covington raised her hand. "Ma'am?" She had a Scottish accent as well, but far more refined. "What about electives? Will two courses be enough?"

Miss Westin fixed her with a stare. "These two classes, I assure you, will be sufficient. One quarter of the freshman class fail and do not continue on to their sophomore year."

The Headmistress pointed to a pie chart and a bell-shaped curve on the blackboard. "Success is based on a strict academic curve and your ranked performance in gym class." She crossed her hands. "At Paxington, only excellence is allowed."

That seemed grossly unfair. If one quarter failed *every* year—Fiona did the math—then only 42 percent made it through to their senior year.

But maybe competition wouldn't be such a bad thing. It would give her a chance to test herself, and prove that she could succeed outside Audrey's protected sphere.

"If you feel the need to be further challenged," Miss Westin continued, "elective courses are available for freshmen who survive their first semester and receive As on their midterms."

Survive?

Fiona and Eliot shared a look. Her word choice seemed deliberate . . . like some students might actually die.

Eliot definitely appeared unhealthy as he digested this statement. Fiona suddenly didn't feel so good, either.

"You will now have a break to stretch and use the restrooms before the next portion of the placement process," Miss Paxton said. "Afterward, you will be given a tour of the campus."

Fiona exhaled and heard the rest of the students do the same.

"This is so weird," Eliot said. He stood and stretched. "I feel like I don't belong here . . . but at the same time, I don't know, it's like we do."

She knew exactly what he meant. Part of her just wanted to go back home and hide. Another part of her wanted to meet some of these people from other magical families. Well . . . except that Jeremy Covington.

The other students mingled and talked, moving through the room like free-floating planets in orbit about one another, and then clustered around maybe a half-dozen individuals who appeared to be the centers of social gravity.

Fiona spotted the boy who had smiled at her and made her feel welcome . . . but he was across the room now, chatting with some other boys and laughing.

Fiona and Eliot stood by themselves.

Would they always be social outcasts? If only the others knew they were in the League of Immortals—that Eliot was an Immortal hero, and she was a goddess-in-training.

But, of course, telling anyone the most interesting thing about themselves was forbidden. So typical.

"We should strike up a conversation," she told her brother.

"What do you want to talk about?" he asked.

"I mean with the others."

"Oh . . . ," Eliot said, looking a tad hurt. "Yeah, sure." He brightened. "You know, I thought I saw someone I recognized." He looked around.

"So did I," Fiona said. "That girl with the brown hair."

Eliot squinted. "No . . . I saw this other girl, a blonde, kind of looked like Julie."

"Julie Marks?" Fiona said, surprised.

Poor Eliot. Daydreaming again.

Fiona then spotted a group marching toward them, and leading them was that redhead and Jeremy Covington.

The last time Fiona had seen Jeremy, he wore a lion mask—which was then knocked off when Robert Farmington plastered him with a snowball. That was in Purgatory, at a cursed never-ending party called the Valley of the New Year.

Jeremy stopped before her and Eliot, and bowed so his long blond hair cascaded off his shoulders.

"Dearest Fiona," he said. "Never in a million years did I expect to see you again. I so wanted to thank you for saving me from my long imprisonment."

Eliot nudged her and shot her a look that said, *Who is this?*

"Jeremy, this is my brother, Eliot."

Eliot offered his hand for Jeremy to shake.

Jeremy clasped it and squeezed. Eliot winced.

"Damn my manners," Jeremy said. "I am Lord Jeremy of the Clan Covington." He gestured to the redheaded girl next to him. "This lass is my cousin Sarah." He spared a glance at the students around him, as though considering whether to introduce them as well, but then shrugged as if they were inconsequential.

Sarah's long hair, elegantly tied up, was the color of tangerines. She had dimpled cheeks, freckled skin, and Fiona could see the effect she had on the boys.

"Post . . . ," Sarah said. "I'm not familiar with your family's name. Were you sponsored into Paxington?"

This sounded like an innocent question on the surface, but Fiona sensed a hint of condescension underneath.

"No one sponsored us," Fiona said. She changed subjects to avoid the

League and its code of silence. "I don't understand something," she said to Jeremy. "You were in Purgatory. There are only supposed to be dead people there. How can you be here . . . alive?"

Jeremy laughed. "No, my dear Fiona. Not dead. Never dead. It would take more than a trifling thing like Purgatory to stop a Covington."

6

NOT A POPULARITY CONTEST

Eliot took a step back from Jeremy and Sarah Covington. They were smiling, but he got the feeling it wasn't because they liked him. More like they were making a joke.

Fiona was no help. She wasn't paying attention to them; instead, she scanned the other students.

"You see," Jeremy said, continuing with his story, "the year was 1853, and I was chasing a leprechaun."

"What's a leprechaun?" Eliot asked.

Jeremy's and Sarah's smiles faltered, and the students around them gave Eliot a weird look, like he'd just asked what oxygen was.

Then Jeremy grinned again. "So true! Who really knows what they be, eh? Pots of gold and three wishes—balderdash, I entirely agree. That's what I set out to prove: The Fey be not the living legends all claim."

Eliot nodded, realizing this was something he ought to have known.

"So the thing led me on a merry chase through every swamp and graveyard in Scotland," Jeremy said. "Thought she could lose me with a romp through the Middle Realms, but I followed her right to the bloody center of Purgatory . . . where I got a bit distracted."

Middle Realms. Eliot made a mental note about that, but didn't ask any more questions. No need to look like a complete idiot.[6]

6. Middle Realms (noun). Archaic usage refers to the Purgatory lands betwixt Heaven and Hell (sometimes Earth, depending on the context). Modern usage expanded to mean *all* realms between the Pearly Gates of Heaven and the First Fathomless Abyss of Hell (considered

"You got trapped in the Valley of the New Year," Fiona said, her attention returning to the conversation.

"Why, yes, dearest Fiona," Jeremy replied. "Then you came along and found the doorway out of that wretched place. Rescued me, body and soul."

Sarah's heart-shaped face brightened, and she reassessed Fiona. "So this is the girl who brought you back? The Clan Covington is in your debt, miss."

Fiona fiddled with her hair. "It was nothing, really."

"Wait . . . ," Eliot said. "You were trapped for over a hundred and fifty years?"

"Aye." Jeremy shrugged. "You might say I'm starting my freshman year at Paxington a tad delayed."

The Headmistress returned. A dozen older students entered with her, and some moved to the windows, drawing long black curtains, while others turned up the gas lamps on the opposite wall.

Miss Westin removed her glasses. She looked different in gaslight: younger, more animated, and vital. A faint smile crossed her pale lips.

"Team selection is starting," Sarah said, and touched Jeremy's arm.

"Aye." Jeremy tensed and cast a quick glance at Fiona and Eliot.

Eliot didn't like the sound of this "team" stuff. He wasn't good in groups.

Miss Westin cleared her throat, and everyone in the room was quiet. "Freshman team selection," she said, "is a tradition that dates to the foundation of this school.[7]

"It tests your skills of diplomacy and strategic thinking. I advise you to combine disparate elements to make something greater than the sum of its parts." Every trace of warmth and color drained from Miss Westin's expression. "This should *not* be a popularity contest."

She motioned to the side door, and more upperclassman entered, carrying claw-footed tables. They set them at the head of the room. On each table were silver trays containing gold coins.

---

the upper and lower boundaries of the known worlds). *Lexicon Primus.* Paxington Institute Press LLC, San Francisco.

7. Freshman team selection at Paxington originates from the gladiatorial arenas of the Roman Empire. Slaves who won their freedom could leave or continue as paid gladiators. Such free fighters would often participate in re-creations of famous battles, but unlike slave gladiators, they were allowed to form their own teams. The victorious teams were glorified throughout the Empire (much like modern-day sports teams), bearing names like Hunting Wolf, Golden Eagle, and the Bloodied Hand. *Your Guide to the Paxington Institute (Freshman Edition).* Paxington Institute Press LLC, San Francisco.

Miss Westin gestured to each tray and said, "Knight . . . Wolf . . . Dragon . . . Hand . . . Eagle . . . and Scarab—in their various incarnations. These will be the symbols about which you must unite with seven other students."

Eliot glanced at the Paxington crest on his jacket. Those same symbols hovered over his heart, part of the school's history.

He looked at Fiona. She shrugged, looking as awkward and uncomfortable as he felt—like they were two guppies in a tank of piranhas.

Jeremy swaggered up to a table. "I, Jeremy Covington, of the Clan Covington, Keeper of the Keys of the Three Stones, hereby claim Scarab as mine." He plucked up one of the coins and showed it to everyone. Upon it gleamed a golden scarab like something lifted off an Egyptian pharaoh's tomb.

Eliot whispered to Fiona, "Are we supposed to go up there and take one of those things?"

Before she could answer, a tall pale boy strode to a different table. "I, Donald of the Family Van Wyck, claim Wolf as my standard."

Sarah Covington moved to Jeremy's side and proudly took a scarab token.

And then another two girls and three more boys moved forward to various tables.

"Logan from the Kaleb brood takes Green Dragon."

"I, Xavier of the DeBoars, claim the Open Hand."

"The Family Pern is Soaring Eagle and challenges all who say otherwise!"

The room erupted into chaos as almost every other student moved for the tables—talking and arguing and snatching up tokens.

Eliot spied that blond girl he had seen before. There was just a flash of her face, and she vanished into the crowds. She *did* look a little like Julie Marks, the girl he had fallen for this summer. Julie was long gone, but he never stopped thinking about her.

Then he spotted another girl with long uncombed brown hair. She looked familiar, too. Maybe that was the girl Fiona had mentioned.

The girl caught Eliot's gaze and quickly looked away.

"Eliot!" some boy called out.

Eliot spun about, trying to locate the voice, but with all the students pushing and embroiled in heated discussions, Eliot couldn't find him.

He was disoriented and completely out of his depth. "This is some sort of test, too," he said to Fiona. "Part of the placement exam."

"I get that," Fiona replied. She wasn't looking at him.

Eliot followed her gaze and spotted a boy who approached Jeremy and Sarah. He had a tousle of curly brown hair, an easy smile, and looked totally relaxed here. He bowed to Sarah and struck up a conversation with the Covingtons.

"Let's see how it's done," Eliot suggested.

But Fiona had already started to move toward them.

The boy told Jeremy, "I was unaware the Covington clan claimed Scarab."

"Goes all the way back to the Freemasons," Jeremy explained, his voice a mixture of insult and amazement that someone would question his claim. He looked the other boy over. "Be that the challenge, Mr.—?"

The other boy spotted Eliot and Fiona as they approached, and his smile warmed. "No challenge," he said. "I'm Mitch from the Stephenson family. I wanted to join."

"Stephenson?" Jeremy's eyes widened a fraction. "Indeed! A family with as noble a pedigree as the Covingtons. It would be an honor, sir." He shook Mitch's hand.

"As noble as they are clever and handsome," Sarah added.

"My cousin Sarah," Jeremy said.

Sarah offered her hand to Mitch, which he clasped. Eliot noted slight disappointment on Sarah's face, as if she had wanted him to kiss it or something.

Fiona pulled Eliot closer and said, "We should join Scarab."

"You told me this Jeremy guy was kind of creepy. I'm not sure he or his cousin likes us."

Eliot glanced around the room. No other team had three people on it yet, and a few of the discussions had evolved into shouting matches.

"But they do seem to know the ropes around here," Fiona said.

Three other freshmen approached Jeremy and Sarah. They spoke briefly, but Jeremy held up both his hands and shook his head. The other students left, muttering a few words that Eliot (even with his extensive vocabulary) had never heard before.

"Definitely Anglo-Saxon etymology," Fiona told him, apparently also curious about these new words. She nudged Eliot. "We should ask them now. I don't want to be the last ones picked."

Eliot reluctantly stepped forward. She was right: Anything was better than getting picked last. Or worse, what if all the other groups became so full that he and Fiona had to go on *different* teams?

"Ah, Fiona." Jeremy extended a hand to her as she neared. "Please join us"—a quick glance at Eliot—"and, of course, your brother."

His gaze, however, slid over Eliot like he was something one saw on a dinner plate, unpalatable, but which had to be tasted in order to get dessert.

Sarah eyed Eliot as well, leaned closer to Jeremy, and said something.

"Yes," Jeremy told her. "I'm quite sure."

Eliot loathed this. Was he getting on the team only because Jeremy liked his sister?

He should've been picked because he was Eliot Post, Immortal hero-in-training, Master of "The Symphony of Existence," son of the Eldest Fate and the Prince of Darkness!

If only he could tell them . . . he would've been their *first* choice.

He could turn them down, too. He would have challenged one of those supposedly blue-blooded mortal magicians, taken one of their big-deal tokens, and started his own team.

But this daydream faded as the girl Eliot had seen before caught his attention.

She walked straight toward him. Her long hair fell into her face, and her gaze firmly fixed upon the floor . . . reminding him of the way Fiona used to be so shy. Yet, without looking, she somehow managed to navigate through the crowds, halting before Eliot. "Hey . . . ," she said. "I never got the chance to thank you or your sister." She looked up, and the hair fell from her face.

The girl was unremarkable save for her eyes. They were dark, wild, and defiant—like black coals, smoldering. The last time Eliot saw them, the world had been on fire, and they were running for their lives through a burning carnival, being chased by madman Perry Millhouse.

"Amanda?" he said. "It's Amanda Lane, right?"

"Yeah." Amanda looked back to the floor.

"Are you okay?" Fiona asked. "We never got a chance to see you after . . ."

"Sure, I'm great," she said, although the way she struggled to get her words out, Eliot guessed otherwise. "Your uncle got me back to my family. He was great. He talked to them. Explained how I got kidnapped. How you guys saved me. I dunno, my parents never mentioned it after that."

Eliot wondered what Uncle Henry had done. He had an uneasy feeling something more was going on with Amanda Lane and the League.

"Then I got the scholarship," Amanda said, "everything paid by Mr. Mimes. He said I belonged here." She looked around. "I'm not so sure this was a good idea."

Something was weird about this. Why would Uncle Henry bring a normal girl here after she'd almost been killed once by the League?

Eliot glanced at Fiona, and she nodded back, thinking the same thing.

"Stick close to us," Fiona whispered to Amanda.

Eliot was going to add his own words of reassurance, but all thoughts drained from his head when he spotted the blond girl who had caught his attention before . . . as she moved toward them.

She most definitely was not Julie Marks, however. This girl was taller. Her hair was pure platinum blond that curled into ringlets about her face. Her skirt seemed shorter than the other girls'. She moved with a liquid grace that made Eliot's heart beat faster.

In fact, every boy watched her as she stopped before their table.

"M'lady," Jeremy said, and bowed ridiculously low before her. Mitch gave her a cordial bow, which provoked a raised eyebrow from this new girl. Sarah and Fiona simultaneously crossed their arms.

"Would you do us the honor of joining our team?" Jeremy asked. "We have two from glorious Clan Covington, a lad from the most ancient Stephenson family, Fiona and Eliot Post . . ." Jeremy searched for some embellishment or title to add to their family name, but failed.

The girl smiled. It was Julie's hundred-watt smile, and yet so unlike Julie's, because while this one was just as dazzling, it was also somehow cruel.

"Your solicitation is as empty as your head," she told Jeremy. "You know not whom you ask, your eyes too full with too obvious intentions."

This insult seemed to please Sarah.

Jeremy opened his mouth to defend himself, but the blond girl ran right over him with her words: "I am Jezebel, Protector of the Burning Orchards and Duchess of the Many-Colored Jungle of the Infernal Poppy King-doms, Handmaiden to the Mistress of Pain . . . and bringer of doom to mortals such as you." Her smile never faltered. "*Now* ask me to join, if you dare."

The room went silent, and everyone watched.

She was an Infernal? Like Beelzebub? Or their father?

Was that why Eliot felt that he knew her? He should be wary, but he was also fascinated.

"Aye," Jeremy said. His eyes could not meet hers. "There's been no In-fernal protégée at Paxington for three hundred years. Your terrible power would honor us, Lady Jezebel."

Jezebel huffed a laugh. "You *are* a rogue, Covington. I appreciate that." She looked over Sarah, moving on quickly, as if the girl were nonexistent. Next she considered Mitch, who had the strength to meet her gaze, and she nodded. She then glanced at Eliot and Fiona—just for an instant, but clearly seeing something in them that she liked, because her eyes widened with interest. Her gaze traversed to Amanda, scrutinizing the unremarkable girl the longest.

"You have an interesting mix of blood and power on this team," Jezebel told Jeremy. "I suppose it will do as much as any other collection of bumbling mortals here."

Jeremy beamed, extremely pleased with this new addition to their group. He shot a glance at Amanda, probably wondering if Jezebel assumed she was on their team . . . and if he had to accept this new unexpected teammate because the Infernal obviously liked her. He sighed and with great reluctance slipped Amanda a scarab token and then looked away.

Jezebel moved to the edge of the table and, with a dramatic flounce, sat on it, crossing her legs so her skirt flashed pale, slender thigh.

A full-blooded Infernal on their team. Eliot could only imagine what kinds of advantages and disadvantages that would give them. On the other hand, he wasn't sure what kind of game they would be playing that they'd *need* an Infernal.

Weren't Infernals supposed to be unpredictable? Cheaters? Dangerous?

Students clambered about their table—all now asking to join. The sheer mass of the crowd pushed Eliot, Amanda, and Fiona back. Apparently, the Paxington students appreciated the power of an Infernal more than they feared one.

"Let chance decide," Jezebel said. She reached for the platter on the table, selected the last golden scarab token from the pile—and flung it across the room.

Before Jeremy could protest, students scrabbled and pushed to get the token as it clattered across the floor.

Jezebel laughed as she watched boys and girls wrestle for the coin.

Eliot watched, too, and saw someone he recognized tossing aside students like he was an experienced wrestler. But the gold coin rolled away from him—kicked back and forth by the others.

This had to be the person who had called to Eliot earlier.

. . . and if he were on Team Scarab, Eliot knew he'd have at least one friend.

Let *only* chance decide? Eliot would see about *that*.

He twisted around, unzipped his backpack, and opened his violin case.

With one eye, he watched the scarab coin wobble along the floor, spinning, then kicked up, bouncing over the desks.

Eliot quietly plucked Lady Dawn's strings.

The heat from his old infection burned along his wrist. He felt air move about him, and saw the coin jump to his notes—ricocheting this way and that—half random, but partially under his command now as well.

It drunkenly rolled toward the boy he knew—who dived for it!

Others leaped for the coin, too, dog-piling into a heap.

Eliot held his breath, hoping.

He quickly surveyed his team: Fiona, his ever-irritating sister; Amanda Lane, more of a social outcast than even himself; Jeremy and Sarah Covington, whom Eliot didn't like one bit; Mitch Stephenson, a nice guy; and the Infernal Jezebel, who stared at Eliot and his backpack, leaning forward, one hand over her throat, fascinated.

. . . and one last teammate.

The boy stood from the pile of students, holding aloft the golden scarab.

He turned and faced them, grinning, blood on his split lip. His James Dean appearance looked out of place in a Paxington jacket instead of his normal leather one.

Fiona gasped.

It was Robert Farmington.

7

THE FOOL'S OPENING MOVE

enry Mimes changed names like other men changed their hats. Along with his nom de guerre shifts, he altered his personality, often becoming the Name.

Earlier this morning, he had been the Messenger. Now, though, as he stood close to Audrey in the private elevator that whisked them to the top of the Transamerica Building, he felt an impulse to try on the Big Bad Wolf.

Audrey wore a dark silk blouse and looked as she had in the old days, clad in similar cold colors, offsetting her alabaster skin. The Pale Rider. She and her sisters were the first of them to show greatness; she was the first woman he had ever called a "goddess."

She ignored him.

Lovely? Yes. Even more important: unattainable. Audrey was as perfect as a woman could be.

Her diamond earrings cast a scattering of reflections over her shoulders and throat . . . her skin was so lustrous. One touch and he knew he could warm that stone-cold flesh. How lonely she must be.

His hand rose toward her.

But he sensed the lines of deadly force radiating from her.

Henry reconsidered and dropped his hand. Perhaps the Fool best suited today's dismal occasion.

"Did you know," Henry asked her, "that San Franciscans call the Transamerica Building—?"

"Pyramid," Audrey corrected him. "It is the Transamerica *Pyramid*."

"Quite right. They also call it the Great Alien Ring Toss. Others say it looks like an ice cream cone stuck into the earth."

Audrey turned, raised an eyebrow, but said nothing.

So much for his attempt to lighten the Lady's mood.

Henry dug into his pocket and retrieved his silver hip flask, unstoppered it, paused to savor the scent of a thousand flowers, and then took a nip. The liquor exploded through his thoughts, leaving curlicues of smoke and memory. He exhaled the vapors.

In truth, Henry's mood needed lightening as much as Audrey's did. He was attempting to think six moves ahead of the Council *and* the Infernal Board—a worthy challenge for any fool.

Or perhaps he was taking this affair with the twins too seriously?

He took another drink and offered the flask to Audrey. This was just for politeness' sake. Never in a million years would Audrey join him. The sun and moon were more likely to unexpectedly eclipse.

Audrey mashed the EMERGENCY STOP button and took the flask.

How wonderful! Someone other than himself had done something surprising.

Audrey inhaled the bouquet, and her pupils dilated. "It would be less dangerous to carry refined plutonium through the city than real Soma." She took a long pull, to Henry's dismay, drinking nearly half. A rare blush spread outward from her neck.

She handed the flask back and said, "I assume you have countless layers of trickery planned with regards to my children?"

Henry put on his best *How could you ever think such a thing? You wound me, woman* look, and then stammered, "If only you knew how much I care for Eliot and Fiona."

"I know," she said, "but sometimes, Henry, people would be better off without any of us 'caring' about them."

She set a hand on his chest—the lightest of touches.

Henry wasn't sure where this was going, for Audrey never casually touched anything. He backed into a corner of the elevator.

Audrey pressed closer and remained with him. Her fingers dug into his black turtleneck. "I sense your heart beating and feeling. You do care for them . . . as much as any of us can."

She grasped a handful of his shirt.

The threads in the weave constricted about Henry's ribs.

"As long as by 'caring for Eliot and Fiona' you mean you have *their* best interests in mind—and not *yours*."

Henry started to protest, but found the air gone from his lungs.

"Did you know Fiona has learned the trick of cutting with string?" Audrey asked. "She has yet to discover that it can also be done with *many* strings at once . . . like woven cloth."

Audrey pulled his shirt taut.

Henry had a sudden vision of Audrey ripping the shirt from his torso—like some stage magician trick—only this would not be trickery . . . and what would remain of his torso would fit though a martini strainer.

Audrey let go.

She tapped the EMERGENCY STOP button. The elevator continued up.

Henry recovered and straightened his turtleneck. He took one more swig from his flask.

The elevator doors parted, and cold fresh air blasted them.

They stepped onto the uppermost secret level of the Transamerica Pyramid.

The aluminum shutters on the angled walls were open, and mid-morning light streamed into the space. This level of the pointy part of the landmark building had been filled with dust bunnies before he'd had it renovated. The space had been redecorated with ultramodern velvet couches (designed in the 1960s, when there actually had been a vision of an ultramodern future).

Of course, the family was already here.

Lucia, Henry noticed first—Audrey's sister, the Middle Fate, and sometimes called (although he thought with the greatest irony), Blind Justice. Then there was Gilbert, known first as Gilgamesh, whom Henry fondly remembered as the Once-King. Kino was next, the Guardian of the Underworld, dour and sour and unsociable as ever. And last was old Cornelius, what was left of the last of the Titans, the once mighty Cronos.

Lucia sat opposite the elevator, a strategic location where she could chastise those who came late. She wore a gray power business suit with bloodred pinstripes. It was conservatively sexy. The steel in her gaze communicated to Henry that she would tolerate none of his usual tomfoolery today.

So he would have to invent all-new tomfoolery for the occasion.

Gilbert crossed the room, a bottle of tequila in one hand, two glasses in the other. He poured Henry a tumbler, and one for himself. "Too auspicious a day to face sober, Cousin."

Henry nodded and took the glass. Gilbert looked disheveled, his golden beard wild and dark circles under his eyes.

But when Henry sipped the drink, he found it disappointingly only iced tea.

Gilbert maintained pretenses, still silently on Henry's side in this matter . . . part of their very, very long-range strategy. Henry was relieved to know that the First King Gilgamesh was still as smart as ever.

"Have you heard?" Gilbert gestured with his drink to a corner bathed in sunlight. "We have a *special* guest with us today."

Henry squinted. Camouflaged in the radiance was Dallas.

Poor Dallas had been kicked off the Council last week, replaced with her older sister, Audrey. Lucia had thought her too soft. That was a mistake, Henry feared, that Lucia would one day pay for dearly.

Dallas wore a sundress of translucent sea green, high-heeled sandals, and carried a Versace clutch. The breeze made her dress and golden hair ripple.

Henry took a step toward her, irresistibly drawn to Beauty . . . but then noted the look in her eyes was pure liquid-nitrogen venom. She was, of course, here under protest at the behest of a Council's summons. Henry understood it all in that instant—her part to play in their schemes and the intersibling politics—and checked his motion toward her.

The door to the emergency stairs banged open, and Aaron entered, lugging a duffel in one hand. He had marched up the forty-nine floors without breaking a sweat.

Aaron made a point of slamming the door. He dropped his duffel with a floor-shaking thud, shot everyone a glare, and then sat across from Lucia, propping his cowboy boots on the couch.

Tall, dark Kino spared him a deprecating glance. He then straightened the lily in the lapel of his black leather overcoat and turned to Audrey. "So good to see you, my dear. I think you shall be a voice of reason among this collection of fools."

"One hopes," Audrey replied as she settled next to Lucia.

"Shall we start?" Cornelius mumbled. "I believe everyone is finally present."

Cornelius was on the floor. He wore an I LOST MY HEART IN SF T-shirt, shorts, and athletic socks embroidered with tiny cable cars pulled up to his knobby knees. Good for him. Playing the tourist, preserving his childlike sense of discovery, was likely what kept the oldest living thing alive.

"Yes, all present," Lucia said, and smoothed back her hair, tying it up in a knot. She rang her tiny silver bell. "I hereby call the Council of Elders of the League of Immortals to order. *Narro, Audio, Perceptum.*"

Lucia set a hand delicately next to Audrey. "Can you give us an update on the twins? Are they well? How have they done at Paxington so far?" The illusion of her concern was nearly perfect.

"Of course," Audrey replied.

Henry drifted from the center of the room to the open shutters for fresh air.

"All has been arranged with Miss Westin," Audrey explained. "I've received word that Eliot and Fiona passed their entrance and placement exams."

"I dislike the twins at Paxington," Kino said, his lips compressing into a line.

"It is neutral ground," Lucia replied, "open only to students and staff. It is the safest place from the Infernals. Besides, Eliot and Fiona may learn a thing or two."

"It is Paxington's neutrality that concerns me," Kino told her. "Now is the time for *choosing* sides—the right side—*our* side! Paxington harbors those who would not join us, and over the centuries, they have grown strong within those walls. Why? To preserve the magical knowledge of the world? Are any of us that naïve? They await an opportune time to strike."

Cornelius cleared his throat. "It is a possibility," he said. "Their Headmistress, however, is the chief enforcer of the 1852 Treaty of the Under-Realms. She alone keeps the peace with the London Confederation of the Unliving. Move against her, and I fear that would be undone."

Kino shook his head. "Even more reason for the twins not to be there: Her kind should never be permitted near a child."

"Do not forget their Gatekeeper, Harlan Dells," Aaron told him. "Quite the feat, dismantling his own bridge as he left us. One does not lightly engage in combat with the One Who Can Be in Many Places . . . not unless you're proposing a full-scale war?"[8]

8. The Bifröst Bridge connected Earth (Midgard) with the realm of the gods (Asgard). It was defended by the god Heimdallr (aka Heimdall, who will alert the Immortals to Ragnarök). Early myths depict the Bifröst Bridge as a shimmering rainbow that can appear and vanish. Modern interpretations suggest a dimensional shift. The theory lends credence to the rumor of the bridge being destroyed and the remnants used in the walls of the San Francisco Paxington Institute (which anecdotally seems to move in and out of phase with this world). *Gods of the First and Twenty-first Century, Volume 6, Modern Myths.* Zypheron Press Ltd., Eighth Edition.

Lucia rolled her eyes. "The Council is *not* debating this. Paxington keeps the mortal magical families complacent. Destroy their precious school, and they might unite, however unlikely, and threaten our power base. No, we require stability at the moment. After we deal with the Infernal issue . . . then we shall revisit Paxington."

Kino sighed, but then nodded.

"What team are they on?" Henry asked, hoping to deflect the subject.

"Scarab," Audrey replied.

"Hmm." Aaron stroked his Genghis Khan mustache. "That's a Covington heritage title. Must be one of those slippery characters in the mix. Not a bad thing: they'll know how to handle the other students. I still dislike the whole point of their gym class, and that Mr. Ma."

"You must get over your competitive streak with that man," Henry told him.

"He and I have unsettled business," Aaron muttered.

"In any event," Audrey continued, "Miss Westin was recalcitrant to keep their identities hidden . . . but she eventually came around to the Council's point of view."

Henry saw in the distance, nestled next to Presidio Park, the Paxington campus: copper-capped spires, the clock tower, manicured lawns, and sparkling quad. A bank of fog rolled past, and the school was hidden again.

Kino was correct: Paxington had its drawbacks. But Audrey was also wise to place the children there. It served many purposes: training them in the realities of their world, keeping them on neutral ground, where they would have the best protection possible . . . as well as being advantageous to *Henry's* schemes.

Henry had also approached the "recalcitrant" Headmistress of Paxington, the lonely and terrible Miss Westin. He adjusted the collar of his turtleneck and shuddered as he considered the price he had paid to engage her services.

"I am worried," Lucia said, "over the lack of Infernal response to our declaration of the twins' indoctrination. There's typically *some* response from their Board—even if it is insulting negation."

"It is the silence of collusion," Kino said, and narrowed his eyes at Henry. "I have no doubt they are taking action against us."

Aaron sat up. "On this I agree. We should act."

"But what action can we take against the other family?" Cornelius asked. "Our own neutrality treaty blocks us."

"We must cement the children's loyalties to the League," Audrey told them. "They are still young and impressionable. You must act to mold them before they are shaped by others."

Kino steepled his hands as he considered this.

Henry saw an opportunity. "I suggest we show the twins how wonderful it can be to be in the League." In a grand gesture he raised his hands to the sky. "So far—and I'm sure, Audrey, you had best of intentions—they have been saddled with nothing but rules and regulations."

Audrey turned to him, and her short silver hair flashed like a halo. The look in her eyes, however, was anything but angelic.

"I offer my humble services to take young Master Eliot under my wing," Henry continued. "Nothing overt, I assure you. Just the odd trip to the ice-cream parlor. Perhaps the occasional man-to-man chat so he has a proper role model."

They all gave Henry a look.

"Oh, very well," Henry said with a shrug. "I'm sure there are others better suited to being a role model. My point is still valid."

"I agree," Lucia said. "We have already done some thinking along those lines. Henry is a suitable choice as emissary to young Eliot."

Henry wasn't sure where Lucia was going with this. Her agreeing with anything he said set off alarm bells.

"Additionally," Lucia continued, "Fiona will need someone to shepherd her, and convince her it is in her best interest to align with the League." She looked pointedly at Dallas. "Someone with a similar youthful exuberance . . ."

Dallas had been pretending to ignore her, looking at the vista of San Francisco, but she turned and said, "Is that why I was 'invited' to this meeting?" She scoffed. "Leave me out of your scheming, Sister. I'm not the Council's puppet. And I have no intention of candy-coating what it means to be Immortal—let alone a member of this League."

"Very well," Lucia replied. "No one is forcing you. We will find someone more willing." She tapped one manicured nail to her lower lip. "I wonder if Ish is available."

Dallas's eyes widened at this, and her hands curled into fists. "That Xanax-popping harlot? You can't be serious."

"We do need someone," Lucia told her. "And she is capable of having fun. . . ."

Dallas stifled a squeak of rage.

Outside the sun grew brighter, and the intense light made the metal walls ping as they heated and expanded.

Henry took a step away from both women.

It had been a mistake to collect all three Fates in one location— explosive, primer, and detonator all in one neat package.

Dallas sighed, however, and hung her head. "Very well. I'll do it."

"Excellent," Lucia purred. "Do I have a second to the motion for Henry to mentor Eliot, and Dallas to bring along Fiona?"

"I will second," Gilbert said.

Lucia looked surprised that her recently estranged lover would so readily agree to her suggestion.

Henry worried that he had overplayed their hand. . . .

Lucia nonetheless continued: "Shall we put it to a vote?"

"Wait," Kino said, his dark, ever-skeptical eyes taking them all in. "Only with honey will you bribe the children? There is a more potent method to convince them our ways are best. With fear."

Aaron stood, color flushing his already ruddy cheeks.

Cornelius made little calming-down motions with his hands. "Let us hear what he has to say."

Aaron nodded and sank back down.

Kino smiled. "Show them the benefit of the League, yes, I agree. But also show them the opposite side of the coin: the *disadvantages* of the *other* family."

Audrey nodded, understanding. "You want to scare the hell out of them," she said. "Literally. Perhaps . . ." Her features hardened. "But *only* scare them, Kino."

The two stared at each other a moment, and then Kino blinked and gave a tiny bow. "Of course."

"And who better to do this," Lucia asked, "but the Lord of the Dead and Guardian of the Gateway to Hell?"

A chill spread down Henry's spine. Indeed, Lucia and Kino had schemes of their own hatching.

But there were worse alternatives to so influencing young Eliot and Fiona—ones no one here spoke of—yet. If the Infernals brought them over to their side . . . the League had signed Warrants of Death for both children.

The bright sunlight faded. Iron gray clouds covered the sky.

This was a possibility Henry would do anything to avoid, or at least delay its inevitability for as long as he could.

TOUR

Fiona waited outside in the courtyard. She welcomed the sunlight on her skin after being cooped up for so long. The classroom in Bristlecone Hall had felt like a tomb.

Without crossing into its shade, she examined the tree in the yard. It was a bristlecone pine with a silver trunk and skeletal arms that only occasionally sprouted a pine needle. This species could live for thousands of years, like her family.

Was she Immortal as well? Fiona couldn't even imagine what it would be like to be 16 years old, let alone 116 . . . or 1,600.

The other freshman teams stood together in loose cliques across the courtyard: Green Dragon, Black Wolf, White Knight, Soaring Eagle, and others. They talked and stole glances at each other.

Sixteen teams. Eight students in each yielded a total of 128 in their freshman class . . . of which a quarter, thirty-two of them, would fail.

Fiona had a bad feeling about this. Why couldn't school just be about reading and learning? Why was it so cutthroat?

She eyed that Jezebel girl, an Infernal—and so did almost every boy. They clustered around her, all smiling and flirting and wanting to know her better.

She did look a *little* like Julie Marks, but this girl was taller and older. Maybe Julie had had an older sister who'd crawled out of Hell.

And why was she getting all the attention? Because she was pretty. Beyond pretty, really: Jezebel had a mystical look, like she had just stepped out of a masterwork oil painting, luminous and perfect.

Fiona smoothed her skirt and jacket, thankful for the school uniforms. If she'd had to wear Cee's homemade clothes, the social chasm between her and the rest of these girls would have been light-years wide.

That may have been the most unfair thing of all. Fiona was a *goddess,* for crying out loud, and yet somehow she still managed to look *less* than ordinary.

Eliot shuffled closer to her. "What kind of mascot is a scarab?" he asked.

She tore her gaze away from Jezebel. "The Egyptian pharaohs used scarabs as symbols of eternal life."[9]

Fiona was about to engage Eliot in debate over hieroglyphics (her knowledge was rudimentary, but Eliot's was nonexistent) when Robert Farmington emerged from the restrooms, cleaned up from the scuffle to get that last token.

She brightened as he walked toward her.

He looked like he owned the entire school. That was so Robert's style.

But he also looked out of place in a Paxington school uniform—like someone dressed for Halloween. She half expected to see his motorcycle parked in the corridors.

Fiona didn't have a clue what Robert was doing here, but she didn't care.

She moved to meet him, and started to reach out and hug him, but that felt wrong in front of all these people . . . and besides, Robert made no such move toward her, stopping a short distance away.

"You didn't call after our vacation," she whispered. "Was there trouble?"

Robert looked away. "Some," he said. "After I got kicked out of the League, I had to lie low for a while. Mr. Mimes says I can't go back to work for him . . . so he got me in here. Kind of a going-away present."

"You're on your own?"

"Yeah," Robert said. "I've always been on my own. It's no big deal."

Robert spotted Eliot and waved. His gaze then fell upon Jezebel and darkened.

Fiona felt something wrong—very wrong—between her and Robert.

---

9. Scarab beetles bury dung balls for later use, which is invaluable, as this removes pest habitat and returns nutrients to the soil. The scarab in hieroglyphics translates as "to come into being," conveying ideas of transformation and resurrection in ancient Egyptian religion and art. Given that the freshman year of the Post twins is cited as their key transformative year, mythohistorians have debated the symbolism, and the coincidence, of their having the scarab as their team symbol. *Gods of the First and Twenty-first Century, Volume 11, The Post Family Mythology.* Zypheron Press Ltd., Eighth Edition.

The week they'd spent on a tropical island this summer was a distant dream. She wanted to take his hand, give it a reassuring squeeze, but the air between them chilled . . . and something inside her protectively curled away from him.

An older boy strode her way. It was the student she and Eliot had met before—the one who *hadn't* helped them find Paxington. His chiseled Italian features broke into a smile as he saw her. "I'm glad you passed the entrance and placement exams," the boy said. "I had a feeling you and your brother would."

Then to the rest of the group, the older boy said in a commanding voice, "I will be your guide today, Team Scarab. I am Dante of the family Scalagari. Please follow me."

Dante turned and they fell in behind him: Jeremy and Sarah Covington introducing themselves to the Scalagari boy, Jezebel parting with her entourage, Mitch Stephenson, and Robert, herself, and Eliot . . . followed at last by Amanda Lane.

"Scalagari is an old family," Robert whispered to Fiona and Eliot. "They weave magic. Usually the best-dressed guys in the place."

"What about the Covington clan?" Eliot asked.

"They're conjurers," Robert said. "Nine times out of ten, troublemakers to boot. I wouldn't waste time worrying about them, though. You've got bigger problems on your team."

He had to mean Jezebel.

Fiona wanted to ask Robert what exactly a conjurer was, but Dante turned, walking backwards, and said, "Paxington was founded in 329 C.E. in Rome by Emperor Constantine. He wanted to study Jewish and Pagan influences on Christianity. Called *Curia Deus Pax*, or 'the Court of God's Peace,' many believed its true purpose was to secretly eradiate those influences."[10]

Sarah Covington lagged behind and turned to Robert (completely ignoring Fiona and Eliot). "I'm Sarah," she said, and smiled so her freckled cheeks dimpled. She held out her hand.

---

10. Emperors Constantine and Licinius in 313 C.E. created the Edict of Milan, declaring the Roman Empire neutral to all religions (this to reverse persecution of early Christians). The Edict was later ignored as Constantine heavily *favored* Christians with his policies, laws, and appointments. *Gods of the First and Twenty-first Century, Volume 2, Divine Inspirations.* Zypheron Press Ltd., Eighth Edition.

Robert took her hand, clasping in a way that was more than a hand-shake . . . and only a little less than an embrace.

"The pleasure is mine," he said.

Fiona felt her blood heat.

"A most impressive scuffle to get our token."

"I do my best," Robert replied.

"Then you'll be an admirable addition to Team Scarab," Sarah said. "I look forward to working together."

Sarah maneuvered past them toward the end of their group, all the pleasantness draining from her features as she approached Amanda Lane.

Amanda tried to move away, but Sarah sidled up next to her.

Their group crossed a quadrangle the size of football field. Its flagstones were quartz with sparkling veins of amethyst and topaz. It was like walking on rainbows.

"I don't recall inviting you onto the team," Sarah told Amanda.

Amanda didn't make eye contact. Her shoulders hunched, and her head lowered as if she were shrinking. "I . . . ," she started. "I was just there, and your cousin gave me a token. . . ."

Fiona wanted to tell Sarah to back off. Amanda hadn't done anything wrong. They were supposed to be on the same side. But she didn't know how to confront Sarah without incurring her anger as well.

Before she could puzzle out the social complexities, Mitch broke ranks and dropped back, walking along the other side of Amanda.

"Did I hear you correctly, Miss Lane?" he asked. "You actually have a scholarship from the League? The League of Immortals?"

Sarah looked over at Amanda disbelievingly.

"It's nothing," Amanda said, trying but failing to keep the hair out of her face.

Fiona was astonished that Mitch had overheard that. More astonished that Amanda was talking about the League in public. Didn't their rules apply to her, too?

"I don't believe Clan Covington has ever received such a scholarship," Mitch said. "Having the blessing of the League, well, that practically makes her a goddess, don't you think?"

Amanda looked up and tried to force a smile on her face.

"Hardly," Sarah said with a snort. She left them, catching up to Jeremy at the head of their group.

Fiona went back to Mitch. "Thanks," she whispered.

"Not a problem." Mitch flashed his easy, reassuring smile. "We're a team, right?"

Before Fiona could tell him that's exactly what *she* had been thinking, Dante pointed to the building on the right: a domed structure that looked like pictures she had seen of the Temple on the Mount in Jerusalem. This building, however, had a pair of red stone pyramids flanking either side.

"Our main library, the House of Wisdom," Dante told them. "It contains the collection preserved from the Library at Alexandria as well as digitized versions of nearly every book in existence."

Fiona was drawn to the building. So many things she didn't know . . . she could probably spend the rest of her life happily reading in there.

Dante, however, veered away and led them through rose gardens in full bloom.

Fiona inhaled and felt drunk with the overwhelming perfume of flowers.

"Constantine's Court of God's Peace," Dante continued, "was infiltrated by Immortals and secretly used to *preserve* the ancient Pagan ways. The League of Immortals, Infernals, and mortal magical families declared the Court a neutral asset, and since then, the Court continued on in various incarnations. In 1642, it officially became Paxington University in Oxford, England. And at the beginning of the twentieth century, for tax considerations, the campus was finally moved to San Francisco."

Jeremy brazenly plucked an heirloom rose and presented it to Jezebel.

She turned her back on him, ignoring the gesture.

Dante led their group out of the garden.

Jeremy sighed and tossed the flower away.

That was destruction of school property. How could a person like Jeremy effortlessly break all the rules—while Fiona would have been caught just thinking about it?

They marched into a grove of towering black oaks, redwood, silver birches, shimmering aspens, and willows. A cobblestone path meandered and branched through this peculiar forest.

"Here," Dante said, and waved at the trees, "is the Grove Primeval. The Paxington Arboreal Society imported famous trees from all over the world, many on the verge of being cut down, and replanted them here for safekeeping." He nodded at a few—"the Hangman of London, the Lady in Mourning, Walking Still Spirit"—and then he moved on.

Ahead Fiona saw a building that looked like the Colosseum in Rome, but a tad smaller, and square instead of oval.

Dante continued his lecture "The Paxington campus appears to the outside world as a prestigious but ordinary private high school. In reality, however, it is where many of the next generation of the world's magical families are trained." He gave an appreciative nod toward Jezebel. "As well as the occasional honor of having a diabolical protégée or Immortal offspring."

Chill bumps pebbled Fiona's arms. Dante hadn't looked anywhere near her when he said this, but it seemed he actually made a point of *not* looking her way. Did he know who she was?

She wanted him to know. She wanted all of them to know.

Just to get a fraction of the attention that Jezebel was getting . . . but there were those League rules, and Fiona knew they wouldn't take her breaking their rules lightly. But hadn't her father said that "everything *was made to be broken* . . . especially *rules*"?

She *knew* she was in trouble if she was even thinking about taking Louis's advice.

"This is where you'll have gym class," Dante said as they approached the archway leading into the coliseum. "The Ludus Magnus."[11]

---

11. The Ludus Magnus was the name of the Great Gladiatorial Training School unearthed in 1937 C.E. adjacent the famous Roman Colosseum, said to have trained countless professional killers. —Editor.

LUDUS MAGNUS

iona peered down a long shadowy corridor that led into the Ludus Magnus. She heard distant cheers, angry shouts, and cries of pain. Part of her was afraid and wanted to run away, but part of her was curious and wanted to see.

Dante led the group into the vaulted entrance, through a passage lined with old bricks and ancient stones—even a few skulls and bones had been cemented into the mix.

They came out on a grassy field half a city block wide. In the center sat the most unusual structure Fiona had ever laid eyes on. It was a lattice of posts and crossbeams, a honeycomb of ladders, ropes, and metal poles. It looked like a crisscrossing three-dimensional web spun by an army of mechanical spiders.

In the lower part of the structure, a person could barely squeeze through, with sinuous crawlways, tunnels that angled underground, even a canal filled with roaring white water.

Higher, however, the structure was wide open and towered six stories tall with ropes dangling, rickety bridges, and wooden spans barely a handsbreadth wide—which all swayed in the breeze.

"This is the gym," Dante said. "It is part obstacle course and part battlefield. You will learn to hate it by the end of the year. Today four sophomore volunteers will give you a demonstration."

Eliot looked sick.

Fiona moved closer for moral support. This "gym" looked like everything her brother wasn't good at—running, climbing, and dealing with heights.

Four students ran onto the field. They wore sweatpants and sneakers. Two wore red T-shirts; the others wore green. They ran past, giving Team Scarab a polite wave, then halted in front of the gym, eyeing one another with mischievous grins.

Dante clapped his hands. A red and a green banner unfurled at the very top of the structure.

"Winning is simple," Dante explained. "Your team must get half their people to their own flag before the other team gets to theirs. Each team has ten minutes to accomplish this, or *neither* wins."

Dante raised his arms. The sophomores tensed.

Dante dropped his hands. Both two-man teams scrambled onto the lattice and climbed.

"You can take a safer but slower route," Dante said. "Or you can go faster, which is more dangerous."

Fiona saw a green-team student stop climbing about a third of the way up and get onto a narrow beam. There was only a slender iron pipe alongside to help him balance.

"Aye, there be a bit more to it than that," Jeremy said, and pointed higher.

Two boys were thirty feet off the ground. Both clambered toward a rope swing.

The red-team boy got there first, leaped for the rope, swung around, and knocked the other boy—

—off the platform. The green-team boy twisted and turned through the air . . . bounced off a ladder . . . landed with a thud in the dirt.

Fiona moved toward him, but Dante stepped in front of her. "No interference," he said. "It has to play out."

"Is he—?" Eliot asked, unable to finish his thought.

They watched as the boy who'd fallen slowly got up, his arm hanging at an odd, clearly broken, angle.

"Apparently not," Dante replied.

"You may use *any* means to get to your goal," Dante continued. "And you can use any means to *prevent* your opponents from getting to their goal—short of bringing weapons onto the field."

Fiona thought it a razor-fine distinction between getting kicked off a thirty-foot-high platform and not using weapons. Both were potentially lethal.

Meanwhile, the boy who'd knocked his opponent off swung across a wide chasm, landed, traversed across monkey bars, and then grabbed the red flag.

"Red wins," Dante announced.

"This will be more complicated," Jezebel remarked, "with two eight-person teams. Sixteen participants. The probability for combat will be much greater."

There was a glint in the Infernal's eyes, and Fiona didn't like that one bit.

Amanda Lane, on the other hand, looked so pale now, Fiona thought she might faint.

"Some students," Dante said without looking at any of them in particular, "leave after they see this . . . or after their first match. It is not for the weak of heart."

Fiona wondered how she would do. Lose or win? Grab a flag in glory— or fall into the dirt . . . maybe breaking her neck? She imagined herself climbing and jumping and swinging through the air high off the ground. It made her blood race.

But there was more to this. Maybe Fiona wasn't the smartest here, or the prettiest, nor did she have a clue about the social mechanics . . . but *this* she understood. She could win here and prove to everyone that she belonged at Paxington.

"I can handle this," she said.

"I bet you can," replied Jeremy, who had moved next to her.

The boys climbed down and helped their wounded classmate get up and off the field—even the boy who had knocked him off. There didn't seem to be any hard feelings.

Fiona wondered how much forgiveness there would've been had the boy snapped his spine.

"Well," Dante said. "Any questions?"

"When is our first match?" Sarah asked.

"That's up to your gym teacher, Mr. Ma. He'll probably run you through practice drills first."

Fiona was relieved. She'd need time to thoroughly understand all this and strategize.

Dante led them back to the tunnel and outside.

They took another path through the Grove Primeval, through a particularly dense and dark section of ancient black oaks, and came out on the far side of the quad.

A fountain splashed nearby, and Fiona welcomed the cooling effect on the warm day. In the center of the water sat a bronze bearded man holding a trident; leaping fish surrounded him—all frozen forever in gleaming metal.

Dante pointed to a row of stately brownstones. "Those are the dormitories for those living on campus." He indicated a larger columned building of gray granite in the distance. "The health center. And over these steps on the hill is Plato's Court, where you'll have most of your freshman classes. "

Robert interrupted. "Hey—what's this?" He pointed back at the fountain.

Two boys stood on opposite sides of the fountain, facing each other across the water. Their Paxington jackets were off, and each held rapiers.

"A freshman duel," Dante remarked. "I supposed I should've covered this. Let's watch."

The tips of their rapiers glistened. One boy was as big as a football player, the other smaller than Eliot . . . even more so because he crouched low.

"Duels are permitted anytime on campus," Dante explained. "But only by mutual consent, of course."

They circled closer toward each other.

The bigger boy rushed his opponent, trying to skewer him through the midsection.

The smaller boy sidestepped and parried—but still stumbled back from the force, and almost fell into the fountain.

"Don't worry," Dante told her, "it's only to first blood."

"But I hear there are always accidents," Sarah added.

Fiona thought it the most barbaric thing in the world. People shouldn't be shoving other people off thirty-foot platforms, and they definitely shouldn't be attacking each other with swords at school.

The small boy parried another attack, riposted—and with a deft twist, skewered the larger boy's hand . . . pushing his blade almost up to the hilt, and then twisting until the larger boy was on his knees.

"See?" Dante said. "Just first blood." He turned away, no longer interested.

Fiona was horrified . . . but couldn't look away.

The smaller boy smiled, accentuating a long scar on one cheek. His opponent was escorted away by two older students.

She wouldn't forget the smaller boy. She might have to face him in gym class.

"Make sure to pick up your reading assignments at the gate," Dante told them, and pointed east. "Miss Westin expects you to be caught up for her first class. You wouldn't want to disappoint her."

"Thanks," Fiona said.

Dante gave her an appreciative nod and then strode across the quad to the library.

"Well," Jeremy said, rubbing his hands together, "we have a fine team. We'll be sure to trounce any competition." As he said this, however, his gaze slid *around* Amanda, as if she weren't there and his description of *fine* didn't apply to someone like her.

Fiona glanced back at the bloodstains by the fountain and then looked over her teammates.

They, in turn, glanced at one another, maybe thinking the same thing she was: Would any of them get challenged to a duel? Would they end up fighting each other? Dante said duels were mutually consensual. No one actually *had to* fight. Or was it trickier than that?

"Yeah," Fiona said. "We're all going to do great."

There was an awkward silence, which Mitch broke. "I don't know about you guys, but I'm getting over to the gate. I've heard Miss Westin assigns a mountain of books the first week."

"We all passed," Sarah said, and casually brushed a hand through her hair. "So what's the worry?"

Fiona had missed almost every question in the magic section on the placement exam. She had a lot of catching up to do.

"I'm out of here." Robert turned and walked toward the gate. He uncharacteristically looked deep in thought.

"Me, too," Amanda murmured, and trotted off to the library.

"We better go," Fiona said, and nudged Eliot. "It was nice—"

Her eyes locked with Jezebel's. It was like staring into clear green water, and drowning. Fiona couldn't quite say it was nice to meet *her*. She had a feeling this girl was going to be nothing but trouble.

She jogged after Robert, calling, "Hey—wait up!"

Eliot came, too. Fiona knew he would, and that was fine because she couldn't leave him alone with *that* group, but she still desperately wanted a few moments alone with Robert. Why couldn't he have figured that out?

Robert had gotten very far ahead of them, although he was just walking. She and Eliot had to sprint to catch up to him as he approached the gate.

Mr. Harlan Dells, the brawny Gatekeeper in the three-piece suit, handed Robert a page-long list of books. Robert scanned it. "I've never read so many books in my entire life," he said.

This was one great difference between her and Robert: Fiona had read almost every book on everything . . . save the one small area of mythology.

Mr. Dells handed her and Eliot their reading assignments. There were titles like *Tanglewood Tales, The Golden Bough* (twelve volumes), *The White Goddess,* and *The Hero with a Thousand Faces.*

Even for her, this might take a little time.

"We need to talk," she whispered to Robert.

"I know," he said, and he pretended to still be looking at that stupid list. "I don't know where to start. Things are so weird."

There was something in Robert's voice she had never heard before: doubt. She wanted to take his hand, but that felt wrong in front of Mr. Dells, the man who said he could hear and see almost everything.

"Walk me home?" she asked Robert.

Fiona nudged Eliot, who for once in his life got the hint.

"I think I'll check out that coffee shop," Eliot said, "just to—"

Eliot's mouth was open, but he was no longer talking. He stared beyond the gate.

A black Cadillac with tailfins rolled to a stop just outside.

Mr. Dells growled and moved toward the gate, shaking his head. "You're blocking the entrance. No one is allowed to park here. Not even you. *Especially* you."

"Oh man," Robert said, "I definitely cannot be here." He walked away.

Fiona started after him, but froze as she saw the car door open and the tallest man she'd ever seen get out. His skin was dark. His smile, cold. His eyes locked on to her and Eliot.

Uncle Kino.

"I am not parking," Uncle Kino told the Gatekeeper. "I'm here to pick up. Them."

10

THE GATES OF PERDITION

Eliot stared at the man who climbed out of the Cadillac. Uncle Kino looked taller than he remembered—like he could step over the walls of Paxington, like he was more shadow cast at sunset than flesh and blood.

He blinked and Uncle Kino still looked tall . . . but no longer unnaturally so.

The last time he'd seen Kino, he and Fiona had just been officially accepted into the League. Kino had made a point of shaking Eliot's hand.

"I am here to take them," Kino again told Harlan Dells.

Mr. Dells crossed his arms over his massive chest. "This is a safe haven. They go only if they want to, Mr. Saturday."[12]

Kino sniffed (this might have been a laugh; Eliot wasn't sure) and donned sunglasses. "There's no trouble here today," he told Mr. Dells. "Why don't you go sweep some hallways, eh, janitor?" He turned to Eliot and Fiona. "Come, children."

Audrey and Cee had drilled into Eliot and Fiona since they were little kids that it was very much *not* okay to accept rides from strangers.

---

12. Kino La Croix (aka Baron Samedi and alternate Voodoo personas, Baron Cimetière, and Baron La Croix. Note: *Samedi* is French for "Saturday.") He is depicted in a white top hat, black tuxedo, and dark glasses. Only rarely seen outside Haiti and other tropical locations. Haitian dictator, Duvalier François, reputedly dressed like Baron Samedi to increase his air of mystery—although some mythohistorians claim the two *were* the same person (for a while). According to Voodoo practitioners, Baron Samedi stands at the crossroads, where the souls of dead humans pass to the nether realms. *Gods of the First and Twenty-first Century, Volume 5, Core Myths (Part 2).* Zypheron Press Ltd., Eighth Edition.

But Kino was part of the League. It would be no different if Uncle Henry had come to pick them up. Wouldn't it?

Eliot tried to see Kino's eyes past the smoky lenses of his sunglasses, but couldn't, and suddenly he wasn't so sure.

"This is Council business," Kino explained. "Your mother sent me. She said to tell you that you will be able to do your chores and homework afterward."

Now *that* sounded right. After entrance and placement exams, a campus tour, a reading assignment that probably would take months, and whatever the Council now wanted—of course there would be chores to do at home.

Eliot looked at Fiona, and she slowly nodded, confirming his hunch.

"Okay," Eliot said.

Mr. Dells uncrossed his arms, flipped the switch on the side of the gatehouse, and the large iron gate rolled silently open.

Eliot took a step toward Kino's car.

"Wait." Kino held up his large hand.

"You *just* said you wanted us to come," Eliot told him.

"You got dice on you? No dice!" Kino said, and pushed his sunglasses farther up the bridge of his nose. "Not in my car."

For a second Eliot didn't know what he meant. He then realized he still had the dice from the Last Sunset Tavern in his pocket. His lucky charms. He'd used them to guess on the last multiple-choice parts of the placement exam he hadn't had a clue about.

He pulled them out of his pocket. "They're just—"

"They're just getting thrown away," Kino declared.

Fiona turned to Eliot and rolled her eyes. That was the look she reserved for when Audrey laid down the law. A look that said, *Shut up and do what you're told, because we're not going to win this one and it's no use trying.*

But Eliot wasn't just going to throw them away. They were his.

He squeezed them in his fist, felt their recessed pips, all those random possibilities contained in his hand. It made him feel in control.

"Toss them here, boy," Mr. Dells said. "I'll hold them for you."

With a sigh, Eliot handed them over.

Mr. Dells rattled them in Kino's direction. The taller man sneered at this and slowly sank back into his Cadillac.

Fiona ran for the front passenger's side door. Eliot sprinted after her.

"The back," Kino told them. "No children up front."

They reluctantly moved to opposite rear passenger doors and opened them at the same time. Eliot paused to admire the way the car's back swept up into two tails.

He then slid inside, and so did Fiona.

The backseats were slick red leather, the interior panels mahogany with chrome accents. There was a smell, not that wonderful new car smell, but more like plastic that had decomposed in the sun.

He and Fiona simultaneously slammed the doors shut.

"Where are we going?" Fiona asked. She nervously plucked at the rubber band on her wrist.

"A short drive to show you children the road ahead," Kino replied. "We want you to make the right decision at the crossroads."

As answers went, this was what Eliot had come to expect from his family: something utterly cryptic.

Eliot eased back and fumbled about for the safety belt. There wasn't any.

"There's no—"

Uncle Kino sped out of the alley and onto the main street without even pausing to look for oncoming traffic.

Eliot and Fiona slid together into the door.

Fiona pushed him away; Eliot elbowed her back.

As he settled back down, he noticed a statuette of the Virgin Mary on the car's dash, her eyes upraised to the pine air freshener dangling from the rearview mirror. All the car's gauges read zero.

They were headed the wrong way to be going home. Instead, Eliot saw the trees of Presidio Park ahead.

"So why no dice?" Eliot asked.

"They are not for us," Kino told him.

"Us? You mean the League?" Fiona asked.

"Dice are an Infernal invention," Kino replied.

"How can that be?" Eliot asked. "Dice have been around forever."

Kino gazed into the rearview mirror. "No good has ever come from dice."

They slowed at the entrance to Presidio Park and turned in.

Eliot had a feeling he should keep his mouth shut, but something bothered him about Kino's distaste for dice. Audrey had a rule for them, too, one curiously devoid of her usual legally verbose wording.

RULE 3: NO DICE.

And when he and Fiona had first been shown to the League Council, they were tested by throwing dice. Everyone had looked so nervous when Henry produced them. What was wrong with dice?

"You've used them before?" Eliot asked.

Kino turned around to face Eliot—no longer even looking where he was driving as he veered onto Lincoln Boulevard. His features could've been molded from cast iron. "No dice," he repeated.

Eliot was used to this stonewall treatment from Audrey. He had his argument ready. "How are we supposed to learn?" he said. "Or make the right choices when we come to this crossroads you're talking about, if no one tells us anything?"

Kino snorted and turned back.

He was silent a moment as he slowly steered the car through the entrance to the San Francisco National Cemetery. Orderly rows of white headstones surrounded them on either side.

"Sure we used the dice," Kino said. "Many, many times in the old days. We loved them . . . too much . . . and made many bad choices."

The Cadillac rolled onto a single lane that turned toward a stand of eucalyptus trees. More headstones and statues of angels appeared clustered in patches of shade.

"The last time we used dice," Kino said, "was after we took the Titans' lands. This was before humans even stepped from the wilderness."

They leaned closer. No one—not even Uncle Henry—had told them about the early parts of their family's history.

Fog swirled through the forest. No big deal in the Bay Area . . . but it was kind of strange at this time in the afternoon. Strong sunlight shone through in patches and made the mists like veils.

"We had all wanted the land," Kino continued. "We argued, used law and logic—but in the end, there were three who would not bend. Three whom men would later call Zeus, Poseidon, and Hades."

"So you rolled for the land," Eliot said, guessing and inching closer.

More trees crowded this part of the cemetery, plunging everything into shadow.

"Zeus rolled the highest, claiming the kingdoms of sky and earth. Poseidon rolled second highest and took the domain of water." Kino gestured ahead. "I rolled lowest and claimed the shadowy lands that were left as my domain."

The Cadillac eased to stop before a gate. It was simple and small: two-by-fours and chicken wire, something you might put up to keep the rabbits out of your garden.

"We knew Zeus cheated," Kino said, sounding bitter.

He got out and went to the gate.

The gate was some sort of optical illusion, though. As Kino stood by the thing, it seemed as tall now as he was—the chicken wire more solid chain-link and padlocked, too.

Kino opened it with a touch and pushed the gate aside.

He climbed back into the Cadillac, and they rolled past the barrier.

"That was the last time we settled *any* matter with dice." Kino lifted a hand off the wheel and made a sideways cutting motion Eliot knew all too well. Audrey had made that gesture countless times—indicating this conversation was over.

Eliot made a note that Kino was Hades. He'd also remember the names Poseidon and Zeus, two more important-sounding relatives he should keep track of.

He had a feeling there was more to Kino's dislike of dice, and much more to the story of how they related to the Infernals, than he was telling. Eliot felt, however, he'd pressed his luck far enough.

Outside, cemetery headstones packed together so tightly in places, they look like crooked teeth erupting from the ground; there were statues and monuments side by side so close that no one could walk through.

They rounded another curve, and the headstones thinned and became orderly again and all had military insignia upon them . . . royal crests and crossed swords and eagles in relief.

Eliot looked back. The gate was far behind them, and it had swung shut.

Kino drove up and over a low hill. There were larger structures: mausoleums, obelisks, crude cairns, and something that looked like Stonehenge. There were rolling fields and poplar trees. Sunlight broke through the fog, illuminating wildflowers and making a distant river glisten.

Eliot was positive there was no such river in San Francisco. This reminded him of one of Uncle Henry's lightning-fast journeys across the world. It had that weird dreamy feel to it.

"This is Elysium," Kino said. "Where the noble dead come to dwell for a time."

"So it's another place?" Fiona asked. "Like Purgatory?"

Kino grunted his assent and continued to drive.

So maybe this wasn't like one of Uncle Henry's rides. Kino was taking them to no place in this world. Did that mean *they* were dead now, too? No . . . Fiona had gone to the Valley of the New Year, which she said was part of Purgatory—and she had managed to get back.

He rolled down his window, scared, but wanting a better look nonetheless. Outside, it smelled of fresh earth and rain. Clean.

Eliot set his backpack on his lap. He wanted Lady Dawn close, just in case.

There were people outside. Some sat in marble pavilions talking, painting, or lounging in hammocks. Others gathered about great barbecues, or tossed Frisbees or collected flowers. Couples walked hand in hand.

"All these people . . . ," Eliot said.

"Dead," Kino told him.

They rode past orchards of cherry trees in full bloom that filled the air with feather white blooms, and over terraced hills with row after row of trellises heavy with bloodred and amber grapes.

How could this be? If this was where the dead really came, shouldn't there be *billions* of them here?

Eliot wanted to ask. But he didn't, not wanting to appear stupid.

The Cadillac picked up speed.

Kino touched a button on his door, and Eliot's window slid up.

He turned onto an unpaved branch off the road. The sky was iron gray.

The car accelerated around curves until this road became a single dirt track. The trees became stunted and small, then there were just grass and tumbleweeds, and then just bare rocky dirt. There were no more people here—and definitely no one tossing Frisbees.

Eliot spied a drop-off in the distance.

Kino pressed his foot all the way to the floor, and the Cadillac leaped ahead, leaving plumes of dust behind.

"What's going on?" Eliot asked.

"Now I will show you the part of the Underworld that belongs to the Infernals," Kino replied, the bitterness thick in his voice, and his eyes glued straight ahead.

Eliot swallowed. That didn't sound good.

The door locks thumped down.

Kino drove and said nothing.

Eliot looked to Fiona, and she gave a slight shake of her head. He wanted to get out, but how? They must be going over a hundred miles an hour—rocketing past jagged boulders—straight toward where the land dropped away.

The Cadillac fishtailed to the left, skating along a cliff—continuing at breakneck speed along its edge.

Eliot slid into Fiona. Neither of them seemed to notice or care; both their faces pressed to the window.

The land plunged more than a mile straight down. A river of molten metal carved through jagged spires of black volcanic rock. In the distance, a desert plain stretched to the horizon. Airplanes, meteors, and flaming debris fell from the sky. Tiny figures swarmed, crowds of people among the rocks and on dunes. They ran, and it looked like they were fighting. Winged creatures circled overhead. One swooped and plucked up a double clawful of people.

Eliot wanted to look away. He couldn't.

"This is what the other family does to the dead," Kino told them. "They torture. Turn souls into wandering insane things. Take a long listen. Remember this next time you hear one of your Infernal relatives and their lies . . . and choose wisely."

Kino rolled down the electric windows.

There was the rumble of distant thunder and volcanoes, and carried on the hot winds were the screams of thousands of lost souls.

Eliot couldn't stand the din. It made him want to scream along with them.

He turned to ask Fiona what she thought, but she was pale and stared straight ahead.

Kino flicked on the Cadillac's headlights. The road they sped along was just a track now through a wilderness of dead twisted trees and whirlwinds of volcanic ash. There was no sun, no stars . . . just darkness.

The Cadillac slowed.

Along the cliff's edge, a fence had been erected. It was giant femurs and rib bones, from dinosaurs, maybe. Concertina wire and long curved talons topped it, pointed away from their side to keep things in Hell from climbing over.

"Why are we slowing?" Eliot asked cautiously.

"The gate is ahead," Kino said without further explanation.

It was the end of the line—literally, as the road curved toward and off the cliff's edge.

Eliot realized one of his hands grasped the leather handle on the back of Kino's seat. He let go.

Mist and smoke parted, revealing a gate the size of their house in San Francisco. It was an interlocked mass of metal and bone and clockwork mechanisms. A half-dozen combination dials sat at eye level. The mass looked utterly impregnable, and like it hadn't been opened in hundreds of years . . . if ever.

"Why would you need a gate here?" Fiona said. "Who in their right mind would want to use it?"

"You would be surprised." Kino pulled up alongside the structure. "Heroes have come looking for lost loves. There are always fools. And the dead are restless." He removed his sunglasses, revealing dark, perhaps sad, but otherwise ordinary eyes. "No one living, not even I, understands what moves them."

The car door locks popped open.

Kino faced them. "This is the Gate of Perdition, where the world of light meets that of darkness. The lands of our family and theirs. When they tell you of the wonders and pleasures of Hell, remember what you've seen here.

"Now," he told them, "get out."

Three heartbeats passed as Eliot and Fiona sat stunned.

"No way," Eliot said.

"I want you to see and hear for yourself firsthand . . . unless you're too scared?"

"I'm not scared," Fiona said. She opened her door and clambered out.

Of course Eliot wasn't scared; his sister was crazy, though, to leave the car.

He sat there a moment, feeling like a total loser and coward. Okay—fine. Eliot couldn't let her go by herself. He opened his door, too.

The only thing that ever felt like this was when he had to open the door to the basement incinerator at Oakwood Apartments. The air was so dry here, it hurt to breathe. He steeled himself, then stepped out.

Kino remained in the car. "Touch the other side," he said. "Feel damnation and the absence of all hope."

"I'm not touching anything," Fiona told him.

Eliot hesitated—but only for a moment. What harm could it do to touch some dirt?

He knelt and wiggled his hand through a gap under the fence.

The earth felt older than anything he had ever touched before. Like it had been dust before the beginning of time . . . totally without life. More dead than dead could ever be.

But it was *not* nothing. Not exactly.

It felt to Eliot more like an empty page: blank, yes, but perhaps the beginning of something. If only the right person would come along, with the right pen . . . they could fill that page up with anything they wanted.

He left the earth where it was and pulled his hand out.

Kino watched him and Fiona. He put his sunglasses back on, and the windows of the Cadillac eased up and sealed with a *thunk*.

Eliot was glad this little demonstration was over.

He and Fiona moved toward the back doors.

The Cadillac's engine revved; the car jumped, fishtailed, and sprayed them with dust.

Uncle Kino sped off.

11

BORDERLANDS

Fiona couldn't believe it. "He ditched us!" she cried.

She picked up a rock and chucked it after Kino's Cadillac. It was a futile gesture. The red taillights winked in the distance, obscured by dust and smoke, then swallowed by shadows.

It was very dark. The only light was from a smoldering river of lava in the valley below.

"Eliot?" she whispered.

"I'm here," he said. "Hang on."

He snapped on a flashlight, the same one they'd had in the sewers when they hunted Sobek.

"You're still carrying that around?"

"A first aid kit, too," he said. "Some water, and a few granola bars, just in case. I even have Cee's lunch if we get *really* desperate."

It was one of the few times her brother had impressed her. Fiona would never in a million years, though, tell him this.

Eliot looked through the gate. "Do you really think it's—?"

She stood next to him. Wind blasted her and carried with it a thousand screams and cries of pain from the depths. A plume of magma blasted from a giant fissure and sent a shower of sparks a mile high into the rust-colored sky.

"What else could it be?"

Eliot held up a hand, fingers outstretched. "I feel it's something terrible," he whispered, "but part of me belongs down there. I can't explain it."

Fiona pulled him back from the gate. The heat must have boiled his brains.

"Are you crazy? Nothing *belongs* down there."

But she felt it, too. A little tug . . . as if just on the other side of this valley of nightmares there might be something terrible *and* wonderful, waiting for them. Or maybe it was that feeling you got when you looked down
from a tall building or bridge, wondering (but never seriously) what it
would be like to jump.

"There!" someone called.

The voice was far away, on the other side of the gate, and so faint, Fiona
wasn't sure if it had been real or not.

It came again, this time more urgent: "A light—I saw a light! Up there!
Quick!"

Shadowy shapes scrambled up the steep embankment toward the gate.
Men and women, wild eyes gleaming, and carrying with them a scent she'd
smelled too many times: on Perry Millhouse, and when Mike Poole dipped
his hand into the deep fryer—burned human flesh.

"We better go," she said.

Two figures ran up the path on the other side of the gate . . . then
six . . . then dozens.

The ground trembled as they stampeded the gate. They cried and
screamed and shouted: *"There! They're opening the gates! Give me that
flashlight! You, come here!"*

Eliot backed up.

The gate look impenetrable by anything less than an atomic bomb . . .
but the adjacent fence was bone and metal and barbed wire heaped
together. Fiona wasn't sure it would stop *all* those people.

She grabbed Eliot's hand and pulled him along faster—running.

A tide of flesh crashed upon the gate and spilled over to the fence.
There must be a hundred people pounding on the gate from the other side.

The bones and rusted barbed wire flexed and groaned and shuddered.

And all those people screamed.

The noise stabbed at Fiona's ears. She dropped her brother's hand and
instinctively covered her head. It felt like her skull split.

Eliot had one hand over his ear, but the other held his violin and
pointed up.

A great bird swooped down from the sky. It was the size of a small air-
plane: a collection of black feathers and outstretched steel claws and
glistening black eyes—and screaming the sounds of breaking glass and
nails on blackboard.

The thing tore through the crowd near the gate. There was an explosion of feathers; bone snapped and limbs tossed into the air.

Fiona's heart beat in her throat.

She and Eliot ran.

Behind them, human cries mingled with the bird's and there was a whoosh of wings.

Fiona looked back.

In the glowing sky, the one giant bird disintegrated into a swarm of swirling feathers and claws like a Salvador Dalí tornado of bird parts. It spiraled up and then toward them.

She looked for cover. Eliot's flashlight illuminated a stand of twisted trees ahead, but that was too far away.

Fiona froze—only for a split second, though. She grabbed and stretched her rubber band. The air about its edge hummed as she focused her mind . . . to cut.

"Come and get me," she said. "Just try it."

Eliot stood next to her, his face flushed, and his violin on his shoulder. Bow on strings, he drew out a long, sad note.

The birds hesitated and lost cohesion hearing this—but their momentum still carried them straight toward her.

Fiona braced.

Countless caws and screechings enveloped her. Grasping claws caught her clothes and hair, but failed to find purchase on flesh.

She cut—bone and sinew and feathers—severed even their screams midair.

Behind her, Eliot played: a song of sorrow that bridged to something lighter.

The birds scattered and fell silent before her brother's music. So did the people on the other side of the gate. Even the erupting volcanoes in the distance quieted. Like the entire world paused to listen.

His song spoke of life and love . . . and hope.

Fiona's picked up their flashlight, looking again for cover or a way out of this mess.

There was no trace of Kino's tire tracks in the volcanic ash. The wind had already blown them away. That shouldn't matter, though; all they had to do was follow the cliff edge back the way they had come.

Those birds, however, would come back if they saw them out in the open.

She cast her gaze to the thicket of dead trees. They looked like skeletons with outstretched arms and fingers. Their shadows lengthened and wavered in the beam of the flashlight.

She spotted another flicker of light deep in the forest.

Eliot stopped playing.

"Keep going," she whispered. "There's someone, or something, coming through those trees."

Eliot shook his head. "I can't do any more. The song hurts too much." He held one trembling hand to his chest.

That hand of his had never recovered from that infection. Fiona knew he should've seen a doctor. She was about to tell him that he'd been an idiot, but decided now wasn't the time for that. Besides, Eliot looked like he was in real pain.

"It's okay." She looped an arm around her brother and helped him toward the trees. "I think someone's coming to help. And if they're not, I can take care of them."

Fiona wasn't so sure. Her legs were leaden, and the adrenaline that had given her strength before was gone.

She waved their flashlight back and forth.

The light in the forest answered, doing the same.

She and Eliot made their way to the edge of the trees and pushed through until they saw a figure with a lantern. It was all shadow first, and then she saw an arm, a body, a man's rugged face.

She knew him . . . but couldn't place exactly from where. The man looked like a retired athlete, with gray hair and hands that could have grasped a basketball as easily as an apple. He wore camo sweatpants, sneakers, and a black AC/DC T-shirt.

She remembered him then: Their last birthday at Oakwood Apartments, this man had dropped by, just as they had been opening their presents.

"Mr. Welmann?" she whispered.

"Miss Post? It's Fiona, right? And Eliot?" He smiled, but it faded fast. "You're not dead, are you?"

"No," Fiona told him, at first thinking this a stupid question, and then remembering where they where.

Mr. Welmann exhaled.

"We just got here," Eliot said. Her brother had recovered from whatever happened to him back there, because he pushed her arm away and set Lady Dawn back in its violin case.

"I saw that damned Cadillac race past," Mr. Welmann said, "and figured there'd be trouble. Come on. The way out of these Borderlands is back here."

As they started walking, Fiona remembered one thing about Mr. Welmann.

He was dead.

Uncle Henry had told them Audrey killed him to keep the League from finding them. She'd done it with the knife they'd used to cut their birthday cake. It was so creepy.

Eliot asked him, "You called this place the 'Borderlands'?"[13]

"Kind of a demilitarized zone," Mr. Welmann said. He broke through the woods and onto a footpath. He looked around as if he expected someone to come along.

"I don't mean to be rude, sir," Fiona said, "but you *are* dead, aren't you?"

"Sure, kid." He shrugged. "It's not a big deal. We all go sooner or later."

"Our mother—?" she started to ask . . . but couldn't quite articulate the entire question: *Did our mother really kill you?*

Mr. Welmann started up the path and answered, "Yep."

They followed his long strides until patches of sunlight broke through the branches and they heard birdsong.

"I'm so sorry," Fiona said, knowing this could never make up for what had happened. "That's horrible."

"I'm not holding a grudge," Mr. Welmann replied. "I got the impression I'd stumbled into a mother-bear-protecting-her-cubs situation. If I had kids, I might have done the same thing. I hope it turned out all right for you two."

"We're in the League now," Eliot told him.

"And Paxington," Fiona added, pointing to the symbol on her uniform.

Mr. Welmann looked them over, nodding. "Yeah . . . I see it in you now. A spark."

Fiona sensed Mr. Welmann's friendly nature cool toward them.

He led them across a grassy field. Dew soaked Fiona's loafers, but she didn't mind. It was clean, and washed away the volcanic ash.

Mr. Welmann waved at a group tossing Frisbees. He caught one of the

---

13. Ye Borderlands be not claimed by good or evil, or anything but whisper and void. Be the wend and winds through the Middle Realms. Shortcut, maze, and dangerous path. Filled with wonders beatific and demonic. Dream and nightmare. Even lost with ye proper guide. Be warned. *Mythica Improbiba* (translated version), Father Sildas Pious. ca. thirteenth century.

flying disks and flung it back. "You must have had some adventures accomplishing all that," he said.

She and Eliot told him everything that had happened that summer: the three heroic trials, the box of chocolates, the return of their estranged father, and the final confrontation with Beelzebub.

Mr. Welmann took it all in without question.

He halted at the top of the hill. Fiona saw the fields stretch out, fading into a distant purple horizon. A river wider than the Mississippi meandered across the plain, seeming from this angle part doodle and part quicksilver reflecting the sky.

"So this is what happens when you die?" Eliot asked. "You come here? And some people go to Hell?"

"I couldn't tell you, kid. I see a few hundred people show up from time to time. The people who go to Hell? I'm happy to say I haven't a clue."

"But that doesn't make sense." Eliot's brows bunched together. "There should be *billions* of people here, then."

"That is *the* question," Welmann said. "Where do they all go?" He knelt, picked a long blade of wheatgrass, and stuck into his mouth. "No one knows. Not me. Not the Infernals." He chuckled. "And certainly not the 'gods.'"

"Someone has to know something," Fiona protested.

"Do they?" Mr. Welmann asked. "Well, the closest thing I have to an answer is that from time to time, the dead move on. Some make rafts and float down the river. Others just start walking." He pointed to the distant horizon. "No one sees them again."

Fiona remembered what Kino had said: *The dead are restless. No one living, not even I, understands what moves them.*

Welmann sighed. "I feel it sometimes. Don't get me wrong . . . all these barbecues"—he cleared his throat—"the company of fine ladies, and all the leisure time is great. But it feels like there *has* to be something more."

He paused and stared miles away. "I'm not sure what 'more' means . . . Heaven, Hell, or oblivion, but I know there's a final destiny waiting for me."

Fiona sensed the weight and the truth of what he said.

They sat quiet for a moment.

Mr. Welmann laughed and got up. "Geez, that's about enough of that. We better get you two back. If half of what I've heard about Paxington is true, you'll have a ton of books to read your first week."

Fiona nodded.

He led them down the other side of the hill. There were mausoleums and obelisks ahead, and the beginning of the graveyards.

"You know your troubles are just beginning, right?" Mr. Welmann said. "The League is dangerous, and three heroic trials or not, it's never done testing you. The other side of your family won't give up, either. It's not in their nature."

Fiona didn't like the way he talked about the League. *They* were part of the League now. But out of respect for Mr. Welmann, she thought about his warning before she answered.

"The League has our best interests at heart," she told him. "And I think our father has gone away. The other Infernals? No one is going to bother us after what we did to Beelzebub."

"Best interests?" Eliot said. "What about what Kino just did to us? In case you didn't notice—we could have died back there."

They came to a stand of headstones so dense, they had to pick a crooked path through them, single file.

Fiona frowned at her brother's assertion. She wanted to say that Kino just meant to show them what the other side of their family stood for. But what about those people on the other side of the fence who had tried to tear them apart? And those birds? Kino had to know about them. He had to know that leaving them there would be dangerous.

Mr. Welmann lifted a foot onto a headstone to tie his shoelace. "Look," he said, "I'm not trying to scare you. Just decide who you trust and who you don't . . . and watch each other's backs."

Of course that's what they'd do. The question was, whom to trust?

Well, each other, of course.

Her mother? As much as Fiona *wanted* to trust her, Audrey had lied to Fiona and Eliot for the last fifteen years. Maybe for a good reason, but she had still lied. There was no reason to think she wouldn't continue to do so.

"Just over there," Mr. Welmann said. "We're almost to Little Chicken Gate."[14]

---

14. Little Chicken Gate is a rickety structure often mistaken for an abandoned garden or a long-forgotten graveyard. Appearing at random throughout mythohistorical accounts, the gate allows the dead one-way passage to the crossroads that lead them to their ultimate destinations. For living travelers, however, these rules of transit may be bent, and passage to the nether realms is permitted (although perhaps not desirable), and there is the possibility of *two-way* travel. Extreme caution is urged. The gate can disappear as quickly as it appears. *A Primer on the Middle Realms*, Paxington Institute Press, LLC.

He slowed. "You two wouldn't know a kid named Robert Farmington? We used to work together. Haven't seen him here yet. I wondered if he was okay."

"Sure, we know Robert," Eliot said. "He's a friend."

"We know him," Fiona echoed, unsure what Robert and she were to each other anymore. He had acted so strange today.

Mr. Welmann, however, did not look happy at this. "He's still driving for Mr. Mimes?"

"Not exactly," Fiona replied. "Uncle Henry fired him. But it's not what it sounds like. He helped us . . . just got into a little trouble with the League."

"He's going to Paxington now," Eliot added.

Mr. Welmann halted and his eyes narrowed. "That can't be right," he said. "No one gets fired from the League and walks away. Robert's a great kid, but he doesn't have the brains or the pedigree to be in a place like Paxington, either. Something stinks. . . ."

"Could he still be working for the League?" Fiona asked. "Watching out for us?"

That would explain his standoffish behavior. As a secret bodyguard, it would be a conflict of interest to get too close emotionally. Her pulse quickened. So it was a forbidden attraction . . . all the more dangerous for them, and exciting.

Mr. Welmann shook his head and started walking again. "The League don't work like that. When they fire you, it's permanent."

"He did mention having to lie low," Fiona said.

"And when Uncle Kino showed up," Eliot said, "did you see how fast he took off?"

"Do me a favor," Mr. Welmann said. He walked up to the Little Chicken Gate and set one hand on it. "Tell Robert whatever he thinks he's doing, he's in way over his head on this one. Tell him to leave Paxington and ride—just ride. He'll know what I mean."

Despite what Fiona had seen before, the gate was only wooden posts and loose chicken wire strung across their path.

Mr. Welmann opened it for them and gestured them through.

"Thank you," Fiona told him.

"You're welcome, kid. Take care, huh? And don't take this the wrong way, but I hope I don't see either of you again."

She nodded and stepped through.

The sun dimmed. The air felt heavier. Every color dulled.

But this *was* San Francisco. Fiona spotted the paved road and the National Cemetery. It would be a long walk home, but at least they *could* get home now.

She turned to thank Mr. Welmann again for everything.

But although there were footsteps in the grass, and even a little swish where the gate had opened—the Little Chicken Gate and Mr. Welmann were gone.

12

HERO-IN-TRAINING

Robert Farmington sat on his Harley Davidson, a curve of blackened steel, dual twin matte black pipes, and the massive *V* of double cylinders between his legs. The ignition, though, was off, and the bike was in neutral as he rode in the freight elevator to the top of this six-story brick building in the Tenderloin District.

There was no way he was leaving his bike on the street in *this* neighborhood. Not that he could have found a parking spot if he wanted to.

The freight elevator ground to a stop.

This had been one giant hassle of a day—but nothing a ride down the coast, a few cervezas, some fishing, and a long nap in a hammock on the beach couldn't fix.

The elevator door rolled up, and Robert pushed his bike into the loft where Mr. Mimes had told him to meet.

The top floor of this building had been one of those industrial sweatshop operations—now stripped, and in the process of being renovated into a tragically hip and overpriced condominium. Ugly brick walls had been meticulously restored. There were tangles of wiring and computer cables and sophisticated halogen lighting dangling from the rafters. Bluestone tiles made a jigsaw on the floor.

Robert pushed his bike ahead, but halted half in and half out of the elevator.

Aaron Sears was in the loft. He lifted a heavy punching bag onto a hook. He was four hundred pounds of muscle poured into jeans, desert combat boots, and a T-shirt that read BEEN THERE on one side and DONE THAT on the reverse.

Aaron was on the League Council, and had wanted Robert punished for his rule-breaking. Mr. Mimes told them he'd taken care of it . . . but if they found Robert here, unpunished, he was a goner.

Aaron was the Red Rider of the Apocalypse, Ares, the god of war, and half a dozen other aliases—all of them potential trouble and a nasty end for Robert.

He spared a glance at Robert. "I suggest you drag your bike in here, young man, before you lose it."

The elevator door lowered. Robert pushed his bike inside.

The door clicked and locked behind him, and the elevator descended, stranding him.

"Ah, Robert—there you are." Henry Mimes was in the kitchen, hidden by the open stainless steel refrigerator door. He emerged with a bottle of wine and a glass.

"New digs, Mr. Mimes?"

"Do you like it?"

Robert shrugged. His eyes were glued on Aaron.

"Don't worry about him," Mr. Mimes said with a careless wave. Wine slopped out of his glass. "He's here to help."

So, they were all friends now? Robert doubted that.

Aaron released the heavy bag on its hook. The beam overhead creaked. It had to be filled with sand and must have weighed half a ton.

Aaron hit it bare-knuckled. The bag deformed and careened back.

"Where's your Paxington uniform?" Mr. Mimes asked.

Robert had stripped out of the jacket and down to his plain white T-shirt the moment he got off campus. Next order of business was to find some jeans and proper riding boots. He hitched his thumb at his saddle-bag, where he had stuffed the blazer.

"It's dry clean only," Mr. Mimes said with a sigh. "Well, no matter. Give us your report."

"Okay, hang on a second. My brain feels turned inside out and wrung dry from the placement exam. I'm glad I only had to do one day of this stuff."

"You *did* have all the answers," Mr. Mimes said, his brows scrunching together with concern.

"Yeah. Those helped. But the answers you gave me weren't in the right order, and guessing which ones went where wasn't easy. Some of the stuff seemed like Greek to me—heck, some of the stuff *was* in Greek."

Robert had cheated under the watchful gaze of Miss Westin. He wasn't sure what she was, but she could give any Immortal in the League a run for their money in the "icy stare" department.

He shuddered.

"And what of the other students?" Mr. Mimes inquired.

"Paxington snobs," Robert said. "Their noses are stuck so far into the air, you've got to wonder how they walk without tripping. Spoiled pukes with a little power inflating their already empty heads."

"As I expected," Aaron grumbled.

"Well, not one girl—that Amanda Lane you wanted me to check out. She's clueless. Made it through her exams somehow, though. I kind of feel sorry for her."

"Ah, good," Mr. Mimes said. "An education is the least we can do for her. The League owes that girl much."

Aaron and Mr. Mimes shared a quick glance.

Robert knew from that simple look there was more to Amanda Lane than they were telling him.

"And the twins?" Mr. Mimes asked.

Eliot and Fiona. A raw nerve twinged in Robert.

He had been glad to see them alive and in good spirits, but the feelings he had for Fiona . . . There was too much there, and it was all so complicated. Robert wasn't built to deal with stuff like this.

"They're fine. Great," Robert muttered. "And, of course, they passed their exams." Robert swallowed, suddenly uneasy. "Only one thing happened at the end . . . Kino." His mouth went dust dry. "He picked them up after school."

Robert was sure he hadn't been spotted by Kino. He'd been just one more clueless Paxington punk in a uniform to him. Robert had gotten out of there quick, though, probably saving himself some fate-worse-than-death League payback.

"Kino moves faster than we thought," Aaron commented. He waved Robert closer.

"Than *you* thought," Mr. Mimes said.

Robert wasn't sure what Aaron had in mind, but he dared not disobey. He moved closer.

Aaron lifted Robert's hands and slipped on lightweight boxing gloves. He indicated that Robert hit the bag.

Robert gave him a *you've got to be kidding* look, but Aaron waited. Robert tried a tentative jab.

The bag was rock solid. Literally.

Aaron frowned, and this made his mustache droop. "With your entire body," he told Robert. "Use your legs. They are your most powerful muscles."

"Now, give me your report from the top again," Mr. Mimes said, "but this time everything about the twins."

Right. The twins. That's what this was all about. Robert was just a spy, a glorified errand boy.

Robert punched. This time he threw his entire weight behind it, and the bag rocked a bit. He shouldn't have been able to do that. He'd never been *that* strong.

Aaron nodded. "Give me twenty like that."

Robert punched as he spoke: "They passed the placement tests. They're both on Team Scarab—the same team I'm on. There's also that Amanda Lane girl on the team. Two from the Clan Covington. One from the Stephenson family. And"—he punched so hard that the bag swung wildly and he had to duck as it came back at him—"an Infernal protégée. A girl called Jezebel."

"Kino is not the only one who moves fast," Aaron said.

"It is nothing unexpected," Mr. Mimes said.

Aaron pushed the punching bag as it swung back—accelerating it to a blur before Robert could react.

It slammed into his face—followed a dizzying moment later by the floor hitting Robert's face as well.

Aaron came over and helped him up, lifting his chin and looking into his dazed eyes. "Should have broken his nose," he told Mr. Mimes. "The Soma appears to be taking."

Robert shrugged off Aaron's hands—got angry for a split second . . . and then cooled down. Getting mad at Aaron, you might as well get angry at a mountain for all the good it would do.

Robert touched his face. It stung, but there was nothing broken. Taking a blow that hard, he should at least have squirted some blood.

"Tell me more about the Infernal," Mr. Mimes said. He had a new glass in his hand, this one with a straw and something that looked like cola inside. He held it out for Robert to sip.

Robert reached for it, but realized he still had on the boxing gloves, so he used the proffered straw.

Whatever it was, it wasn't cola. It was liquid fire and curlicues of multi-colored smoke that blasted through his thoughts. It was velvet and honey and a thousand open flowers . . . and sulfur, too, like someone had lit a match under his nose.

Robert exhaled, felt bubbles popping, and the sensations faded.

He'd had this stuff before. Mr. Mimes gave him some when he'd been sprung from that Immortal prison cell.

Was that was Aaron was talking about? What did he call it? Soma? He'd said *"the Soma appears to be taking."*[15]

"Ah, yes," Mr. Mimes said, noting the quizzical look on Robert's face. "I took the liberty of stocking the refrigerator with a few bottles of this for you. It will do you worlds of good. Now, the Infernal? What did you call her? Jezebel?"

"She's pretty, like you'd expect," Robert said. "Drop-dead pretty, in fact. She had titles . . . Protector of the Burning Orchards, Handmaiden to the Mistress of Pain. Gave me the serious creeps."

"Sealiah's minion," Aaron said. "There will be subterfuge as well as blood."

"Don't sound disappointed," Mr. Mimes said. "The snakes in the grass will make themselves known soon enough—then you can cut off their heads."

"I don't understand how you know who this Jezebel even is," Robert said. "She could be *any* Infernal."

Mr. Mimes cocked one eyebrow. "How so?"

"Well," Robert said, "Lucifer—what did you call it—he 'cloned' me last summer. Made himself look like me to trap Fiona in that Valley of the New Year. Infernals can look like anyone they want to, right?"

---

15. Soma is a ritual drink associated with divinity among early Vedic and Persian cultures, thought to have been prepared from an (as yet) unknown rare mountain plant. Soma is analogous to the mythological Greek ambrosia—what the gods drank and what made them deities (which also appears to have addictive properties). While mortals have struggled for millennia to find the correct plant(s) to brew Soma, and others, most notably the alchemists of the Ancient China and Middle Age Europe, have tried to invent the famed Elixir of Life, none have succeeded. It remains an open question if the correct formula can be discovered—or if it *has been* discovered but does not have the desired effect on mortals. *Gods of the First and Twenty-first Century, Volume 4, Core Myths (Part 1).* Zypheron Press Ltd., Eighth Edition.

"No," Aaron said as he pulled on boxing gloves. "Most have only the humanoid and combat forms."

"To be precise," Mr. Mimes added, "only two Infernals could ever shift their shape like that: Lucifer and the great Satan. The latter is long departed, his bones dust. And I doubt this Jezebel is Louis in disguise. Even he wouldn't be able to fool the Headmistress and certainly not Paxington's eagle-eyed Gatekeeper."

Robert agreed. That Gatekeeper was an Immortal. Harlan Dells had that look of righteous condescension and unquestionable superiority. It was interesting, though, that he wasn't in the League . . . or that there could even be Immortals *outside* the League's control.

Aaron approached. He wore boxing gloves now and had his hands up.

"You have got to be kidding," Robert said.

"I don't 'kid' when it comes to combat," Aaron said. "Defend yourself."

He jabbed Robert. It was bullet fast.

Robert sidestepped and swatted the fist away at the absolute last split second. It felt like a steel piston, and would've taken off his head if it had connected.

"Hey!" Robert shouted.

Aaron circled. There was no escape. No way Robert could turn and make it to the elevator.

Mr. Mimes leaned against the wall, watching, and took a sip of wine. "Now, Robert, I want you to tell me about Fiona. How do you *really* feel about the girl?"

"Feel? Wha—?"

Robert never finished the thought. Aaron's fist impacted his gut, squishing the soft bits. Something popped.

There was blackness.

Robert found himself peering through a tunnel, and a high-pitched ringing filled his head. He kneeled, blood streaming from his mouth.

"I said *defend* yourself, boy."

Robert stood.

Slowly stood. But he shouldn't have been able to.

At best, he should barely be able to crawl toward the phone and dial 911 after a sledgehammer punch like that.

"Okay," he said through gritted teeth. He clenched his hands so tight, the knuckles popped.

Aaron came at him again—right and left and straight punches.

Robert intercepted them with strikes of his own. The force knocked him back, but he kept his head down, as Marcus Welmann had taught him.

He kept fighting. Faster and harder.

One of his jabs caught Aaron in his ribs.

Aaron grunted, grimaced . . . and then he smiled.

There was motion—not even a blur, really—just a flicker in the corner of Robert's vision.

. . . When he came to this time, he was flat on his back on the floor.

It felt like his body had been hung up and both Mr. Mimes and Aaron had hammered on it for a few days.

Aaron reached down and hauled Robert to his feet. He turned to Mr. Mimes and said, "He has the potential." Then to Robert, he said, "I shall set up a schedule for you and me to train."

"Excellent," Mr. Mimes said, raising his glass to toast Robert. "Now, Robert, the girl—you're about to tell me how you feel. . . ."

"Oh, man," Robert said, regaining his wits enough to understand what Mr. Mimes was asking. He took a few steps back from Aaron. "Okay. Fiona. I don't know." He felt his insides tighten. "I like her. But it's not that simple. She's in the League."

"Of course it's that simple," Mr. Mimes countered. "You're a boy. She's a girl."

"Yeah, I got that part. But she's a girl who could get me killed."

"How is that different from any other girl in the world?" Mr. Mimes asked. "Do you love her?"

The question caught Robert as off guard as when Aaron had sucker-punched him. "Love?" Robert laughed. "Come on, man. That stuff is for kids!"

There was no way Robert bought into all that. Love was one of two things: what you saw at the movies (fantasies of what girls thought guys should act like); or it was like his mom, who had worked her way through half a dozen boyfriends and stepfathers by the time Robert left home. Even with all the slammed doors, the shouts, the bruises and busted lips—she had "loved" them all.

Any way you sliced it, love was a slippery, dangerous thing.

But Fiona wasn't like any other girl.

There was something more there. She was a goddess . . . maybe . . . and Robert couldn't figure out how that fit into the whole boyfriend-girlfriend thing.

"Yeeeees," Mr. Mimes said. "I see the flames inside you."

Robert shook his head and held up his hands. "Come on, Mr. Mimes. Just tell me what my next assignment is. I need to move, get out of this place."

"Tell him, Henry," Aaron said. "The boy deserves a piece of the truth."

"Hmmmm." Mr. Mimes smiled. "Let me ask you one more thing, Robert. Forget Fiona for a moment. What do you think of Paxington?"

Robert snorted. "It's okay if you like a bunch of stuck-up rich kids and wannabe sorcerers. And if you like book dust and being bored to death in some musty lecture hall. Sure, it's *great*."

"And gym class?" Aaron asked him.

"Cakewalk. I could take those guys without even trying. But like I said, I'm just glad I had to be there only for the one day."

Aaron nodded to Mr. Mimes.

"Robert, my dear boy, I am pleased to tell you that your next assignment *is* Paxington." Mr. Mimes gestured grandly about the half-finished loft. "And this is now yours, along with a generous allowance."

"I don't get it," Robert said. "You want me to set up surveillance on the place? Telephoto lenses and stuff like that?"

Mr. Mimes's ever-present smile faded. "I'm afraid not. This will undoubtedly be your hardest assignment. You're going to go to Paxington. Really go. No more cheating. Musty books, boring lectures, gym class—all of it. You must go for the entire year, Robert. And you must pass."

13

JUST THE START

Eliot walked fast. The sun had already sunk behind the eucalyptus trees in Presidio Park, and the last thing he wanted was a moonlit walk with Fiona through a graveyard.

He just wanted to get home and have this day end.

"You think . . . ," Eliot started. He had a hard time saying it: it was so stupid. "You think that was really Hell?"

"Yes," Fiona replied. "It felt like the Valley of the New Year. Like a dream. But different from a dream, because you felt more awake there."

Eliot nodded.

If their father was Lucifer, he had come from someplace, right? But Hell?

"So there must be a Heaven, too, right?"

Fiona ignored him as she rummaged through her book bag.

Maybe it didn't matter if there was a Heaven or Hell, as Mr. Welmann had said . . . just that there was something else out there, a greater destiny waiting for him.

Or maybe he should stay focused on this world's problems.

Like his hand.

Eliot flexed his fingers. They didn't hurt anymore, but earlier, when he played "Julie's Song" to stop those birds and the people at the fence, the pain had flared so bad, he had to stop. It felt like fire, burning him to the bone. All he'd been able to do for a full minute after that was hold his arm to his chest and let the agony pulse away.

Earlier this summer, a snapped violin string had cut his finger and it became infected.

Eliot, however, no longer thought this was a simple bacteriological infection. There was a connection between the pain and his music. Or maybe the connection was to Lady Dawn. Sometimes when he touched the violin, the infection in his hand felt normal, sometimes even better than normal . . . but sometimes when he played her, it hurt more, too.

Her? Why did people always refer to musical instruments with gender? And why female?

Lady Dawn. This was obviously a girl's name . . . which made sense because he'd always had trouble with girls.

The violin was safely tucked in his backpack, and Eliot was in no hurry to take her out and experiment with what made him hurt and what didn't.

"This is ridiculous," Fiona said. She'd retrieved their Paxington required reading list. She shook the pages at Eliot. "Do you know how long it's going to take us to get through all these?"

Eliot glanced at list. There had to be a hundred books, and only two—the King James Bible and *Bulfinch's Mythology*—did he recognize from the references they'd seen in other literature.

The rest were probably things Audrey would never have let into their house because of Rule 55, the "nothing made up" rule, which covered books on mythology, legends, and fairy tales.

Despite this rule, however, he and Fiona *had* learned things—from snippets of overheard conversations, people on the radio, and bumper stickers. Things like, HAVE FAITH IN GOD, THE DEVIL MADE ME DO IT, SINNERS AND DEMOCRATS BURN IN HELL, and WALK GENTLY ON MOTHER EARTH.

"It's like her entire plan to keep us 'safe' totally backfired," Fiona said as if she were reading his mind.

"That's why she's sending us to Paxington," Eliot said. "To fill in the blanks."

"More like *we* get to make up for *her* mistakes."

They turned the corner. The entrance to Paxington should have been just down the street, but he couldn't see it yet—not that Eliot had any desire to go back to school today. He just wanted to rest after this too-long, dangerous, and completely weird day. Still, it was fascinating that the entire campus was close: tucked in some in-between place in the middle of San Francisco.

A black cat sat in a doorway, staring at them. When Eliot met its amber gaze, the cat looked away, preened itself, then left, tail flicking in irritation.

"Maybe," Eliot said, "it doesn't matter anymore who, if anyone, is to blame. What's the point? We've got homework to do tonight. We should concentrate on that."

"It should matter," Fiona said. "Why are you always so eager to please her?"

"Me? You're the prenatal *Vombatus ursinus*."[16]

Fiona pursed her lips and slowed. She knew exactly what he had meant—that she was tied to Audrey like some suckling baby. Not adult enough to make her own decisions.

"At least," she said. "I'm big enough to come out of the pouch."

Eliot halted in his tracks. That wasn't playing fair. Vocabulary insult was about clever etymologies and double entendres, not simple putdowns like that.

And besides, he was only an inch or two shorter than she.

Eliot didn't feel like playing vocabulary insult. He walked ahead of her.

Fiona trotted up to him. "I'm sorry. I didn't mean that."

"Whatever," he said.

Eliot glanced across the street, still not seeing Paxington where it should be—then in a flash, the alley aligned and tunneled to fill his vision. Eliot got a glimpse of the café and older students chatting at tables under a blue canopy decorated with a river of glowing stars, sipping coffee, and reading books or scrolls. Beyond this he saw the gate. Mr. Harlan Dells was standing there, arms crossed over his chest, smirking as if he had eavesdropped on him and Fiona.

Streetlights flickered on, and Eliot blinked.

The slice of sideways reality extending into Paxington vanished.

Seeing his new school reminded Eliot there were plenty of other things to worry about besides a reading assignment. That would be the easy part.

"What are we going to do about gym class?" he said. "It looks like a person could get seriously hurt."

Fiona marched alongside him awhile before she answered. "Don't worry. I'll watch your back."

"So you think *I'm* going to need watching? You think I'm helpless?"

"No." She glanced at him, and then at his backpack. "Far from it."

16. *Vombatus ursinus*, the common or "coarse-haired" wombat. The wombat is a marsupial indigenous to the cooler, wetter regions of Australia. They gestate a single offspring (a *joey*), which spends nine to eleven months within its mother's pouch. —Editor.

There was a tentative quality to her voice that Eliot had heard only rarely . . . as if she was scared.

Eliot quickened his pace. He didn't want to think about why his own sister would feel that way about him. It wasn't like *he* had conjured a fog filled with the dead or made the sun rise early on command. That had been the music, out of control—not him.

"I just meant that we're a team," Fiona said. "And people on a team watch out for each other. That's all."

They rounded a corner, turning onto their street. Even though it was still a block away, Eliot spied the highest window in their house. A candle burned there, a beacon for them. Cee must have lit it.

"I don't think Jeremy or Sarah Covington are concerned about being team players," he said.

"At least they know how things work at Paxington," Fiona replied. "We can learn from them. I'm more worried about that Jezebel."

The Infernal. The Julie Marks look-alike.

"You've got that stupid look on your face," Fiona said, "like you think she's going to date you." She shook her head. "Listen, she's dangerous. We just walked back from the brink of Hell—that's where people like that come from. She's evil. Stay away from her, okay?"

Eliot stopped and crossed his arms. "We're part Infernal, too. Does that mean we're evil?"

"We're Immortals," Fiona told him. "The League said so."

"Then why did Kino make such a big deal about telling us we might have a choice? Why drive us right to the Gates of Perdition and ditch us? He was obviously trying to scare us into choosing his side."

Fiona considered this.

"Maybe . . . ," she said, and she started walking again.

"Don't worry about Jezebel," Eliot told her. "It's not like she's even noticed me."

"True," Fiona said with a hint of sarcasm.

She didn't have to agree so easily. "So, what's the deal with you and Robert?" Eliot shot back.

"That's none of your business."

"Sure it is. He's on our team now, isn't he? I thought you two were, I don't know, closer."

Fiona sighed. "We were. But now I don't know what to think. He got into trouble because of us before. Because of me. If he gets noticed by the League . . . you know what they'd do to him."

They turned off the sidewalk and mounted the stairs of their porch.

Cee opened the door and beckoned them inside. "Come in, my darlings! Congratulations! We ordered Chinese to celebrate your first day, and we wouldn't want it to get cold." She trembled with excitement. "I'm so glad you passed all your tests."

Eliot glanced at Fiona, sharing a quizzical look. Cee already knew how they did on their tests?

Of course they knew. Audrey would have called Miss Westin.

They followed her inside, and Eliot detected the savory scents of Mongolian beef, five-star golden shrimp, and pot stickers.

He and Fiona dropped their bags and raced upstairs.

On the dining table were white cardboard boxes overflowing with noodles and rice, steaming vegetables and dumplings. Eliot and Fiona grabbed plates and piled the food high.

Eliot devoured one entire plateful, went back for seconds, and then finally looked up.

Cee watched him and his sister with rapt attention. "Tell me everything," she said.

Eliot wanted to tell her about the exams, how Paxington was hidden in plain sight, the duel they saw, and the students he'd met. It was all so different—scary and wonderful . . . mostly scary.

But what to tell her about Uncle Kino, their drive to Hell, getting ditched, and then Mr. Welmann's—the dead Mr. Welmann's—timely rescue?

Cee knew about school already. She might even know about Uncle Kino.

But the stuff Mr. Welmann had told them about what happened to the dead . . . that somehow seemed like a secret.

He glanced at Fiona.

She'd had eaten only a few morsels off her plate and was in the process of pushing the rest around. She looked up. She narrowed her eyes slightly to let him know they had better keep that information to themselves . . . at least until they had a chance to figure it out.

"It was great," Eliot told Cee. "But we're beat and we have tons to read tonight."

"There's this list of books," Fiona chimed in. "You wouldn't believe it."

"You were late," Cee said. "We weren't sure what happened to you."

Eliot felt like he'd been stuck with a pin, and he sat up straight.

Cecilia's words were wrong. On one level, they were just normal words like he'd heard a bazillion times before from her . . . but there was also an undertone: reflected mirror images of words, shadow words, whispered backwards and upside-down words.

They were *lies*.

Cee knew exactly where they had been.

Eliot didn't know how he knew—but he was sure she wasn't telling the truth.

Why would Cee pretend not to know? Just to get more information out of him?

Well, two could play that game. Eliot's gaze returned to his food, and he prodded a dumpling with his chopsticks. He didn't answer her question; instead, he asked, "Have you heard anything from our father? I mean, since Del Sombra? I thought he'd have called or written . . . or something."

"Of course not," Cee said. "There's not been a single word from the scoundrel. And we're lucky for it."

Eliot discerned only the truth from her words that time.

"But he is going to show up again, isn't he?" Fiona asked.

Cee licked her lips, gently patted Fiona's hand, and replied, "I know he is your father, my dove. You must have feelings for him, but best to let them go."

A shadow appeared in the stairwell, and Audrey spiraled down from her upstairs office. She carried a cigar box in the crook of her arm. "Good," Audrey said, "you're finally home." She settled at a table and poured herself a cup of green tea. She took a sip, all the while watching them, and then said, "I'm very proud of you both for passing the entrance and placement examinations."

That wasn't what Eliot had expected. He and Fiona had received Cs on that placement exam. Well, he got a C+. In this household, the *only* passing grade was an A.

"I spoke with Miss Westin," Audrey said. "She was impressed with you . . . considering the challenges we had with your homeschooling."

"Challenges?" Fiona dropped her chopsticks.

Before Fiona could start protesting, though, Audrey cut her off. "I see you have the reading list." Audrey nodded at the pages near Fiona. "Two sets of those books are being delivered by courier this evening. I didn't want either of you to wait another instant to make up for lost time."

Fiona reddened.

Audrey continued, holding out her hand to forestall her. "I know what you're going to say—the lies, the deliberate obfuscation of our family's history, and how it is 'not fair'—and then I would tell you it was for your own good, and life is never fair, and that we should focus on our present duties. So, let us imagine we've already covered that well-trodden territory, so I may give you your gifts."

Fiona blinked.

Eliot didn't understand. Their dangerous journey today seemed almost par for their new lives. And the mountain of reading they'd have to do seemed right, too. But Audrey accepting a C on tests? Even being proud of them? And now presents on a day that wasn't their birthday?

That was just plain weird.

Audrey said to Cecilia, "Go prepare dessert."

"Oh yes, yes." Cecilia said, and backed toward the kitchen. "Yes."

"And," Audrey called after her, "do not *add* anything to it." She turned back to Eliot and Fiona. "It's ice cream and cake from the Whole Foods Market."

She opened the cigar box she had carried down. Audrey removed two cards, setting one before Fiona, and then Eliot.

He stared into the card's gleaning stardust platinum surface. It had raised numbers and in capital letters, his name: ELIOT Z. POST. He'd seen these before, working at the pizza parlor, but he never believed he'd have a real credit card himself.

Audrey handed him a ballpoint pen. "Sign the back," she said. "That's very important."

Eliot obeyed, and then handed the pen to his sister. Fiona looked dumbstruck.

"You'll need a thousand little things for school," Audrey explained. "More books, clothes, athletic equipment, or the occasional snack. You are to use these for all your expenses."

Eliot picked the card up. It seemed heavier than plastic, like maybe it was real platinum.

"These cards are financially backed by the League," Audrey told them, her voice solidifying into its normal somber tone. "I therefore expect you to use them responsibly."

"We could buy anything?" Eliot asked.

"If you need," Audrey said. "Yes."

Before, Eliot always had to scrape together spare change just to buy some juice. Limitless money? It seemed like another test. Like that never-ending box of chocolates his sister had gotten.

"There is a number on the back of the card," Audrey told them. "Call it if the cards are lost or stolen. It is also the number to call if you need to contact the League for any emergency. Program it into your phones to-night." .

From the cigar box she removed two contoured black shapes and gave one each to Fiona and Eliot.

It easily fit his hand, and his thumb naturally found a recessed button. He pressed it, and the shape clicked open. There was a tiny keyboard, a number pad, and computer screen that lit up.

"I understand that no respectable teenager today is without one of these contraptions," Audrey said. "I left the phones' instruction manuals in your rooms."

"Wow!" Eliot breathed. "Thanks, really!" He got up and gave Audrey a hug.

"Thank you, Mother," Fiona said. She got up and gave Audrey a hug as well.

"Now, go wash up." Audrey brushed volcanic ash from Fiona's skirt. "I cannot believe Cecilia allowed you to the dinner table in such a filthy state."

Eliot and Fiona obeyed and ran to the bathroom.

Fiona got there first, and started washing her hands.

"This is great," Eliot told her as he examined his new phone.

"Don't be a dork," she replied, scrubbing her face.

"What's your problem now?"

"We wouldn't be getting all these things unless we're going to need them," Fiona said. "Unless there was *real* trouble coming. Like our heroic trials this summer. Paxington, the League, our father's family—Mr. Wel-mann was right: This is going to be a lot harder than we thought."

The happiness drained from Eliot.

His sister was correct. Today with the tests, that preview of gym class, the duel they witnessed, and the ride to Hell and back—all that had happened on their *first* day of high school.

With a sinking feeling in his stomach, Eliot realized that ahead of him was an entire year of days like this.

RIGORS OF ACADEMIC LIFE

14

BLOOD PEDIGREE

Fiona and Eliot strolled into the Hall of Plato. One hundred and twenty-six students, the entire freshman class of Paxington (minus themselves), filled the amphitheater seating of the classroom. The gaslights were lowered. It smelled of chalk dust and old books.

Miss Westin stood upon center stage and peered at them over her glasses. Her gaze chilled Fiona to the bone.

Heads turned their way, and everyone whispered.

"Master and Miss Post," said Miss Westin. "How good of you to join us again." She stepped to the lectern, opened a black book, and made two marks.

There had been some confusion this morning because Eliot's rusty alarm clock had finally busted, and the grandfather clock in the dining room had been sent out for cleaning. Fiona could have sworn they were an hour *early* . . . which was why they had dawdled, wandering the halls of Paxington, admiring the murals and mosaics that covered the walls. The ones in Plato's Court showed gods, their battles, and wondrous pastoral scenes with eighteenth-century ladies in flowing dresses.

"Find a seat," Miss Westin said. She turned to blackboards suspended by chains from the ceiling. They were covered in her perfect cursive script, and one board had the title, *Origins of the Modern Magical Families (Part One)*.

Fiona looked for seats. There were concentric circles of fold-down seats and desks, but all were taken.

In the dim light, she saw Mitch Stephenson and Robert; either boy, she bet, would have given up his seat . . . which would have been nice, but she didn't want to make any more of a scene than they already had.

"They're all full," Eliot whispered. He donned his glasses and looked around the lecture hall. "Should we stand in the doorway?"

How humiliating. Their first real class, and already they looked like total dorks.

"I guess so. . . ."

As she turned, however, Fiona spotted Jeremy and Sarah Covington waving to her. They pulled off backpacks and jackets they had set in adjacent seats.

"Ugh . . . ," Eliot said.

"Don't be that way. Come on."

She clambered down toward the Covingtons, but hesitated. Did she sit next to Jeremy, who had once tried to kiss her? Or next to Sarah, who, for some reason, intimidated her even more than Jeremy did?

Jeremy patted the seat next to him and smiled.

Fiona sat next to Sarah (who scooted away from her).

"Thanks," Fiona whispered.

"You are most welcome, teammate," Jeremy said.

Eliot and Jeremy exchanged awkward smiles, and then Eliot took the seat by him.

"About time," said the boy in front of them, clearly annoyed by this disruption.

"Shhh." Jeremy's stare bored into the back of the boy's head.

Miss Westin cleared her throat. "Before we start our lecture on the modern families, we shall review the origins of various magical lines."

She pulled down a section of blackboard, revealing a gorgeous illustration of an oak tree in cross section—like those diagrams showing the evolution of protozoa, dinosaur, bird, chimpanzee, and finally modern man.

In this diagram, however, Fiona saw leaves and intricate wood grain, and upon the tips of the upper branches were neatly printed names, and on the lower branches Greek symbols, cuneiform . . . and then older unrecognizable symbols.

"The ancient forces," Miss Westin lectured, "the Old Ones, the gods, Infernals, and the Fey—these are our murky past, and much of what we know of it are lies. As you review the texts, note the obvious embellishments and question all 'truths.'"

She gestured at the lowest branches, the ones gnarled and clearly dead.

"We merely mention the existence of the Primordial Ones from before time. All are dead or forever banished—incomprehensible now and forever-more to mortals and Immortals alike. We leave their delicate and dangerous studies for your junior and senior years."

The symbols on those lower branches were lines and dots and tangles of geometries that compressed to points as Fiona stared at them. She felt suffocated—strangled. She blinked, and the symbols were once more flat and plain chalk.

She should be writing this all down. Fiona fumbled out her notebook, accidentally nudging the boy in front of her.

The boy turned around. "Do you mind?" He was pale; his hair, dark and straight and falling in a neat angle across his glare.

"I'm so sorry," she whispered.

"Eyes up front, cad," Jeremy spat back.

The boy snorted, but nonetheless turned back to face the lecture.

Fiona's face burned. She was glad she was in the shadows. She nudged Eliot so he, too, could take notes, but his eyes were riveted on the black-board to where Miss Westin next pointed.

"The Titans," Miss Westin said. "Their origin and connection to the Old Ones is murky at best. This branch, with one notable exception, is now ex-tinct."

Fiona squinted. She read crossed-out names on that branch: Oceanus, Hyperion, and Tethys. The one not crossed out was Cronos, the Harvester, Keeper of the Sands of Time, founding member of the League of Immor-tals, aka Cornelius Nikitimitus.[17]

Uncle Cornelius? The frail old man on the Council was one of the old-est living things in the world?

Fiona scanned the other names, followed a side branch, and her breath caught in her throat as she read: (Son of Iapeuts) Prometheus, Bringer of Fire, aka Perry Millhouse.

Perry Millhouse had been a Titan, too. Nausea rolled inside her as she remembered how it had felt to cut through him.

"The Titans," Miss Westin continued, "were the progenitors of many of

17. Cronos the Titan is often differentiated from the Chronos, the Greek deity and personifi-cation of Time. Modern mythohistorians, however, now believe they were the same entity, this later persona created for Cronos when he joined his offspring in their rebellion against the ancient Titans. *Gods of the First and Twenty-first Century, Volume 4, Core Myths (Part 1)*. Zypheron Press Ltd., Eighth Edition.

the gods of the prehistoric and classical eras. Their children rose up to challenge them, recruiting some to their cause—but in most cases eliminating their parents altogether."

Fiona's mouth dropped open, horrified. Uncle Henry, her mother—they had *murdered* their own mothers and fathers? Was that what they were afraid Eliot and she might do one day? Was that the reason Immortals treated their offspring so badly? Because they were afraid of them?

"This transition from Titan to the Immortals," Miss Westin said, "occurred circa eight thousand years B.C.E."

That was *ten thousand* years ago. They were all so old. Fiona felt suddenly insignificant. Was that what she glimpsed when she looked into her mother's eyes? The experience and knowledge of millennia judging her fifteen years of attitude and arrogance?

She searched the next branch—the Immortals—and found two familiar names: Hermes, messenger/spymaster for the League of Immortals, aka Henry Mimes; Ares, League of Immortals Warlord, aka Dr. Aaron Sears.

There was another branch next to this—connected only by a dotted line and punctuated by a question mark.

On this offshoot were three names: Atropos, Lachesis, Clothos.[18]

"Atropos," Fiona whispered to Eliot. "Audrey . . . Post."

He nodded.

She wanted to ask Miss Westin what that dotted connecting line meant. Fiona started to raise her hand, but she hadn't seen anyone else interrupt the lecture. She'd wait until the end of class.

Miss Westin indicated another branch. This one coiled up from the base, a snaking vine with a dozen names, like Sealiah, Leviathan, and several that had been crossed out, such as Satan and Beelzebub (which sent shivers down Fiona's back).

One name was most peculiar in that it had been written, crossed out,

---

18. The three Moerae, the Norns, or the Fates are Clothos, the youngest Fate, who spins the thread of a person's life; Lachesis, the middle Fate, who measures the length of a person's life; and Atropos, the oldest Fate, who cuts the thread of life. Their origin is unclear. In many accounts, they are the daughters of Zeus; in others, they are the daughters of Nyx (the primordial Goddess of Night). As Norns, the three are described as maiden giantesses who simply arrived in the hall of the gods in Asgard and marked the end of the golden reign of those gods. Whatever their source, it was soon proved that they held the (not-so) metaphorical threads of fate for *both* mortals and Immortals. Even the gods feared the Fates. *Gods of the First and Twenty-first Century, Volume 4, Core Myths (Part 1).* Zypheron Press Ltd., Eighth Edition.

and then rewritten: Lucifer—the Prince of Darkness, the Morning Star, aka Louis Piper, her father. . . .

"The Infernals are the exception to the preclassical cutoff date for living immortal beings," Miss Westin explained. "Many of the fallen angels are still active in their Lower Realms . . . and occasionally venture to the Middle Realms as well.

"Other immortal branches"—Miss Westin gestured to a half dozen others, grayed out—"the Fairies or Folk of the Aire, the King's Men, Atlanteans, and the Heavenly Angels are all thought dead or departed."

Jeremy leaned over Eliot's lap, closer to Fiona. "The Fairies be hardly gone," he said. "I've seen them—chased the little buggers, even held their gold. That's how I came to find myself in the Valley."

Sarah sighed as if she had heard this a hundred times.

Fiona nodded to be polite, but she really wanted to hear Miss Westin's lecture, and wished he would shut up.

"Now," Miss Westin said, "on to the *mortal* magical families."

She pulled down a section of the adjacent blackboard. On it was a detailed expansion of the younger, topmost branches with dozens of names, including Van Wyck, Covington, Kaleb, and Scalagari. There were also more cryptic titles like "The Dreaming Families" and "Isla Blue Tribe."[19]

"The thing about Fairies," Jeremy continued to tell Fiona, oblivious of the lecture, "is that they didn't want anyone to know they're still alive. They had it in for me because I knew. Lured me with a trail of gold . . . just to shut me mouth. What they didn't know was—"

The pale boy in front of them turned and quietly but firmly told Jeremy, "Too bad they couldn't keep it shut, Covington. Close your piehole, before I close it for you."

Jeremy considered this threat, and his lips curled into a cruel smile.

"Here we go," murmured Sarah. She closed her notebook and set down her pen.

Jeremy eased back in his seat and held up both hands. "Of course, laddie. My apologies."

19. There are two dozen major, and a score of lesser, mortal magical families. Among many interests, they control global pharmaceutical conglomerates, diamond mines, crime syndicates, and political infrastructures. Although nowhere near as powerful as the Infernals, or as influential as the League of Immortals, they collectively control one twelfth of the world's assets. *Gods of the First and Twenty-first Century, Volume 14, The Mortal Magical Families.* Zypheron Press Ltd., Eighth Edition.

The boy glared at him a moment and then turned back to the lecture.

Jeremy picked up his copy of *Bulfinch's Mythology*—and slammed it into the back of the boy's head.

The boy reeled forward, scattering his papers onto the floor.

Fiona was stunned. She knew there could be fights at Paxington; she'd seen that duel the very first day . . . but in class?

Miss Westin clapped her hands once. That instantly got the entire room's attention. Even the boy who'd been clobbered looked at her, and didn't move or say a word.

Miss Westin took a deep breath and in an even voice said, "Mr. Covington, Mr. Van Wyck—if you have differences to work out, do so outside my classroom." She looked them over a moment, a gaze that reminded Fiona of glacier ice, utterly cold and unstoppably crushing. "I sense your blood is up, however, so the lecture will be suspended for ten minutes. Resolve this. Now."

"Suits me perfectly," Jeremy said, and stood. "This Van Wyck cad should be taught some manners, using such language before a lady." He gave a quick bow in Fiona's direction.

Fiona pushed herself deeper into her seat. She felt as if everyone were staring at her.

Jeremy hit him on her account? Or was that just an excuse?

The other boy got up.

Although he was on a lower row in front of them, he stood taller than Jeremy by a full head and was so bulky, it looked like he could, and would, pick up Jeremy with one meaty hand and crush him. "Okay, Covington, you're on." He stalked out of the lecture hall.

Jeremy pushed past Fiona. Sarah got up to follow her cousin.

So did Eliot . . . and then Fiona . . . and then everyone in the class.

Outside they all crowded about Jeremy and the Van Wyck boy. Looking at the ludicrous size difference between the two, Fiona was seriously worried Jeremy was going to get killed.

The Van Wyck boy looked down on Jeremy, pausing . . . because perhaps he was wondering what it would prove to beat up someone in such a mismatch?

"Why don't we forget about this," the Van Wyck boy offered. "There's no point in fighting. Unless you were going to use only magic."

Robert Farmington sidled up next to Fiona. At first she didn't recognize him in his neatly pressed school uniform. He had gotten a haircut, too.

"I've been wanting to talk to you," Robert whispered to her.

"Me, too," she said. "But now's not the time."

"Right."

Robert sounded disappointed. But how did he expect her to talk when Jeremy was about to get pounded flat?

Jeremy stuck his face a hand's span from the other boy's. "You want to see me magic? Well, here's some."

Jeremy spit into his face.

The Van Wyck boy turned red. He stepped back, cleaning off the spittle with one quick angry wipe. "Okay, Covington—you asked for it!"

Jeremy backed off, smiled, and danced back and forth as the other boy started shrugging off his jacket.

Jeremy didn't wait. He socked him in the nose.

Bone and cartilage cracked.

The Van Wyck boy fell backwards into the wall, both hands covering his face, tears gushing from his eyes.

The students cheered and yelled.

Jeremy punched him in the gut. He lashed out with his foot, connecting with the other boy's knee.

The Van Wyck boy doubled over. His leg crumpled.

Jeremy kicked him once, twice.

Fiona felt something greasy in the back of her throat and thought she might be sick.

Miss Westin watched impassively, arms folded over her chest, almost as if she were grading the boys on a test.

If no one was going to stop this—Fiona would.

She pushed her way through the crowd.

Jezebel, though, got there first. The other students let her pass, seeming to fear getting in the way of an Infernal. She stepped between Jeremy and the Van Wyck boy just as Jeremy brought back his foot for another kick.

"You've won," Jezebel said.

Jeremy blinked, and the rage faded from his eyes. "Do you think so?" He drew back, smiling, for one final coup de grâce.

"First blood"—Jezebel nodded to the downed boy—"is as far as they allow in campus duels."

Jeremy lost his smile as he watched his opponent cough a globule of blood and snot from his face.

"Continue if you want," Jezebel nonchalantly told him, "but it would be a shame to have a team member suspended over such a trivial rule." She glanced at Fiona. "And over such a *slight* reason."

Jeremy straightened his jacket and brushed back his silky blond hair. He knelt and told the boy, "That should teach you a lesson. Next time, mind your manners when in the presence of a lady."

Jeremy then bowed to Fiona, and although he faced her, he seemed to be performing for the watching crowd. "Your honor be upheld, fair maid."

A few girls giggled.

Fiona wanted to slap Jeremy's grin off his face . . . but there'd been enough violence for one day.

Miss Westin, without comment, turned and marched back to class. Most of the students took this as their cue to leave as well.

Fiona went to the Van Wyck boy to help him up, and even though it wasn't her fault, she thought she should apologize.

The boy's bloodshot eyes stopped her cold, however; it was pure spitting-cobra venom.

He blamed her. And there'd be no explaining or apologizing it away.

Fiona also knew that somehow, one day, he was going to get even with Jeremy . . . and with her.

15

THE TRUTH WILL HURT

Jezebel stepped off the Night Train, slipped off her loafers, and set her bare feet upon the black loam of the Poppy Lands of Hell.

She wriggled her toes, felt her blood pulse, and felt the warmth and life flow back into her bones.

Although she wore the uniform of a Paxington schoolgirl (not the pantyhose, however; there were limits to what she would endure), and although she looked much like a mortal girl (albeit one of extraordinary and enchanting beauty), within her heart beat pure poison and hellfire.

She was Infernal. This was her domain.

They belonged to each other.

Jezebel inhaled the pollen-laden air, tasted the odors of vanilla and honeysuckle, the sweet decay and mold spore.

Behind her, the train hissed and screamed and pulled out of the station house.

Jezebel picked up her book bag and strolled to the adjacent stables.

Servants bowed and scraped before the Duchess of the Many-Colored Jungle and Handmaiden to the Mistress of Pain.

They handed her the reins of the readied Andalusian mare.

The snow-white beast neighed, stomped with razor-shod hooves, and then bowed its head as well, recognizing her status.

Jezebel mounted, wheeled about, and galloped toward the Twelve Towers to make her report.

The Poppy Lands lay in perpetual twilight. Luxuriant fields of color spread in all directions; opium flowers and orchids looked like a galaxy of fallen stars.

Between thunderous hoofbeats, she heard the endless churning of worm and cockroach through the rich soil. In the distant hills rose the jungle, thick and dark, covered with vines and moldering with resplendent fungus.

She dimly remembered what it was to be mortal in this realm, and she recalled being repelled by the narcotic decay and the overwhelming vapors.

This was a dim memory, though—the vestiges of her hope-filled human soul.

It hurt to remember.

Her Queen had told her if she ignored it, it would soon go away—like the summer sniffles.

Indeed. She was Jezebel now, filled with the power of Hell, primordial and more intoxicating than the opium to which she had once been so addicted.

The serfs of the fields genuflected as she rode past.

They did not tend to the poppy harvest as usual, but rather cultivated spear and pike thickets, rolled spore cannons upon the backs of the giant bats as the animals hissed and squeaked in protest, and propped suits of plate armor among the twining bramble . . . which would coil and fill them and bring them to life.

As she neared the cliffs of the Twelve Towers, she saw engineers strengthening its fortifications. Antiaircraft artillery squatted upon the ramparts. The walls were heavy with creeping death vines, which bristled with thorns and oozed a flesh-corrosive toxin.

Even the land prepared for inevitable war. The Laudanum River that wound through the valley rainbowed with oily slicks as the jungle that had overgrown its banks wept poison to make it a moat of death.

Jezebel clattered up the cobblestone road and through the castle's raised portcullis.

Guards in thorn armor and flower-laden lances saluted her and helped her dismount. The Captain bowed and indicated the Queen awaited her pleasure in the Chamber of Maps.

She raced up the stairs of the Sixth Tower, the so-called Oaken Keeper of Secrets.

It was not wise to keep the Queen waiting. Ever.

She paused outside the chamber to adjust her skirt and smooth her Paxington jacket, to make sure her hair was just right.

Jezebel sensed Sealiah near. They were connected through the Pact of Indomitable Servitude, the oath that broken and damned Julie Marks had taken to transform herself into Jezebel. It made her a part of Sealiah's will, Julie's soul consumed and replaced by the shadow of the Queen of Poppies. Jezebel felt this in her very atoms. She did not struggle against it. One might as well try to struggle against breathing.

She entered the chamber, bowing low, not daring to look upon her Queen before instructed to.

"I shall tend to you in a moment," Sealiah said. "And rise. Submission becomes most young girls . . . but not you."

The Queen of Poppies had dressed to kill today. A sheath of gossamer metal clung to her curves—liquid dark-matter silver that had been in existence before the mortal Earth had been dust gathering in void.

Jezebel's gaze settled on the emerald that sat in the delicate V of Sealiah's collarbone. This stone was the personal symbol of Sealiah's power. It pulsed, daring any who desired it to try to rip it from her.

Jezebel had a sliver of that stone within her left palm—a gift and living link to her Queen.

Her fingers rolled into a fist. How she would love to taste more.

She averted her eyes from this obvious temptation, however, and her gaze landed upon the curved daggers, Exarp and Omebb, strapped to Sealiah's thighs . . . as well as the broken Sword of Dread, Saliceran, sheathed on her hip.

That terrible blade was said to have been broken as it struck the Immovable One in the Great War with Heaven. It had killed thousand of mortals and Immortals. The metal wept venom equal to the rage of the one who wielded it.

Jezebel then turned her attentions to the map table. It was a model of the Poppy Lands from the Valley of the Shadow of Death across the Dusk End of Rainbow to Venom-Tangle Thicket. Miniature infantry and fungus bat squadrons, Lancers of the Wild Rose, and Longbow of the Order of Whispering Death guarded key strategic locations . . . waiting for the enemy to make its move.

Bumblebees flew from open windows and landed upon the table. Covered in pollen and sticky with nectar, they waddled, buzzing among the unit markers and pushing them to their latest positions.

Sealiah plucked up one black-and-amber insect, its stinger half the length of its squirming body. "Tell the Lancers to pull back to the Western Ridge. Bury antipersonnel mines as they go." She then blew on the creature, and it took to the air.

"Now," Sealiah said, and finally turned to Jezebel, "how was school?"

Her Queen was, as always, breathtaking: bronze skin, her hair gleaming copper and streaked with platinum, and eyes that knew the depths of seduction and addiction.

Jezebel had to resist the urge to fall down in worship. "I passed entrance and placement exams without incident, my Queen."

The entrance to the Paxington Institute had been obvious to her Infernal senses. And between the answers provided for her, as well as weeks of intensive study from tutors, Jezebel had earned a B+ on the written exam, of which she was extremely proud.

Her former incarnation, Julie Marks—when she bothered to go to high school at all—had scraped by with Cs.

"Of course you passed." Sealiah arched one delicate eyebrow. "Or you would dare not show your face here."

Jezebel felt her cheeks heat, and she carefully averted her eyes so her Queen did not see the hate within.

"Tell me about the twins," Sealiah ordered.

On a side table, the Queen unrolled the circular mat for a game of Towers, a game that to Jezebel seemed part checkers, part chess, and had a long list of rules that seemed improvised half the time.

"They passed their tests, too. We are on the same team: Scarab." Jezebel continued with a narration of their first day, explaining the composition of their team (including a report on Robert Farmington, who surely worked for the League), their tour of the Paxington campus, and the Ludus Magnus.

She told Sealiah how Fiona and Eliot reacted to it all. How they were so naïve about everything. It was pathetic.

"You think your Eliot Post is weak, then?"

"No, my Queen. There is something still to the boy. I can feel it growing within him. Something that . . ."

Jezebel couldn't find the words. She wasn't sure how she felt about him . . . something no doubt left over from her weaker, mortal self.

"You are drawn to the boy?" Sealiah narrowed her eyes at Jezebel as she searched her heart. "Beyond his mere power?"

Jezebel opened her mouth to deny any attraction.

But that would be a lie. One her Queen would instantly detect. Such simple deceptions were the greatest insult one Infernal could give to another.

So she said nothing.

Sealiah inspected her nails: bloodred and pointed. She then set a handful of white cubes upon the Towers game mat. "Does he suspect who you were?"

"He may." Jezebel fidgeted. "He looks at me—I mean, like all the boys, of course. But, I think he sees a shadow of . . . she who I was." Jezebel couldn't speak her former name aloud. She loathed the weak creature she had been. "It shall not be a problem. It will be child's play to deflect his questions."

Sealiah stroked Jezebel's cheek with one fingernail, cutting the flesh. The sensation sent shivers through Jezebel. "You will tell him the truth if he asks," Sealiah said. "All of it. Even, and *especially,* about Julie Marks."

Jezebel inhaled and took an involuntary step back.

"I don't understand," she said. "I thought I was to get close to the twins. Help them so they would be sympathetic to our cause. Wasn't I going to be friends with Fiona? With Eliot? How will the truth help that?"

Jezebel realized too late that withdrawal from her Queen's presence, questioning her orders—either could be reason to be annihilated.

Sealiah, however, merely smiled and tilted her head. "These are still our goals, my pet. But Eliot is far more Infernal than any yet suspect. I have reports of his music quelling the borders of the disputed Blasted Lands."

Eliot had been to Hell? Jezebel wanted to ask how and when and what he had played.

For a terrible moment, she was Julie Marks again, yearning to hear *her* song once more. Her heart filled with hope and love and light.

She quickly snuffed those weaknesses before Sealiah saw them—and ripped them from her chest.

Still . . . she didn't understand.

Sealiah must have seen the confusion on her face, because she said, "If the boy continues to develop his stronger, Infernal nature, then he will certainly be able to do what any young lord of Hell can: sort lies from truth."

Jezebel wrestled with her Queen's command to tell the truth. Deception had been the entire basis of her relationship with Eliot. He had fallen for sweet, innocent, and vulnerable Julie Marks, the new manager at Ringo's Pizza—not runaway, died-of-a-heroin-overdose Julie Marks from the alleyways of Atlanta, not Julie Marks who had made a deal for her life and soul in exchange for seducing him into damnation everlasting.

"Shhh," Sealiah said, "quiet your thoughts." She looked down upon her, her features a mix of pity and disgust. "Since you have yet to be trained on the higher arts of trickery, our young Eliot will sense any attempt to hide the truth—so do not. It would backfire and further alienate you from him."

"I shall do as you say, my Queen," Jezebel said. "But . . . won't he hate me?"

"Oh, my precious dear—of course he will. How much you have yet to learn of men."

Sealiah drew Jezebel closer and slipped her arms about her shoulder. This felt wonderfully warm and comforting and yet terribly dangerous at the same time.

"Eliot *will* hate you, at first. But you will then have the boy's interest . . . which, when mixed with his good intentions and budding manly concerns, will curdle into love."

Jezebel understood. She didn't like her part it in, but she nonetheless appreciated the cleverness of the ploy—both dreaming of *and* dreading what would happen to her and Eliot when it came to fruition.

"Then," Sealiah said, glancing at her game of Towers, "we will have him."

16

BREAKFAST SPECIAL

Eliot ran along the sidewalk. Fiona raced him to the spot on the granite wall where the entrance to Paxington hid in plain sight.

He'd gotten a few paces ahead of her because she had to dodge a flower cart parked on the sidewalk (and she was too prissy to run around it on the street—even a few feet).

He stopped at the wall, touched it, and panted.

She shrugged as if to say, *Whatever—I let you,* but couldn't speak because she was breathing too heavily.

Eliot knew they wouldn't be late today—absolutely not.

He'd learned how to set the alarm on his new phone and gotten up extra early. He hadn't wanted to take any chances, though, so he and Fiona raced all the way from the breakfast table down through Pacific Heights, onto Lombard Street to here.

Eliot opened his phone, double-checking that they had plenty of time to make it to class. They did.

He found the crack in the wall, focused on it, and this time it was easy to slip around the corner that shouldn't exist.

It still felt weird.

Fiona came in right behind him.

The alley to Paxington was shaded, and the ivy-covered walls cooled the already chilly air. Café Eridanus was full, the outdoor tables taken by older students eating pastries and drinking lattes before school started.

Eliot paused and inhaled scents wafting from the café: freshly ground coffee and steamed milk, a slightly charred citrus odor from flaming crêpes suzettes, melting butter, bacon, and sourdough bread just out of the oven.

"Come on," Fiona said, and moved toward the gate.

Eliot's stomach complained, and he lingered. He would die if he had to sit through an entire lecture, or at the very least, he wouldn't be able to hear Miss Westin speaking over his grumbling digestive tract.

"Just a sec," he said. "I'll grab a bite—"

Eliot's mind halted mid-thought. Even his stomach stopped rumbling.

His father sat at one of the outdoor café tables under the sky blue canopy. Three older Paxington boys stood around him, so Eliot hadn't seen him at first.

The plates and coffee cups at his table had been shoved aside. Louis moved his hands over the tablecloth, shuffling three cards.

"Don't take your eyes off it this time," Louis told the boys. "Not for an instant!"

Eliot edged closer. Fiona was right behind him.

Louis's cards were facedown on the table, and each creased down the center so they could be easily manipulated. One was dog-eared. Another had a water spot in the center.

Eliot felt something off . . . and understood Louis was trying to fool the boys by making the shuffling look so simple and the cards so easy to identify.

"Now," Louis asked the boys. "Where is the Queen of Spades?"

"That one." A boy pointed to the center card.

Another told him, "No, it's the one on the right."

Louis smiled. "Are you *sure*?"

He looked up as he said this, and caught Eliot's eyes. Something passed between them, a slight tilt of the head, recognition, and an invitation to watch and learn.

"I'm sure," the boy said, "the center card. Flip it already and pay up."

Louis obliged. The card was the three of hearts.

"I'm sorry," Louis said, genuinely sounding sad. "You'll get it next time, I'm sure." He scooped their money off the table.

The boys asked for one more game, but Louis said no. "I have other customers this morning." He gestured at Eliot and Fiona.

The three boys left, muttering and arguing over how they had lost track of the queen.

Eliot and Fiona moved to the table.

"You came here to see us, didn't you?" Eliot asked.

"Of course, my boy." Louis clasped him warmly by the shoulder. "You look dashing in that uniform, by the way. The girls shall swoon."

Eliot felt instantly two feet taller.

Louis turned to Fiona. "And you, my dearest Fiona, you look . . ." He gesticulated with his hands, but couldn't find the right words as he looked her over. "So nice."

Fiona crossed her arms over her chest. "You're not supposed to be here."

"True," Louis said. "I am often not where I am supposed to be. And your mother *has* promised to kill me if I ever came near you again." He shrugged. "But she does not know of this meeting, so the point is moot." He stood, pulled out a chair, and gallantly offered it to Fiona.

Fiona remained standing and glared at him.

Louis was unfazed by this. He looked for the waiter, saying, "Let us not dwell on the ugly past and all these wretched parental custody issues, shall we? Let us just forgive one another, order breakfast, and chat. There's so much lost time to make up for."

"Forgive each other?" Fiona said. "What have *we* done that needs *your* forgiveness?"

Louis raised a finger. "Tut-tut. I won't hear of it. All is forgotten and pardoned."

Eliot sat.

Sure, he was still mad at Louis for using them as bait to lure Beelzebub into a trap (a trap, by the way, that hadn't worked). Only by the narrowest of scrapes had they not been killed. And sure, Louis was an Infernal, the Prince of Darkness, and perhaps evil incarnate. But he was their only relation who had ever given them straight answers. Something in very sort supply these days.

Besides, Eliot was hungry.

A waiter came and took out a notepad.

"Shall it be two or three specials?" Louis asked Fiona.

She toyed with the rubber band on her wrist, and then reluctantly settled into the chair.

"Ten minutes," she told Eliot. "No more. If we're late again for class . . ."

"Yes," Louis purred, "Miss Westin once had a guillotine for her tardy students." He looked utterly serious and he made a chopping motion onto the table. "Three specials," he told the waiter. "Make it a rush."

"Oui, Monsieur Piper."

Eliot studied his father. He looked so different from the dirty homeless person he'd been just a few months ago . . . and definitely different from the bat-winged fallen-angel woodcuts he'd seen in *Paradise Lost* (part of last night's reading assignment). Louis wore black slacks and a black silk dress shirt undone to his sternum (with buttons that looked like real diamonds). Eliot thought this might be what a stage magician would look like.

But it was Louis's face that fascinated Eliot most. His eyes sparkled as if he had just been laughing; his nose was crooked and hooked at the end; his thin mustache and goatee were immaculately trimmed and pointed; and his silver-streaked hair had been pulled back. It gave him an air of casual grace, elegance, and above all else . . . mischief.

"What do you want?" Fiona asked their father.

"What I want?" Louis got a faraway look in his eyes and stroked his chin. "I want my family to be whole and happy. I want you two to graduate from Paxington *maxima cum laude,* bar none, *merito puro*! I want to sail a galleon of solid gold upon a lake of jewels in my treasure kingdom the size of Nevada! I want the love of a beautiful woman. All women! I want the respect and adulation of billions. I want the world to be my pearl-stuffed oyster!"

Louis made eye contact with the waiter. "Although," he said with a sigh, "I'd settle for a cup of this establishment's wonderful Turkish coffee. What about you, darling daughter?"

"I want you to stop calling me that," she said.

"I want answers," Eliot chimed in before his sister worked up a head of steam.

Louis brightened and turned to him. "And so you shall have them, my boy. Ask! Anything. I shall be your unbiased oracle."

The waiter brought coffee and orange juice and a basket of steaming blueberry muffins drizzled with butter.

Eliot tore into a muffin, drank half a glass of juice, and then said, "Uncle Kino drove us to the Gates of Perdition. To show us where Infernals come from. Was it really Hell? Is that where you live?"

Louis considered for a moment, and slipped four sugar cubes into his coffee. "He showed you . . . yes, but only the absolutely most wretched part. It's like driving through the worst sections of Detroit and being told that is America. Why, you'd miss out entirely on Disneyland and Las Vegas."

"Please," Fiona scoffed. "Are you saying there are *nice* parts of Hell?"

"There are forests, jungles, and cities filled with exotic delights," Louis said. "There are circuses, meadows of flowers, castles filled with lords and ladies—realms beyond imagination."

Eliot leaned forward.

He half hoped Louis would invite him to see for himself. He'd never take him up on such an offer, not after they'd seen what lay beyond the gate in the Borderlands . . . but still, it'd be wonderful to learn a little bit more about his father's side of the family.

And just for a moment, Eliot considered the possibility of life beyond his mother's influence. He and Louis could be adventurers, pirates on the high seas, travelers and explorers.

Fiona, however, looked unconvinced.

"None of that matters to us," she told Louis. "We're in the League now." She kicked Eliot under the table. "Both of us. I'm in the Order of the Celestial Rose. And Eliot is an Immortal hero."

"Congratulations," Louis said without enthusiasm.

Breakfast arrived: plates with a stack of crêpes drenched with brandied sauce, a side of sizzling bacon, and steaming fresh croissants. The waiter set the bill next to Louis's plate . . . which Louis ignored.

Eliot tasted the bacon. It was crisp and salty and wonderful. But something stopped him from enjoying it: Fiona's assertion that they were in the League. Around a mouthful, he said to her, "Okay—so we're part of the League of Immortals . . . but why does that mean we're *not* part of the other family? That makes no sense from a biological point of view."

Fiona glared at him, but for the moment, she had no answer.

It occurred to Eliot that he was breaking a rule by talking of the League in public. Then again, no one here seemed to be listening. Nor could this alley outside Paxington truly be considered a public place.

Or was it just easier for Eliot to break rules when his father was near? Louis had once told him: Everything was made to be broken, especially rules.

Right now, Eliot didn't care; he just wanted answers.

"You are both," Louis told them. "Immortal *and* Infernal."

"That's not what the League's decided," Fiona said.

"I'm afraid the facts speak louder. You, my darling daughter—" Louis stopped, remembering that Fiona didn't like him calling her that. "You killed Beelzebub."

Fiona paled.

Eliot lost his appetite as well when he remembered how she had sev-ered Beelzebub's head.

"There's a neutrality treaty between the League and us," Louis said, "which prevents any such physical interventions."

"But it was self-defense," Eliot said.

"Of course it was," Louis replied. "The reason is irrelevant. My point is that you must *be* an Infernal to *kill* another Infernal. And you must be an Immortal to be legally accepted into the League of Immortals. These are immutable facts with a single conclusion. . . ."

"That we're both?" Eliot tentatively offered.

A faint smile spread across Louis's face.

"So what?" Fiona said. "We decided to stick with the League. It's our choice."

"And an admirable choice it is," Louis replied. "But I'm afraid there are those who will not care what you have chosen. Some think you are the means to unravel our neutrality treaty. Some believe that one day you will lead one side to war against the other."

War? Louis had to be joking.

But for once, he looked absolutely serious.

"We would never do such a thing," Eliot whispered.

"Never? Really?" Louis asked. "Not even in self-defense? Could you en-vision some unscrupulous character manipulating you into a situation where conflict might be inevitable?"

Fiona was quiet, probably reliving that moment in the alley when she had decapitated the Lord of All That Flies.

Eliot wanted to say that he'd never kill anything or anybody . . . but then he remembered that to save Fiona, he had summoned a fog filled with the wandering dead. It was a mistake the first time, but he'd known what he was doing the second time, and he'd still done it. He *had* killed. And it'd been his choice.

Eliot knew he would do it again if Fiona's life were at stake.

He pushed his plate away, no longer hungry.

"So what do we do?" Eliot asked.

"What you think is right," Louis told him, leaning closer. "You two are smarter and stronger than anyone in the families knows. You would do best not to listen to deceitful characters who would try to influence you. Be-sides, of course, your father."

When Louis turned to Fiona, his expression sobered, and he searched for the right words, finally saying, "Within you burns the fury of all the Hells, unquenchable and unstoppable . . . and yet you somehow manage to rein in that power. Truly impressive, my daughter."

"Thank you," Fiona said. "I think."

He turned to Eliot. "And you, my son, have a talent the likes of which the world has never before seen. Not even my humble abilities come close. When you play, the universe holds its breath . . . and listens."

Eliot wanted to say so much more, ask Louis so many things, but it felt as if he'd just swallowed too much information, and it stuck in his windpipe.

Louis stood. "You two are going to be late if we sit all day chitchatting like sparrows over crumbs." He dug into his pockets. "Before I depart, I wanted to give you some trinkets I had lying about."

He tossed one of the playing cards to Eliot.

It fluttered, and to Eliot's utter astonishment, he snatched it out of the air with nimble fingers.

The card was the Queen of Spades, but not a normal one. This queen held a sword like a suicide king—stuck through the side of her head. Most intriguing, though, there were tiny lines and dots scribbled upon it.

Notes. Musical notes.

"'The March of the Suicide Queen,'" Louis told him. "It's an old song that you may find useful."

Eliot touched the notes, and heard them whisper their tune to him.

He tucked the card into his pocket for a closer look later. He wanted to thank Louis, but then remembered that the other songs he'd gotten from his father had led to death and destruction.

He kept his mouth shut and simply nodded.

"And for you, Fiona . . ." Louis smoothed a silver bracelet over the table-cloth. Its slender twisted links reminded Eliot of a snake. "This was made from the last bit of metal that fell from the sky millennia ago. Archon iron."[20]

Fiona picked up the bracelet and examined it. "I don't know what to say. Thank you!" She frowned. "Is it *supposed* to be rusty?"

---

20. Archon iron. A mythohistorical metal said to have fallen from Heaven—literally fallout from the war between God and his rebellious angels, preceding their fall from grace. The metal was an ingredient in the manufacture of the chain binding the wolf Fenrir (prior to its release during Ragnarök). See also Volume 11, the *Post Family Mythology*, for more on this wondrous and terrible element wielded by Fiona Post during the Last Judgment War, which ended the Fifth Age. *Gods of the First and Twenty-first Century, Volume 4, Core Myths (Part 1)*. Zypheron Press Ltd., Eighth Edition.

"The price of antiquity, I am afraid," Louis assured her.

Their father bowed, clasped Eliot's shoulder once more, and gently patted Fiona's hand. "We will meet again soon, I hope. Now you must pardon your poor misremembering father, but he has other business to attend to."

And with that, Louis plucked up his jacket, strode out of the café, turned onto the main street, and was gone.

Fiona gazed at the chain. "We need to think about what he said . . . everything."

"So maybe Louis isn't all bad?" Eliot asked her.

She looped the bracelet around her wrist and did the clasp. "Maybe," Fiona said.

Was it possible this was the beginning of a real relationship with their father? So what if he was an Infernal? Maybe even a man who was supposed to be living, breathing evil could still care for his son.

Eliot and Fiona got up to leave. They miraculously still had plenty of time to get to class.

As they started to go, however, the waiter followed them, clearing his throat. In his hand was the bill that had been left untouched on the table.

Fiona's face darkened, and Eliot took back all the nice things he had thought about Louis.

He'd stiffed them for breakfast.

17

FRIENDS AND ENEMIES

Fiona was mortified. Nothing like this ever happened in homeschooling. She'd never had to undress in front of other people.

She was grateful she hadn't worn her gym shorts and T-shirt *under* her school uniform. That's how she thought it might work. She'd tried it at home, but the extra layers only added to the wrinkled appearance of her jacket and skirt.

The Paxington girls' locker room had only the illusion of privacy. There were rows of benches and lockers so you couldn't see *everyone* at the same time. But still, within the range of a casual glance, dozens of girls laughed and chatted as they stripped out of their uniforms like this was the most ordinary thing in the world.

Fiona didn't think she could blush any harder as she struggled with the buttons on her shirt.

Maybe it was a lifetime of eating Cee's home cooking, maybe it was her severed appetite, but she felt so skinny, so . . . unendowed, compared with the other girls.

Plus all these other girls had perfect manes of hair. Fiona's hair (thanks to the foggy morning) was all frizz.

Not to mention they all wore makeup. They had purses bulging with lipstick and powders, liners and every brush imaginable.

Fiona had used Cee's homemade soap, which efficiently removed dirt (and your first layer of skin), but didn't really enhance anyone's beauty.

Fortunately no one noticed her.

She looked at her feet and focused on slipping out of her skirt and into her gym shorts as fast as she could.

Fiona would have done it with her eyes closed if she wasn't afraid she might have done something dorky like put them on backwards.

She'd never look like these girls. They'd had fifteen years to perfect their looks. They had every modern product and advantage.

She'd just have to be happy with who she was and how she looked . . . though that was easier said than done. Who was she, really? Immortal? A goddess-in-training with the League of Immortals? Or an Infernal? The daughter of the Prince of Darkness?

Both?

But then why did she still look like Fiona Post, shut-in, social and beauty moron?

Louis showing up this morning had thrown her off. She hadn't expected to feel anything for him . . . or if she had, she expected it would have been contempt. He still sounded half crazy, but there was something else there: a spark of wit and intelligence.

He was her father, and she *wanted* to feel a bond with him. She wanted to have something approaching a normal relationship . . . at least with one of her parents. Was that too much to ask?

Jezebel sauntered into the locker room. The girls fell silent.

The Infernal stepped up to the locker next to Fiona's, opened it, and removed her jacket.

Fiona started to say hi, but Jezebel (although she had to see her; she was standing right there) acted like she was completely alone in the locker room.

Jezebel shrugged out of her top and bra.

Fiona quickly turned away.

But not before she caught a glimpse of Jezebel's snow-white porcelain skin, ample curves, and taut stomach. Like pictures Fiona had seen recently in her mythology books—that's how goddesses were *supposed* to look. Or demons.

A girl approached Jezebel and cleared her throat.

Jezebel ignored her.

The girl was tall, tan, blond, and athletic. Fiona remembered her from team selection. She was on White Knight.

"Hey." The girl confidently leaned on a nearby locker. "I'm Tamara. A bunch of us were going to grab coffee after class today. You want to hang out?"

"I don't care who you are," Jezebel told her. "What makes you think that I have need for coffee . . . or the company of mortals?"

Tamara's features bunched together in outrage. "Why, you little bit—!"

Jezebel turned.

The air was charged with tension. The hair on the back of Fiona's neck prickled.

Jezebel's shadow crossed Tamara, darkening her face.

But that was wrong. Fiona checked her own shadow—yes, the overhead lights cast several weak shadows in various directions. Jezebel's shadow somehow defied the optics of the situation, and had collected into a single slice of dark.

Whatever Tamara was going to say, she didn't. The breath seemed to have evaporated from her lungs.

"You will find that I have no tolerance for trifling," Jezebel said. "Decide now if you wish to live."

Tamara took two steps back. "Never mind," she whispered.

Jezebel's shadow returned to normal.

Fiona exhaled.

Tamara managed to regain a bit of her composure, although her healthy tan seemed to have drained away. "Whatever . . ." She walked off—banging her shin on a bench.

Jezebel gave a stifled laugh, then opened her locker and primped the curls of her hair (although it didn't need it), and then continued ignoring the rest of the world.

Fiona made a mental note: *Do not make small talk with an Infernal*.

She smelled mint and turned. Sarah Covington stood next to her. Sarah's red hair had been pulled back and tucked up under a white baseball cap. "Don't worry about that," Sarah said conspiratorially. "Tamara's just sussing out the pecking order."

Sarah offered Fiona a stick of gum, which she accepted to be polite, but didn't unwrap.

"I'm dying to know about the girl who saved my cousin," Sarah said. "No one is *supposed* to come back from the Valley of the New Year. You said your family name was . . ."

"Post," Fiona said, nervous, as if this were the answer to a pop quiz.

"As in 'as dumb as'?" Sarah smiled and laughed. "I'm just jesting, my dear. You must take care not to take any of that nonsense from the other girls, or they'll walk all over you for the next four years."

Fiona didn't like being called dumb—even as a joke. Especially as a joke.

Despite Sarah Covington's outward kindness, Fiona didn't think that's what her teammate had in mind by coming over here and chatting. Her instincts told her this was another test. Not an official Paxington-sanctioned pencil-and-paper test. One more important.

Fiona straightened. "The last person who tried to 'walk all over' me and Eliot . . . didn't do *any* walking afterwards."

Fiona had to soothe the anger coiled within her like a sleeping dragon, knowing how easily it could be aroused . . . knowing, too, that despite her dorky appearance, she *was* special . . . powerful . . . and if she had to be, dangerous, too.

The smile on Sarah's freckled face faded. "Yes, I can indeed see a bit of the spark that got you and my cousin out of Purgatory." She looked as if she had more to say to Fiona, but her gaze then caught something intriguing across the locker room. "Excuse me. There's a bit of unfinished business to take care of."

Fiona watched Sarah flounce off.

Jezebel glanced at Fiona—with neither approval nor disdain—which Fiona guessed was what passed for a friendly gesture in Infernal circles.

Sarah moved to where Amanda Lane was awkwardly trying to tuck her T-shirt (which was three sizes too big) into her baggy shorts.

Fiona hadn't seen Amanda when she came in. She had mastered social invisibility, and Fiona understood why. If no one ever saw you, you didn't have to struggle to find the right words, and then stumble and stutter them out in the unlikely case someone actually spoke to you.

She knew all this because that's just the silent subspecies of nerd she had been only a few months ago.

In many ways, she still was, and everything she was trying to be—poised, confident, and likable—was just an act.

"I don't recall inviting *you* to Team Scarab," Sarah told Amanda so sweetly that she could have been talking about the weather.

"I didn't . . . ," Amanda started. She swiped her straggly hair out of her face, but it fell immediately back. She looked at the ground. "I mean, my name was on the roster posted outside."

"Then that's a mistake," Sarah said, jabbing at her for emphasis. "You need to find another team. And quickly, so we can find a suitable replacement."

"But, I thought . . ." Amanda's voice faded to nothing.

"You said you were sponsored to Paxington by the League?" Sarah asked. "Of Immortals? Truly? Not the League of Losers? Or is this one of the gods' practical jokes?" Sarah grabbed a handful of Amanda's T-shirt, yanked it out of her shorts—then shoved her. "Or are you just a liar?"

Amanda banged into her locker and winced.

Fiona took an involuntary step closer. Her first instinct was to rush over there and stop this.

But she halted. Part of her wanted to know why Amanda was here, too. She knew Amanda wouldn't lie about the League sponsorship. Why had they sent her here?

Sarah pressed on, however, before Fiona could act. She grasped Amanda by her arm and shoved her into the showers.

The other girls watched, some laughed, but most just kept doing what they were doing.

"No," Amanda whimpered. She didn't even look up, her eyes firmly glued to her feet, unwilling—or maybe unable—to stand up for herself.

Amanda stumbled onto the tiled stalls. "Please don't," she whispered to Sarah.

"'Please'?" Sarah said, mocking her. "Please help you get clean? Help you wash that rat's nest hair? Why, certainly."

Sarah twisted on a cold water spigot. A shower nozzle sputtered and shot forth streams of water.

It hit Amanda, and she yelped, then jumped out of the way.

Sarah tapped the pipe. All the cold water spigots turned by themselves. Icy water rained and filled the entire shower section of the locker room.

Amanda backed into the corner, but still got drenched.

"St-st-stop it," Amanda sobbed. "Please."

Fiona had watched enough. Someone had to stand up for Amanda. And someone had to take that horrid Sarah Covington down a few notches.

She marched over to them. "Turn it off," Fiona told Sarah.

Sarah looked around the gym, pursed her lips, and appeared for a split second as uneasy with this cruel prank as Fiona . . . but then she shook her head.

Fiona reached for the water faucet—Sarah stepped in front of her.

Fiona wanted to punch Sarah right in her petite button nose, freckles and all.

But she checked the impulse as she remembered how she had fought

Beelzebub. She'd hit and been hit with enough force to smash concrete. If she hit Sarah *that* hard, the girl might not survive.

And as tempting as that was, at this particular moment, Fiona knew violence was wrong.

So instead she reached for the main pipe, her fingers slipped over the beads of condensation on the metal, and she closed her hand—crushing the steel as if it were an empty aluminum can.

The water in the pipe squeaked and squealed and shuttered to a stop.

Louis had told her: *"Within you burns the fury of all the Hells, unquenchable and unstoppable . . . and yet you somehow manage to rein in that power."*

. . . Maybe not *entirely* reined in at this moment.

Fiona released the mashed pipe and turned to Sarah. Her hand slowly clenched into a fist in front of Sarah's face. "She's on our team," Fiona told her. "But if you don't like it—*you* don't have to be."

Sarah glanced at the crushed pipe, seemingly unimpressed, then looked at Fiona's fist. Her eyes narrowed a tad. She didn't look frightened, but nonetheless she snorted and backed off a step, then returned to her locker.

"'Just sussing out the pecking order,'" Fiona muttered after her.

Fiona might never be Sarah's social equal at Paxington—but if she could help it, she wasn't going to be bullied or let her bully anyone else.

Fiona went to Amanda.

The girl stood shivering in the corner, wet hair plastered over her face. She tried to control her sobs, but they still came out in little gasps.

Fiona was about to offer her hand to the girl . . . but then thought better of it. Probably not the smartest thing to do after she had just crushed the pipe in front of her.

For a moment she wondered if Sarah hadn't been right in one sense: Amanda didn't belong here. She was going to get hurt. Or worse.

Why had the League sent her here anyway?

"It's going to be okay," Fiona said, amazingly sounding like she meant this.

"Th-th-thanks." The word shuddered out of Amanda's body.

"Let's get you toweled off," Fiona suggested. "I have an extra set of gym clothes you can borrow."

Amanda nodded and skittered out of the showers.

Fiona considered what she had done by saving Amanda: she'd have to watch out not only for herself and her brother—but now a third clueless person as well. That was going to be trouble.

These thoughts came skidding to a halt, however.

The water at Fiona's feet steamed.

It wasn't cold the way it should have been. It bubbled, boiling hot.

18

THE UNPREPARED TEST

Eliot had changed into his shorts and gym T-shirt (which had a nifty gold scarab embroidered on the right breast) and now stood on the field before the six-story-high obstacle course in the Ludus Magnus coliseum.

If there'd ever been a jungle gym event in the Olympics, *this* would have been it.

There were simple things like stairs, slides, and monkey bars—most of which were fifty feet high, though. There were less childlike things: rope bridges, balance beams, and zip lines. Then there were the things that looked dangerous: barbed wire mazes, and platforms held by single poles that swayed (even in no wind).

Eliot took a deep breath. He wasn't afraid of heights . . . but even unafraid, you'd have to be nuts to climb this thing.

He'd had a week to prepare for his first gym class, a week he had spent with his nose stuck in books on myths, gods, and demons. He'd learned tons, but he should have been jogging, or doing push-ups or something to get ready for this.

One good fall and a busted neck . . . and all that reading would be moot.

Next to him, Jeremy Covington droned on to Mitch Stephenson about classic winning strategies on the Ludus Magnus course.

Mitch caught Eliot's uneasy look and, with a flick of his head, invited him to join them.

Eliot waved back but didn't approach.

In the last week, Jeremy had barely said five words to him. The Scotsman was a bully. He'd been in three fights—won them all with kicks to the groin and thumb jabs to the eyes. Eliot was also pretty sure he smelled whiskey on his breath yesterday, too.

Mitch, on the other hand, got along with everyone. He always said hi, had something cool to say, paid attention in class—he'd even protected poor clueless Amanda from getting hassled. But Mitch also kept everyone at arm's length, like he used his friendliness as an invisible shield.

Standing to Eliot's left were four boys. Eliot had seen them on campus, but didn't know them.

On these boys' black shirts was a different symbol: a white sword crossed over a white lance. They were Team White Knight.

Eliot had read that White Knights were supposed to be the good guys. The polite thing to do would have been to introduce himself . . . but from the boys' cold assessing looks, he didn't think they were here to rescue any damsels or do good deeds.

They whispered and nodded at the jungle gym—from the snippets Eliot overheard, coming up with a strategy to beat Team Scarab.

Eliot kept his distance. He wanted to be friends with everyone, but something told him that being friends might get in the way of winning.

It seemed Paxington had been engineered to promote a philosophy of "win at any cost" with its duels, academic bell curve, gym class, and social pecking order. But Eliot didn't want to win if so many others had to lose.

Robert came out of the boys' locker room and jogged over to Eliot. "Almost didn't get here today," he said. "Slept in."

He had a faded bruise around one eye, like he'd been in a fight recently. His T-shirt was taut and flexed with muscle. He must be working out.

"I've been trying to catch you all week," Eliot said, "but you're gone as soon as the class bell rings."

"Just studying," he said without meeting Eliot's gaze. "That reading stuff comes easy for you . . . not so much for a guy like me."

All this was true, but it felt a bit off, like Robert had left out one important fact.

Eliot guessed what it was. "Are you avoiding Fiona on purpose?"

Robert took a big breath and sighed. "Probably," he said. "Some folks in the League think I got off too light for breaking their rules. I could get Fiona in trouble just being seen with her."

Eliot had figured as much. He wanted to have a long talk with Robert. Partially because he thought of him as a friend. Partially because Eliot needed someone to talk to . . . someone who wasn't getting more and

more concerned with how they looked, staying locked inside the bathroom every morning. It was like Fiona thought her hair was more important than school.

Before he could say more to Robert, however, four girls marched onto
the field. They stood with the White Knight boys and eyed Eliot and
Robert with a mix of curiosity and contempt. The White Knight boys
spoke to the girls, pointing up the gym structure.

Jezebel then emerged from the girls' locker room, followed a moment
later by Sarah Covington.

"We'll talk," Robert said, "but later. Catch me after gym today, okay?"

Eliot nodded.

"Does the Infernal . . . ," Robert whispered. "I know this sounds nuts,
but she looks like that girl you hung out with this summer. What was her
name?"

"Julie Marks."

Eliot had thought it was just him, but she really did look like Julie. Un-
curl her hair, add a little color to the dead white skin, and she could have
been Julie's twin.

But believing that was wishful thinking. Julie had been mortal; the only
extraordinary thing about her was that she had liked Eliot. She even kissed
him, before she'd left Del Sombra for Hollywood. Remembering made
Eliot feel wonderful and miserable all at the same time.

Sarah Covington waved Eliot and Robert over to where the girls, Jeremy, and Mitch now stood.

Eliot grabbed his pack off the grass and they joined his teammates.

"Where's Fiona and Amanda?" Eliot asked.

"There was a wee issue," Sarah told him, and tucked a strand of red hair
into her cap. "A girl thing. They'll be out in a jiffy."

Jeremy cleared his throat. "We need to be thinking up a strategy," he
told them. "First, we pick the Team Captain."

"You?" Robert snorted.

"Who else?" Jeremy said. "I've studied freshman gym extensively. I
know all the tactics."

The thought of taking orders from Jeremy made Eliot's skin crawl.
"Seems simple to me," Eliot countered. "Get to your flag before the others do."

Sarah looked at Eliot like he was a bug. "You think it so simple? I can't
wait to see how you do up there."

Eliot matched her stare. "Sure, it's going to be harder than that. But what about Robert or Mitch . . . or Jezebel? It'd be nice to have someone leading us who—I don't know—knows something about modern technology, like cell phones, for instance?"

Jeremy's smile vanished.

"What do cell phones have to do with gym?" Mitch asked.

"Field communications," Robert said, nodding. "We can get a conference call going. We should get headsets, too."

"Perhaps," Jezebel told Eliot, "you should be Team Captain."

She said this without inflection. Eliot wasn't sure if it was a joke. Her jade green eyes were not like Julie's clear blue eyes at all . . . yet they had the same sparkle.

"Please m'lady," Jeremy said. "We need someone with experience in these matters. Someone maybe who has struck another in anger before? . . . In case such a far-fetched possibility occurs."

"So fighting's the goal?" Eliot spat back. "Or getting to our flag and winning?"

If Jeremy wanted his résumé on fighting, he could tell him about the ten thousand rats he and Fiona had faced in the sewers, or Perry Millhouse, or an entire air force base, or the Infernal Lord of All That Flies.

Fiona and Amanda stepped out of the girls' locker room, and seeing those two halted Eliot's thoughts.

Amanda wore a stunned expression. Her hair was wet as if she'd just taken a shower. But *before* gym class?

Eliot caught Fiona's eyes and she gave a shake of her head. Something had happened, but she couldn't tell him—not now.

He met Fiona halfway and said, "We're trying to figure out a strategy. Jeremy wants to pick a Captain first. It's so stupid."

"*He's* so stupid," Fiona said. She turned to Amanda. "Can you do this? Maybe you better sit it out."

"No." A spark of life returned to Amanda's dark eyes. "I'm okay."

Fiona stalked over to the rest of their team. She was mad, at whom Eliot didn't know, but he felt the anger coming off his sister in waves.

"Ah, Fiona, me darling," Jeremy said, "we be ready to vote for a Captain. I know I can count on your support."

"You don't have a Team Captain yet?" one of the girls from White Knight said. She was tall, tan, and stood with her hands on her hips—and she had obviously been eavesdropping. "What a bunch of losers."

"Mind your own business, Tamara," Sarah told her. "We'll see who'll be losing soon enough."

"What do you expect?" one of the White Knight boys with a shaven head remarked. "They have an Infernal on their team. They've got to be disorganized."

Jezebel turned to see who had said this, but her expression didn't change, nor did she say a thing.

Somehow this scared Eliot more than if she had threatened him with hellfire.

"Hey!" Robert yelled back. "You're going to sound pretty funny with a mouthful of fist, buddy."

"Bring it," the boy said, taking a step forward.

Mitch set a hand on Robert's arm. "Save it for class," he advised.

The air stilled and Eliot felt something. *Felt,* however, wasn't quiet right, because this was just an itch below his threshold of conscious detection . . . a whispered warning that danger was near.

He, Fiona, and Jezebel turned.

A man walked onto the field. He held a clipboard and stopwatch. He wore black sweats with the Paxington crest. He moved with strength, confidence, and grace. He was darkly tanned and trim and very old. Deep laugh lines and wrinkles made a spiderweb of his face. His hair was white, thick, and gathered into a long tail.

Eliot felt the weight of the Ages on this old man. As if he'd seen everything and that nothing Eliot could do would ever impress him.

"I am Mr. Benjamin Ma," the old man said. "You shall call me Mr. Ma or simply Coach." He didn't speak loud, but his voice was commanding. "I shall review the rules. Team Scarab and White Knight will then mount the course for their first match of the year."

A lump of ice materialized in Eliot's stomach. A match on their first day? He'd expected a warm-up.

"That's not fair," Mitch told Mr. Ma. "No one told us. We're not ready."

Some of the students on Team White Knight snickered.

Mr. Ma looked Mitch over, and then replied, "That is too bad, young man. In life we often find ourselves unprepared. How you perform in such circumstances is the only true test of one's abilities."

Mitch looked like he wanted to protest more, but he only nodded.

"Rule one," Mr. Ma told both groups. "Half of your team members must get to their flag to win. These four must be moving under their own power."

He nodded at the jungle gym. On the very top, two flags unfurled and fluttered, one with a golden scarab, the other with the helmet and lance of White Knight.

They were at least forty feet off the ground.

"Rule two," Mr. Ma said. "You have ten minutes to reach your flag. If neither team gets four members to their flag, then *both* teams record a loss. If both teams get four across, then the team with the lowest time wins."

Eliot knew that winning meant more than just bragging rights. The lowest-ranked teams were cut, and didn't go on to their sophomore year.

"Rule three," Mr. Ma continued. "You may use any means to cross the course. You may use any means to prevent your opponents from doing the same. Magic is allowed, but no weapons, specifically *no* guns, *no* blades, and *no* explosives." His black eyes bored into them. "If I find such contraband, I shall use it *on* the offender."

Eliot was sure he wasn't kidding.

"Questions?" Mr. Ma asked.

"I have a question, sir," Eliot said. He shifted his backpack and unzipped it.

He was the only student who'd brought a pack. He'd had to. At first he'd left Lady Dawn in his locker, but that felt wrong, and when he tried to walk away, his hand burned with pain and the old line of infection reappeared up to his elbow.

Eliot pulled out the battered violin case and opened it for Mr. Ma. "Is *this* a weapon?"

Jeremy and Sarah rolled their eyes.

The people on Team Knight laughed. "Going to play 'Mary Had a Little Lamb'?" one of them asked.

Mr. Ma reached to touch the wood grain, but hesitated.

"Powerful." He assessed Eliot with a look that made him feel like all his secrets were being turned inside out. "But not a weapon, technically, in my class, Mr. Post. She is approved."

The chuckles from the White Knights died.

Eliot took Lady Dawn out. That Queen of Spades playing card was tucked inside the case. He'd put his father's gift there for safekeeping.

He retrieved it and scanned the notes written on it. "The March of the Suicide Queen," Louis had called it.

Eliot hadn't had a chance to play it yet, but the song nonetheless came unbidden to his mind: a fanfare of horns, a swell of strings, and bass kettledrums. It was a military march. He imagined troops gathered upon a field of battle, soldiers with bayoneted rifles and horse-drawn cannon.

He unthinkingly plucked Lady Dawn's strings.

The Ludus Magnus and the rest of the world fell away, and Eliot was alone in the darkness of his imagination, a single spot light illuminating him. A choir of baritone men joined, singing:

> *Off we go and march to war*
> *sing our song to bloody chore*
> *shoot and stab and rend and kill*
> *Live to march o'er one more hill*

Eliot stilled the strings, and the world came back into focus.

The gym structure swayed to the march's rhythm, and then the entire thing leaned toward him as if it wanted him to play more.

Eliot wouldn't, though. That song was too dark. It was about war and killing . . . and while he was certain it could help Team Scarab, it'd be like using artillery at a game of darts.

Everyone stood speechless, staring at him.

The White Knight boy with the shaven head whispered to his teammates, and they nodded—all of them watching Eliot like he was the most dangerous thing they'd ever seen.

Eliot had a bad feeling about that.

Jezebel had held out one hand to Eliot. She retracted the gesture, curling her fingers inward to her chest, and she quickly looked away—but not before Eliot saw her eyes. They were now blue, the color of clear water. Like Julie Marks's had been.

"Team Knight and Team Scarab, ready yourselves," Mr. Ma said. He took out his stopwatch. "Get set. Go!"

19

TEAM SCARAB'S FIRST MATCH

Team Knight and Team Scarab ran for the jungle gym.

Adrenaline pulsed and pounded through Fiona's blood. She raced ahead, and she easily outdistanced them all, except Robert.

He got to the obstacle course first, clambered up a ladder, and turned to make sure she was right behind him.

Fiona grabbed the ladder, but then looked back.

Jeremy and Sarah Covington, Jezebel, Mitch Stephenson, Eliot, and Amanda Lane had scattered across the field. It was total chaos. Eliot had a hard time running with that stupid pack of his.

Team Knight was different. They ran in formation—two four-person teams. One angled left, and one split off to the right side. They had a plan.

"Come on," Robert said. "We need to get up as fast as we can." He scrambled up the ladder.

Sarah and Jeremy ran up to her but ignored the ladder. Instead they tromped along the adjacent spiral that went up a ways and then wormed into the center of the structure.

"Hey!" Fiona said. "Stick together!"

"Middle path, me dearie," Jeremy called back. "Hurry. Knights be taking the high and low paths."

Fiona saw the Knights had done precisely that. One group ran up along a zigzag of stairs—almost as high as Robert now despite his head start. The other team—she just caught a glimpse of them in the lower portion of the course, and then lost them in a tangle of hanging chains.

Jezebel, Mitch, then Eliot, and finally Amanda caught up to her.

"It's a maze," Jezebel said, scrutinizing the structure. "Not all paths lead to our goal, I bet."

"Then which way?" Mitch asked, looking up and squinting.

Amanda was so out of breath, she couldn't speak. She knelt and panted.

Eliot hefted Lady Dawn, and said, "I've got an idea."

Fiona's gut reaction was to tell him to stop playing with that silly violin, that they didn't have time. But with everything she'd seen Eliot do with his music, she figured it was worth the gamble of a few seconds to see what he had in mind.

Jezebel didn't wait, however. She found a knotted rope and pulled herself up hand over hand.

Mitch glanced at her and then to Fiona, indecisive which way to go. He smiled and took a step closer to her. "I'll stay with you guys, if that's okay."

"Great." Mitch hadn't said much to her since school started, but whenever he was around, he had a way of making her feel comfortable. She was glad he was here now.

Eliot ran a thumb over the Lady Dawn's strings and then plucked out a whimsical tune.

Fiona smelled popcorn and the burned sugar scent of cotton candy, and then heard on the wind a distant calliope join Eliot's song.

This had something to do with that carnival they'd been in, where they'd fought Perry Millhouse, and where they rescued Amanda.

Amanda went white. Her eyes widened. She backed away from Eliot.

The song was a little musical phrase that repeated and then reflected and inverted and bounced around in Fiona's head. A wonderful invention.

"Where did he learn to play like that?" Mitch asked in awe.

Fiona didn't have an answer for him.

She saw multiples of Eliot prism, as if her eyes were full of tears. She saw the obstacle course blur with a hundred different twisting paths. It was like the mirror maze in the carnival; that's what Eliot's music was about.

The jungle gym creaked and pinged. The scuffed aluminum ladder shone like it was new—and then a dozen rungs up, there was a set of monkey bars whose tarnished brass cleared and gleamed as if just polished—and where those ended, a balance beam of scuffed and scratched wood smoothed into gleaming mahogany as she watched.

He was finding the path through the course.

"The quickest way to the flag," Eliot said as he played. "Go. Quick. I'll keep playing."

Mitch started up the ladder, and then waited for Fiona and Amanda.

Fiona wasn't sure. It was a great idea, but she didn't like leaving Eliot by himself.

How else were they going to win, though?

She and Eliot locked eyes. It'd be okay; they both knew how to take care of themselves if they had to.

"I can't do this," Amanda whispered. She looked miserable, sick from the brief sprint, terrified at the height of the imposing course, one hand clutching the side of her head, trying to block out Eliot's music. "Let me stay. I'd just slow you down."

"Keep your eyes open at least," Fiona told her . . . a little more nastily than she had intended.

Fiona and Mitch then mounted the ladder, climbed up—and then swung onto the monkey bars, following Eliot's gleaming path.

Mitch got onto the balance beam, braced one hand on a railing, and extended his other hand to Fiona.

She took it and felt perfectly safe with him here—she looked down—even though "here" was a precarious twenty feet high.

They stepped across the beam, followed its arc shape up and then down in a half-moon trajectory and landed on a platform held by a steel pole. The thing swayed but held their weight.

Eliot looked small on the ground, his music tinny and far away . . . but it still worked: Among the tangles of woven rope netting that went up from the platform, one section looked new, its knots squared and firm and sturdy.

"Your brother's a miracle worker," Mitch said, and started up.

"He's something, that's for sure," she replied.

If they'd been smart, they would have had Eliot find the path ahead of time, and they could all have gone up together.

Fiona scanned the course and spotted Jezebel ten feet higher, where her rope ended in a solid concrete ceiling. She was stuck.

Robert was very high now . . . almost to their flag. Good for him.

Should she have gone with him in the first place? That would have given them two at their goal. Nearly half a win. She didn't see Jeremy or Sarah.

Half of Team White Knight, though, were almost to their flag. They worked together, helping each other along, and they were all looking for the best path . . . keeping an eye out for an attack from Team Scarab as well? It was a smart strategy.

Fiona clambered over the top of the cargo netting and into a tube made of chain link. It was rickety, sloped down and then up and then sideways, spilling out into a series of hand-powered lifts: a bucket and rope and pulleys that would carry them almost to Robert's position.

In a minute, they could be all caught up.

A breeze rocked the gym. Fiona clutched onto the chain and felt her stomach in her throat.

She looked down, for a moment not being able to see Eliot . . . then she found him. Tiny and playing and still there.

But she saw something else that made her heart skip a beat: the missing half of Team White Knight. They were on the ground and moving toward her bother.

In a flash, she understood. Their strategy was to send one half up—fast sprinters—and let one half lag behind to slow down the opposition. And right now, the most vulnerable target was her trouble-magnet of a brother.

They were going to clobber him.

"Eliot!" she yelled.

Her voice was lost in the breeze. Eliot kept his head down, playing.

"I see them, too," Mitch said, his normally reassuring tone heavy with concern. "There's no way to get to him in time."

The Knights moved carefully . . . probably because they knew magic when they heard it and didn't want to give Eliot a chance to turn on them.

Amanda just sat there, listening. Utterly useless.

Fiona's anger came. It spilled through her blood, molten and pulsing and erupting along every nerve.

She turned to Mitch. "Get to the flag. You can't follow the way I'm going."

Fiona stretched the rubber band on her wrist and sliced through the wire cage.

Without a moment's hesitation, she jumped—free fall for a heartbeat—then impacted on the platform below.

The wood splintered and cracked. Pain exploded along her shins, and her shirt ripped.

These distractions were quickly blotted out by her swelling anger.

Her father's words echoed in her mind once more: *"Within you burns the fury of all the Hells, unquenchable and unstoppable."*

She flipped around to the underside of the platform, grabbed the supporting pole, and slid thirty feet down. She landed so hard, her sneakers made craters.

She stalked onto the field.

"Hey!" Fiona shouted at two closest Knights, a boy and a girl.

They turned, shock on their faces; then the boy regained his wits and spoke to the girl. It was Tamara from the locker room. She smiled and moved to Fiona while the boy continued toward Eliot.

Amanda heard Fiona's shout, however. She glanced about wildly, now seeing the danger: three White Knight boys had her and Eliot surrounded. She screamed.

That scream broke Eliot out of his trance. He looked up, turned all around, taking in the three boys closing in. He hesitated; his fingers twitched.

Meanwhile, Tamara blocked Fiona's path and set one hand on the ground. The grass where she touched turned gray and crumpled to dust— a circle of death that spread outward.

Around Fiona, however, the yellowed grass greened, wiggled, bursting forth with life, and growing in thick tangles about her feet.

She took one step, but the grass snaked and laced about her, holding fast.

Tamara laughed.

Fiona knelt to cut the offending runners, but as soon as she did, shoots gripped her thigh, pulled the one hand she'd set onto the ground, holding it.

She tugged. The grass ripped out . . . but immediately grew new, stronger roots.

Tendrils wormed along her wrist and up to her elbow. She yanked as hard as she could, but she felt the anger slipping from her . . . becoming panic, hot in her throat.

Fiona glanced up. The three boys were almost on Eliot.

Eliot flicked his fingers over his violin, and a dissonant chord distorted the air between him and the closest boy—throwing the boy backwards as if he'd been swatted with a giant invisible hand.

But that's all the chance the other two needed to rush in.

One tackled Eliot; the other kicked Lady Dawn from his grasp.

Tamara walked near Fiona. As she did so, the grass pulled harder, pulled her closer to the ground, and twined about her neck. Tamara was going to make her eat dirt . . . or strangle her.[21]

"Remember, little dung scarab," Tamara said, "in gym class, we can use *any* means to stop our opponents—even if that means *killing* them. Bet you wish you had that Infernal with you now."

She was bluffing. Had to be.

Try as she might, though, Fiona couldn't summon her hate again; it was like trying to make herself hiccup.

She strained against the pulling grass . . . helpless.

Fiona heard a girl's voice: "The Infernal *is* here, fool."

She turned her head. Jezebel was five paces away. Her expression was cool and implacable—save her eyes, which boiled with caustic venom. The grass around her, instead of grabbing, bent toward her and bowed in supplication.

Jezebel crossed the distance to Tamara in two quick strides and backhanded her, sending the girl end over end through the air.

Tamara landed in the sod and didn't move.

"Help," Fiona whispered.

Jezebel looked down with contempt. "Help yourself. You have all you need at your fingertips." She moved toward Eliot. "Do what you do best and *cut*."

Cut? There was nothing at her fingertips besides grass.

. . . Which were very much like threads. Heck, they were even called *blades* of grass. She'd been such an idiot.

Fiona focused, felt the edges of every grass shoot touching her, saw their delicate edges—and pressed until they sharpened and focused to a laser-thin line—

—that cut—each other—the ground—everything, slicing itself into a million wriggling shreds of confetti.

Fiona got up and ran to Eliot.

One of the boys sat with his full weight on her brother's shoulders, pinning him facefirst in the grass. The other boy strode to Lady Dawn. And the third boy moved toward Amanda . . . who, to her credit, was at least *trying* to outmaneuver the bully around a pole and get to Eliot.

21. Tamara Pritchard, part of the Dreaming Families, and infamous for her use of Life/Death dual magics, was born with gifts we could scarcely imagine. Had her focus been magical rather than social engineering during those early years . . . she would have been a real threat to us. *The Secret Red Diaries of Sarah Covington, Third Edition,* Sarah Covington, Mariposa Printers, Dublin.

The boy on Eliot reared back to hit his head.

Jezebel got to him first—tackled the boy—a blur of motion—they rolled together once on the ground. There was the snap of breaking bone.

The Infernal got up. The boy didn't move.

Eliot shakily got to his feet.

Fiona joined him. "You okay?"

"I think so," Eliot grunted, rubbing the back of his neck. "If my head's still on straight." He gazed riveted on his violin. "Hey! Don't touch her!"

The other boy picked up Lady Dawn.

A string snapped and sliced the boy's arm—cutting the vein at his wrist.

"Holy—!" The boy dropped her and clutched his wrist, blood dribbling out.

A whistle trilled, and that sent shivers down Fiona's spine.

Mr. Ma had appeared on the field (although Fiona had not seen him anywhere close). "That is the match," he declared. "Halt all activities."

Mr. Ma pulled out a handheld radio and called for medics. He went to the bleeding White Knight student and sprinkled a powder on his wrist, which staunched the flow of blood.

"Thank goodness it's over," Fiona breathed.

She turned to thank Jezebel, but the Infernal was already walking off the field.

"Did we win?" Eliot asked.

Mr. Ma now had an extinguisher in hand. He blasted a jet of frozen carbon dioxide at a fire licking a wooden pole on the obstacle course.

Had one of the White Knights tried to burn something? Fiona hadn't seen any of them set it, but who else? What wouldn't these people do to win?

The other four White Knight boys and girls slid down ropes in formation.

Robert, Mitch, Jeremy, and Sarah clambered down along different routes . . . and from the long looks on their faces, Mr. Ma didn't have to say who'd won.

How could this have gone so wrong?

"What happened?" she asked Mitch.

"Didn't get there in time," he said with a shrug, but otherwise seemed unfazed. "Once the music stopped, it took me longer than I thought to find the right way."

Sarah stalked up to her. "Next time you be halfway to the flag, I suggest—

strongly suggest—you keep going. The match would have been over in a blink if you'd let them have your brother a wee bit." She trounced off.

Fiona was too shocked to reply.

She couldn't image what those four White Knights would have done to Eliot. They would have put him in the hospital for sure.

Maybe that was the point.

A few broken arms, and you could reduce the number of opponents on the other team—maybe permanently, so if you had to play that team again, there'd be fewer of them, and a better chance to win.

Logical. And horrifying.

Robert, covered in sweat, came up to her and Eliot. "You guys all right?"

"We're fine," she told him.

Why hadn't Robert stayed with them? Had he wanted to win so badly that he'd forgotten everything else?

Looking at him as he stood panting, soaked, a faint bruise under one eye, she wondered again just what he was doing at Paxington. He wasn't interested in books and learning. Robert lived to ride.

Before she could figure out how to even ask Robert about any of this, Mr. Ma spoke.

"Three at Scarab's flag," he announced. "Four for White Knight at seven minutes thirteen seconds. A moderately good time. Win for the Knights." Mr. Ma nodded at their team, and then looked over to Fiona and Eliot. "A loss for Scarab."

The White Knight boys and girls exchanged high fives and went to their injured teammates to help the medics dress wounds and get them off the field. None of them spared Fiona another look.

And why should they? They'd lost.

"Too many weak links on this team," Jeremy said bitterly, and walked off the field.

Eliot looked like he'd been struck.

Fiona didn't like the way Jeremy had said that . . . it sounded like a threat, and she wondered if the students on the other teams were the *only* ones she'd have to worry about.

20

LITTLE WHITE LIE

Eliot was sure Jeremy and Sarah Covington blamed him . . . with their averted glances and cold shoulders all week. And yet, they still spoke to Fiona, and Jeremy always tried to open doors for her.

As far as they were concerned, he was just her "little brother," the kid with the violin who had caused half their team to lag behind and lose their first match.

He sat in the back of Miss Westin's Mythology 101 class. This week she continued her lecture of the mortal magical families. He'd learned about the Kaleb clan and the Scalagari family.[22]

Everyone at Paxington was special in their own way. Some families had political clout, others had powerful magic, and some had a pedigree that stretched back to antiquity.

And while Eliot, at least in theory, had *all* these things, no one could know (thanks to the League's stupid rules).

Even if there weren't rules, Eliot wasn't sure it would matter. If people knew who and what he was—*especially* if people knew who and what he

---

22. The Scalagari family is renowned for its weavers and fine tailors. They employ highly guarded methods to weave magical aspects into cloth. Their camel hair overcoats, for example, are impervious to bullet or blade, and are said to have the "strength and weight" of an entire mountain woven into their feather-soft fabric. The Scalagaris also have a darker side, reputably connected to the criminal underworld. From ancestral estates on Sicily and the isle of Nero Basilica, it is said they operate gambling, extortion, and smuggling rings (under constant investigation by Interpol; no charges, however, have ever been bought to court). *Gods of the First and Twenty-first Century, Volume 14, The Mortal Magical Families.* Zypheron Press Ltd., Eighth Edition.

was—that would just make it worse. He'd be the Immortal hero kid with all the power, family, and political connections who *still* lost the match for Team Scarab.

Miss Westin ended the lecture and wrote an extra-credit reading assignment on John Dee on the blackboard.

Fiona sat next to Eliot. While she was completely absorbed, scribbling this down, he grabbed his notes and slunk out of class.

"Wait a second," Fiona hissed after him.

Eliot kept going. He wanted to be alone.

Slipping through the blackout curtains and double doors of the auditorium, he blinked in the too-bright sunlight after being in the shadows for the last two hours.

Or maybe losing the match *wasn't* his fault.

What if everyone on his team shared the blame? What if losing was as much Jeremy and Sarah's fault for not meeting ahead of time and coming up with a plan? They were the ones who were supposed to know everything.

Eliot had actually helped Fiona and Mitch find the right path before getting ambushed.

What if Team Knight had just been better prepared?

As his eyes adjusted to the noontime sun, he saw that he wasn't the only one to have left early.

Jezebel was here as well.

Last week, when she had looked at him as he held Lady Dawn—at that particular moment—Jezebel had looked *exactly* like Julie . . . down to her blue eyes.

The fantasy of Jezebel being Julie vanished as Jezebel tilted her head, blinking in the sunlight, getting her bearings. Her features were too sharp, cheekbones pushed up higher . . . and, of course, she was an Infernal protégée.

Julie had just been . . . well, Julie. Normal. Mortal. Nice.

Concern creased Jezebel's otherwise smooth forehead as if she was worried she would be seen. Then she spotted him. Her eyes narrowed with disgust. She turned and walked off in the opposite direction.

But that look—it was the same annoyed, you're-under-my-skin-look that Julie had given him . . . just before she had kissed him the first time.

Eliot was totally confused now.

He followed her. "Jezebel!" he called out.

Her stride faltered, only a single step, but it was enough to know she'd heard him.

She continued walking, increasing her pace.

Eliot trotted behind her. "Thanks for the other day. You know . . . gym class. You saved my neck."

"Begone, wormfood." Her voice was full of icy indifference. "I've nothing to say to you."

He'd expected this. He'd be defensive, too, if everyone treated him the way the other students had treated her—all the whispering, the leering, and the innuendo—just because of her family.

Eliot had, however, seen Hell for himself. Maybe there was a good reason to treat her differently.

But wasn't he like her, too? At least part Infernal?

Maybe it was time to trust someone . . . introduce himself. There were no stupid League rules that prevented him from telling anyone about his *Infernal* side. He and Jezebel might even be distant cousins, for all he knew.

"I'm Eliot Post," he said, this time quietly. "I'm half Infernal. On my father's side."

Jezebel slowed. She still didn't look his way, but she pursed her lips as if deciding something.

"Lucifer's son," he said.

They entered the corridor that led to the quartz-paved quad. Columns of veined marble cast crisscrossing shadows along their path.

"You are a fool, Eliot Post." She quickened her stride.

Eliot's strength left him. How much rejection was a guy supposed to take before he finally got the hint?

"Okay, no problem," he said. Then so softly that even he barely heard: "You just reminded me of someone I cared about. A lot. Someone I miss."

Jezebel halted half in and half out of the shadows.

She trembled. One hand made a fist. One hand reached out, fingers splayed.

Eliot felt a tug in his center: a connection.

Something inside him was drawn to something within her. . . .

"Julie?" He took a tentative step toward her. "It *is* you, somehow, isn't it?"

A shuddering breath escaped her, and she turned to him. Her fist clenched tighter, knuckles popping. But her open hand reached for him.

Her face quavered with rage *and* longing; one eye was green—the other blue, and from it, a single tear marked her cheek.

"Maybe," she said.

The effort of that one word seemed to quench her anger. "Once I might have been Julie, but you don't know what I've done since then—or plan to do," she said, her words intensifying. "Or what I really am now."

Eliot met her hand with his, and took it. Her flesh was warm and soft and yielding.

Her face was a mix of Infernal and mortal, Jezebel and the Julie Marks he knew.

He wanted to tell her how much he had missed her. How wonderful that she was here now with him.

The thing in his center, pulling him closer to her, however, cooled and curled inward—repulsed.

"You lied to me." He dropped her hand. "I mean, you are Infernal. There's no way you could have lied about *that* in front of Miss Westin and got away with it. So that means in Del Sombra you weren't really Julie Marks?"

Her blue eye dissolved into translucent green once more. The tear upon her human flesh evaporated.

"There is *no* Julie Marks," she told him, her voice hoarse.

"You pretended to be the manager at Ringo's," he said, "and said we'd run away together to Hollywood." Eliot's tone hardened. "Was *everything* a lie, then? Did you ever even like me?"

Jezebel's open hand closed, and trembled, as if barely restraining it from violence. Her gaze dropped to the floor.

"Tell me the truth," Eliot demanded.

The shadows in the corridor deepened and angled—became bands of absolute dark slashed by golden sunlight. Eliot stood half in and half out of the shade. Jezebel, however, was now fully immersed in the darkness.

"You want the truth?" she whispered sweetly, but there was cruelty in her voice as well.

Eliot had a feeling this was much more than a simple question. It was something Infernal. A ritual he didn't understand, like signing a contract in blood. It was dangerous.

He couldn't stop himself, though. He had to know.

"I do," he said.

She glared at him for a heartbeat. Her hands dropped to her side. The air chilled. "How can you be so smart and so stupid at the same time?"

Eliot had often wondered this very thing, but wasn't about to admit it.

"I was Julie Marks long ago," she told him. "I lived in Atlanta, ran away, made many foolish choices, and died of a heroin overdose. I wasted my life."

To hear her speak of her death so casually horrified Eliot.

A boy and girl from their Mythology 101 class passed by, shot curious glances their way, and hurried along.

"I died," she continued, "and I went to Hell, the Poppy Lands of Queen Sealiah. I won't bore you with the torment heaped upon my unworthy mortal soul there, but just know that I was picked by my Queen and given a chance to live again."

The chill from the shadows made Eliot shiver.

This *was* the truth, though— he sensed that much—and it tasted addictively sweet to him.

More students passed them, and gave Jezebel a wide berth, wanting to avoid those preternaturally cold shadows.

"That is when I came to you, Eliot, darling." She inched closer, the shadows dragged along with her, and her voice rose over the murmurs in the corridor. "I was sent to seduce you, to trick you to come back to the lightless realms. I was bait, which you so eagerly tasted."

Eliot took a step back.

"But you left . . . without me."

She paused; confusion crossed her features, then it cleared. "Yes, another in a long string of mistakes I've made. Instead of seducing, I was seduced by your music . . . into believing there was something more, something better."

"It's not too late," Eliot told her. "There's still hope. There's always hope."

"Like there was hope when I ran away to protect you? When they caught me and dragged me back to Hell? Like there was hope when they did so many unpleasant, unspeakable things to me to repay my hope-filled *kindness*?"

Jezebel laughed. It was the sound of breaking glass and ancient glacier ice crackling. It was a thousand prancing, dancing booted feet that crushed dreams.

"There is no hope in Hell, Eliot Post. And there is no longer hope in my heart. I am a creature of the Lower Realms, reborn into the Clan Sealiah. The venomous blood of the Queen of Poppies forever flows through my veins. Dare not tempt me with your vile hope ever again, if you desire to draw another breath."

Every student in the hall had stopped to listen to this.

Eliot retreated another step and backed into a column.

Jezebel leaned closer. "You are a complete, utter moron. A fool of such sterling caliber, you could be the Prince of Incompetence. I wish I'd never met you."

Eliot felt as if he'd been struck—not because of her stinging words, but because of her declaration. Her words had been like Cee's were that one time: backward sounding, turned inside out, made of smoke, and reflected in the mirrors in his thoughts.

A lie.

"That's not right," he said. "I mean, probably not that other stuff you just said, but that last bit . . ."

"What are you babbling about?"

Jezebel appeared outwardly confident; however, the shadows about her had lost some of their chilled solidity.

"You said you wished you never met me," Eliot whispered, ignoring the gathering students. "That was a lie."

Jezebel flushed and locked gazes with him.

The crowd about them fell silent, and stepped back.

"You *dare* accuse me of . . . of . . . lying?" she breathed.

Her skin reddened, both hands arched into claws, the air about her shimmered like a mirage.

Eliot held his ground, though.

He was tired of being lied to. Everyone had lied to him his entire life. And now he had this gift to hear pathetic, lousy mistruths. He wasn't about to let it pass.

"It was obvious," he said louder, crossing his arms over his chest.

Jezebel shook with rage.

The people around them backed away, some tripping over one another.

Jezebel screamed, drew back her fist, and punched the marble column over Eliot's head. A spiderweb of cracks shattered its polished surface and blasted chunks out the other side.

Eliot flinched.

She turned and, without another word, stomped off.

The students around him spoke to one another. Eliot ignored them all, trying to make sense of what had just happened.

Should it even matter? Eliot should just stay far away from Jezebel—Julie Marks—or whatever she was. He couldn't believe he'd really cared for her. She was trouble. Sent first to trick him to Hell. And now what was she doing at Paxington?

Eliot hated the fact that he'd been so easily manipulated. Whatever was going on . . . he swore he'd get to the bottom of it.

21

UNEXPECTED RENDEZVOUS

The gaslights brightened, and class was over. Fiona gathered her things and left.

She blinked once in the strong sunlight, but welcomed the warmth after sitting in that chilled room for the last two hours. Miss Westin kept the place like a tomb.

Fiona walked away quickly. The Headmistress gave her the creeps—more even than Uncle Kino. Something *inside* that woman was a lot colder than her classroom.

Despite the gloom of the place, Fiona had wanted to linger, though. She had yet to talk to Robert and find out how he was coping now that he wasn't in the League. He could be so stoically stubborn sometimes. Where was he living? How did he eat?

But maybe it was better to stay apart a little longer . . . as painful as it might be. If Robert attracted any League attention, she had a feeling that even Uncle Henry wouldn't be able to get him off the hook this time.

Beside, she had to catch Eliot. He bolted before he'd written down tonight's reading assignment—something he never forgot. He was so distracted lately.

As she tromped down the corridors, one archway caught her eye. It wasn't a real passage, but rather a mural that gave the illusion of depth. The mural was a Picasso: cubist students with too many arms and legs, their faceted heads listening with disjointed ears to a lecturing stick figure Plato.[23]

The real reason she had to find her brother, though, was that he—without fail—got into trouble without her watching out for him.

Like in gym class. She should have known better than to leave him behind.

"Fiona?" a voice squeaked behind her.

She turned. Amanda Lane trotted up to her. Ever since Fiona had stopped Sarah from tormenting her in the locker room, Amanda had decided they were best friends and stuck close.

Like Fiona needed another person to look after.

Amanda's school uniform was a mass of wrinkles. She carried a pile of books, and her backpack was filled to the bursting point. Fiona felt bad for her. Amanda's eyes rarely left the ground, she wasn't able to talk to anyone, and her hair has half tangle, half cowlick.

"Hey," Fiona said. "What's up?"

Amanda tried to brush the hair from her face, but couldn't with her arms full. "Headed to the library?" she asked. "Maybe we could compare notes? I'm in the middle of Lovecraft's unpublished *Languorous Lullabies*. His histories of the Dreaming Families are so poetical. Did you know that parts can be read backwards for an entirely different meaning? It's called reflective/reflective style."[24]

For someone never exposed to magic before, Amanda seem to have a knack, if not for its practice, then at least its study.

---

23. Painted by Pablo Picasso in the fall of 1921, the arch was acquired by the Paxington Institute for an undisclosed amount in a 1940 auction (just before the Nazi occupation of Paris, where the arch originally resided). The arch is unusual in that it incorporates classical Renaissance elements—only deconstructed. Art historians cite as the piece's major influence Picasso's marriage to ballerina Olga Khokhlova, who introduced him to the high society of 1920s Paris (at odds with Picasso's core bohemian aesthetic). Close friends cite Picasso calling this piece a "mistaken dream" that was destined to be destroyed by evil. –Editor.

24. The Dreaming Families exist on Earth and in a middle realm known as Meriden, or the "dreaming lands." Every night when they sleep, they enter that world, and when they sleep there, they dream of Earth. This dual existence is said to be the reason for their unusual dual magic. Some speculate that never truly sleeping affects their mental stability. *Gods of the First and Twenty-first Century, Volume 14, The Mortal Magical Families*. Zypheron Press Ltd., Eighth Edition.

"I read those," Fiona told her. "Eliot and I still needed to tackle the *Canticles of the Clan*."

Fiona had to study the canticles, not only for Miss Westin's class, but also because it was *practical* knowledge. They told (in excruciating minutia and with endless commentary) the political intrigues among from the nineteenth- and twentieth-century mortal magical families.

Covingtons, Scalagaris, Pritchards, Kalebs—these families taught their children fencing, etiquette, the art of small talk, poisons, and assassination from the time they were toilet trained. Politics that translated into duels and alliances and vendettas here at Paxington.

She had a lot of catching up to do.

Fiona snapped her fingers. "There's one thing, though, we have to do before we hit the homework: find the others on our team and talk strategy."

"Oh . . ." Amanda drew her books closer and dropped her head.

"Slip too far in the rankings," Fiona explained, "and all the studying in the world won't matter."

Amanda curled even farther behind her books and said, "I'm really sorry about what happened."

"Don't worry about it," Fiona said. "We'll *all* do better next time."

Amanda brightened.

She was a real liability. If only Fiona could boost the girl's confidence, she might actually get her *onto* the obstacle course next time. Funny how Amanda seemed to have no trouble relating to Eliot. Maybe they had an equivalent nerd quotient.

Amanda glanced past Fiona. "There's your brother and that Jezebel. Let's go say hi."

"Jezebel?" Fiona whirled about. She squinted through archways and spotted them in the adjacent corridor.

Just as she had feared: Eliot in trouble again.

This was 100 percent weirdness. Why was he pushing his luck and talking to that thing? And why was Jezebel even listening to him?

And yet there they were.

This was typical Eliot: making well-intentioned but stupid friendly overtures. Probably still thought she was related to Julie Marks. He'd be lucky if the Infernal didn't kill him. But what could Jezebel do to him here out in the open? Challenge him to a duel? Even her brother wasn't foolish enough to accept an invitation to fight an Infernal.

The worst that might happen is a wounding of her brother's ego.

But they were still just talking. It felt like a private moment between them, though . . . almost intimate.

Fiona's face heated. "I guess it's him," she told Amanda. "Whatever."

She turned away and marched toward the gate.

"I thought you wanted to talk about gym . . . ," Amanda said, running after her.

"Sure—with Robert or Mitch, even Sarah or Jeremy. But I can talk to Eliot anytime. And I'm not going to waste time with Jezebel. Not with a million things to read."

They crossed the quad, and the sparkling quartz flagstones dazzled her. Fiona veered by the fountain of Poseidon and let the spray cool her face.

"You never said why you're here," Amanda said. "You and Eliot, your Uncle Henry . . . you're not part of any of the magical families we're studying." She continued with difficulty, forcing the words out: "But you're not normal, either, are you?"

Fiona glanced at the fountain and the marble face of the dead god who had the same high forehead as her mother and her. "Not exactly," she told Amanda. "It's complicated."

"So what isn't?" Amanda said, and retreated behind her disheveled hair.

Maybe it was time to open up—not break any League rules, of course, but just share stories about families. It'd be a breath of fresh air to talk to someone other than her brother.

"Let's grab something to drink at the café," Fiona said. "We can talk."

Amanda tilted her head up. "Really?"

"Sure. Iced Thai coffees. My treat."

Eliot could waste his time with the Infernal all day if he wanted to— and he could figure out the reading assignment on his own, too.

Fiona turned. She felt a cold sensation at her back, like the shadows behind them had somehow darkened. She resisted the urge to look, however, and mounted the steps, making her away along the path to the front gate.

Mr. Harlan Dells stood there. The large man wore a suit that matched his blond beard and hair. He smiled at her and Amanda.

"Miss Post . . . Miss Lane, I hope you girls are doing well with your studies. Not letting *too* many boys distract you?"

Amanda convulsed with what might have been a silent giggle.

Fiona felt like he'd stabbed her in the heart, and her lifeblood pumped out there in front of the iron gates, spattering over the cobblestones. She thought about Robert. Deep inside, she wanted to be with him . . . but not if it got him into trouble . . . or killed.

"No," she told him, "no boys. Just books."

He looked into her eyes and said, "That is for the best. Trust me."

"Yes, sir."

She took a little step toward the gate, but Mr. Dells didn't open it.

"One more thing, Miss Post." His voice deepened. Fiona sensed a weight settle about his person like he could've halted her and Amanda and an entire army with one upraised hand. "Please tell your family not to block my driveway again. There is a fire code, and I will have them towed."

Fiona glanced around his massive bulk.

A sleek black ultra-modern Mercedes limousine sat in the alleyway. It looked like one of Uncle Henry's.

"Pass along my deepest and warmest regards to your relation," Mr. Dells told her.

"Sure," Fiona said.

He flicked a switch and the gate rolled back.

Fiona ran to the limo.

The driver's door opened and a man in a black jacket and cap climbed out. It was the same uniform Robert had worn when he'd been Uncle Henry's Driver. But this man wasn't Robert. He was old and wrinkled. He bowed to Fiona and opened the back door for her.

"Thank you," she said. She leaned into the back section. "Uncle Hen—"

Inside, Fiona saw slender toes slipped from a high-heel sandal, attached to a shapely tanned calf, and a leg and a black skirt. A smile and dimples flashed from the shadows, and a tousle of honey blond hair shook free. A woman grinned at her.

"Aunt Dallas?"

"I hope you weren't expecting someone else," Dallas said. "I have a surprise for you this afternoon." She tilted her head and looked out the window. "And your friend, too. If you're game."

22

A PROBLEM NEVER MEANT TO BE SOLVED

Eliot watched Jezebel tromp down the corridor. The students who had gathered to watch them fight moved on as well.

He had to find Fiona and tell her everything. They were smarter together. They could figure out what Jezebel, Infernal protégée, once Julie Marks, was doing here at Paxington.

He backtracked to the lecture hall and spotted familiar faces from class, but no Fiona. Maybe she had gone to the library. He turned and marched toward the Hall of Wisdom.

He thought about calling her, but remembered the "no cell phone" rule in the library. The staff confiscated them if they rang, and he wasn't sure Fiona would have turned hers off.

There were so many little things like their phones they still had to get used to . . . let alone the big things.

Like Jezebel being Julie.

Eliot's instincts about her had been right all along. But she wasn't really Julie anymore. She was an Infernal. Dangerous.

But was all of the Julie he'd known gone? There was hope, wasn't there, that there was still something between them?

Or was he just an extreme loser, and that was nothing but wishful thinking?

Eliot sat on a bench. He set his roiling emotions aside—he'd try to sort through the facts.

First, Jezebel was an Infernal. That's how she'd announced herself at

Paxington, and he believed Miss Westin wouldn't let her lie about something like that.

Second, she admitted she'd been Julie Marks.

Third, she had told him the truth . . . except when she told him she wished she'd never met him.

Eliot *knew* it was a lie. How he knew exactly, he wasn't sure. But from her reaction when he'd accused her, he was certain.

All this left him with one solid speculation: The Infernal families were involved again in his and Fiona's lives. They were using Jezebel . . . or Julie as a piece in some game whose rules he didn't know.

And he knew this game could be deadly. Julie had been punished for her failure with him: killed again, dragged to Hell . . . and tortured.

Eliot's mouth went dry.

His first priority had to be to learn something about the Infernals' game. Then he'd move a few pieces of his own. Defensive moves. And maybe, just maybe, learn how to capture Julie and bring her over to his side of the board.

He got up and strode to the library to find Fiona.

A few students had gathered to chat by the Little Faun Pool, where several bronze statues of dancing fauns and satyrs, giant mushrooms and gigantic flowers were artfully placed about a reflection pool filed with lotus and koi.

Eliot recognized students from Team Wolf there. They'd won their first match in gym in six minutes four seconds, and inflicted three broken limbs on the other team to do so.

He hoped Team Scarab got their act together before they faced *them*.

Eliot veered away, not wanting any more confrontation today, and angled toward the House of Wisdom.

Within the library's twin sandstone pyramids and under its glittering golden dome, Eliot and Fiona had gotten lost twice so far this year in the stacks. Someone should have handed out maps. There were hundreds of thousands of medieval books; illuminated manuscripts; ancient Roman, Greek, Chinese, and Egyptian scrolls; and first-edition Shakespeare folios with stories Eliot had never even seen cataloged.

They'd found weirder things, too: thin volumes that wavered as if they were mirages (he didn't touch those), one room with marble busts whose eyes definitely followed him, and plenty of off-limits sections. Eliot wondered if there was a section of Infernal books.

Eliot spotted Robert Farmington on the long sweep of library stairs. He spoke to a girl (not Fiona) who had her back to Eliot.

He flashed Eliot a look of recognition and a warning to not interrupt.

Eliot nodded, understanding as he saw the girl's hair: a tangerine color that could belong only to Sarah Covington.

Eliot didn't want to cross paths with her. She'd been nothing but mean to him. He wondered how she had any friends at all—and yet, maybe being cruel was the secret to popularity at Paxington, because Sarah had dozens of admirers who surrounded her, smiled at her jokes, and hung on her every word.

Eliot could pass Immortal heroic trials and survive Infernal plots, but he flunked the basics of how to get along with people.

Robert and Sarah finished their conversation. She laughed and waved good-bye, and wandered up to the library without turning to acknowledge Eliot.

Robert trotted over to him.

"Hey," Eliot said.

"What happened to you?" Robert asked. "You look like you got hit by a truck."

"It's complicated." Eliot glanced up the stairs at Sarah Covington. She joined with a group of girls, and laughing, they entered the library. "Why were you talking to her? She's not . . . very nice."

Robert wriggled uncomfortably inside his Paxington jacket. "You'd be surprised. She acts one way in public. I think it has to do with her family— so prestigious, they're not supposed to bother with lesser people like me. Get her alone, though, and she's nice enough."

"I'll believe that when I see it," Eliot replied. "You think Jeremy's like that?"

"No way. *That* guy is pure grade-A jerk."

"Agreed," Eliot said. "Have you seen Fiona?"

"No . . ." Robert looked around, uneasy, and Eliot knew there was something wrong between those two.

Apparently even Robert, who had been all over the world, and probably had had a dozen girlfriends, still had problems with girls. Somehow, it was reassuring.

"You headed out?" Robert nodded toward the front gate. "I've got to go. Too many people around for me to think."

Eliot decided he could talk to Fiona tonight about Jezebel. Finding

Robert in a talkative mood was a rare thing, and he wouldn't waste the opportunity.

"Sure," Eliot said. They walked together down the steps. "Maybe you can help me out. You ever been with a girl you thought hated you . . . but she really liked you?"

Robert laughed. "All the time." He sobered. "Very recently, in fact—"

"You mean Fiona. She's just worried about how the League would react if, you know, they found out about you."

"I figured that out," Robert said. "Figured, too, that there might *no* way for me to be with her . . . and keep my skin in one piece. It sucks."

Eliot felt weird talking about his sister this way. Romance and boys and Fiona weren't *supposed* to go together.

Maybe everyone had trouble when it came to intimate relations. Heck, if supercool Robert got his heart stomped . . . what chance did Eliot have?

They walked in silence, crossed the quad, and approached the main gate.

"So," Eliot started again, "what do you do if you think you found the one special girl?"

Robert halted and looked him, one eyebrow arched. "We're not talking about Fiona anymore, are we?" He smiled—but that vanished quickly when he saw the seriousness on Eliot's face.

"Not Fiona," Eliot admitted.

Robert started walking again, his hand cupped to his chin. "I've found lots of girls I've liked, and a few who have even liked me back. Nothing *has* to be complicated about it."

Eliot wanted to believe that, but given his recent experience with girls—all one of them—he wasn't sure.

"But," Robert continued, "the problem is, I've never figured out how to get the 'one special' girl. *That* always ends up complicated." He sighed. "But it's the complicated ones who get you going, huh? The ones that keep you up at night thinking about them. Maybe that's the way it supposed to be, I don't know."

Mr. Harlan Dells stood by the gatehouse. "Gentlemen," he said, and flicked the switch that made the gate roll back.

As they walked through, Mr. Dells remarked to no one in particular, "There are some problems never meant to be solved: the philosophical struggle between good and evil, the many-body problem in classical mechanics . . . and women."

He shut the gate behind them, leaving them to ponder this.

"Need a ride?" Robert looked at Eliot, decided something, and then added, "I'm headed to my place. Why don't you come with me? We could burn a few hours on video games or something."

Eliot started to say no; he had enough homework to drown in.

But who was he fooling? His brain couldn't focus on mythologies and ancient families no matter how hard he tried. Not with Jezebel rattling about inside his head.

"Sure," Eliot said.

Robert nodded down the alley in front of Xybek's Jewelers, where he'd parked his motorcycle. The double-twined exhausts of his bike were mirrored chrome. The rest of the machine was a curve of black steel, looking like it was ready to pounce on prey.

Robert opened a saddlebag and pulled out a spare helmet for Eliot.

Eliot wormed the helmet on, which mashed his ears, then got on to the Harley.

Robert kicked over the motor and the bike thundered to life.

Everyone in the alley looked their way, startled—then annoyed at the ruckus.

Robert revved the engine in defiance and peeled out.

They rocketed out of the alley and onto the street—so fast that the air in Eliot's chest got squeezed out.

At the intersection Robert turned on a red light without pause, leaning so low Eliot thought they were going to scrape asphalt.

It was terrifying. And fun.

Up a hill they raced—airborne for two wild heartbeats . . . in which Eliot believed he'd left his internal organs behind—then they were back on the ground, tearing down the street.

Before Eliot could get used to the neck-snapping acceleration, however, Robert slowed and turned into a driveway. Robert reached into his jacket, clicked a garage door opener, and the rolltop door before them squealed up, revealing a freight elevator.

Robert drove in, turned the bike around, and killed the engine.

"Hit six," Robert told Eliot.

Eliot removed his helmet (almost scraping off his ears) and tapped the top button.

They rode up in that awkward elevator silence; then the car wrenched to a halt and the safety door rolled up.

Robert pushed his bike into a corner of his loft, which was combination parking stall, motorcycle lift, and machine shop. A thousand chrome tools glistened on racks.

In the center of the apartment was an entertainment center bolted to the brick wall. It held the biggest television Eliot had ever seen, music equipment he didn't have a clue about, and a dozen speakers—from tiny cubes to floor-to-ceiling towers.

The kitchen beyond was all stainless steel and littered with empty energy-drink cans, chips bags, and pizza boxes.

One wall had three wide windows that overlooked rolling hills, the Transamerica Pyramid, and sailboats in the distance.

The place was open, and light, and there' wasn't a bookshelf in sight.

Eliot stepped off the elevator—an instant before the safety door slammed shut and the car simultaneously lowered.

"Grab a bean bag," Robert said, kicking one toward him, and moved to the television. "I got all the latest, greatest games. Martial arts stuff, first-person shooters—whatever floats your boat."

Something else caught Eliot's notice, though. Tucked in the far corner were punching and speed bags. The floor was padded. There was a pole with wood arms and legs jutting out from its center. On the wall was a rack of free weights . . . along with swords, clubs, knives, and shuriken.

"You work out?" Eliot asked.

"A little," Robert replied.

Eliot felt drawn to the equipment. His blood raced. His hands clenched into fists, and it felt good.

"And you're training to . . . fight?"

Robert was silent a moment then carefully said, "Paxington's a danger-ous place."

Why hadn't Eliot figured this out before? He didn't have to be the smallest, weakest, dorkiest kid. Why not study how to move and fight just like he studied ancient Roman history? Could boxing be any harder than trigonometry?

Eliot turned to Robert. "Forget the games. Can you show me? I mean how to make myself stronger. How to fight?"

The cautious look on Robert's face broke into a grin. "I'd love to."

Eliot grinned back. He had a feeling he was going to leave here bruised and battered tonight—and he very much looked forward to it.

23

SHOPPING FOR TROUBLE

Paris. That's where they were going.

Fiona had always wanted to see the City of Lights. She'd dreamed she would go one day as a college student, alone in a city filled with art and style and wonderful romance.

But not with her aunt as chaperone.

And definitely not with Amanda Lane tagging along.

They rocketed through forest and over roads barely visible on tundra plains, past oil-drilling derricks, and then back again into Sitka spruces . . . only the stars wheeled overhead instead of the sun.

"This *is* one of Uncle Henry's limousines, isn't it?" Fiona asked Dallas.

No other car could break a half dozen laws of physics, drive faster than the speed of sound while being whisper quiet, and get you from one side of the world to the other in a few hours.

Dallas shrugged. "He lent it to me," she said. "Henry's a darling and does whatever I ask."

Fiona imagined that no man could refuse her aunt Dallas anything. She had a perfect geometry of dimples, cheekbones, and mouth—which all animated into a dancing smile that made you want to smile along with her.

Everyone seemed to like her . . . which, ironically, made Fiona suspicious.

Amanda had her face plastered to the window, gawking at the blurry scenery.

They flashed by billboards covered with the backward Яs of Cyrillic writing. They had to be in Russia.

"How long now?" Amanda whispered.

"Just a few minutes." Dallas poured them both more iced tea from a silver thermos.

Earlier, when Fiona had protested that she needed to study, Dallas told her that she was right: She really didn't need a shopping trip to Paris. She said that Fiona looked *almost* perfect in her Paxington uniform, and that she was *nearly* the flower of womanhood.

Fiona got the message.

Almost. Nearly. Two lousy adverbs that communicated loud and clear that she still was awkward and nerdy, and likely a total embarrassment to the League of Immortals.

So here she was, getting a stupid fashion makeover on a school night.

She looked over at Amanda to watch her expression at their magical journey. But she wasn't blown away like when Fiona and Eliot had first ridden in one of Henry's cars.

Had she driven with Uncle Henry before? Maybe when he took her home after they'd rescued her? What did Amanda's parents think of her going to Paxington? They were probably normal people. So why did they let her go to a dangerous school full of magic and Immortals?

"So where do you live?" Fiona asked Amanda.

Amanda turned from the window and looked at the floor. She paled and twisted her hands. "In the dorms on campus," she murmured. "It's easier that way. For everyone."

"We're there," Dallas said, and her eyes sparkled. "Driver, slow down. I want them to see absolutely everything."

Smears of head- and taillights resolved into traffic. The limousine turned onto the Boulevard Périphérique. Strings of lights draped over manicured trees and the classic architecture of every building. Statues glowed as if dipped in silver.

They angled onto Avenue des Champs-Élysées and Fiona's breath caught as she saw the towering Arc de Triomphe, gleaming a rosy gold in a column of illumination.

Dallas sighed. "There's no time to see it all. And I think your mother would kill me if I got you home too late. A pity." To the Driver she said, "Take us to *Art d'air*."[25]

The car turned onto smaller and smaller streets. Only the occasional

---

25. "Art of the Air." Translated from French. Also a play on words, as often pronounced as "Art Dare" in English. —Editor.

lamppost punctuated the darkness now as they twisted onto byways so narrow that Fiona feared they'd scrape the walls . . . although the Driver managed to squeak through somehow.

The buildings here weren't classic architecture or decorated with gold lights; they were crumbling brick and leaning against one another as if too tired to stand by themselves.

The limo halted before a storefront, its windows partially boarded. A spot of light cast from a wrought-iron lamppost revealed a sign over the doorway with curling vapors rising about a cavorting nymph.

"We're here!" Dallas said gleefully.

She started to get out.

"I thought we were going shopping," Fiona said.

"My dear, I could have taken you to Gucci or Prada, but this is where *those* designers come to steal their best ideas. I wouldn't dream of giving you *more* secondhand things to wear."

She meant Cecilia's clothes: hand-stitched with love but also with an amazing lack of skill . . . things she had found at deep-discount stores and then altered to fit . . . or not fit, as the case might be.

The older Driver held out a hand and helped Dallas out, then Fiona, and Amanda.

It smelled like someone had urinated on the nearby wall.

Down the street, a group of boys eyed them. There were seven of them. They looked dangerous and hungry. They spoke to one another, and one called out to them—French so gutturally accented and drunkenly slurred that Fiona couldn't decipher a word.

Dallas shouted back—the same primitive dialect—and then made a rude gesture.

The boys all laughed at the one who had yelled at her.

"They won't bother us," Dallas said, and entered the store.

Her Driver remained with the car and polished the side mirror.

Fiona glanced one last time at the gang—she didn't like their looks—and then hurried Amanda in front of her into the shop.

Inside were mirrors: silver dusted and gold variegated, lit with soft lighting and angled so Fiona couldn't help but look at a dozen copies of herself and Amanda. Aunt Dallas smiled at herself and preened.

Between the mirrors hung red curtains and velvet wallpaper. There were racks of clothes as far back as Fiona could see. Everything emitted a faint flowery perfume.

A model runway ran down the length of the store. Floor lights flickered on, and an old woman hobbled down the raised platform. She was impeccably dressed in black slacks and shirt and high heels that barely brought her up to Fiona's chin.

"We're closed," she croaked in a thickly accented voice and shooed them away. "Forever closed! Go away."

Her scowl dropped as she saw Aunt Dallas. "Oh, it's you, Lady. A thousand apologies. Come in, come in." She smiled and bowed. "Can I have coffee or tea or perhaps some *Kirschwasser* brought out for you?"

"Nothing for me, Madame Cobweb. We are working on my niece tonight." She nodded at Fiona. "And her charming friend, Miss Lane."

The old woman's eyes grew wide. "*The* Fiona Post? Yes . . . I see the resemblance. To the mother as well. Stunning. Grace and beauty just now budding." She fumbled the glasses on a silver chain about her neck and donned them, taking a more careful, much longer look.

Fiona felt like she'd been set under a microscope and every pimple and too-large pore exposed.

"Yeeees. Exquisite material. Both of them. But Paxington girls? Those uniforms—something must be done." Madame Cobweb said *Paxington* like it was a rare tropical disease. Like she and Amanda needed to be quarantined.

"Maybe this wasn't a great idea," Amanda whispered, and took a step back. "I'll just wait in the car. . . ."

"We shall hear none of that," the old woman said. "Beautiful girls must wear beautiful things. Come, I measure you."

Dallas wrapped her arms around Amanda and Fiona and drew them along to Madame Cobweb. "It won't hurt," she said. "Much. Probably."

Madame Cobweb took out a tape measure and zipped it across Fiona's shoulders and down her back, making tut-tut noises. "They should not have been let out in these rags." She turned her about and measured her chest—first above, then directly over, and then she measured under as well. "Needs lifting and definition," she said.

Fiona's face burned, but she endured the handling rather than letting any of them see how self-conscious she was.

"You know how that horrid Miss Westin is with her tweed and slavish devotion to Victorian styles," Dallas said, rolling her eyes. "We're lucky they're not in whalebone corsets."

Madame Cobweb measured Amanda, who let her move and pose her like a doll.

She then examined the numbers on her notepad. "I have many things in their sizes. My latest creations."

"Very well," Dallas said, and tiny frown appeared on her lips. "But you will make a few things, just for them, no?"

"But of course, M'lady. Originals. Only the best." Madame Cobweb moved to the back of the shop. "One moment, please."

Fiona turned. "Aunt Dallas, this is great. Really. But we're wearing uniforms all day. When are we going to need anything else?" She made a little frustrated motion with her hands.

"And their wretched uniforms!" Dallas shouted back to the old woman. "They will need three new ones that actually fit."

"*Oui, mademoiselle,*" Madame Cobweb called back.

Dallas turned her attention back to Fiona. "There are always occasions to dress up, darling. Dances and parties. I'll see to that."

"Maybe we should just try on a few things," Amanda whispered. "It *could* be fun." She brushed her hair to one side.

Dallas stepped closer. "Let me, please." She grabbed a clip off a nearby rack of rhinestone encrusted hairpins and tucked Amanda's hair back and fussed over it. She did the other side of her head then and turned her back to face Fiona. Amanda's hair was *finally* out of her face, artfully swept up, and highlighted with tiny sparks.

"Why, Miss Lane," Dallas said. "You are lovely. The world can be such a dreary place; you should help light it."

Amanda blushed so hard, Fiona felt the heat on her skin three paces away.

Before Fiona could figure out how that was possible, there was a great crash outside.

She went to the window and glanced between the boards.

That gang of boys threw rocks at a tiny car that sputtered by on the street. They shouted after it, and then all laughed and took swigs from bottles wrapped in paper bags. What a bunch of creeps!

Amanda, however, was too busy admiring her new hair to even notice.

Madame Cobweb returned then, wheeling a rack loaded with dresses and slacks, gossamer blouses, and carrying a separate tray of necklaces, bracelets, and earrings.

"*Pour les belles jeunes dames.* Miss Post"—she gestured to the right side of the rack—"and Miss Lane"—she waved to the left side. "Please, help yourselves. The dressing rooms are this way."

Fiona and Amanda exchanged a look and then shrugged, grabbed an armload of clothes each, and stepped into the dressing rooms.

If Fiona tried on a few things to appease Dallas, then maybe they could find a moment to have a *serious* talk with her aunt about the League and what it meant to be a goddess . . . surely more than fancy clothes.

She got out of her uniform and wriggled into a gown of gray silk that flared about her ankles.

A perfect fit.

Fiona had never had clothes like this—no puckering, not too long or too short, no binding in all the wrong places. It felt better than her own skin.

She added a string of jade beads and turned to the full-length mirror. Her breath hiccupped in her throat. She looked great. Like a model.

Sure, she was still stuck with her unmanageable hair and her face . . . but that almost didn't matter with *this* dress. The silver made her skin look luminous.

She wanted it. And she wanted to wear clothes like this all the time.

She twirled, and smiled, and then stopped.

So why did it also feel so weird? So wasteful?

"This is great," Amanda whispered from the adjacent changing room. "Let me see."

They both stepped out. Fiona was dumbstruck.

Amanda wore spike red heels and a red skirt that fell to her knees and clung about her slender waist, a white silk blouse, raw rubies that flashed against her skin, and a smart little jacket to match. She had auburn highlights in her hair that Fiona had never noticed before. When she smiled, she looked like a princess or a model on the cover of a magazine. She wasn't exactly beautiful, but she had *something* that had eluded Fiona.

"Wonderful!" Dallas clapped her hands. She hugged them both. "Try something else."

There was a scratch at Fiona's wrist: the price tag.

She looked and gasped. Dollar or euros, it wouldn't matter, this one dress cost more than she made working all last summer at Ringo's Pizza Palace.

She had the credit card Audrey had given her. That was supposed to be for school supplies and emergencies. Did this qualify as school supplies?

Hadn't Aunt Dallas said there might be school dances? Maybe her clothes were a justifiable fashion emergency?

No. It'd be breaking a rule.

"I'll just change back," she murmured, so softly that she thought only she heard.

"Oh no no no," Dallas said. "Don't worry about price." She waved her hand toward Madame Cobweb. "Put it on my account."

"*Oui, mademoiselle.* Very generous."

Amanda trembled with joy and took Dallas's hands. She looked like she was going to cry.

"Thanks, Aunt Dallas," Fiona replied. "I don't know what to say. . . ."

She really didn't know what to say. She was grateful, more than she could express, and she *did* want the clothes—all of them—but wanting them felt a little like those truffles that she had gotten this summer— delicious and sweet . . . and poisoned. It was too much, too perfect.

Audrey's often-repeated mantra came to her: *Too-generous presents come with strings.*

Outside the store came muted shouts.

Fiona moved to the window as Dallas and Amanda fell on the rack of clothes, riffling for a new selection.

Those boys again—only this time, their attentions were focused on an old woman carrying two bags of groceries.

They pushed her down. One boy grabbed her bag and scattered vegetables across the sidewalk, stomping on tomatoes, laughing.

Fiona was horrified.

Dallas came to Fiona's side.

"We have to do something," Fiona told her.

"Why?" Dallas said. "I told you those boys wouldn't bother us."

"But that old woman . . ."

"She will be fine," Dallas reassured her, and gently tugged on her arm. "It's just a few tomatoes."

Fiona pulled away.

Her anger kindled. It had been banked and ready to be blown into a full raging inferno . . . and this time Fiona welcomed it.

She *was* mad.

She'd been mad for a while, and it was time she admitted it. She was mad that Team Scarab had lost their first match. Mad at her brother for always getting into trouble. Mad at Amanda for being sad, pathetic, and looking *better* than her in her dress. And most of all mad at Aunt Dallas for wasting her time and not doing anything to help that old woman.

"Is this what the League does?" Fiona whispered. "Let people get hurt . . . while *they* shop?"

Dallas gave her a look as if to say she should grow up. "My sweet, the 'people' always get hurt, and they never appreciate help. There is nothing that can be done for them."

"Yes, there is."

Fiona stalked out of the shop.

Only distantly did she realize she must look ridiculous in this wispy little dress and in her bare feet. The cool night air whipped about her. She crunched over broken glass, and it didn't hurt.

The boys hadn't seen her—they still taunted the old woman while she wept on the ground.

"Hey!" Fiona yelled.

Fiona shoved the limo out of her way. It had to weigh two tons, but it felt like cardboard.

The boys turned, shocked to see her push aside a car, more shocked to see the look of pure hatred in her eyes.

"You want to fight a woman? Try me."

In her hand, she clutched the slightly rusted chain Louis had given her. One moment, it had been on her wrist, an ordinary bracelet; the next, a *real* chain—six feet long and heavy. It scraped and sparked along the ground, every link twisted to lie flat, angled to a fine sharpened edge—the entire length feeling like an extension of her arm.

She hadn't recalled unclasping the thing, but there it was. It felt like it had always been there, too: a part of her.

Fiona whipped the chain around her once—and then lashed it toward the lamppost.

It wrapped around the sculpted wrought iron.

She glared at the boys, who, astonished and openmouthed and frozen, could only stare back.

She imagined her chain wrapped about their necks—and then yanked.

The metal cleanly severed.

The light went dark. The lamppost twisted and fell into the street with a deafening wrench.

The gang of boys stood for a heartbeat . . . then ran—almost knocking each other over to get away from her.

Fiona smiled. That had felt good. Not just saving the old woman from further indignity, but the primeval urge to cut something, too. To tear and rip and rend; she felt it surge and sing through her blood. She wanted more.

The old woman got shakily to her feet. Her eyes were wide and dark, like some deer about to be eaten, as she stared at Fiona . . . like she was looking into the face of Death.

She backed away, then turned and ran, crossing herself, whimpering . . . leaving her groceries scattered on the street.

Aunt Dallas, Madame Cobweb, and Amanda stood behind Fiona in the doorway of the shop.

"That was the most amazingly cool thing I've ever seen!" Amanda cried, clapping her hands.

"*That's* what you could have done," Fiona told Dallas.

Dallas sighed and shook her head, but nonetheless looked the tiniest bit impressed. "*Just* like your mother," she whispered.

Fiona stood taller. Dallas's words—obviously not a compliment—for some reason made Fiona feel better than any new clothes ever could.

ADVERSARIES

24

FIRST STEP ON A CROOKED PATH

Eliot walked alone to school on Halloween morning. Most houses in Pacific Heights had carved pumpkins on their doorsteps, leering at him as he passed.

He was sure no one was going to let him dress up in costume and go out this evening. It was a school night and candy wasn't allowed in the house. There wasn't a rule about candy, per se, but Cecilia claimed her peanut brittle was better than anything you could buy . . . and if you liked eating reinforced concrete, she was right.

Eliot tromped along, doing his best to ignore the festive decorations. He was by himself because Fiona was still taking her time trying on all her new clothes—not just the new dresses Aunt Dallas had bought her, but her new custom-tailored Paxington uniforms.

He tugged on his own Paxington jacket. Still too big.

But it *was* starting to fit better.

For two weeks he'd gone to Robert's after school. Eliot was on a new physical regime of tai chi, calisthenics, and free weights. Robert had also taught him the basics of fighting. Every muscle ached, and the ribs on Eliot's left side hurt where Robert had left a tattooing of bruises.

Eliot curled his hands into fist and flexed his forearms. It'd been worth it, though. He felt stronger.

Near school, Eliot saw more students. Some walked alone like he did, although most collected in groups of three or four, chatting along the way. Others sputtered by on motor scooters.

Funny how on that first day he'd seen only one or two other students—

now he saw them everywhere. Had they all been here and he'd never noticed? Was it something about the uniform that made them blend in?

He spotted the Paxington entrance half a block away and went to it. He touched the rough granite blocks . . . and hesitated.

He should go inside. He'd heard there might be a field trip today. He also had to cram for a rumored pop quiz in Miss Westin's class. But it didn't feel right entering without Fiona.

Then there was the matter of Jezebel, which remained *completely* unresolved. The revelation that she had been Julie Marks, and was now an Infernal . . . he hadn't told anyone.

The problem was he still didn't know much about Infernals. Their studies in Miss Westin's class hadn't covered them in detail.

And Eliot hadn't had a chance to talk again with Jezebel. She disappeared after class. And in gym—they'd been so busy drilling for the handful of remaining all-important matches, there'd never been a chance to get her alone.

If this was some Infernal game of chess with Jezebel as a living pawn . . . he had to make sure he made the right move.

Telling Fiona would be a move; it would set her in motion, possibly provoking a confrontation between the two girls.

He wasn't ready for *that*.

And telling Robert? He'd wanted to at first. But now it felt like a family matter . . . dangerous . . . and private.

He sighed, feeling completely alone—and walked through the there-but-not entrance to school.

Off the main street there, Paxington students browsed store windows, ogling the jewelry, watches, and latest computers. There were fashion boutiques with gaudy dresses and flashy tuxedos and the zombie, vampire, and robot costumes for Halloween. Café Eridanus was packed.

A man sat at one of the café's outdoor tables. He waved Eliot closer.

Eliot's spirits soared as he recognized him.

"Louis!"

He was the one person he could talk to about this stuff.

Eliot tried to sit next to his father, but as he pulled out a chair, he saw a black cat curled upon it. Amber eyes blinked at him. It didn't move, and returned to its nap.

Eliot thought about petting it or lifting it over to the next chair.

"Ignore that wretched animal." Louis gestured to the seat on his left.

Eliot sat there. "I'm glad to see you."

Louis smiled warmly, but that happiness faded as he gazed at Eliot. "What has happened?"

"There's so much," Eliot replied. "But I don't want to be late for class."

He took out his phone and set it on the table where he could watch the time. "You're just *not* late for Miss Westin's class more than once."

"A new phone? A gift from your mother? Or, perhaps the League?" Louis reached for it. "Do you mind?"

"Sure," Eliot said, pushed it closer. "It does everything."

Eliot regretted letting the phone out of his grasp the second Louis touched it. If anything happened to it, Audrey would kill him.

Louis poked and turned it this way and that. For an instant the phone seemed to vanish—but that was just a trick of the light, because then Louis immediately set it back on the table.

"I must upgrade mine one of these days. Now, explain what weighs so heavy upon your heart."

Eliot told Louis about Jezebel—that she was an Infernal like him—then backtracked to when she'd been mortal Julie Marks at Ringo's Pizza Parlor, and how she'd been nice to him, and how they'd been at the Pink Rabbit and he'd serenaded her.

"I have heard that melody," Louis said, wistful. "A lovely thing. Ripe with hope. So tragic."

"Yeah," Eliot whispered.

Thinking about her song made him sad. Like there was no longer any hope for the Julie Marks he'd known . . . and there was even less hope for *them* now that she was the Infernal Jezebel.

Louis made an encouraging gesture, indicating that he go on.

Eliot then told how Jezebel had arrived at Paxington, her titles, how she looked so much like Julie, and so much *not* like her, how she fought and saved him in gym class . . . and then how he had confronted her about the truth, and how she had revealed everything.

"She lied to you?" Louis asked, bemused. "And you told her as much? You know, there is no greater offense for an Infernal to be caught in a lie." He smiled, but there was a hint of malice to it.

"Her lie . . . ," Eliot said. "The words sounded hollow. I don't know. I could just tell."

"Of course," Louis replied. "Any Infernal can hear *obvious* lies."

The black cat seated next to Louis looked up and glanced at Eliot, ears flicking forward.

"How is that possible?" Eliot asked.

"How does a dog hear the faintest whisper? How do bees see ultraviolet? Superior senses, my boy."

Eliot remembered what his father had told him long ago: *that the truth would be best between them.* He wondered now if the reason for that was entirely moral . . . or if it was just good Infernal politics.

"Can the others, the Immortals, hear lies, too?"

"No more than any other person with a modicum of wit." Louis chuckled. "They are entirely different creatures."

This halted Eliot's thoughts cold.

"Wait—if you're different species, how'd you and my mother . . . ? I mean, Fiona and me . . . how'd you . . . ?"

Eliot blushed, unable to finish.

Louis held up both hands. "How foolish of me! I am sorry, Eliot. I should have realized your education in this would have been conveniently 'forgotten' by Audrey. I shall give you all the details."

He dug into his pocket and pulled forth a string of individually wrapped foil packets, each the size of a half dollar.

Condoms.

Eliot's blush heated to a blazing intensity, and he quickly waved them away. "That's okay," he said. "Cecilia covered basic, uh . . . reproduction last year."

"A pity." Louis looked disappointed as he shoved the condoms back into his pocket.

Not that any contact with the opposite sex had been possible with Rule 106, the "no dating" rule in effect. Still, Eliot had had to learn everything about reproduction: earthworm sex organs, chromosomes, and the inherited hemophiliac anomalies of Russian royalty.

"So . . . I'm a mule?" Eliot whispered. Mules were a sterile hybrid and a genetic dead end.

Louis frowned, and sparks danced in his eyes. "No. You and your sister are hybrids akin to the mighty griffon—half eagle and half lion—noble, powerful, and awe-inspiring. No Infernal has *ever* been anything less!"

Eliot's pulse quickened as he listened, almost believing that he could be special. "So why are Infernals different? I've seen Miss Westin's family tree. Infernal, Immortals, even the mortal magical families, they all have a common origin."

"Oh . . . that," Louis said, and sniffed. "Well, we have evolved. *We* have land. The others do not."

Eliot crinkled his forehead. "Land? Like office buildings? Uncle Henry has land."

"No," Louis said, drawing out the *o*. "We are *monarchs* of the domains of Hell, the benevolent kings and queens over the countless souls who are drawn there to worship us. *That* gives us true power. Without land, we would be the lowest of the low."

Eliot pondered this comparison of formidable Uncle Aaron or even Audrey to the "lowest of the low."

And yet, he sensed no *outright* lie in Louis's words.

But if true, why didn't the Infernals overthrow the Immortals? Rule everyone? Why have a neutrality treaty at all?

And who ruled that blasted landscape and all those people who had rushed the gate in Uncle Kino's Borderlands? None of them seemed "benevolently ruled." Something wasn't right with Louis's picture.

"Do you have one of these domains in Hell?" Eliot asked.

Louis eased back. "Ah, well, regrettably there were setbacks to my personal portfolio when I was demoted to mortal status." He set a long hand atop Eliot's and patted it. "Worry not. I have plans in motion to reclaim what was once mine.

"But let us talk more of *your* problem," Louis said. He twisted off his pinkie ring. It was a battered gold band with a clear crystal cabochon. He held it up to the light and squinted. "I believe I have met your Jezebel once before. Observe."

A tiny figure appeared in the ring's stone . . . which reflected and wavered in the water glasses on their table . . . then in the curves of the spoons and forks . . . and then along the inner curve of Eliot's glasses.

Everywhere Eliot looked: there was Jezebel.

She stood with head lowered, wearing a black velvet cloak that highlighted her pale skin and platinum locks.

Eliot stopped breathing.

"I see the reason for your interest," Louis whispered. "But there is another to focus your attentions upon."

A second woman appeared in the ring. And as impossible as it seemed to

Eliot, she was more beautiful than Jezebel, with copper red hair and feral eyes. She radiated power—waves of the stuff that made Eliot's pulse quicken.

She was intoxicating and overwhelming.

"That *creature*," Louis explained, "is Sealiah, Queen of the Poppy Realms and your poor unfortunate Jezebel's mistress. She is the reason for her being at Paxington. A rather clumsy attempt to seduce you . . . one that I fear is working, however."

"Yeah, I know," Eliot sighed. "But there has to be a way to save Jezebel while not falling into the trap." He gazed up at his father, every fiber of his being hoping Louis could help.

Louis tapped his pointed chin, thinking. "I admire you wanting it all. . . . I shall consider the situation and concoct something."

Eliot nodded, truly grateful. He was completely out of his depth. Any advice would be welcome.

He tried to envision that family tree Miss Westin had drawn in class and where this Sealiah, Queen of Poppies fit. He couldn't remember— although now that he reimagined it, there was something else that had nagged him about the Infernal family tree.

"I keep seeing this name come up in class," Eliot said. "One Infernal who might or might not be dead? No one seems sure. Satan?"

Louis's face went rigid. "Oh . . . him." An eyebrow twitched in irritation. "Do you know people *still* confuse the two of us?"

"What happened? His name was scratched off the family tree, not erased like if he'd died."

Louis shrugged. "He left. Said he grew tired of the endless bickering. Can you imagine?" He picked up a napkin and made a great show of wiping his hands. "Who can say if he lives or not? When a puppy goes missing for ten years, one assumes it was run over by a truck, no?"

Eliot remembered what Mr. Welmann had said: That the dead grew restless and moved on. If Satan were dead, where would he move on to? Did Infernals go to Hell if they died?

Louis tapped the table. "Remain focused on our relations in the here and now, my boy. The ones trying to stab you in the back, eh?"

Eliot nodded.

"For now," Louis said, "watch your Jezebel, but keep your distance. Neither be cool nor solicit her attentions. And tell no one of *my* involvement. I fear your sister and mother would not understand what is clearly an Infernal family matter."

Not telling Audrey—that would be easy. She might take the matter of Jezebel up with the League. That could get messy, fast. But not telling Fiona felt wrong.

He decided, though: He'd trust Louis this once.

Eliot held out his hand for his father to shake. "Deal."

Louis's face split into a crooked smile, and he grasped Eliot's hand.

It felt as if Eliot grasped lightning and raw pumping blood and had a tiger by the tail all at once.

But it also felt good—like he and his father were now in this together.

Sure, it was stupid and dangerous to trust his father, the self-admitted Prince of Darkness, but at the same time, it also felt like the smartest, most important thing Eliot had ever done.

25

STONES THAT WEEP

Fiona stepped off the bus with the rest of Team Scarab.

It had been an awkward hour-long ride from Paxington through hills of central California.

First, on this small bus, she had had to sit behind Miss Westin—not the ideal location for gossiping or discussing with Eliot the politics of their Immortal relatives.

Second, Miss Westin had segregated the boys from the girls. Amanda was on Fiona's right, face plastered to the window, alternately too shy to speak, and then exploding in rapid bursts of enthusiasm over her new clothes and Aunt Dallas, and when was she going to show up again after school?

Behind her sat Sarah Covington and Jezebel, who exuded icy silence at one another.

Thank goodness Mitch Stephenson had the seat across the aisle—and while not daring to cross the gender boundary that ran down the center of the bus, he nonetheless managed to occasionally communicate with her with a smile and roll of his eyes as Jeremy Covington went on and on next to him about his life and exploits in the nineteenth century and how the twenty-first century had gone to the dogs without servants and a rigid social order.

Robert and Eliot seemed to be having a normal conversation in back. Fiona caught only snatches of what they said. She thought they might have been talking about a video game because there were lots of gesticulations with fists and karate chops.

Sometimes they could be so foolish.

Eventually Fiona opened her copy of Homer's *Odyssey*. She read (or rather tried), managing to reread the same paragraph about Circe about twenty times over the bumpy roads.

She gave up when the bus pulled onto a dirt road. They bumped along for a few more minutes and eased to a halt.

The door folded open, and Fiona stepped off after Miss Westin.

There was nothing here, just rolling hills, golden grass, and the occasional orange poppy that trembled in the breeze. The bent black oaks seemed to wave to her.

"Clear the bus," Miss Westin instructed. "We have another group coming through."

Fiona marched out the door, to the rear of the bus, and leaned against it. Another group of students marched toward them, escorted by Mr. Ma, who held his usual clipboard. It was Team White Knight. They queued in front of the bus's doors.

The Knights glared at Fiona and the rest of Team Scarab; Fiona returned the favor.

Tamara Pritchard still sported a black eye from their match. Good.

Miss Westin and Mr. Ma carefully checked off names in her black book and on his clipboard, comparing notes . . . as if someone was going to get lost in all this open expanse of nowhere.

Fiona wanted to ask again what this was all about. She'd tried before when they'd been herded onto this bus from Miss Westin's classroom earlier that morning.

Miss Westin had told her: *"Words are . . . insufficient."*

Eliot was last to tromp off the bus.

Miss Westin then instructed Team White Knight to board the bus.

Mr. Ma moved between the two groups and crossed his arms (Fiona suspected, to make sure there was no trouble of outside of gym class between Team Scarab and the Knights).

Tamara Pritchard snorted as she passed Jezebel. "We told the Wolves all about your little tricks." She sneered. "They'll be ready for you."

"Oh, really now?" Jeremy quipped. "We face Team Wolf next?" He tilted his head in mock appreciation. "Thank you very much, lassie, for the information. We'll be well prepared, then."

Tamara's face contorted into a scowl as she got onto the bus.

The slightest smile appeared on Jezebel's lip, and she told Jeremy, "I am so glad you are on *our* side."

Fiona wished the freshman teams weren't kept so isolated. Surely they could all learn better together.

Why make *everything* so competitive?

Or was there a reason? What if the mortal magical families were just as aggressive outside school? Then it made sense that Paxington had to prepare its students not only for magic—but also for cutthroat business and political realities.

It all seemed endlessly Machiavellian.

She sighed and made a mental note, however, to find out more on this Team Wolf.

Mr. Ma and Miss Westin spoke in hushed tones. The two teachers couldn't look more different.

The Headmistress had on a black dress with a lacy collar. She wore a hat with mesh across her face, held a tiny black parasol, and had donned dark sunglasses.

Mr. Ma wore slacks and a polo shirt, and looked like he had spent his entire life playing golf, with dark golden skin and a picture-perfect physique (even at his advanced age).

Eliot sidled next to her. "Hey," he whispered.

"You hear what this is about?"

He shook his head.

Fiona was relieved that Eliot wasn't holding a grudge for this morning. Something had felt a little "off" between them for the last couple of days—actually since their first gym match. This morning hadn't helped matters.

Fiona had had to try on all six uniforms that Aunt Dallas couriered over. Each fit, but had been designed for a different look . . . some scandalous, with how short the skirt had been raised and the jacket engineered to push up her chest. She settled on a "normal" uniform that simply fit. It was a huge improvement over her too-small uniform, and gave her an enormous confidence boost. She hadn't realized how little she'd been able to breathe.

Also, she got a bit distracted with all the other clothes that Dallas had sent: dresses and new jeans and twenty pairs of shoes (none of which Fiona seemed to be able to balance in).

It'd been fun to look at them, even try a few on, but it all reminded her how trivial her aunt could be.

Weren't Immortals supposed to do heroic, important things? Why was Aunt Dallas wasting time and money on that stuff?

"About me being late this morning," she murmured to Eliot. "Won't happen again."

"It's cool," he whispered back.

He sounded like he meant it, too. No quips. No vocabulary insults.

"We have a special All Hallow's Eve treat for you," Miss Westin said to them. She tilted her parasol so her pale face revealed itself. "Today we conjure the dead."

Fiona shivered.

"Not a literal summoning of the deceased," Mr. Ma added. "But a re-creation of memories. We shall watch the last great battle between the Infernals and a collection of Immortals that would precipitate the founding of the League of Immortals—circa 336 C.E."

Fiona's heart jumped. They were actually going to see Immortals fighting?

Robert raised his hand and asked, "It's like a movie, then?"

"No." Miss Westin pointed to the hill behind her. "We have transported stones from the ancient battlefield. They remember all that occurred, and on All Hallow's Eve, we can coax them to share their recollections." She nodded to Mr. Ma.

"Let us talk as we walk," Mr. Ma said, and strode up the hill along a faint path.

Grasshoppers took to the air and whined about him.

Fiona and the others fell in behind him.

Mr. Ma explained, "The stones are said to be ancient beings, petrified and set to guard some priceless treasure—or some unspeakable horror—from ages long past. Or maybe they are just stones, who can say?"

She squinted. There were yellow rocks on the hilltop, nothing extraordinary like the monolithic Easter Island carvings, although some were the size of a car, and a few did stand upright.

"We will stand in the center to start," Mr. Ma said. "Then I shall awaken our friends, and the battle will occur on the far side of this hill. We shall watch and *not* interfere."

They mounted the hilltop.

"Feel free to examine the stones," Mr. Ma told them.

Fiona noted that the stones made a rough ring. No grass grew between them. The earth there was hard and cracked. It reminded her of the steril- ized dirt in Hell, and she suppressed a shudder.

Jeremy went to one stone and reached out to touch it . . . hesitated, then pulled his hand back.

Mitch took out an art pad and, and, examining one severely cracked stone, started sketching. Amanda stood close and admired his work.

Jezebel bowed to one of the monoliths with grave solemnity.

Fiona and Eliot inspected one that stood upright, a pillar that could have been a sandblasted termite mound.

"I feel something," Eliot whispered.

Fiona took a deep breath and inched closer. There *was* something. Al- most not there . . . something . . . sleeping?

She held out her hand.

She had no intention of actually touching the stone, and yet her finger- tips pulled closer and did just that.

The rough texture became smooth like polished marble, then yielding like flesh. For a moment, Fiona could make out features, faded and forgot- ten and dreamlike: the suggestion of a cheek and eye where she touched, and there a leg, part of an armored chest, the barest outline of a broken, square-tipped sword.

This felt *older* than stone.

She blinked, and the stone was just rough sandstone. And she wasn't touching it, either.

Yet the feeling of its different smoothness lingered on her fingertips.

"Weird," she murmured.

"You heard it, too?" Eliot whispered. "The crying?"

"What are you talking about?"

"Never mind," Eliot whispered. He looked pale in the sunlight.

Before she could ask him to explain, Mr. Ma came to them. He smelled of exotic black tea. "I ask that you keep your violin in its case," he said to Eliot in a hushed voice. "These memories need no further coaxing." Although his voice was friendly, his eyes were dark and deadly earnest.

"Yes, sir," Eliot immediately replied.

"You are a good boy," he said.

Fiona and Eliot shared a confused look.

Mr. Ma went to center of the circle. "We begin," he announced. "Stay within the circle as I awaken them." His spread wide his callused hands.

Team Scarab gathered closer around Mr. Ma.

Fiona noted that Robert stood opposite her, trying not to look her way. With his hair wind-tousled and in his eyes, he appeared every bit the rebel despite the Paxington uniform.

Was this where they were now—not even looking at each other?

She had done everything this week to avoid thinking about Robert— even reorganized the books in her room thematically instead of alphabetically.

Maybe there wasn't a solution to the problem of her being in the League of Immortals and Robert being an outcast from the League.

Best to rip their relationship apart—quick, like a Band-Aid off a fresh scrape.

Sarah Covington moved closer to Robert. "How exciting," she whispered to him with that slight Scottish accent that all the guys went crazy over (and Fiona bet wasn't even real). She was standing way too close to him.

But if Fiona was letting go of Robert, then what did that matter? She narrowed her eyes and gritted her teeth. Sarah took no notice.

Mr. Ma inhaled and held his breath. The wind stilled.

A sound started from the inside of Mr. Ma, a deep bass hum that he twisted into some eastern Indian dialect that was part song, part funeral dirge, part wail. It made the hairs on her arm stir.

Clouds covered the sky. They boiled away and left night overhead, stars shining, but not the ones Fiona recognized in the normal summer sky; these were brighter and a hundred times more numerous.

Fiona heard crying. She cast about to see who it was, but it was no one from Team Scarab.

The sound came from the stones.

She felt their sorrow and the pain wash through her. It was the first time in months since she had felt so much or so deeply. Droplets of rain appeared and trickled down the sides of the rocks.

Fiona wanted to go to them, touch the stones, and comfort them . . . but she felt to do so would break the spell.

So she waited and watched.

The sky lightened. The sun broke over the horizon.

Mr. Ma ceased his chant and drew in a long breath. "We now share their dream," he whispered. He went to the edge of the circle of stones and pointed. "The memory of the memory of the Great Battle at Ultima Thule."[26, 27]

In the valley stood rows and ranks of a thousand men in ancient armor. There were chariots and phalanxes, their long spears gleaming in the dawn. There were armored elephants, companies of archers, and catapults.

Standing front and center of all this was a man—even at this distance, unmistakable to Fiona, his breastplate dull rusted iron, his thick mustache drooping, just as it had been when she last saw him.

"Uncle Aaron," she whispered.

There were others she recognized. Cousin Gilbert wore a robe of gold and carried a gold shield that caught the sun's warmth.

She squinted. Three women stood together at the far edge of the army. One had long glowing golden hair that flowed from her helmet. One held three lions on the leashes. The last wore armor made of bones; her white hair fell to her waist, and she wielded curved knives.

"Dallas?" she murmured so softly that only Eliot heard.

"And Lucia," Eliot breathed.

And together they whispered, "Mother?"

Fiona struggled to make sense of this. Intellectually, she understood the possibility that their mother and their relations were old, even ancient. But to see her here like this—in this page from history come to life—it was more than she could fathom.

"Observe." Mr. Ma pointed to the far side of the valley. "The opposition takes the field."

26. Thule is a mythic land, whether wholly fabricated or based in fact is a matter of continued debate. Ancient peoples described it as an island north of Great Britain. In the Middle Ages, it was thought to be Iceland, Greenland, or Svalbard. Confusing this issue is the use of "Ultima Thule" in medieval geographies to mean anywhere beyond the edge of the world. Nazi mystics believed Thule real, the Nordic equal to Atlantis, where once dwelled a race of supermen. *Gods of the First and Twenty-first Century, Volume 9, Mythic Places*, Zypheron Press Ltd., Eighth Edition.

27. "The blood spilt that day we used to write the *Pactum Pax Immortalis*. Were we craven? Or wise? Constantine united East and West under Holy Christian rule . . . did we creatures of light and dark see doom for all? Stop warring long enough to fight the greater foe? Only the truth be certain slain on that battlefield." Coded passage, page 48, deciphered and translated from the original Greek, *Mythica Improbiba* (Bezzle edition), Father Sildas Pious. ca. thirteenth century.

A crack parted the earth. Steam hissed forth as a dozen figures emerged.

They looked like men and women . . . although it was hard to tell because they were obscured by the mist.

Jeremy said with a little laugh, "A dozen against hundreds? Those unfortunate souls are going to be trounced."

"Incorrect on many counts," Jezebel replied. "Those are the Infernal Lords of Eld."

"How can the Immortals lose?" Amanda asked Jezebel and Mr. Ma, twisting the ends of her hair. "I mean . . . they are gods down there, aren't they?"

"Some are gods, so-called," Mr. Ma answered. "Some heroes. Some merely brave fools. But there is one thing that you have yet to appreciate, Miss Lane. The Infernals are led by the Great Satan himself."

The man in front of the Infernals screamed. Talons grew from his hands; curved ram horns burst forth from his head; skeletal bat wings cracked and popped from his spine.

He grew . . . taller and larger than any man could be . . . grew until he was six stories tall . . . skin darkening to amber and orange and finally electric crimson . . . and then he burst into flame.

The Great Satan roared a deafening challenge to the army of gods. Then he charged.

26

THE BATTLE OF ULTIMA THULE

It happened fast.

Fiona was so filled with raw adrenaline, though, that her mind slowed everything.

Satan crashed toward the Immortals on the field.

The only thing she had ever witnessed to compare to this creature was seeing the bones of a *Tyrannosaurus rex* in a museum. But the dinosaur was close only in size and the head full of teeth—it wasn't moving, screaming, and filled with flaming violence.

Satan was a true nightmare.

Seeing it made her wanted to whimper and hide.

As he ran, the fire in one hand solidified into an iron lance, pitchfork tipped and white hot.

Following his lead, the other Infernals took shape.

One lay down and transformed into a serpent, longer and fatter, and swelled into a form that dwarfed Satan . . . corpulent coils of scaled flesh that wormed forward, crushing the rocks before it to dust.

Another strode forth, each step growing in size until it was a giant that cast shadows in all directions; at its center darkness that defied the sunlight. Fiona saw its smile, however, swimming suspended in the black nothingness, fanged and full of malice. It dragged a chain whip the size of a tank tread with fishhook barbs.

Mitch stepped next to Fiona and furiously scribbled this into his sketchbook. "It's not real," he whispered. His voice wavered, unsure.

But Fiona couldn't answer. It felt like there was no oxygen in her lungs.

A bat-shape cloud took to the air, screaming, and leaving a trail of crows and insect clouds and smog.

There was a clockwork man with bladed arms, a woman who dripped boiling poison and left a sizzling trail of lava in her wake, a three-headed hound with black eyes, a dragon, some shapeless tentacled horror, and centipede with a million needle legs.

Fiona forced herself to look away—or she would have frozen completely solid with terror.

She turned to the Immortals.

They stood tall and held their formation. They braced lance and spear and held their shields before them, ready for the onslaught. None broke ranks.

Uncle Aaron shouted orders and raised an impossibly large sword. His army cheered.

Fiona's heart leaped with joy. *Yes!* She felt the courage and the power and the nobility flowing though her blood as well. Her fear evaporated. She gathered herself and stood taller. She would have given anything to be with her family on that field.

Immortal archers loosened arrows; a cloud of spines filled the air, arcing up and toward the enemy.

One archer held back his shot, however. He wore silver armor, so mirror-polished that he blended with the background. He ran onto the field, bow held out before him.

He launched a sliver of light from his bow—its trajectory flat and so fast, it streaked under the other arrows.

The Great Satan dodged—surprisingly even *faster* than this arrow—although the projectile grazed his side and left a scar of blue flames.

The arrow continued on course, rocketed toward the Infernals, and struck the monstrous serpent in the right eye—obliterating the socket and exploding out the back of the angular viper head.

The serpent hissed and thrashed, its coils smashed trees and hills, blocking the advance of the other Infernals.

The other arrows landed, some sticking the Infernals and drawing blood, most harmlessly bouncing off or shattering upon their bare skin.

"One lucky shot," Mr. Ma said, "or perhaps it was not luck, may have decided the battle before it started. The mighty Leviathan was distracted. The Immortals would have not survived a direct confrontation with the Beast. Learn the lesson: Remove your largest opponent if you are able. You might be as lucky."

Fiona spotted a man in the chariot by Uncle Aaron's side. He was older, handsome, with a curled white beard. He shouted orders, and Aaron nodded with grim determination, looked once upon Satan bearing down on them, and stepped aside, ordering the soldiers nearby to do the same.

She saw now that the older man was larger than Aaron, muscular, and regal. Four white stallions drew his chariot. Within the chariot's carriage were metal coils and spinning armatures that sparked and arced electricity and connected to the lance held by the man.

The apparatus spun faster, and the air about the chariot wavered and smoked.

The man spoke to his horses and they snorted with fear, but nonetheless pulled the chariot ahead.

He shouted and flipped a switch on his lance.

Electricity chained along the length of metal.

A flash. The air cracked. Lightning leaped from the lance's tip and struck Satan.

The monster writhed in agony, dropped its pitchfork, and fell to its knees.

But then the lightning diminished and sputtered and died.

Satan was smaller now, perhaps only three times the size of an ordinary man. The warrior in the chariot barked orders, and Uncle Aaron and soldiers ran forward.

Satan looked up, smiling, and from his knees jumped upon them.

The monster ripped limbs from men and tossed broken bodies about like toys.

Uncle Aaron deflected claw and lashing tail and bat wing with his sword, but even he was driven back.

The man in the chariot fired his weapon once more, but the charge was a fraction of the original blast, and it only momentarily slowed Satan . . . before the monster turned and came for him.

The charioteer snapped the reins, and his warhorses galloped forward. He swerved at the last moment and jumped from the chariot—

—as it crashed headlong into Satan.

The electrical apparatus exploded in a cloud of sparks and arcs and gears and coils and chariot wheels, and left a cloud of dust, obscuring all. Four horses emerged unscathed and bolted across the field.

The charioteer, spear held before him, moved forward into the cloud.

"What's going on?" Fiona cried. "I can't see any more."

"Something I have never seen," Mr. Ma remarked as he stroked his chin thoughtfully. "The angle is different this time. This is when Zeus and Satan met in deadly combat. Later, leaderless, both sides were too disorganized to continue their war. It was the single most important factor responsible for their neutrality treaty."

"Wait," Eliot said. "You're telling us those two are going to die? I mean, they did die?"

Fiona had been so engrossed, she hadn't even noticed Eliot and the rest of Team Scarab pressed close around her.

Mr. Ma nodded as he squinted into the rising clouds of dust on the battlefield. "Observe how both sides now engage."

Infernals clambered or flew over the bulk of the writhing Leviathan, and attacked the army of Immortals.

Dozens of heroes enveloped Infernals, but the fallen angels were too powerful and they killed many, leaving a trail of broken and wounded gods and goddesses.

Across the field, one group of Immortals rallied. Aunt Dallas led them, a golden sword in each hand, fending off a giantess Infernal with flaming hair and dripping poison from her claws.

The warriors at Dallas's side fell one by one, but she fought on, determined and fearless.

This was not the Dallas that Fiona knew—not the shoe-shopping, care-about-nothing socialite. This was Dallas the *goddess*.

More wind and dust whipped across the field, and Fiona couldn't see her anymore.

"Curious . . . ," Mr. Ma remarked. "This is not like the other times."

"I have to know what's going on," Fiona whispered. She moved toward the ring of weeping stones.

Mr. Ma set a hand on her arm. His flesh was immovable iron, and he checked her motion.

Fiona turned to him. Mr. Ma's eyes were unyielding—but so were hers. In her veins raced the blood of the Immortals. She felt ten feet tall. She felt a sense of pride and purpose that she had never before experienced.

"I *have* to go to them," she whispered. "And I will." Her gaze dropped to his hand.

Mr. Ma looked about . . . perhaps to see where Miss Westin was, but not seeing her anywhere, he sighed and released Fiona.

Did he know what she was? Surely the teachers at Paxington had to know that she and Eliot were half Immortal. He had to know that it was her family out on that battlefield.

"Very well," he said. "I, too, wish to see what is happening. We shall investigate this anomaly together. You *will* stay behind at all times . . . or I can and will carry you back here, child. You understand?"

She nodded.

They started down the hill.

"Hey!" Eliot said, trotting after them. "If you're going, so am I."

"I will accompany you as well," Jezebel declared, stepping forward.

"I'll go, too, if that's okay." Mitch flipped over a new page in his sketchbook.

Mr. Ma sighed, shook his head, then looked to the rest of Team Scarab.

Amanda stood behind one of the stones, barely peeking out, trembling.

Robert sighed and looked at Amanda, then said, "I'll stay here and watch."

Jeremy crossed his arms. "I have no desire to see the blood and guts of gods and devils, up close, thank you very much."

Sarah Covington glanced uneasily from the battlefield, to Mr. Ma, to her cousin, and then whispered, "I guess I'll be staying here as well."

Mr. Ma turned to the rest of them. "Stay close to me, then, and always behind. I will tolerate no wandering off." Then more to himself, he said, "Something is very wrong."

He strode down the hill, and they followed.

Eliot trotted next to Fiona, apparently just as curious about their family, although he was looking more at the Infernals. She was fascinated with them, too . . . in a grotesque, can't-take-your-eyes-off-it-because-it's-so-horrific way.

How could she and Eliot be related to them? And how could they look so human one moment and so completely monstrous the next? Which was their real form?

Overhead, flocks of crows and vultures circled.

Was their father a man or that thing they'd caught a glimpse of standing over Beelzebub as Del Sombra burned down around them? A bat-winged nightmare?

Mr. Ma led them past heroes who fought valiantly, picking a path through the debris of broken catapults, and gingerly avoiding where the earth smoldered as cooling lava.

The fog parted before them.

Immortals and Infernals clashed in combat, but moved out of their way with perfect timing as if these memories were squeezed aside by the presence of real people.

Fiona wanted to touch something, pick up a sword and fight—help her family somehow. But if this was just a memory from the weeping stones, she couldn't interact with anything here—and vice versa.

So why, then, was Mr. Ma looking so concerned? He paused and surveyed the battle through the mist and smoke.

A stone's throw away, Aunt Dallas battled for her life against the Infernal with flaming hair. Her enemy was smaller now, but Dallas fought alone. Every soldier that had been in her group lay in the dirt with throats and arms and chests torn out.

"That is Abaddon, a Destroyer," Jezebel dryly commented. "A match for any god."

The Infernal slashed. Her nails scraped down the length of one of Dallas's swords as she parried. The metal sparked and shattered at the hilt.

Dallas stabbed with the other sword, and penetrated the monster's heart. It didn't slow her down.

Abaddon drove her back against jagged rocks, forcing her to her knees. Dallas fought on, tears of rage streaking her face, and would not give up.

The Infernal was going to kill her.

Fiona had to do something.

She glanced back at Mr. Ma, who had his back turned, surveying the far side of the battlefield.

Fiona wasn't stupid enough to break her promise and run off on her own, but she had to do *something*.

She knelt, grabbed a fist-sized rock, and threw it.

The stone hit Abaddon on the side of her head and bounced harmlessly off . . . but it *did* connect.

And it got her attention. She turned.

"You shouldn't have been able to that," Mitch whispered.

The Infernal turned back to Dallas . . . then halted again and cocked her head as if hearing something.

Fiona felt motion in the air—like an arrow's whistle or a blade just before it cuts.

The woman in bone armor emerged from the mist. Audrey was wide-eyed, long white hair flowing over her shoulders, teeth bared, and holding twin curved daggers of sharpened tooth and tusk.

She slashed at the Infernal so fast, feinting and weaving a razor pattern in the air.

Abaddon hissed fire.

Audrey ducked, rolled, the flames unfurling over her head, and then she bounded forward again—slashing.

The Infernal held out a hand to block.

Her pinkie severed and wriggled upon the ground. She screamed and took three strides backwards. Abaddon glared at her opponent . . . then turned and fled into the smoke.

Audrey helped Dallas to her feet.

They hugged—then Audrey wheeled about, staring straight at Fiona.

Mitch stepped next to Fiona, touched her lightly on the shoulder, and whispered, "Don't move. You hit that Infernal with a rock . . . maybe they *can* interact with us."

She raised her jawbone visor and stared at Fiona and Mitch, Eliot and Jezebel. Really seeing them.

To witness her mother like this. . . . Not Audrey Post, but Atropos, a primitive goddess, fighting, full of life and battle lust. It was so unlike the stately woman she thought she knew, and yet so like her mother, all her iron will and inner strength.

Fiona reached out—stopped.

Her mother's eyes hardened into a cold deadly glare.

Mr. Ma stepped in front of Fiona.

The connection broke.

Audrey shook her head as if clearing a dream and returned to her sister's side. They joined Uncle Aaron and other Immortals that formed a phalanx against a single Infernal, the mechanical man with bladed arms.

Mr. Ma gave Fiona a look that promised a long lecture about following the meaning of his instructions.

"Observe," he said, nodding toward the regrouped Immortals. "They work collectively against a superior foe. Alone, the Infernal—even though it has more power—cannot penetrate the formation. This is the one of the key philosophical difference between them."

The battle slowed.

The Infernals retreated back to their hellhole.

Heroes gathered wounded comrades and limped toward the hills.

Fiona felt the dream begin to fade, the ancient memories submerging into shadow and silence.

"I lost Zeus and Satan," Eliot said, looking around. "Mr. Ma, you said they died? Where are their bodies? Satan should have left a big smoking crater."

Mr. Ma cast his gaze about. "Indeed. Not this time . . ." His voice trailed off as he pondered. "Come." He indicated they follow him deeper into the fog.

Fiona would have given anything to see Zeus one more time. She'd look up everything there was on him in her books tonight. How had one Immortal ever led the League when the modern Council of Seven Elders could barely decide anything?

Things were different back then—that's why. Even Dallas had been a real warrior.

Mr. Ma found Zeus's broken chariot: coils and copper-wound armatures still arcing and smoldering. There were great gashes in the earth, and blood—splashes of crimson and tar-black ooze everywhere.

But no trace of either Satan or Zeus.

"History tells us they *did* die," Mr. Ma whispered. "At this very spot." He knelt and touched the earth and blood. "And yet so much is different— more real—in this version of the dream." He looked at Fiona and Eliot. "I wonder . . ."

He stood.

"The demonstration is over." Mr. Ma strode back toward the hill and the circle of stones.

The fog cleared, and overhead it was a sunny California afternoon again.

"You will each write a three-thousand-word paper," Mr. Ma told them, "comparing and contrasting the fighting and philosophical styles of the two sides. Due Wednesday."

They'd just relived one of the most important battles ever . . . and he was assigning homework? Fiona wanted to do something *significant*: wage a battle, lead an army, change the world, be a real goddess.

Fiona kicked the dirt in a futile act of rebellion.

Mitch trotted alongside her. "I sketched their formations," he said. "You want to hang out after school? Have some coffee and compare notes?"

Fiona's thoughts completely derailed. She almost tripped. "Coffee?"

"Sure." Mitch smiled his reassuring smile that made Fiona feel like she'd known him forever. A smile that could even make her forget she was mad.

She glanced at the hilltop where Robert was, and that ruined her mood again. *He* wasn't going to ask her out for coffee any time soon. Things were so different now between them.

Her analysis of how she was so *not* like the ancient gods would have to wait. So would obsessing about how she and Robert could fit together with the League always between them.

The real world had to take priority, and right now that meant homework . . . and maybe being friends with Mitch.

"I'd love coffee," she said.

27

A WRONG TURN

Eliot and the rest of Team Scarab got on the bus and got driven back to Plato's Hall.

There Miss Westin lectured on the ramifications of the Battle of Ultima Thule . . . how the then leaderless Immortals and Infernals signed a neutrality treaty (the *Pactum Pax Immortalis*) in 326 C.E. . . . which provided stability for the mortal magical families to surface and thrive . . . and prompted a fragile cooperation between mortals, fallen angels, and Immortals to preserve the ancient knowledge in Emperor Constantine's Court of God's Peace . . . which made the Paxington Institute possible . . . and was the indirect cause of the modern political balance between mortals and Immortals everywhere . . . and the reason they were all here today.

The *Pactum Pax Immortalis* was the treaty that Louis had mentioned, the one he said Eliot and Fiona might unravel.

If they undid that, what happened to the world?

On top of all that, Eliot couldn't stop thinking about Jezebel. Compared to everything else, his personal problems *shouldn't* matter.

And yet, Jezebel sat just a few seats away . . . and it very much *did* matter.

The scent from the battlefield was still with Eliot—all the smoke and blood and dust, but Jezebel's perfume—vanilla with hints of cinnamon—overwhelmed him.

All he could focus on was how she had lied about wishing she'd never met him.

Miss Westin dismissed class. Everyone filed out; even Robert and Fiona left without him.

Eliot lagged behind.

Miss Westin gave him a long look, nodded behind her glasses as if she understood everything . . . and then left the room as well.

He was alone.

That suited Eliot fine. He'd slink home and get that paper done for Mr. Ma—maybe even dig out his old *Mythica Improbiba* and see what it said about old Satan and Zeus. It would feel good to do almost normal homework for once.

He wandered out of the classroom and across campus, not looking where he was going until he was near the front gate.

Jezebel was there, walking along the same trajectory . . . but not alone.

Dante Scalagari and that tall Van Wyck boy Jeremy had trounced the first day (who still had his broken nose taped), walked with her. They showed great interest in everything she said.

Well, of course, every boy at Paxington would be interested in her.

Something sleeping stirred inside Eliot, however: a heat that sparked and kindled. His hands curled into fists.

He took a deep breath.

There was no way he was going to march over there and try to insert himself in their conversation . . . and yet, he found himself doing precisely that.

"Hey . . . ," he said.

The boys' smiles faded, and Jezebel's face turned to stony disdain.

"It's our young Master Post," Dante said with a polite tilt of his head.

"I was wondering if we could talk," he said to Jezebel. Eliot's ears burned, but somehow he pressed on, getting the rest of the awkward words out as quickly as he could. "About gym class. Strategies for our next match, I mean."

"The way I heard it," Van Wyck said, flicking his angle-cut hair from his face, "a good strategy might be for you to sit out the next match."

"Donald, there's no need for that," Dante said to his friend, and gave an apologetic shrug to Eliot.

Jezebel's gaze fell upon Eliot. "I must speak with the boy," she said. "If you two wouldn't mind." She flashed them her patented hundred-watt smile.

"As you wish, lady," Dante said. He and Donald van Wyck bowed, and they left (although not before Van Wyck gave Eliot a withering look).

Jezebel's smile vanished. Her eyes narrowed to slits. "For being the son of the Great Deceiver," she whispered, "you, Eliot Post, are a rotten lair."

His head snapped up, and he returned her hateful stare. He wasn't lying—well, he was . . . about wanting to talk about gym class. But hearing how pathetic a liar he was coming from *her*—that just fanned the flames inside him.

Eliot flushed, but it wasn't from embarrassment. This was some animal instinct to move and take her in his arms and . . . what? It was so much darker than his normal high-adventured daydreams, it startled him back to normal.

Louis had said how Infernals could easily tell lies from the truth. He must have just insulted Jezebel with that little white lie.

He exhaled. "Yeah," he whispered. "Sorry about that. The truth between us would be best."

Jezebel's eyebrows flicked up. Her glare eased a notch and she was silent a moment.

"No," she said, turned, and headed for the gate. "I believe that it would be best if there were *nothing* between us." She didn't say this cruelly, but as if it broke her heart.

Eliot watched her leave.

He should drop this and let her go. How much clearer could she be on what she wanted?

But that wasn't the issue. It wasn't what she wanted that he needed to know; he had to know how she *felt* about him.

Eliot followed after her to the gate.

Jezebel walked faster . . . but then they both had to stop.

Harlan Dells, as ever, stood at the gate. He looked them both over with that microscopically penetrating gaze that made Eliot feel naked and helpless.

"Hey, Mr. Dells," Eliot said.

Jezebel curtsied, lowered her eyes, and said, "Hail, Keeper of the Gates."

Mr. Dells smoothed his tasseled beard, then turned and gazed into the alley.

"Something wrong?" Jezebel asked.

"The shadows a moment ago," Mr. Dells replied. "Just a flicker. Half a wavelength. A trick of the fog and light . . . perhaps." He turned back to them, his face clouded. "Take care to walk the straight and narrow on the way home today, children."

Eliot wasn't sure what that was all about, but he replied, "Yes, sir."

Harlan Dells opened the gate and watched them pass.

"Look . . . ," Eliot said, trying to keep up with Jezebel.

She ignored him and trotted ahead.

He knew it was rude, and he knew she could probably knock his head off if she wanted to, but he had to talk to her. Eliot reached out and touched her hand.

The effect was immediate.

She whirled on him, the hand he had touched curled into a clawed strike.

"I'm sorry," he said quickly. "For everything. And I mean *everything*. How you got involved with the Infernals. How I should have figured it all out in Del Sombra and done something more to help. And how you gave up your freedom for me, and had to go back . . . to Hell."

Jezebel's mouth dropped open. "How can you be such a fool?" she breathed.

"Fiona asks the same thing," he said. "Maybe I am a fool to want to help you. I know you're part of some plot involving me. But that doesn't matter. We had something real in Del Sombra. My song for you didn't come from nowhere. I could never have composed that on the spot for you if there hadn't been a connection between us."

"There was no connection," she whispered.

Eliot sensed that lie.

And she knew that he knew, too.

"I *can* help you." Eliot held out his hand.

She looked at him and then at his proffered hand.

Jezebel slowly turned away and continued down the alley. "You understand nothing."

Although the alley had been full of students just a second ago, it was empty now . . . which was fine, because Eliot wanted to be alone with Jezebel.

Still, it was strange. Where'd everyone go?

He walked alongside her, and this time she let him.

Jezebel kept her head lowered, not looking at him, and edged closer until their shoulders almost touched.

"This is not a game with the Infernal clans," she said. "My Queen is at war with Mephistopheles. Only one side will survive. Help me and you become *his* enemy. He will destroy you." In the tiniest whisper, she added: "I cannot let that happen."

"None of that matters," he told her.

That fire that had been inside him before rekindled through his body, burning away his fear and doubt.

He spoke in a deeper voice: "It matters not if all the demons in Hell, every angel in Heaven, or the gods themselves stand between you and me. Nothing will keep us apart." The heat inside Eliot cooled—but it *had* been there. It was real. His Immortal side . . . or his Infernal blood surfacing?

He felt the old connection between him and Julie—like the day he had played her her song, when she had poured her soul into his.

Overhead, however, electrical lines hummed, and Eliot felt vertigo . . . like he was in a falling elevator . . . a sensation not unlike the first time he and Fiona had found the sideways passage into this alley.

He looked about.

They were still in the alley—but it was wrong.

He and Jezebel stood in a deserted side passage off the main thoroughfare. Eliot hadn't seen this before.

And he sure didn't recall turning down it.

Jezebel whirled around. "A trap!"

She glared at Eliot, angry, then took her eyes off him and searched the passage . . . whose entrance now turned away at a right angle . . . an angle that hadn't been there a moment ago.

The shadows in the alley grew longer.

The buildings leaned toward one another, limiting how much light filtered down. It was as if the space around them was as pliable as molding clay.

"See?" Jezebel said. "I told you! They've come for me. Run—while you can."

He reached into his pack, flipped open his violin case, and grabbed Lady Dawn. Eliot set bow to strings, and the air stilled.

"I'm sticking with you," he told her.

"I cannot believe how stubborn . . . ," she muttered under her breath, gritting her teeth until they ground out the rest of her words.

They were no longer alone. Eliot could feel the presence in the shadows surrounding them.

A dozen black eyes stared from the dark—pulling themselves from the flat dimensionless shadow planes.

These things had long limbs that terminated into chitinous points. Where they touched brick and asphalt, they left gouges and sounded like a herd of cats running over blackboards. Their heads were smooth and tapered and split open to reveal a grin of countless shark teeth.

Jezebel faced them. Her hands up in a fighting stance, she stepped next to Eliot so they stood back to back.

"Droogan-dors," she whispered. "Do not let them pierce you. Their poison turns flesh into smoke."

For a heartbeat, Eliot froze, wanted to do nothing but run—but there was no way he was leaving Jezebel to fight alone.

He played the first thing that sprang into his mind, the "The March of the Suicide Queen." He jumped to a part about a third of the way into the piece—allegro—bowing until his fingers blurred—the battle charge: it spoke of horses racing toward the enemy line, knights with lances leveled—impacting upon the enemy and breaking bodies, splintering wood, shattering bone, trampling deeper into the fray.

In his mind he heard those soldiers sing:

> *We shall never show mercy*
> *We shall ask no quarter.*
> *We spill rivers of blood*
> *Gallop through blade and mortar.*

Hoofbeats echoed off the alley walls. The dust stirred and white ghost horses appeared with headless riders charging at a full gallop—passed *through* Eliot and Jezebel—but solidly tramped over the nearest creatures.

The Droogan-dors went down, stabbing the phantom horses and knights.

The horses screamed as gaping holes of darkness appeared, consuming them . . . but not before they trampled the creatures, with shell-splitting crunches and wet grinding splats.

Two of the creatures jumped at Jezebel. She slashed out—her fingernails now long claws.

The Droogan-dors reared back, the cuts along their bodies swelled and blistered from poison. They writhed on the ground, screaming, and turned to smoke.

The remaining Droogan-dors backed off, whispering among themselves.

"They're leaving," Eliot said. "We can get out."

"No," Jezebel said, "there are never so few. That was merely a test. There is no way to survive this."

The shadows multiplied with blinking eyes, scraping, rasping points, and leering smiles . . . and Eliot saw a hundred more of them . . . all smiling from the dark.

28

SHADOW LEGION

Fiona returned from the girls' restroom and found Mitch where she'd left him on the library steps. Robert was there talking to him.

Her first instinct was to walk away. She and Mitch were supposed to get some coffee and swap notes—all innocent enough, but how could she do that in front of Robert, with him and her all tangled up in League politics? He'd get the wrong idea.

But maybe it wasn't the wrong idea.

She *did* like Mitch . . . although at this point, it was more of a theoretical "like" than anything else, because they'd never really had a chance to talk.

And there was an ugly reality that neither she nor Robert was facing: With her in the League, and him out, there was no way they could be more than friends. Even that might end up being dangerous for Robert.

She tried to smile as she walked up to them, but couldn't quite make herself.

"Fiona." Mitch looked up and smiled. "Robert and I were going over the battle. He's got some insights into the Immortals' tactics. Did you know that he actually worked for the League for a time?"

"Yeah, that's great," Fiona said.

Robert looked away and took a deep breath.

Mitch sensed something wrong. He missed only a single beat, though, and then set a hand on Robert's shoulder. "You want to join us? Fiona and I were going to grab coffee and compare notes."

"You had plans . . . together?" Robert looked up, unable to hide the surprise on his face—then quickly recovered. "That's cool, uh, but no, I've got places to be this afternoon. Thanks anyway." He nodded to Fiona (without looking at her) and made a hasty exit.

Fiona watched him go, her heart breaking. That *had* been necessary, hadn't it?

She realized that her posture had slumped over and she looked, and felt, very much like the old always-too-shy Fiona Post.

Yeah, it was necessary.

Robert had to know they couldn't be together anymore. The sooner they *both* adjusted to that reality, the better for everyone.

She stood tall again.

"There's something between you two?" Mitch asked, an uneasy expression crossing his face. "I like Robert. He's a good guy."

"Ancient history," Fiona replied. "Coffee?"

"Sure."

Mitch smiled again, and Fiona knew it was going to be okay. Eventually.

They walked across the quad, close, but not touching. Mitch smelled faintly of cloves.

He paused at the fountain of Poseidon and tossed a quarter into the waters. "Tribute for dead gods," he told her. "Brings luck—at least, that's what my father told me."

Poseidon was dead? Fiona filed that fact next to the possibly dead Zeus, and kept moving.

"You believe in luck, then?"

"Not really, but the Stephenson family can't afford to take chances."

They started to walk again side by side.

"The Stephensons—Miss Westin hasn't covered them in lecture yet."

Mitch chuckled. "She probably won't. We're not that important. Never been politically connected or financial powerhouses like the other clans."

"Your family's name sure managed to impress Jeremy and Sarah Covington, though, at team selection. That's no small trick."

"Oh, that. I guess that's the one thing we Stephensons have going for us: a reputation. It's no big deal. My many-times great-grandfather was Dr. Faust."[28]

---

28. Dr. Johan Georg Faust, a fifteenth-century alchemist and astrologer, who became the origin of the Dr. Faustus literature (notably Marlowe's *The Tragical History of Doctor Faustus* [1604] and Goethe's *Faust* [1808]). Papal investigations confirmed that Johan Faust did make an Infernal pact, gained fame and fortune, and fathered a dozen bastard children before his demise. One of these children was born of the Lady Dorchester Stephen, the progenitor to

Fiona nodded, like she got this "Faust" reference. Thankfully, Mitch continued, so she didn't have to ask a slew of embarrassing questions.

"Everyone thinks Faust really did make the best deal ever with the devil—if that's not an oxymoron—and became the most powerful sorcerer of the age. Of course, he then squandered that power showing off."

"So," Fiona said, growing concerned, "what kind of reputation does your family have?"

"That's a fair question." Mitch sobered as if Fiona had touched a nerve. "After Faust died, some of his power passed to his children. They had a hard time, persecuted as witches, and then hunted by the Vatican. That changed when the Inquisition recruited them and trained them to use their power to fight evil. Since then, they've become the greatest practitioners of white magic in the world."

This fascinated Fiona. Not just his story, although it was interesting, but also that Mitch knew so much about his family. It must have given him a sense of stability to know where he came from. It was something she envied.

"Is that why you were so interested in the Infernals at Ultima Thule?" she asked. "Taking notes on how to fight them?"

"Not exactly," Mitch said, mounting the steps before the front gate. "It was more like being a marine biologist swimming in a tank with a megalodon. I never imagined that I'd get close to a *real* Infernal like Jezebel."

Fiona tried to puzzle this out, but couldn't. "Shouldn't you two be mortal enemies?"

"No, thank goodness. All that devil-fighting stuff stopped centuries ago. Probably extended the longevity of my family. We still have a talent for white magic, exorcisms and stuff like that, but as far as the Infernal Lords are concerned—and certainly Jezebel, a real Duchess of the Poppy Lands—we're small fry."

Fiona studied Mitch. There were nobility and kindness in his face: high cheekbones, straight nose, hair the color of mahogany, and smoky eyes she could drown in.

They halted at the front gate.

Harlan Dells had his back to them, staring into the alley.

Mitch cleared his throat.

"I know you are there," Mr. Dells grumbled. "Be quiet." He took in a deep breath and held it, waited, and then finally said: "I can no longer hear them."

"Who?" Fiona asked

Mr. Dells turned, his face more serious than usual. "Your brother, Miss Post. He and the Jezebel girl entered the alley . . . and they have taken a wrong turn beyond my senses."

"Wait a second," Fiona said. "I thought you said you could 'hear grass grow on the other side of the world'?"

Mr. Dells stiffened. "I can, young lady." His eyes narrowed. "In *this* world." He flicked the switch that operated the iron gate, and it rolled aside. "I suggest you find him."

Fiona and Mitch shared a glance wrought with concern.

The wrongness she had felt a second ago crystallized into fear. First, Eliot was with Jezebel. She couldn't begin to count all the things that could go wrong with *that* situation. And second, there was no place to make a "turn" in the alley. It led straight out into the street.

This was just the kind of trouble only her stupid brother could get into.

"Please come with us," Fiona asked Mr. Dells.

"My duties do not permit me to leave the campus." Mr. Dells looked into the sun without blinking. "You need to hurry . . . before their light goes out altogether."

Fiona wasn't sure what he meant, because the sun was nowhere near setting, but it chilled her blood.

She and Mitch ran out into the alley where Mr. Dell had stared.

There was Xybek's Jewelry and an Apple computer store for Paxington students—but no place where Eliot could have turned.

"How can you turn on a straight line?" she whispered.

Mitch cocked his head as if listening. "You add another line—another dimension." He moved to the brick wall and touched it.

Fiona followed, hearing something, too: a violin, distant dull explosions, thundering horse hooves, the crash of metal, and screams.

Fiona swallowed. She understood now.

Eliot had taken a "wrong turn" as they had that first day when they found this alley. Normally, you weren't supposed to be able to see the entrance, because it was hidden "sideways" from the perspective of normal three dimensions.

But there was no reason strange extradimensional passages couldn't be hidden anywhere . . . *everywhere*, right in plain sight.

Maybe even ones you could've stumbled upon *without* wanting to.

She ran her fingers over the wall, searching.

She brushed over Mitch's fingers and felt an electric thrill. Embarrassed, she almost jerked her hand away, but the sensation had been real . . . and not just because she'd touched Mitch. There was something there, underneath.

Fiona pressed harder, feeling a bump in the fabric of existence.

She let her vision drift out of focus; she felt a loose thread and pulled it out.

Fiona's ears popped. She fumbled for Mitch's hand and grabbed it.

She felt as if she were descending fast in an elevator.

Behind her, a long brick-lined passage stretched back toward the alley—and stretched farther as she watched, curving out of sight. Overhead buildings leaned closer.

Shadows were everywhere.

Fiona couldn't see a thing. She felt like she was suffocating.

Mitch held his free hand up. A ball of light appeared in his palm—as brilliant as an arc welder. He gritted his teeth in pain.

The shadows retreated about them . . . screaming.

Mitch's light revealed hundreds of creatures climbing over one another to retreat from the brilliance.

There were more of them, pushing and oozing to a point a quarter block ahead.

That's where Fiona spied Jezebel and her brother.

The darkness crowded about them and obscured her view. She heard Eliot, though, playing Lady Dawn . . . something muffled by the smothering layers of shadow.

She and Mitch shuffled carefully forward.

The shadow creatures looked like man-sized bats (specifically the pug-nosed *Desmodus rotundus,* vampire bat). They dragged themselves on too-long skeletal limbs that ended in three curved talons. Their claws trailed an oily darkness like squid ink in water. When they smacked open their mouths, more teeth than should have been possible to fit inside their heads flexed outward.

One rushed Fiona, despite Mitch's light, claws reaching.

Fiona lashed forward—finding her father's gift, the bracelet about her wrist, once more transformed into a full length of real chain.

She cut the creature in half.

It hit the pavement with a wet splat . . . apparently more than mere shadow, reeking of hot gasoline and ozone.

Fiona gazed at the partially rusted chain and vowed to thank Louis if she ever saw him again.

She turned to Eliot. They had to get out before they got lost in the encroaching darkness.

Next to her, Mitch stared openmouthed at the severed monstrosity that oozed black blood at her feet . . . then to the chain she held. The color drained from his face.

She nodded to his upheld hand and the ball of intense light. "Can you make it brighter?"

"I can try," he whispered. He licked his lips and concentrated.

The light blazed like a tiny sun. He grunted in pain and his hand blistered.

The shadows about them backed away, their edges sizzling in the intense illumination . . . clearing a path to Jezebel and Eliot.

Fiona now clearly heard Eliot's music. It was the song he'd played at their first gym match. Only then, he had cautiously plunked out the song. Now he bowed with vibrato, and Fiona felt the music resonate in her bones; it made her want to march forward.

She resisted, though, because she didn't understand what she saw.

Eliot and Jezebel stood in the center of a hundred shadow creatures that wheeled about them, circling closer.

Jezebel's hands had finger-length needle claws that dripped venom. Where it spattered on the ground, the asphalt dissolved. Her arms were still slender and porcelain white, but her veins stood out, vinelike and pulsing. Her face was drawn, mouth filled with serrated teeth. But her eyes—they were wild and solid green, glimmered as if faceted emeralds . . . and reminded Fiona of the emotionless gaze of a praying mantis.

A shadow rushed Jezebel, its mouth extended in a gruesome smile.

Jezebel struck—so fast, Fiona barely saw the motion.

The creature fell screaming, withering, clutching at the holes that once contained its eyes, and then it died.

Only then did Fiona see dozens of liquefying corpses about the Infernal Jezebel, dribbling away to the drain in the center of the alley.

An overpowering scent of vanilla reached Fiona's nostrils. She almost gagged.

Fiona had seen Infernals more disgusting at the Ultima Thule battle, even faced horrific Beelzebub in combat, but she hadn't seen one part transformed, half human and half nightmare . . . and definitely not someone who sat next to her in class.

Maybe as Louis had said "the fires of Hell" burned in Fiona's blood as well—but if being Infernal meant unleashing the monster within, then Fiona never wanted to let that side of her take control.

But more than Jezebel . . . it was Eliot that *really* threw her.

Eliot's hands were blurs as he played. His eyes were unblinking, staring off into space. About him fog swirled, and Fiona glimpsed a battlefield beyond and hundreds of red-coated soldiers stepping into the alley, bayonets fixed upon rifles, firing in time with the music, and marching forward to battle the shadows. The soldiers fought blade to claw. They died, dozens of them—and still they materialized from the music, never broke ranks, never cried out or showed any emotion . . . like windup toys.

And they sang:

> We live to fight until we die
> Queen and country and flags to fly.
> Brothers and sons a'glory sought
> Our silent graves what we wrought.

Eliot bowed faster, his head bobbing. Horses rode from the fog into the alley. Their headless riders were armored, holding shield and lance. They charged into the fray, scattered the shadow monsters, impaling some, then slowed as they faced overwhelming numbers, switching to sword, horse rearing . . . but all falling in the darkness.

Eliot tapped his bow upon the strings.

Black iron cannon mounted on wagon-wheel bases maneuvered to the front—and fired!

Six flashes of thunder and smoke filled the alley. Blasts that blew shadow and flesh and claw to bits, battered brick walls down . . . and revealed more darkness beyond . . . a thousand shark-tooth grins . . . and an endless starless night.

Fiona had never seen her brother like this before. He'd been stupidly brave, sure. But not the center of a battle and conducting troops like some general. It was like one of his daydream fantasies come to life.

But it was strategically stupid to fight here.

It wasn't just the shadow monsters—although their numbers seemed endless, and certainly any one of them looked like they could tear them to pieces.

It was this alley. It was a sideways passage through nothing. A void in space that, if they weren't careful, they'd get lost in and never find the way out.

Already Fiona felt her sense of direction swimming.

"Eliot!" she shouted.

Eliot jerked away from the reloading cannon crews, squinted as he finally noticed Mitch's light, nodded, but kept playing.

"This way," Fiona called.

The shadows about them pushed in.

Fiona wouldn't let them stop her—not when she was so close.

She turned to Mitch and told him: "Duck."

Confusion washed over his face—but only for a moment—then he understood. He crouched and held the ball of light before his body.

Fiona spun her chain overhead and let out the full length.

Where whirling metal touched shadow and flesh, there was smoke and blood and shrills of pain . . . and the enemy moved back.

Fiona and Mitch crept forward past outstretched talons and hissing maws.

Jezebel moved to the other side of Eliot, her pale arms reddening as if severely sunburned by Mitch's white-magic light.

"You can't keep fighting," Fiona told Eliot. "We've got to get out—while we still can."

Rather than be delighted at his rescue, Eliot looked annoyed.

"She is right," Jezebel said, blinking in the strong light. "The Shadow Legions are endless in their realms . . . which are near. I can feel them, and I can feel us getting pulled deeper into the darkness."

Eliot looked around them. "Okay. But which way is out?"

Fiona turned and couldn't see the exit.

She had, however, left a trail of fallen monsters. Connect any two points, and you had a straight line. In theory, anyway . . . in normal space. She wasn't sure if the geometry she knew applied here.

"Back this way."

Fiona led them—Mitch next to her, his light brighter than ever; Eliot next, who continued to play (although his music changed, sounding like a retreat now); and Jezebel last, walking backward so she faced the tide of creatures that followed.

Eliot left his cannon crews behind.

They fired together once more—a storm of smoke and screams and shouts—then shadows covered them, coinciding with the end of Eliot's song.

Fiona saw a sliver of light overhead, and the buildings tilted back to their proper standing positions. Then the passage straightened and she spied the Paxington alley.

She broke into a trot and they followed, emerging in the warm afternoon.

Jezebel looked as she had in class: no claws, her praying mantis eyes back to normal.

Fiona, though, would never forget the monster inside the girl.

Mitch closed his hand and his light winked out. "Apologies," he said to Jezebel.

"No need. Your white magic was necessary to keep the Droogan-dors at bay," Jezebel replied, unperturbed. "I am in your debt, Stephenson."

"Those creatures were from the Shadow Legions," Mitch told her. "Beelzebub's operatives, right?"

"Your intelligence on Infernal affairs is outdated," Jezebel replied. "Urakabarameel and Beelzebub are dead"—she paused to make eye contact with Fiona—"and with these forces leaderless, *any* Infernal Lord could now command them."

"But why attack you and Eliot at all?" Fiona asked.

"I was their target," Jezebel said. "I tried to explain to Eliot that my Queen is at war with Mephistopheles. It is not wise to be near me—save on the Paxington campus, where the school's magics keep all but students and instructors out."

Eliot set Lady Dawn back in her case and shut it. His eyes were ringed with dark circles. "None of that matters," he said. "We're all safe." He turned to the side passage—or rather where the side passage had been—and touched the solid brick wall.

"Thanks," he said to Fiona. "Another few minutes . . . I don't know what would've happened."

He looked like Eliot again, her little brother, normal and nerdy.

But in battle, he'd reminded Fiona of how the Immortals had been as they faced overwhelming power of the Infernals at Ultima Thule, and she felt a surge of admiration for his courage—however stupid he'd acted.

"I must take my leave," Jezebel said. "Again, my thanks." She nodded to

Fiona and Mitch. To Eliot she said, "This incident should prove how much of a fool you are. Stay away from me."

With that, she turned and marched out of the alley.

"What's her problem?" Fiona asked.

Eliot shook his head. "A lot's happened," he whispered. "A lot I need to tell you."

"Sounds like you two need to talk," Mitch said, and his easy smile returned, like nothing had ever happened. "How about a rain check on our date?"

Date?

That caught Fiona off guard. They were going to have a date? It was not an unwelcome surprise . . . it just complicated everything.

"S-sure, that would be nice," Fiona managed.

"Let me walk you to the street," Mitch said, glancing over at the still-solid brick wall. "Just in case."

"Thanks," Fiona said, feeling a blush color her face. Then she turned and whispered so only Eliot could hear: "Whatever is going on—whatever you need to talk about—it'd better be *good*!"

29

DECEPTION BY MOONLIGHT

Eliot explained everything to Fiona as they walked home: how Jezebel had been Julie Marks in Del Sombra; how the Infernal Queen, Sealiah, had used her to try to get to him—but instead Julie had saved Eliot . . . got dragged back to Hell and punished for it, too.

He went on telling how Sealiah was probably trying *again* to use Jezebel to get to him. Eliot owed it to Jezebel this time to help her, save her somehow.

It felt good to share this with someone. Fiona would, of course, believe him. And she had to sympathize with Jezebel; see that she was as much victim as they were in the Infernals' schemes.

Fiona listened, looking shocked, angry, and incredulous by turns.

As they rounded the corner to their street, Fiona said, "I think Jezebel . . . Julie—whatever you're calling her—was right."

"Jezebel," Eliot told her. "Right about what?"

"That you're an idiot, and you should stay away from her."

Eliot halted and crossed his arms.

He detected no lie in Fiona's statements—which really irritated him—but Eliot didn't think his half-blooded Infernal lie detector covered insults from a sibling (which would have been *half* of what Fiona said).

"She was bait for the Infernals," Fiona said slowly as if she were explaining this to a moron. "She admitted it. You saw what it's like in Hell. How can you want to get mixed up in that?"

"Because she needs our help," Eliot said.

Fiona looked unbelievingly at him. "It's just part of their plan. Make you feel sorry for her. Draw you in deeper."

"Maybe," Eliot whispered. "But I can't ignore the other side of our family any longer. I want to learn their game and play it to my advantage."

Fiona's mouth dropped open. "It's no game. And they've been doing this for thousands of years. You can't 'play' with them. Stay clear of Jezebel or"—Fiona hesitated, choking her words out—"or I'll tell Audrey."

Eliot stared at Fiona, shocked.

She stared back.

The world felt as if it had stopped spinning. Birds ceased singing. The traffic quieted. ·

Don't tattle to Audrey or Cecilia: this was the one brother–sister protocol that they had never, *ever* violated. Why bother? Audrey always found out anyway.

"Do that, and I'll tell about you and Robert," Eliot blurted out.

Fiona shrugged. "What's to tell? It's over. Probably best for Robert if the League knows we're not together, anyway."

"So, I'll tell Audrey about Mitch and your 'date' today. You could bring him home for her to meet."

Fiona paled.

That hit a nerve. Eliot would never really have mentioned Robert or Mitch. He liked them both, and drawing either to Mother's attention was dangerous. But it had been worth lying to see Fiona's face, let her know how it felt to have people you care for get in the way of Infernal, or Immortal, forces.

"Okay!" She held up her hands. "You win. Do what you want—just leave me out of it."

"Whatever," Eliot muttered, and then because he still couldn't believe she had seriously considering telling on him, added, "Onychophagist Phasmida."

That was a not-so-clever opener for vocabulary insult.

Onychophagist meant "nail biter," a reference to the old pre-goddess, nerdy Fiona. She used to bite her nails all the time. And Phasmida was the order of stick bugs, a shot at her too-slim figure.

Fiona reddened, angry and embarrassed, as she puzzled out the meanings. She narrowed her eyes and told him, "I wouldn't talk with your mouth full, merdivorous *Microcebus myoxinus*."

Okay, Eliot admitted his insult had been a *little* mean. Fiona's, though, was cruel.

Merdivorous meant "dung eating" (he'd seen that one a bunch of times,

looking up scarab references recently). And *Microcebus myoxinus* was the
pygmy mouse lemur, the smallest primate in the world—with eyes so large,
they looked as if they wore oversized glasses. Most lemurs were herbivo-
rous, or occasionally insectivores, so that dung eater was just gratuitous . . .
although the alliteration was a skillful twist.

He scoured his brain for some word he'd saved for a special occasion to
blast Fiona back—then he spotted a Brinks armored truck in front of their
house.

Two guards got out and walked up to the front door. One carried a box.

Eliot and Fiona glanced at each other—communicating this game of
vocabulary insult was now paused—and raced toward them.

They met the guards on the porch just as Audrey open the front door.

Audrey eyed the men suspiciously, and then stared at the package.

Both guards looked uneasy. "Delivery for Ms. Audrey Post?" one said.

"I am she," Audrey told them.

"Would you sign, ma'am?" One guard offered a clipboard with forms in
triplicate.

"What is this?" she asked.

"Special delivery," the other guard said, looking at Eliot and Fiona as if
this explained everything.

Audrey continued to stare at the package and signed without looking at
the forms. "Set it on the stoop, please."

They did so and the guards left, practically running back to their armored car.

Audrey waited until the truck drove off. She then asked Fiona and Eliot,
"How was school today, children?"

"Fine," Fiona said, and shot a glance at Eliot.

It was a lot weirder than "fine," but how could Eliot even start to explain? Even for them, it had been an unusual day.

Eliot decided to add nothing by way of explanation, and instead asked,
"Is that package for us?"

Audrey continued staring at the box as if she could see through it. On it
were labels with Cyrillic lettering and a dozen overlapping customs stamps.
"No," she said. "For me."

"Are you going to open it?" Fiona asked.

Audrey picked it up, shook it gently, and turned it over and over. "I believe so." She went inside.

Eliot and Fiona followed her upstairs.

Audrey set it on the dining table, took out a pair of scissors, and sliced through tape and paper.

Inside were Styrofoam peanuts and a tiny egg.

It was a Fabergé. Eliot had seen pictures of them in encyclopedias. This one was the size of a hen's egg. It had to be authentic, because it glimmered with inlaid diamonds and flowing sinews of sapphires, which gave the impression of water flowing over its surface.

Audrey inhaled and her eyes widened. "Lovely . . . ," she whispered.

Fiona, also apparently touched by its beauty, reached for it.

Audrey moved it away.

"Sorry," Fiona whispered. "It's just so . . ."

"Yes," Audrey replied. "*Too* entrancing, I'm afraid." She frowned and removed the manifest from the box, scanning it.

"Who's it from?" Eliot asked.

"A private collection in Bangkok," Audrey relayed, reading the manifest, "the director of antiquities in Moscow, and then to an art house in Paris . . . but these are just half truths."

She returned to the egg and touched a sapphire on its equator. There was a click, and the top portion hinged into seven slices that opened like the petals of a lotus.

Within was a minutely crafted scene of a gondola sailing down a canal—the entire thing made of gold and silver, lapis lazuli and aquamarine, and sparkling diamonds everywhere, so it looked like moonlight and stars reflecting on nighttime waters, tiny fish frolicking alongside the boat, a boatman with pole in one hand, his passengers a man and woman embracing.

There was a tiny whir, and music tinkled from within the egg.

Audrey stared somewhere else, far away and long ago. Emotion trembled upon her lips. She whispered, *"Quasi una fantasia."*[29]

---

29. Italian for "almost a fantasy" aka the Piano Sonata No. 14 in C-sharp minor by Ludwig van Beethoven, more commonly known as the "Moonlight Sonata." The piece is said to be inspired by moonlight on the Lucerna River, or perhaps Beethoven's unrequited love for the Countess Giulietta Gucciardi, or some claim that it is closer in mood to a solemn funeral hymn, which had been inspired by the death of a close friend of Beethoven's. Speculation of the meaning of this music continues—given the importance of this egg upon the Post family history (and indeed the subsequent history of the entire world). Mythohistorians believe it was not only a love token from Louis Piper to Audrey Post, but also a direct warning of the coming trouble for their family. *Gods of the First and Twenty-first Century, Volume 11, The Post Family Mythology.* Zypheron Press Ltd., Eighth Edition.

She looked on the verge of tears, but she blinked and was back in the present.

Audrey snapped the egg shut. "It is from your father," she said, her tone frigid.

Uncle Henry had once told them how their mother and father met at the Carnival in Venice. Both masked, they had fallen in love before they knew each other's true identities.

Audrey tore through the pages of the invoice. "How did he find us?" Her finger traced through shipping codes and credit card information—halting at a phone number. She slammed the pages onto the table.

Eliot jumped, startled by the sudden violence.

"This . . . ," Audrey said in a deliberately calm voice, "is *our* phone number. Our *very* unlisted phone number. Only those in the League have it." She cocked her head, thinking, then turned to Fiona and Eliot. "May I see your phones?"

A peculiar numbness tingled through Eliot's extremities, and it felt like the floor dropped from under him. He hadn't done anything wrong, had he?

"Uh, sure," he said.

He and Fiona got their phones and set them on the table.

Audrey glanced at Fiona's, then nodded, and made a little *take it away* gesture.

She stared at Eliot's twice as long, then picked it up with two fingers as if it were a stinging insect. After looking at it, this way and that, she set it on the table and grasped her scissors.

Faster than Eliot could follow, she snipped at the phone—cutting it in half.

He felt something pass through *him* as well, a sensation of lightning from his throat to the base of his spine, followed by a nerve-jangling shudder. His heart pounded in his chest, and he found himself unable to take a breath.

And his phone . . . it wasn't *his*.

The two halves on the table were from a smaller, older phone. The beige plastic was well-worn, dirty, and missing half its number buttons.

"Your phone was stolen," Audrey explained. "This is a cloned copy, from, I'm almost certain, Louis." She spat out his name and turned her glare fully upon Eliot. "Where and when did you see him?"

Eliot had seen Audrey serious, maybe even angry before, but not like this. The world closed in around him. There was a gravity to her words that he seemed to fall into. But he managed to take up a breath and gather his courage. He wouldn't let himself be bullied.

"At the café," he told her, "just outside Paxington."

Next to Eliot, Fiona shifted nervously as if he might mention she was with them.

But Eliot was talking about this morning when he'd been alone with the Prince of Darkness.

Eliot remembered how fascinated Louis had been with his new cell phone, too . . . how he had picked it up.

That's when he must have made the switch.

Louis had played him for a fool as easily as he had so many others.

"Eliot," Audrey said, her words softer now. "You must be careful. Louis speaks the most delicate mix of lies and truths. You will not be able to discern one from the other with him. He is called the Great Deceiver for good reason."

Eliot nodded. Louis obviously hadn't lied to him. He of all people would know Eliot would be able to sense outright lies. He'd known Eliot would rely on his new ability . . . and completely fall for his more sophisticated mistruths.

Audrey turned to Fiona, asking, "How could you let your brother talk to that creature? I thought *you* knew better."

Fiona inhaled, but before she could answer, Eliot cut her off. "She wasn't there," he said.

If anyone was going to get into trouble for talking to Louis, it would be him. Just him. Fiona had encouraged him *not* to speak to their father.

"Very well," Audrey said with a sigh, "let me see your credit cards."

Eliot and Fiona dug through their bags and retrieved their platinum charge cards.

Audrey scrutinized Fiona's, then flicked it back to her. She examined Eliot's. "Both are real. At least Louis did not gain access to the League's discretionary funds. That is some conciliation."

With her scissors she cut Eliot's credit card into a dozen pieces.

"What did you do that for?" he cried.

Audrey arched one of her eyebrows at his outburst. "Because you have let your father take advantage of you. You should never have spoken to him against my wishes. You should not have any interaction with that side of your family. They will destroy you. Or worse, they would use you to destroy others."

Eliot's outrage cooled.

Use him to destroy others? Isn't that what Louis had told him, too? That both Infernal and Immortal families would try to use Eliot and Fiona to circumvent their neutrality treaty and start a war?

Could *some* of what he'd said been the truth?

Audrey swept the credit card fragments into her palm. "You have a great deal to learn. And until such time, you cannot be trusted with such valuable League assets."

Like Eliot had even used the stupid credit card—like he ever would have a chance between all his studies, gym class, getting dragged to Hell, and fighting in alleys.

Audrey plucked up the priceless Fabergé egg, stormed in the kitchen, and came back with the trash can. She hesitated only a moment as she gazed once more at the egg—then dumped it.

Eliot glared so hard at her, with so much anger, that it felt like his gaze bored right through his mother.

For one moment, Eliot let his anger take him, and the blood burned through every vein and artery . . . and then he cooled it and contained it all, compressing it to a white hot spark deep within his core.

"I'm going to my room," he muttered. "I've got homework."

Fiona tried to say something, but Eliot walked away.

Once in his room, he closed the door and slid a few boxes of still-unpacked books against it.

Then he fumed.

But what good was getting angry, unless you did something with it?

He set his pack on his bed, pulled out Lady Dawn, and tried a few notes of that song the egg played. They flowed like water over his hand and strings; moonlight danced and reflected off his walls. The song was a little sad.

It soothed his soul.

He was about to grab the bow and really play, when his eyes lit up on his bookshelf. Wedged between volume seven of *The Golden Bough* and *Languorous Lullabies* was a thick segmented book spine covered in dark gray leather.

Mythica Improbiba.

He was sure he'd deliberately *not* unpacked this book. He'd found it in their old basement, just before their first heroic trial. It was the most unusual collection of fairy tales, maps, poems, and anecdotes from all history—and he had very much wanted to keep it hidden.

He was certain Cee or Audrey hadn't unpacked it for him. That would be cleaning up his mess for him (which *never* happened in *this* household).

Eliot moved toward it, drawn to the mysteries between its covers . . . remembering the hand-scrawled note on the first page: "mostly lies."

Well, that's all either side of his family seemed capable of.

Eliot had work to do. He had his Paxington homework, learning about the mortal magical families, and the immortals that were his family.

He grabbed *Mythica Improbiba* and flipped through the pages until he found that medieval woodcut of the Great Satan.

He also had to learn everything he could about the other side of his family because the game was on . . . and he'd lost the first move.

30

CAPTAIN

Fiona waited alone on the field and studied the jungle gym. She was aghast.

The last two weeks in gym, they'd drilled: going up ropes, sliding down poles, balancing on narrow beams, and scrambling over cargo nets like monkeys. She had memorized five different ways to the top.

All useless now.

Mr. Ma had changed everything: ladders and spirals and chain-link climbing walls had been jumbled—some gone altogether and replaced with new features; there were spinning tubes; a chasm with a rope dangling in the middle (with an impossible reach from either side); and ramps too steep to climb without rappel lines.

Like they *needed* to make it harder for Team Scarab after their first loss.

Fiona hadn't had a lot of time to dwell upon their failure. She'd been busy. Miss Westin had piled on the homework. And with gym practice three times a week, she was mentally and physically exhausted.

She'd also been by herself. Amanda and Mitch had been just as busy.

Eliot had become a recluse as well. He went over to Robert's every day after school. He said to help him study . . . which could have been true, but Fiona sensed it wasn't *all* of the truth. When he came home, he locked himself in his room.

Maybe that rebuke from Audrey over the stolen phone had pushed him away. Fiona should've said something, but it *had* been stupid to talk to their father alone.

She took in a deep breath.

Her thoughts focused back upon the imposing six-story structure, and the fact that Team Scarab had its second match today. Mr. Ma hadn't told them against whom, just to "be ready."

They needed a win. Two losses would drop them to the last quarter of the standings . . . well on their way to flunking out.

She checked the tension of the rubber band on her wrist. Taut.

She'd removed the bracelet her father had given her because she wasn't sure if Mr. Ma would classify it as a weapon, and she didn't trust anything from Louis anymore.

Fiona was as ready as she'd ever be. It was the rest of her team, how'd they work together (or not), that had her worried.

Amanda, Sarah, and Jezebel marched out from the girls' locker room.

Sarah looked ultra-confident as usual. Was that just an act? Fiona doubted it; Sarah seemed to be good at everything.

Jezebel limped onto the field. She hadn't been injured in that fight in the alley, so this was something new. Fiona wanted to speak with her about leaving Eliot alone—but Jezebel seemed to be doing that all by herself these last two weeks, so maybe it was better to have as little contact as necessary with the Infernal.

Amanda bounced on the field last, looking better than she ever had, her hair pinned up, and her face freshly scrubbed . . . deflating only a little at the sight of the newly configured gym structure.

The boys then walked out.

Mitch was first. His eyes instantly found Fiona and lit with delight. Fiona smiled back. She was looking forward to their rain-checked coffee study date (if they ever got a break in their schedules).

Jeremy jogged onto the grass after him. He mistook Fiona's smile for him and waved to her.

What a jerk. He probably thought she liked him.

Robert was right behind Jeremy and took no notice of her.

Eliot came out last. He stopped and studied the new gym structure. He looked a little scared, as he had that first day. She hoped he was up for this.

She didn't understand her brother. She never had, really, but this was a different level of not understanding. How could he fend off an army of shadow creatures almost single-handedly with Lady Dawn . . . be so heroic one moment . . . and then at times like now seem like her little brother, nerdy, vulnerable, so . . . Eliot?

They gathered in a loose circle.

"First things first," Jeremy said. "We need a Team Captain. We can't ignore it." He puffed out his chest, tried—and didn't entirely fail—to look dashing.

Fiona rolled her eyes. "Do we really need to go through this? We have a new jungle gym to figure out before the match starts."

Mitch shrugged. "We lost the first time because we had no leadership."

"We could pick a captain randomly," Eliot suggested. "Roll dice. That'd be fair."

Sarah scoffed. "We choose based on qualifications. I suggest the Lady Jezebel. She is the strongest amongst us, no?"

"Not today." Jezebel rubbed her elbow. She cast a warning glance at them all. "There's been . . . trouble at home."

"Trouble" like the war she'd mentioned before between her clan and Mephistopheles? How did the Infernal even get to Paxington from Hell with a war going on? Certainly not the way she and Eliot had: the Gates of Perdition and the Elysium Fields—it would take her half the day to get to school.

Fiona almost asked how hurt she was, and if she was up for gym today—then stopped. It was probably an act to get Eliot's sympathy. That'd be a very Infernal thing to do.

"I suggest Fiona," Jezebel said.

Fiona blinked, surprised. "What? Me? Why?"

Jezebel assessed her in a slightly less than condescending manner. "You are now the strongest here. You think clearly in battle. And there is no fear in your heart."

"She gets my vote," Eliot chimed in.

Eliot and Fiona hadn't been on the best of terms lately, so for him to so openly support her (even though being Captain was the last thing Fiona wanted) meant a lot to her.

"Mine, too!" Amanda added.

"I agree," Mitch said. "Fiona can think on her feet."

"Why not?" Robert added, and kicked the sod.

Fiona wanted to say thanks to Robert, but things had been so strange between them lately. So awkward. She simply nodded at him, unable to say anything.

With a sigh, Jeremy said, "Very well, Fiona it be for this match. But should we lose, we revisit who's Captain."

Fiona held up her hands. "Hey, I didn't say I *wanted* to be Captain."

Eliot pointed to the top of the gym structure. "Has anyone noticed those?"

Two flags had unfurled on opposite top corners of the jungle gym. One was their golden scarab on a black background. The other was white with a red leaping wolf.

"Team Wolf," Jezebel whispered.

"That be trouble," Jeremy added. "Wolf won their last match with very aggressive tactics. Some say they cheat."

"We've taken the liberty of learning a bit about the other teams," Sarah said. "Wolf wastes no time eliminating their weakest opponents." She cast a quick look at Amanda and Eliot, then to Fiona and said, "And immediately target their enemy's Captain."

Fiona was about to protest again that she wasn't Captain—but then something clicked in the social order on the field. They all looked at her expectantly, like she was supposed to come up with some winning strategy on the spot.

"There be one more wee thing," Jeremy said. "Wolf may have a grudge to settle with Scarab."

"Why would anyone have a grudge against *us*?" Fiona asked.

Team Wolf strode onto the field and she had her answer.

The student leading them was tall and pale, and his dark hair fell at an angle over his eyes . . . the same person Jeremy had challenged that first day in class: Donald van Wyck. His nose was slightly crooked from where it'd been broken. He smiled a predatory grin as he saw Jeremy and the rest of them.

And more trouble: The others in Team Wolf were tall, lean, and looked like they could run circles around them.

Except one boy. He was smaller and had a long scar on his face. This was the student she'd seen duel by the fountain on the first day of school. Fiona recalled how he had won and twisted the rapier that had skewered his enemy's hand . . . and had enjoyed it.

"So what's the plan?" Robert whispered. "You've got maybe thirty seconds before Mr. Ma gets out here."

Fiona struggled with the notion of her being Captain. She could argue the point and waste their time—or she could lead. Wasn't that what she'd wanted to do ever since she'd seen the Battle at Ultima Thule?

Her mind embraced the problem: a team of superior opponents and a new and dangerous terrain. Her hands flexed. She could almost feel it under her fingertips: the weave of a tapestry.

Scarab had one advantage: No one knew who their Captain was.

If Sarah's data was right, Wolf had one potential disadvantage, too: they predictably went after weak members of the opposing team.

Fiona had studied every battle from Agincourt to Waterloo, thanks to Audrey and Cee's homeschooling. She knew about passive lures and overlapping fire—and something more than tactics whirled inside her . . . as if she had done this a thousand times before.

A plan crystallized in her mind.

She motioned them closer, and they huddled together. "Okay, this is it. Just listen. We don't have time to argue. Mitch, Jezebel, Amanda, and Robert go high as fast as you can. You might get lucky and find a quick way to our flag. If you do—go for it. Four is a win."

Fiona didn't explain that their real purpose was to move Amanda along and keep her safe. While she'd be an obvious target, Wolf wouldn't go after one so well protected.

She turned to Jezebel and told her, "Keep on eye on the rest of us. Drop back when trouble starts, and stop as many Wolves as you can."

Jezebel tilted her head. "A pleasure."

"Our second unit will be Jeremy and Eliot."

They both recoiled and looked at each other with disdain.

"Don't complain," Fiona told them. "Just pick any path. And Eliot, don't play your violin. I need you to keep moving fast."

Fiona knew that Wolf would go after their other obvious weak target: Eliot. And with Jeremy being marked for revenge, it was a safe bet that they'd draw three, maybe more, of the Wolves . . . which was precisely what she wanted.

They were bait.

Fiona loathed using Eliot as bait, but it was the best plan. Besides, she was going to be there, too.

"Sarah and I will be the third unit," she told them. "We'll circle around, and when Wolf comes, we'll close ranks. Jezebel has our backs." Fiona chewed over the irony of trusting her and continued. "That gives us three going straight for the goal, a sizable rear defensive force"—she looked at Jeremy, Eliot, Sarah, and Jezebel—"and one of us should be able to break out and get to the flag for the win."

That was it: the best, most flexible thing she could come up with on the spot.

Her team digested the strategy.

Mitch grinned and gave her a thumbs-up. Amanda swallowed, looked frightened, but nonetheless nodded. Robert scanned the jungle gym, looking for a route to the top.

"Bloody hell," Jeremy said with a sigh, and then added, "okay, we'll give it go."

Mr. Ma walked onto the field and blew his whistle. "Teams, make two lines!" he shouted. "Prepare to start."

"We can do this," she told them.

They lined up.

Eliot moved close to her. The look in his eyes was pure concentration. Fiona had seen him like this before—in that alley as he fought a hundred shadows, and when he had faced the Infernal Lord of All That Flies, Beelzebub.

He looked like a hero.

31

WHAT MATTERED TO ELIOT

Eliot set his pack down on the sidelines.

Inside was Lady Dawn. Fiona was right—speed would be the key to winning this match. Playing a violin while balancing on some platform didn't make a lot of sense.

As he let go of the pack, though, his hand twinged. He tried to will the pain away, telling himself that he'd be close to his violin soon. It ebbed, not entirely subsiding, though.

He ran back to Team Scarab.

Mr. Ma gave him a look, communicating volumes of irritation.

Jeremy muttered, "Try to keep up with me, Post."

"Just worry about yourself," Eliot snapped back.

He had confidence, thanks to Robert. Training every day after school had more benefits than new muscles and learning how to throw a punch. Sure, Eliot *did* know how to hit and kick and stand without getting knocked down—but there was a lot more to fighting. Mainly not being scared.

He glanced at Team Wolf. A rough bunch. Mean and lean, and that near-albino Donald van Wyck snapped his teeth at them like they were fresh meat.

Whatever. Psyching the other side out was obviously part of this game, too.

He smiled back . . . and Van Wyck's grin faded.

Mr. Ma raised his starting pistol and fired.

They ran.

Robert, Mitch, Jezebel, and even Amanda sprinted ahead of everyone else.

Sarah and Fiona circled to his left, clambering up a cargo net.

They were bit too far away for comfort, but Eliot trusted Fiona. She'd get to him quickly, when he needed help.

Jeremy took the lead and Eliot followed him to a wooden ladder. It was a good choice, because it was a straight shot halfway up through the jungle gym . . . but the end dangled three body lengths over their heads.

"What're you doing?" Eliot asked, panting. "We—can't—reach that."

Jeremy's hands moved fast, fluid motions like the sleight of hand Louis had made with his three playing cards—then he pulled a hemp rope . . . from nothing.

Eliot blinked as he remembered the Covingtons were conjurers.[30]

Jeremy threw the rope and it swished over the lowest ladder rung, lashed about, and knotted itself with a bowline. Jeremy flicked it once and the rope knotted for climbing as well.

"Hurry," Eliot whispered.

Jeremy scrambled up the rope.

Two remaining members of Team Wolf spotted Eliot and ran toward him.

He went up the rope while Jeremy was still on, and sent the line spinning.

His progress wasn't great, but he got up out of the reach of the boy and girl from Team Wolf just as they got to the rope.

They started up after him.

Fiona and Sarah, however, had circled around to intercept them.

Eliot focused on climbing. He couldn't stop and help. As much as he wanted to fight (for the first time in his life) and test himself, that wasn't his job. He was supposed to draw as many of Team Wolf away as possible, let the rear defenders take them out . . . and if he got the chance, get to the flag.

He grasped the lowest ladder rung and scrambled up to the top.

Jeremy gave him a hand onto a platform connected by four chains.

It swayed and tilted. Eliot grabbed one of the chains for balance. He looked down.

30. There are four stages of expertise in the art of conjuration. First is simple molecular manipulation, which can heat or cool matter. The second stage is the movement of matter, i.e., basic telekinesis. Third is the transmutation of elements, which if the student has mastery of they may conjure items from thin air. NOTE: It is *notoriously* difficult to transmute into heavier elements, especially gold. The fourth stage is almost never attained: the creation of living matter such as plants, and only with extreme rarity, sentient animals. *Gods of the First and Twenty-first Century, Volume 14, The Mortal Magical Families.* Zypheron Press Ltd., Eighth Edition.

Sarah had conjured a web of ropes spread between her and the other students. Fiona grasped handfuls of the lines. Where strands wrapped about beams, they severed, collapsing in a heap before the other students, blocking them.

"That way." Jeremy pointed to a series of platforms similarly hung by chains.

Each was an easy jump, no more that a body length apart. Landing would be tricky. Those platforms would swing all over the place.

Eliot glanced up, but saw no sign of Robert or the others.

A quick glance down; he couldn't see Fiona or Sarah, either . . . but he did notice then that he was three stories up. A chill ran along his spine, and he got angry at himself for it, and stepped forward.

"I'll go first," he said.

Jeremy raised an eyebrow. "Be quick about it." He nodded to another sequence of platforms. Three from Team Wolf jumped along them, moving to catch up, Donald van Wyck in the lead.

Eliot bolted off their platform—fast, before he lost his nerve.

The platform shot backwards as he pushed off.

What an idiot! Newton's third law: Every action has an equal and *opposite* reaction.

He bounced onto the edge of the next platform, half on, half off.

Luckily it had swung toward him . . . or he would have missed.

As he pulled himself up, Jeremy landed next to him. He didn't help Eliot, but kept running, jumped off, and landed on the next platform.

This left Eliot behind on a crazily gyrating platform.

Not nice. But it *was* an effective tactic.

By the time he got to his feet, Jeremy was two jumps ahead, and the three Team Wolf interceptors were halfway to Eliot.

Eliot had to figure how to move fast, or he'd get taken out.

But *everything* moved—this way and that, up and down, ropes and platforms and chains. It seemed like the entire jungle gym was alive.

Eliot heard it, too. The squeaks and groans and clinkings and rattles . . . they sang to him. Each motion, the vibrating ropes, the pendulum arcs . . . those were beats, plucked notes, all combining into the phrases of a chaotic clash of noise. A symphony.

The gym was an instrument. Not one that Eliot could play by himself, but he could play a part like one person in a larger orchestra.

His body moved in time to this motion, and in response the platform under him synched and swung harmoniously.

He jumped—the action timed at the precise moment dictated by the gym's song—landed perfectly on the next platform—jumped easily to the next, and again, until he had covered half the distance along the platforms.

Team Wolf was right behind him, however.

He ignored their curses and threats and kept moving.

They'd catch up; he was dead unless he did something. But without Lady Dawn, what could he do? Fight three against one? Robert had taught him that even fighting two on one, no matter how good you *thought* you were, was a bad idea.

Eliot landed on the last platform—one bolted to massive timbers that went all the way to the ground and was rock solid.

A curve of chain-link fencing arced up from this. Jeremy had already scrambled partway up. It was loose and swayed, however, so Jeremy's progress was slow.

But he was ahead of Eliot, and that was the only thing that mattered.

The three boys from Team Wolf, led by Donald van Wyck, were one jump away.

Something thudded softly next to Eliot—he turned.

Jezebel. Beautiful, radiant, and utterly unperturbed.

Eliot froze, shocked speechless at her sudden appearance.

This seemed to please her because a slightest smile flickered on her lips.

She had landed so quietly and with such grace that it almost seemed as if she had stepped down, instead of—Eliot glanced overhead three stories—made a jump that would have broken an ordinary person's legs.

"This fight is my job," she told him.

The Team Wolf boys hesitated at the sight of her. They whispered to one another.

"No way," Eliot said. "I'm staying with you. Like in the alley."

"One day you will no longer be a fool," she muttered. "I hope I live to see it." She turned to him, glowering. "I have no wish to lose *another* match. Go and win it. Win it for me, if you need a reason."

Jezebel touched his arm. A simple thing, but to Eliot it was electric. It was like they were back in Del Sombra, that he was just normal, nerdy Eliot, and she was sweet, mortal Julie Marks.

She withdrew and was hard, cruel Jezebel again. She turned to Team Wolf. "Or stay," she hissed. "I shall not be responsible."

Although it went against every instinct, Eliot climbed the chain link. He'd trust Fiona's plan . . . and Jezebel's ability to take care of herself.

The Team Wolf boys jumped, landed on the platform, and circled her.

Eliot scampered up to Jeremy, who flashed him a look of annoyance.

"Come on," Eliot urged. "We're almost to the top."

The ribbon of chain link had been nailed to a wooden beam overhead. That beam, in turn, ran straight to a zigzag of stairs . . . that would take them to the top, and Team Scarab's flag.

Robert, Mitch, and Amanda, already limped up those stairs.

They were close to winning. Once they got to their flag, all it would take was either him or Jeremy—it didn't matter who—to get there as well.

That would make four. The match would end.

Maybe Eliot could stop this before anyone else got hurt.

He glanced down.

The Wolf boys had Jezebel surrounded. She held her hands up in a martial arts stance.

A thin fog blew in and vapors swirled around her.

The smallest Wolf boy (Eliot recognized him from the duel by the fountain) had a wooden club. He darted in, struck her leg—and danced out of her reach.

She fell to one knee, but didn't cry out.

"Jezebel!" Eliot cried.

Another boy stepped closer, grabbed her injured shoulder.

Jezebel winced, shrugged off the boy's hold, and backhanded him—off the platform.

She whirled toward Eliot. "Stick to the plan!" she shouted.

Van Wyck moved in—his hand ghostly insubstantial, the bones within visible, his motion trailing increasingly thick fog vapors.

Jezebel deftly avoided his grasp.

She shot Eliot a hate-filled glare. "Go!"

Nothing was worth this, Eliot decided—not winning—not even if it meant flunking out of gym class. Seeing Jezebel fight alone, already injured, he couldn't stand it.

He started back.

The chain link that Eliot and Jeremy clung to, however, pinged, and the nails holding it to the beam popped out.

They plunged—jerked to a halt and dangled . . . one corner tenuously secured by three nails in the beam overhead.

Eliot's heart hammered in his throat, but still all he could think of was Jezebel.

He searched for her. The fog below, however, made it impossible to see the platform. He heard the Wolf boys moving, grunting; there was the cracking of wood.

There was no choice on which way to go for him, though; he was certain he wasn't over the platform anymore. Eliot pulled himself up, hand over hand.

Jeremy hauled himself up, too. "I'll be first to the flag," Jeremy whispered.

Eliot straddled the beam and offered Jeremy his hand.

A curious look narrowed Jeremy's eyes as he reached forward and clasped Eliot's hand.

Eliot pulled.

Jeremy gripped the beam with his other hand and pulled himself up—yanking Eliot *hard*.

The unexpected motion threw Eliot. His hand slipped from Jeremy's sweat-slick grasp . . . and Eliot tumbled off.

Airborne, panic spiked through Eliot. He was in free fall, arms and legs thrashing.

Three fingers dragged along the chain link—grabbed—and he whipped around, slamming into it.

Overhead, two more nails screeched out.

Jeremy had pulled him off *deliberately*.

He'd said he had to "be first to the flag." Was winning so important to Jeremy he was willing to *murder* Eliot? Maybe. Then he could find a replacement for Eliot on the team, too.

Eliot scrambled up onto the beam.

Jeremy had already made it halfway across the beam to the stairs. He had his hands outstretched for balance.

Eliot ran. He didn't worry about balance. He was concerned only with momentum. He plowed shoulder-first into Jeremy—shoved him off the beam. Not so hard, however, that he'd go flying off as Eliot had, but enough so he fell down.

Eliot stepped in the middle of his back and ran over him.

He didn't look back. He'd wasted enough time and breath on Jeremy Covington.

Eliot bounded the stairs three at a time—just like he was racing Fiona at home—until he emerged at the top of the jungle gym.

Wind whipped his face. There were layers fog and cloud, and far overhead, crows circled and cawed. Eliot saw the entire campus, and beyond, all the way to Pacific Heights and the bay.

Robert, Mitch, and Amanda yelled to him and waved.

Eliot snapped out of it and sprinted for the flag.

It seemed like he ran forever . . . never quite making it to his goal . . . never getting closer . . . like some nightmare. Then his hands brushed the black silk.

Far away on the ground was a gunshot: Mr. Ma's signal to end the match.

Mitch clapped him on the back. "Well done! You won it for us, Eliot."

Amanda gave him a hug, blushed, and withdrew.

Robert nodded to Eliot. His eyes, however, warily locked on Jeremy as he climbed the last of the stairs and joined them.

Jeremy smiled like nothing had happened. "Excellent," he said, and then added softer, "Sorry we got bunched up back there. No hard feelings, eh?"

"Sure," Eliot said with a smug shrug.

"As long as we won," Jeremy murmured, "what does it matter."

Eliot didn't need any Infernal senses to weigh Jeremy's sincerity. It did matter. There was something driving Jeremy far beyond healthy competitiveness.

This wasn't over between them. Not by a long shot.

Eliot glanced down through the jungle gym. His heart ached, hoping Jezebel was okay.

If he could have, he would gladly have taken her place—fought Van Wyck and the others—knowing he'd lose. It'd be worth it to spare her.

He could almost hear Jezebel telling him he was a "fool" for such thoughts.

But Eliot couldn't help it. The only reason he'd come up here was to stop the match by winning it. To keep her safe.

She mattered to him . . . more than any stupid gym match . . . even more than Paxington.

32

BOY TROUBLE

Fiona sat on the edge of her seat. This was the most fascinating stuff in the world . . . no, that wasn't right; it was the most fascinating stuff *out* of this world.

Miss Westin had finished her lectures on the magical families yesterday, and today had moved on to a new topic in Mythology 101. On the blackboards of Plato's Hall were maps of the Purgatories, the Borderlands, and more places that she called the "Middle Realms" between Earth and the end of places known.

Fiona had always wanted to travel, and last summer she had seen Greece and the Bahamas. She'd even been in Paris.

These places were different, however. What would it be like to go to wander among the Lost Floating Gardens of Babylon? Snorkel among the ruins of Atlantis? Or find the Temple of the Fountain of Youth? Or glimpse dread R'lyeh?

Or maybe not. Her enthusiasm was tempered by her recent visit to the Valley of the New Year, where she'd almost gotten stuck forever. And her visit to the Borderlands near the Blasted Kingdom of Hell—that was a place she could do without ever seeing again.

"Travel to the Middle Realms is perilous for mortals," Miss Westin lectured. "Humans were not meant to exist there. An analogy would be deep-sea diving or a journey to the moon. These things are possible, but complicated . . . and if mistakes are made, lethal."

Fiona struggled to keep up, take quick notes while she tried to copy the map of the Butterfly Vales of the Fairylands.

She imagined herself there, splashing her toes in Gabriel's Wishing Well and exploring the Cavern of Floating Lights that connected their world to hers—places just on the edge of imagination that beckoned.

"Some realms," Miss Westin said, indicating the map, "*are* mere legend. For example, the Fairylands or the Land of Gray and Gold has never been visited by any human . . . or if they have, they have not returned."

Fiona frowned at this and made a note.

Miss Westin pulled down a new blackboard covered with mountains among a Milky Way's worth of stars. "Others, such as Heaven, seen here as portrayed by Dante Alighieri's first crude map in his *Paradiso*—have not been visited by mortals since the fourteenth century, and may be forever closed to two-way, living travelers."

Eliot sat next to Fiona in the dark classroom, head propped lazily in his hands. He wasn't taking notes. He wasn't even paying attention.

Fiona didn't understand him. Just last week, he'd been fascinated with stupid Hell.

Ever since their last match, he'd been moping around. He'd won the match for Team Scarab! What more did he want?

Okay, so that match hadn't been all roses and sunshine. Gym was tough. Fiona was horrified at the carnage and mayhem. They'd all gotten cut and bruised. Sarah had a few busted ribs. Donald van Wyck and two other Team Wolf members had torn kneecaps and dislocations.

But Team Scarab's record was now one win, one loss—50 percent, which placed them far from the bottom of the freshman team ranks. A few teams had two losses and might not graduate to their second year.

At least she wouldn't have to worry about that . . . for a while.

Just as important to Fiona, her plan had worked. She shouldn't feel good about it; it was really Eliot and a lot of luck that got them the win, but she couldn't help it. Her teammates had followed her strategy. Maybe she *could* lead them.

"Today I end with a question," Miss Westin said. "One that we may never find an adequate answer for, but is nonetheless worth pondering." She pushed her glasses higher up on her nose. "If so dangerous, why travel the Middle Realms at all? Why have so many tried and failed, so many tried and died, but we are all still drawn to these most exotic of places? Why . . . when it is not only life and limb in peril, but one's very soul?"

Fiona thought the answer was obvious.

What was the point of *any* travel? The thrill of finding someplace no one had ever been before. You could learn new things and meet new people. Maybe someone could start some trade between realms.

But that remark about peril to one's soul bothered Fiona.

What if she had never escaped the Valley of the New Year? Would she have gone crazy with its never-quite-done New Year's Party? Forever stuck in Purgatory with Jeremy Covington? Ugh. She shuddered.

And how did this all fit with Mr. Welmann's claim that even the dead didn't stay in those places forever? Where did they all go?

"I'll expect an essay on this," Miss Westin told them. "Two thousand words by Friday. You are dismissed."

The gaslights in the room warmed and the students filed out. Fiona packed up her notes.

Eliot grabbed his books and bolted out like he'd been a caged animal.

"Hey, wait!" she called after him, but he ignored her and was out the door.

Fiona finished packing and pushed her way outside.

She didn't see Eliot . . . but Fiona did see Amanda, Sarah, and Jezebel standing together by the Picasso Arch.

Sarah beckoned her over.

Fiona approached, her eyes on Jezebel. The Infernal had fallen three stories off the jungle gym and walked away without a scratch . . . well, other than a torn uniform and deep lacerations on her shoulder (and those she claimed had been from her clan's war in Hell).

Was being invulnerable to cuts and broken bones an Infernal thing? Fiona might have inherited some of that from her father—her blood pounded and pulsed as she remembered how she had been tossed twenty feet through the air by Beelzebub, hit a car headfirst, and had been able to shrug off her injuries.

She calmed herself. She didn't like being able to get angry so easily. It felt powerful, but she gave up too much control.

"What's going on?" Fiona asked.

"We need your opinion, my dear," Sarah said with a mischievous grin. "Perhaps you can settle a difference of opinion."

Fiona drifted closer. What dire circumstance could gather together these three who had absolutely *nothing* in common? It had to be trouble.

"We were just trying to figure out," Amanda whispered, and fidgeted as if saying this was painful, "which boy on our team is the cutest."

Fiona crinkled her nose.

They had to be kidding. Here they were, learning about dozens of new worlds, every kind of magic known, and the secret history that had shaped the entire modern world . . . and they were worried about *boys*?

"Well, you can forget Eliot," Sarah remarked. "Obviously."

"Why?" Amanda asked, her dark eyes smoldering. "I think he's nice. Cute, even."

Someone thought Eliot was cute? Fiona might have believed dorky or clueless . . . but cute? She wasn't sure what was more shocking: hearing this . . . or hearing it from Amanda. She sure had come out of her shell since that shopping trip to Paris.

"If you like a puppy dog that trips over its own paws," Jezebel remarked. "Perhaps when he grows up . . . No, for pure aesthetics, I have to stick with Jeremy."

Sarah tilted her head appreciatively. "But for attitude and old-fashioned chivalry," she said, "I'd take Robert Farmington. There's something about him so deliciously rugged. Wouldn't you agree, Fiona?"

Fiona opened her mouth, but found herself unable to speak. With Sarah's perfectly styled red hair and her oh-so-cute freckled peaches-and-cream features . . . she was so *not* Robert's type. But while Fiona knew Robert could outdrive and outfight any boy on campus, when it came to Sarah, would he be able to recognize that she was a viper in disguise?

Sarah's eyes widened a fraction. "Oh, I didn't know, dearie. Are you and he—?"

Fiona blushed, both embarrassed and angry—fought to control it—which only made it worse.

After an awkward moment, Fiona whispered, "Last summer there was something. But it's over now."

The three girls exchanged looks of curiosity, disbelief, and envy.

Fiona didn't want to talk anymore. This entire conversation was disgusting.

But she couldn't just walk away. It would seem like she was running away because Sarah had asked her about Robert, so she added, "Mitch gets my vote. Everytime he smiles, I don't know, it makes me happy."

Jezebel scoffed. "A man's smile is like a dog wagging its tail—before it bites."

"No." Sarah held up a finger. "I have to agree with Fiona. I've seen that smile—devilishly charming, it is. Mitch is handsome. Oh, perhaps in need of a haircut and a bit of grooming, but a fine specimen nonetheless."

"Eliot still gets my vote," Amanda muttered, now looking at her feet. "He's so . . . deep, you know?"

Jezebel nodded across the courtyard. "Speaking of our young Master Post. It looks like he is deep. In trouble."

A crowd of students had gathered around the Contemplation Pool of the Faun, a koi pond with bronze statues of fauns and satyrs and enchanted mushrooms.

Fiona spotted Eliot there—face-to-face with Donald van Wyck.

Donald still had his left arm in a sling from their last gym match. That didn't stop him from shoving Eliot.

"Oh no." Fiona marched toward them.

Jezebel, Sarah, and Amanda trotted behind her.

Fiona hoped Eliot wasn't stupid enough to get baited into a duel.

But Fiona caught the look in Eliot's eyes—pure hatred—and she knew there'd be a fight.

Another boy from Team Wolf, however, the dangerous short one with a scar on his face, joined Van Wyck and they *both* faced Eliot.

Fiona was too far away to stop whatever was about to happen.

But Robert wasn't. He appeared from the crowd and stepped next to Eliot. He dropped his pack and halted the approaching boys with his no-nonsense glare.

"Two on two, then?" Van Wyck laughed.

"Why not?" Robert said, flexed his fist, and popped his knuckles.

But the other six from Team Wolf then appeared behind Van Wyck, making sure Robert and Eliot stayed outnumbered.

Fiona and the girls finally got to them.

Donald Van Wyck looked them over, swallowing at the sight of Jezebel. "So you need your girlfriends to help you out?" he asked.

Fiona stepped up before either Eliot or Robert could answer. "No one's doing anything," she told him. "You can't *make* anyone fight on campus. Duels are by mutual consent."

Van Wyck snorted. "So they are. Fine, we don't settle this here. It's a short walk to the gate. We'll wait outside for you . . . where there are no rules about stopping at first blood." A smile spread over his thin, pale lips.

Fiona went cold.

He was threatening her, her brother . . . everyone on their team. Could he get away with that?

She knew people like Donald van Wyck; they always got away with things like this.

Unless she did something to stop him. Now.

Fiona took a step back and peeled off her jacket. She no longer felt cold. Her blood was hot and pounded through every cell. "Fine," she said. "You *have* to fight? You fight me then."

"I don't think so," Robert said, looking just as mad.

"Yes," Fiona told him. "You voted me Team Captain. Well this is a team decision."

"Let her fight," Jezebel told Robert, looking pleased at the potential for violence. "I shall be her second."

The glee on Van Wyck's face drained at this. He glanced at his team, and they nodded back. "Okay," he said. "Suits me. A Captains' Duel."[31]

Robert gritted his teeth, but said nothing more.

Eliot stood by Robert, looking ready to kill . . . either Van Wyck or her, Fiona wasn't sure.

She'd intervened in his behalf to *save* him, but Fiona also knew that Eliot probably resented it, thinking he was "man" enough to handle this himself.

Sure, he could have handled it.

To win against Van Wyck and his wolf pack, though, Eliot would use his music. And if he pulled Lady Dawn out and played it on campus—Fiona was sure something bad would happen as it had at Groom Lake . . . something that would have ended with *more* than first blood. People might get killed.

This fight required force, but the right amount of it. It had to be swift and decisive, but more than anything, *controlled*. First blood, that's all.

One cut.

A girl from Team Wolf opened a case and handed Van Wyck the gilded rapier within. It glistened needle sharp.

Fiona unzipped her book bag. She undid the clasp on her bracelet and dropped it inside. She didn't want to use the chain. It cut too easily—almost like it wanted blood.

She touched the rubber band on her wrist and shuddered, recalling how she had used it to slice Perry Millhouse in half. That wouldn't do, either.

Fiona spotted something round and wooden at the bottom of her pack: a yo-yo.

31. A Captains' Duel shall adhere to all previously described rules for duels with the following provisos (1) Terms must be mutually agreed upon by the Captains. (2) Terms must be adhered to by the Captain's *entire team*. (3) Captains' Duels are not allowed within the Ludus Magnus nor shall affect the outcome of any gym match. *Your Guide to the Paxington Institute (Freshman Edition)*. Paxington Institute Press LLC, San Francisco.

Uncle Aaron had made a gift of it last summer. It was the first weapon she'd ever used in a fight; its string had taught her how to cut.

That *would* do.

She looped the yo-yo's string about her middle finger and faced her opponent.

Several students laughed.

Van Wyck looked at her and blinked. "Are you kidding?"

Fiona flicked the yo-yo. It ran down the string and twanged—for a split second she felt the urge to cut run though her and along its taut length. The air pulsed with raw energy.

That shut them all up.

"Try me," she whispered.

All mirth vanished from Van Wyck's face. He slashed his rapier back and forth—and attacked.

33

THREE WORDS THAT CHANGED HER LIFE

Van Wyck struck at her.

It was a crude attack; Fiona easily sidestepped. She'd sparred with her uncle Aaron, the supposed God of War, Ares. Van Wyck was no master swordsman.

Almost too quick to follow, however, he angled his rapier up and it plunged straight at her heart.

Her last step had left her flat-footed, off balance.

Fiona twisted awkwardly aside.

The tip of the rapier grazed her jacket, neatly puncturing the heavy wool. Van Wyck ripped it free.

Too close. Fiona wouldn't underestimate him again.

Sure this was to first blood . . . and if his one and only "first blood" wound pierced her heart, it might be okay as far as the rules covering Paxington freshman duels were concerned . . . but Fiona would be dead.

A smiled flickered over his face.

He was toying with her. Enjoying this.

Well, Fiona wasn't about to let him play a lengthy game of cat and mouse.

She flicked out her yo-yo.

The smirk on his face vanished when he saw how fast it came at his head. He parried the wooden disk expertly . . . with the precise minimal deflection require so his rapier still pointed at her. This made the yo-yo's string slide alongside his blade.

As Fiona had hoped.

She yanked the yo-yo. The string caught and wrapped about the blade at the guard.

Fiona focused her mind along the string's length; it narrowed, almost vanished to a one-dimensional edge that left a wake in the air—as the string cut through the steel blade.

The students around them gasped.

Van Wyck, eyes wide, stared at his lovely weapon . . . now a useless stub.

Fiona stepped back three paces and took the opportunity to rewind her yo-yo.

She saw a crowd had gathered.

Van Wyck shook off his surprise, tossed the rapier aside, and raised his hands.

The color faded from the world about him. His fingertips went ghostly, and Fiona glimpsed flickers of his bones as if they were being X-rayed.

Technically, magic was permitted within the Paxington duel guidelines, but Fiona felt a lance of fear stab at her resolve because he was using the magic of the Van Wyck family: necromancy.[32]

Whatever happened, Fiona couldn't let him touch her. Miss Westin had been explicit on this point when she had lectured on the necromancers: it was simple for them to drain a person's *entire* life force . . . easier, in fact, than draining a little.

They circled each other.

Fiona refocused her thoughts . . . not just on the yo-yo's string . . . she became aware of the bumps and slick patches of cobblestones under her feet . . . of the air flowing over her sweaty skin . . . of her tensing muscles . . . of her quickening breath.

Van Wyck feigned right, then left.

Fiona moved in—straight.

His hand grazed her chest.

It was a cold the likes of which she had never experienced—not even

---

32. There are four orders of necromantic power. The lowest allows communication with the dead. The next level enables the transfer of life essence (not to be confused with the Life/Death duality magics of the Dreaming Families). The third tier of mastery preserves life past injury, disease, and extreme age. The last order is the ability to raise and possibly command the dead. Other powers exist, but are secrets known only to practitioners—notably the Van Wyck family. The Van Wycks are also known for their pharmaceutical conglomerate. *Gods of the First and Twenty-first Century, Volume 14, The Mortal Magical Families.* Zypheron Press Ltd., Eighth Edition.

the bone-numbing cold of the Valley of the New Year. This chill went beyond physical. It touched her soul. It fired every instinct within her to curl into a ball and shiver. To give up.

But her blood heated, resisting.

She blinked and regained her focus.

Fiona punched him in the jaw. Pain exploded down her hand and arm, and she stumbled back.

So did he.

She hadn't hit him hard—but hard enough to break his concentration.

Before he recovered, before he could touch her with that awful magic again, she lashed out with her yo-yo.

It whipped forward.

Donald reacted, instinctively reaching to stop it with an outstretched hand.

And did so, catching the string.

Fiona jerked it. The string whipped through two of his fingers—severed them at the knuckles. She felt no resistance as it passed though his flesh and bones . . . but something vibrated though the string as it cut away the magic in his hand.

Fiona then swung the yo-yo and looped it about Van Wyck's neck.

And then she stood stock-still, held her breath . . . and they faced each other.

He clutched his wounded hand. Blood streamed from it.

His magic was gone. His eyes were wild.

The crowd of students fell silent.

"That's first blood," Fiona whispered. "Now, you leave me and my brother, and my team alone . . . or I will end this. Permanently."

She gave a tiny tug at the string about his neck.

Van Wyck didn't flinch. Amazingly, he smiled weakly through his pain.

Did he think she wouldn't go through with it?

Fiona wasn't sure, either. She had killed before to defend herself and Eliot. This was different, though. Van Wyck was human. And the Paxington rules said she couldn't go further than first blood.

On the other hand, she had to end this here and now.

Van Wyck didn't sense her equivocation, or maybe he just wanted to live, because he finally sighed and said, "Very well, Fiona Post. I accept your terms. I pledge a truce between myself and your team." His faint smile vanished as he clutched his maimed hand tighter. "Until, of course, we meet in gym."

The students around them jeered and groaned . . . a few chanted, "Cut—cut!"

Fiona exhaled and relaxed her grip.

The small boy on Team Wolf grabbed the severed fingers off the ground. Others from Team Wolf wrapped Van Wyck's hand, and they hurried him away.

As she watched them leave, she wondered if this would really be the end of their conflict.

She hoped so . . . but had a nasty feeling the answer was no.

Before she could figure it all out, everyone pressed closer, asking how she'd cut like that—what kind of magic it was—where her family came from—they'd never heard of the Post family before.

Eliot pushed closer to rescue her from all these impossible-to-answer questions.

Jezebel cleared her throat and said, "You've never heard of her family before?"

Everyone turned to her.

"Oh, you are all such idiots!" Jezebel continued, a sneaky grin creeping across her face. "Don't you know? She's a goddess."

The students stood stunned and looked back at Fiona, examining her, some nodding, others mouths open.

Fiona couldn't believe she had said that.

Jezebel knew? Of course, if she was working with the Infernals—they knew. And no League rules prevented *her* from just blurting out the very thing that would have landed Fiona or Eliot into serious trouble.

"Fiona Post," Jezebel said with theatrical flair. "The daughter of Atropos, the Eldest Fate, the Cutter of All Things."

Fiona started to protest, but everyone began talking at once, suddenly fascinated with her.

Jezebel, with those three words, *"She's a goddess,"* had forever changed Fiona's life.

And, having gotten over the initial shock of this deepest secret uncovered, feeling the admiration and instant popularity from all the students . . . Fiona thought that maybe it wasn't such a bad thing, after all.

Until she saw Eliot.

Fiona tried to move toward him—but Tamara Pritchard and group of her girlfriends cut her off.

Completely ignored by the other students, he skulked away. The expression on his face was one of wounded pride . . . and something else . . . something dark.

34

OUTSIDER

Eliot left campus but didn't walk home. He picked a direction at random—crossing two busy streets, down an alley between houses, and then angled north until he smelled the ocean.

He took this route so Fiona wouldn't be able to catch him. Not that she was trying. She had been swamped by students—all asking questions and looking at her as if they'd just seen her for the first time, enamored by her presence.

Eliot hadn't been able to stand it.

He tromped down a staircase and onto a smaller street, where the houses had tiny co-op gardens for front lawns. It was November and the squash and peas had long been harvested. A vine-strangled scarecrow with button eyes stared at him.

This afternoon had been nothing but one disaster after another. It started when Van Wyck had called Jezebel Team Scarab's "succubus."

Eliot had studied enough in Miss Westin's class, and read the "Tale of the Amber Vixen" in *Mythica Improbiba,* to understand the reference. Succubi were demons that used love and sex to steal souls and make people do terrible things (although the succubus in the "Amber Vixen" had turned to ash rather than betray the human she'd fallen in love with).[33]

---

33. "Ordered to slay Master Raimes / She fled a'cross the River Thames / She could not stay, she could not run / She waited and watched the rising sun / Love did bloom within her heart / T'was then did flames crackle a'start / Love did kindle and love did burn / Flames to flesh and ash she turned / Last upon her lips / A prayer for her love did slip." *Mythica Improbiba* (translated version), Father Sildas Pious. ca. thirteenth century.

He'd let Van Wyck's casual, non—vocabulary insult get to him.

Eliot paused to admire an antique white car parked a half block away. It was one of those long-nosed things from the 1930s. It was sleek and the silver trim gleamed like liquid mercury.

He shuddered, dismissing the sudden chill from the encroaching fog, and he moved on.

Eliot should likewise have ignored Van Wyck's rude comment, but he'd seen himself as a knight riding to the defense of a lady's honor.

Jezebel was no lady, though. She was Infernal and certainly capable of defending herself.

Eliot had been no knight, either.

He would've used his music, and who knew what would have happened. While his power seemed to increase every time he played, his *control* hadn't. He'd probably have summoned a skeletal dinosaur or something equally weird, hurt lots of people, and gotten expelled.

But then the worst thing was that Fiona had stepped in and fought *for* him.

Eliot wasn't buying her "Team Captain" excuse. She was trying to protect him, her little brother.

It was humiliating.

And to top it all off, Jezebel spilled the beans about Fiona being an Immortal.

Fiona's social status had gone from nobody to instant celebrity.

They'd all made so much over her. Nobody even made the connection that he might be an Immortal, too. Maybe if he'd stuck around to bask in her glow, someone would've noticed—but he hadn't been able to stomach all those fawning people.

Eliot glanced about. He'd lost sight of the bay. He was surrounded by old warehouses, and nothing looked familiar.

Great, add to his list of things gone wrong today: getting lost.

He reached for his cell phone. He'd use the global positioning to find out where he was . . . only Louis had stolen his phone, and Audrey had declared him too irresponsible to be given another.

He sighed. Could this day get any worse?

As if in answer, Eliot spotted that weird white car, parked ahead on the corner.

What were the odds of seeing two identical antique cars within a block? And even more astronomically impossible—what were they odds of two long vehicles like that finding parking spots in San Francisco?

Eliot marched toward it, suddenly angry.

Whoever it was—Immortal, Infernal—it didn't matter. He'd demand to know what they wanted. He was tired of not being able to stand up for himself.

As he got closer, he saw the silver figure on the car's hood: a woman with wings swept back and arms held forward. His eyes slid off the snow white surfaces, unable to find any angular features.

He blinked, strode up, and rapped on the driver's window.

A window in back *thunk*ed down.

"Eliot." Uncle Henry's voice drifted from inside. "Get in."

Eliot relaxed a notch. He didn't trust Uncle Henry; he always seemed to be up to something, but he had tried to bend the League's rules for him and Fiona. And although Eliot would never guess at the motives of a god, he believed Henry actually liked him.

The back door opened and Uncle Henry sat inside, wearing a white linen suit that matched the white leather interior. He smiled. "I was look- ing for you . . . but I sensed you needed time with your thoughts."

"Yeah." Eliot shrugged. "Not so much anymore, though."

He glanced down the impossibly smooth length of this car, remembering how Robert had destroyed Henry's last limousine, the black Maybach— crashing it into Beelzebub.

"Do you like it?" Henry asked. "She is my 1933 Rolls-Royce. We call her Laurabelle. I've given the girl a tad of engine and body work so she could keep up." He patted the car lovingly.

"She's great," Eliot said. "Could you give me a lift home?"

"Unquestioningly. If you don't mind a *slight* detour?"

"As long as it's not like last time—Uncle Kino drove me to the edge of Hell."

Henry tilted his head. "No. It's not far. And it's nothing dangerous."

Eliot believed him. He got inside and sat opposite, facing Uncle Henry.

The Rolls-Royce accelerated and the streets became a blur—and then they were speeding though rolling hills of gold.

"So how are you?" Uncle Henry said. "Tell me everything—absolutely everything."

Eliot did. He sketched his school year so far: the exams, gym class, his girl troubles (although he was vague about who and what Jezebel was), how Fiona was now Team Captain, and how Eliot seemed to be the social equivalent of a flaming leper.

Uncle Henry nodded and made sympathetic noises, but asked no questions.

Outside, coastal waters flashed. The road then plunged into green shadows.

"The worst thing," Eliot said, "is all the fighting."

He struggled with his words. Eliot wanted to talk about this, but he didn't want to sound like a whiny kid.

"I mean, I know the Immortals and Infernals were at war, then there was the battle at Ultima Thule, and then the treaty, the *Pactum Pax Immortalis,* but there's still violence and plots . . . as if both sides *want* to fight. Like it's part of what they are."

Eliot was careful not to say "what *we* are" because he still wasn't sure how he fit within the Immortal and Infernal families.

Henry leaned forward. "Go on. . . ."

"It's not only the families," Eliot whispered. "It's Paxington, too. Gym class is a battlefield. There are duels every day, and the other students are beyond competitive. Why is it that way?"

Henry considered this, tapping his lower lip. "We are creatures of struggle and strife, my dear Eliot. We kill to live, and some of us live to kill. Many have tried to make a lasting peace, but they perish, their words soon all but dusty histories. Those who fight, win and survive."

Eliot sensed this to be true. Why then did it feel so wrong?

"We *have to* fight?" he asked. "There's no other way?"

Henry eased back. "All living things fight to survive. Even gods." He sighed. "Especially gods. Or perhaps"—a sly smile appeared on Henry's lips—"there is another undiscovered way? Waiting for someone to find it?"

Eliot didn't understand this, but he didn't immediately ask what Henry meant. Something secret and powerful echoed in his words just then. Something that was part puzzle, part prophecy, and part, Eliot was sure, something even Henry didn't quite understand.

The Rolls-Royce slowed.

Outside were palm trees and white sands, and a flock of red parrots took to the wing. The air conditioner kicked on.

Eliot had ridden with Uncle Henry before. His car could get anywhere in the world in a matter of hours. They could be in Florida, or Mexico, or farther.

Henry looked up. "We've arrived."

Smears of the surrounding countryside resolved into sand dunes, plantain trees, and a wide river. Laurabelle ran along a four-lane road crowded with chemical tankers and older sedans—all of them bearing a molecular logo that had planet Earth as one of its atoms.

They turned a corner and the world changed.

A chunk had been ripped from the tropical landscape. For miles in every direction were stumps and smoldering fields.

Nestled in the center of this hell on earth (and Eliot thought he was qualified to make that distinction having recently been there) squatted a refinery. A multitude of towers shot flames and oily smoke into the air. Pipes wormed from every crevice, leaked sludge, and tinged the nearby ocean red.

The Rolls-Royce turned into a parking lot and pulled into a space marked DIRECTOR MUY ESPECIAL.

Eliot opened the door.

The smell overwhelmed him: burning plastic and sulfur and something so repugnant that his nose shut and he gagged. He was barely able to get out and stand.

"Ah," Uncle Henry said, "that." He covered his face with a handkerchief. "A rather unfortunate side effect of the manufacturing process. Come, let us retire to my office. My secretary makes the most wonderful iced tea."

It was so hot, the pavement stuck under Eliot's loafers. He shrugged out of his wool Paxington blazer, his shirt beneath already soaked with perspiration.

"Wait," Eliot said. "Why'd you bring me here?"

Henry waved dramatically about. "For what every young man needs: a part-time job."

Eliot blinked rapidly. "I don't understand." He had the same feeling he had had as he watched Louis shuffle his three cards at the café, like some misdirection was occurring.

Uncle Henry slipped out of his white jacket and unbuttoned his shirt. "I know you feel bad about Fiona's rising prestige, especially within the League. I also heard from your mother how you lost your phone. So, I wanted to give you a chance to restore your confidence. 'Step up to the plate,' as the Americans say. I do love all their wonderful sports metaphors . . . and let you 'knock it out of the park.'"

"Still not understanding," Eliot said, getting annoyed.

"This place makes things," Uncle Henry said. "Oh, I don't know all the specifics—petrochemicals, pasta, plastics—something that begins with a *p* that the world simply cannot do without. It employs thousands of workers whose families would otherwise starve. And I am giving it all to you, my boy."

Eliot stared at the place, revolted by the mess, the odor, and the devastation of the land . . . but trying nonetheless to see the good that Uncle Henry spoke of.

"Run it on behalf of the League," Uncle Henry whispered. "Use its profits to buy a yacht or two—or reinvest the capital and transform it into whatever you desire." He patted him on the shoulder. "I have faith in you."

"Thanks . . . ," Eliot reflexively said. Audrey had taught him to always thank everyone for everything, no matter if he wanted it or not. "I'm busy with school, though."

"Oh, you don't *actually* run it." Uncle Henry laughed. "You have other people do that for you. You just make the big decisions."

Eliot imagined himself sitting in a boardroom wearing a white suit and executives hanging on his every instruction.

Why not? Maybe he could turn this place into something better. Prove to the League that he was . . . what?

Responsible? Capable? One of them?

Like Fiona?

Something inside Eliot writhed and rebelled against this idea.

Eliot didn't want to be molded into someone else's notion of what they thought he should be.

He wanted . . . What? He wasn't sure. But this factory wasn't it.

And yet, he couldn't just refuse and leave this place as it was. Uncle Henry was right on one count: It needed help.

"I appreciate the offer," Eliot said, "but it's not going to work for me."

Uncle Henry's face fell. "My boy, this corporation is worth a great deal. Millions . . . or billions . . . I forget."

Money didn't mean much to Eliot. When did he have time to spend money?

"I'm still saying no, Uncle Henry, but"—Eliot returned to the Rolls-Royce and got his backpack—"I think I can do something for you."

"Oh?" Uncle Henry's eyebrows quirked.

"Just come with me and listen."

Eliot marched to the corner of the parking lot and mounted a sand dune to get a better view. The land was surrounded by a fringe of burning jungle. There were acres of plastic-lined pits holding pools of fluorescent lime and yellow chemicals. Eliot set one foot on a pipe that jutted from the earth and got his violin case.

He pulled out Lady Dawn and stroked her amber grain. "This time," he whispered to her, "we work together."

"Eliot?" Uncle Henry said, a slight unease creeping into his voice. "What are you doing?"

Eliot held his violin bow between Henry and himself, brandishing it like a conductor's baton. "You said you wanted me to 'step up to the plate' and 'knock it out of the park.' That's what I'm going to do."

Eliot turned his back to him and focused.

He'd only been able to make little things happen *on purpose*: finding the crocodile, Sobek, in the sewers and Amanda Lane in that burning carnival— that dissonant chord he'd struck and sent a Team Knight student flying backwards.

The big things he'd done . . . summoning the dead, battling Beelzebub, and calling forth an army . . . those were from songs already written: "Mortal's Coil," "The Symphony of Existence," and "The March of the Suicide Queen."

He closed his eyes and set his bow to Lady Dawn's strings. Under his fingertips, she pulsed.

For what he wanted to do now, Eliot would have to use bits and pieces of songs he knew, and invent new musical phrases as well.

He took a deep breath. He could do this.

First, the poisonous air, the layers and lakes of toxic chemicals—they had to go.

But not merely moved somewhere else. That would just poison another place. Eliot had to destroy the stuff . . . *un*make it.

There was only one thing that would do: "The Symphony of Existence." There was a bit toward the end about the death of the universe—where matter compressed and heated, atoms disassociated into mist and void.

It was powerful music to start with, perhaps too powerful.

Eliot banished that thought. There would be no room for doubt.

He played notes so low, they trembled on the subsonic threshold, notes so terrible and bloodcurdling, the earth cracked in a spiderweb pattern about him. Clouds covered the sky and cycloned about Eliot. Lightning flashed.

Eliot felt poison drawn from the air, water, and the earth. Rivers of the stuff flowed into the freshly created fissures, steaming and hissing and dissolving soil as it went.

He pushed the notes deeper and darker, pulled the material down—past surface layers and bedrock—he bowed faster, and the heat and subterranean pressure rose—burning and decomposing what it could, oxidizing the remaining toxic metals.

The music wanted Eliot to keep playing . . . to the very end . . . like a swimmer caught in a river rushing toward a waterfall.

He resisted, though, and deftly transitioned to a major key.

Lady Dawn heated under his fingers. He felt tiny crackles along her length.

The notes sweetened as he wove in strands of "Julie's Song."

The land had to be cleaned, but it also needed more. It had to be nurtured. "Julie's Song" was the only thing he knew that so sounded full of love and light and hope.

He'd composed that song, however, when he was a different person. A boy in love.

He tried to be that again and gave his heart to the land, felt its suffering, and soothed its wounds.

It started to rain, pelting dust and sand, washing away debris, and extinguished distant jungle fires.

Eliot's thoughts drifted from the land . . . to Julie . . . and then to what she had become . . . Jezebel.

The music shifted, a subtle dissent into a minor key, something that spoke of wild growth and decay, jungle loam and running creepers and opening blossoms—a cycle of life *and* death.

Eliot smelled fresh vegetation, rich turned earth, and honeysuckle.

He pulled the song back . . . sensing something *diabolical* in the mix.

He was angry. Eliot didn't want to depend on trivial musical phrases, silly love songs, and music others had written. He wanted his *own* grand music—sonatas where air and light and birds mixed in fantastical aerobatics, symphonies that touched the stars and spoke of love and loss and the redemption of gods and angels.

He played with fury—the notes nothing he'd ever dreamed of before.

He put his soul into his music.

Live, he urged the land.

And the lands that had once been beautiful called back to him: the phantom songs of a hundred birds and a million insect chirps and whines, the breeze and every rustling leaf that had once lived beckoned, wanting to be once more.

Eliot mourned it all, and he knew then that he *had* to bring it back.

Somehow. No matter what it took.

He felt a part of himself slip into the land . . . and made a connection.

He lost himself, played until he turned everything he was inside out—cast it forth—gave it all.

And then he slowed . . . and plunked out the last notes . . . and stopped.

Eliot fell to his knees.

Sweat dripped from him, tears streamed from his eyes . . . and all mingled with the blood that ran freely from his fingers.

Eliot barely felt Henry's hand on his shoulder.

The earth was black, and mangrove trees sprouted and grew as he watched, vines wrapped around trunk and branch. There was a rich scent of cut grass. Orchids bloomed. Beetles buzzed. With a rainbow of fluttering feathers, flocks of birds alighted in the treetops, twittering with excitement. Shadow and sunlight angled under the rising jungle.

The factory had changed as well. Rust and corruption had become gleaming stainless steel and green plastic.

Workers ran out and looked with fascination, many making the sign of the cross.

"That . . . should . . . do," Eliot breathed, barely able to get out the words, he was so exhausted.

He fell and Henry caught him.

"Do?" Henry's voice was full of wonder. "Indeed that shall."

Eliot tried to laugh, but ended up coughing.

He had done something the entire League had been unable—or more likely, unwilling—to do. They were all too selfish to act beyond their personal interests.

And Eliot, at that very moment, realized he would never be one of them.

FRESHMAN MIDTERMS

35

FATHER–DAUGHTER CHAT

Fiona walked alone down the street. She loved the blinking Christmas lights. In the early morning fog, they glowed like the ghosts of fireflies.

There were no such lights on *their* house. That was covered by her mother's Rule 52.

> **RULE 52:** No Christmas, Easter, St. Valentine's Day, Hanukkah, Kwanzaa, or any other religious or mass-market orchestrated celebrations that include the rituals of unnecessary gift-giving and/or decorations.

That's what she and Eliot called the "no holiday" rule. They'd never had a Christmas tree or been on an Easter egg hunt, and they were forbidden to wear green on St. Patrick's Day.

Her mother didn't even like those holidays mentioned. What history was there between the League and the world's religions to make Audrey dislike them so?

Fiona could pretty much guess what the Catholic Church would think of her father. . . .

Fiona frowned and focused her thoughts on a problem within her control—like why being popular was not what she had expected.

She was glad to be walking to school by herself this morning. As soon as she got to Paxington, all the students would want to small talk their way around what they really wanted to know: What was it like to be in the League? Did she know this god or that goddess?

Fiona had quickly learned she could use the League's rules of secrecy to hide behind. She really didn't know anything about the League. Nor did she know who most of its members were, with their ever-shifting aliases. She hadn't even known her who mother truly was until a few months ago.

Still, it was nice that everyone wanted to get to know her.

Fiona had always dreamed of that kind of attention. Did it matter that it was *only* because of her League connections?

She knew the answer and shuffled her feet on the sidewalk.

Those people didn't want to get to know her, share her problems or her feelings; they just wanted to be friends with a "goddess." They just wanted to be friends with her fame.

Complicating this fame—and she was still mad at Jezebel for outing her without asking—was that now Fiona hardly saw the people she considered her real friends, like Mitch and Amanda.

And then there was Eliot.

He'd done his best to hide on campus. And lately, she didn't even see him at home. He'd come home late from Robert's, go straight to his room to read or practice with Lady Dawn (now with his door shut and locked). He spoke only in monosyllables . . . if at all.

Eliot hadn't even responded when she called him a *Fuligo septica*.[34]

This morning she'd wanted to talk to Eliot, waited for him to drag himself to the breakfast table, only to find that he'd already left the house.

Eliot getting up early had to be a sign of impending disaster. The way the universe was *supposed* to work was that he was always late for everything.

Fiona wondered if Eliot's evasiveness had something to do with Jezebel.

In the last few weeks, the Infernal had been to school only two or three times—and then, only to turn in her homework before she vanished again. When Jeremy asked, she had told him to mind his own business, and that it was an "internal Infernal affair."

Fiona almost stumbled into a man. She'd been so absorbed in her thoughts, she hadn't seen him.

Blushing, she looked up to apologize—and stopped.

"You!" she said.

Louis wore a soft camel-hair coat, which on this foggy morning made

---

34. *Fuligo septica* the scientific name for a species of slime mold more commonly called the "scrambled egg" or "dog vomit" slime mold. —Editor.

his outline a blur. He stood tall and confident. His long dark hair was streaked with sliver. He had a smile that would have disarmed her . . . had she not known him.

"Me." Her father held up his hands in a gesture of peace.

Fiona's blush of embarrassment turned into a flush of anger. "I've got nothing to say to you—not after you stole Eliot's phone! And certainly not now." She maneuvered around him and kept walking. "I have midterms today."

Louis strode alongside her. "Have I told you lately how much you remind me of your wonderful mother? But yes, midterms, precisely what I came to discuss."

He waved at the fog ahead and it curled and spiraled like the ocean surf . . . hypnotic.

Fiona blinked.

"Stop it," she hissed.

She touched her wrist and the rubber band there. Louis's silver bracelet was still safely tucked into her bag. It seemed to have a mind of its own, and she no longer trusted it.

"Just leave me alone," she said.

"I wanted to talk about your potential," Louis said, ignoring her request, "within the League . . . and outside of it."

She scoffed. "You mean with your side of the family. No thanks."

She thought about Jezebel, so effortlessly stunning and confident, and she also remembered how she *really* looked as an Infernal: those inhuman eyes and claws—a monster.

"We've been over this," Fiona said. "The League's declared me an Immortal—not Infernal. Everyone knows that."

But something in her words rang hollow in her ears.

"Yes, I've heard. And how do you like your new fame at school?"

There was a sarcastic edge to his tone that made the back of Fiona's neck prickle with irritation.

"How did you know . . . ?"

"I hear things. Like how you dealt with that trifling duel, so wonderfully ruthless and humiliating to the Van Wyck boy. A very Infernal thing. But as much fun as it might have been, you should have cut off his head. Now you have an enemy for life."

Fiona slowed. Donald Van Wyck had vowed never to come after Team Scarab. Well, of course, except in gym—where she suddenly remembered there *weren't* rules about first blood . . . where he and the rest of Team Wolf could kill them.

The ire drained from her as she realized her miscalculation.

But what alternative was there? She wasn't about to just kill someone.

Louis held out an arm in her path.

She halted, only now noticing she had almost walked off the curb into a busy intersection.

"Red light, my dear." He waggled a finger. "Mustn't jaywalk. What would your mother say?"

Fiona pursed her lips at this taunt. She shouldn't let Louis get to her so easily. But he did. Just as Audrey always got under her skin. It must be a skill they teach parents.

Well, she couldn't do anything if Louis wanted to walk on this sidewalk. It was a public place. She just wished he would shut up.

"Enough niceties, eh?" Louis's smile faded a bit. "I came to warn you about midterms. Some Paxington students will do whatever they must to pass . . . even cheat."

Fiona dismissed this notion. She imagined Plato Hall, the entire class bent over their tests—all under the unnerving gaze of Miss Westin. There was no way anyone was cheating. The Headmistress had made a special announcement about her zero-tolerance cheating policy last week—all the time looking at Jeremy and Sarah Covington.

"Let them try," Fiona said. "They'll get caught."

"But there are other ways to influence Paxington's precious grading curve," Louis murmured. "For my sake, please keep your eyes and ears open for danger. What harm could that do?"

"I suppose. . . ."

Fiona got the feeling that Louis knew more than he was telling, and just as important, that his concern for her was genuine.

She sighed. "I want to believe you. I want to trust you. You're just so . . . *un*trustworthy! Why did you steal Eliot's phone? He got into massive trouble."

Louis's smile entirely vanished and his gaze dropped to the ground. "Oh, yes . . . that. It was the only way I could reach your mother. She is good at covering her tracks, and I needed to know where you lived."

He took a deep breath and continued. "So when I saw Eliot's phone . . . I borrowed it." Louis looked up, and there was none of the usual mocking in his eyes. "I had planned on returning it the very next time I saw him . . .

but that never quite happened. His phone, though, it had your address programmed into its tiny brain. That's how I sent the Fabergé egg. I had hoped Audrey might remember how it was between her and me once . . . and perhaps . . ."

Louis shook his head, and his hand curled over his heart. "But I supposed she has already dashed the lovely thing into a million pieces, hasn't she?"

Fiona didn't have the heart to answer. She stared at him, which was enough to communicate all that had happened.

He stood mute.

She knew a little of how this must feel—not being able to be with the one you felt the most for. But she couldn't imagine what it would feel like to have that person utterly reject you.

"Maybe I could talk to her," Fiona said.

Louis chuckled. "Oh no, my dear. Audrey would never hear of it. And I'm sure she would find some suitable punishment for speaking on the behalf of such a disreputable character."

"But if you still love her—?"

"Some things are beyond the reach of even love," he whispered. He hesitated, opened his mouth, stopped, but then finally said, "Just one more thing before I leave you this morning. About Eliot. The boy should not be alone. Things will be tricky for him. Stay close."

Fiona believed that Louis truly cared for Eliot.

Quite possibly her, too.

And most especially Audrey.

They were *so* close to being a real family . . . and yet it felt like they were light-years apart. Why was it so hard?

Yes, Louis was the Infernal Prince of Darkness, and yes, he was truly a monster with bat wings and horns and talons, and utterly disgusting. But he was also her father, wasn't he? That had to count for something.

Louis leaned closer, gingerly took her chin, and tilted her head down. He kissed her on the forehead.

It felt like a warm autumn breeze, like sleeping on soft blankets, like . . . like coming back to a home she had only dreamed of before.

Fiona looked up

Only the fog remained.

To her disappointment—and her relief—her father was gone.

36

CRAMMING FOR THE MIDTERM

Robert focused on the five two-by-fours he'd duct-taped together and set on cinder blocks. He knelt before them as if in prayer.

One such board, even two would have been easy to break if you were trained or even if you wanted to "brute force" it and bruise your hand.

Sure, it was a stupid test. In their sparring sessions, Aaron had disdained such tricks. *"Breaking wood—fah! Useless. How many boards ever fight back?"*

Robert struck.

The boards broke like eggshells.

He gathered the pieces and stacked them again, ten high.

He hit once more without hesitation.

The boards shattered—so did the cinderblock. The floor cracked, too.

Now *that* was more than a stupid test.

Robert flexed his fist and examined it. Red, but otherwise not a mark.

There was a lot more to Aaron's lessons and Mr. Mimes's Soma liquor than he'd first guessed. He knew he was part of some larger scheme they'd hatched—and he hated being used by them . . . but he couldn't complain about the results.

That had been the deal, too, when he was a Driver for Mr. Mimes. There'd been danger and intrigue, but a heck of a benefits package that included near total freedom and an unlimited expense account.

His gaze fell on the stack of books by his futon. He should have been reading and taking last-minute notes for today's midterm. That stuff was so dry, though. So many dates and facts to memorize. Besides, he figured he knew everything he was going to. Five more minutes wouldn't . . .

Something was near. He sensed it in his apartment.

Robert whirled about, standing, and raised his hands . . . and found Mr. Henry Mimes leaning against the wall.

"Shall I send a carpenter to fix that?" Mr. Mimes nodded at the broken floor.

"No, thanks," Robert said, hiding his astonishment at yet another of Mr. Mimes's miraculous entrances. "There's leftover bamboo from the re-model. I can handle it."

"As you wish." Mr. Mimes stood and rubbed his hands. "I just popped by before school for an update on young Eliot." He waved at the two-by-fours. "Can he cause such destruction, too?"

"No, but he's coming along. You wouldn't think it to look at him, though. Kid's full of surprises."

"So you're teaching him everything? Boxing? Grappling? Knife and clubs?"

"All the basics," Robert said.

Mr. Mimes suddenly looked serious. "But?" he said. "There was a 'but' in there?"

Robert shook his head. He didn't want to rat Eliot out, but Mr. Mimes would get it out of him anyway.

"Eliot is really smart," Robert told him. "The guy can learn anything he puts his mind to, but it's *why* he's learning that bugs me." He frowned. "There's more to it than just not getting his head bashed in at school."

Mr. Mimes brightened. "A girl, I hope? Is she pretty?"

Robert chewed over those questions. "Kind of. I mean kind of a girl. Pretty? Yeah—she's off the charts. He doesn't talk about her, but I've seen him looking at her . . . Jezebel the Infernal."

Mr. Mimes tapped the tip of his nose, thinking.

"Eliot's always been a little on the quiet side," Robert said, "but now—geez. He mopes around in a constant funk. Not like any ordinary guy with an ordinary crush. This is different and darker. I'm worried that he might be drifting over to *their* side."

"The Infernals?" Mr. Mimes laughed. "No, no, no, the symptoms you de-scribe are that of *any* normal teenager. You think them extraordinary only because you yourself have never suffered those feelings."

"I wouldn't say that," Robert muttered.

Mr. Mimes looked him over. "Oh, I am sorry. I forgot. But keeping your distance from Fiona is essential at the moment. So much depends on it. Not least of all your personal safety."

Robert was going to say thanks . . . for nothing, but his mind stuttered about the "so much depends" part of what Mr. Mimes had just said.

What plans did he have for the twins? He bet nothing the League was involved in. And if the League was willing to throw Robert in prison for a hundred years, or burn him alive forever, or something just as nasty for him breaking some *little* rule like kissing Fiona—what would they do to one of their most trusted people who pulled a *serious* fast one?

Mr. Mimes stepped closer to Robert and set one hand on his shoulder. "Best not to trouble your mind with such things. Keep on your studies, stay in the shadows, watch and protect . . . especially in light of Fiona's new popularity. Remember, misdirection is most easily accomplished with a beautiful, shiny object."

Robert nodded. He was used to taking orders. What choice was there? Cross Mr. Mimes?

Marcus Welmann's famous last words echoed in his thoughts: *"They're more force of nature than flesh and blood. Lose sight of that, cross them once . . . and you might as well try talking your way out of an tidal wave for all the good it'll do you."*

But Robert was stronger now than Marcus had ever been. Strong enough maybe to stand on his own two feet and not take orders?

He buried that thought deep. Mr. Mimes had a way of guessing what you were thinking, especially when it involved him.

Mr. Mimes pulled out his silver flask and uncorked it. He took a sip and then handed it to Robert, saying, "For what ails you."

Robert spied the liquid inside. Soma was what Mr. Mimes and Aaron had called it. The liquid gleamed like molten gold and reflected off the mirrored walls of the flask. In Miss Westin's Mythology 101 class, Robert had learned a little about the drink.

"Mostly mythohistorical lies," Miss Westin had said. But Robert had figured out two things. First, over time it turned normal guys like him into the equal of the gods. And second, it changed who they were, made them more assertive and dominant.

Both of which went along perfectly with his plans.

He tipped the flask into his mouth, drank deep, and drained it.

Robert's mind exploded, and he could see every memory, every sensation, and every nerve down to the primitive animal level. A sulfurous fire burned his throat and stomach. Vapors blasted through his lungs . . . and he exhaled, blinking away streaming tears.

"What's in that stuff, man?"

"Sugar and spice for girls; snips and snails and puppy dog tails for you." Mr. Mimes took the flask, frowning at its now empty state, and tucked it away. "But nothing illegal or even alcoholic, sadly. A few herbs, filtered water, the odd vitamin or two."

As Robert regained his equilibrium, he asked, "So what do you want me to do about Eliot? I can introduce him to a lot nicer class of girl. Human, for starters."

Mr. Mimes sobered. "I wouldn't do that, Robert. I appreciate your concern, but if this Jezebel reciprocates Eliot's affections, well, you would not want to deal with an Infernal woman scorned. *That* is on my list of the eleven most dangerous things in the universe—right after trying to balance a national economy by printing money."

He leaned closer and whispered, "Besides, the Post children have a knack to twist fate to their own ends, regardless of what either Immortal or Infernal family desires, eh? Those two—by themselves—may represent an entirely new force for us to consider."

"What's that supposed to mean?" Robert asked, suddenly feeling protective of his friends.

Mr. Mimes stood straighter and brushed some imaginary dust off his silvery gray sports coat. "Oh, just silliness, a bit of random number mathematics I was toying with. Nothing at all for you to worry about."

When Mr. Mimes said don't worry like that, Robert *really* started worrying.

He filed that clue about the twins and them being a "new force" under stuff to follow up on later with his own investigations.

Mr. Mimes glanced at his watch. "Where does the time go?" he muttered. "I need to ask Cornelius. I must be off. So many things to attend to down in Costa Esmeralda."

"That's in Central America right?" Robert asked. "Near Panama?"

Mr. Mimes cocked his head, looking surprised at Robert's grasp of geography.

"I rode through there once. Nice place. There some Mardi Gras or something you have to be at?"

"Something like that," Mr. Mimes replied with a smirk. "In the late spring. You should visit."

It must be a heck of a bash if Mr. Mimes recommended it. Robert made a note of that, too, filed away under Things to Do/Party/Spring.

Mr. Mimes paused. "One more thing, Robert. Midterms are today, are they not?"

"Sure. You got some more answers to Miss Westin's tests for me?"

"Not quite. That was a one-time arrangement we made to get you inside Paxington. The rest is up to you, as I said. Besides, even I would not cross Lucy Westin on her home soil."

"It's cool," Robert said, hiding his disappointment, and allowing his appreciation for Miss Westin to rise a notch. She intimidated even Mr. Mimes. "I've hit the books. I'll pass."

"Perhaps," Mr. Mimes whispered. "But to be on the safe side . . . pack your brass knuckles today, my boy."

37

PRE-TEST JITTERS

handful of the popular girls circled Fiona. They nodded as they walked by, but this morning everyone was too nervous to talk to Paxington's newest social pinnacle.

Fiona pinned the silver rose token to her jacket lapel. She'd started wearing it last week. It had been given to her by the League when she was inducted into the Order of the Celestial Rose. She still didn't know what that was, but it was pretty, part alive, and part silver, and it smelled as fragrant as the day it'd been given to her.

The entire freshman class had collected outside Plato's Hall. The doors were shut and locked, and a sign rested on the handles:

MIDTERMS TODAY
Wait Outside for Instructions

Fiona was as nervous as everyone else, but because she was a goddess, she didn't feel she ought to show it, like that might reflect poorly on the League.

She paused by the Picasso Archway. The portrait had been painted to resemble a real archway that led to a courtyard where anatomically jumbled students listened to a lecture and took notes. It was fascinating, but it also gave Fiona the creeps. Like someone had taken those people apart and put them together . . . wrong.

Fiona turned from it and smiled, hoping this masked the fact that she quavered inside. She wondered if she had time to go the girls' restroom one more time.

Midterms were one third of her grade. Fail this, and she might as well not bother coming back tomorrow.

Where was Eliot?

She scanned the courtyard.

Team Wolf was in the far corner, and they all looked away when she glanced at them. Fiona was sure Donald Van Wyck was plotting something.

She moved her eyes away, searching for her brother. Eliot didn't exactly pop out of a crowd, but she should have seen him by now. He'd skipped breakfast again this morning and left early. Was it possible he'd chickened out and wasn't coming?

"Hey," Eliot whispered.

He hadn't sneaked up on her; Fiona just hadn't seen her brother and had almost walked right over him. She didn't jump, but for a split second she was speechless, thinking she'd seen his ghost.

Eliot stood in the shadows. Something was darker about him, and not just the ambient light.

"Where were you?" she whispered. "I was worried."

Eliot shrugged. He glanced at her silver rose pin and frowned.

She wanted to say so much. About needing to stick together because they were stronger. How when she studied alone, it was like she had lost half her brain . . . well, maybe a quarter. How she had actually missed her brother these last few weeks—and what was he thinking always wandering off on his own?

But she could never say any of those things in public without dying of humiliation.

Why couldn't Eliot say something? Why was it always she who had to do the talking? After all they'd been through together, he should just *know* how she felt.

"Let's stick together today," he whispered. "I have a weird feeling about this test."

Fiona exhaled, relieved that no one had to admit to any stupid emotions—now of all times.

"Good idea," she said. "I've got a funny feeling, too."

Behind them, the archway clicked and slowly swung outward. Behind it was a doorway that so perfectly mimicked the arch in the painting, Fiona had to blink twice to make sure it had depth and was real.

Miss Westin emerged and glanced over Eliot and Fiona. "The Post twins," she remarked. "What a pleasant surprise to find you on time for *this* exam."

Fiona shivered. Beyond the now-open secret door was a passage of rough, wet granite that spiraled underground.

Miss Westin cleared her throat. "Your attention, students."

Those in the courtyard who hadn't noticed Miss Westin turned at the sound of her commanding voice and instantly stopped talking.

"Midterms are one third of your total grade," she continued, "and there will be *no* makeups."

Fiona swallowed and wondered what happened if you were sick today.

"There are three rules for today's tests," Miss Westin said. "First, your performance will be individually graded and mapped to a so-called bell curve as follows: For every one hundred students, there will be ten As, fifteen Bs, and fifty Cs." As she said "C," she looked as if she had just tasted one of Great-grandmother Cecilia's home-cooked spinach casserole specialties.

"And, of course, the last twenty-five will be Ds and Fs."

At this, the respectful silence of the gathered students crystallized into palpable terror.

And something else . . . everyone glanced suspiciously at one another.

The camaraderie that Fiona had felt a moment ago for her fellow students—the fact that they had helped one another and studied side by side for weeks—all that vanished.

It was everyone for themselves.

No, actually, it was worse than that: It was everyone against everyone. Twenty-five of them were going to *fail* this test, largely determined by how the best students performed, because of that bell curve.

It was bloody unfair . . . but there was no way Fiona was going to be one of those failing twenty-five.

As if a magnetic force had been turned on, the crowd of students shuffled apart from one another.

Fiona fought that feeling, though. She took a step *closer* to her brother.

"Second," Miss Westin said, "students shall assemble as I call their teams before the midterm entrance." She gestured to the now-open Picasso Arch. "This, however, is only to prevent bottlenecks during the examination."

Fiona understood what Miss Westin said, but not what it meant. Bottlenecks during the exam? How could there be a bottleneck?

"Third," Miss Westin continued, "answering a question incorrectly may be dangerous. I advise that you *not* risk guessing. If you do not know an answer, move to another path, or if you find yourself at a dead end, you may stop the examination by raising your hand and declaring yourself 'done.' You will be removed and your score tallied."

These new facts sent waves of murmurs through the gathered freshmen.

Maybe because the notion of giving up was abhorrent to this crowd of overachievers. Or maybe, like Fiona, it was the idea of being utterly mortified by being "removed" from the exam in front of everyone.

Or just maybe it was because Fiona couldn't imagine how putting down a wrong answer could be *dangerous* . . . although she took Miss Westin at her word.

This test obviously wasn't going to be a normal pencil-and-paper, multiple-choice type thing.

Miss Westin opened her little black book and ran a bony finger down the page. "Ah, yes," she said, "first up—Green Dragon. Gather before the entrance now."

Eight students pushed forward through the crowd.

Eliot and Fiona got out of their way before they got trampled.

Green Dragon had some big people on it. The boys looked like seniors—giants compared with Eliot. Even the girls were all a head taller than Fiona. They shot one another sidelong glances and elbowed each other for the best forward positions.

Fiona didn't get it. Okay, sure, they were all competing for the same good grades. But the people on Green Dragon had fought together in gym class. Didn't that count for anything? She couldn't imagine being so rude to anyone on her team . . . not even Sarah or Jeremy.

The Dragons nervously bounced on the balls of their feet as Miss Westin checked off their names in her book. She removed her silver pocket watch and made a note of the time.

"You may proceed," she told them. "Good luck."

They rushed the archway—pushed and shoved down the tight corridor, and then were gone.

The tunnel swallowed the sounds of their passing.

Fiona shivered.

Miss Westin flipped a page in her book and declared: "Team Scarab. Gather before the entrance."

Adrenaline shot through Fiona. She wasn't ready. She should have reread the *Clan Canticles* this morning. She definitely should have gone to the girls' restroom one last time. Everything she had learned this semester seemed to be gone from her memory.

Eliot nudged her.

She turned on him, irritated.

Worry creased his brow as well, but amazingly, he looked ready to do battle. It was the same stoic concentration she'd seen when he fought those shadow demons in the alley.

Fiona snorted. Well, if he could keep his cool, then so could she.

Together they stepped toward Miss Westin.

The Headmistress gave them both a tiny nod of approval. Her gaze then darkened as it fell upon the rest of Team Scarab.

Behind them gathered Jeremy, Sarah, Mitch, Robert, Amanda, and last, Jezebel.

Jeremy and Sarah looked impeccable in their freshly pressed Paxington school uniforms. Both had their long hair pulled back tight and had looks of total focus on their faces. But they weren't together like her and Eliot. They stood on opposite sides of the team, deliberately not looking at each other.

Amanda brushed aside her hair, spotted Fiona, and gave her a confident smile.

Fiona reciprocated the gesture, relieved that at least one other member of Team Scarab wasn't putting friendship before grades.

Why was it an either/or choice? Fiona didn't accept that to win this battle, one of her friends or someone on her team had to lose because of the grading curve.

Mitch and Robert simultaneously noticed her; Mitch grinned, Robert frowned—then they saw each other looking at her and quickly diverted their gazes.

She'd have to have a talk with Robert soon. This limbo state they were in relationship-wise was doing neither of them any good.

Fiona shook her head to clear those thoughts. She had to stay focused on how to help out her team while winning at the same time.

Jezebel limped up to join them.

She was, as ever, lovely and poised as a porcelain doll with perfect platinum curls . . . but broken, too. One arm hung in a sling, and tiny drops of black blood seeped through. There was a bruise on Jezebel's check (although somehow its placement actually enhanced her strange attraction).

For the first time, Fiona felt something close to sympathy for the Infernal. To have to go through midterms injured like that . . .

Fiona wondered what on earth could have done that to her. She wanted to go over there and offer her help.

There was no way, though, that proud Jezebel, Infernal Duchess of the Grand Whatsits was going to accept help from anyone, least of all her.

Eliot took a tentative step toward her, his face lined with concern.

But he halted when he saw her expression—just a quick glance at him, full of steel and venom and hurt—like if he took one step closer, she would either punch him in the face . . . or cry.

Jezebel then looked purposely away.

Eliot sighed and stepped back.

Fiona wanted to say something to her brother, but what? How did you help someone who didn't want help?

The answer to everything came to Fiona: not only how to help Jezebel—but everyone on the team—and Eliot—*and* herself.

"Hey," she whispered, and motioned Team Scarab closer.

Jeremy sniffed, and the rest of them looked about unsure. None of them moved an inch.

"Come on," she chided, and then in a low whisper so only they could hear: "I've got a way to boost everyone's grade on this thing."

"Oh, very well," Jeremy said, moving closer, acting like he was doing her the biggest favor in the world.

The rest of them followed, except Jezebel, who remained on the outside of their huddle. Fiona had no doubt, though, that with her Infernal ears, she'd be eavesdropping.

"I think we should work together on this," Fiona started.

"Just as I said," Jeremy whispered to Sarah, scowling. Then to the rest of the team, he muttered, "Don't you understand that be the *one* thing we cannot do? Help one person, as well meaning as that might seem, you hurt yourself. That's the way this grade curve works, lassie."

Mitch looked sheepish and chimed in, "I hate to admit it, but he's right. It's a mathematics thing. Not personal."

"It might be 'right' by the numbers," Fiona shot back, "but you're missing the bigger picture."

Jezebel inched closer.

"And what is that?" Sarah said, managing to sound sweet and condescending at the same time.

"We've all studied the same stuff in Miss Westin's class." Fiona leaned in closer. "But each of us has an edge in a different area. Me, Eliot, and Robert know a lot about the Immortals and the League."

She had spent most of her time learning about her relations so far this year. A little obsessed, really. Robert had a bunch of firsthand experience. And Eliot? Fiona just assumed that's what he'd been studying, too.

"The Covingtons and Mitch know tons about the mortal magical families," she added. "Jeremy especially has firsthand experience with the Middle Realms. . . ."

She added that bit to pander to his ego. She didn't really count getting *lost* in the Valley of the New Year chasing some leprechaun as "experience."

"Amanda has studied harder than anyone in the entire class," Fiona continued. "She knows something about *everything*."

Amanda looked down, blushing.

Fiona paused to glance over at Jezebel, who had her head turned away (but was obviously paying attention).

"So you're saying we're smarter together," Robert said.

"Exactly," Fiona replied. "We can help one another and, yeah, we'll shift the grade curve . . . but because we're *all* going to get higher grades."

Sarah tapped her lips thoughtfully. "As long as the others don't chance upon this bit of trickery," she whispered, "it might work."

"Isn't it cheating, though?" Amanda squeaked.

Jezebel finally joined them. "It is not," she answered. "Miss Westin said we would be *graded* individually, but there was no specific prohibition against *working* together."

"Geez," Robert noticed Jezebel's injuries. "What happened to you?

Jezebel shot him a withering glare. "Nothing that concerns you, mortal."

Mitch cleared his throat. "Okay, sure she didn't specifically say we *couldn't* work together . . . but that's splitting it pretty fine, don't you think?"

"They're such sticklers for following the rules at Paxington, it'll work," Fiona countered. "Trust me."

"I guess," Mitch admitted, sounding entirely not convinced.

"Then we're agreed," Fiona said. "We work together on this?" She made eye contact with each of them, trying to look and feel as confident as she could.

They nodded.

"Team Scarab," Miss Westin said and made a note of the time in her book. "Enter the Midterm Maze—now."

They scrambled through the open Picasso Arch and into the dark passage . . . twisting around, descending.

38

MIDTERM MAZE

Fiona and the others ran down the spiral passage and found themselves in a large cavern. The ceiling had dripping, teethlike stalactites. Pools of water on the cobblestone floor reflected the wavering light from torches on the walls. Between the flickering flames were arches with closed portcullis.

They spread out.

"Over here." Robert said. "There's a brass plaque by this gate. It's got a question on it."

"Here, too," Mitch called out. He started reading it. "Seems easy enough." He reached to touch it.

"Hang on," Fiona told him. "Miss Westin called this the 'Midterm Maze.' We shouldn't just pick one at random. We could get lost."

"How does that work, then?" Sarah asked. "Is it best to find the longest path and answer the most questions? Will that get the highest score? Or are we supposed to find the shortest path?"

"Or maybe," Amanda whispered, "we're supposed to go until we chicken out and say were done."

Yells echoed from the distant passages . . . someone far away screamed. Then it was quiet.

"Was that a wrong answer?" Jeremy whispered with a nervous laugh.

Fiona wondered what nasty surprises Miss Westin had engineered for them. "There has to be a clue to the *best* path," she murmured.

"Or we just pick one at random," Jeremy said, and strode toward that farthest gate.

"Wait." Eliot withdrew Lady Dawn from his pack. "There *is* a way."

Jeremy looked at Eliot with obvious jealousy. "I don't think now be the time to break into song."

Jezebel moved to Jeremy and held up one finger, commanding his silence. With a flick of her hand, she indicted that Eliot continue.

Eliot nodded to her and set his violin to his shoulder.

Fiona wondered what was going on between her brother and the Infernal. It was hard to tell if Jezebel liked or hated him half the time. All the glares and warnings for him to stay away . . . and then she did stuff like this. Maybe she was just being practical.

Or maybe it really was part of some Infernal plot to draw him closer to that side of their family. Fiona would have to keep a careful eye on this situation—especially with Eliot getting deeper into trouble.

Eliot set his bow on Lady Dawn's strings and the air stilled.

The song was slow and steady and classically styled.

Fiona smelled chalk dust and the pages of old books and that weird pine antiseptic odor that permeated the Hall of Wisdom. She blinked, understanding that Eliot's song was about class and them studying.

He turned, facing one arch, then another, frowning at each. His music shifted, even slower notes, sad too, and then an unexpected pizzicato phrase that sent Fiona's heart skipping.

She felt a rush of shock and disappointment . . . exactly what she had felt when she saw that C on her placement exam.

Eliot quickly turned to the remaining arches. He then halted and wavered between the last two. He changed his music again: Faster, notes light and springy.

In her mind, she imagined that she'd gotten an A+ on that placement test. Fiona couldn't help but grin.

She glanced at the others and they smiled, too.

Except Jezebel, whose gaze was firmly locked on Eliot. Jezebel looked softer, almost human as she watched him.

Jezebel then noticed Fiona staring, and her features hardened to alabaster.

Eliot halted.

The rest of the team snapped out of their trance.

"That one." Eliot pointed to the farthest arch. "That's the path that leads to the best grade. At least potentially."

"That was my guess originally," Jeremy muttered. He strode toward it.

They crowded about the brass plaque on the wall and read:

Order from the oldest to most recent these mortal magical families: Covington, Scalagari, Kaleb, Van Wyck, De Marco, Janis, and the Isla Blue Tribe.

This was followed by a blank space on the plaque. "Kaleb," Amanda and Sarah said together.[35] Amanda took a step back, blushing. Sarah touched the name.

The raised brass letters of "Kaleb" sank through the other letters, and settled to the top of the blank space. Sarah then pursed her lips, concentrating, and twined a lock of her red hair as she considered the other names.

"Oh, get on with it," Jeremy hissed. "It's Kaleb, Isla Blue, Van Wyck, Scalagari, De Marco, Covington, and then Janis."

Sarah took a deep breath and held it, as if to keep the words she wanted to say to her older cousin contained. She quickly touched the names in the order Jeremy suggested. They sank and arranged themselves in a list.

As the last one fell into place, there was a *click*.

The portcullis noisily ratcheted up.

"Now what?" Robert asked.

"I believe I go through," Sarah replied.

She sashayed through the arch, but as soon as she crossed the portcullis, it slammed down behind her.

They all jumped.

"Remember Miss Westin said we'd be graded individually?" Mitch whispered. "I think we each have to answer to get through."

Fiona saw the ordered list of families on the plaque vanish . . . and the names return scrambled to the top portion, except the Janis family became the Clan Soto.

"Ah," Jeremy said, leaning over her shoulder and noting this as well. "Nothing to it." He rattled off the proper sequence.

Fiona touched the names, the gate rose, and she marched through—then the gate slammed shut after her.

---

35. Clan Kaleb are renowned for magic that enhances their fierce combat abilities. They receive extensive martial arts, blade, and marksman training prior to reaching puberty. Childhood mortality is common. The clan originates from nomadic desert tribesmen and can trace their lineage to 2600 B.C.E. There is an ancient saying about Kaleb warriors: "Only fools battle the desert winds." *Gods of the First and Twenty-first Century, Volume 14, The Mortal Magical Families*. Zypheron Press Ltd., Eighth Edition.

Sarah exhaled, relaxing now that she was no longer alone on this side of the arch.

One by one they went through, Jeremy finishing last and following.

"So far so good," Fiona declared.

The room they stood in was lined with brick and looked like the interior of a blast furnace, with scorch marks and patches white from extreme heat. Fiona didn't like it . . . wondering if the place would fill with fire if they missed an answer.

No way. She couldn't believe they'd really hurt students who failed. Miss Westin had to be psyching them out. That's all.

Still . . . she had no intention of finding out.

There were three exit arches.

"So which way?" Robert asked Eliot.

Eliot nodded to the gate on their left.

Fiona examined the plaque by it. There was the impression of a tree with many branches, each with a tiny blank rectangle. At the base of the tree trunk like so many fallen apples lay jumbled the names of gods and goddesses.

This would be easy.

She directed Amanda how to arrange the names in the family tree of Immortals.

. . . even the Fates on their own separate branch.

The portcullis rose.

There was a commotion in the main cavern. The next group had entered. They scattered—each student running toward a different gate and question plaque, and each covering their answers so none of the others could see.

One boy from Team Eagle ran toward the gate that led to this room, but seeing them *all* inside, he halted, confused—and then turned away.

"Hurry," Sarah rasped to Amanda. "Before the others understand what we are doing."

Amanda moved through the arch, and the portcullis dropped behind her.

Fiona watched as the names in the brass trees fell to the bottom. "Aphrodite" faded, and "Loki" appeared in its place.

But Fiona knew them all still, and she helped the rest of her team through.

She paused just before she walked through. This was easy. *Was* it cheating?

She didn't think so. As Jezebel had said, Miss Westin hadn't prohibited them from pooling resources. Maybe no one at Paxington had thought about it because working together for a common good was an alien concept for them.

So selfish.

Team Scarab efficiently moved through four more passages and four more rooms.

There were questions covering the development of alchemy, the rise and fall of the now-extinct gypsy shamans in Eastern Europe (which was a trick question because they hadn't covered that yet in class—but Mitch knew anyway), the Battle of Ultima Thule, and the Treaty of the Under-Realms.[36]

As they entered the fifth room, however, Fiona noted it had but one exit—so they had to get the question on the brass plaque to proceed.

It was on the Angelic Alphabet.

Jezebel was the closest thing they had to an expert on the subject . . . but she puzzled a long time over the odd language which comprised lines, arcs, circles, and tiny squares.

Fiona had seen those letters before. Once in class—just a passing reference by Miss Westin, and also in that book Eliot had been so excited about this summer, *Mythica Improbiba*.

She also vaguely recalled some extra credit reading on John Dee, but she'd skipped the footnotes on all his variations of the invented languages of the angels.[37]

36. In 1852, the war between the London Confederation of the Unliving (a loose alliance of undead factions) and mortal magical families (Covington, Gower, and Van Wyck) halted after three hundred years. The League of Immortals brokered an armistice for the living to retain possession of their Earthly realm. The Confederation of the Unliving were given dominion over the London Warrens and the adjacent Gloom Lands. Earth, while open to visitation and even residency, remains off-limits for predation by the undead. Although breaches do occur, the Confederation maintains an internal enforcement division to police offenders. *Gods of the First and Twenty-first Century, Volume 7, Those That Live Not.* Zypheron Press Ltd., Eighth Edition.

37. Although many variations of the "Alphabet of the Angels" appear in medieval grimoires, perhaps most notably in the infamous Beezle edition *Mythica Improbiba* (Taylor Institution Library Rare Book collection, Oxford University), none have authentically been deciphered. Those that claimed to have were all denounced later as fakes. Catholic Church officials claim that one must be blessed, i.e., be a saint or of angelic origin, to read the script. *Golden's Guide to Extraordinary Books*, Victor Golden, 1958, Oxford.

"Very close to Infernal dialects," Jezebel murmured. Concentration furrowed her brow. "But their grammar . . . so many rules."

Mitch peered over her shoulder but quickly moved back, shaking his head. "Way out of my league," he whispered.

Eliot moved to her side and asked, "Do you mind?"

"If you think you can," Jezebel snorted, "be my guest."

Eliot set his palms over the raised symbols as if it were Braille, closed his eyes, and traced their edges.

"I have it," he whispered to her. "I'll need your hands."

She looked at him and then her hands, confused. "I . . . I don't know. . . ."

"Here." Eliot gently took them and moved them over the letters.

She inhaled sharply—but before she could say anything, he was helping her move the scrambled letters like the pieces of a jigsaw.

Jezebel's eyes widened. Her colorless cheeks tinged pink.

Fiona took a step back. It felt weird . . . almost intimate to see the two of them, hands atop one another.

Eliot finished. He quickly removed his hands and without a word took a step back.

The portcullis rose.

Jezebel looked at the deciphered passage—and then covered her eyes as if she'd just stared into a flashbulb.

The text, apart from looking like a geometry problem, didn't look like anything legible to Fiona.

An English translation, however, emerged at the bottom of the brass plaque:

> *Be sober, be vigilant; because your adversary, the Devil, as a roaring lion, walketh about, seeking whom he may devour.*[38]

"How did you do that?" Jezebel whispered to Eliot.

"You better go on," Eliot told her. His eyes were darker than usual, the color of blue smoke. "I'll need to get the next person through."

Jezebel moved to the other side and watched intently as Eliot helped the rest of the team.

Fiona noted that Eliot didn't touch anyone as he had Jezebel, rather just instructed them where to place the odd geometric letters.

---

38. *Holy Bible,* King James translation, 1 Peter 5:8. —Editor.

Eliot went through last and told them, "I think there's only one more question ahead."

"About bloody time," Jeremy replied. "Men weren't meant to be underground like so many rats."

"No worries," Fiona said, trying to sound confident. "One more gate. We get through and we're finished."

"Come on." Robert grabbed a torch off the wall and led the way.

The tunnel angled up, zigged and zagged, and then a light appeared far down the passage.

It was blurry and dim, but definitely the same fog-covered sunlight she'd seen earlier this morning. And there was no gate!

They broke into a trot.

Fiona's heart raced. They'd done it. Made it through the entire maze— got every question right! They'd all get As and show the rest of the class what teamwork could accomplish.

The light brightened, and Fiona found herself blinking as she ran out onto grass.

She whooped and cheered and whirled around.

. . . but her victory dance spun to a stop.

They were inside the Ludus Magnus.

The jungle gym loomed before her. It was taller now, eighty feet high. She saw the balance beam she had crossed a few weeks ago had spiked weights that swung back and forth so you'd have to dodge. The chain-link fences had barbed wires woven through them. And higher, there was a sloped bridge of solid ice, dripping in the overcast sky—impossibly slick.

They'd made the course *harder*.

Eliot jogged up to her, skidded to a halt, and took in the sight.

"This is wrong," she whispered.

"Very wrong," he said, and nodded to the far side of the coliseum.

Team Green Dragon had gathered there. They spotted Fiona and Eliot and moved toward them . . . a slow trot, and then a faster run.

And just emerging around the opposite side of the jungle gym was Team Wolf . . . Donald van Wyck at the head of his pack.

Mr. Ma was nowhere in sight.

"This is not good," Robert said, joining them.

Jezebel limped up next to Eliot. "As you said . . . there *was* one more part of the test to pass."

"How can that be?" Sarah asked. She stood with them in a line, facing the other teams. "There can't be *three* teams on the field at once."

Van Wyck called as he approached, "Has to be a mistake, huh? Green Dragon *and* Wolf matched against Scarab?" His pale face split into a wicked grin, and he turned to the Dragons. "Whatever shall we do about it?"

The Captain of the Dragons was a boy who looked like a weight lifter. "Rules are clear," he said. "If there's a Dragon flag, we're going to get to it—and stop our opposition from getting to theirs."

Van Wyck halted and turned to the jungle gym.

The Wolf flag unfurled next to the Dragon's . . . and on the opposite corner, the Team Scarab banner appeared, rippling in the wind. .

All the joy Fiona had felt a moment ago curdled. She remembered Van Wyck's promise never to hurt anyone on her team—*except* in gym class, where violence was encouraged . . . and lethal violence allowed.

Jeremy and Mitch trotted up last, joining the rest of Team Scarab on the field.

"We won't play," Fiona told them. "They can't do this."

"They *are* doing it," Jeremy declared, "whether we play or not, dearie."

Mitch said nothing, but moved to Fiona's side. A ball of white-blue light appeared and smoldered in his clenched hand.

Fiona's mind floundered. There were outnumbered, outpowered, about to get pounced on and torn to bits.

Eliot was unfazed. He took out Lady Dawn and set the instrument on his shoulder. "I'm ready to fight," he told her. "Tell us what to do."

Eliot's unwavering confidence snapped Fiona out of her panic.

"Okay," she told them. "I've got a plan—listen."

Just then, however, Van Wyck took out Mr. Ma's starting pistol.

If that was supposed to scare Fiona, it wouldn't. That thing fired only blanks.

But he didn't point the gun at her; instead, he aimed it into the air and—with the remaining three fingers on his hand—fired.

39

TWO AGAINST ONE

Team Dragon and Team Wolf sprinted toward Eliot and the rest of Team Scarab.

Eliot wasn't scared. He was ready to fight.

Robert had taught him how to stay cool and not burn through his adrenaline reserves when they'd sparred. He'd also learned when to move quick, strike, and finish an opponent before they knew what hit them.

The other teams spread out and slowed, making sure Team Scarab couldn't escape.

One worry: Eliot had learned to fight only one-on-one.

How did you protect yourself against *sixteen* enemies at once? Or protect everyone else on your side?

Especially Jezebel. She looked like she'd already been through one major battle today.

For all Eliot knew, that could be true. Had she crossed some battlefield in Hell just to get to Paxington for midterms? He wished she'd open up and tell him.

Too much thinking. They had to take the initiative—or lose it.

"Fiona?" he whispered. "What's the plan?"

She tore her gaze from the onrushing teams. She blinked, and her features screwed with intense concentration. "Right—the plan is to get to the jungle gym and our flag."

Robert whispered, "You're actually going to *play* this stupid game?"

"It be the only way," Jeremy told him. "End the match, and then there's no fighting allowed."

"*If* that'll stop Dragon and Wolf," Mitch countered.

"At least on the gym, we'll have some cover," Sarah said, panic creeping into her voice.

Amanda's hands were at her throat, too scared to add an opinion.

Fiona turned to Eliot. "Get us some cover to cross the field."

Eliot nodded. He understood what she asked of him.

He might hurt the others. Or worse. But Van Wyck was out for *their* blood. Eliot had to defend himself and his teammates . . . whatever that took.

"Leave them to me." His voice sounded hollow and cold and not his at all.

Eliot tapped his bow on Lady Dawn's strings, the opening of "The March of the Suicide Queen," and skipped a third of the way into the piece— where shrieking notes built to a crescendo: the entrance of the cannoneers.

He cast three shadows upon the grass, and through them wheeled forth cannon pushed by crews in mud-spattered blue uniforms with white bandoliers.[39]

Their appearance from nowhere stopped the charging Dragons and Wolves dead in their tracks.

Van Wyck, after only a heartbeat to assess the situation, shouted, "Scatter! Quick! Circle around!"

The cannoneers lit the fuses while they sang:

> *Keep the powder dry*
> *there's little more dire*
> *Watch your step, laddie*
> *lest your boots a'mire*
> *Stuff the wad with care*
> *load the grapeshot, squire*

---

39. At the Battle of Waterloo, the field was muddy, and recoil caused cannon to bury themselves after repeated firing. One British squad known as the "Roaring Devils" remained to prevent French infantry from advancing, firing, according to legend, until three cannoneer teams perished, drowning in the mud. They were never found, but occasionally over the years, cannoneers in muddy uniforms are seen wandering under full moonlight—firing artillery at unseen foes. *Gods of the First and Twenty-first Century, Volume 6, Modern Myths.* Zypheron Press Ltd., Eighth Edition.

Damn the devil back to hell
and let the cannons fire!

Flame and thunder belched from open metal maws.

A girl on Team Dragon motioned as a cannon ball arced toward her. The black iron blurred translucent and passed through her and into the earth.

Elsewhere, though, lawn exploded twice and cratered, and dirt showered into the sky.

Two on Team Wolf were blasted backwards—landed, bounced, and slowly crawled off . . . out of the fight for now.

Eliot worried how badly they were injured, but nonetheless played on.

His cannoneers tried in vain to reposition their artillery as the rest of Dragon and Wolf flanked them.

Well, Eliot could change tactics, too.

"Get ready to run," he whispered to his team.

Only now did he look at his teammates. They watched the other teams, arms raised defensively . . . except Sarah and Jeremy, who stared at Eliot, astonished and openmouthed.

It was almost worth it to see their faces.

Eliot sank back into his music and played "The Symphony of Existence"—the part where you died and some spirits wandered aimlessly in limbo, forever lost.

Cannons and crews faded to shadow.

The air thickened as veils of haze collected into tendrils and then condensed into impenetrable fog.

"I'll be right behind you," he told them.

"Go, go!" Fiona urged.

Eliot heard their padded footfalls over the grass.

He did his best to keep the fog from closing on them, but the music was elusive and slippery . . . and the air filled with glowing eyes, outstretched skeletal hands, curling ropes of vapor . . . and drifting bodies that moaned.

Eliot paused and looked up.

Lost in the pea-soup-thick fog, he heard Van Wyck cry out, "Make fire. Call the winds. Anything to get rid of this stuff! And watch out for ghosts!"

Several of his Wolf teammates called back, unafraid.

It was only a matter of time before they undid his efforts. Every one one of them had magic. Eliot had to escape while he had a chance.

He started toward the jungle gym—but stopped, seeing that behind him was Jezebel.

She stood still, head cocked as if trying to pinpoint every sound whirling about her: spirit and flesh.

She hadn't run with the others.

He took one step closer, hoping, his head spinning about one possibility. "You . . . you stayed?" he whispered. "For me?"

But the instant Eliot said it, he knew that was wrong.

Her eyes snapped open, jade green so intense, they seemed to smolder, and then her beautiful lips parted in a mocking smile.

"Young Prince Eliot Post," she said, "so like his father, ever the hopeful romantic." Her smile turned into a snarl.

Eliot's face burned. He'd thought she cared enough to stay with him, endangering herself to do so. How did she always do this to him? Make him think she liked him, when she . . . what? Hated him?

But Eliot also burned on the inside . . . from the attraction he felt for her even now. In the middle of a pitched battle, surrounded by death and students who wanted to kill him, Eliot wanted nothing more than to embrace and kiss her.

This feeling sang in his blood and called to something in her blood. Something on fire. Something that moved and pounded and pulsed in time to her pulse.

Something diabolical.

Jezebel's eyes widened. "Stop," she breathed. "Do not. You do not understand."

Eliot tried to heed her words, but found himself stepping closer. He could smell her cinnamon and vanilla perfume.

"Then explain," he demanded in a hushed voice.

"You feel my . . ." Her gaze dropped and she flushed. "I *do* care," she murmured. "But you feel my blood not because . . . because . . . of that, but because I give myself to the hate that burns within."

That stopped Eliot.

He blinked, indeed now feeling the screaming rage mixed with the passion swirling between them.

Eliot thought he understood. What he'd mistaken for an attraction . . . was not quite right. It *was* animalistic, primitive, and unstoppably building within her.

But it wasn't lust. It was *blood*lust.

"You're going to fight them," he said. "All of them."

"My injuries will only slow you. I choose to stand my ground."

"They'll tear you apart. I won't let you."

She laughed. "You *still* know nothing. I have been holding back. This seemed prudent, as Miss Westin and I had an agreement. But that pact was under normal circumstances . . . and this is very much *not* normal."

Eliot felt her heat intensify, pulsing in waves.

Jezebel's claws extended and fangs filled her mouth.

Mr. Ma had called it the "Infernal combat form."

He took an instinctive step back. "Don't do this," he said. "Please." He held out a hand, beckoning her to him.

"Run. Eliot," she said. "Run while you can." Jezebel's voice deepened and darkened and seemed to echo from within a great space. *"Run before my rage blinds me. Before I consume all the living flesh that dares corrupt my dreadful presence!"*

The air about her moved and charged with static. Her shadow spread outward in a black circle.

Jezebel's claws dripped venom that hissed as it burned the sod. The faint blue-green veins under her skin bulged and twisted, some sprouting free as vines that twined with budding orchids. Delicate horns curled from her head, and snow-white bat wings ripped through her T-shirt—all swelling and unfolding, until she was twice his height.

She continued to grow, and Eliot stepped back, trying to see . . . losing her in the fog, making out only a winged silhouette towering thirty feet over him.

This was really Jezebel, Protector of the Burning Orchards and Duchess of the Many-Colored Jungle of the Infernal Poppy Kingdoms—terrible and magnificent.

Eliot felt hate flood and burn through his blood.

Was this what she truly was? Some fallen angel so far removed from the girl he thought he'd known?

He sighed, realizing his hate wasn't for her. It would physically hurt Eliot to hate her. What she looked like didn't matter.

She was willing to sacrifice herself for them. Maybe it was a rage-filled Infernal motivation, but she was going to throw herself at their enemies— vanquish them or, in turn, be vanquished.

Eliot wanted to join her. That's why he felt the anger burn within. He wanted to be like his father, like her: Infernal, horrific, glorious—and destroy everything he touched.

ERIC NYLUND

Then reason returned and his blood chilled . . . and he was ordinary Eliot Post once more.

Team Dragon and Wolf were closing in.

Fiona and the others would need him.

He ran for the jungle gym.

40

GRUDGE MATCH

Eliot caught up to his teammates one story up on the jungle gym. They were on a landing and faced the balance beam bridge.

The beam was a single handsbreadth wide. There was no railing. Spiked steel balls swung over it, so to cross without getting your skull bashed in and then knocked off, you'd have to time it just right.

"Where's Jezebel?" Fiona asked. She looked concerned, confused, *and* relieved that Eliot was alone.

Eliot shook his head, unable to explain, still trying to cool his blood.

He didn't have to say anything, though. On the field, there was a thunderous roar and screams. Streaks of fire lit the fog, and a giant silhouetted shape moved.

"The Infernal combat form," Jeremy whispered in awe.

"She's buying us time," Robert said.

Fiona gazed into the murk and bit her lower lip. "Okay—we have to go *now*. No more debate."

Eliot looked away from his sister. Jezebel was strong, but she faced *two* teams. With her injuries, he wasn't sure she could stop them all . . . or even survive. He wished he had stayed with her.

"Let me go first." Sarah set a foot on the balance beam. "I'll clear the way."

Fiona frowned, but nodded and motioned her ahead.

Sarah pulled back her hair and tied into a knot. She walked onto the beam as graceful as a ballerina.

She approached the first deadly pendulum . . . took a deep breath, and then stepped *into* its path.

Eliot and Robert both involuntarily started toward her.

"No," Jeremy warned. "Donna break her concentration."

Sarah faced the spiked ball rushing toward her, one slender hand held to ward it off.

There was no way she'd stop it. The steel ball was as big as her head.

Her face was a mask of pure focus.

Inches before the ball struck Sarah—it burst into a cloud of confetti and fluttered to the ground in a thousand flashing colors.

"Bravo!" Jeremy cheered.

Of course. The Covingtons were conjurers, able to sometimes transmute one thing into another.

Sarah continued along the beam, confident now, pausing only to alter the deadly steel weights into more confetti, a splash of water, and a shower of tiny glittering garnets.

Robert, Fiona, and Mitch then crossed, using the now dangling lengths of chain for balance.

Amanda hesitated before the beam. Eliot thought she was going to chicken out, but she glanced back at him, turned, and stepped forward—not looking back.

Then Eliot went. It was like crossing the stone bridge from Uncle Henry's island to the Council's amphitheater. He moved without fear and found himself stepping onto a bamboo platform on the opposite side.

This new landing had ropes that ascended into the fog.

Jeremy was right behind him.

"Up!" Fiona told them—then she whirled around.

Donald van Wyck and four bruised members from Dragon and Wolf teams clambered onto the deck on the far side of the beam. They glared at Team Scarab across the distance.

Eliot looked behind his opponents to the field below.

The Infernal combat form of Jezebel took to the air, white bat wings beating in a vain attempt to fend off a pillar of fire on one side, a whirlwind on the other. Three students lay motionless on the ground, tangled in masses of flowering vines.

Eliot reached into his pack for his violin. He wouldn't stand by and just watch her be hurt.

Fiona clamped a hand on his shoulder. "No way," she whispered, and then as if knowing his thoughts, said, "The best way to help her now is to get to the flag. End the match."

Eliot tore his gaze from the battle and nodded.

A boy from Green Dragon with military-cropped hair ran across the beam.

"He's a Kaleb," Jeremy whispered. "Don't let him get close."

"I've got him." Fiona plucked the rubber band from her wrist. "Go!"

Eliot grabbed a rope and pulled himself up, hand over hand—a feat that a month ago would have been impossible. Robert was next to him on an adjacent strand. Mitch, Jeremy, and Sarah were behind them. Amanda struggled, but at least she was trying.

Fiona knelt and with one quick thrust severed the foot-thick balance beam.

The Kaleb boy and the timber fell into the fog.

Van Wyck pursed his lips and nodded to his teammates—one of whom vanished. The rest of them backed down. They'd have to find another way around.

Eliot climbed up onto the edge of straight runway. It was thirty feet long, five wide, and made of worn planks.

This gave him pause.

There was no trap to block their way . . . just a wide path that led to a wrought iron circular staircase.

At least there were no *obvious* obstacles.

Robert got up next, and together they helped the others climb.

Eliot and Robert, though, actually had to pull Amanda up. She clung to the rope stubbornly, her hair in her face but her mouth set in a grimace of determination.

Fiona joined them and marched forward.

"Wait. . . ." Mitch set a hand on her forearm. "It's too easy."

Eliot reached into his pack and strummed Lady Dawn.

The air along the path wavered. Spiderweb-fine wires appeared, resonating in sympathy with his violin.

These wires crisscrossed up and down and side to side, so it'd be impossible to pass. They were so thin, they'd have tripped over them—so razor sharp, they'd certainly have been sliced.

"What's Mr. Ma, trying to do to us?" Amanda set her hand to her throat.

"Apparently," Sarah replied, "amputate a few arms and legs."

Eliot wondered if Sarah was serious or just trying to scare poor Amanda.

"I'll cut them," Fiona said.

"You might not see them all," Eliot countered.

He withdrew Lady Dawn and plucked three crisp notes.

Every wire twanged in sympathetic vibrations—and each one snapped, under so much tension that as they broke the air "cracked."

Sarah hadn't been kidding about amputation. Whoever engineered this had upped the stakes of gym class.

Robert took a careful step forward. "All clear. Should be easy from here on—"

Van Wyck and six more students swung through the fog on ropes and landed before them, on the far side of the runway.

He grinned as he approached Team Scarab.

"Finally," Van Wyck said. "No more running. We settle this." He snorted. "Although contrary to my best efforts, it appears we are evenly matched."

"They just want a fight; they're not even trying to win," Fiona whispered. "The way to the flags is right behind them." She looked to Robert and Jeremy and told them, "So we three will give them their fight."

Then she glanced at Eliot, Amanda, Mitch, and Sarah. "And you guys get to the flag."

Eliot started to protest.

But Van Wyck and the others charged.

Robert rushed to meet them. Fiona was right behind him. Jeremy, however, hesitated, and slinked to the edge of the runway.

Robert leaped, hitting Van Wyck and two other boys. They all went down in a heap of arms and legs. Eliot caught a glint of brass held in Robert's hands as he punched one boy so hard, he broke the boards of the runway underneath.

Fiona skidded to a halt, both fists held out before her—her rubber band stretched between them.

Two girls and one boy stopped before her, confused, not knowing how to approach without getting cut.

Jeremy, meanwhile, touched the seasoned wood of the runway. The outer boards creaked and groaned and split away—the braces and supports beneath extending shakily outward along with them.

He turned and winked at them. Then, laughing, he jumped in the melee pile with Robert.

"Go!" Sarah urged. "He's made a way around."

Eliot jumped to the extended path. It was only a foot wide, and shuddered under his weight.

He held out his hands to Amanda (making sure he was braced).

She gulped, but jumped into his arms.

Mitch and Sarah leaped onto the boards as well, and they all ran past the fight.

A boy from Green Dragon pulled free of Jeremy's grasp, whirled, and jumped into Eliot's way.

The boy teetered, slightly off balance. He was twice Eliot's size.

Eliot made a fist . . . shifted his center of gravity lower and hammered his fist upward, using his leg muscles to add to the force.

He felt the bone in the boy's jaw crack.

The boy toppled, dazed, but managed to grab the edges of the board.

Eliot leaped over him and kept moving—

—until the entire jungle gym wrenched to the right.

Eliot dropped to all fours to keep from falling off.

Amanda toppled, but Eliot's hand shot out and grabbed her.

The combat form of Jezebel crashed into the structure, snapping platforms, chain link, and oak support beams. One snowy white bat wing was on fire; the other bent and broken. In either massive taloned hand wriggled a member of Team Wolf, screaming as if their souls were being ripped from their flesh.

Two other opponents clung to Jezebel's back. They blasted her with lightning, leaving craters of smoldering blackened flesh. Arcs of electricity played along her spine.

She stumbled, shattering the corner of the jungle gym to splinters.

The back part of the runway broke.

Eliot rocked forward. With one hand he gripped the plank; with the other he held on to Amanda, and they both stayed on.

Jezebel roared and tumbled to the ground.

Eliot felt his stomach fall with her. His fear and dread crystallized into raw determination, however. Eliot stood, pulling Amanda up with him. There was nothing he could do for Jezebel now except end this by winning.

He ran.

Sarah and Mitch followed his cue and they raced for the stairs.

Behind them, Van Wyck shouted, "Stop them. Quick, you fools!"

Eliot mounted the wrought iron staircase, circling up and around the spiral, practically dragging Amanda behind him.

He emerged on the top of the gym. Clouds raced alongside him. Hurricane winds whipped about and stung his eyes.

He spotted their flag—a fluttering black length and a flash of scarab gold.

Eliot ran for it . . . and with an outstretched hand, grabbed a fistful of silk.

So did Amanda. She shouted a primal victory scream.

Mitch and Sarah crashed into them, not bothering to slow down, grasping the flag as well.

A gunshot rang out.

The winds ceased.

The shuddering jungle gym stilled.

Van Wyck scrambled up the stairs and stopped. Rage colored his face as he saw them and realized that against all odds, Team Scarab had not only *survived* his cheating two-against-one grudge match . . . but they'd *won*.

41

EXPELLED

Fiona stood on the field of the Ludus Magnus with Team Scarab. She shifted nervously. This wasn't over yet.

Everyone on her team had made it . . . well, except Jezebel, who lay on a stretcher ten paces away, being treated by Mr. Ma.

The instant she'd seen Mr. Ma, Fiona suspected he had *let* Donald van Wyck do this. How else could a student engineer such a colossal two-against-one cheat in the middle of midterms with everyone watching?

Had Mr. Ma colluded in this scheme? Or had he just looked the other way? She'd probably never know.

One thing she was sure, though: Mr. Ma wouldn't have shed any tears if Team Scarab had lost.

It was strange looking at them. Mr. Ma was so dark and Jezebel so pale. He was old and wise . . . while Jezebel would likely be forever young and, just as likely, forever irresponsible.

She was a total mess, her chest and arms bandaged. Fiona didn't know why she hadn't been carried off in the ambulances with the other seriously injured players.

At least, to Fiona's relief, there'd been no casualties during this mismatch.

Mr. Ma helped Jezebel sit upright and whispered to her. She nodded while Mr. Ma shook his head. He then helped her stand, which she shakily managed, and then he escorted her to stand with the rest of Team Scarab.

"Bloody glorious work back there," Jeremy said to her.

"Yeah," Robert added, "uh, very nice."

Jezebel nodded to them, apparently too hurt even to come up with her normal condescending replies. She locked eyes with Eliot, but neither of them said a word to each other. Jezebel limped away from Eliot and stood next to Amanda.

Behind them was the jungle gym . . . well, what was left of it. The area had been cordoned off with yellow HAZARD tape. Half had been demolished in the match. Parts were on fire. A dozen workers in hard hats chainsawed and bulldozed over the rest because it had been declared unsafe by Mr. Ma.

She thought this ironic, since it'd been engineered to be "unsafe" in the first place.

At the far end of the field, Miss Westin spoke to Harlan Dells. The Headmistress had her back turned to the students. Mr. Dells faced them, however, his eagle eyes on every student. From his narrowed glare, it was clear how displeased he was.

Miss Westin turned and strode toward them.

Fiona tensed and felt like she might be sick.

The other students being treated for minor cuts, burns, and broken bones also got to their feet and quickly shuffled toward their teams.

Teams Dragon and Wolf stood facing Team Scarab.

Green Dragon was down two members. They stood stoic with eyes fixed straight ahead.

Team Wolf was down three members, and Donald van Wyck's head hung low.

"Breaking rules at Paxington is never tolerated," Miss Westin said as she walked between the teams. Her words were like stones dropped from a great height; each felt like it thudded into Fiona's stomach.

Miss Westin glanced at the carnage behind them, and then turned to scrutinize them, taking her time, allowing her silence to smother their thoughts. She inhaled a deep breath, seeming to decide something, and let out a great sigh.

This struck Fiona as odd because she'd never seen Miss Westin sighing . . . and now that she thought about it, she wasn't sure she'd ever seen her breathing.

"But before we talk of rules . . . and punishment," Miss Westin continued, and nodded to Mr. Ma as he joined her, "Mr. Ma and I have discussed this so-called midterm match and have come to a decision."

Fiona stood taller, proud that Team Scarab had not only survived two-to-one odds, but won.

"I declare this match invalid," Mr. Ma said.

"What? . . ." Fiona whispered, her high spirits deflating.

"No supervisors," Miss Westin said. "An inappropriate match." She cast a haughty glance at Jezebel. "Illegal metamorphosis."

Jezebel tilted her head in defiance.

"But," Fiona countered, ". . . that's not fair."

Miss Westin wheeled toward her. "Fair? Life is not fair, Miss Post. Ever. Not for mortals or young goddesses. Be thankful you learn this lesson when the stakes were merely your team's rank and their lives."

This sounded like something Audrey would say. *Merely our lives at stake?* What more could be at stake?

Fiona wanted to shrink back, but she fought the impulse and remained standing tall. What she really wanted to do was give Miss Westin a piece of her mind. And yet Fiona sensed something important in the Head-mistress's words . . . so she kept her mouth clamped tight.

A slight smile rippled over Miss Westin's pale lips as she watched Fiona's internal struggle. And then, seeing her student hold her temper, the Headmistress nodded.

"Team Scarab," Miss Westin continued, "for their valiant efforts, however, will be given a 'non-grade' for the match. Their midterm grade will be based wholly on their *individual* accomplishments in the Midterm Maze . . . which I note are miraculously identical scores of A-minus."

Fiona took that in, stunned, but quickly recovered.

Okay, so they wouldn't get the win, but it wouldn't count against them, either, in gym. She could live with that. Still, that left Scarab in a precarious position of having one win, one loss, and a draw.

It was, however, nice that they'd gotten an A on their midterm. Eliot had really pulled off a miracle in the maze, and yet, it irked her that it was an A–. What was the *minus* for?

She knew better, though, than to let out even a squeak of a complaint in front of Miss Westin.

Fiona shot a quick warning glance to the rest of her teammates—especially bigmouthed Jeremy Covington.

Miss Westin turned to face the other students. "Team Dragon."

The Dragons stood at full attention.

"You were slated to compete against Team Scarab," Miss Westin said. "I accept that you were led astray by unscrupulous influences, so we shall record the loss of this match on your gym record."

The Green Dragon students stiffened as if struck.

The huge boy who was the Green Dragon Team Captain ran a hand over his crew cut and answered, "Yes, ma'am. Thank you."

Miss Westin then strode to Team Wolf, slowly pacing before them.

They looked as if they were about to be executed, shuffling feet, the color draining from their faces; one girl looked as if she were hyperventilating.

"Team Wolf," Miss Westin said. "We shall also mark you down as a loss for this match." She halted before Donald van Wyck.

He looked up, but reluctantly, as if he had no choice in the matter, and whispered, "May I speak, Headmistress?"

"No. I have spoken to your family," Miss Westin told him. "They lobbied quite vigorously on your behalf, but you sealed your fate when you diverted Mr. Ma's attention and arranged this demonstration of your 'superiority.' Pride, arrogance, and underestimating a worthy opponent—these are among your many failings."

Van Wyck remained standing, but his shoulders slumped.

If Fiona hadn't hated him so much, she would have felt some pity.

"These personality traits we might have addressed and corrected here at Paxington, given enough time," Miss Westin continued. "But broken rules? *That* I will not abide."

She turned her back to him.

"You are hereby *expelled*."

Donald van Wyck looked up, eyes wide. He tried to speak, but nothing came out. He glanced helpless to his teammates, but none of them would look his way.

Harlan Dells moved to his side and set one massive hand on his shoulder.

Van Wyck looked at Fiona, eyes pleading.

Maybe she should say something.

No—he'd tried to kill her, Eliot, and everyone on her team. Fiona's glare sharpened. He was getting off easy.

Miss Westin nodded to Mr. Dells, and the Gatekeeper marched him off the field.

Fiona watched until they vanished into the tunnel.

Miss Westin withdrew her tiny black book and made a note within.

"There," she said. "I believe that ends this matter. Students, you are dismissed."

The Dragons and Wolves skulked off the field.

As they left, Jeremy whooped and danced a celebratory jig. He hugged his cousin Sarah.

Robert and Mitch exchanged a more reserved high five.

Fiona should have felt like celebrating, too. Instead, she was wary, as if something else bad were about to happen.

Eliot stepped next to her and whispered, "I wonder if we'll see him again." He gazed at the dark tunnel through which Donald van Wyck had left.

"I don't know," she said. "I hope not."

Had they won today? Or made an enemy for life? Or with his Van Wyck necromancy . . . had they made an enemy for eternity?

Fiona's attention turned as she saw timid Amanda Lane approach Jezebel, working up the courage to speak.

Fiona marched over to them and heard Jezebel reply, "I need no mortal's assistance."

The Infernal glared at Amanda, who took a step back.

Jezebel glanced at Fiona, and in a less threatening tone, said, "No help. Thank you." She picked up an abandoned Paxington blazer off the grass and snugged it about her shoulders—wincing. A dot of blood seeped through.

"There is only one place that can help me," Jezebel murmured. "Home." She limped off the field.

Robert and Mitch joined Fiona and Amanda, and they watched her stalk off.

"Is she going be okay?" Robert whispered.

"I don't know," Fiona said. "But I know there's nothing we can do for her—not when she's so . . . I don't know what she is."

Mitch shook his head as he watched Jezebel leave. "Don't let her get to you. We did good today."

Fiona felt a twinge of irrational anger toward the Infernal. She wasn't sure why. Jezebel had made it possible for them to win the match. Maybe even saved all their lives by nearly throwing hers away. And yet . . . something was so wrong about her.

Fiona turned to ask Eliot if he had a clue.

But Eliot was nowhere on the field.

42

CONSEQUENCES BE DAMNED

Eliot tried not to think about what he was doing . . . but that wasn't his best thing.

Getting into trouble, Fiona would say would've been his best thing.

Rescuing the damsel in distress, Robert might tell him.

Or perhaps as Louis would declare, *Rushing in where angels fear* . . .

But this was none of those things. Eliot followed Jezebel because he had to. Something inside him pulled him along the sidewalk, a magnetic force he was helpless to resist—but something also repelled him from her and held him back from rushing to her side and wrapping his arms about her broken body.

Jezebel walked ahead of him half a block. She had someone's oversized Paxington jacket on. She half stepped, half stumbled along, and then paused to lean against a building.

Other people didn't notice. Tourists with Chinatown maps, a bunch of older women complaining about the President, and a policeman on bicycle—none of them offered to help or even ask if she was okay.

Of course, if they had tried, Jezebel, the Protector of the Burning Orchards and Handmaiden to the Mistress of Pain, might have torn their throats out . . . so it was probably some primitive human instinct for self-preservation that made them shy away.

Self-preservation instincts that apparently Eliot lacked, because he had slipped out of the Ludus Magnus when he overheard Amanda and Fiona talking to Jezebel, and her adamant refusal for help.

He knew she'd never let anyone help her. Just as Eliot knew that she desperately *needed* help.

Eliot was determined to make sure she was okay. Even if that meant sneaking out ahead of her, lurking in the shadows, and then following her like some creepy stalker.

Although he wasn't sure what he was going to do. Make sure she got home okay, he guessed—make sure she got there without bleeding to death in some gutter along the way.

Why was she *so* stubborn?

She trudged ahead, south one block down Webster Street, east one block along Golden Gate Avenue, and then zigging back south. If she kept going, they'd end up in the Mission District.

The sun broke through the fog and painted the streets with lines of light and shade.

Eliot drifted into the shadows to stay unnoticed.

Jezebel mirrored his steps, clinging to the darkness.

Eliot let her get a bit ahead as he waited to cross busy Van Ness Avenue, and then hurried just as the stoplight changed.

As he set one foot into the street, however, it felt as if he plunged into warm running water. It didn't slow him as normal water would, but it felt very different from the space he'd been in.

As he crossed back onto the sidewalk, the sensation vanished.

Eliot stopped and looked around, perplexed.

Then he spotted the difference: The crosswalk was in sunlight . . . and he stood once more in the shadows.

Although the fog softened everything, the edge where light met dark was razor sharp to his eyes.

Everyone on the sidewalk went out of their way to step around the shadows, like they were too cold. None of them looked at Eliot either as he stood in the shade. They strode past him, ignoring him as they did Jezebel.

Eliot stepped into the path of a girl walking a Yorkshire terrier.

The tiny dog's head snapped up and it barked, startled, at Eliot. It hadn't seen him.

Eliot had an urge to kick the miniature canine. He didn't like dogs.

"Sorry," Eliot whispered.

The girl smiled and moved on, jerking the dog along—not really wanting to interact with him, but at least *seeing* him.

Eliot slinked back into the shadows.

Weird.

He could live with weird, though; he had for a while. And today he preferred to be in the shade. To be unremarkable. Invisible almost.

He followed Jezebel like that for another block, keeping to the dark, and then they turned onto Hyde Street.

She was headed downtown. Buildings towered over them and the sidewalk was red brick. The people here had to enter the shadows (or end up walking in the street), and as they did, they shuddered, pulled up their collars, and sped along to the next patch of sunlight.

The only exception was a velvet black cat that sat on a trash can, watching Jezebel, him, and then its amber eyes locked back on to her—crossing in front of, and almost tripping, her.

Jezebel hissed at it.

The animal hissed back and scampered across the busy street—ignoring traffic—making it to the opposite side.[40]

Jezebel watched it go, then walked fast, turning onto Market Street ahead of him.

Eliot followed, but Jezebel was gone.

There was a bus stop, but there were people still waiting. There was a theater she could have ducked into. And just in front of it, stairs that angled under the street: A BART station.

That had to be it.

He hurried down the steps into a vast open space well lit with flickering fluorescents. There were token vendors, automated turnstiles, bike racks, and information kiosks directing people to all the places the Bay Area Rapid Transit system could take them.

It was deserted.

There were three escalators to the next level. One had an OUT OF ORDER sign and yellow warning tape draped across it. The tape dangled, torn.

Eliot went to it and saw the escalator was still. It was dark down there.

He took a deep breath—not quite sure he was doing anything remotely

---

40. Black cats have historically been associated with witchcraft, luck (both good and bad) and/or evil, and hundreds of other superstitions. A black cat crossing one's path is almost universally considered bad luck, however. Black cats were also believed to be shape-shifters—witches transformed, traveling incognito, and doing evil. *Gods of the First and Twenty-first Century, Volume 5, Core Myths (Part 2)*. Zypheron Press Ltd., Eighth Edition.

smart, but knowing he couldn't stop now. He crept down the motionless escalator. The edges looked disturbingly like metal teeth.

He emerged onto a wide hallway. Only every fifth fluorescent light overhead was lit.

Eliot's eyes adjusted to the gloom. A yellow stripe divided the white tiles where people were supposed to wait well away from the sunken tracks of the BART train.

As above, there was no one here on this level. No train, either.

And still no Jezebel.

Had he made a mistake and lost her? Jezebel could have spotted him and broken that tape on the escalator to throw him off her trail.

A single black dot caught his attention. It was tiny, but obvious on the white tile. It called to him, sounded like a perfect note plunked in his mind.

He glanced once more down the platform and then crept to the spot.

Eliot reached out and touched it. The spot was liquid, tarlike—half-congealed. It smelled of vanilla and cinnamon and rust.

Blood. *Her* blood.

She *had* been here.

The question was, where had she gone?

She hadn't been so far ahead of him that a train could have come, picked her up, and left without him hearing.

He spied another drop of blood. This one was by the tracks.

His gaze continued, and he spotted a third drop on the far side of the train tracks . . . right under a shadow. The shadow looked just like the dozen others on the far side of the train tracks . . . only it fell *directly* under one of the fluorescent lights overhead.

Eliot moved to look at it from another angle.

It looked like any other shadow, translucent, and flickering with the same frequency as the lights. Only there was nothing between it and the light to cast it.

This shadow fell directly between two concrete squares, and as Eliot turned his head back and forth, he caught a glimpse of more: a darkness that stretched beyond the flat plane of the wall.

A doorway.

If that's where Jezebel went, he'd follow. Maybe she was hurt and had crawled in there to rest or hide from more of those things that had jumped them in the alley outside Paxington. Or maybe she had gone in there like some wounded animal to die.

Eliot held his breath and listened for any rumble that might indicate a train. He heard only his heart thudding.

With extreme care, he crept past the yellow safety line. Eliot then eased over the edge onto the channel with the train tracks.

He swallowed and gingerly stepped across the electrified third rail—pressed himself against the cool concrete by the fake shadow.

If a BART train came by now, he'd get pasted.

Eliot inched to the shadow. So close, it was easy to see how it extruded deeper into the wall, a passage that sloped at a steep angle. There were stairs and handrails. He twisted closer to looked straight into it; there was a flicker of amber light at the end . . . a very long way down.

He hesitated on the threshold.

Some part of him screamed that if he went down there, he wasn't coming back. Ever.

As surely as he knew this could be a one-way trip, though, he also knew Jezebel needed him. Like every daydream he'd ever had: The hero charged in to save his lady in peril, no matter what.

More realistically . . . he knew Jezebel—or more accurately, the part of her that was still Julie Marks—was the key to unraveling the Infernal plots circling about him. She still cared for him. She was still his friend . . . and possibly, hopefully, more.

He pushed into the darkness.

Eliot reached and pulled his pack around. He undid the top flap and opened Lady Dawn's case. He wanted her handy. When things got this weird, they usually got dangerous, too.

He moved down the stairs.

As he neared the bottom, Eliot smelled moisture and brimstone and mold. He saw red and gleaming gold.

There was a rumble in the distance and a train's whistle—that wasn't a single shrill note, but rather a collection of tortured human screams. It got louder. It cut through him and twisted his insides. Eliot wanted to clap his hands over his ears and curl into a ball.

But he'd heard this noise before. In Kino's Borderlands . . . at the Gates of Perdition.

His father's words came back to him: *"We are monarchs of the domains of Hell, the benevolent kings and queens over the countless souls who are drawn there to worship us."*

Countless souls.

Knowing what the sound might be, though, didn't make it any less horrific, but Eliot was able to set it aside in his mind. He could be scared *and* keep moving forward.

He got to the foot of the steep stairs and peeked around the corner.

A room stretched as far as he could see, another train station, but not like upstairs. This place looked like it was from the late nineteenth century. Red and gold tiles covered the floor and had a million cracks, as if the place had survived the Great San Francisco Earthquake of 1906 . . . or maybe it hadn't and had sunk down here. Columns of carved teak and inlaid ivory stood like a dead forest. There were stained glass windows (bricked up on the other side) and tarnished silver candelabras set out here and there, flickering with smoking candles.

The screams grew to a crescendo, and bright light flashed from within a tunnel and filled one end of the station, illuminating a crisscross of train tracks.

Billows of steam blasted forth, and a train engine appeared, chugging, wheels screeching to a long agonizing halt.

The main cylinder of the engine glowed red. Black smoke billowed from twin stacks. Three coal cars were pulled behind this, and after them were passenger cars with rich wood paneling and gilt scrollwork that curled about picture windows. Red velvet curtains framed those windows and hid the interiors.

Eliot squinted at the first passenger car and saw lettering in ornate silver cursive: *Der Nachtzug, Limited*.[41]

With one last massive sigh, the engine came to a full stop and the tortured voices fell silent.

Jezebel stepped out from behind one of the columns. She'd been waiting there for the train. She staggered and barely made it to the first passenger car. She hung her head and leaned against it.

An old porter emerged. He bowed before Jezebel and then set down a tiny step. He took her hand and gently helped her up and onto the train.

Jezebel had said there was only one place where she could get help for her injuries: home. Eliot hadn't taken her literally when she said that. He thought she'd head to an apartment in the city.

. . . Not actually return to Hell.

---

41. "The Night Train," translated from German. —Editor.

The old porter glanced about the station, looking for other passengers.

Eliot ducked back into the stairwell.

Now what?

Three options occurred to him.

Eliot could let her go. Jezebel had to know what she was doing. But hadn't she said her clan was fighting a war? He had a feeling she was headed into even greater danger.

The second option was to talk to her, try to get her to stay. There had to be someone here who could help her.

Of course, that would involve Eliot actually speaking to her and her responding in a rational manner. That never seemed to happen. Whenever they interacted, it seemed to be charged with emotion . . . and anger.

That left the last option: Go with her and help her.

That thought turned to ice inside Eliot.

Go to Hell *on purpose*?

The locomotive hissed. Its wheels squealed to a slow start and sparked along the tracks.

Louis had said Sealiah was Jezebel's mistress . . . and that she was Queen of the Poppy Lands of Hell. Poppy Lands. Eliot wasn't sure he liked the sound of that.

He decided not and turned back.

At the top of the staircase, light and shadows flashed: A BART train had entered the normal human station.

Normal. Human. A world he was feeling more and more apart from.

Besides, hadn't he *really* decided when he ventured down here? To find out more about the Infernals and their plans? Wasn't he committed to helping Jezebel? That was the right thing to do—no matter where it took him.

Eliot ran back.

The train picked up speed, cars accelerating past his view.

He ducked his head and sprinted after the last car as it raced toward the tunnel.

His hand caught the railing—he leaped—swung himself up and onto the swaying floor.

There. He'd done it.

Now he really was a hero rushing to the aid of his lady . . . the consequences be damned. Maybe, this time, literally.

43

A MATCH

Fiona and the others walked through the deserted corridors of Paxington. It was eerie. They were the only ones there. Everyone else must still be taking midterms.

She felt like she'd been through war, and couldn't even imagine what *finals* would be like.

Her footsteps echoed on the flagstones. The lords and ladies, gods and angels painted on the nearby murals seemed to disapprove of her for making so much noise.

"I thought it was great," Amanda whispered, breaking the spell of silence. "We creamed them." She smiled, but it was short-lived.

Sarah rolled her eyes.

"She's right," Mitch said. "We should be celebrating, not moping around like we've been to a funeral."

"Could we at least make that a wake?" Jeremy asked, perking up.

Fiona tried to smile, but couldn't manage it.

Why not? There *was* cause to celebrate. They'd all gotten As (well, okay, A–s) on their midterms. They'd done it as a team, too—not giving in to the prevalent "win at any cost" attitude of Paxington.

What was dragging her down?

She glanced over her shoulder: Robert lagged behind.

He glanced at her for a fraction of a second—their eyes locked—then he looked away, shifted his backpack, and rummaged through it . . . falling farther behind the group.

Only Robert never fell behind. Was this a magnanimous gesture? Acknowledgment that he knew Fiona and he couldn't be around each other?

"Hey." Mitch gently jostled her elbow. "I thought maybe I could use that rain check and have our coffee date now?"

Fiona blinked, not understanding.

Then she remembered that after the field trip to Ultima Thule, she and Mitch had been going for coffee—before they got seriously distracted rescuing Eliot in that "side" alley from an army of shadow creatures.

How typical was that?

And Fiona also recalled that Mitch had called it a coffee date then, too.

Was the emphasis on the *coffee*—as in two students going to grab something to drink and go over homework? Or was the emphasis on the *date*? As in a boy-and-girl type thing? (And still technically forbidden by Audrey's Rule 106.)

"I don't know," Fiona whispered. "After everything that happened this morning, maybe we should lie low for a while."

"If you never let yourself have any fun," Mitch teased, "you're going to end up as dried out as Miss Westin."

He grinned. Fiona could never resist it and found herself smiling, too.

Besides, she'd never heard *anyone* make fun of Miss Westin. She half expected the Headmistress to appear, standing behind them all this time—glaring right through them like they didn't exist.

But Miss Westin wasn't there.

And Mitch's smile could have lit a pitch-black room.

"Okay," she said, ducking her head in a half nod. "Coffee it is."

She was careful not to say this was a coffee *date* . . . not yet anyway.

Jeremy angled toward them. "Aye, coffee with a wee nip o' whiskey would hit the—"

Sarah and Amanda stepped in front of him, Sarah elbowing him in the ribs as the two of them jostled Jeremy back from Mitch and Fiona.

Sarah quickly whispered to her cousin.

Jeremy shrugged, then gave a conspiratorial nod to Mitch.

"We're heading to the library," Sarah said, a little too loud. "Must return a few books."

She and Amanda pushed Jeremy. Fiona heard him muttering: "The library? Gods! Couldn't you think up a better excuse?"

Fiona would have to thank Amanda and Sarah later. The last person she wanted tagging along was Jeremy Covington.

And Robert? She glanced back over shoulder.

Robert was gone.

She and Mitch crossed the silent campus, seeing only a few older students, who looked more harried than they did. Fiona didn't want to think about what senior midterms were like.

Harlan Dells waited for them at the front gate as if he had never left his post. He nodded to Mitch and gave a tiny bow to Fiona.

"Congratulations," he said as calmly as if they had just taken an ordinary paper-and-pencil test. "A-minus. Most impressive." He added with a chuckle, "Mr. Ma will spend all week rebuilding his pet monstrosity obstacle course. I believe he is quite . . . cross."

Fiona wasn't sure what to say. "Uh, thanks," she tried.

Mr. Dells's laserlike gaze flickered over her head and then returned, his expression cooling a bit.

"You two have a wonderful time." He opened the gate for them.

Fiona turned toward the direction he'd looked. In the shade of a cedar tree along the path to Bristlecone Hall sulked the unmistakable silhouette of Robert Farmington.

Mitch saw, too. "Did you want to ask him to join us?" His tone was polite, but he managed to say it such that it was clear he was *only* being polite.

She couldn't believe it. Robert following them? Was he jealous? Spying on them? Fiona thought they were getting over this.

She wandered through the gate and into the alley. "He's *not* joining us," she said, clenching her jaw.

Fiona tried to smother her mounting anger. She didn't want to show that side of herself to Mitch.

She couldn't stop Robert from watching her. He was quick, and all Drivers were trained to track by the League. He'd be there in the shadows while she and Mitch sat and sipped coffee at the Café Eridanus.

He was going to ruin it for them.

"It'll be fine," she said.

Mitch read her expression and glanced back at Robert. His smile reappeared. "We can do much better than 'fine' today." He held out his hand. "Trust me."

Fiona forgot her anger, suddenly curious but also wary. Her hand hesitated halfway toward him. "What are you going to do?"

"Give us a little space," he replied. "It doesn't always work—only when things are perfect . . . and only if I'm with the right person."

He stared deep into her eyes and took her hand.

Mitch's skin was soft and warm, but there was an underlying strength, as well. He pulled her gently along, three steps down the alley and around the corner—only it should've taken more than three steps to get there—and they turned onto the sidewalk.

There was the sensation of extra motion, like when you step on an escalator or moving sidewalk—then a sudden halt.

She stumbled. Mitch steadied her.

Fiona blinked. They weren't near Presidio Park as they ought to be. They were still on a sidewalk, but the road now twisted and turned, switch-backing down a steep hill among picture-perfect gardens and houses.

This was Lombard Street . . .

. . . which was halfway across the city.

"How'd—?"

Mitch held up her hand, still twined within his. "Magic," he whispered. "A gift a few in my family have . . . which seems to be working much better with you along. At heart, I guess, I'm nothing but a show-off."[42]

Fiona grinned, not completely understanding, but nonetheless thrilled at what had just happened.

It was more than just moving miles in a single step. And it was more than holding hands with Mitch (although that was nice). It was that she'd left Paxington and all the stress and worries behind. Not just physically . . . but in her head, too.

Apparently, the universe had other plans: A counterbalance to her rare moments of happiness . . . because a few blocks away, she heard the rumble of an all-too-familiar Harley Davidson racing toward them (a motorcycle crafted by Uncle Henry to go faster than the speed of sound).

Mitch cocked his head, also hearing. "Robert hasn't given up."

"In more ways than one," she muttered to herself.

---

42. Although translocation (aka teleportation: an object moving instantaneously across a distance while not crossing the intervening space) has been attempted and pretended by mystics and stage magicians for millennia, there are no documented accounts of the phenomenon ever occurring among mortals. The infamous Dr. Faustus (Johan Georg Faust) did appear in two places at once, but it is hypothesized that he was cloned or doubled (with the aid of his Infernal sponsor, Mephistopheles) and did not translocate. The ability is also unknown among Immortals (although some have mastered the trick of *bending* space to travel across the world in astonishingly short times). True and instantaneous translocation, as yet, seems to be the sole purview of select gifted Infernal clans. *Gods of the First and Twenty-first Century, Volume 13, Infernal Forces.* Zypheron Press Ltd., Eighth Edition.

Mitch tugged on her arm. "Want to try again?"

"Can we?" Fiona replied.

Mitch gestured ahead, and they strolled together down stairs, past pots of Christmas poinsettias and ferns. His forehead creased with concentration as they crossed into shadow—

—and turned. The sun was brighter and higher overhead. The sidewalk was now paved with pink bricks, and on her right was a wide canal filled with sailboats. There were bridges and hotels and restaurants everywhere.

"We're in Texas," Mitch explained, exhaling as if he had just lifted a great weight. "Would you care to find someplace to sit?"

She squeezed his hand. "Let's go farther."

Mitch considered her a moment, his grin widened, and he squeezed her hand back. "Very well. Let's tempt fate."

He gripped her hand harder, as if he was afraid she'd slip free. Maybe there was some chance that this was dangerous—that if he let go, Fiona might land someplace between steps. Or maybe he just wanted to hold her.

She gripped his hand just as tight.

She wasn't afraid . . . although her blood pounded . . . and it wasn't her all-too-familiar anger, either. This was excitement and elation, and maybe a dash of infatuation.

Fiona leaned in closer to him as they turned into the shadows, stepped—

—through darkness for a moment, so cold and empty, she found it hard to breathe. Like she'd frozen solid. But then they stepped out—

—and the light had dimmed and turned gray. Skyscrapers reached for the clouds; there were six lanes of patched asphalt filled with cars on her right. People were everywhere, none of them looking their way.

Mitch seemed perfectly at ease, knowing exactly where he was and where he wanted to go. He kept her hand in his and led her around the corner, where she spotted a piece of sidewalk art: large red three-dimensional letters, *L* and *O* balanced atop a *V* and *E*.

"Is this Manhattan?" she whispered.

He nodded and pulled her to a hot dog vendor on the corner.

"You take yours with mustard?" Mitch asked, fishing out his wallet. "Or relish? Or plain?"

Fiona finally had to let go of his hand.

"Mustard, please," she replied, eyeing the hot dogs suspiciously as the vendor pulled them out of a steam cabinet. Cee didn't let this kind of "preprocessed poison" into her kitchen.

ERIC NYLUND

Mitch paid for two dogs with mustard and two lemonades.

To be polite, she took a bite of the thing.

It was delicious.

She took three more bites, then felt full. That had to be the continuing side effect of her severed appetite.

"Another?" Mitch asked, giving her a paper napkin.

She dabbed her mustard-smeared mouth. "No, thanks. This is good for now."

Mitch offered his hand. "Let's see Central Park, then."

Fiona took it and they strolled down the Avenue of the Americas.

"You've never said anything about . . . ," Fiona started to say. "I mean, ever since Jezebel told everyone . . ." She stopped, remembering there were rules about her talking about her League side of the family in public.

"Ever since she told everyone about your mother? Atropos?" Mitch shrugged, but offered no further comment.

Suspicion gnawed at Fiona. Had Mitch insisted on their coffee date to-day because of her new social status? Like everyone else, was he attracted to the League's power?

"It's just that everyone treats me differently."

He laughed softly. "Oh, your paparazzi?"

"They're not fans, so much," she countered. "They just hang around and ask about my relatives."

Mitch made a noncommittal murmur.

She wasn't getting anywhere with this. Mitch was either being evasive or dense, or, astonishingly, he really didn't care about her League connections.

Fiona just had to know—so she blurted out, "Doesn't it make a differ-ence to you who my family is?"

Ahead were the trees and rolling lawns in Central Park. There was a huge dog show in progress: hundreds of people and just as many yelping canines.

"Ugh," Mitch said. "Not exactly what I was hoping for." He gripped her hand and tugged her toward a shadow. They crossed the plane of darkness—

—and this time, when they stepped out it was dark . . . but a normal nighttime dark.

As her eyes adjusted, she saw they stood upon wide flat stones. On the horizon were the crisscrossing silhouettes of spires and columns and the broken spans of once mighty bridges. Farther, there was a jagged outline of a pyramid. Wind whipped through this place, crying like a wounded animal. It chilled her.

"The Gobi Desert," Mitch whispered. "This city has never been found by any archaeologist. It was here before the Xia Dynasty. Been buried and uncovered by desert sands countless times."

"It's so dark," Fiona whispered back. "I wish I could see."

"Dark is why I brought you here."

Mitch gestured over their heads.

It was a moonless night, and more stars filled the sky than Fiona had ever dreamed possible. The band of the Milky Way dazzled her with colors she'd never seen at night.

"Miss Westin talks about the Middle Realms," Mitch said. "How great they are. But I think this world has wonders to match anything out there . . . especially with the right person."

Fiona got dizzy looking straight up in the dark, and she leaned against Mitch almost without thinking about it . . . as if this was the most natural thing in the world for her to do.

He pulled her slightly closer to him. "I don't care," he whispered.

Mitch was warm, and shielded her against the cold night air.

"Don't care about what?" she asked.

"Your family," he murmured. "You asked before if it made a difference to me. You're probably wondering if that's the reason I wanted to go out with you." Mitch was so close, she felt his breath rush along her neck. "It's not."

Fiona's heart pounded and she found it impossible to concentrate on the stars. "Why, then?"

He hesitated. She felt his heart beating, just as fast, next to hers.

"It was that first day," he said, "at the placement exams. When I saw you . . . I knew."

Fiona shook her head, not understanding.

"My family's magic lets us look at people, and sometimes we get a glimpse of what's inside—a person's soul—if you believe in that sort of thing."

Fiona became very still, remembering that first day, how scared she been, but resolute to do her best.

"What did you see?" she asked.

"A right person," he whispered, ". . . for me."

She knew what he was talking about, because she'd been thinking the same thing: She and Mitch fit together. Two puzzle pieces, ones she'd thought were different shapes and colors, and never in a million years supposed to be put together, but when she'd turned them this way and that, suddenly they aligned, and she realized they were *supposed* to be together all this time.

Mitch leaned back against a wall, and his hand found hers.

Fiona snuggled up against him, warmed by his body, not wanting to be anyplace else in the entire universe at that moment.

They held each other and watched the stars until the sky warmed in the east.

44

INFILTRATION

The Night Train entered the tunnel. The chugging screams from the engine echoed undiminished. Standing on the rear platform, Eliot choked on the brimstone-laden smoke that swirled in the train's wake.

He cupped his hand to see through the window into the last train car.

The gas lamps on the wall were turned down to flickers, but there was enough light to see no one else was inside. Perfect.

He entered the car and eased the door shut.

It smelled of rose water and cigar smoke. It was quiet, too; the only suggestion of the train's thunderous passage were faint clacks under his feet.

Eliot fumbled for the valve on the lights and turned them up.

There were tables with green felt tops and trays of poker chips. Black velvet wallpaper covered the walls, and intricate mahogany curls framed a fresco on the ceiling: a cloud-fringed view of Heaven . . . with an exodus of angels leaving their friends behind. Many angels left behind wept or beckoned to those leaving, but the departing ones had their backs turned to them in disgusted indignation.[43]

Eliot swallowed, looking for his father in the painting.

---

43. Flocks of creatures are often designated by a special words, e.g., a "murder" of crows or a "pod" of whales. Groups of Infernals (fallen angels) are called an "exodus" of angels (or Infernals). Although this grammatical designation has entered the vernacular, it remains controversial and contested by the Catholic Church for two reasons: first, Infernals almost never group (making the term largely hypothetical); and second, it suggests that the "fallen" angels' exit from Heaven may not have been the result of an expulsion after losing a war, but instead, a *voluntary* departure. —Editor.

Something else caught his attention, though: in the train car ahead—the lights brightened.

Eliot turned down the lights and retreated to the back door. He slipped onto the rear platform, holding his breath.

Outside, the train continued to screech through the dark of the tunnel, but there were things in the darkness answering that screeching now.

Eliot reluctantly closed the door and crouched to hide.

The lights in the last car turned up again, and Eliot saw it was the same old man who'd helped Jezebel board. The man was bent with age. He had a black cap and uniform with gold braids on the shoulders. He wore white gloves, and on his belt was a tiny brass clockwork mechanism.

Eliot had misjudged the size of the man. He was not hunched over from age, but because his head would otherwise have bumped the ceiling.

The man cast about, mumbling. He sniffed the air, looked behind a table, then turned—only just remembering to turn down the lights as he left.

Eliot exhaled with relief (and because he was running out of air). He waited until the lights in the second and third cars also dimmed, and then he crept back inside.

That had been close.

Eliot collapsed into an upholstered chair at a poker table.

He had to find Jezebel and talk to her. Or should he keep following her and learn more before he made his move? In truth, he hadn't thought that far ahead.

He should have. But when it came to Jezebel, he was finding it harder to think and too easy to let his emotions drive him.

That's the way it'd been with his music . . . all passion in the beginning. He reached into his pack and reassuringly touched Lady Dawn. Only now did he have even a little control. And how many people had he hurt in the process of learning that? How many times had he almost been killed?

It wasn't a fair comparison, though. Lady Dawn, despite her namesake, wasn't a real girl.

Then again, technically, neither was Jezebel anymore.

His eyes fell upon the poker chips on the table. They gleamed with inset rubies, sapphires, and diamonds. There were plastic-wrapped decks of cards, too. And there were dice—dozens of pairs of dice: ivory, some clear red plastic, others black iron.

He unthinkingly reached for them. He could let chance decide what he should do next. . . .

The door to the rear platform opened—slammed shut.

Eliot jumped up and turned.

The old man in uniform stood behind him, his arms crossed over his chest. "Ticket, young man?" he demanded.

Eliot backed up, almost falling over his chair. "I . . . I didn't—"

The old man leaned over him, and a jagged smile broke his face. "Just pulling your leg, sonny."

He offered a hand to shake, but there was no way Eliot was touching him, so he stepped back out of reach and politely nodded.

"So," Eliot asked, "you don't need a ticket to ride?"

"Oh, you most definitely *do*." The man's bushy white eyebrows arched. "But not for the trip going in. . . ." He winked. "It's the return trip that'll cost."

A chill shuddered up Eliot's spine.

The man set his thick fingers on the tiny typewriter apparatus on his belt. "Name?"

"Uh . . . Eliot Post."

The man froze. "Not Master Eliot Zachariah Post, by any chance?"

Eliot nodded.

"A thousand pardons, sir." The man eased to one knee and bowed so low that his bones creaked. "Allow this lowly Ticket Master to welcome you aboard *Der Nachtzug,* Limited Express to the Outer Domains of Hell, O Mighty Infernal Lord."

Eliot wasn't comfortable with this genuflection. "Sure. Thank you. Uh, get up, please."

The Ticket Master obeyed. His expression was one of utter respect, and he rubbed his gloved hands together. "How may this most unworthy one be of service? A drink? A companion, perhaps?"

Eliot wasn't about to disagree with someone mistaking him for a real Infernal Lord . . . especially someone who was big enough to flatten him with one fist. And besides, Eliot might be able to use this case of mistaken identity to his advantage.

"How about some information? Can you tell me what stop is—?" Eliot searched his memory. Louis had shown him an image of Jezebel in his ring, and her Queen Sealiah, and then he'd mentioned the name of the realm she ruled. "—the Poppy Lands?"

The Ticket Master flinched. His gaze darted to the front of the train.

"Stop after next, young Master." He swallowed. "After the Slag Mountain Station in the Blasted Lands."

Eliot followed his gaze up the train, seeing nothing. "Is there a problem?"

"The Protector of the Burning Orchards is also on board," the Ticket Master whispered. His rubbing hands stopped. "Her clan and your father's . . . I wish there to be no trouble."

There was already trouble. Eliot was on a train to Hell. There was no guarantee of him getting back. No one knew where he was. How Jezebel reacted when she finally discovered him tailing her . . . that, at least, might be trouble he could delay.

"There won't be any," Eliot told him, "as long as she doesn't find out I'm here." He tried to sound elegantly threatening just as his father sometimes could.

The Ticket Master took an involuntary step back.

Eliot felt bad, so he added, "If you don't mind, please."

"It shall be as you say." His hands smoothed over one another again. "If you require anything"—he gestured to a silver noose hanging on the wall—"pull that. I will come."

The Ticket Master then bowed and bowed again, backing toward the door, and left.

Eliot sighed with relief . . . but then started to worry. What if the Ticket Master found out he wasn't really an Infernal Lord? Did they let just anyone ride this train? He bet not.

Light flashed from the cars ahead, closer and closer—then sunlight streamed through the windows. This light was the color of blood and so bright that Eliot had to squint and blink away tears to see outside.

The landscape looked like a newly formed planet Earth. There were rivers of lava and exploding volcanoes. It rained fire and ash. Clinging to raftlike islands of rock were screaming people—fighting one another for space.

Air-conditioning whispered on within the rail car, blowing cool air on his face.

He reached toward the window, but had to halt because it was too hot.

The train plunged into darkness—another tunnel—and then emerged in desert where it continued to rain smoldering ash. Meteorites fell from the sky, too. In the distance, zeppelins crashed, blossoming into fire. Eliot counted one, two—then three airplanes plummeting from the black clouds, crashing and tumbling into flaming wreckage.

He stared, horrified, eyes wide, unable to move.

The Blasted Lands . . . aptly named.

The Night Train raced through this terrible place, faster than the falling jets. One tiny bit of wreckage on the track, though, and that would end the breakneck ride.

There was no debris on the tracks. Even the falling ash seemed to avoid it. It was a clean line of crushed gravel and iron rails that ran through the desolation.

A single red mountain sat among distant ashen dunes, and pink-tinged whirlwinds screamed about it.

As they got closer, Eliot saw the mountain wasn't natural; rather, it was piles of old cars, steel girders from bridges, countless tin cans, cut-up oil tankers, and miles of unraveled wire—all corroded and melting into piles of rust.

The train slowed. Their track joined dozens of others, and then the Night Train entered a huge metal station roundhouse. They eased to a stop with a scream and a hiss.

There were dozens of trains here. Most were junk heaps, billowing black smoke and barely able to pull themselves along the track. One, however, was a sleek silver bullet that levitated over the tracks.

"Slag Mountain!" The Ticket Master cried, walking alongside the cars. "Five minutes, Lords and Ladies! Apologies, apologies—but there is an unbreakable schedule to keep. Slag Mountain! The Blasted Lands! All depart who so wish. Abandon all hope."

Shadows and shapes left the cars ahead. Eliot sat alone in his chair, trying to look invisible.

After five minutes, there was a tug from the engine, and they moved again.

There was more desert and desolation, and fierce winds tore at the land. Hot air balloons and gliders and kites and even people tumbled in the tornadoes that passed.

The Night Train slowed as it crested a hill, and then tilted downhill and accelerated. Streams of muddy water flowed, then there were tiny twisted trees, and then meadows and thicker forests that became overgrown with ferns and hanging moss and fungus that grew in the gloom.

As before, the train tracks remained clear, cutting through otherwise impenetrable jungle.

Occasionally a shaft of light pierced the canopy . . . but it was not sunlight, rather a gray half twilight.

The Ticket Master returned, bowing as he closed the door behind him.

"Your stop is next, young Master," he told Eliot. He hesitated, then added, "The Duchess is near the head of the train in our most luxurious quarters, naturally. If it is still your intention to depart, I suggest you wait until the train is leaving . . . to minimize any potential conflict."

"Thanks," Eliot said.

"If you do not mind me asking, are you here because of the war?" The Ticket Master's gaze fell to the carpet. "Queen Sealiah and your father's clan have always had the most delicate of . . . relations, but I never envisioned the twice-fallen Prince of Darkness daring to align himself *against* the House of Umbra."

House of Umbra? The name made Eliot's breath catch. *Umbra* was the darkest portion of a shadow . . . like those shadow creatures that had attacked him and Jezebel in the alley?

Eliot didn't like the Ticket Master's sudden interest. He twisted around to get a better look at the man's eyes. Something glittered in them, sharp and dangerous.

The Ticket Master lowered his gaze even more.

Eliot felt an unfamiliar heat build within him.

"How easy it must be to get information along your route," Eliot said. "And how many must ply you for such trinkets of truth. But I wonder how easy it would be with your tongue removed from your head?"

Eliot blinked, startled at the ferocity of his words. It was as if someone else had said them.

The effect, however, was immediate. The Ticket Master bowed so low, he touched the floor with his giant hands.

"I beg your forgiveness, young Master. The House of Umbra pays for any information pertaining to the Poppy Lands with whom they have sanction to wage open civil war. All know this."

Eliot was once again in way over his head, but at least the Ticket Master had laid out the major players: Queen Sealiah of the Poppy Lands on one side, the House of Umbra and Mephistopheles on the other.

"Silence can be rewarded, as well," Eliot said. "Consider *discretion* an investment should Queen Sealiah prevail, eh?"

Eliot marveled at how much he sounded like his father, and was worried by it, too.

"Thank you, young Master Post." The Ticket Master rose. "So it shall be."

The train slowed and entered a station the size of an aircraft hangar made from panes of frosted glass like a hothouse.

"Your stop, sir," the Ticket Master said.

Eliot slipped out the back. The air was so humid, he could barely breathe. It smelled of decay and freshly turned earth.

After a moment, the train started again to move. Eliot jumped off.

As he landed, his fingers lightly brushed the dirt. As when he had felt the earth of the Blasted Lands, reaching through the Gates of Perdition, it felt alien . . . but as desolate as that place had been, this earth felt full of life to the bursting point.

Eliot spied motion beyond the frosted glass of the station house, a figure whose stride he knew well: Jezebel.

He followed her.

Outside, there were more buildings, and one that looked like a stable, but they'd all been boarded up and abandoned.

The smell of the air was like Jezebel's perfume: vanilla and cinnamon and a hundred other exotic spices. It was like trying to inhale underwater, only instead of drowning, Eliot felt intoxicated.

A road of worn gray stone wound between hills and through the jungle. On a distant hill, fire flashed. Eliot had seen this before: cannon. The echoing thunder confirmed his suspicion. There was the retort of gunfire and the curling smoke from a hundred rifles that illuminated swords and spears and claws.

It was war. So close.

Was this what Jezebel had to go through every day to get to school?

Eliot no longer saw her.

He'd been a fool, sightseeing while she'd moved on.

He jogged down the road.

As he rounded the first curve, jungle gave way to a field of tall grass and red opium blossoms.

Part of the field, however, had been burned, the soil turned over, and heaps of salt scattered upon it. In those places were shadows—crisscrossing where they had no business being cast.

Eliot was afraid. Not for his own safety, but for Jezebel's.

There was no sign of her anywhere, and from his vantage, he could see the curve of the road for miles. There was no way she could have gotten so far ahead of him. Something had happened to her.

He ran—

—but made only a few strides before a crushing force hit him from behind, lifted him off the road, and into the tall grass, rolling over and over with him.

Something smashed against the side of his head.

Eliot shrugged off the weight on his chest, scrambled to his feet, and raised his fists.

Jezebel lay before him, her hair tousled over her face.

Next to where she'd pinned him was a pulverized rock. Eliot touched his head, and pebbles of granite fell free.

"You hit me?" He rubbed his head. There was no blood . . . but his skull should've been crushed from that blow.

"You!" Jezebel whispered, brushing her curls aside, her eyes wide.

His anger vanished as he saw that her bandages had sloughed off in their tumble. Her wounds from earlier today were only pale scars on her arms and shoulder.

She stood and smoothed out her tartan skirt.

"You're better," he breathed.

"The land," she said. "Every Infernal is connected to their land . . . and it to them. It is the source of our strength."

She came to him and touched his head. "I'm so sorry. I thought you were one of them," she whispered. Her fingers combed through his hair. She was Julie Marks once more: eyes blue and pale and her face soft and all human.

But her touch turned rough as she examined him. "That rock should've killed you," she growled. "So you are truly Infernal, after all." Her face hardened and her eyes crystallized, becoming the color of raw emeralds. "Why did you follow me?"

"To help?"

"*You* came to the Poppy Lands to help *me*?" She laughed.

But her laugh died as the grass withered and turned to dust, and shadows sprang up in their place.

From this darkness, a shape pulled itself free: as in the alley, a Droogandor with pointed limbs and needle teeth. But unlike in the alley, this shadow creature was bigger . . . the size of a car. Cold radiated from it that chilled Eliot's soul.

"Still the fool!" Jezebel took his arm and drew him closer, hissing, "They've seen you. You've doomed us *both*!"

45

SHADOWS, HONEY, AND BLOOD

Eliot watched the Droogan-dor push itself out of the shadows like some sticky birthing . . . unable to comprehend the geometry of the situation—until his brain unfroze.

He pulled Lady Dawn from his pack.

"Don't worry, we've fought *hundreds* of these things before," he reassured Jezebel.

Jezebel grabbed him by the shoulder and pulled him back into the tall grass. "But not in Hell. Here they are stronger." She let go of him, and her hands became venom-dripping claws.

"It's just a—"

The words died in his throat. The just-freed creature was now the size of an elephant, with ten pointed crablike limbs.

The Droogan-dor lunged at them.

Eliot instinctively flicked his fingers over his violin strings. There was an earsplitting twang.

The air between him and the creature blurred with energy—cracking the thing's exoskeleton, splitting open the ground and making its front legs stumble.

Jezebel darted in and clawed its eyes.

The Droogan-dor reared back, screaming, shaking its upper body, pushing forth *two* new heads from the holes Jezebel had carved out.

It pulled free from the cracks in the earth.

Jezebel was right: This wasn't like the things they'd fought in the alley. It was growing, as large as a bus, getting bigger as more shadows adhered to it.

It stabbed at Jezebel.

She dodged and rolled. Its claw left an impact crater where she'd stood.

"Run, Eliot!" she cried. "I'll delay it."

"Not this time," he murmured. This wasn't like a gym match, where all you do is get the flag and end the battle.

Eliot drew out his violin's bow and tossed aside his pack.

He played "Julie's Song." It was sweet at first, then turned dark and sorrowful. He kept playing because he knew it would change into the weapon he'd need. He played and remembered her smile, how her human laugh had sounded like tiny sleigh bells, and how he had played her song that summer day . . . and made the sun rise early just for her.

The Droogan-dor screamed, rearing back, flailing its needlelike legs at him, but not daring to come closer to the music.

Eliot was on the right track. He had to focus, couldn't be afraid. He had to make the song right.

But the right notes felt very far away. Neither light nor hope nor love belonged in this place. It was like forcing oil and water to mix.

He stayed and he played. He had to. For her.

The Droogan-dor snorted, shook its heads to overcome its aversion, and charged Eliot. It was a dozen pointed limbs and tons of black armor rushing headlong to crush him.

And still Eliot played . . . with nothing but hope to shield him.

Jezebel watched, horrified, her mouth agape.

Eliot felt the connection: it all poured from him—no distance could keep him away and no darkness could prevail against his unwavering hope.

Sunlight streamed from the cracks in the earth, from his eyes and fingertips, and made the very notes from Lady Dawn waver in the air like heat.

The Droogan-dor's wailing pitched to a panicked ultrasonic cry. Its exoskeleton bubbled and steamed and popped, and it disintegrated into dust and ashes before Eliot's feet.

The song ended and Eliot fell to his knees, spent.

The light went out and the darkness rushed in like a cold tide.

There was a soothing, gentle rocking motion. Somewhere far away, Eliot heard his name called by the sweetest southern-accented voice imaginable.

Eliot . . . Eliot, honey, snap out of it.

The gentle rocking became urgent.

"Eliot!"

Pain lashed across his face, sharp and electric. His eyes flew open in time to see Jezebel raising her open hand for another slap.

He blocked her swing and caught her. Wrapping his fingers about hers, he got up and didn't let go.

"I'm fine," he whispered. There was an edge in his voice that he hadn't intended.

Jezebel stared at him, then at their intertwined hands. She wasn't angry as usual; rather, her forehead wrinkled with worry.

Eliot touched her captured hand lightly . . . then released her.

"We have to move," she said, and nodded across the road.

Eliot blinked, trying to see what she meant, still recovering from his performance. His eyes focused, and he instantly understood: The fight was far from over.

The battle on the distant hills had spilled into the meadow. Hundreds of knights in thorn-spiked plate mail slashed at a handful of giant Droogan-dors, impaling the creatures upon lances; cannon fired puffballs of fungus that exploded and showered spores that took root and dissolved all in their path; legions of foot soldiers armed with lanterns and flaming oil sprayers made lines of light in the gloom . . . but the creatures from the House of Umbra were too strong. They stabbed and crushed everything within reach.

"They shift shape so easily," Eliot murmured. "Why are they so strong now?"

Louis had told him Infernals normally had only two shapes, one humanoid, the other a "combat" form.

"The Droogan-dors have no shape to begin with." Jezebel glanced about. "And as for their strength . . . all creatures of the dark are stronger in Hell, strongest of all on their lands."

Lands. She meant the domains of Hell.

Was Eliot, son of the Prince of Darkness, a creature of darkness stronger here, too?

He gazed once more at the battle. Where the shadow creatures killed and advanced, the land changed. Grass and flowers died. The bare earth dried and cracked, and jagged spikes of black rock grew in their place.

Like the place was becoming another land.

"You said you're connected to land," Eliot said, "but the connection goes *both* ways, doesn't it? The land is connected to you?"

"Yes," she said, grabbing his hand and tugging him along. "We can discuss it while we're running for our lives."

She pulled him through the fields, running parallel to the road, still on "her" side, where the land was full of life, where Eliot guessed she'd be the strongest.

Farther ahead, though, the road wound about more hills . . . upon which more battles raged.

Eliot halted, stopping Jezebel her tracks. "Wait a second," he said. "Where are we going?"

"Doze Torres." She yanked him back in her direction. "My Queen's castles. We shall be safest there."

Eliot didn't budge.

He scrutinized what lay ahead, not liking what he saw. In some battles, Queen Sealiah's forces outnumbered the shadows three to one and pushed them back. In a few cases, her forces lit the fields on fire to drive the shadows away (at best, a delaying tactic). But in the majority of the battles, it was an even match . . . with lots of casualties on either side.

Eliot wasn't sure what happened to the souls of the dead when torn apart by shadow creatures—if they ceased to exist, regenerated, or just lay there in pieces for all eternity.

He was pretty sure, though, he knew what would happen if *he* got torn into tiny pieces.

"That way's too dangerous." He drew Jezebel closer to him. "The safest path is back." He pointed over his shoulder. He could just see the top of the train station's glass spires.

"No," she insisted. "I cannot leave. I must fight."

"No, you don't," he told her. "Come back with me. We'll get you a dorm room at Paxington. The Droogan-dors would never dare come there."

"Where I'd be safe?" Jezebel dropped his hand, and her face turned cold. "Where I would slowly die?"

Eliot looked at her. That was no lie—but he was light-years from understanding what she meant.

"The land," she said, growing annoyed with him. "You saw the connection."

He nodded, starting to get it. When the Droogan-dors won, they took the land and made it Mephistopheles'. And logically, the more land that Infernal Lord had, the stronger he became . . . while Queen Sealiah lost her land and grew weaker.

"What happens if you lose?" Eliot whispered. "Lose all the land?"

Her hand rose to her throat. "There would be no more Jezebel. At best, the soul of Julie Marks would belong to Mephistopheles. But in all likelihood, as a Duchess of the Royal House of Poppies, I would be destroyed."

Eliot refused to accept that. His father had lost all his lands and not been destroyed . . . but he was the Great Deceiver, and a full-blooded fallen angel. Jezebel wasn't.

"Okay," he said, "that's it, then. I'm staying and fighting."

"No, no, no." She pursed her lips. "We're only going to the castle so I can be safe and you can get an escort out of here. I won't let you die for me."

He crossed his arms. "I'm not leaving you."

Cannon fire lit the nearby ridge, and bioluminescent puffballs whooshed overhead, lighting the sky like ghostly meteors—impacting and exploding on the opposite side of the valley with flashes of pastel lights, illuminating the solid wall of onrushing shadow.

Jezebel balled her hands into fists. "You—are—so—stubborn!" she said through gritted teeth, and she shook her platinum curls.

She grabbed his hand and raced back the way they'd come. "Fine. The train, then. My orders definitely do not cover this."

As they ran, her wounds bled once more. Was it the sudden motion? Or was it because Queen Sealiah was losing?

Eliot risked a glance back.

Knights upon giant centipedes charged downhill; monster bats screeched overhead, dropping lines of phosphorescent napalm—and rushing down the opposite hill against these forces, a tide of dark, full of limbs and jagged maws and a thousand unblinking eyes.

Eliot turned and ran faster—and slowed only once they got inside the great glass station house.

"How long?" he panted. "Until another train?"

"*We* do not wait," Jezebel replied.

She went to a wrought-iron pillar and opened a call box. Inside was an ancient phone. She turned a generator crank and spoke into the fixed microphone: "Ready the *Poe*. No delays."

Jezebel replaced the earpiece and closed the box. She then moved to his side, seemed to deflate, and rested her forehead on his shoulder. "I was going to tell you you're a fool," she said, "but I think you already know that."

Eliot held her lightly.

She let him, leaning closer. "I . . . I just can't believe you came for me," she whispered. "I tried so hard to push you away. Why didn't you go?"

Eliot tilted her chin up and looked into her eyes. They were a shade of blue-green he hadn't seen before—part Jezebel, part Julie.

He wanted to tell her that from the moment he first played her song, learned what she was inside and out and what she could be, he had loved her.

But until he had come to Hell to save her, even Eliot hadn't quite realized that. He just didn't have the words . . . so he opened himself to her, let her look through the windows of his eyes into the depths of his soul.

Jezebel stared deeper and deeper; she held her breath, and held him, her hands clutching his jacket tighter.

The moment was broken as an engine chugged and strained against inertia, pulling three rail cars from the roundhouse.

She released him and took a step back; her hands, however, still rested lightly on his chest as if she couldn't let go.

The train and its cars were all polished brass and gleaming rosewood. As it pulled in front of them, hissing steam, Eliot smelled lilacs and a hint of sulfur.

A bald porter emerged, set down a step, and bowed before Jezebel. With a flourish, he waved them both into the car. "Destination?" he asked.

"Market Street BART station, San Francisco, the Middle Realm of the Earth," Jezebel commanded. "And relay my wish to the conductor to make no stops along the way."

"It shall be as you command." The bald porter hurried off.

Eliot followed Jezebel into the rail car.

The wall panels of the car were silver dust mirrors veined with filigrees of gold. The ceiling was Tiffany stained glass with lilacs and dragonflies, but along the edges were mushrooms and crystalline millipede motifs with tiny real bones. There were bloodred silk lounges, and a desk with modern computers and phones, and along the wall a bar with cut crystal decanters. In the back were red curtains, slightly parted, and within he spied the ruffle of a round bed.

"All the conveniences one could desire," she told him.

There was velvet in her voice. It was nice. Not a lie per se . . . just something wrong nonetheless that heightened Eliot's awareness.

She shut the door, moved closer, and her hand pressed against his chest, slowly running up and tracing his contours with her nails.

About them, dozens and hundreds of reflections of him and her all mirrored their touching. The air within the rail car turned hot.

Yes . . . something was very wrong; at least the rational encyclopedic part of Eliot's mind was screaming that to the rest of him (and being ignored).

Her fingernails slipped inside his shirt and scraped along bare skin. It was electric.

Eliot set a hand on the small of her back and pulled her closer.

Jezebel sighed. "If only . . . ," she whispered.

"What do you mean?" Eliot asked.

"I mean," she said, taking a deep breath, "you may be perfect, Eliot Post, Son of Darkness, but you're not the only one capable of sacrifice for"—she struggled with her next words—"the ones they care for."

Eliot crinkled his brow, confused.

She leaned closer and kissed him. It was soft; then she pressed harder, her lips urgent.

Eliot caressed her and tasted honey. He drowned in that sensation, dizzy, only with her while the rest of the universe vanished.

There was a stab inside his cheek. Like a needle. It was lightning fast, the prick gone as fast as the sensation had registered.

Heat and pain lanced through his mouth and then his throat, pumping down the vein in his neck.

Eliot staggered back, one hand making a choking motion about his throat, the other brushing across his lips . . . and coming away bloody.

His lips went numb. Then his face.

Jezebel stepped out of his reach. She took out a handkerchief and wiped the blood—his blood—off her perfect, smiling lips.

"Ghhahh . . . ," was all he managed.

She watched him, her features cold and calculating.

Eliot tried to grab her and demand to know what she'd done, but he couldn't raise his arms. His legs didn't respond, either. He crumpled to the carpet.

Only when he lay immobile and helpless, did she finally approach. "I had to," she said with a tremulous whisper.

He never heard the rest of her words, because the darkness swallowed him.

———

Eliot's face throbbed as if he'd gone a few rounds sparring with Robert . . . leading with his nose instead of his fists.

His heart fluttered, and his pulse pounded rhythmically through his fingertips.

No, it wasn't his pulse. His hands rested on the floor, feeling the *clack clack clack* of the train beneath him.

The *moving* train.

There was a handkerchief stuffed into his hand. It was white linen embroidered with a single lacy rose that bristled with a dozen thorns. Impressed upon the field of white were a pair of bloody lips. Jezebel's lips. His blood.

He remembered.

Her kiss had poisoned him.

He got to his feet, wobbled, and slumped next to a window. The train was definitely moving—the *Poe Express* chugged through fields of red opium poppies as battles raged alongside and fires licked the sky.

No!

Eliot pulled himself from the lounge to the wet bar, staggering, and then to the back door of the rail car, pushing his way through and almost tumbling off the rear platform.

The effort had been almost too much. He slumped to the floor, his heart in his throat, almost passing out again.

But not before he saw her.

Growing smaller as the train accelerated, standing on the edge of the Great Glass Station House, watching him go, her chin tilted up in defiance and pride was Jezebel.

. . . tears spilling down her cheeks.

46

CONCLUSION MOST DIRE

Audrey wondered what it was about the male psyche that made them want to build everything so big.

She sat in the "intimate" living room of Aaron's log cabin. The rafters were mammoth tree trunks that soared three stories. The sun filtered in through tiny square windows, making a mosaic of the twilight. Candelabras made of antlers hung there as well, their candles lit in anticipation of a long night ahead.

On a more human scale, down at ground level, three river-rock fireplaces roared with scented cedar logs. Audrey sat by herself, as close to the flames as she dared.

The Norwegian winters were very cold.

This was the house Aaron had hand-built, a log cabin in the remote forest. Part hunting lodge, part palatial fortress, his "man hut," as Dallas called it.

Audrey glanced outside, through the triple-pane insulated windows. The sunset made the snowdrifts look bloodied.

Aaron sat across the room, host of this Council meeting, which meant that everyone had their own tray of liquor and a platter of sizzling barbecue. He was happy, bottle of vodka in one hand, a skewer of charred meat in the other.

Henry sat between them, uncharacteristically only nursing a martini.

Dallas sat close to Henry, giggling at his endless jokes. She wore a collar-to-tiptoe-length mink and little else. She reminded Audrey of a playful ferret, and she wondered if her sister took *anything* seriously anymore.

Kino stood across the room, away from the fires. His towering figure seemed dwarfed in the great room. His suit was white, and his skin was a shade paler than midnight. Both portents of ill fortune.

Lucia finally breezed in. "Apologies for my lateness," she said, "but there is a storm front moving in, and Gardermoen Airport in Oslo has all these ridiculous rules."

"I did offer you a ride," Henry said with a hint of sarcasm.

Lucia frowned at him and settled into a leather chair, her pink dress flourishing about her. She stretched and curled her long legs under her body. "Where are the others?" she asked, looking about.

"Gilbert and Cornelius send their regrets," Kino muttered. "We, however, still have a quorum."

Lucia pondered this . . . just as Audrey had when first told.

Gilbert attended every Council meeting because he'd been Lucia's loyal supporter. After their recent falling out, though, in both politics and the bedroom, Audrey wondered if his absence today was for personal reasons. On the other hand, Gilbert seemed more like his old self: a fighter and a king. If so, then his absence had meaning beyond some mere lovers' quarrel.

And Cornelius . . . he had founded the Council in the fifth century, and had missed only three meetings: the night before the coronation of Charlemagne, when Archduke Ferdinand had been assassinated, and the evening of the Trinity nuclear bomb test.

Lucia sipped a flute of honey liquor and nibbled on a carrot stick, her eyes dark with concentration.

"Well," Lucia said, "let us begin. Thank you for hosting, Aaron."

Aaron raised his bottle in salute and took a deep draft.

Much to Audrey's annoyance, Lucia found her tiny silver bell and rang it thrice, its tinkling notes grating on Audrey's nerves.

"I call this session of the League Council of Elders to order," Lucia announced. "All come to heed, petition, and be judged. *Narro, Audio, Perceptum.* I move to skip last meeting's minutes and proceed directly to the Balboa business."

"Second the motion," Henry said with a wave of his hand.

They all nodded their assent to skip the minutes.

"Thank you, Henry," Lucia said. "I believe we were discussing whether to support the current dictator, Balboa, in his civil war or overthrow him and install a democratically elected leader of our choosing."

"Democracies are so tedious," Henry said.

"And ultimately just as corrupt," Kino added.

Aaron set his bottle aside and looked serious. "But I dislike this Balboa. He kills for pleasure. He is a beast that must be put down."

Kino shrugged to Aaron, the closest thing to assent Audrey had seen from him. Curious. Had the two made overtures to peace? That was a highly unusual move for Aaron.

Dallas shifted in her furs. No longer a member of the Council, she wasn't allowed to speak without permission. She was here only to report on her efforts with Fiona—a topic Audrey was far more interested in than the fate of one little Central American country.

"We remove Balboa," Audrey said. "I have already made up my mind."

Lucia sighed. "We do prefer to debate the issues *before* we vote, darling Sister."

"My mind is decided," Audrey repeated.

Lucia threw up her hands in frustration. "Do you understand that beneath the soil of this country, right where Henry has perched his little refinery, is more light crude oil than in the entire Fertile Crescent? That in thirty years, we shall 'discover' it and change the socioeconomic balance of the world? Besides filling our coffers, it will give humanity the cushion they will need to ease into a non-petroleum-based infrastructure and prevent a worldwide economic disaster?"

"Not with Balboa in charge," Audrey said. "He has already sent geologists looking for gold in the region. He will discover the porous rock formations long before we want."

Lucia's mouth fell open; then she recovered and asked, "And how did you learn this?"

Audrey spread her hands, her fingers delicately moving as if over the weft and weave of some invisible pattern. "I *looked*, Sister," she said, a cutting edge of steel to her voice.

Lucia pursed her lips and shot her back an irritated *Of course I knew that* look.

Aaron snorted a laugh. "Motion to vote, then. We kill Balboa."

Henry sighed. "Ah well, I shall miss my golf games with the man."

Kino nodded.

"Fine," Lucia said. "Let the record show, we sanction the death of V. C. Balboa. Aaron, please see to the details, would you?" She smoothed the fabric of her dress. "Next item on the agenda: Eliot and Fiona."

They all turned toward Dallas and Henry. The sun had set, and in the dimming light, the two were silhouetted by flames.

This is what Audrey had come to discuss—why she'd maneuvered her sister off, and had maneuvered herself onto, the Council.

Her children. Their fates. To defend them, if possible . . . and if not both, perhaps one of them could be saved.

She felt cold inside. Absolute zero cold.

She had to be. She had to think her way through this, for if she felt anything . . . blood would be spilled. And despite her certainty that oceans of blood *would* flow one day . . . that could not be today.

She *prayed* not today. She just needed a little more time.

Dallas broke the crystalline silence that hung in the air. "So I should talk?" she asked, dripping with sarcasm. "Now? Why, I'm not sure I have it all straight in my head."

"Do not play games with this Council," Lucia murmured.

Dallas stood and sneered at Lucia. "You're no fun."

She practically danced to the center of the room, and cleared her throat. Fire illuminated her on all sides. She smiled. "Fiona is with us. More than 'with.' I think one day she'll be *leading* us."

Dallas turned to Audrey. "Oh, and you should see how she looks! She could be on the cover of *Teen Vogue*." She laughed. "And the best part, she doesn't even know it. Beauty and modesty—the rarest of combinations."

She paused, touching a finger to her lip, thinking over the self-directed irony of her words.

Audrey hissed an exasperated sigh.

"We care nothing for such silliness," Kino interrupted, folding his arms over his chest. "The only things that matter are her deeds and moral center. Assuming she has one at all."

Dallas snorted. "You wouldn't call it silliness if you saw her cleaned up, old prune."

Tension crackled between Kino and Dallas—which vanished as she flashed her dimples at him. Even the Keeper of the Dead could not stay mad when she fought dirty like that.

"And as far as her moral center is concerned," Dallas continued, "it is far more intact than any in this room. She protects the weak, fights evil, and has a certain . . . je ne sais quoi, a character that reminds me of the days when Zeus fought for this family, instead of against it."

Kino stroked his chin. "Interesting . . ."

"We look forward to reading your full report," Lucia told her.

"Oh, was I supposed to write this down?" Dallas asked, batting her eyes.

Lucia gave her a stony glare, which was wasted because Dallas turned and flounced back to the fireplace.

"Henry?" Lucia said. "What of Eliot? How did he react to the gift of the corporation and his new responsibilities?"

Henry stood and smiled.

Something was wrong. Audrey spied his still-full martini glass. His eyes were narrowed with an uncharacteristic concentration.

"Oh, I wish I could call the lad my own." He bowed to Audrey. "Such a good boy with a sterling conscience."

"So he accepted the chairmanship?" Kino asked.

"Well, no, not precisely."

"Either he is running Del Mundo Pharma Chemical on our behalf," Lucia said, leaning forward, "or he is not."

Kino huffed. "Perhaps even this honorary position was too much responsibility for the boy, a sure indication that chaos runs through his blood."

Audrey made no move. In truth, she wanted to know the outcome of Henry's experiment as much as the rest of them. Was Eliot more her son . . . or his father's?

"It most certainly was not 'too much' for him," Henry said. He approached Lucia and handed her a file folder of glossy photographs. "The exercise was to see if Eliot could do something to improve the refinery—to keep it literally from sinking into a pool leaking financial resources and toxic wastes."

Lucia's face went blank as she shuffled through the photos. "What am I looking at, Henry?"

Kino came closer and looked as well, then passed the photos to Audrey.

Audrey scrutinized the aerial photographs. The land was green and lush as land was when the world was new. The only features that marred this Eden were a four-lane freeway and a sprawling complex of stainless steel and green plastic buildings, which from ten thousand feet looked like an open flower.

"That *is* Del Mundo Pharma Chemical," Henry told them.

None of them could do that. Or more accurately, those who might were unwilling to put so much at risk to do so.

Her Eliot had power . . . and apparently no compunctions against unleashing it. What had this cost him?

Audrey ran her fingertips over the picture. This had a hint of the diabolical, though. The Infernals and their land . . . their connections were always closer than any of the others, but that connection had ever remained in their Lower Realms . . . not on Earth.

Was it possible for an Infernal to claim land here? Bring Hell to the living?

Minutes ticked by as they examined the photographs: acre after acre of impenetrable jungle, spotless white beaches, and an improbable five-kilometer spiral of river that disappeared into a sinkhole.

"So . . . ," Henry continued, "I would say he passed my little challenge."

"He solved the problem," Kino whispered, "but the way he did so, it is not *our* way. When it is discovered—"

"It will not be." Henry waved his concern away as if it were a buzzing mosquito. "Not like that. I made sure the face of the Madonna appeared on a Del Mundo Pharma Chemical stucco wall. The locals have already proclaimed it and the clean land a 'miracle.'"

Audrey read the faces of Kino and Lucia: They were uncertain about Eliot.

"But," Lucia said, "he did not stay to run things."

"Too committed to his studies at Paxington, I'm afraid," Henry offered.

"I like not that both twins are still so firmly entrenched at that school," Lucia said. "How have they done on their midterms, Aaron?" She turned to him. "Have you heard yet?"

Aaron stood and grinned. "Eliot and Fiona—their entire team—all received As!" He smashed one fist into his open hand for emphasis. "And destroyed Ma's precious obstacle course in the process. Ha!"

"A-minuses," Audrey corrected.

"Still," Aaron said, "they used teamwork to achieve that grade. And that is a trait of *this* family."

"Could it not have been solely Fiona's influence?" Lucia asked.

"*Paxington.*" Kino said this word as if it had a sour taste. "I do not trust anything that happens there. How can we, when no League member is permitted on campus?"

"Nor any of the Infernal clans," Henry countered.

"Technically neither of those statements is true," Lucia told them. "Any student who passes the entrance and placement exams may go to Paxington. Both Eliot and Fiona are from the League. The Infernal protégée, the Handmaiden to the Mistress of Pain, also attends Paxington."

"We should have taken that place long ago," Kino muttered.

"Perhaps you would storm the gates," Henry said, "as Harlan Dells defends his wall, fights, and dies in his many incarnations as he did in the old days against the giants? Or perhaps you would test pernicious Miss Westin—who can become shadow and mist and summon her hordes from the darkness? Or would you challenge the unbeatable Ma? Even though killing him would mean death for us all?"

Aaron flinched at those names.

Kino scowled.

"We're getting off topic." Lucia tapped the pile of Henry's photographs. "Have we come to a consensus on Eliot's inclinations?"

Henry shook his head. "I move that we continue to watch Eliot. Personally, I find him quite fascinating."

"How long can we watch?" Kino took a step closer to Henry. "Until it is too late? Until he is one of them?"

Audrey observed Aaron, but the man did not stir. He simply watched Kino and then Henry, unmoved by this debate that could decide if Eliot lived or died.

This was one more thing that was off today. Aaron had always jumped to Eliot's defense before.

"What do you think, Audrey?" Lucia asked. "You know the boy better than any here."

"I think . . ."

What she thought was largely irrelevant. These facts were inconclusive. But what she felt—*that* was another matter entirely. When she imagined her Eliot, she saw him in shadows now.

"I think a brief recess would be beneficial." She stood. "I find it too stuffy in here." Audrey stared into Lucia's eyes as she said this, and her gaze softened. It was a silent plea; she had to leave this room, the heat, and the swirling thoughts of the others.

Lucia sighed. "Very well. Thirty minutes." She shook her tiny silver bell.

Audrey had to be alone for a moment . . . to think . . . to find a way to logically avoid coming to the same conclusion that Kino had: that Eliot was drifting to the other side.

As part Infernal–part Immortal, Eliot could bypass the neutrality treaty that kept the families from murdering one another. They'd already seen this was possible: Fiona had decapitated Beelzebub.

The opposite had to be true: If Eliot went to their side, became an Infernal Lord . . . he would be able to kill Immortals.

Their discretion now would save countless lives later. But that meant her son had to die.

47

TIPPED BALANCE

Audrey crunched over the ice-crusted snow into the woods. The spruce and pine were dense and deep and full of gloaming shadows.

This was what she wanted: to be alone, and cold, and in the dark.

She had to think things through with great care . . . and with no dangerous emotional responses.

Audrey extended her arms and felt everything hanging in balance in the weave of the world. It wasn't just Eliot. He was a catalyst, but it all teetered: alliances and treaties, the entire League, and the fate of every creature in this realm.

The smallest action at this point—even her feeling the surface of the weave—could potentially tip it all one way or the other.

And she instinctively knew that once that happened, such an imbalance would accelerate, every thread would pull against the other and tangle and snap and snarl . . . and then the only way forward would be to *cut* it all to shreds.

She let her arms drop.

It started to snow; the flakes made a million downy impacts about her.

Henry had, of course, tried to come with her on this walk, but she'd firmly declined his offer of jabbering company. He was part of the problem, too.

As Audrey arranged her thoughts to encompass more factors, she realized that Henry might be a *real* problem.

Henry . . . and Aaron . . . and even Gilbert.

Henry was charming, and always scheming, and ever elusive. He was holding something back about Eliot and his transformation of the Del Mundo Pharma Chemical plant. And there was the matter of his no-longer-in-the-League Driver, Robert Farmington. Henry had somehow finagled him into Paxington . . . as his spy?

Audrey had been keeping tabs on Mr. Farmington, at first thinking he was at Paxington to keep track of Fiona. But now Eliot was going to his apartment almost every day after school. There was more to Henry's agent, and she would have to investigate further.

Her conclusion, however, was the same: Henry was taking a too-personal interest in the twins.

To what end? Certainly not to help the Infernals, but it seemed he wasn't really helping the League's interests, either.

She considered questioning him directly, but that had never done any good. Henry was too slippery.

She set him aside in her thoughts and moved on to the next factor that made little sense in all this—Aaron.

He had initially taken such great interest in Eliot and especially Fiona. But now? He seemed to be maintaining a distance from them . . . or at least made it *appear* that way.

And then there was Gilbert, the Once-King, who was not here today. He, too, had been such a supporter of the twins. Why abandon them now? Gilbert had never walked away from a fight.

Unless he had chosen to fight on another *unknown* front?

Yes. Henry, Aaron, and Gilbert—all three of them were in this, working together. That was a dangerous possibility: brains, strength, and courage allied.

But again, to what end? It was unlikely they would move against the will of the League. They all had signed the Warrants of Death, in case one of the children turned Infernal.

Audrey felt a choking in her throat, and her hand covered her heart.

She was feeling. Despite her cut maternal ties, emotions churned inside her, acidic, boiling, so deep and powerful she dared not let them take control.

She squeezed her eyes shut and banished them . . . but not entirely.

Her thoughts remained clouded.

There was doubt now. Where was her sense of right and wrong? What happened to the certainty that her children should die, if necessary, to prevent war between Immortals and Infernals?

She had known exactly what the possibilities were the moment she realized was she pregnant . . . and who the father was.

Audrey took a deep breath, held it, and exhaled, regaining a bit of her icy control.

Eliot and Fiona had grown up all too quickly. Their roles within the families would soon be determined—a continuation of order within the League or a place in the Infernal clans, where they would be used to shatter the long peace.

That was the *only* factor to consider. The only reason to embrace Fiona and Eliot—or to destroy them. The choice and consequences were all clear.

Why, then, was this so hard?

Wasn't it utter insanity to consider any other options?

Audrey then realized that she—as with everything else surrounding the twins—was also in balance. All she had to do was tip one way or the other . . . life or death for her children, ignore her feelings or embrace them . . . and the entire weave of the world shifted.

Which way?

Her front pocket buzzed, startling her. Her phone.

Who would dare call now? Henry, trying to cajole her into further discussion? Lucia, wanting her back . . . but it wasn't time yet to reconvene. Or Cecilia with some new emergency at home?

Feeling a flutter of precognitive alarm, she pulled out the slender black phone . . . but hesitated. The icons indicated there was no service here, no satellites overhead to bounce a signal.

So *how* was her phone ringing?

Warily, she pressed the TALK button. "Hello?"

"Audrey, my darling . . ."

It was Louis.

The control Audrey had so carefully collected shattered at the sound of his voice. It was rich and dark, and without a trace of remorse for his countless deceptions.

"Did you get my gift?" he asked. "I do hope you remember Venice. It meant so much to me."

As if she could ever forget . . . the only time anyone had ever fooled her so completely.

"I know you're still there," Louis continued. "I hear you breathing. Ah, you're still angry at me. I don't blame you. Tell me, though, what did you do with that egg? Dash it upon the floor? Throw it in the Dumpster?" He chuckled. "You know it was priceless. At least, in sentimental value."

"Yes," she finally answered. "To all your questions."

That was not entirely true. Yes, the egg's sentimental value was beyond measure, as was its monetary value. And while she had thrown it in the trash, after the children and Cecilia went to bed, she had retrieved it.

It was foolish to remember their time in Venice.

"My dear," Louis cooed. "I wonder how we can care so much for each other, and yet find so much pleasure at this torture? Why we cannot speak about how we feel? But"—his tone brightened—"that is not why I called."

Audrey gritted her teeth. He was toying with her! Making a game of her emotions.

Her hands balled to fists. No. She would not let him get the better of her.

Audrey did not understand how he was connecting, but she suddenly understood where he had gotten her number: Eliot's stolen phone.

As if reading her mind, Louis said, "I want to talk to you about the children. First, this business about Eliot's phone. Don't blame or punish him. He is a lamb among a pack of wolves. Borrowing his phone was only so I could reach out to you."

Audrey took a deep breath and felt a bit of her control return. While every word Louis spoke was a potential lie . . . this was a rare opportunity to find out what he was up to.

And how she could stop him.

"Speak plainly, Louis," she said. "What is it you want?"

About her, the snow fell thicker and the temperature plummeted.

"I . . . I do not know," he said.

For the first time, Audrey heard a hint of uncertainty in his voice, something possibly even bordering upon sincerity.

"I find myself oddly unmotivated by self-interest," Louis mused. "Or rather, I'm more interested in finding a way to protect Eliot and Fiona while gaining all the usual advantages. It is most curious. Besides you, I have never even considered the well-being of another. . . ."

"You want to protect Eliot and Fiona?"

Audrey voiced this as a question, but it was not entirely directed at Louis.

A long time ago, she, too, pondered what was best for them without any other considerations. That was sixteen years ago. She had loved them all. The dream of a family, her and Louis and the children, it was still a possibility, then—something resembling a normal life—the twins not in constant danger, not forever tested, and not inevitably marching toward bloodshed and war.

She had had hope—

—until she realized what and who Louis was, that his love for her, despite all his promises, was a charade.

For no Infernal had ever truly loved. And certainly none had ever loved an Immortal.

All contrivance.

"No, Louis," she whispered. "I don't believe you're capable of thinking about anyone's well-being but your own."

"The obvious assumption." He sighed. "I had hoped you would risk believing otherwise."

Audrey moved her thumb over the END button.

She had to terminate this conversation before he tricked her again.

For some reason, however, her hand froze.

She hoped . . . what? That she'd been wrong so long ago? That creatures such as they, whose families had been enemies for centuries, held apart from bloodshed, and by the most tenuous of treaties, could actually feel for one another?

"Don't go," he said. "Please . . ." Louis struggled with his words as if each weighed a ton. "I had to tell you that, no matter what, I . . . love you, Audrey. The children, too. Against all reason, I love you."

There was no mockery in his tone. His words were clear and unadorned. It was the truth. At least, she so wished to believe it was the truth from him.

It felt as if a hundred daggers plunged into her heart, and her blood flowed out of the rivers.

She pressed her thumb on the END button and dropped the phone into the snow.

Audrey sank to her knees and let out a tiny gasp.

Accursed weakness!

Only Louis could do this to her. She was still so vulnerable to him. Why had she not killed him when she had the chance?

She gazed up into the night, watched the spirals of falling snow stretching to the infinite, and let tears spill down her cheeks.

A moment of truth. For Louis. And for her.

With her emotions freed, she realized that, severed maternal ties or not, as impossible as it was, she loved her children and wanted them both to live.

No matter if the cost was every soul in every realm.

And there was one other thing she knew.

Louis loved her still . . . and she loved him, too.

SECTION

V

———

THE SEMESTER OF FIRE AND BLOOD

48

WHEN THERE WERE STILL LOTS OF OPTIONS

Fiona organized the pile of three-by-five cards on the dining table.

Some semester break. She'd done nothing but study for the quiz Miss Westin was going to give when they came back.

A spring-semester orientation package had been sent the first day of vacation as well. In the accompanying letter, Miss Westin had congratulated Fiona and Eliot for passing their winter freshman semester . . . what an honor it was . . . and blah blah blah.

It also said the grade bell curve had been "severely skewed" during midterms. A correction would be required, namely, a quiz covering Zulu mythologies and the lost histories of the Gypsy Clans.

Fiona glanced at the grandfather clock: Fifteen minutes before they had to leave.

To make matters worse, Audrey had been gone the entire week. "Council business," Cee had said. But that could mean anything.

She'd so wanted to impress her mother with her midterm grade. If anything could have cracked Audrey's diamond-hard exterior, that A– might have.

Fiona sighed, and then inhaled the orange zest and cinnamon wafting from the kitchen. At least she'd get a good breakfast.

Aunt Dallas had arrived at dawn in cutoff shorts and a red tank top, carrying a double armful of organic groceries. She announced that they were all getting a grand meal to start the new semester.

Cee, of course, had protested.

Dallas just danced into the kitchen, ignoring her, and proceeded to take out every dish, turn on every burner, and then shooed them all out—even Cee (who Fiona had thought unshooable).

Feathers ruffled, Eliot had tried to soothe Cecilia with that stupid Towers game they'd started playing this week. The circle mat sat on the other end of dining table. He and Cecilia had been there for an hour, moving stone pieces, building towers, and then toppling them over one another.

Fiona had more important things to do—namely, cram . . . and pick a new class.

The very first day, Miss Westin had explained that they had to take Mythology 101 and Mr. Ma's gym class (still true for this semester). But if they made it to the second semester, they could also take an *elective* course.

Her hand rested on the Paxington catalog that had come in the orientation package. Bound in leather, the pages were whisper fine and translucent. Printed in tiny handset type was a description for every course at the school.

When she had first seen the catalog, Fiona laughed—like she had time for a third class.

It was only after she'd watched Eliot flip through the thing for an entire day that she grew curious.

There were the classes she had expected, like Introduction to Alchemy. Take that, and you'd learn how to manipulate the mythical elements and combine them with the mundane ones—brew universal solvents, dreaming potions, and similar stuff.

She could just see setting her hair on fire, or spilling the universal solvent, alkahest, on her books and dissolving them all.

No thanks.

But there were also ones like Mythic Forging Techniques, where you could learn how to blacksmith the Four Winds and the might of volcanoes into a blade. That sounded cool. Naturally, though, the prerequisite was two semesters of alchemy.

There were dozens of exotic languages that intrigued her: the ancient rune scripts of Atlantis, Egyptian hieroglyphics, and the anti-poetical cadence tongues of the Ancient Ones. (Although for that, you had to pass a psych evaluation, be at least eighteen years old, and sign an insanity waiver!)

It figured that the best classes were open only to juniors or seniors or had ludicrous requirements like "must have tamed animal spirit" or "endure trial by fire" or "must provide documentation of wilder ancestry" (whatever that was).

The one that really intrigued her, though, was a class called Force of Arms.

> **FORCE OF ARMS:** A series of weeklong intensive instructions, sparring exercises, and field trips to train the already proficient warrior in hand-to-hand techniques, fencing, athletic prowess, and strategies, with an emphasis on defending against magical techniques with physical force.

This was exactly what she needed for gym—which had seemed more battlefield than obstacle course during midterms. It was also a perfect fit for her after-school lifestyle—having to fight off an army of shadows or something else every other day.

She glanced at Eliot.

His eyes were on the Towers board, flicking among the stacks of stones Cecilia had on her side.

"This game would be better," he murmured, "if there was an element of chance."

"It has been suggested more than once," said Cee without taking her gaze off the board.

"Something like dice."

Cee looked up. "Your mother would not approve."

"So what else is new?" Eliot moved a stack of three inward toward the center of the circular board.

Cee's brows furrowed. ". . . Unexpected."

Eliot brushed the hair from his face. It'd been a while since he got his hair cut—that is, since he let Cecilia put a bowl on his head for one of her trims.

Grooming habits weren't the only thing changing with him. His already dark mood had gotten gloomier over break. He hadn't gone over to see Robert once; he hardly studied; he just moped about pretending to do his chores; or occasionally he'd plunk out some sad little tune on his violin.

It was getting on Fiona's nerves.

The only clue he'd given as to why was when he got home late that first night of vacation. Audrey was gone, and Cee was already in bed—or else Eliot would've gotten grounded. He'd told her that he tried to follow Jezebel and help her . . . and that hadn't gone as planned.

Great. So her brother was still following the Infernal around, working overtime to find more trouble. Jezebel wasn't some stupid, simple crush to him. Eliot was really hooked on her. And Jezebel was—by her own admission—trying to seduce him to the other side of the family . . . maybe drag Eliot down to Hell with her.

A confrontation was inevitable between Fiona and Jezebel.

If Eliot got any worse, Fiona would consider breaking their unbreakable rule about never telling on each other—and snitch to Audrey.

That'd put an end to Jezebel once and for all.

One day, though, Fiona was going to have to let Eliot solve his own problems.

Or maybe she should just let him be sad for the rest of his pathetic, moping life—if that's what he really wanted. Talk about picking the absolute wrong person to fall for.

She'd never make that mistake.

Fiona's fingers brushed the envelope she used as a bookmark. Inside was Mitch's letter. She'd never gotten a real personal letter before. (That card on the cursed box of chocolates earlier this year didn't count.) She had it memorized.

> *Fiona,*
> *Hope you're having a great break. I'm visiting family, catching up with old friends, but wishing I was there with you.*
> *What's with Westin's pop quiz? Check out* Our Shadows Wander, *by the way, for essays on the extinct Gypsy Clans.*
> *It's so obvious that she's trying to make up for everyone on Team Scarab getting an A. Well, it's Westin's school and her rules, but if we stick together, she won't be able to beat us.*
> *I enjoyed our walk the other day. I hope we get to do it again.*
> *M.*

His letter was friendly, but not friendly in the way Fiona was hoping for.

Their walk around the world had ended in an embrace, but maybe it had been Mitch just trying to keep her from shivering to death in the chilled Gobi Desert night.

They'd watched the stars fade into the dawn. It was the most romantic thing that had ever happened to her . . . but he *hadn't* kissed her.

She was ready for it. Wanted it.

But he'd just taken her hand and then they'd "walked" back to San Francisco. There hadn't even been any awkward abortive attempt to kiss her at the end of it all. Wasn't that the way these things worked? She just didn't know.

If she'd made the move, would he have gone for it?

Or was he too much of a gentleman to kiss on the first date?

Or was it a sign that he wanted to be friends? And *just* friends?

No way. All that talk about "looking into her soul" and "knowing she was the one for him." That was not "friend" talk.

Maybe if they went out again . . . he'd kiss her. Really, what was the rush?

She fidgeted and sighed, exasperated.

The kitchen door swung open—kicked by Dallas as she entered with both arms loaded with plates. The sun broke through the Bay Area fog, and golden light filled the room.

Her aunt *did* know how to make an entrance.

She set the plates on the table.

There was wild mushroom quiche and crêpes suzette, steaming cinnamon buns with icing, fresh squeezed juices, croissants that smelled divine, artful arrangements of sliced fruits and cheeses, and for each of them— Fiona, Eliot, and Cee—their own steaming cups of cappuccino with heart shapes swirled in foam.

"It's not much," Dallas apologized, "but it was the best I could whip up in your dinky kitchen."

Cee made a strangled coughing noise, poked a croissant, and then retreated back into her kitchen.

Eliot dug in.

So did Fiona. "M-thanks," she said as she chewed fluffy egg and chomped drizzled cinnamon glaze.

Fiona's stomach rumbled, feeling already full, but she forced herself to eat more. It was good.

Dallas sat cross-legged in the chair next to hers and grinned.

Fiona wanted to tell her that she could come over anytime, cook for them morning, noon, and night if she wanted to, but didn't. It would've crushed Cee.

Eliot rolled his eyes. He was in the same predicament, not being able to thank Dallas properly—but not pausing in his feeding to do anything about it.

Fiona took a gulp of pomegranate juice.

"Thanks, Aunt Dallas," she whispered.

Dallas nodded, but her attention was on the school catalog, reading it upside down . . . and her fingers touched Mitch's letter.

Fiona wanted to snatch it away. But that would be rude, especially to someone who just cooked you the best breakfast ever. So instead Fiona gingerly tried to pull the catalog and letter across the table. "That's nothing," she told Dallas. "I was just worrying about classes this semester."

"Anything you want to talk about?" Her tone indicated that she meant things more important than school. Dallas kept one finger on Mitch's letter, as if she could discern the contents within the envelope through her fingertips.

Dallas considered, smiled, and released Mitch's letter. "It's nothing to be ashamed of. I was dizzy and confused the first dozen or so times I got married."

Confused didn't begin to cover how Fiona felt. What she didn't know about boys could fill books, volumes—libraries, even. Someone should've told her how complicated it all got.

On the other hand, if she told Dallas about Mitch, wouldn't that be like telling the League? Would they take an interest in him . . . make sure he was safe and appropriate for their youngest goddess?

And what if they found him wanting? Fiona shuddered.

What was Dallas? In cutoffs and a tank top, she looked more like her older sister than the goddess who had wielded two golden swords and stood toe-to-toe against Abbadon the Destroyer.

Fiona took another sip of juice to clear her throat. "No, I'm okay," Fiona said, but then changed her mind. When would she ever get a chance to talk to an expert on boys? "Well, maybe . . ."

Fiona cast a frustrated glance at her brother.

He sighed, understood that she wanted him gone, and in a rare magnanimous gesture, Eliot excused himself to go to the bathroom.

When Fiona was sure he was out of earshot, she continued, "There's one boy."

Dallas's eyes widened. "One you like, I take it?"

Fiona nodded, feeling the heat rise in her face. Why did she always lose her cool when it came to boys?

"What's stopping you?" Dallas asked.

Fiona huffed out a tiny laugh. "The League. Mother. Who knows what they'd do if they found out I wanted to—"

Fiona couldn't finish the thought. She wasn't sure what she wanted from Mitch. To go out on more dates? To be his girlfriend? And then what?

It was crazy. In her life, with people trying to kill her, how was she supposed to ever have a normal relationship?

"Wait." Fiona's smooth forehead wrinkled with bewilderment. "*You* were married before? To people in the family?"

Dallas laughed. "Never to an Immortal, baby. Don't get me wrong: some of your cousins and uncles are fun"—she looked away, distracted—"and *incredibly* talented, but that's not what I need in a partner. I need someone who can appreciate me for me, not my power, or how being with me alters the politics of the League." She sighed. "Not that it's *ever* uncomplicated. I just get a better connection with a mortal."

"And the League doesn't mind?"

Dallas stiffened. "It's none of their damned business."

Fiona was stunned at this revelation.

Her aunt was 100 percent correct: It *was* none of their business. Fiona had rights as well as responsibilities in the League.

"For people like us," Dallas whispered, "there come too few chances at bliss. You find something that makes you happy—grab it with both hands and don't let go."

Fiona had a lot to process. Like how to balance her life in the League and at school . . . with having a life *at all*.

"Thanks, Aunt Dallas. That helps. A lot."

Dallas smiled. "It's cool. Anytime."

Eliot came back then (his entrance so well timed that Fiona suspected the sneaky *Rattus rattus* had been eavesdropping).

"Oh—there's one more thing that's been bugging us," Fiona said. "Maybe you can clear it up."

Eliot starting eating—then stopped, picking up on Fiona's train of thought. They'd discussed this at length: What had happened to the ancient families' leaders? Satan and Zeus?

"Oh yeah," he said. "At the Battle of Ultima Thule, when you and the others were fighting the Infernals."

"What really happened to Zeus?" Fiona asked. "Mr. Ma said he died there. But there was no body. It was like he walked off or something."

Fiona had a fascination with Zeus. He was the only one ever to lead the *entire* League of Immortals by himself. She'd studied everything there was about him in their assigned textbooks, and had checked out the more obscure references from the library (although there hadn't been any time to crack them) like: *Lightning Eaters and other Tales of the Titans, The Seven Forbidden Lovers,* and *Divum sub Terra.*[44]

At the mention of Zeus, however, her aunt's smile vanished. Outside, fog swallowed the sun.

"Oh, him." Dallas sneered. "The greatest womanizer in all history."

Fiona knew what she meant—all those classical stories about his seductions, the transformation into swans and showers of gold (whatever that was).

"He had to be more than that, though," Fiona whispered. "We saw him leading you. He looked so brave. He was willing to die to save you."

Dallas waved her hands, dismissing those words. "In the old days, maybe. So far back, who can remember?"

"But he did lead the League," Eliot pressed. "Before there was even a Council?"

The light outside further dimmed, and rain pelted the metal roof of their house.

"Yeah." Dallas's face hardened, and she sounded more like Audrey as her tone chilled. "He was a different man—organizing us against the Titans, saving us all . . . before the age of treaties and politics . . . before he grew fat and lazy and lecherous and forgot what he was."

"Did he die?" Fiona asked.

Dallas was quiet a long moment, and then whispered, "I don't *think* so. He was wounded at Thule . . . but he limped off the battlefield. After we started to talk peace with the other family, though, he said his time had

---

44. *Divum sub Terra* (Latin for "Sky under Earth") transcribed from scrolls (ca. 500 B.C.E.) and spirited away from the Library of Alexandra, lost, and then rediscovered in the walls of a Benedictine monastery and translated by Sir Eustace De Vires. The book details the sacrificial rites and prayers of the popular cult of Zeus prominent throughout classical society (*Zeus Olympios*) as well as the more secretive forms driven into hiding, but which survived well beyond the advent of the Christian era. One such cult was dedicated to the "underground" Zeus (*Zeus Katachthonios*) where the deity is often represented as snakes and a man intertwined. The book was ordered destroyed by Papal authority, but two copies survived the 1677 Great Burning in Wittenberg, and found their way to such collectors as Oliver Cromwell, Napoléon Bonaparte, and Charles de Galle, who have praised it for its insights into the philosophies of leadership. *Golden's Guide to Extraordinary Books,* Victor Golden, 1958, Oxford.

come and gone . . . that things were changing, and he no longer wanted to change with them. He left us. Maybe to go die."

The grandfather clock in the hallway chimed out a half hour.

Cecilia came out of the kitchen. "Your lunches! I forgot."

"Oh, stop clucking," Dallas said, and her smile returned. "They're made."

On the table by the stairs sat two paper bags. Scribbled with crayon upon them were masterwork impressionistic scenes: one of the dark forest, the other a seascape.

"A little something for my favorite niece and nephew," Dallas explained with a wink.

"Then off to school with you both," Cee exclaimed. "Miss Westin will skin you alive today if you're late."

Fiona jumped to her feet, not sure if Cee was being literal or not.

Eliot raced for the stairs.

Fiona hesitated, glancing back at her aunt.

"You're just like him," Dallas whispered, ". . . minus the lechery."

Fiona detected a bit of regret in her aunt's eyes, and something else burned inside that she had seen in the Dallas who on the battlefield was fighting for her life—a fire full of power and life and passion.

Then Fiona blinked . . . and noticed the table by the stairs was empty.

She raced after her brother. That rat! He'd grabbed *both* lunches!

49

ELECTIVES

Eliot and Fiona entered the Grand Spring Ballroom. It was the size of an aircraft hangar, filled with crystal chandeliers and miniature lights that mimicked the stars on a clear summer solstice night. Floor-to-ceiling tapestries of courtly dances, pastoral scenes, and major battles covered the walls and made the place seem even larger.

Freshmen usually weren't allowed in here. Eliot shuddered. Good thing, too—because some freshman girls might get the idea they were supposed to have dances.

Miss Westin probably wanted her freshmen focused on studying (and surviving) their first year. For once, Eliot was grateful for homework.

In the center of the ballroom sat a dozen executive desks spaced ten paces apart. Around them students queued, waiting to sit and talk to the adults at the tables. It wasn't just freshmen here, but Paxington upperclassmen, too.

He spotted Amanda, hair in her face, not exactly confident as she'd been the last time he saw her in gym glass—but still a long way from the shy and scared creature she'd been that first day of school.

He'd heard one of the dorms had caught fire over the break. Three students had been hospitalized. Amanda stayed in the dorms, and he was glad to see she was okay.

Eliot and Fiona started toward her, but then it was Amanda's turn in line and she sat at one of the desks.

Eliot examined the adults at the tables. They were dressed in business suits, and each possessed that indefinable air of superiority he'd come to associate with people of power.

"Those must be our counselors," Fiona whispered.

"Teachers?"

"I don't know," she replied. "We've never seen the other teachers before, though. I mean other than Mr. Ma and Miss Westin."

Jeremy and Sarah Covington sat at one table. Jeremy spoke vigorously to the little old man on the other side of the desk. Jeremy stood and paced, gesticulating wildly . . . although still smiling. The old man smiled, too, but kept shaking his head.

Sarah fidgeted in her seat. She made eye contact with Eliot and looked away.

The funny thing was, Eliot didn't *hear* anything from their table . . . none of them, actually. Like the sound didn't travel.

A group of girls spotted Fiona. "Oh, Fiona!" one called out. They all moved toward her.

That was her pack of admirers. They were always trying to make small talk and find out what it was like being a goddess in the League.

Fiona sighed, but nonetheless smiled and waved back to them . . . trying to move on, but she was too slow and they intercepted her.

Eliot dropped back.

How was it that everyone loved Fiona (or at least loved the fame, money, and immortality they thought she represented) but not one of the students at Paxington had made the connection that Eliot, her brother, her *twin*, might be in the League of Immortals, too?

It was like last week when he had followed Jezebel to the Market Street BART station. When he stayed in the shadows, no one saw him. Like he was invisible.

At school . . . he wasn't invisible, not optically anyway. For some reason, though, he seemed to be *socially* transparent.

Maybe it was some Infernal power, a sort of mental sleight of hand that he was doing without thinking about it.

He looked for Jezebel, but saw not a trace of her platinum curls among the crowds. Jezebel didn't blend well. She would have had a crowd of boys around her. That would be okay with Eliot—just to know that she was here, safe.

No luck.

And no Robert, either. Although if *he* had wanted to blend, Eliot was sure he couldn't have spotted him. He made a note to ask how Robert did it . . . and compare notes on social invisibilities.

"Hey!" someone called out.

Eliot looked. Across the room, Mitch Stephenson waved at him.

So much for the "invisibility" theory. Mitch saw him just fine.

Eliot waved back.

That was a mistake, a humiliating one. Mitch had waved to get Fiona's attention—not his.

He noticed Eliot waving like a complete dork, though, and shifted his glance a notch. His waved at Eliot, too, trying to make it look like that's what he'd been doing.

Eliot appreciated the gesture, but didn't feel any better about his near-zero social status.

"Mr. Post?"

Eliot turned to the deep baritone voice behind him.

Harlan Dells stood there, his hands clasped behind his back. He looked like a funeral director today in a black suit and tie, his blond beard braided into a single tight cord.

"Uh, hey, Mr. Dells. How are you?"

"Fine, young man, but you and your sister have an appointment now. And your counselor is not known for her infinite patience."

Mr. Dells gestured to Fiona. She saw him even while surrounded by her pack. The other girls saw the Keeper of Paxington's Gate as well, and all simultaneously shut up.

Fiona trotted to Eliot's side. "Hello, Mr. Dells. What can I do for you?"

"There." Mr. Dells nodded to the far corner of the ballroom. "Do not keep her waiting, more than you have already."

Eliot squinted into the shadows. There was some light in the corner: four candles floated in the gloom. No . . . as his eyes adjusted, he saw the candles sat on the corners of large desk, almost hidden in the folds of black curtains.

And sitting, watching them, her glasses reflecting flames, was Miss Westin, her hands steepled on the desk.

"*She's* our guidance counselor?" Fiona whispered.

Miss Westin looked like a spider in the center of a dark web . . . one that no student dared get close to. Just like the repellent field that Eliot seemed to have around him. Maybe he and the Headmistress had something in common, after all.

"Come on." Eliot crossed the room, moving deeper into the dark, away from the crowds. He settled into one of the high-backed chairs across the desk from her.

Fiona caught up and sat in the other chair.

"Good morning, children," Miss Westin said. She pulled out two file folders with their names printed on the sides and set them down.

"Good morning, Headmistress," they said in unison.

"No sound may leave the confines of this desk," Miss Westin said. "This session is completely confidential even from your parents."

Eliot glanced at Fiona and she shot back the same curious look. Why the secrecy? It was just their class schedule. Like Audrey wouldn't know what it was in a few hours anyway.

But maybe that was the point: Their mother would know *in a few hours,* after they'd signed up for their elected classes . . . and too late to make any objections. This would be entirely their choice. How often did *that* happen?

"Miss Post first." Miss Westin opened Fiona's file.

Miss Westin scanned her official Paxington record. From across the table, Eliot saw an account of her duel with Donald van Wyck, and photographs of her looking ferocious in gym class.

"Your performance last semester was remarkable," Miss Westin said.

Fiona sat up straighter, basking in this rare praise from the Headmistress.

"Most freshmen, however, fail to maintain their grades in the second semester," Miss Westin went on without looking up. "They are either too stupid to keep up with their studies, or more concerned with their social agendas to grow and excel.

"So," she said to Fiona, "shall I sign you up for Mythology 102 and Mr. Ma's classes and call it good?" There was a challenge in her voice.

It was wasted on Fiona, of course, because she had already decided to take that advanced fighting class, Force of Arms.

"No, ma'am," Fiona smugly replied. "I've already picked out an elective." She opened the catalog and turned it for Miss Westin to see.

Miss Westin smiled.

That smile chilled Eliot to the core. The only thing that came close was the lethal permanent grin of the crocodile oracle, Sobek. There was nothing unusual in her smile—just perfectly white and straight, but ordinary teeth, and yet Eliot sensed death in her bite.

Miss Westin glanced at the catalog. "Force of Arms?" One eyebrow arched.

"Is that a problem?" Fiona asked.

"There are prerequisites." Miss Westin flipped to the next page. At the top, the Force of Arms entry continued.

Fiona looked startled, as if she hadn't seen this before.

It read:

> **PREREQUISITES:** For sophomores or older students. Must have parental/guardian consent. Must pass a test of minimal expertise.

"Oh . . ." Fiona started to pull the catalog back, and her forehead wrinkled.

Miss Westin, however, kept the book, pinning it to the desk. "Perhaps," she said, "in light of your record, it would be appropriate for me to waive to sophomore requirement . . . if you could manage to pass the qualifying test and obtain a signed permission slip."

Fiona licked her lips. "I can pass any test, ma'am."

Fiona, though, made no comment on the signed parental permission slip. That would be the tricky part.

Miss Westin made a few marks on Fiona's record. "Very well. Let us hope that your talent for passing tests translates to real-world challenges."

Miss Westin then closed her file and turned to Eliot's.

Eliot had near identical grades. There were photos of him in gym class, too (although he looked more clueless than heroic somehow in *his* shots). There were also several handwritten notes on Paxington stationery. The script was too tiny for him to make out . . . but Miss Westin made disappointing clicking noises as she read over them.

She looked up. Because they were both sitting, and because the angle was just right, for one brief moment in the candlelight Eliot saw behind her glasses. Unfiltered by the lenses, her eyes were not their usual brown. Instead, the irises were clear and brilliant like cut diamonds.

"And for you Mr. Post? What shall it be? Trivial social pursuits? Or would you like to learn something this semester beyond the bare minimum and keep pace with your sister?"

Eliot bristled at that.

He wasn't going to take any class that got him bruised and battered any more than he was already getting in gym (and with Robert after school).

"No, ma'am," he replied. "I mean, yes, I'll be taking an elective class." He nodded at the catalog. "Page twenty-three, if you wouldn't mind."

Miss Westin ran a finger along the edge of the catalog, flipped open to the precise page, and scanned the class descriptions.

"Extraordinarily dangerous," she murmured, and tapped her lower lip thoughtfully. "Are you absolutely sure?"

"What is it?" Fiona leaned forward.

Miss Westin turned the catalog to face him. "This one, correct?" She pointed to

THE POWER OF MUSIC: Seminars discussing music as applied to theoretical magical structures. Practice for instruments and/or voice held twice a week with emphasis on emotive control. Periodic evaluation before live audiences. Prerequisites: Must pass an audition. Signed waiver for the student's soul.

"For the soul?" Fiona whispered. "What does that mean?"

"The class is far more perilous than any physical combat," Miss Westin explained. She turned Eliot. "But you know that already, don't you?"

"Yeah," Eliot whispered.

When he first read that part about the soul, Eliot had thought it was a joke. But it wasn't. It's what he felt every time he played—and something weird and strange and wondrous happened. There was a connection between the magic and the music and his soul—and risk as well. He knew that his soul teetered on the edge of some unknown precipice when he played . . . and he had to know why.

Next to him, Fiona shuddered. She opened her mouth as if she had something to say, but couldn't articulate it, and then after a moment, she whispered, "Are you sure about this?"

Eliot met his sister's concerned gaze.

There was another reason to take the new course. Last semester, he and Fiona had had every class together. These electives would separate them. Cee had told them, and it'd been proved over and over, that they were stronger together.

But that was the point.

Eliot sometimes felt like he was *only* strong with his sister. He couldn't go through his entire life depending on her. He had to stand on his own feet.

"Yeah," he whispered back. "I'm sure."

Worry and then resolve flashed over Fiona's features, and she nodded . . .

maybe even on some level understanding him for once, for once even *agreeing*.

Eliot guessed she had come to similar conclusions about the two of them—maybe she would be happy to finally be getting rid of her "little" brother . . . or maybe she had something to prove as well.

Miss Westin signed the bottom of Eliot's record and closed it. "I do believe," she said, "you will have a most enlightening experience this semester—provided you two survive."

50

NO MATCH FOR HIS CHARM AND INTELLECT

Louis Piper took one of the many twisty and illegal passages that led to the main entrance thoroughfare of the Paxington Institute. He had to squeeze through shadows and push past trash cans and those homeless wretches who belonged neither in the Middle Realms nor in the island of space that Paxington occupied.

Bums. Beggars. Prostitutes.

Myths and heroes and nightmares who'd fallen on hard times: Mordred . . . Mr. Nox . . . the ever-blinded Gorgon. Why couldn't they respectably crawl into a bottle and try to make themselves disappear as *he* had?

He avoided their lecherous, leprous touches and piteous calls, turned the corner—

—and emerged in the sunlight and relatively fresh air behind the Café Eridanus.

Louis glanced at the Dumpster but avoided it (although old habits died hard and he *was* famished). Best not to tarnish his image further, however. He sniffed at his shoulder to make sure he was unscathed by the unwashed in the alley.

In truth, his dapper appearance was for once not foremost in his thoughts. That honor was reserved for his beloved Audrey.

He had been thinking of her much—too much, such that it now interfered with his normal scheming. It was painful to dwell upon her. She was so lovely. And this entire affair so charged with unexpected nauseous sentimentality.

Who could've ever predicted he could still be in love? Or was it lust?

No. His lust was simply (if only ever temporarily) satiated.

But there was no cure for his desires now . . . to hold her hand . . . to be with her . . . those wants *never* ebbed.

He hissed out a sigh of frustration. See? Such reminiscing clouded rational thoughts—interfered with his making of plans most intricate.

And *that* was the kernel of the matter: He had spent considerable energy on figuring out ways to increase his power, gather lands, and rule all the realms . . . but at the same time, he sought benefit for his fledgling, broken family—Audrey, Eliot, and Fiona.

Well, at least to keep them from harm.

Or, perhaps, try not to get them all killed.

Why was it so difficult to think clearly?

Direct deception and intervention had not worked. That last call to Audrey—what had he been thinking? Confessing his love like some besotted teenager? He had almost died from mortification after she had rightly hung up on him.

So, no more of that—thank you very much.

A roundabout approach was his next-best option.

Louis smoothed out his camel-hair coat, straightened his black tie, and strode from the alley's shadow.

He surveyed the few students sitting beneath the star-covered canopied tables outside the café. One boy caught his eye, a mortal with brown hair that curled down to his shoulders. He flashed a winning smile at the waitress as she served him cocoa.

Louis recognized him from Amberflaxus's reports. This was the mortal he'd come to see: Mitchell Stephenson.

The boy stirred the whipped cream atop his hot chocolate. There were two empty cups on the table. Was he waiting for Fiona? Young Mr. Stephenson picked up the bill, considered, and then took out some cash and set it down for the waitress.

What delightfully perfect timing.

Louis whistled and strolled forward, waving away the hostess as she tried to seat him.

Mitch Stephenson hadn't yet taken notice of him. Odd, given that the Stephenson family was infamous for their practice of white magic. Their attempts, for a mortal family, against Infernals was admirable . . . not because they had been successful, but rather that they had managed over the centuries not to be exterminated. According to Louis's sources, the lad had gifts as well as training. Radiant conjurations. A flicker of witch sight, too.

One would think, then, he would know when the Prince of Darkness was in his midst.

The boy's mental thickness was a small disappointment. But then again, it would be nice to interact with a mortal who was no match for his charms and intellect.

Louis cleared his throat.

Mitch looked up, and confusion wavered over his face. Perhaps Louis's power and grace had overwhelmed the boy.

"Can I help you?" Mitch asked.

"You may indeed, young man. I am Louis." He extended a hand to shake. "Louis Piper."

Mitch's confusion congealed into wariness, and he stared at the offered hand.

"Louis Piper," Louis repeated. "Fiona's father?"

"Ah!" Mitch smiled. "Fiona's family."

Louis instantly revised his opinion of the lad. That smile . . . Perhaps he was a little dense, but there was some quality about him that was endearing.

"Wait—her *father's* side of the family?" Mitch's grin disappeared, and he nodded dismissively at Louis's hand.

Louis withdrew, wounded, his blood rising.

But then he understood. Mitchell Stephenson would, of course, know Infernal customs: They never shook hands unless the circumstances were extraordinary. One might lose fingers, arms . . . one's soul if not careful.

Louis chuckled. He knew better now than to ask for a seat, so he took one across the table.

Mitch set both his hands on the table.

Excellent. Another proper Infernal custom. Hands in the open—a gesture to indicate that no weapons were being readied under the table, a prerequisite to any serious discussion. Louis mirrored the gesture.

What fun. This was like a game of chess with a Grandmaster on one side, a child on the other. Amusing, for now . . . although Louis feared it would soon grow dull.

Louis decided to play along and honor human customs as well. He would start with small talk and break the ice, the unnecessary social fluff that all humans seemed to enjoy.

"Isn't the weather pleasant today?" Louis asked. "I've heard wonderful things about you, young man. An A-minus on your midterms—wonderful!"

One corner of Mitch's mouth twitched, and he eased back into his chair.

This was so easy. Humans were ever so willing to be buttered up. Perhaps the Stephenson family was not all their reputation had led him to believe.

"Say what you came to say, Deceiver," Mitch spat out, somehow managing to sound repulsed and polite the same time.

Louis blinked. The boy had some spine somewhere in all that base human flesh, after all.

"Very well," Louis said. "Cards on the table, as you people say. I came to discuss my daughter."

Mitch snorted. "You know she hates you Infernals? Every time they're mentioned, her hackles rise."

Louis quickly stopped a scowl from creasing his face, and hid his true feelings behind a smile.

Was this mortal baiting him? And why did his words sting so?

Fiona didn't *hate* him, did she? No—they had had a wonderful discussion when last they spoke . . . although perhaps she was uneasy with Louis's new and magnificent presence.

"Be that as it may," Louis said with deliberate calm, "I thought it high time to speak to the young man courting her."

"If you think I need your approval to go out with Fiona, you've wasted your time as well as mine."

How had this conversation turned? The boy should not be acting like this. He should be charming and gracious, humble—or, at least, terrified of Louis. What were they teaching teenagers at Paxington these days? Whatever it was, he approved.

Or was there something else to this mortal?

Louis forged ahead. There were ways to appeal to young men, especially shrewd young men such as this.

"Of course," Louis agreed. "Fiona knows her own mind. I could see she has chosen wisely. No, I came to offer *you* a deal."

Mitch's eyes flickered with interest, and he leaned forward. "What precisely are you offering?"

Louis had him now. He had but to tease just a bit more to set the hook. It was almost too easy . . . but that was fine. Louis could enjoy a small, simple victory, a long overdue sign that his luck was changing for the better. He'd purchase this boy's soul with some trinkets and use him to worm his way into Fiona's good graces.

Louis's hands curled slightly on the tabletop, his nails scratching the glass in anticipation of victory.

"Why, I am offering you the world, young man," Louis whispered with utmost sincerity. "Money, power, and all that goes with it. As much as you dare grab with both hands."

Mitch cocked an eyebrow and leaned even farther forward. "And in return for these grand boons, sir, you expect . . . what?"

Louis almost laughed out loud at someone calling him "sir." This was perfection.

"Just a trifling thing: an alliance of a sort."

Mitch looked unconvinced, but he turned over one hand on the table, the traditional signal of his willingness to bargain.

Louis nodded at the empty cocoa cups. "It is obvious you require help with my daughter. If you truly knew her, you'd realize that the mere smell of chocolate is enough to make her disgorge her breakfast."

Mitch's eyes widened. "I hadn't realized."

"It's the little things in romance that women notice," Louis told him. "Details count. I have a nearly infinite amount of experience in these matters. Let me help you."

"So you're giving power and money and help with Fiona?" Mitch murmured. "But you mentioned an alliance? . . ."

"Only the smallest of considerations in my behalf," Louis said with a careless wave. "Fiona and I have had our moments, but there are so many family matters we have yet to settle. Her mother has made things most difficult."

"Still confused over here," Mitch said, his eyes narrowing.

Something about this boy was achingly familiar. Had they spoken before? Louis searched his memory: there was nothing but suspicion.

"After I have helped you secure your relationship with my daughter, from time to time I would have you mention—as a natural part of the conversation, mind you—how misunderstood I am. As a Stephenson, being an authority on such things, you can just let it slip out that among the Infernals I am the noblest, kindest, and most generous of their ilk."

"I get the idea," Mitch said. "You want me to lie."

Louis frowned. "'Lie' is such an overused word. But no, never lie to Fiona. She would know the instant you spoke such a thing to her."

"She can hear lies already?" Mitch whispered.

"Yes, yes," Louis continued. "All you need do is tell her the truth about me . . . perhaps embellish as you see fit. I do have her best interests at heart."

Mitch stared into his eyes, searching. "Astonishing. I believe you do." Then he blinked and was all business again. "So you don't want my soul?"

Louis laughed. "No, what would I want with your soul?"

The point was moot. If young Stephenson made this deal, upon his death his soul would naturally seek Louis's realm (provided he had land by then). Of course, there was no need to mention this detail.

Louis spread his hands to the edge of the table. "All that is within my power to give shall be yours."

Mitch considered this a moment; then his smile returned.

Louis grinned as well. So easy.

Mitch lifted his hand off the table and reached across toward Louis.

Louis did the same. All that formal business with written contracts and blood signatures could wait—a handshake would suffice and be binding for now.

Mitch, however, didn't clasp his hand. He instead grabbed the saltshaker off the table. With a flick of his fingers and some sleight of hand trickery, the top popped.

Mitch upended it and dumped a line of salt on the table between them.[45]

"May you one day choke on the truth," Mitch said.

Most vile of insults! The boys *did* know their customs. Louis's claws found purchase and cracked the glass tabletop.

He took a deep breath . . . resisting the impulse to remove the young man's head. Not here. Too many witnesses. Someone would escape. And with his luck, Fiona would find out, and one more plan would backfire.

"So you, too, wish to bring Fiona to your side, Old Scratch?" Mitch

---

45. Salt appears in many world religions as a bane to evil. Since ancient times, bowls of salt were placed by the door to keep the devil at bay (until he had counted every grain). It is used in contemporary religious rites such as the Traditional Latin Mass, exorcisms, and in the Shinto purification rituals of sumo wrestling rings prior to a match. The substance's effectiveness has diminished since ancient times (if it ever existed). In Infernal parlances, the use of salt, especially when relating to business, is considered a grave insult because it infers that the insulted Infernal is so weak as to be affected by such a common substance. *Gods of the First and Twenty-first Century, Volume 13, Infernal Forces.* Zypheron Press Ltd., Eighth Edition.

laughed. "As always, behind the curve on such things. Fiona is her own side now. She doesn't need to join yours."

Louis hardly heard, so strong did the blood thunder through his body. Fiona her own side? What nonsense . . . and yet, he detected no lie.

"Clearly you are addled," Louis whispered. "Or suicidal. Those are the only reasons for you being so reckless with such opportunities."

Louis pushed away from the table, glaring at the salt between them. He reached out and scattered the offensive substance—as if such a trifling thing could ever stop him.

"When next we meet," Louis growled, "there will be no table between us, young man. No veil of politeness, either. No deals. And no witnesses."

Mitch nodded, unfazed. "I know. And I look forward to it, Deceiver."

The boy smiled again, that same welcoming, warming smile Louis had first seen—only now there was an edge to it.

Outrageous! Louis strode back into the alley, where he could properly fume.

He had been a fool to deal with this boy. He should've realized that a practitioner of white magic would've been confused by Louis's advanced sense of flexibile morality.

This left only one roundabout option . . . perhaps where Louis should've started in the first place: with his own kind. They, at least, would recognize the value of a double deal and proper backstabbing when presented with one.

Yes, he would approach Eliot's potential paramour, the delectable Jezebel.

Although this would mean a trip to the Poppy Lands and a smoothing of things with Sealiah. Perhaps it was not a bad idea. He had dwelled far too long in the world of light. A trip to the old country would be rejuvenating.

And he could use Sealiah to forget, he hoped, Audrey.

Besides, providence had provided the cash for the train ticket and all appropriate bribes. He opened his hand and counted the money that young Mr. Stephenson had left on the table for the waitress—the money Louis had snatched as he scattered the salt.

One never turned one's back on so simple an opportunity.

Such a large tip! Indeed, how was Louis supposed to do business with such fools?

51

NO MORE JUST FRIENDS

Fiona staggered into the locker room, half-dead.

Mr. Ma had made them do calisthenics and reflex drills all afternoon.

It hadn't helped when Fiona asked why they had been singled out for this punishment, and Sarah added that it was unfair because their parents spent fortunes to send them here and this wasn't a prison camp, and Amanda had even asked why Teams Dragon and Wolf weren't doing the same exercises.

By way of answering, Mr. Ma made the girls run around the coliseum five times, while the rest the team was dismissed.

The man was a sadist.

She would've been angry . . . had she the energy. As it was, she was barely able to stand and let the shower run over her body.

Fiona toweled off and sat on the bench by her locker.

Amanda came out of the shower a moment later, her towel tight about her body. Sarah followed, towel wrapped only about her head, unabashedly glowing and looking refreshed as if she'd just taken a light jog.

Conspicuously absent was Jezebel. No one had seen her since the new semester started, an entire week ago.

Amanda pulled away the hair plastered to her face, and followed Fiona's gaze to Jezebel's locker. "You think she's okay? She didn't look so great after the midterm match."

"I don't know," Fiona replied.

"Jezebel is an Infernal," Sarah said, "and she's shrugged off damage that would have shattered a normal person's bones. But she better get back soon." She took out her blow-dryer and shook out her mane of red hair.

"Team Scarab is down its strongest fighter." She turned on the dryer and preened in front of a mirror.

Sarah was coldheartedly pragmatic, but correct.

If Jezebel never came back, Fiona better think up new strategies for how to win matches. By the rules, they had to get half the team to their flag to win. With seven on their team, was half three or four people, then? She bet Mr. Ma would round up to four.

And what about Eliot? It wasn't exaggerating to say he might have a "fatal" crush on the Infernal. Would he get over her? Or would his darkening mood just get worse? Or maybe, if Jezebel never came back, it'd be the *best* thing for him.

Fiona glanced at Amanda and wondered if she'd ever tell Eliot she liked him. It was so obvious . . . even to Fiona, who—let's face it—was no expert in boy–girl relationships.

On the other hand, if Amanda told him, and then Jezebel came back . . . who knows what the Infernal might do to her. Probably laugh. Or kill her.

Poor Amanda. Poor Eliot.

She had a feeling that no matter what, they were going to get hurt.

It was the same with Robert. Sometimes she wished he'd just go away. That sounded cruel, but it was true.

Anyway, she had Mitch now.

Sarah finished her hair: it shone and curled with expert precision in a completely relaxed and natural-looking way. She looked over at Amanda and her tangles, frowning, but not offering any advice.

"How do you know a boy likes you?" Fiona asked Sarah.

Sarah blinked. "With your looks and social connections, I wouldn't worry. *All* the boys like you."

Fiona blushed and started to get dressed, suddenly feeling a little too exposed.

"I mean," Fiona continued, "say a boy likes you, you think, but you're not sure how much . . . or what exactly his intentions are."

"Oh . . . ," Sarah said, "a coy one, then, is it? They're the most dangerous of all."

Out of the corner of her eye, Fiona noted that Amanda eagerly listened, soaking up any boy advice that might accidentally drift her way.

"We are talking about Mitch, then?" Sarah asked.

Fiona's blush deepened.

"Well, he likes you. It's obvious. Don't be so thick."

"He smiles at everyone," Amanda added, "but the way he smiles at you . . . no one but you gets *that*."

"Really?" Fiona suddenly felt out of breath.

"But that's a problem," Sarah said as she tied her hair up with a royal blue velvet ribbon. "You hinted there was something between you and Robert last summer?"

"That's none of your business," Fiona snapped.

"Don't get your feathers ruffled." Sarah patted the bench next to her. "It is my business. All of ours, in fact."

Fiona sat.

"Mitch is a wonderful lad, and so is Robert," Sarah said, "but if you pick one over the other, then what happens to the team? Would Robert want to get even with Mitch? At the very least, they wouldn't be working *together* when we needed them to in a match, would they?"

Fiona wasn't sure. Robert was above that sort of thing, wasn't he?

And Mitch? He'd acted like nothing but a gentleman (which was part of the problem).

Fiona had a vision of the two of them dueling with sabers on campus. She shook her head to clear it.

"I'd never tell you how to run your personal affairs," Sarah whispered. "Just be careful. We have three more matches to get our rank high enough to graduate. You might want to be nice to *both of them*. For a bit longer?"

Fiona didn't know. That wouldn't be fair to Robert; it might actually be dangerous for him. And it certainly wouldn't be fair to Mitch. Or her.

"Let's get some coffee," Amanda suggested. "We can figure it all out to-gether."

"Coffee?" Fiona stood bolt upright. "I was supposed to meet Mitch at Café Eridanus half an hour ago!"

Fiona grabbed her Paxington jacket, hesitated, and then told Sarah, "Don't worry. It's just coffee."

Sarah nodded, although she did not look at all convinced.

"See you!" Fiona waved to Sarah and Amanda and ran out of the locker room.

She burst out of the Ludus Magnus and almost ran over Mitch in the bone-encrusted entrance tunnel.

"Whoa!" He dodged her—without dropping the take-out coffee cups in his hands.

"I'm so sorry," Fiona said.

"No harm." He flashed his smile—that *special* smile that he had only for her (or so Amanda thought).

True or not, that grin warmed her more than any run around the coliseum or hot coffee ever could.

"I thought we were meeting at the café?"

"I was going to suggest we take another walk," he said. "The café's too crowded."

"A 'walk' like last time?"

Mitch handed her one of the coffees and then offered her his free hand. "A walk *better* than last time. I've got a few surprises scouted out." His smile intensified.

Fiona almost dropped the coffee. Her legs wobbled, but he didn't notice.

"Sure," she said, managing to sound causal—as if she took strolls around the world with boys who might like her every afternoon. Her pulse thundered in her ears.

He took her free hand in his and started down the winding path to Bristlecone Hall.

But after a dozen steps, nothing happened. They were just walking.

"Oh, I thought—"

"We are." He gave her hand a squeeze. "But we can't leave Paxington like that—some security feature. Mr. Dells had a talk with me about it."

Fiona nodded. No one but students and staff were allowed on campus by foot or by car, and apparently there were restrictions on the use of magic, too, to cross its boundaries. As if Paxington were its own little country. She remembered how Dallas and Kino had waited for her outside the school gates, which made sense only if even the gods were forbidden from entering.

What kind of agreement did Paxington have with the League and the Infernals and the mortal magical families that let them operate with that kind of autonomy?

She turned her attention to the warmth flowing from Mitch's hand into hers. He'd picked the long, roundabout way to the gate. Was that because he had *wanted* to hold her hand for the pleasure of holding it? Wanted, as she did, to make it last as long as possible?

She squeezed his hand back. "Hey, normal walking—just fine with me," she said.

"You looked like you had a lot on your mind coming out of the coliseum."

"Oh, the girls and I were talking about our last three matches—trying to come up with strategies to deal with our missing Jezebel."

Fiona omitted their discussion of the boy–boy–girl dynamics of Team Scarab, and how her personal relationships could potentially sink their team's ranking.

Mitch nodded. "Jezebel missing isn't a huge problem. Not anymore. Every team in second semester is down at least one person. Dropouts, injuries—happens every year."

The walked past the pedunculate oak called the Hangman of London. Its giant shadow crossed their path, and fog blew through its twisting branches. It reminded her of the misty graveyards that led to the Borderlands.

Fiona definitely preferred the sunshine these days. She took a sip of the coffee to warm her. It was perfect: lots of cream and no sugar. Just how she liked it.

"If teams get too small, people get reassigned," Mitch continued. "I have an aunt who's a Paxington alumna, and she explained it all to me."[46]

"You mean they could break up Scarab?"

What if she and Mitch, Robert, Amanda . . . or Eliot got reassigned to different teams? How could she ever compete *against* any of them?

"No worries. We're only down *one*. And theoretically, Jezebel could show up any time. If she doesn't, it's more likely Scarab will pick up a straggler from another team."

Then maybe Jezebel going missing could turn out to be a good thing. As an Infernal, she was the strongest person on their team, but that didn't make up for being a monster. Not to mention the effect she had on Eliot.

The sun broke through the fog as they emerged near Bristlecone Hall, and they strode along the cobblestone path to the front gate.

It might all actually work out for the best. Fiona playfully swung her arm with Mitch's.

Mr. Dells opened the gate. "Have a wonderful day, kids." His laserlike gaze, however, carefully tracked Mitch as they left.

"We will," Fiona told him.

---

46. Genevieve Stephenson-Hines, one of the longer-lived of the Stephenson clan, retired from the practice of white magic at the age of 106. Whereabouts unknown, but no record of her death exists, so she may still be alive. —Editor.

As they approached the end of the thoroughfare, Mitch whispered, "Here we go. Hang on." His smile vanished and intense concentration crossed his face.

There was vertigo, a flash of light, and a step—

—and the concrete sidewalk they were just walking upon was a path of granite strewn with pebbles and dust.

The air was clean and fresh and cold. Fiona blinked to adjust to the brighter light; she saw that they were on a mountain path. Flags and streamers fluttered along the precipitous edge. Titanic granite ridges jutted into a startling blue sky, and *below* them roiled clouds.

"Listen," Mitch whispered.

Fiona cocked her head. In the distance echoed bird cries.

A flock of cranes broke through the clouds—hundreds of flashing wings and gray-blue feathers streamed up toward them, and then over their heads.

"It's their spring migration," Mitch explained. "They go right over the top of the Himalayas. Reminds me of what we do at school. All of us trying to get to the top."

Fiona watched the flock flap through the thin air, higher and higher.

"Every year," he said, "they struggle to get over this mountain. Some don't. Some die. Are we the same? It's great we're learning, but why? Graduate with honors? Be like our parents?"

The flock crested the ridge. The cranes called out once and then glided effortlessly, silent, exhausted, and vanished.

"I definitely don't want to be like *my* parents," Fiona replied.

That would be a choice between her emotionally distant mother, and her father, who was . . . what? A monster? At best, a liar and thief.

"Not knowing what I want to be is part of the reason I'm at a Paxington," she said. "I need to get my bearings and figure a few things out."

That wasn't the entire truth, though. Fiona had something to prove at school, too: that she was as good as anyone else—not only at school, but at the League as well.

"I guess," Mitch said. "I just wish they gave us some breathing room in our schedules." He exhaled. "Speaking of breathing"—he pulled her along—"we should move. It's not good to be at this altitude for too long without oxygen."

They trudged along the path, Fiona started feeling a bit dizzy now, and they rounded a ledge and into shadows—

—and stumbled over roots and underbrush, and a flock of butterflies took to the air, making a storm of confetti-like flutterings.

"This way," Mitch said, pushing branches out of their way.

Fiona struggled to breathe the now heavier, moist air. She got her bearings and saw the faintest of trails snaking through the jungle. There were stone heads as big as houses and overgrown with hundred-year-old tree roots. Those idols stared at her with blind sockets.

Ahead was the sound of water churning and crashing.

Mitch stopped abruptly and parted ferns for her.

They stood on the edge of a river that plunged into a kilometer-wide sinkhole. Along the steep edges, trees and vines grew at precipitous angles. The water never seemed to hit the bottom—instead it vaporized into rainbows.

"Down there is the Cavern of the Six Fairy Kings," Mitch whispered in hushed awe. "There's supposedly a trail leading down . . . somewhere. I've never found it. The cave is one of the fabled gateways to the Faerie Lands—if you believe that sort of thing."[47, 48]

"Jeremy would give anything to see this," Fiona whispered.

"Like I'd ever bring *him* here." Mitch said.

So many places, and so many fantastic sights, and being with Mitch—it was disorienting, but Fiona nonetheless managed to pick up their conversation where it left off. "So, Mr. Stephenson," she said, "why are *you* at Paxington?"

Mitch's smile faded. He let go of her and laced his hands, thinking. "At first, because it's what was expected of me. I studied for years, sacrificing, and taking tests."

He fell silent; his gaze drifted to the waterfall.

"But?" Fiona asked.

47. The mythohistorical origins of fairies remain inconclusive, although there are many theories: the dead, angels (demoted or otherwise), elemental forces, transformed mortals, baby's laughs, or pagan gods. Supposedly fairies live in a realm severed from the remote nether realms, borderlands, and purgatories. To travel to, and more notably *back from*, their realm is fraught with danger even by nether realm standards. Journey is never by happenstance, and beings only rarely depart by special permission (e.g., the Faery Queen's Silver Bough, which must be held at all times to avoid the glamours and charms of her realm and subjects). *A Primer on the Middle Realms*, Paxington Institute Press, LLC.

48. "When I trod to Avalon / not did man come back anon. / 'Tis not me now writing this. / My soul lost, a' wander bliss." *Mythica Improbiba* (translated version), Father Sildas Pious. ca. thirteenth century.

"But . . . it's not like I thought it would be. Paxington. The people there. Even this world we live in. It's more complicated than I thought, terrible— and wonderful, too."

For the first time, she saw Mitch struggle with some inner turmoil. "I want to change it all," he told her, and looked into her eyes. "Immortals and the magical families, the way they run things . . . it's all so political and greedy. It's about power and not about people or principles."

Fiona nodded. "I think I know what you mean. The League of Immortals used to stand for something—order and fighting wrongs, but that seemed to end with a treaty with the Infernals. All that's left today is posturing and politicking. Where did all their greatness go?"

They both fell silent, the only sound the thundering of the water.

"So let's change it together," she suggested, and found his hand again and wove her fingers through his.

He didn't object, and he looked at her hand, turning it over.

"No," he told her. "What I want to do one day . . . it'll be stupid . . . and probably dangerous."

"I'm willing to do stupid, dangerous things, as long as it's with you." A smile crept across her face.

"Maybe," he whispered. "I still have to figure a few things out." He shook his head, looked up, saw her smiling, and mirrored it. "Hey, let's just get through our next match and then we can plot to change the world."

"Sure."

But Fiona was already dreaming about what it would be like to make the world a better place. How would they begin? With magic? Politics? Something subversive?

Mitch led her down the path until it faded, and then through the deep shade of a banyan tree—

—and they stepped from its shadow to one cast by a lamppost onto Pacific Avenue in San Francisco.

"There we go," Mitch said. "A few blocks from home, all safe and sound."

Fiona bit her lip. That was it?

Then she stopped her pout. Mitch had just revealed one of his deepest secrets to her, taken her to the Himalayas, probably to Indonesia, and back here. She was getting spoiled by all the magic . . . and all the attention Mitch was giving her.

He stepped closer, still holding her hand, and said, "Don't tell anyone how I feel about Paxington and the families. I can imagine what they'd think or do if they knew I was such a rebel."

She touched his lips with her finger, silencing him. The softness of his flesh sent a ripple of electricity along her arm.

"I won't tell—even though I think what you've said is the noblest thing I've ever heard."

He nodded and pulled back a tiny bit. "Well . . ." He cleared his throat. "I guess we better hit the books, huh?"

Fiona wasn't letting him slip away this time.

She grabbed him and pulled him back—her lips met his, and she melted into his arms as he wrapped them about her.

Whatever happened next . . . let Robert and the rest of them sort it all out. Let Team Scarab crash and burn and fail, for all she cared.

What she had here and now was everything she wanted.

AUDITION OF STARS

Eliot followed the map he'd been given by Mr. Dells. *"For your audition to-day,"* Mr. Dells had said, and then told Eliot that he had to go alone. Mr. Dells had handed Fiona a similar map and wished her luck.

It was weird—Eliot and Fiona going to different courses—but Eliot couldn't imagine Fiona in a music class, and there was no way he was signing up for *more* organized mayhem at Paxington. Gym class and boxing lessons with Robert were enough.

The map was crudely drawn. The Ludus Magnus was an oval, and the paths around squiggles. The way he was supposed to take was indicated by a stick figure. That path supposedly wandered through the Grove Primeval . . . only there wasn't a path there. He knew, because he'd walked this way a hundred times and never seen it.

And yet, when he approached the spot marked on the map where a willow tree everyone called the Lady in Mourning stood—there it was, another path paved with worn black stones.

That was so typical of Paxington.

There were areas hidden, he guessed, from freshmen, and maybe for good reason. Things probably got rougher for the upperclassmen, which probably would have been lethal for him. That would explain why Eliot only rarely saw older students on campus.

Just how big was this school, anyway?

Eliot walked onto the new path.

The trees grew larger here, oaks with ancient black trunks that twisted upward into the sky.

The forest gave way to lawn with a sculpture of a Dixieland band playing. The path circled about the sculpture, and then descended into an entrance underneath.

Eliot paused a moment to stare at the frozen bronze figures, smiling, with drums and horns—all of them looking like they'd been captured having the time of their lives.

He entered a steep tunnel. Gas lamps flickered along the rock walls, and after twenty paces, Eliot stood before a marble arch three times his height. Set within this arch was a double set of mahogany doors, and upon them carved scenes of a rock concert, a stage magician sawing a girl in half, and acts from Shakespeare's plays.

Running along the edge of the arch were the following words: MUSES UT RIDEO RISI RISUM, TRIPUDIO, PLORO, INTEREO, QUOD NASCOR DENUO.[49]

Eliot consulted his map. This was the end of the line, literally—with an X marked and a scrawled note: "Grotto of the Muses."

He took a deep breath and pushed through the doors.

Beyond was a cavern. In the center sat a platform lit by stagelights and additional spotlights above. Four columns—where stalactite and stalagmite had melded together—stood equidistant about this stage. Also ringing the stage were seats of violet crushed velvet with padded armrests.

A dozen students milled near the stage, whispering to one another. They had instrument cases from piccolo- to tuba-sized.

The acoustics were amazing. Hushed murmurs across the room echoed and bounced and sounded as if Eliot stood right next to the others.

As quietly as he could, he approached the stage . . . and felt the first stirrings of butterflies in his gut.

Eliot recognized two students from his Mythology 101 class, but no one he had ever actually ever talked with.

He almost tripped when he spotted Sarah Covington.

Great. All he needed were her snide remarks before his audition.

She'd pulled back her hair into a tight bun, wore none of her usual makeup . . . and looked as nervous as Eliot felt. She didn't have an instrument case, though. So what was she doing here?

She saw him, smiled, and walked over. "I was hoping you'd try out," she said. "It's good to see a familiar face."

---

49. "Muses to laugh, to leap, to lament, to perish, and to be born anew." Translated from Latin. —Editor.

Eliot blinked and resisted the urge to look over his shoulder—to see if she spoke to someone behind him. That's what usually happened. But no . . . she stared right at him. Audrey and Cee had drilled years of polite responses into him; otherwise, he'd have floundered.

"Thanks," he said. "Good to see you here, too."

And it was. If Sarah Covington of the haughty Clan Covington was here and just as nervous as he was, then maybe it was okay to feel like he was going to throw up.

"I've admired your playing," she whispered, and bit her lower lip. "You're good. I just wanted to say that before we started."

Eliot waited for the punch line—*you're good . . . for an amateur*—or *good . . . for someone with eight thumbs*—or *for a rhonchial musicaster.*[50]

But she said no more, instead turned as the stage lights dimmed and the spotlights brightened.

Eliot and Sarah sank into two adjacent seats.

Why was she being nice after an entire semester of being mean? Girls were so weird.

A curtain rustled stage left, and a flowing silhouette appeared among the shadows. A spotlight snapped on, revealing a deeply tanned woman in a gold dress. She was elegant with diamonds adorning her fingers, wrists, and neck; but wild at the same time, with her dark hair a frenzy of curls. With one graceful step, she was on the stage.

Four more spotlights angled on her, making her sparkle. She smiled at her audience, and it was more dazzling than any gold or diamonds. She had that unassailable confidence that every Immortal had, but more: she had the glamour of a star.

"Welcome, students. I'm Erin DuPreé. In my class, you call me Erin or Air, but never teacher or Ms. DuPreé or ma'am or any of that other nonsense. There's too much real stuff going in here to mess with such silly formalities."

Eliot liked her. He relaxed into his seat.

Next to him, though, Sarah tensed and gripped her armrests.

"I don't care about your technical skill," Ms. DuPreé told them in a lowered voice. "Oh, that's the easy part, baby. If you came thinking you're going to learn to play Mozart better—you go take lessons somewhere else and practice your scales."

---

50. *Rhonchial* means "pertaining to snoring," and *musicaster* is a mediocre musician, so in this context "one who's moderate musical talents sounds like snoring." —Editor.

She sat on the stage's edge, leaned closer to them, and whispered, "We're going to get what's inside you out into the world. Make *real* music. Make people *feel* something." She rolled her hands in dramatic flourishes. "And do magic that'll make all that other stuff seem like three-card monte."

The spotlights on her focused. "I'm talking about the music in your souls, kids." She made a fist and held it over her heart.

Eliot sat on the edge of his seat. That's what he wanted . . . but then he remembered the permission slip in his backpack, and his excitement cooled.

It read,

I, (FILL IN COMPLETE NAME), hereby relinquish any claims and responsibilities of the Paxington Institute with respect to the class known as THE POWER OF MUSIC for damages to my psyche, soul, and mental state for the duration of the semester, and if I continue to practice the musical arts, *in perpetuity*. All mental aberrations, diminishment of spirit, lost faith, substance abuses, and other similar conditions are solely the undersigned's responsibility to avoid and, if possible, correct.

(SIGN FULL LEGAL NAME HERE) / (DATE)

He'd signed it, of course. It wasn't such a big deal. Eliot knew he was already in over his head with his music . . . so much so that his soul burned a little every time he played.

So let it—even if there was nothing left but ashes. He had to know how far he could take it, if his music would eventually save him . . . or destroy him.

Ms. DuPreé clapped her hands. "So," she said, excitement gleaming in her eyes, "you got what it takes to be a great musician? You got real soul?" She stood and waved toward them. "Who's going to show me first? Someone make me laugh. Someone make me cry."

A boy stood and walked onto the stage. He was a junior or senior, with a goatee and a long black braid down his back. He carried an electric guitar.

Ms. DuPreé motioned, and stagehands quickly set up amplifiers and speakers. Then with a bow, Ms. DuPreé turned the stage over to him, backing to the shadowy edges.

Eliot couldn't help but stare—not at the boy, but at his guitar. It was solid black with silver rivets, powerful and masculine, everything dinky Lady Dawn was not.

The boy took a deep breath and then played a rock 'n' roll riff—tough and rough and shifting keys fast and furious as sound distorted through the speakers, so loud it made the hairs on Eliot's arms dance and his insides quaver.

The boy's face contorted with exultation and agony, as if this song caused him joy *and* pain.

Eliot clenched his hand into a fist. He could relate.

But more fascinating than the music was the guitar: Eliot wished he had something that . . . well, wouldn't embarrass him every time he took it out to play in public.

Lady Dawn was a beautiful instrument. Eliot loved her. She had been his father's heirloom before given to him, and he respected the music they made together.

He squeezed the never-quite-healed wound in his palm where Lady Dawn had cut him with a snapped string, and remembered there was a price to pay for playing her, too.

The boy onstage finished with a screaming crescendo and slid onto his knees.

Eliot and the others clapped. He was great.

How was Eliot going to pass any audition following that act?

The boy grinned and stood, and he held up one hand to the applause in mock modesty.

Ms. DuPreé clapped as well, but slow and without enthusiasm as she walked toward him. "A technically perfect performance," she purred. "High marks for showmanship, too." She moved closer and whispered to the boy—but with the perfect acoustics, Eliot still heard: *"But you didn't move me, kid. So go live a little, and then show me something next year."*

The boy's smile contracted to a grimace, but he nodded, seeming to take her criticism seriously. He gave her a bow, picked up his guitar, and left without looking back.

Ms. DuPreé addressed the remaining students, "Somebody make me *feel* something," she told them. "Don't just perform—*move* your audience." She looked at each of them. "So who's next?"

Sarah stood, trembling. "I'll go, ma'am, I mean Erin, if you please."

"Show me what you got, kid."

Eliot touched her arm lightly and nodded to her.

Sarah nodded back.

It was a simple gesture between them, but genuine: his reassurance and hope . . . her gratitude for the kindness.

Sarah walked to the stage with slow deliberation. Ms. DuPreé offered a hand and helped her up.

Sarah had no instrument, nor did Ms. DuPreé signal for any to be brought out. Instead Sarah clasped her hands in front of her and sang.

Eliot didn't understand the words, not even the language, Gaelic maybe. But while the words didn't mean anything to him, the song did.

She sang of marshes and glens and trees and birds. He could almost see the land, and almost smell the heather and the ocean in the distance. He knew how she felt, that her heart was still at home. How she missed it all. How she loved that place.

Sarah finished and looked down.

No one clapped.

Not because it was bad, but because Eliot and the others were in shock. He'd never realized the human voice could be so lyrical and evocative.

Ms. DuPreé came to Sarah, took one of her hands, and petted it. "Very nice."

Sarah managed a tight smile.

Ms. DuPreé waved her back to her seat and then looked to the rest of them. "That's what I'm talking about. Who's next?"

Sarah shakily sank back into her seat. She looked ill.

Eliot understood how music like that could drain you. He wanted to tell her, too, that's how it was for him when he poured himself into his music.

"No volunteers?" Ms. DuPreé sounded disappointed.

A spotlight snapped on Eliot.

Adrenaline flooded through his body, and he cringed in surprise.

"How about you, then, Mr. Post? Why don't you show us all what you're made of?"

Eliot froze as if he were a deer in the headlights of an onrushing truck. Everything he knew about music was suddenly gone from his head.

Sarah whispered to him, "Go show her a thing or two." There was a bit of her usual sarcasm in her tone, although Eliot didn't think it was directed at him this time.

It was strange: Eliot's confidence returned (what little of it there was) because he didn't want to let Sarah down. He didn't understand why he should care what *she* thought, but he did.

Well, he'd come to audition. He'd give it his best shot.

He grabbed Lady Dawn's case, plodded to the stage, and stepped up without taking Ms. DuPreé's proffered hand.

Ms. DuPreé gave him a wry look. "Well, Mr. Post, I've heard you got a spark in you, but so did the boy up here before you. Do you have soul? Can you make me cry?"

Eliot snorted. He felt irritation prickle at the back of his neck.

She wanted him to make her feel something? He flipped open the violin case and removed Lady Dawn, set her on his shoulder, grabbed the bow . . . then stopped.

He had to play a song that meant something to him, though. It couldn't just be "Mortal's Coil" or "The Symphony of Existence" or the "The March of the Suicide Queen." They were great pieces, but they were other people's songs.

Even "Julie's Song" wasn't Eliot's. He'd taken what was inside Julie, turned it inside out, and added a melody, that's all.

This had to be all *his*. Like Sarah had sung about her home, revealing a part of herself he would never have guessed existed . . . exposed herself in front of all of them.

He swallowed.

There was one nursery rhyme he recalled—or thought he remembered. It was like fog in his memory, shifting—there but ghostly, something he thought his mother might have once sang to him. Maybe the only thing she had ever sung to him.

Eliot set aside his bow. He wouldn't need it.

He cautiously plunked out the tune.

A girl in the audience snickered. "That's 'Twinkle, Twinkle, Little Star.'"[51]

Someone shushed her.

Eliot paid them no attention and kept playing. This song, whatever it was, was his and his family's. It was the mother he'd had, if only for a moment, before Louis left and everything changed—before Audrey severed

---

51. "Twinkle, Twinkle, Little Star" was first published as "The Star" by Jane Taylor in 1806. It is sung to the French melody "Ah! vous dirai-je, Maman." The older French lyrics (among many variations) are translated here as: *"Ah! I shall tell you, Mum, / What causes my torment. / Papa wants me to reason / Like an adult / I say that candy / Is better than being right."* Perhaps closest to the original source is this couplet from the obscure Benedictine Hymn scroll, *Obsequium Angelus*, authored by Father Sildas Pious ca. thirteenth century: *"'Ware young child the Morning Star. / Look away and you'll go far. / Like a jewel ablaze in dark, / fallen angel casting spark. / 'Ware the dark and 'ware the light. / Naught but trust in God at night."* *Origins of Art and Power in Music*, Erin DuPreé, M.F.A, Ph.D., Paxington Institute Press, LLC.

her connection to him and Fiona. A connection he'd never get back . . . that he mourned over.

The song was simple, slow, and full of that loss. Each note was leaden and painful in the still air. He felt completely alone up on the stage.

It was a stupid little baby thing . . . but it was his.

He put himself into the song, all the love and happiness of his perfectly imagined family that had never been: growing up with a real father and mother . . . having Audrey's tenderness, Louis's guidance—not 106 rules.

But that was a lie. The notes soured under his fingers, and he shifted to a minor key.

About him, the spotlight flickered and dimmed.

He'd never had real parents. Nothing about his family was normal. He cast aside his dream and faced the fact that he was the son of the Eldest Fate, Atropos, and of Lucifer, the Great Deceiver. Maybe that made Eliot a freak, or a nerd, but something in him had to be part divine and part darkness.

The simple song under his fingertips now spoke of the heavens wheeling overhead, and among them a boy . . . ascending to stars—or falling like his father, crashing and forever burning.

One day he would be very much more than simple Eliot Post.

He finished, the last notes echoing throughout the grotto like the beating of his heart.

There was no clapping.

Eliot couldn't see any faces in the dark.

He trembled from the exertion and from the humiliation that he'd put everything he was out there for strangers to see.

Ms. DuPreé set one hand on his shoulder. "That was good," she whispered. "Real good, kid." She smiled and her eyes sparkled. "Stick with me, and one day I'll make you a star."

CHALLENGE

Fiona followed her stupid map to the far side of the Ludus Magnus. She was irritated they thought she needed a map when she'd been wandering around here for a half a year already . . . more irritated that she *had* needed the map.

Although she had seen the far side of the Ludus Magnus before, had even had a bird's-eye view from the top of the obstacle course, she'd never noticed this tiny sister coliseum.

Instead of columns, giant statues stood along curve of its outer wall: an armored knight, a one-breasted Amazon, and a gladiator with trident and net.

She passed through the wide entrance. The inside training grounds were the size of a softball field, with sand and mud and grass and concrete surfaces, dotted with wooden practice dummies; steam-powered, multi-armed robots; barricades of spikes and razor wire, racks of swords and shields and spears—and lots of open space to fight.

In the center stood Mr. Ma. About him in a loose circle were ten boys in their Paxington school uniforms (not gym sweats).

Fiona's heart skipped a beat. Of course Mr. Ma would be the combat instructor. Who else but sadistic, by-the-book Mr. Ma?

She did a double take, though, as Mr. Ma laughed and smiled and patted one of the students on the back. He seemed more at ease here than in gym class. Maybe she'd catch a break and he might actually be *nice* to her. Unlikely.

ERIC NYLUND

The boys in the class were bigger and more serious than the ones she usually saw on campus. Upperclassmen. Two of them she recognized from that first-day demonstration of the obstacle course; one had had a broken arm, but he looked no worse for the injury today.

Fiona worried that she might be late—despite having made sure that she had an early start this morning. It was one of those things that just seemed to happen to her: misreading the grandfather clock at home, class getting moved up . . . Eliot doing something to mess them up, like start a small war.

She checked her phone. No, she still had ten minutes.

As Fiona walked toward them, however, she noticed one more thing different with this picture.

Robert Farmington.

He stood with the other boys (just as tall but not quite so filled out), and he looked completely at ease—as he always did. He had a black eye, but nonetheless laughed along with Mr. Ma, and grinned—until he saw her.

His smile dried up. The others turned.

Mr. Ma's smile similarly vanished, and he was once again the same stern figure who made her life miserable in gym.

"Good morning, Miss Post," he said.

The way he said it, though, was laced with disapproval—as if what he meant to really say was: *Good morning, Miss Post, and notice that while you're on time, you're not early . . . indicating that you don't have the dedication to the martial arts that these other fine young men do, so why don't you go back to bed and get your beauty sleep and not worry your not-so-pretty-little head about such things?*

Imagined or not, irritation made her neck flush with heat.

"I've come to learn how to fight," she told him as confidently as she could (which sounded more like a squeak to her).

"I'm sure you have," Mr. Ma replied. He nodded to Robert. "But as you can see, I've already had one freshman who has contested the prerequisites for this course. I have no desire to babysit *two* such fledglings. It would not be fair to the others."

Robert looked at the ground, unable to meet her gaze.

The prickly heat on her neck spread across Fiona's chest. Anger or embarrassment or both—she wasn't sure.

It was completely unfair. Just because Robert had gotten here a few minutes earlier and passed Mr. Ma's stupid test? A test she was sure she could pass, too.

"Miss Westin said I could challenge your prerequisites." Fiona had wanted to say this calmly and logically, as if Mr. Ma had just overlooked some bookkeeping error, but it came out sounding petulant.

"I'm sure she did. But Miss Westin's influence stops at the entrance of this hall."

Fiona pursed her lips. Something solidified in her . . . a titanic, immovable mass of stubbornness.

"I *will* challenge your prerequisites," she told him. She had made that sound exactly as she wanted this time—as if she were contesting Mr. Ma personally.

The other students collectively inhaled and held their breaths.

Mr. Ma narrowed his eyes slightly as he took her in, and then after a moment said, "A challenge, is it?" He chuckled. "What would be the point, Miss Post? You need a signed permission slip first."

He turned back to the others.

"I have one." Fiona got out the piece of paper and handed it to him.

Mr. Ma looked at the permission slip—which covered all the things she had expected: a dozen hypothetical near-fatal injuries, and the four *D*s (death, decapitation, dismemberment, and disembowelment) . . . as if there weren't already a million different ways to get beaten, broken, or killed in Paxington.

What was absolutely fascinating to Fiona, though, was that Audrey had signed it.

Fiona had gone back and forth on the best way to approach her mother—how learning to fight would actually increase the odds of her graduating—it was better to learn in a structured and supervised environment where there were medics nearby rather than doing so outside of classes where *anything* could happen.

Audrey hadn't listened. She had simply taken the permission slip and signed it.

On the signature line of the page, her mother had printed *Audrey Post,* and then next to it she had drawn an infinity symbol with a line stricken diagonally across.

Mr. Ma gazed upon her signature, and his face crinkled so hard in concentration that it looked like a prune with two deeply set dark eyes. As he continued to gaze at it, Fiona saw the ink was thicker than she recalled, almost bulging off the page . . . and it scratched deeper into the surface than it ought to have without tearing through.

He ran his thumb over the symbol. Mr. Ma then folded the paper and tucked it into his warm-up jacket.

"So be it," he whispered. "I accept your challenge."

One of the older boys stepped forward, but Mr. Ma held a hand up at him and shook his head. "I will do this."

The other students looked amongst themselves, confused.

Robert's eyes widened. "Don't fight him, Fiona," he said. "It's a trick."

A smile creased Mr. Ma's wrinkled lips. "Listen to your friend, Miss Post. He is correct: I *do* intend to trick you."

Fiona saw real concern on Robert's face. But Robert was always over-protective . . . and he didn't know what she was capable of anymore. Besides, if *he* had done this to get into the class, so could *she*.

"You can try," she told Mr. Ma.

Mr. Ma looked her over and gave a snort.

He stalked to a rack of weapons, considered the sticks and shields and practice swords, and then selected a pair of wooden samurai swords, *bokken,* and tossed one to Fiona.

She hefted it. Heavy.

From her studies of kendo, she knew these solid wooden swords couldn't cut. They had a simple chiseled simulated edge, but nonetheless had enough weight to bruise quite effectively, break bones . . . or even bludgeon a person to death.

Her confidence flagged and her stomach flip-flopped.

What did she think she was doing? Mr. Ma had a million times more fencing experience than she had.

No. She'd sparred with Uncle Aaron and did okay (and she bet Aaron could have walloped Mr. Ma). And when she had fought the Lord of All That Flies, Beelzebub, she'd held her own . . . for a while. At least the Infernal had treated her as a *real* threat.

Not like a joke, as Mr. Ma did.

Fire sparked inside her and the fear evaporated.

Mr. Ma held the tip of his *bokken* up. "Come at—"

Fiona lunged.

He deflected her point and whipped his sword around.

She blocked—but the force of his blow sent her skidding sideways in the dirt, and pain shuddered up her forearm bones.

The old man was stronger than he looked. Faster, too.

She feigned high, drop the tip of her sword—thrust up toward under his chin.

Only Mr. Ma wasn't there. He'd sidestepped a split second before, and his sword was a blur coming toward her.

She twisted out of the way.

Too slow.

The *bokken* hit her side. Ribs shattered. Every particle of air blasted from her lungs.

Fiona crumpled . . . although somehow stayed on her knees and didn't sprawl facefirst into the dirt.

She also managed to hold on to her *bokken*. A small victory.

Necessary, too.

Because Mr. Ma didn't show mercy. He swung his *bokken* in a double overhand stroke.

Through a haze of agony, she lifted her sword to block—barely. The impact sent new lightning strikes of pain shuddering through her bones.

She fell, dropped her *bokken,* and panted in the dust. Helpless.

Mr. Ma stood over her.

Fiona couldn't breathe, it hurt so much. She couldn't move. He had her.

"That," Mr. Ma said, looming over her, "should be quite enough, I think. Go away, Miss Post . . . or you will lose your head."

His tone was irritatingly polite with just a hint of pity. He turned and walked back toward his students.

No one, but no one, *ever* turned their back to her in combat. She was Fiona Post, daughter of Atropos and Lucifer—daughter of Death incarnate and the Prince of Darkness. She was a goddess in her own right . . . and more.

The world tinged red through her eyes. She welcomed the pain of her broken ribs. Let it set her mind aflame. Let it burn.

Fiona grasped her wooden sword.

She stood.

There was more pain, but it didn't matter. The pain was in some other Fiona Post, one she'd pushed deep inside. Some new Fiona surfaced. This other Fiona said: "You should've finished me when you had the chance, old man."

Mr. Ma halted and cocked his head.

The other students, even Robert, stared, astonished . . . and backed farther away.

Mr. Ma slowly turned, his eyes narrowed, and he nodded. "Perhaps I should've at that."

He lunged at her; she met him.

He struck three times. Her arms moved on their own—without thought—and parried. She riposted, but he just as effortlessly deflected her blows.

Mr. Ma slipped inside her guard and struck her dead center in the chest. The force shattered his *bokken* into splinters.

The impact pushed Fiona backwards into a crouch.

It had force enough to shatter a person's rib rage and liquefy a human heart.

Fiona gritted her teeth. Fortunately, she wasn't feeling very human at the moment. She smiled. His strike hadn't even bruised her.

The world to her looked as if it were on fire—all brilliant ruby red and tinged with the blood that pounded through her, blazing with anger.

Mr. Ma backpedaled as she approached. He grabbed two new *bokken*s off the weapons rack.

Fiona swung with wild abandon, screaming her rage.

He parried each blow. His defense was solid . . . perfect, in fact. She would never get through. She would beat on him until he wore her down, and then she'd make a mistake, or collapse from exhaustion, and she'd lose.

Her anger doubled and redoubled, and it felt as if her world would explode.

But the other, submerged Fiona started thinking again. She had to get around that perfect defense of his somehow . . . from behind? Under? No, those wouldn't work.

Maybe the way around his defense was *straight through*.

Fiona stepped back and gazed upon the chiseled wooden surfaces of her bokken, and forged her hate into something stronger: resolve.

The planes and fibers of the wood stiffened, and the length of the *bokken* hummed with power. The rounded notched surfaces smoothed to a clean edge, a line that seemed to slide in and out of her vision, it was so fine.

A *cutting* edge.

Her rage subsiding, she strode toward him, her *bokken* held high—and brought it down.

Mr. Ma must have sensed a flaw in his perfect defense, some danger—even before her *bokken* touched his, because his ever-calm expression puckered and she saw the tiniest flicker of fear in his eyes.

Her *bokken* passed through his as if it weren't there, cleaving the wood in two.

Mr. Ma leaned back.

Not far enough, though.

The tip of Fiona's *bokken* crossed his face . . . and she felt resistance along her cutting edge—something hard, so she pushed *harder* with her arms and her mind—and his flesh yielded.

It was nothing serious. She hadn't wanted to cut off his head. It was just a reminder that he should *never* turn his back on her again: a nearly microscopic slash curved from his cheek to chin.

She stepped back.

Mr. Ma felt the wound, and his fingers came away a tiny smear of red. He stared at it for the longest time.

The other students stared, too.

Fiona no longer felt the anger; she wasn't even glad that she'd given Mr. Ma a taste of his own medicine.

Something was wrong.

It felt as was if she'd broken a rule—and not just some Paxington rule that might get her expelled. *This* rule felt like it should not have been able to be broken, like gravity. The entire universe felt as if it might unravel because of what she'd just done . . . starting from where Mr. Ma stood . . . from that one tiny cut.

Mr. Ma curled his fingers into a fist and took a breath. The wound on his chin stopped bleeding.

He moved toward Fiona.

The *bokken* slipped from her grasp. She started to say she was sorry—but halted herself. She wasn't sorry, and she wouldn't lie about it.

Mr. Ma gazed into her eyes. He wasn't angry. It was as if he were searching for something that he'd misplaced a thousand years ago.

And then he blinked and nodded. "Very nicely done, Miss Post. Come, we were covering the basic fighting stance . . . which I note you could use some improvement on." He motioned for her to join the other boys, and very much made a point of not turning his back on her.

Fiona hid her surprise. So now he was actually inviting her to join the class? She didn't understand, but she wasn't going to question it, either.

As she joined them, though, the other students shuffled away. Not one of them offered their congratulations or would look her in the eye. Not even Robert.

Fiona stood by herself.

Mr. Ma showed them how to stand and fight, how not to lose one's balance as they shuffled their feet.

She watched and listened and learned, but felt hollow inside, as if she were alone in the world . . . as if she'd severed much more with that one little cut than she had meant to.

————

"Robert! Wait." Fiona jogged after him along the trail through the grove, catching up. She grabbed the sleeve of his jacket. "Robert, please. What'd I do? Is it because I'm the only girl in the class?"

Robert stopped, looked at her, but didn't say anything.

It felt weird trying to get Robert to talk to her, almost pleading, after working so hard to put some distance between them. But he was in her class now. They'd have to talk, wouldn't they? *Not* talking would be weirder.

She waited for Robert to explain, but instead he turned and walked away.

He stopped after two paces, sighed, and turned back to her. "It's not that." He shook his head, but then seemed to decide something. "You *cut* him, Fiona."

"That was the point, wasn't it? Show him I was good enough to get into the class? It's the same thing you did."

Robert paled. "I didn't fight Ma. I wouldn't have the guts to try."

"Okay, so one little paper cut."

Robert stared at her, unblinkingly. "You really don't know, do you?"

Fiona shot him the look that she usually reserved for Eliot, the *obviously you're being too stupid for me to understand* look.

"I guess not," Robert said. "It's in *The Mahābhārata*."

"East Indian mythology? Miss Westin hasn't covered that yet, so how could I know?"

Robert blinked. "It was a movie. Pretty cool one, too. Look, sorry, I just assumed everyone knows this stuff. . . ."

Fiona crossed her arms over her chest. "Did you forget that until last summer, Audrey kept Eliot and me isolated? As in a total-vacuum-of-all-things-diabolical-and-divine type isolated?"

"Okay, it's just that Mr. Ma is an Immortal, and has the power to choose when he dies."[52]

"So what?" Fiona demanded. "No kidding: he didn't die today."

"He's not supposed to," Robert explained. "Not until the end of things. He's not supposed to get touched. Not a bruise, not a chipped tooth . . . not even one little cut."

"One little cut . . . ," Fiona echoed, and her stomach twisted into knots. "I still don't see the big deal. So I caught him off guard with—" She stopped. "Wait, what do you mean 'until the end of things'?"

"Mr. Ma is supposed to get hurt only at the end . . . of everything."

That sense of wrongness was back. As if when Fiona had cut Mr. Ma, she'd broken something unbreakable . . . that couldn't be repaired.

"The end of days," Robert whispered. "Ragnarok. Armageddon. That's what everyone's freaking out about. They think because you hurt him, well, maybe you might have *started* it."

52. Benjamin Ma (aka Bhishma and Mr. Ma), gym teacher and combat instructor at the Paxington Institute before the end of the Fifth Celestial Age. May be the same Immortal warrior from the Sanskrit epic, *The Mahābhārata*, who took an unshakable vow of celibacy and was thereby gifted by cosmic forces with the power to choose the time of his death. Reputedly killed in the climatic battle of *The Mahābhārata*, however, similar warriors and yogis appear later in history, and this famous death may have been faked (certainly he did nothing to dissuade the useful rumor). The prophecy of his death triggering the end of things, of course, was proved true—foreshadowed when Fiona (ironically sent with permission slip in hand by Death incarnate) drew his blood that fateful day. *Gods of the First and Twenty-first Century, Volume 11, The Post Family Mythology*. Zypheron Press Ltd., Eighth Edition.

54

MUSIC TO END THE WORLD IF THOU DESIRE

Eliot sat cross-legged on his bed. He had a lot to do. He'd tackle the hard stuff first: tonight's music homework.

He had to play his violin for fifteen minutes without repeating himself. Ms. DuPreé said he had to or "the bit of creativity that hadn't been sucked out of him yet would solidify like concrete."

But repetition was part of the music Eliot knew. Self-taught with "Mortal's Coil," "The Symphony of Existence," and "The March of the Suicide Queen"—those pieces had ordered stanzas and repeated phrases that built on each other.

How did you make music *without* repetition?

He pushed his violin case away. Maybe he'd get to that later.

The next problem on his list was Fiona. He'd hardly seen his sister this semester. She came home late from her Force of Arms class, showered, slept, and then got up at 3 A.M. to do homework. She was such a zombie by the time they walked to Paxington in the morning, he barely got a grunt or two out of her.

Which normally would've been great . . . except he had a feeling they'd need to work together more than ever to survive the rest of the school year.

Any free waking moments Fiona had between classes, she spent with Mitch. Not that it was any of Eliot's business, but Robert was hanging out less with their group because of it. He couldn't decide if Robert and Fiona not being together was a good or bad thing.

Which brought him to the next problem to solve: gym class.

Team Scarab practiced like their lives depended on it. Sarah was great. She'd learned how to harmonize with Eliot's music, and together they could shatter a three-foot-thick beam halfway across the course. Fiona and Robert were just as impressive, stronger and faster than they'd ever been . . . although there was definitely some unresolved tension between Mitch and Robert. The only one who didn't seem to be trying so hard was Amanda. Jeremy shot her glances that could kill, and occasionally he'd lose his temper and stomp out of practice.

The problem with gym wasn't them, however, or even the competition. It was the unfair ranking system.

The lowest-ranked team had been dissolved: Team Soaring Eagle because of a disastrous accident during their first match this semester. Six deaths.

He'd thought about quitting that day. No school—no matter how fantastical or magical—was worth dying for.

But Fiona convinced him it was just an accident, a terrible accident, but one that could happen anywhere.

Maybe. But it wasn't just anywhere where you had to dodge spears and swords sixty feet off the ground.

The result of Eagle's dissolution hadn't been a review of safety rules, a suspension of play, or the academic bell curve normalizing. Instead every team slipped *down* in the ranks one notch (sliding the entire freshman population that much closer to flunking). To make the cut and graduate, Team Scarab *had to* win two of their remaining last three matches.

Of course, gym would be a lot easier if they had their strongest player. Jezebel's presence, however, would generate a whole new set of problems . . . but they'd be problems Eliot would *want*.

He dug through his pack and found Jezebel's handkerchief, still stained with the blood from when she kissed him, still smelling like vanilla and cinnamon.

She hadn't been at school since the start of the semester. Two weeks and no trace.

How long before they kicked her out?

It'd be the least of her worries, though; it meant the war in the Poppy Lands was still on.

Where she'd be fighting . . . or hurt.

Or dead.

His blood chilled at that thought.

So why was he here? He should've been back on the Night Train and helping her—whether she wanted it or not.

Was it because he knew they'd get in a big fight and she'd just try to get rid of him again?

Or was he just the world's biggest chicken?

He swallowed, remembering the swarms of Droogan-dors that had enveloped Queen Sealiah's knights . . . and left only frost and shadow in their wake.

Eliot made a fist, crushing her handkerchief, and then tossed it over to a corner of the pack.

His skin itched just thinking about her. She was so obstinate.

He was getting nowhere with these human relationship problems. Like music, they had patterns: attraction, coming together, fighting, breaking up—wash, rinse, and repeat.

Eliot pulled his violin case closer. Maybe he could make some progress on Ms. DuPreé's assignment. He got Lady Dawn and admired her fiery wood grain that looked like molten gold and amber.

He played slow and strived to define his confused feelings. It swelled from him, roiled and swirled about him in the room, making homework pages flutter and books tremble on the shelves.

But it felt dangerous, too, like he was tapping into emotional waters deep and dark.

As he started thinking about how to express himself, his fingers fell into old habits, and they repeated a phrase, and built upon it.

He stopped.

That *was* right. That was how the music *should* be played, but it wasn't the assignment.

He hissed his frustration.

Why was it that the others in music class never had these problems? They just played. They just did it. Their passion flowed from them effortlessly.

David Kaleb had a silver horn that flashed the reflected spotlights like his own light show. When Sarah Covington sang, she seemed warm and friendly (everything she actually wasn't). And the older boy who had auditioned, his guitar had been bold and strong and big. Masculine.

Eliot glanced at Lady Dawn. Was he outgrowing her?

When he practiced in front of the others, he'd been embarrassed. Lady Dawn was the instrument a "good little boy" would play.

There was something else. When he had summoned the dead that first time at Groom Lake, she'd snapped a string. He curled his hand, still feeling the pain. It was as if she had done that on purpose because she disapproved . . . like she was alive.

Eliot had to be just imagining that.

He set aside the violin and stared past the gleaming surfaces, trying to feel more.

She was quiet. There wasn't even that subsonic hum he usually sensed about her. She was sulking.

"It's time I tried something else . . . ," Eliot told her. "I mean—"

He couldn't continue. What if she were really alive? Hadn't he seen crazier things? It didn't matter, though—real or imagined, the problem between him and her would still be there.

"It's not like we're breaking up or anything," he continued, fidgeting his hands. "Look, I just need to try out a few other instruments. Something a little more . . ."

Eliot searched for a rational excuse (flimsy or not) to tell her.

"I'm tired of living in my dad's shadow," he said. "The violin is *his* instrument. I need something that belongs entirely to me."

Lady Dawn just sat there.

Eliot couldn't stand it. He picked her up, set her in her case, and slammed it shut.

Okay, so he *was* losing his mind. Maybe. But tomorrow he was going to find a new instrument to play.

He opened the giant tome he'd checked out from the Hall Of Wisdom. It was Volume Twelve of the Copper-Prince edition of *The Mahābhārata*, tonight's assigned reading. Miss Westin had jumped ahead in their syllabus and had them working on Eastern Indian mythologies all of a sudden.

He read about battles, and betrayals, and family politics, stuff that usually interested Eliot, but he felt guilty about setting aside his trusted violin.

Eliot pressed his forehead to the page and groaned.

He just needed to clear his head, rest his eyes for a moment, and then he'd read . . . and make a few notes. . . .

————————

This was the most moronic dream Eliot had ever had. He dreamed that he slept in his bed. No dragons to slay, no being late for some midterm he'd never studied for . . . just drooling on his pillowcase, snoring gently, books pushed aside.

Did he really look like such a dork when he slept?

The lamp was off to his room, but light streamed in from under his door. Half shadows gave his room a weird underwater feel.

There was a sigh nearby, and Eliot knew he wasn't alone in his dream.

A person stood by his bed . . . a girl.

Eliot was wide awake now (at least in his dream) as he sat up and saw this girl wore nothing—just a silhouette of skin and long hair that was half pinned up, half escaped in loose curls.

She was too small to be Jezebel or Sarah. Maybe Amanda?

The girl stepped closer.

"Look into mirrors," she whispered, "and thou beholdest not what is before your eyes, Son of Darkness."

Definitely not Amanda, either. This girl's voice was silk smooth and sounded *so* familiar.

The girl leaned against his bed, planted one knee, and eased onto his legs.

"For thou would I do anything, *be* anything," she said. "Thou art the one I have waited for."

Eliot wanted to say something—but his tongue wouldn't work.

She slid onto his body. Her flesh was warm and she didn't stop until her face was directly over his.

Eliot finally saw her. Beautiful didn't describe her features. She had something beyond human, Immortal, or Infernal beauty. Her eyes were amber flecked with gold and blazed wild with passion.

"Not since before time was, doth I so offer myself," she said, her breath tickling his neck. "Thou art the one I was created for, and thou created for me."

Eliot could no longer breathe.

Her lips were directly over his. Every curve of her body pressed into his.

"No other hath ever made me feel like thou dost. Not even thine father."

She kissed him.

Eliot tensed and pulled her closer, smothered in sensation. Every nerve flamed. Color flashed across his closed eyes.

He'd never been kissed like this—not Julie's urgent passion—not Jezebel's narcotic sting. This was high art and animal instinct blended. This was beauty and lust and heartbreakingly perfect. It was what every kiss should have been . . . but *never* could be.

The girl pulled away, panting.

"We shall together make music the likes of which even God has not yet dreamed," she whispered. "Music to end the world if thou desire."

She pressed her lips back to his. They embraced and burned.

———

Eliot bolted upright.

He was drenched in sweat, and sheets tangled about him. His face hurt as if someone had punched him, bruised, and his lips felt sunburned raw.

Eliot got up and noticed, much to his mortification, something amiss with his groin. He grabbed a pillow to hide the state of his physiology there.

Pulse still pounding, he remembered the dream—especially the girl. How could he forget? And yet, the details were fading fast.

He fumbled for the light on his nightstand, found it, and snapped it on.

Homework papers and books lay scattered on the floor. It was as if someone had come in, tossed it all, and then danced in the mess for good measure.

His violin case wasn't there.

Eliot dug through the debris. Panic shot through his heart as he found the violin case—just the case neck, busted off and smashed flat.

He held his breath. Was it possible he'd done this? Subconsciously re-pressed all the anxiety about his music and taken it out on poor Lady Dawn? Crushed her in his sleep?

He tore through the mess, searching, and found more bits of cardboard and leather from the case, but no trace of his beloved violin.

Eliot breathed again.

Okay, it had to be somewhere. He riffled through the papers, piling them on his desk. He looked under the bed, too. The violin wasn't there, either.

He'd never forgive himself if he'd damaged Lady Dawn. His father had given him the instrument.

His father.

Eliot remembered something the dream girl had said. It was hard to re-call much more than her kiss or the way she'd pressed into his body, but hadn't she said that he made her feel like no other had . . . not even his father?

Eliot would have to review his Freud to figure *that one* out.

He paused, suddenly wary. *Anything* involving Louis, dream or not, had some trick to it.

Eliot froze as he realized there was something in his room that hadn't been there when he'd fallen asleep. It stood, propped against the corner bookcases.

A guitar.

It wasn't just any guitar, either, but an electric guitar. Its wood gleamed amber and gold and brass fittings glistened like crystallized sunlight. The fingerboards were ebony with mother-of-pearl inlays in the shapes of stars and swords and crows. There was a bar to adjust string tension on the fly, and six knobs and a few switches along the bottom that he had no clue what they did.

Eliot did know, however, he wanted nothing more than to pick it up, and play it.

But he halted as he recognized the wood grain pattern . . . so mirror-smooth that he saw his face reflected in its flaming colors. He'd seen it countless times before.

Lady Dawn.

"No way," he whispered.

But why not? What if, in dreaming, he had done this? Played some song of transformation. The Covington conjurers could change one thing into another . . . so it was, in theory, possible.

Eliot didn't think *his* magic had ever worked like that. And it'd never worked with such precision.

If he hadn't done this, though . . . that left only one logical conclusion.

Her.

The dream girl had said: *"For thou would I do anything, be anything."*

Could she be real? Alive?

Was that dream even a dream? The thought of an instrument who was also a young girl—who'd been in his father's hands for so many years—it sent a shiver of revulsion down Eliot's spine.

Still . . . he reached out and held his fingers a hairsbreadth over the guitar, feeling a subsonic thrum of her power, of anticipation for his touch.

Eliot took her and slung the guitar over his shoulder.

She was a perfect fit.

His fingers slid along the six steel strings. Different from his violin. Familiar, though, too. Definitely weird.

"We shall together make music the likes of which even God has not yet dreamed. Music to end the world if thou desire."

Not yet.

Eliot was going to track down his father first. Louis had questions to answer.

55

UNDERESTIMATION OF HIS CUNNING

Louis puffed on a cigar he had borrowed from the Night Train's humidor. He opened a window. These cars were stuffy with the sweat and fear of its usual passengers.

The engine's screams echoed through the tunnel.

Amberflaxus licked its black fur in the seat next to him. It flicked its ears forward, thinking that noise was prey.

Louis felt better away from San Francisco, no longer obsessing over Eliot and Fiona, and his beloved lost Audrey. How wonderful to be away from the world of light and love!

He was annoyed that he was even thinking of the *memory* of their memories . . . and yet, he found it nearly impossible to stop.

Louis exhaled smoke and watched it mingle with the steaming screams outside.

But stop he must and concentrate on his deceptions, namely how to play with Sealiah and Mephistopheles.

Manipulating mortals was one thing, even Immortals, but his Infernal family? That was ten times the danger. He had to proceed with great care.

Should he betray Sealiah? Or side with her against Mephistopheles?

He chuckled. As if the Queen of Poppies would *want* him on her side, as if he would stick his neck out and actually stoop to physically fighting anyone in her war.

No, the best option was to play both sides against the middle, and then pick over what was left. To accomplish this, however, Louis would need leverage, some fact about the tactics and plans of one to ingratiate himself with the other—just long enough to get into the proper position to backstab and double-cross.

Sometimes the most clichéd schemes were best . . . because they worked.

He marveled at his willingness to embrace the simple truth of it.

The huge Ticket Master entered the car and bowed. He then adjusted the slightly out-of-place tassels of his uniform's brocade and brushed a bit of ash from the black fabric.

"May I approach, O most noble of deceivers?"

"No," Louis muttered. "I need nothing."

"Yes, Lord," he said, smoothed a hand over his bald head, and then added, "your stop is next, the Poppy Lands."

Louis cocked one brow. "Oh? I don't recall saying that was my destination."

"No, my lord. It's just your most illustrious offspring was here. . . ."

"Yes, yes," Louis said with careless wave.

Eliot had been to the Poppy Lands?

"Had been" being the operative verb tense, because Amberflaxus spotted the boy just last night entering that Pacific Heights hovel of his—no doubt to dutifully practice his violin or do his Paxington homework.

But he obviously was not the good little boy everyone believed. He had not consulted Louis as he had promised, and any visit to the Poppy Lands had to have broken dozens of Audrey's rules. How delightful.

Louis smiled at this new development.

Sealiah's plans involving Eliot had to be further along than he had dreamed.

But when had he crossed? And more curiously, *how* had he returned?

All this Louis considered in a heartbeat.

"My business today takes me past the Mirrored Realms," he told the Ticket Master.

The Ticket Master looked disappointed, for he hadn't tricked any salable information from him.

The Night Train's last stop was the Mirrored Realms—and anything past that in the Hysterical Kingdom was only the business of the fool who attempted such a journey.

Louis had spoken the truth: He *did* have business past the Mirrored Realms with Mephistopheles . . . just not at this time.

The Ticket Master bowed again, left, and the train slowed.

Louis glanced outside at impenetrable jungle. The only path was the train tracks that cut through. Every flower was in full bloom. Every fungus clouded the air with spore. How deadly. How lovely.

The Night Train pulled into the station house, paused only a moment as required by the Infernal Transportation Pact, and then the brakes released, and the engine chugged ahead.

No one either had departed or gotten on.

Louis looked into the car ahead. No sign of that gossip-mongering Ticket Master.

He turned to Amberflaxus and held one a finger. "Stay," he ordered.

The animal continued to lick itself, pretending (as always its habit) not to notice him.

Louis borrowed a small bottle of whiskey from the wet bar, and then from the poker table scooped a handful of diamond-studded chips along with a set of dice—the minimal supplies one might need in the wilderness.

He slipped out the back and off the train . . . and infiltrated the Poppy Lands.

The hothouse train station had been shelled, and most of the frosted panes were shattered. A billion bits of glass glistened on the ground.

Of course, the station would be an obvious target. It was only a matter of time before Mephistopheles cut the train tracks as well.

Louis had to act with haste, gather information, and then be on the next train out.

He wrapped his cloak about him and walked in the ditch alongside the road toward Sealiah's Twelve Towers, her so-called Doze Torres. She would no doubt make her stand in her castles, where she felt safest.

The poppy fields were on fire: violet, lemon, pink, and crimson blossoms withered in the flames. Green smoke drifted over the lands and flashed with hypnotic phosphorescence.

Louis held his breath.

Droogan-dors fought on the distant hills and valleys, flitting wraiths among the gloaming.

A mere league to his left, hundreds of shadow creatures swarmed and circled a legion of Sealiah's noble knights, the Order of the Thorn. The dark tore at the warriors . . . then their fires burned out . . . and the shades moved in. Frost crackled over the ground there, killing all traces of vegetation.

Mephistopheles was no fool. He carefully whittled away parcels of her land, gathering strength while Sealiah lost hers.

But Sealiah was no fool, either . . . and Louis wondered what trick she had yet to play.

Motion ahead on the road caught his attention: a fat shadow writhed between a dozen poorly defined shapes—rat—crow—worm—camouflaged in the blackness.

Louis slowed, creeping artfully so that nothing should be able to detect him.

A black eye materialized in the mass of the Droogan-dor, however, tracking him, the body underneath coiling to pounce.

He smiled at the creature. "Nice doggie," Louis whispered. "Just a neighborly visit from a neutral observer. Nothing to raise one's hackles over."

It sprang.

Louis sidestepped its charge and dug his nails deep into the shadow flesh, clenched his fists—ripped hide free from flesh and bone.

The thing screamed as it dissipated into an oily mist.

Louis grinned and his pulse pounded. Such wonderful violence. He had not felt the thrill of destroying a lesser opponent in a long time.

Such trivial pleasures would slow him . . . still, Louis paused to admire the black velvet sheen of the Droogan-dor's skin.

He started again—then halted as he saw how seriously he had miscalculated.

About him, growling and crouching, were a dozen Droogan-dors—each the size of a house, each growing rows and rows of dagger teeth.

"Now boys." He held up both hands. "Can't we all be *friends*?"

The monstrosities all took a step back, simultaneously shaking their heads to clear the confusion from the hell-blaspheme oath. *Friends* was not a word uttered without some effort in the depths.

Which is when Louis attacked them.

He didn't transform . . . not entirely. That would've garnered him too much attention. But just a partial shift, claw and fang and wing of bat—to rip and rend and slash.

How could he pass up such fun?

He paused, panting, and realized there was nothing left to fight . . . only shreds and quivering pieces that lay about him.

And curiously, a single cut ran down along his forearm. A trickle of black blood congealed there.

Careless of him.

Or had Mephistopheles' minions gathered power enough to actually hurt an Infernal Lord?

Indeed. He snugged his cloak tighter and trotted. Time was far shorter than he had realized.

Miles ahead, he spied the tallest tower of the Sealiah's castles, burning bright with beacons and the swoop and swirl of armored bat defenders flying about.

Skirmishes raged upon the plains and hills and what was left of the jungles, but Louis noted a procession of knights had the right idea . . . as they steadily limped down the road back to the castle, dragging those too injured to walk on their own.

A retreat? So early? It seemed unlikely, yet the evidence was before his eyes.

The damned of Hell mended bone and flesh after a long painful process. Wounded typically were not removed from battlefield. It was a measure that smacked of desperation—not mercy—for there was only one reason to bother: to deny Mephistopheles converting even the weakest of her warriors to his cause.

It also presented Louis with an interesting problem. He slowed his pace and hid in the ditch. Sneaking past so many numbers would take time.

He glanced about, seeking opportunity.

And he found it: a battle had taken place here recently. Among broken lances and smoldering opium stalks, one knight lay in three pieces, each part struggling to find the other and its missing head.

Louis removed the warrior's thorned mail. "Might I borrow this?" He then kicked the knight's head across the road into the far ditch. "I thank you, brave sir."

He donned the armor—a tad loose for his frame—and then shuffled forward along the road, joining the ranks of despondent soldiers marching toward their doom.

Through his spiked and slotted visor, Louis watched as the twelve towers of Sealiah's fortress loomed larger. Atop each flickered a tongue of flame to keep darkness at bay. This fire was ghostly blue . . . marsh gas piped in from the surrounding flooded lands. In their murky waters, tangles of razor vine squirmed and thrashed and waited for something to wander into their hungry embraces.

More soldiers joined their ranks—hundred and hundreds, but not the numbers that he knew Sealiah had at her disposal.

How badly had Mephistopheles beaten her?

This concerned Louis, not because he felt any pity for his most beautiful adversary, but because it would not give him the chance to take advantage of her *first*.

Or perhaps there was more to this? Certainly Louis had no monopoly on deception (even if he was the *best* at it).

He and the others marched along drawbridges that spanned the wide black waters of the Laudanum River. Along the banks, barrels of oil sat half-buried, awaiting the torch to transform them into floating sheets of fire—unassailable proof against the dark . . . for a time.

Louis then stood before the base of the towering mesa that held Doze Torres. The wisteria-covered earthen ramps that had once zigzagged along the cliff face had been torn away, leaving only sheer rock.

He looked straight up and saw industrial cranes perched on the castles' walls. On their steel cables, a lift descended that could carry three hundred soldiers.

Louis got on with the others, and it rose into the air.

From this aerial vantage, Louis saw not hundreds, but thousands of soldiers and wobbling cannon and catapults and wagons piled high with soldier pieces struggling back toward the castle from every direction. Most of these ragtag lines came under attack from the darkness.

Louis heard their distant screams and futile shots.

Although if he hadn't just walked through the killing fields himself, he would have sworn it all had an air of theater to it.

The crane lifted his platform over the ramparts.

A silk spider line brushed Louis's face, and he absentmindedly brushed it away.

Louis then saw a pleasant surprise: the art of the Poppy Queen's duplicity.

Within the outer walls surrounding the Tower of Whispering Lilacs, camped under tarps to shield their glow, were ten thousand knights—each with gleaming silver rifle-lances and phosphorescing fungus sprouting from their armor and flesh. There were lines of spore catapults, steam-powered missiles, and squadrons of hanging cluster bats. Firepower to *not quite* assault the Vaults of Heaven . . . but enough to have given them a run for their money should they dare.

Certainly equal to any force Mephistopheles could muster.

He glanced back at the devastated, deflowered Poppy Lands.

All a calculated lure? He didn't quite think so.

Sealiah's lands (much like herself) had admirable natural defenses, ones she would not have so casually abandoned. The fact that she had chosen this particular deception was telling.

It was also information that Louis could sell—perhaps so ingratiate himself with the Lord of the Mirrored Realms that he could learn something of *his* plans . . . and in turn sell that information to Sealiah for her most delectable favors.

All the while eroding any advantage either might have over the other, so when the final battle came, the victor would be weakened.

He licked his lips. So dangerous. But so tempting.

The crane set him and the other knights down and they limped toward the Tower of Nightshade, darkest among its fellow flowering structures.

Louis fell behind.

There were precious few shadows in the courtyards with all the pink and lime green and robin's-egg blue light pulsing from the fungus that grew everywhere. He found a sliver of shade, however, entered its welcome depths, and slinked away unnoticed toward the Oaken Keeper of Secrets.

That was where Sealiah's map room was (if he remembered correctly). All her plans would be laid out there for the taking.

He almost giggled. How easy this would be.

Of course, she would not expect such a skilled infiltrator—and not him of all her relations. Who was he? Lowly Louis? The earth under her feet? It would not be the first time others had fatally underestimated his cunning.

Louis passed the guards and triple-locked outer door of the keep without notice, and glided up the stairs.

The map room would be on the third floor, where her winged insect spies brought the latest intelligence from the field.

He set one finger on the living wood of the map room's tiny door.

No pulse beyond. It was empty.

He then undid the puzzle knots that would have given any mathematician specializing in topology psychotic fits. He slipped inside and ever so carefully eased the door shut.

Louis was grateful for the cool darkness within. The only light twinkled from the map table in the center of the chamber. From the decided lack of echoes, he felt of the dimensions of this place were larger than he recalled.

No matter. He tiptoed closer and saw the snaking Laudanum River and the Valley of the Shadow of Death, smoldering jungle and patches of black silk draped over fields that marked the locations of Mephistopheles' armies in the Poppy Lands.

He also noted with great interest that a game of Towers had been set up alongside the map table, white and black cubes stacked and arranged to fight, and a handful already removed from play.

How intriguing.

Torches whooshed to life—thirteen fiery brands about the perimeter of the room—each held by a Champion of the Blood Rose, Sealiah's personal guard.

Sitting upon a tiny throne, orchids twinning along her arms, was Queen Sealiah in armor that appeared as if it had been painted upon her body—curves of dark silver that flashed with light and shadows and reflections of fire . . . and pulsing a nacreous green from the emerald set upon her exposed throat. She was all the more lovely because her features also smoldered with the angry passion that came from bloodlust . . . and lust . . . and anticipation of the kill.

She held a sliver of dark-matter steel that had existed before the mortal Earth had been dust gathering in void: Saliceran—the broken sword. Its blade wept poison from its Damascus metal folds that had sent many to a painful demise. She pointed the jagged tip at his neck.

"Welcome, Great Deceiver," Sealiah said in a mocking tone. "Welcome to your death."

56

TWO MORE PIECES IN PLAY

Sealiah, Queen of the Poppy Lands, raised one finger, and her thirteen personal guards set their torches in wall sconces and lowered their rifle lances at Louis. They would not miss.

"Not a word from you," she cautioned Louis.

She held her rage in check only because she felt the smug satisfaction of being right.

Louis had come. He had tripped but a single of her black widow warning lines that crisscrossed every square meter of her castles' walls. Even without the warning, though, she knew he would eventually have tried to enter *this* room. It was too much of a temptation for one so far fallen from glory.

And for once, the crowned, clown Master of Deception had been caught red-handed. Perhaps weakened by his association with too many mortals? Or had he only allowed himself to been captured . . . part of some more intricate ruse?

Nothing was ever what it seemed with this one.

Louis sighed and nodded his head in the slightest of bows. The rogue even had the temerity to smile!

She admired such daring. *Almost* enough to forget he had come to betray her and sell her battle plans to Mephistopheles.

Would the slightest of dalliances hurt? Louis was handsome and cunning once more—all the things she remembered that had once attracted her to him. And he was never more attractive than when in the midst of his duplicity.

But such thoughts made her vulnerable. She exhaled. If she took advantage of his weakened position for her pleasures, she would be exposed in their intimacy . . . and he would take advantage of her as well.

Perhaps mutual vulnerability was the very definition of "intimate."

Louis opened his mouth.

Sealiah held up one hand and stood, keeping the jagged end of Saliceran pointed at his throat. She walked over to him.

Louis shut his mouth, no longer smiling.

"Your words are too sharp," she whispered. "So I shall not give you the chance to cut me."

She motioned and three of her champions searched him. They found wallet, cell phone, handkerchief, poker chips, dice, and bottle of Irish single malt whiskey—but no weapons.

"His cloak," she said. This was a game for her now. Certainly Louis would not be here without tricks up his sleeves.

Her champions ripped it off and examined it: ordinary black wool.

Louis held up his hands in mock surrender.

As if this would make her think him defenseless. She knew better than to fall for his simpleton's misdirections.

She looked from his hands, to his animated angular face, to the floor— to the flickering shadows cast by her guards . . . to the decided *lack* of any shadow attached to Louis's feet.

"Of course," she said, "you would not risk coming with it. But where I wonder does your shadow *now* roam?"

Louis shrugged, and the simpleton look of innocence on his face told her no answers would be soon forthcoming.

"So be it." She moved to his back and raised Saliceran.

One thrust and she could forget Louis. That would be best.

Under normal circumstances, having him underfoot was dangerous. In wartime, leaving Louis alive could be a fatal oversight.

And yet why did she still imagine him joined with her? Was that *so* impossible? Him by her side as Urakabarameel once had stood?

Yes.

And a thousand times no.

It had been so long since she trusted another. This above all else was why the Post twins fascinated her: brother and sister, part Infernal, and yet they worked together. It was such an obvious strength, something her kind had long forgotten.

She lowered Saliceran (although the blade twisted in her grasp, sensing her equivocation—and sensing that it would not taste Infernal blood tonight). ·

"Take him to the Well of Mirages," she told her Captain. "Set three guards to watch him at all times. Have them stuff beeswax in their ears so he may not trick them with his silvered reptile tongue."

The Captain grabbed Louis by his shoulders.

"I yet have a use for you," she said.

Louis's smile returned—that smirk all men don when coming to the *wrong* conclusion.

Sealiah was all too happy to deflate his zeppelin-sized ego. "Not for that, my unlanded and unimportant cousin. I would not stoop so low for so quick a snack."

His unassailable grin faded.

"I have another use for you . . . involving your family."

Louis eyed her with suspicion, and he twisted in her Captain's grasp. "Eliot is mine," he growled. "Leave him to me."

The Captain struck the back of his head with a mailed fist, and Louis fell to his knees.

Sealiah laughed. It was good to see him so clueless. There was no greater satisfaction than hoodwinking one's relations. She ran a razor-edged fingernail down his chin . . . careful not to break the skin because the scent of his blood would drive her crazy.

"Not Eliot, my dear Dark," she whispered. "I already have the boy well in hand."

Louis's face registered confusion for one instant, then crystallized into an unreadable mask. He was quickly analyzing and recalculating his plots.

But too late. The Deceiver was no longer playing in this game.

"There'll be none of your usual tricks," she said. "The Well of Mirages has once more been repaired and will not bend or fold to your will. Glow fungus covers its walls, so there are no shadows to slip through, either."[53]

---

53. The magic (or wishing) well is common in fairy tales, often depicted as granting three wishes, dispensing healing waters, or giving (all-too-often unheeded) advice to young heroes. The earliest stories of these wells, however, contain sinister forces: trolls or imprisoned spirits eager to pull in unsuspecting children. Many of the tales relate that these wells were conduits to hell or the Fairy Lands. Coins were dropped into their depths in the hopes of appeasing the evil within. *Gods of the First and Twenty-first Century, Volume 5, Core Myths (Part 2).* Zypheron Press Ltd., Eighth Edition.

Sealiah ordered her Captain, "Make him comfortable."

The Captain nodded, understanding that she meant the opposite. He dragged Louis off, and the Deceiver did not even struggle.

In fact, his smile returned.

Perhaps she should have skewered him while she was in the mood. Well, if he turned into his usual annoyance, she could always fill the Well of Mirages with molten lead. Let him grin at that!

But such pleasantries aside, she had more serious matters to consider. Time was short, and Mephistopheles moved closer with every heartbeat—to either destroy her or be destroyed by her trap.

Sealiah turned to the map table and examined the pieces in play. Mephistopheles's shadows were near the station house. A few more hours and he would cut the rail lines.

Her trap was not merely the hidden army within Doze Torres. Even those forces would only make the final battle more bloody; their two sides were too evenly matched.

Two more pieces have yet to be brought onto the board—figuratively and literally.

The timing was delicate; she had to wait until the last possible moment to maximize the drama. That was a necessary risk. Sealiah knew the hearts of men and how to manipulate them, but she also had to make up the mind of a young woman—and that was a much more difficult task.

She withdrew the letter she had written weeks earlier, and made sure all was in proper order and her signature and seal were intact. All as it should be. No need to let some fussy Paxington protocol stop her greatest ploy.

She gestured at the ceiling, and a tiny mouse-tailed bat spiraled down. It lit onto her cupped hand.

She rolled the letter into the tube fixed to the creature's leg. "Take this to the Ticket Master. Caution him to tamper not with the seal. He would not wish to irritate the intended recipient. Few survive the disapproval of Miss Westin."

The bat chirped once, understanding.

She tossed it into the air and the bat fluttered out the window.

So much in balance. Forces of destruction and love and betrayal orbiting her the likes she had not seen since the War in Heaven. She smiled, tasting the anticipation of victory on her lips.

Sealiah turned to her guards and, with a nod, singled out their shortest member.

Her champion came to her, kneeling on one knee, head bowed.

Sealiah gestured for the spiked helmet to be removed.

Jezebel shook loose her platinum curls. Her eyes burned with hate and she quickly lowered her gaze. "He is dangerous, My Queen. I beg you; give me the order to destroy the Deceiver."

Sealiah smiled. "Not yet, my pet."

She appreciated her protégée's viciousness. Under normal circumstances, she would have agreed with her. It was an instinctual reaction: erase one's smartest enemies when the opportunity presented itself, and allow the stupid ones to live to breed inferior competition.

But instinct changed and evolved or a species perished. Even for the Infernals. Especially facing the new order heralded by the Post twins.

Sealiah lifted Jezebel's face. The girl's shattered bones had mended, and her battle-won bruises all but faded. Only the slightest imperfection marred her features, but for what Sealiah needed her for next, her broken doll had to be perfect.

"We must make you ready." The bones would have to be rebroken and properly aligned. Sealiah brushed a finger over her cheek.

Jezebel stiffened and stood straighter, and a flicker of horror flashed across her features.

"Are you ready for the next act of our little drama?"

"Yes, My Queen," Jezebel relied. "I will perish for the cause if so ordered."

"Very good," Sealiah whispered, "because that may be precisely what I require."

57

HOW TO FOIL A DEATH TRAP

Fiona stood in the middle of a war zone.

Not entirely unexpected . . . not after the last few times when Mr. Ma had ramped up the difficulty of the obstacle course, but this was ridiculous!

She ducked—a jet of flame roared over her head.

Eliot knelt next to her and pointed his guitar at the pipe hissing fire. He twanged and held a single note, made it waver and warble and growl with feedback.

The pipe sputtered and sparked. It exploded, extinguishing the flames.

She twisted the shutoff valve closed.

Fiona wasn't sure where Eliot had gotten his new instrument (or, for that matter, how an electric guitar made so much sound without any wires or an amplifier). He'd just showed up at the start of gym class today with the thing. No explanations.

Time for question and answers later . . . if they made it through today's class. She scanned the course, trying to reorient.

They were thirty feet off the ground. The ramp she crouched upon was aluminum, fireproof thankfully (one of the modest safety considerations Mr. Ma had allowed for his reconstructed course), but the surface reflected heat so she felt as if she were in an oven.

Mitch was at the top of the ramp. So was Amanda.

Twin waters cannon pelted her teammates with high-pressure streams—forcing them into a corner to keep from getting blasted off the edge.

Mitch tried to shield Amanda from the worst of it, but they both looked as if they were drowning.

"Are you sure this is the *easiest* way?" she yelled at Eliot over the noise.

Eliot gave her that *I know what I'm doing* look, but nonetheless strummed his guitar, turned back and forth, and nodded his head.

Fiona squinted through the smoke and mist. Lines of fire crisscrossed the obstacle course. She didn't see any trace of Team Falcon . . . or how far ahead of Scarab they'd gotten.

Team Falcon was the number one team at Paxington. They'd taken an early lead on the course—and then disappeared.

But there'd been no gunshot signaling the end of the match . . . so Scarab still was in the game.

"We've got to free them up!" Eliot yelled and pointed to Mitch and Amanda.

Fiona nodded, but stayed where she was, thinking. She didn't want to rush up there and have the cannon turn on them—get knocked off this slick-with-water ramp.

She traced the water pipes as they snaked back around the supports.

She leaned over the ramp and with care looped her rubber band about the two-inch water main. She eased back, focused her mind along the edge—made the cut.

The pipe ruptured.

Steel twisted into a jagged flower. Pressurized water sprayed high into the air and arced onto the field below.

"Fiona!" someone called from above.

She shielded her eyes from the sun. Jeremy and Sarah were twenty feet above her on the next level. Jeremy's hands were pitch black.

"We're stuck," Sarah cried. "Everything up here is covered with tar! You'll have to go around."

For the bazillionth time today, Fiona wished Jezebel were here. Infernal schemes or not—even with all the drama between her at Eliot— it would've been worth it. She could've easily gotten up there, freed the Covingtons, and then they'd have three team members close to the top. Almost a win.

But no use wishing. It was a fact Scarab was down its best player. Fiona's job was to figure out how to win anyway with only seven.

Seven: Her and Eliot . . . Jeremy and Sarah . . . Mitch and Amanda . . .

She turned to Eliot. At the same time they both asked, "Where's Robert?"

"Here!" Robert called. He extended a hand up and over the edge of the ramp; Eliot then helped Robert onto the steaming aluminum surface.

"Are you okay?" Fiona crouched next to him.

She wanted to touch his arm, just to reassure him, but with all the weirdness between them lately . . . and all the stuff happening between her and Mitch, she decided not to.

"I'm just peachy," Robert muttered. He slicked back his wet hair. "Nice plan—charge straight into a trap."

She glared at him. "I didn't see it. And Eliot said it was the way."

"It *is* the way," Eliot replied, annoyed. "I keep telling you."

"So we keep going," Fiona said, and then to Robert, "and try not to fall off this time, okay?"

"I didn't fall." Robert frowned and his brows knit together, uncharacteristic worry lines creased his forehead. "But we've got to go back." He pointed over the edge. "Team Falcon is there. They're down."

Fiona stood and set her hands on her hips. "If they're down, isn't that a good thing?"

Robert shook his head. "They cut a gas line to stop the fire . . . and there's no shutoff valve. They've passed out."

"You've got to be kidding," she whispered.

Robert narrowed his eyes. "Come on. They might be dead already. I need your help. I can't do it myself."

Mitch and Amanda trotted to them. "What's going on?" Mitch looked back and forth between her and Robert.

"New plan," Eliot told him.

Fiona's face burned—not from anger, but from shame that she had actually considered moving ahead and capturing their flag . . . at least getting four of them up there, instead of going back to help people who were dying.

This was not a war. This was just a class. Everything at Paxington was warping her sense of right and wrong.

"Okay," she said. "New plan."

Fiona figured they'd been on the gym for about five minutes (she made a note to buy a shockproof, waterproof watch after this). So there'd be time to do the right thing *and* win. But there was no time for Team Falcon if they were breathing methane—so they were the priority.

"Robert, Eliot, and Amanda get down there," she said. "I'll be right behind you. Go!"

The boys nodded, Eliot slung his guitar over his back like a samurai sword, and they clambered over the side.

To Mitch she said: "Get up to Jeremy and Sarah. They would have transformed that tar if they could have, so something's stopping them. Get them free, and then get down to help us."

Fiona tried to communicate all her concern and her confidence in Mitch with a nod, and failed miserably, she was sure, but Mitch smiled anyway.

"I'm on it," he said.

Amanda looked at her feet. "I can't go down there," she mumbled. "Not near the gas."

Was Amanda really so much of a coward that she'd let people die? Maybe she was more shaken from those water cannon than Fiona had realized—almost getting knocked off the course and then nearly drowning.

"Okay," she told her, "go help Mitch."

Fiona scrutinized the course, a lattice of supports, ramps, stairs, and moving clockwork parts—and the plumes of water and fire that filled the air, mixed smoke and mist . . . and then she glanced down. Somewhere down there a cloud of natural gas billowed and expanded, complexly invisible . . . and lethal.

The encyclopedic part of Fiona's mind clicked on. Natural gas was primarily methane, and lighter than air, so it would be rising. If it didn't ignite off the open flames, it'd displace the oxygen and asphyxiate them all.

Either way—*this* was not the place to mull over what to do next.

She eased over the edge and climbed down.

Methane was odorless, but the gas companies added mercaptans as a safety feature so it smelled like sulfur.[54]

She hesitated, only a second, but the fear washed over and through her all over again.

No. She had to do this.

---

54. Sulfur (aka brimstone) is often cited in relationship to evil within the Bible, and it is implied that Hell smells of brimstone (hence "fire and brimstone" sermons). In fact, sulfur is odorless. Its characteristic smell comes from hydrogen sulfide (the odor of untreated sewage, and flatulence [along with sulfur-containing mercaptans]) or sulfur dioxide (from burnt matches). Early Chinese doctors used sulfur for medicinal purposes (WARNING: See toxicity tables in Appendix), and gunpowder was likely discovered by Taoist monk-alchemists searching for the elixir of immortality. The fifteenth-century Swiss alchemist Paracelsus believed sulfur embodied the soul (along with the emotions and desires). *Primer of Alchemical Elements: Truth and Myth*, Dr. Kensington Park, Paxington Press LLC.

That's what Mr. Ma had been teaching her in the Force of Arms class—to push past doubt and fear on the battlefield—to keep thinking and trying and moving even if it looked like you were going to die.

She continued down. The fear was there, but she could deal with it.

She stepped onto a bamboo platform.

Eliot and Robert were waiting.

So was Team Falcon. All of them passed out (or dead, it was hard to tell) on the floor ten paces away. Near them, but too deep to reach in a tangle of pipes, a ruptured gas line hissed.

Eliot was on one knee and strummed his guitar. Robert stood by him. The notes were a simple scale, but they make the air swell and ripple about them.

Fiona got dizzy.

She ignored the urge to run as fast and far away as she could from the danger, and instead joined Robert and Eliot.

The stink cleared. The air within the circle Eliot had created smelled sweet.

"Can you make this area of clean air bigger?" she whispered. "Or move closer?"

"Methane concentration too high closer," Eliot said, through gritted teeth. "Trying to expand the circle from here. Still getting used to the steel strings. The methane in the air is . . . slippery."

Fiona stopped asking questions. Eliot had tried to explain the intricacies of his music, and it'd been as enlightening a square trying to explain "corners" to a circle.

Robert looked at her expectantly, and then stepped toward the fallen members of Team Falcon. "They can't wait any longer."

Fiona grabbed his arm. If Robert charged in and tried to pull them out one by one, and she'd end up rescuing him, too.

"Agreed," she said, "but that way is too slow. She nudged Eliot. "Strings?"

Eliot paused a beat. The odor of sulfur rushed back. He ripped off a tiny envelope taped to the back of his guitar and handed it to her. After Lady Dawn had busted a string, he always carried spares.

Eliot went back to playing. The air cooled and the noxious odor again vanished.

Fiona took two strings from the envelope, uncoiled them, stared along their lengths—and the steel wire stiffened straight.

She looked up into the lattice of the course and spotted Sarah, Jeremy,

Mitch, and Amanda as they clambered to a pole and slid down to safety. Good. Four less lives to worry about.

"We do this my way," Fiona said. "Get the rest of them down all at the same time—fast."

Robert nodded. "A twenty-foot drop." He looked over the platform that held Team Falcon. "Four supports," he said. "I'll take the closest. You get into position near the far two."

"Then we go together."

Robert held her gaze. Emotions flashed in his normally too-cool-to-let-anything-show eyes. There was courage and determination . . . and worry.

At that moment he had never looked like more of a hero to her, and she knew that she still cared for him.

Fiona looked away. There was no time to feel for Robert now, though.

She took a huge breath and ran.

She jumped over the prone bodies of her classmates and stopped on the far side of the platform—between two telephone poles that held up the bamboo floor.

Robert darted to the other corner. He dropped to all fours, stared at the foot-thick posts, lashing, and bamboo . . . and drew back his fist.

He struck.

The wood shattered.

Robert rolled back as the platform, now free from the support, dipped toward the mangled corner.

The brass knuckles he'd worn when he'd displayed such feats of strength before weren't there. Robert had done that *bare* fisted. He was stronger, and tougher, and it wasn't just from the training they were getting in Mr. Ma's class. Something else was going on with him.

Robert knelt by the post on the far side and looked to her.

Fiona, still holding her breath, nodded.

She held one stiffened steel string in each hand. She looked along one, then the other; the metal glistened. She fixed them both in her thoughts, imagined them thinner and thinner until their leading edges were so fine and sharp that they flickered in and out of existence.

She lashed out—both arms at once, angled to intercept the floor, ropes, and two supporting telephone poles.

Robert punched.

It sounded like shotgun fire—three shells simultaneously blasted as wood cracked, bamboo fractured, and ropes snapped.

The platform hitched and dropped.

Fiona fell along with it and lost her focus. The bamboo floor rushed up and swatted her. She crumpled—hard—and bit her tongue. The edges of her vision blurred.

She spit and shook her head to clear her confusion.

Dust filled the air, but it no longer stank of sulfur.

She shakily stood and saw Robert dragging two Team Falcon boys away by their feet.

Eliot dropped down, too, and helped by picking up and carrying off one of the unconscious girls.

Fiona grabbed the nearest limp body, a boy, and pulled him by his armpits to the relative safety of the grass—far enough from the jungle gym so if it blew up there was a decent chance they wouldn't all get incinerated.

Mitch, Amanda, and Jeremy and Sarah (both covered in black splotches) appeared as well, and got the remaining members of Team Falcon away from the danger.

Fiona checked the pulse of the boy at her feet. It was weak, but steady. Would there be brain damage?

How could Mr. Ma do such a dangerous thing?

Robert started mouth-to-mouth, and got one boy breathing again.

The other Falcon team members groaned, threw up, and slowly regained consciousness.

"That was too close," Eliot whispered.

Jeremy glanced at his wristwatch. "Saving these folk be all well and good," he murmured, "but there be three minutes. We can still get the flag."

A gunshot cracked through the air.

The arcs of water and fire on the obstacle course stopped and only swirls of smoke and fog remained.

Mr. Ma strode onto the field. He clicked his stopwatch, made two marks on his clipboard, and then announced: "That is time."

Fiona approached him. She felt dizzy again, her feet uncertain. Maybe she'd gotten a lungful of that gas . . . but *something* definitely felt wrong.

"Mr. Ma, there has to be a mistake," she said. "We have three minutes."

"I do not make such mistakes, Miss Post." He narrowed his dark eyes to slits.

"No, sir," Fiona said. There was no way she was going to say he was wrong. She glanced back to Jeremy, who looked incredulous, shook his head, and pointed emphatically at his watch.

Jeremy might have been sneaky enough to set back his watch, but there was no way he'd be stupid enough to try such a simple lie on Mr. Ma.

"Could you please check again?" Fiona asked.

Mr. Ma stared at her. It felt just like when he stared at her that first day in the Force of Arms class—when he'd fought her.

"No," he said.

"That's not fair!" one of the boys from Team Falcon said. "We had a perfect record."

"*Had.*"

Fiona understood then what felt so wrong. The rules of gym class were brutal, but in their own way fair (even if Mr. Ma was apparently *cheating*). The rules stated that if neither team reached their flags before time ran out, then *both* teams tallied a loss.

A loss for Falcon was no big deal. A little wounded pride. They were still at the top of the rankings.

But for Team Scarab, a loss bumped them below the passing/failing cut off.

She turned to the teammates. Robert glared after Mr. Ma. Eliot shook his head and wandered back to the locker room. Amanda slumped to the ground. Mitch ignored them, and kept helping some of his still-groggy classmates. Jeremy and Sarah crossed their arms and looked at Fiona as if this were her fault.

It was. She was their team captain, after all. It had been her decision to save lives instead of going for some stupid flag.

And what if she had gone for the flag? She'd bet Team Falcon would have died . . . and that gas would have ignited and blown them *all* to smithereens.

There had to have been a way to win, though.

Or did there? What if Mr. Ma was just trying to kill them?

There was only one thing she knew for sure: They *had to* win the next match, or they would flunk out of Paxington.

DITCHING

PERFORMANCE

Eliot stood on the sidelines. He was scared. There was no shame to admit that . . . not under these circumstances.

He'd faced Lords from Hell, stood up to a gigantic crocodile, the Hordes of Darkness, and a mother who was Death incarnate, *and* put up with a sister whose abrasive personality was probably what she used to cut through high-carbon steel.

This was different.

This was a *live* audience.

Eliot had watched the other students go first. It had all been arranged by Ms. DuPreé. One by one, they were supposed to go onstage between sets at the Monterey Jazz Festival . . . in front of people who knew music and had just listened to professional signers, jazz quartets, and the most inspirational folk singers that Eliot had ever heard.

Eliot reread the program clutched in his sweaty hands: "Hear California's finest young musicians sing and play their souls out for you!"

Eliot hoped that was a metaphor. Although given the way things worked at Paxington, he wasn't taking *anything* for granted.

"Practicing alone is one thing, playing for your classmates another," Ms. DuPreé had told them on the bus ride out. *"But when you stand in front of a real audience—you're going to sink or fly, baby."*

So here Eliot was: On a sunny day in the wings of the open-air theater, waiting to go on next—just him, about a billion stage lights . . . and three thousand people in the audience.

Ms. DuPreé stood next to him and listened, as entranced as he, to Sarah Covington onstage, singing what she'd described as a "torch song."

Sarah wore a dress as red as her hair. The fabric was tight and sparkled. A bass and piano accompanied her as she lamented about a man who had treated her so badly, but he could make her shiver with pleasure, and how she still loved him.

It was sad. It felt *real* to Eliot, as if Sarah had been through it all and still wanted to love this guy—even if it was a doomed relationship.

She held one last long note, reached out to the audience, and hung her head.

The crowd gave her a thunderous round of applause. Many stood.

When she looked up, though, all traces of her agony had vanished and she smiled and waved to her admirers.

There were hoots and yells for an encore.

Ms. DuPreé leaned close to Eliot so he could hear her over the noise, and said, "That is how it is done. She gave them everything, lost nothing, and got something more precious than gold."

Eliot shot her a quizzical look back.

"Her moment in the spotlight, completely loved by them all," Ms. DuPreé said as if this answered everything.

Eliot examined the audience and saw they did love Sarah at that moment.

He was also certain that clapping and love could easily turn to disgust and boos if they didn't like someone's performance.

Sarah bowed once more, and then exited the stage. The curtain fell behind her. She sauntered to him and Ms. DuPreé, all sparkles and grinning. She smelled of perspiration and Brandywine perfume.

"Knock 'em dead," she told Eliot. "You're better than all of us put together, you just don't know it." She said that like it was part compliment, part annoyance—and then she smiled at Ms. DuPreé and whirled back to the dressing rooms.

Ms. DuPreé gave him a gentle push forward.

Eliot moved, although his legs now seemed to be glued to the floor. It took all his strength to walk to the curtain, and then push through . . . where he froze.

The three thousand people who had been applauding before looked expectantly at him. There was a polite smattering of claps.

Which stopped as Eliot continued to stand there.

Like a complete dork.

What was he doing? Sure he could play. If you needed the dead conjured, gravity warped, or a legion of Napoléon-era soldiers to blow something up—then he was your guy.

But play for people? Be entertaining? Move them? No way.

He wasn't like Sarah. She had a gift with people (even if she was really cruel when you got her alone). That was *real* talent.

And before her, David Kaleb had wowed the crowd with his silver horn flashing like a mirror under the lights; the audience had gotten to their feet and danced even!

Sarah and David had had fun with it. Music used to be something Eliot had fun with, too. Now, though, it was a constant struggle to do better, to control the wild magic in him and Lady Dawn.

And why in the world had Ms. DuPreé made him go last?

The people in the audience whispered as he stood there. Some got up and left.

Eliot watched them and narrowed his eyes.

No one walked out on him—not before they'd *heard* him, at least.

He marched out front and center on the stage.

There was more polite, encouraging applause.

But there ended his bravery. . . .

And Eliot was stuck again—in front of all those people—them waiting for him to impress them—and him unable to move. So he did the only thing he could. Stall.

He fiddled with the knobs on the lower edge of his new Lady Dawn guitar. He then checked the cable plugged into her socket—a cord that ran backstage but actually connected to nothing. It was just for looks.

By adjusting the dials, flicking a switch or two, his new guitar could sound like an ordinary unpowered instrument one moment, then blast out amplified noise with reverberating electronic feedback the next . . . all without having anything plugged in anywhere. Flip another switch, twist a dial, and the guitar echoed with the deepest bass notes.

He played it almost as well as he did the violin. It was like switching between writing in cursive script to block letters. It was something he could do without thinking about it.

His fingers drifted to the steel strings and twitched over them.

Faint sound pulsed. Pure and simple.

He'd start there.

He played the "Mortal's Coil" nursery rhyme—straight up, one note

ERIC NYLUND

after another, just like the first time he'd heard Louis play in that Del Sombra alley.

He kept his eyes on the strings, focused, and shifted notes up and down the scale. He made the sweetest sound, and there was a slight echo . . . as if there were another guitar accompanying him.

Eliot looked up.

The audience nodded and moved to the rhythm. They weren't exactly captivated as they had been with Sarah or David, but that was okay. He didn't entirely suck.

Now he had to up the stakes—get these people really excited. Like Ms. DuPreé had been trying to teach them: put his soul into his music.

But why?

He stopped. Right in the middle of the song. His hair fell into his face.

Why *was* he doing this? Really? He didn't want to be here. He'd never wanted to impress anyone with his music.

He slammed his hand across the guitar stings. The sound that came out was odd and dissonant and abrupt.

The audience jumped.

It startled him, too.

He hadn't known he could do that—scare people. Without magic.

Maybe that was the best magic of all. . . .

He played—and didn't even think about it—just moved fingers over strings. It was classical, a bit like Mozart. It reminded him of the way he felt the first day at Paxington, at least, the way he thought it was *supposed* to have been: learning about mythology and his family, surrounded by books and other students just as smart and dedicated.

That music was too predictable for his mood, though . . . and it seemed like a lie to force himself to play it that way.

Eliot flipped a switch and the sound looped. He riffed over the piece, shifting to bass notes.

He picked up the pace and his music felt like all the fighting that went on at Paxington—the duels and the team battles in gym class.

It was rock and roll (one of several terms he had studied in class last week) and he made Lady Dawn snarl.

He dialed up the feedback and sound tore through the air.

Head down, he focused on the notes, no magic, no ghosts or chorus of kids singing along. He was alone and that suited him fine.

He even tuned out the audience. He didn't look. He didn't care.

Lady Dawn heated under his hands, her wood flashed like liquid fire, and her strings felt sharp as if he were pushing her past her engineered limits.

He shifted back and forth between styles that he'd just discovered—mariachi to bluegrass—classical Chopin to jazz to the ancient ballads of Charlemagne and then with a long slow grinding changeover, he beat out some heavy metal.

He wasn't playing to *do* anything. No miracles. No life-or-death situations that he had to save himself from.

He wasn't playing *for* anyone, either. Not to impress Julie, or Jezebel, or Ms. DuPreé.

He just played.

Music—for the thrill.

Because he wanted it.

Lady Dawn resonated and flexed under his hands, soaking up all his anger and frustration and power, amplifying it . . . and wanting more.

He blasted out the last power chord, flourished with the phrase of a little lullaby, and stilled her strings.

He was bored with this . . . and done.

He finally looked up.

Not a single person in the audience moved. They sat and stared open-mouthed.

Far away, dogs barked and howled and a dozen car alarms warbled.

Eliot didn't care what any of them thought. He turned and started to walk backstage.

Ms. DuPreé waited in the wings; Sarah had come out to listen to him as well, and both their eyes were wide at his audacity.

They hadn't liked it? Maybe Ms. DuPreé would kick him out of her class. It seemed so silly and trivial now to play for her approval.

Eliot had almost reached the curtain's edge when the applause came—waves of it along with wild cheering and calls for more.

He turned. Every single person in the audience was on their feet, clapping and waving their lighters in the air.

They'd loved his music and him.

And none of it mattered to Eliot.

He went to Ms. DuPreé and Sarah. The applause behind him intensified. The look on Ms. DuPreé's face shifted, and her mouth snapped shut. She wasn't astonished anymore; the narrowing of her eyes signaled something closer to disapproval. It was hard to tell.

Sarah's mouth, however, remained dropped. Then she blinked and shouted to him over the applause, "That was the most amazing thing I've ever heard."

"Do me a favor?" he shouted back.

"Anything!" She seemed out of breath.

"Borrow your phone?"

Sarah frowned, like this wasn't what she'd wanted him to say, but nonetheless, she turned and rummage through her backpack. She handed Eliot her phone.

Eliot dialed, held the speaker to his head, and stuck his finger in the other ear.

There was a connection. The person on the other end picked up on the first ring. "Yeah?"

"Robert?" Eliot yelled as loud as he could.

"Geez," Robert said. "I can barely hear you. Speak up."

Eliot ended the called and texted Robert instead: *need 2 get out of here. give me a ride?*

send gps, Robert texted back. *ill get u—where 2?*

anywhere, Eliot thumbed. *just need to ride.*

59

PRACTICE DOESN'T MAKE PERFECT

Fiona crackled her knuckles and stretched. Team Scarab had the gym for an hour of practice, drills, and figuring out the new course. It was a golden opportunity and couldn't be wasted.

She squinted though the hazy morning air at the new eight-story obstacle course. There were coils of razor wire and nozzles that belched frozen carbon dioxide. Chain-link ramps swayed in the breeze. Two new top levels rippled, swathed in plastic, and had OFF-LIMITS signs all over them. Inside workers hammered and sparked with arc welders. More surprises courtesy of Mr. Ma.

But the course wasn't the only thing they had to figure out. They had to fight and win now against the grade curve, too.

Not only had Team Soaring Eagle been disbanded because of their disastrous accident . . . but Team Red Dragon, too; they'd been declared ineligible because they had too many injured players—and their remaining members had been picked up by other teams down a person or two.

The problem was that these two disbanded teams got *removed* from the ranks. All the other teams slid down—without moving the cutoff point for failing.

This morning when Fiona checked the roster, Team Scarab was now well below that cut.

She turned to face and rally her team . . . at least, the half of her team that was here.

Robert, Jeremy, and Amanda sat on the bleachers.

Amanda scanned a moldy book called *The Non-Illusion of Law* as she weaved her hair into a braid.

Jeremy peered into a little book, jotting the occasional note.

"We have to win the next match," she told them. "Let's get up there and practice."

"We're going to practice without everyone?" Amanda asked. "Let's compare notes on Miss Westin's last lecture instead. I'm not getting this whole 'dharma' thing."

"What do you want us to do, Fiona?" Robert said, and picked at a crack in the wood. "Run a few laps?"

Fiona frowned and crossed her arms.

Eliot and Sarah were on a field trip for their music class. She didn't blame them; they had to keep their grades up. It still irked her, though, knowing they were off having fun while the rest of them had to work.

Jezebel was still missing. Six weeks and she hadn't even shown up at Paxington. Was she dead on some battlefield in Hell? They might be permanently down one team member.

And Mitch? He was missing, too.

"Did you try Master Stephenson's cell phone?" Jeremy asked without looking up from his notebook.

"Twice," Fiona said. "No answer. Just a text."

He'd sent her a text message a few hours ago:

> FIONA
> I'LL BE LATE FOR PRACTICE. START W/O ME.
> FAMILY STUFF TO DEAL WITH.
> COFFEE LATER? A WALK?
> MITCH

When she'd tried to call, she got the "subscriber out of service area" message. And when she texted back, there'd been no response.

Mitch had never missed a practice. It worried her. This "family stuff" he had to deal with . . . was that the same problem he'd hinted at over winter break?

Whatever the reasons for their missing teammates, Fiona got why no one wanted to practice: They needed one another.

Without Sarah here for Jeremy to boss around and show off in front of, he seemed more lazy than usual (if that were possible). Fiona made a mental note to ask Sarah later if they were first cousins or more distantly related. He was from the nineteenth century; Sarah from the twenty-first. Their relationship had to be . . . complicated.

And without Mitch, Robert seemed more rude than usual (which was *not* so hard for her to imagine). It was as if he acted civil these days only with Mitch around. What was up with that? Some too-cool alpha male thing? She doubted she'd ever understand the boy psyche.

Fiona had to do *something* to motivate her team, though.

"We should look at the new parts of the course," she said, "see if we can figure out what tricks Mr. Ma has planned."

"Wouldn't that be breaking your sacred rules?" Robert said, arching one eyebrow.

"They're not my rules," she replied. "They are *the* rules—and those signs up there just say 'off-limits,' not 'don't peek.' Besides, I'm willing to test the boundaries of the rules if it means saving the necks of my teammates."

Amanda shook out her hair and closed her book. "Sure—let's go," she murmured. "I can't wait to see if we're going to get frozen solid next time or chopped into bits."

Jeremy smirked. "A tad dark for you, lass, no?"

Amanda turned and held Jeremy's gaze until he looked away.

Robert jumped off the bleacher suddenly, startled, and reached into his pocket. He pulled out his phone.

"You brought that to practice?" Fiona asked.

Robert shrugged. "I have people that need to get ahold of me."

Fiona didn't like that. Who needed to stay in touch with Robert so desperately that he couldn't leave his phone in his locker for one hour? Was he still spying for Uncle Henry? Or maybe it was as simple as him having other friends she didn't know about. Perhaps a girlfriend? Well, he was certainly entitled to have a life outside school—the only reason it irritated her was that it was cutting into *their* practice time.

Robert pressed the phone to his ear.

Amanda moved closer to Robert. "Is it Mitch?"

Robert held up a finger and shook his head. "Geez," he said into the phone. "I can barely hear you. Speak up."

He then looked at the phone's screen, started to close it, then paused. "Not Mitch," he told them. Robert texted whoever it was, waited, texted again—then snapped the phone shut.

He looked at Fiona and pursed his lips. "I've got to go. Sorry."

"What!" Fiona said. "We've got the course for thirty more minutes. You can't leave."

Robert squinted at her, and his face flushed. In a low voice, he said, "I don't work for the League anymore. You can't order me around."

It felt like he'd slapped her in the face.

She wasn't ordering anyone around. She was just trying to win—so they could *all* graduate.

But before she could say any of this, Robert walked away.

She watched him go. Furious. Helpless.

Jeremy came to her side. "Let him go, lassie. There be no point in practicing today with so many missing, anyway."

He stood so close, Fiona felt his body heat, too near for comfort. She took a step away.

"Whatever . . . ," she muttered, trying as hard as she could to sound like she didn't care.

"It only goes to show how unreliable some members of this team are." Jeremy tapped his notebook. "I've been so bold as to prepare a list of suitable alternatives."

"Alternates?" Amanda jumped up and came over. One of her tiny hands had balled into a fist. "You can't just kick people off the team."

"Don't interrupt me," Jeremy told her.

Fiona made a *calm down* gesture at Amanda. "It's okay," she said. "I think I know what he means. Planning ahead, right?"

Something had happened to Amanda over the break. She would've never stood up to Jeremy Covington like that before. Was it that dorm fire Fiona had heard about? Three people got hurt. Maybe Amanda had rescued them, and that had boosted her self-esteem. Fiona should've hung out with her more to find out . . . but oddly, Amanda hadn't even tried to speak with her since the start of the new semester.

"Precisely," Jeremy replied. "Planning ahead. What shall we do if our esteemed Infernal teammate never returns? Or Mitch? What if he has met some unpleasant fate? Or Robert . . . what if he just rides off one day?"

Now it was Fiona's turn to glower at him. Mitch had *not* met some unpleasant fate. And Robert wouldn't just ride off and leave them. But he did have a point about Jezebel.

Jeremy leaned closer and his silky blond hair fell into his face in a distractingly attractive way. He touched one finger to his lips, trying to hide the smile growing there. "Just in case . . . ," he whispered.

Fiona glanced at his notebook and the list of names in neat calligraphy.

"We should start talking to some of the other students," she said. "The ones on teams down two or three members already—before someone else snaps up the best of them."

"Aye," Jeremy said. "That be where my expertise is pure gold. I'll be able to sort through the chaff for ye."

Amanda gave a dismissive snort.

Fiona agreed with her assessment—at least that Jeremy was a relic, rude, chauvinistic—but she also saw the truth of the situation. The maneuvering for replacements, the politics of picking new teams; Mr. Ma had to have known this would happen in the later half of the year. She saw that this was part of gym class, too. Fiona had to learn how to recruit and, at the same time, stop other teams from getting *her* best players.

She imagined this process only accelerated as finals drew near. For most Paxington students, their loyalties would dissolve the instant they thought they were on a losing team.

"We'll have to act quick," Fiona whispered, more to herself than Jeremy. She was about to ask him what he had planned when she spotted someone on the far side of the field.

Mr. Ma emerged from the locker room. He wasn't in his usual Paxington sweats. Today he wore camouflage fatigues, a khaki shirt, black combat boots, and a red beret. He looked all business, grim, and his dark eyes fixed upon her.

"Miss Post," he said, as if her name were an accusation.

"We were just going to start," she said, feeling suddenly guilty about not being on the gym.

But she stopped herself, disgusted at feeling so weak—when she'd done absolutely nothing wrong. Fiona stood straight and told him: "We're just about to figure out the best strategy to get to the very top of the new course."

A flicker of irritation passed over Mr. Ma's face as he turned and glanced up to the top of the gym structure. He then looked over Jeremy and Amanda.

"A fine idea," Mr. Ma said, "but there will be no practice for you today. Where is Mr. Farmington?"

"No practice? We need it," Fiona protested. "Team Scarab was signed up for this time."

She decided not to say anything about Robert's phone call and his ditching. Why she was protecting him, though, she had no clue.

"Team Scarab, yes," Mr. Ma agreed. "But *you* are coming with me. There's a special field trip for the Force of Arms class today."

"A trip?" Fiona said. "Where?"

"South," Mr. Ma told her. "We have a chance to study a revolutionary war in progress . . . firsthand."

60

THE TROUBLE WITH TRUANCY

Eliot had never ditched before, and he wasn't sure what he was supposed to do. Study? That was the only thing that came to mind . . . but it sure seemed to defeat the purpose.

It was nice to be out of class and in the sunlight, though. And when Robert had picked him up (in a sidecar attached to his Harley) outside the Monterey Fairgrounds, the outraged look on Sarah's face had been great. Ms. DuPreé, though, had said nothing, looking almost as if she approved of this rebellion.

He was sure he'd pay for it—but for now, he'd enjoy it while it lasted.

Robert slowed his bike as they got to the exit of the fairgrounds' parking lot. "So where to?"

Eliot tried to think of something he'd always wanted to do, but never had the time or freedom for.

"How about miniature golf?"

Robert gave him a *you've got to be kidding* look.

Eliot shrugged, a little embarrassed. "I'm open to suggestions."

Robert snapped his fingers. "There's a Mardi Gras—a real blowout bash. Just a bit south, if you don't mind the drive to Costa Esmeralda."

There was something funny in Robert's eyes, though; like this Mardi Gras thing was a deep memory surfacing . . . as if he was in a trace.

"Sounds good," Eliot replied.

"Cool." Robert grinned, and the look vanished. "Hang on."

They drove fast—same as when Robert had chauffeured Uncle Henry's limousine—breezing down the California coast to the border in ten minutes—then they blasted down the Pan-American Highway past cars and trucks, and through Mexico City traffic like it was frozen in amber.

Rocketing just a foot off the ground in the sidecar was scary *and* fun. Eliot might as well have been strapped into the front seat of a first-class roller coaster that never stopped (not that he'd ever ridden a roller coaster, but this was how he imagined it'd feel).

"That exit there!" Eliot shouted, and pointed.

Robert veered onto the off-ramp. They raced past a sign that read

COSTA ESMERALDA, CENTRO DE CIUDAD 8 KM

Eliot recognized this stretch of jungle coastline. It was the same place Uncle Henry had driven him a month ago, crowded with palm trees and ferns and flowers, and flocks of parrots that called out to him. In the roar of the wind and surf, he heard his rejuvenating song echoing still.

His guitar was wedged next to his thigh. He'd never be able to play such a delicate song on this new version of Lady Dawn, and almost regretted her transformation.

Eliot ran his hand over the mirror-smooth wood, the bold brass fittings, felt a thrum with her coiled steel strings. But there was more power in her now . . . or in him, and that was a good thing.

The jungle thinned; there were patches of bare dirt, and then pavement, and small buildings that crystallized into suburbs: tiny houses with dark metal roofs. Clean, too—not a speck of trash or pollution.

As they sped on, the houses became factories and then rose into clusters of office towers arranged in orderly rows.

And all of them without color: faded black asphalt, concrete sidewalks and walls, bare iron pipes and lampposts—everything shades of gray. It was depressing.

The strangest thing, though, was the traffic. There were three lanes full of honking cars and trucks, but all going north. On the southbound lane that they traveled on . . . it was empty.

Pretty weird, if there was a Mardi Gras.

Robert slowed as they approach the end of the off-ramp and looked around. Down either side of the street was a towering canyon of office buildings. The only movement was papers blowing in the gutters. No people.

"Are you sure this is the right place?" Eliot asked.

"Positive," Robert answered, annoyed. He sounded unsure now about the reliability of his *sure thing* Mardi Gras tip.

A few blocks away, thumps echoed from the city center.

"Come on," Robert muttered. "Sounds like *something's* going down. Maybe the party's started or it's a parade."

Eliot nodded, but he detected something in Robert's voice he didn't often hear: worry.

Eliot's hand rested on Lady Dawn's strings, just in case.

Robert eased the Harley into gear and went slow, the bike's engine shaking the frame.

Eliot had an urge to get out and walk, so, if nothing else, he could properly hold his guitar. It was claustrophobic in this sidecar. Sure, the leather padding was comfortable . . . but it kind of reminded him of a coffin on wheels.

On the other hand, maybe it was best to stay in the vehicle that could accelerate past the sound barrier—in case they had to make a quick exit.

They moved closer to the downtown office towers, each with the same dirty square windows, the same square entryways. There were, however, splotches of color here and there. Plastered on the walls were posters. In them, a man stood in a heroic pose holding a pistol in one hand, a sword in the other. He was drawn in angular red, white, and black lines. A red flag waved behind him. At the bottom of each poster, black bold letters proclaimed: COL. V. C. BALBOA. PRESIDENTE DE POR VIDA.

This guy gave Eliot the creeps.

Robert pulled up to a four-way stop and predictably rolled through the ALTO sign into the intersection. This gave them an unobstructed view into the center of Costa Esmeralda.

And they saw exactly who was throwing this "Mardi Gras."

There were hundreds of soldiers. They wore faded green uniforms and held rifles with bayonets. A few hefted bazookas. Squads moved among the buildings, rounding up civilians and ordering them to stand against a wall.

One man shouted at the soldiers—and got clubbed to the ground for his trouble.

Eliot's hands rolled into fists. Seeing this enraged him more than anything, even the unfair, potentially lethal classes at Paxington—those students were there because they wanted to be. They knew the risks. This was just a bunch of bullies picking on people.

Eliot wanted to climb out, grab Lady Dawn, and . . .

All his heroic thoughts ground to a halt.

On a corner three blocks away squatted an armored tank, its muzzle pointed down the street at head level . . . at *them*.

Robert gunned the Harley, spun around, and roared down a side street.

They went fast, but it was *just* fast. Not the fast that Eliot knew they could go—fast that made the rest of the world stand still.

They raced for two blocks, screamed around three corners, and Robert skidded to a halt. He doubled over, examining the bike's exposed V-pistons.

"Something's wrong," Robert murmured.

A block behind them, two primer gray Humvees careened through an intersection.

Gunshots cracked.

Holes chipped in the wall over Eliot's head. "No kidding something's wrong! Just go!"

Robert twisted the throttle and they sped off, quickly outpacing the larger vehicles—slalomed around two corners—then down an alley.

Rolling to block the alley's exit, however, were two more Humvees. These had their tops off, roll bars exposed . . . with mounted fifty-caliber machine guns. They fired.

"Holy—!" Robert ducked, spun them around, and peeled out, scraping the alley's wall.

Behind them, gunfire chewed through the concrete. Eliot instinctively crouched deeper into the sidecar (as if the fiberglass were going to stop a bullet).

Robert plowed through a row of trash cans.

Sparks flew and bullets puckered the metal . . . both cans and the bike's frame.

Then the Harley was around the corner.

Robert accelerated to ninety miles an hour . . . still nowhere near the magical speed Eliot *wished* they were going.

Four blocks away, a helicopter skimmed over the rooftops. It rose, spun, and angled toward them.

Robert spotted it, too. He pressed his body low and went faster.

But there was no way they'd outrun a helicopter. They needed another option.

Eliot gripped Lady Dawn. He could summon Napoléon-era cannoneers and cavalry. Or that ghostly fog. At least that'd give them some cover.

But nineteenth-century artillery and soldiers on horseback against au-

tomatic weapons, bazookas, or armored tanks? They wouldn't last two seconds. Fog would get blown away by the helicopter, and besides . . . the
spirits inside that fog wouldn't care if they attacked soldiers or civilians.

The Harley flashed through an intersection.

Eliot looked for more Humvees or tanks. The adjacent street was a blur
of concrete gray and iron black—except for a spot of gleaming white and
chrome.

He knew those colors. Not *what* specifically they belonged to, just that
he *had* seen them before.

He tapped Robert and made a *circle around* motion.

Robert nodded. He braked, turned, and gunned the bike back the way
they'd come.

The helicopter thundered overhead, overshooting their position.

Eliot pointed down the side street. Robert leaned the bike into the turn
so far that the sidecar wheels lifted.

One building on this street was different. It was three stories, and on
top was an enclosed glass atrium, gleaming in the tropical sun. There was
an iron statue in front: the same gun and sword-wielding Presidente in the
posters. Red flags fluttered alongside the wide stairs that led to steel double
doors.

But this is not what Eliot had recognized, not what now made his heart
catch.

Parked in front of the building was a 1933 Rolls-Royce limousine, all
white curves that seemed to never end, chrome that looked like dripping
quicksilver, and the woman-with-wings-swept-back-and-arms-held-forward
hood ornament.

It was Laurabelle. Uncle Henry's car.

"Hang on and duck!" Robert shouted.

He veered past the limo's bumper—over the curb, shot up the stairs,
and crashed though the double doors.

The Harley flopped over and skidded into a wall. The engine coughed
and died.

Eliot tumbled out, Lady Dawn in one hand . . . the room spinning.

He was in was a lobby with more flags and oil paintings of Colonel V.
C. Balboa, *Presidente de por vida,* but otherwise it was deserted.

Robert went to the doors that hung askew in their frames and shoved
them back (more or less) into place.

Eliot looked over his shoulder. There was a thump as that helicopter passed overhead and faded—then the shadow of a jet flashed across the street and there was a teeth-shaking rumble—followed by three Humvees that rolled by. They didn't stop.

Eliot sighed and opened his mouth to ask Robert a million questions.

Robert shook his head. He pulled out a gun from the holster in the small of his back. He pointed his eyes the up and down the lobby.

Eliot nodded, hung back, and slung Lady Dawn over his shoulder . . . fingers just over her strings.

Robert checked one end of the lobby, then came back and motioned Eliot to follow.

Eliot took one last glance outside. He didn't see any pursuing soldiers.

He and Robert entered an abandoned courtroom. They crept past rows of seats, flags and official seals, and through the curtain behind the raised judge's bench.

They found an office with walls of legal books. There was a mahogany desk upon which sat a drained bottle with hand-painted gold leaves embellishing a label that proclaimed: TEQUILA.

Robert nodded toward stairs that led up. A second bottle lay on the steps, liquor spilled, smelling smoky and pungent.

Uncle Henry had to be up there, or someone, at least, who had his car. Either way, there were answers, and maybe a way out of sunny, festive Costa Esmeralda.

They climbed up. Robert swept his aim as the stairs angled back and forth.

Two more flights. This reminded Eliot of the obstacle course in gym, and adrenaline surged though his blood and his fingertips lit upon Lady Dawn's strings. The barest subsonic resonant thrum came in response to his feather touch. The paint on the walls crackled.

Robert looked at him, but said nothing.

They eased along the last steps to a glass door, pausing to let their eyes adjust to the sunlight.

On the other side was a garden of palm trees, cacti, and bromeliads with flowers like fanged mouths. There was a table with shade umbrella, and lounging there with his back to them was Uncle Henry in his white suit (his jacket off) and straw hat, shot glass tilted in his hand, its contents dribbling down his arm.

Robert eased open the door, scanned the garden right to left.

There was no one else there, but he didn't lower his aim.

Eliot didn't understand. It was Uncle Henry. He tapped Robert and gave him a *What are you doing?* look.

Robert shrugged him off and shot back a glare that could have given Fiona a run for her money in the withering-flesh department.

Without turning, Uncle Henry said, "Robert's quite right to be wary, Eliot. This is a war, after all." He gave a dramatic wave that sloshed out the remains of the tequila. "Dangerous elements loose in the streets . . ." He reached for the bottle and knocked it over. "Can't even trust one's liquor to stand still at such times."

Robert sighed, clicked on his gun's safety, and lowered it.

They went to Henry. Eliot plucked up the bottle and set it right.

"You're drunk," Robert said.

"I certainly hope so. Otherwise a perfect waste of several bottles of Tequila Casa Noble Extra Anejo."

Eliot surveyed the city from behind the glass walls. Tanks and Humvees rolled into the city center where he and Robert had stopped. There were more people in the streets, and more soldiers shoving them around, and one thing he hadn't seen on the far side of the city's center square: an older section with a cobblestone courtyard and church that looked like it could have been built by the original Spanish missionaries. Dozens of people streamed toward the church, taking shelter within—scared people, crying people, children, and women carrying bundled babies.

Eliot set a hand on the glass, wanting to help them.

"You said this was going to be a party . . . ," Robert told Henry, stabbing at him with a finger.

"Did I?" Henry crinkled his brow. "Oh, perhaps I did at that." He frowned. "Really, Robert, you know better than to take me literally. This is more of a wake for a friend, actually."

Eliot turned. "Why is the League doing this? Why are you *letting* them?"

It was just a guess the League was involved—but a darned good guess in Eliot's estimation. All the organized violence. Uncle Henry here, doing . . . whatever he was doing.

"I had not the time or the strength to stop them," Henry whispered. "They're right, of course: Balboa must go. But you're right, too, Eliot; there were other ways for those with patience." He shook his head. "And I have so few friends left. Even if the Colonel had all those nasty habits— suppression of free speech—communism—a taste for women a tad too young."

Henry took a deep breath and continued. "Alas, he committed the one unpardonable sin: not following the exact letter of the League's bidding."

He studied his empty shot glass, surprised it was no longer full. "And communism—ha!—that has never worked among mortals. Even among the Immortals—Zeus and his 'fair' autocracy . . . what a farce. Only the Bright Ones ever came close."[55]

Robert's eyes widened with realization. "Balboa has one of *your* cars."

"Yes," Henry said with a sigh. "The 1970 Shelby. So naturally, the League sent me here to prevent him from spiriting away."

"That's why the bike didn't work," Robert muttered to Eliot. "Henry's blocking."

Eliot didn't understand completely, but he did enough to know they'd be stuck here until Uncle Henry let them go.

"If this is a League-sponsored revolution," Eliot asked, "why use the military? Why not just let people vote?"

Uncle Henry wobbled to his feet and joined Eliot by the glass wall. "I do love you, child, and your idealism. It is one of the few fragile joys left to me."

"You could've taken Balboa out neat and easy," Robert spat out. "The only problem is, it might've left tracks—and the League couldn't have that. Nothing covers tracks like a little blood, huh, Mr. Mimes?"

Uncle Henry sobered. "Yes. And even better than a little is a lot. I do wish there was a way to stop this, but set in motion, these things take on a life of their own, I'm afraid."

Eliot didn't know what to think. He detected no lie in Uncle Henry's words. And he did indeed look remorseful (or maybe he was just drunk like Robert said). Still, this situation seemed utterly wrong.

"Look here," Uncle Henry said, and fished a scrap of paper from his shirt pocket. It was a stamp, triangle shaped, with a pineapple printed on it. He ran a finger over its perforated edges. "Every conflict between two forces has three outcomes. One side can win. Or the other side can."

He placed the stamp in Eliot's hand and closed his fingers over it.

"What's the third option?" Eliot asked.

"Haven't a clue," Henry replied. "But I do know there's *always* a third option. People just never seem interested in looking long enough to find it."

Eliot didn't understand . . . but his hand closed about the stamp. He'd keep it.

---

55. "Bright Ones." A seventeenth-century colloquialism for "fairies."—Editor.

He turned and watched as soldiers moved toward the church. One of them shot at a shadow moving behind a stained glass window. Rainbow fragments littered the ground, out of place in this city of gray.

Eliot stomach twisted. He turned Robert. "I have to get down there and stop them. They're going to kill those people!"

Robert pressed his lips into a single white line. Through gritted teeth, he told Henry, "Unblock my bike, man. We can save them."

Uncle Henry hesitated and then, "I cannot. I want to, but the League would know." Henry then cocked his head and looked at the courtyard. "How refreshingly unexpected!"

Eliot stared unbelieving as a single person strode into the courtyard—blocking the soldiers' advance on the church.

It was Fiona.

61

WHAT LITTLE GIRLS ARE MADE OF

Fiona stood on a rooftop and watched soldiers in the courtyard below. They went from building to building, searching, pulling people out into the street. It was awful.

Behind her stood six boys from the Force of Arms class, wide-eyed, also watching with fascination. Among them was also the upperclassman who had given her a tour the first day at Paxington, the handsomely chiseled Dante Scalagari.

Mr. Ma observed as well, impassive, arms folded over his chest.

Fiona just wanted to leave.

She glanced back at the Paxington helicopter perched on the roof. It had whisked them from the landing pad behind the Ludus Magnus over the Pacific—then the turbines had kicked in and blasted them through the sound barrier.

They'd flown south at that terrific speed, so Fiona guessed they were somewhere near the equator from the position and strength of the sun overhead.

. . . Sunlight that clashed with the chilling events in the streets.

The boys whispered about how the soldiers covered each other with overlapping patterns of fire. There was a nervous edge their voices. They were worried, too—for the people down there or for themselves, she wasn't sure.

Mr. Ma had briefed them on the flight. They were to observe a coup d'état, the beginnings of a democratic revolution. If, he had stressed, none of the heroes of the *revolución* got greedy and seized the dictatorship for themselves. It would be a chance for them to watch urban combat tactics, and to witness the rarer occurrence of ideologies clashing on a battlefield.

Fiona didn't understand that last part. All she saw were people getting pushed around.

"This situation has similarities to the battle of Ultima Thule," Mr. Ma said. "Instead of Immortals and Infernals, however, there are many lightly armed rebels fighting a lesser number of soldiers who are better trained and armed."

On the street, a squad of soldiers shoved a family out of their apartment building. There were older men and women and a dozen children—all so scared, they stumbled and huddled together for support.

This wasn't even close to Ultima Thule. The few armed nonmilitary men she'd spotted had been running away. Meanwhile, the soldiers had automatic weapons and an armored tank on the corner. Similarities? Mr. Ma was crazy.

He was stone-faced, though, and his dark eyes were as unreadable as two blank blackboards.

Fiona felt sick.

She didn't trust him. With six upperclassman boys here (charming Dante Scalagari or not), well outside the watchful eye of Miss Westin and the regulations of Paxington, Mr. Ma could do . . . she wasn't sure . . . something awful to her . . . or, at least, try to.

Fiona took two steps away, and only then did she return her attention to the street (still keeping Mr. Ma in her peripheral vision).

The soldiers herded the civilians from the apartment building toward another group. They made them stand against a wall and turn around.

The people weren't fighting back. How could they? There were kids in the line of fire.

But then again . . . there were little kids there. How could they *not* fight?

"W-what are they going to do?" Fiona whispered. Her knees shook. She locked them, forcing them to still.

"What do you *think* they're going to do?" Mr. Ma replied without glancing at her. "What would you do if you had your enemies helpless before you?"

Fiona sure wouldn't line helpless people against a wall and threaten to execute them.

"We have to do something."

"Yes," Mr. Ma said. "We watch and learn what we can. But only that."

"What!" She turned. "Why?"

The boys in her class stepped back, astonished that Fiona had questioned Mr. Ma. Dante nodded, apparently sharing her sentiments, although not daring to offer an opinion.

Mr. Ma twitched a single eyebrow. "This is a League matter, Miss Post," he said. "Paxington's charter states we must preserve our neutrality among the Immortals, Infernals, and mortal magical families. Staff and students are not allowed to interfere . . . regardless of how much we wish."

"The League's doing this?" Fiona asked, but more to herself than to Mr. Ma.

She was part of the League of Immortals—but only because the Council had decreed it so—not that she actually worked with them. They never even told her *what* they did. She chewed her lower lip. She wasn't sure why they'd do this, but if they had a reason for a civil war here, the League was capable of making it happen, she bet . . . and make it appear as a military coup.

Mr. Ma looked back to the courtyard and continued his vigil.

Uncertain what else to do, Fiona turned and watched, too.

A mother and her child sneaked away from the others. They made a run for the church at the opposite side of the courtyard. Several others rushed though its doors, too, seeking refuge.

"This is no Ultima Thule," Fiona declared. She heard the rising indignation in her voice and couldn't stop it. "Those people will be slaughtered. Is that what you wanted to teach us today?"

Mr. Ma gripped the metal railing on the edge of the rooftop so tight, it creaked. "Perhaps," he said.

Fiona's jaw clenched. "I'm going down there and stopping them."

"I have told you," Mr. Ma said with strained patience, "I cannot permit school staff or students to—"

Fiona shrugged out to her Paxington jacket. "Then I'm ditching."

Without waiting for him to tell her to stop, or some acknowledgment that she was doing the right thing from Dante or any of the other boys— Fiona jumped over the railing onto a fire escape.

She padded down and around the ladders and landings . . . pausing on the last.

She'd need a weapon. She unzipped her book bag.

What was she was doing?

She should have thought this through. These weren't shadow creatures or Paxington students with swords. They were men with guns that could kill her before she got close to them.

Her hand closed about her wooden yo-yo. What good was that going to do?

She had to do *something,* though. What was the point of being a real goddess—of everything she'd learned at Paxington—all that training in gym class, if she couldn't put it to use?

She touched cold metal and jerked her hand from the book bag.

Her father's gift, the slightly rusted steel bracelet, had wrapped itself about her wrist. The bracelet had unclasped and grown to a heavy chain before, its links tapering to razor edges . . . it had lengthened a dozen feet and whipped through a Parisian lamppost.

It was magic. An Infernal thing. A thing to cut.

And precisely what she needed.

Okay. Mr. Ma was training them to fight. So she'd fight.

She squeezed the metal. It warmed, squirmed, and heated . . . just like her blood.

Infernal or Immortal rage, that didn't matter, and it didn't matter that the anger was the *only* emotion that seemed to come easily to her these days. Right now, she was going to use it to do some good.

Fiona slid down the last ladder and strode across the courtyard. She walked straight toward a soldier who watched the church. He shielded his eyes to see through its stained glass windows, raised his Kalashnikov machine gun, and shot at the shadows.

Part of Fiona knew not to be afraid. She was half goddess, and half . . . whatever her father was.

But she was afraid.

She was still the same old Fiona Post.

And yet, there was something else in her: a fighter. Something extraordinary. She clung to that—and strode forward to find which Fiona she would become.

She uncoiled the length of chain now in her hand and loosed a slur that would have never qualified for a round of vocabulary insult with Eliot. "Hey!" she called out. *"Perro que come excremento!"*[56]

56. Translation from Spanish, "excrement-eating dog."—Editor.

The soldier wheeled.

Fiona lashed her chain at him.

Before the chain struck, however, he shot her.

A staccato burst: three rounds in her chest and gut.

The impact blasted her back; she spun and bounced and flipped and skidded along the cobblestones to a halt . . . facefirst.

The pain was beyond anything she'd felt. It was lightning that flashed and unfurled from her belly button to sternum to her spine—bone shattering, organ shredding—it ricocheted teeth to toes.

She lay still. Dead.

Boots on cobblestones approached.

She had to be dead . . . didn't she? Of course.

So why then did she feel her heart thump—pumping, faster, until blood thundered through her veins?

She got up.

The man who'd shot her stood there, mouth open, blinking. He raised his Kalashnikov.

Fiona didn't give him another chance. Chain wrapped about her fist, she slugged him.

His head snapped back, and he fell, and didn't move.

Three holes smoldered in her shirt and skirt. Her belly was a solid bruise, but it *was* in one piece . . . which was more than she could say about her uniform. Custom fit by Madame Cobweb—how was she going to replace it?

Heat surged through her and seared away the pain.

Six more soldiers saw her over their fallen comrade. They ran at her, yelling, and leveled their weapons.

She moved toward them.

They opened fire.

This time the bullets felt like wasp stings. They hurt. A lot.

But Fiona shrugged them off.

She whipped her chain around—it elongated, links clinking—and cut through black gun metal, wooden stocks . . . fingers, and hands.

The soldiers screamed and writhed on the ground. The smell of their blood repelled her, and, at the same time, it was intoxicating.

When she'd cut Perry Millhouse in half, that had been a different Fiona Post. She'd actually mourned the death of that killer.

These men were murderers, too. They would have killed innocent people. Little kids.

The only thing she felt for them was contempt.

She stepped over them—left them crawling, in shock, bleeding—and strode toward the church.

Every soldier in the courtyard saw her now, though. There were two dozen of them. They screamed. Some made the sign of the cross. Others ran away.

Most opened fire.

They couldn't touch her. She was no longer Fiona. No longer susceptible to mortal inconveniences like death. Power and hate pulsed through her every fiber—

A monstrous diesel engine coughed to life behind her.

Fiona froze. She'd forgotten one very important thing.

She whirled and her overblown ego deflated . . . along with her sense of invulnerability.

The armored tank on the corner belched black smoke from a tailpipe. Treads chewed through cobblestones as it and its turret rotated and the main gun arced toward her.

Stupid. Stupid!

How could she have been so blatantly arrogant to turn her back on an armored tank?!

Three options flashed through her mind.

First, she could stand here like an idiot and get blown to bits (an option her body seemed to favor at the moment because her knees wouldn't un-lock). Not that it even had to hit her to kill; the overpressure blast from the cannon could do that without ever touching her.

Two, she could run. She was sure, though, all that would accomplish was to get her blown up a few paces from where she stood. Great.

Or three . . . she could do what she came down here to do: fight.

Her body moved before she finished that last thought—as it had when she'd fought Mr. Ma. Her muscle and sinew knew more about saving itself apparently than her brain.

Fiona sprinted *toward* the tank. The chain played out through her grasp.

The turret locked on her dead center.

She jumped and flicked the chain forward. The slender bracelet that had loosely fit about her wrist was now five times her body length, each link as large as her fist, the edges razor sharp. It wrapped about the tank's turret—whipped around and lashed twice about the main gun's muzzle.

Fiona felt rapid pings through the metal in her grasp . . . the shell click-ing into the tank's firing chamber.

She grasped the chain with both hands and pulled.

Infernal metal shrieked through hardened steel. The turret slid apart at an angle where it'd been severed; half the muzzle clattered to the ground.

The tank fired.

Turret cut in half, firing mechanisms no longer aligned, the shell exploded *inside* . . . along with the rest of the tank's munitions.

The air filled with firecracker flashes, each as bright as the sun.

Fiona only distantly registered this as she was hurled back, felt a thousand stings—and then a section of steel tread hit her.

There was blackness. . . . It was quiet. . . .

That was nice. Peaceful.

But then a ringing intruded on her rest, which started faint and then turned up to an ear- and then skull-splitting intensity.

She blinked. There was a dull blur. The sky? Clouds?

Yes; they were nice. Fluffy. That one looked like a hand. Those, a flock of white crows.

She rolled over. The courtyard where she and the tank had been a moment ago was a crater of smoldering bits of metal and shattered cobblestones.

Everything hurt. Fiona was cut and bleeding and a slash in her side bubbled as she tried to inhale. It felt as if she were drowning.

At least she stopped those creeps before they killed anyone . . . except, maybe, her.

She laughed. That hurt, too.

She spotted three soldiers. They'd retreated into an alley and peered at her, astonished at what she had done . . . and that she still moved. One held a radio, spoke into it, looking at her—then up at the sky—back and forth.

She didn't want to die here. The anger that had made her so strong before, though, was nowhere to be found. All she felt was her pain and a bitter cold as shock set in.

She hallucinated that Eliot and Robert stood by her. Oh—how she wished that were true. She would have given anything for Robert to take her hand and help her up.

She got to her knees. Hallucinations or not—she wouldn't lie here and bleed to death.

She had to defend herself. Or get back to Mr. Ma.

Or, if she couldn't do that, she'd at least be on her feet if this was the end.

Dizzy, Fiona pushed on her knees and rose. She looked at the clouds again. A line in the sky flattened and arced toward the street.

That was a contrail made by jet engines. She squinted and saw a Korean-war era warplane: a MiG-15. They had two 23 mm cannon.

It was doing . . . what was it called? A strafing run.

Funny how her last thoughts were from the old encyclopedia-loving Fiona Post. Maybe that's what she truly was made of after all.

That was okay. She liked *that* Fiona Post.

She clutched the chain in her hands. She had no regrets about what she'd done. It had been the right thing—the only thing she could have done.

Fiona stood tall and proud and faced death as it rushed at her.

COLLATERAL DAMAGE

Eliot hung onto the sidecar for his life.

Robert's Harley clipped an overturned car, and then narrowly missed several people (civilians and soldiers) running from the courtyard.

He swerved around a burning pickup, and Eliot realized that their insane speed was warranted. Maybe . . . they'd even gone too slow. In the center of the courtyard, Fiona stood nose to nose with an armored tank.

Eliot blinked to make sure he saw that right.

Fiona crouched and jumped at it, lashing forward with a thick chain. The chain wrapped about the turret and muzzle.

She pulled—severed metal from metal.

The tank exploded. Inside.

Steel and titanium mushroomed out—and a dozen detonations followed and lit the courtyard—blasted the armored tank to smithereens, as well the ground for twenty feet in every direction.

Fiona tumbled through the air, bounced, rolled . . . and lay limp in the dirt.

Was she dead? He and Robert should've gotten there faster. Done *something*. A cold, hard shape took form in Eliot's mind—a dangerous thought that if his sister was gone, a lot of people were going to pay for it . . . starting with Uncle Henry and the League.

Robert ducked but didn't slow as molten metal and shards of stone whizzed past them.

He skidded sideways next to Fiona.

Eliot jumped out of the sidecar, guitar in hand.

Robert stayed on the bike, pulled his Glock 29, and aimed at the three soldiers huddled in the alley.

One of the soldiers spoke into a handheld radio and pointed at the sky. The other two had Kalashnikov machine guns. They looked stunned, at least for the moment.

Eliot's reached for Lady Dawn's strings.

Robert was faster. He shot three times—one round cratered the wall over the soldiers' heads. Two bullets hit the Kalashnikov stocks and shattered wood.

The soldiers dropped their weapons and ran.

Fiona moved . . . got to her knees, and slowly stood.

"Are you okay?" Eliot asked, helping her up.

This had to be the stupidest thing he'd asked in weeks, because blood trickled from Fiona's ears and nose. She ignored Eliot and looked with glazed eyes up at the sky.

. . . To the same spot where that soldier had pointed.

Eliot turned. A MiG-15 jet dived toward them on what had to be a strafing run.

Robert stood next to Fiona and propped her with one arm. She must really have been hurt because she let him touch her, even leaned against him. She tried to raise her hands, but the chain she clutched seemed too heavy for her to lift. Robert had his Glock and frowned at it. Useless against a jet.

Eliot stepped in front of her and Robert and whispered, "I got this one."

Fight or run—there wasn't much of a choice.

The MiG would close in seconds, not enough time to cross the courtyard.

And there wasn't just him and Fiona and Robert to protect; there were all those people in the church in the line of fire. Eliot was partially responsible for them, too. Not just because he wanted to save innocent people, but because *he* was connected to this: Uncle Henry had said the League engineered this war—Robert's "party tip" to drive down today—and Fiona (what *was* she doing here?). It was too much of a coincidence . . . like the League had pulled a fistful of tangled strings to trick them into coming. Why? So he and Fiona could pass another of their cruel tests?

It was like Area 51 all over again. People getting killed because of them; only this time, he'd do something to save them.

Eliot heard the roar of the jet. Felt the rumble in his bones.

Its dive leveled and it angled on a straight shot through the open street of Costa Esmeralda's cityscape canyon.

Eliot gripped Lady Dawn, his hands sweating, and he played.

There was no time to warm up with nursery rhymes. He needed raw force—fast—enough to *destroy*.

He flicked out a bassy power chord, throwing the strength of his arm into it. The notes resonated from Lady Dawn's body and shook the dust off the cobblestones and blew away smoke and ash.

The jet wobbled on its trajectory, but kept coming—and shot. Twin cannon spit fire and death at them.

Bullets sparked in the air between him and it, bouncing off a wall of sound, peppering buildings, tracers making spirals.

Nothing got through.

But as the jet streaked toward him, Eliot's barrier shuddered and contracted—force meeting force.

Eliot needed more power.

He double-pumped the strings and danced his fingers up the scale, back and forth; wavering mirage air and water vapor flashed outward.

The MiG spun, righted, and ceased the machine gun fire.

It launched two missiles.

Lady Dawn jumped under his hands—and his fingers stepped up the register—a lightning-fast bridge, found, and held, a high C.

Out of the corner of his eyes, Eliot saw the shadows in the alleys lengthen and sharpen into slices of darkness that cut through the noontime light . . . and sway as if they danced to his music.

The missiles streaked at them, hit the wall of noise, and blossomed in sparkling rosettes, shattering glass and blasting apart the steel frames of nearby office buildings.

The jet was almost on them. It shuddered, a blur, and its metal skin peeled—wingtips fluttered to pieces. The fuel tanks breached and ignited.

The pilot ejected, a plume of white smoke that arced from the craft.

But the flaming, out-of-control MiG fighter aircraft was still on course, plummeting straight at Eliot.

He let go of the single note and flicked the strings—power chord upon power chord, building upon their resonant echoes, increasing in pitch and intensity, sucked in the air from the courtyard, blasted out feedback-laden notes, waves of pressure, and lines of force that seemed to emanate through and from his body as much as Lady Dawn's.

It was as if they were one, rocking back and forth, playing together.

Glass ruptured off every building for six blocks. Asphalt bucked and crumbled. Water mains burst and showered into the air.

The MiG-15 exploded: fire and spinning metal and burning fuel still on an impact course.

Eliot pounded on Lady Dawn as hard as he dared . . . and then as hard as he *could*. Her strings cut into his fingertips.

Before the jet crashed into him, Eliot found the strength for one last downward power stoke.

Buildings on either side of the street shook and cracked, and two toppled over.

The tumbling wreckage of the MiG-15 detonated *again*—driven back as if someone had blown out a lit match.

Confetti bits of metal and trails of oily smoke drizzled down . . . harmless.

Eliot exhaled. He shook out his numbed hand and arm.

"Very cool," Robert murmured.

Fiona shook her head as if just now seeing them. "What are"—She looked back and forth between them—"*you* two doing here?" Her brow scrunched and her expression was a mix of confusion . . . and, as she concentrated on Eliot, annoyance.

She doubled over in pain.

Robert caught her and his hand came away bloody. He scrutinized the seeping, bubbling wound on her side. "She needs help."

Fiona went limp.

Eliot took a step forward, feeling helpless to do anything, forgetting everything he'd ever read in *Marcellus Master's Practical First Aid and Surgical Guide*.

"Shock," he said. "Her pulse is strong, though. That's a good sign, but we've got to get her to a doctor."

A crowd emerged from the church and stared at them.

Eliot called out, pleading, "Is one of you a doctor? *Hay un médico?*"

The people gaped, pointed, and they ran away.

How could they not help them after he'd just saved all their lives?

Eliot felt, then heard, subsonic quaking and thunderous crashes behind him. He wheeled and watched every office building for three blocks collapse into dust and rubble—a swath of destruction *he* had caused.

Those people in the church might have been grateful, they might have helped . . . if they hadn't been scared out of their minds.[57]

Eliot touched Lady Dawn, ran his bloody fingertips over her fiery wood grain. He smiled. He liked this new incarnation of the violin. She no longer fought him. How much power could they together summon?

He had also enjoyed the destruction and havoc they'd wreaked.

The smile on his face vanished. Fiona was in shock and bleeding to death—what was he thinking?

"Get her into the sidecar," he told Robert. "I'll ride on the back. Just go slow until we get on the highway."

Robert lifted Fiona into his arms. She yelped, but clung to him and let him carry her toward his bike.

The power when Eliot had played was seductive. He had felt glee as he blew the jet apart, rapture at seeing buildings fall at his whim . . . and was horrified that he wanted to do it all again.

"Put her down," someone behind Eliot commanded.

Mr. Ma dropped off the last rung of a fire escape, followed by six upper-classmen Paxington boys. Dante Scalagari was there, and he looked grim, made a move toward Fiona—but Mr. Ma checked his motion with a hand on his shoulder.

"I shall take Miss Post," Mr. Ma told them. He pointed toward the roof of the building he'd climbed down. A jet helicopter sat there, blades spinning up to full speed.

Robert glared at Mr. Ma and held Fiona tight.

Mr. Ma continued toward him. "You cannot jostle her on a motor bike with a punctured lung," he said, glancing down at her, "and likely other internal injuries."

57. Buildings in a four-block radius were declared structurally unsound and ordered demolished by the newly elected Costa Esmeralda Parliament. Miraculously, the church in the adjacent courtyard was unscathed, save a single shot-out window (and this even miraculous in that witness and photographic evidence corroborate that for three days after, sunlight passing through the open frame was colored as if the window were intact). Given these miracles—and, of course, the fact that this church was later the location where the Divine reentered the mortal world (see *Volume 11, The Post Family Mythology*)—the church was rechristened Bastion of the Herald of Light and selected by the New Catholic Church of the Sixth Celestial Age as the site to rebuild the Vatican. *Gods of the First and Twenty-first Century, Volume 2, Divine Inspirations*. Zypheron Press Ltd., Eighth Edition.

Robert's glare faded and the color drained from his face.

Mr. Ma stopped before Robert and held out his arms. "We have medical supplies on board. I can stabilize her."

Robert looked to Eliot.

Eliot wasn't sure. How much did he trust *any* Paxington teacher? Especially one who tried to kill them every few weeks? Enough to literally place his sister's life in his hands?

But Mr. Ma was right: On the bike they might hurt Fiona more. And if the unthinkable happened . . . the League would kill Robert for trying and failing to save her life.

"You won't hurt her?" Eliot asked.

Mr. Ma blinked. "No."

Eliot listened with great care. There were no weird echoes or any backward whispers that he detected from the lips of liars.

Eliot nodded to Robert. Robert passed Fiona to Mr. Ma.

Mr. Ma held her as if she weighed no more than a feather.

"I'm going with her," Eliot told Mr. Ma. "We're stronger together." His tone left no room for discussion on the matter.

Mr. Ma looked at him a moment, then nodded.

The Paxington helicopter lifted off the roof, turned, and lit in the courtyard.

As they walked toward the craft, Eliot glanced back at Robert. Worry and helplessness etched his friend's face, and Eliot understood that pain. He'd felt the same thing for Jezebel . . . and he knew at that moment that Robert loved Fiona.

Near the helicopter, Mr. Ma ducked, and held his unconscious sister closer.

Eliot barely made out his whispered words over the noise of the blades. "School rules give me no choice in the matter." Mr. Ma told her. "You get an F for today's lesson."

But then for the first time, Mr. Ma's craggy features softened, and tiny laugh lines crinkled the corners of his eyes. "And even though I must hate you, young lady, for we appear to be on opposites sides of fate . . . for dueling an armored tank to save people that meant nothing to you, you *deserve* an A-plus."

WOLF UNDER THE WAVES

Henry Mimes tried on the captain's hat and regarded himself in the mirror bolted to the wall of the guest quarters. The pilfered cap was a tad too big, and the golden fringe and black canvas didn't look right with his silver hair. Not his colors, alas.

It was just another reminder that he was a mere passenger on this submarine.

He twirled the hat on his finger. It was hard to let go of the rudder, even among friends, when one was used being the Captain.

A fluted speaker whistled to life. "Mr. Mimes?" said a tinny voice. "They're ready for you, sir."

"Tell them I'm on my way," Henry replied.

He left his cramped quarters and entered an equally cramped corridor. Two uniformed ladies bumped into him.

Henry smiled, did his best to bow, and greeted them both.

They returned his salutations . . . and his promising smile.

"Would you lieutenants be good enough to take this to the bridge?" He handed the hat to the athletic brunette.

They said they would. There were more smiles and flirtatious glances, and then they went on their way, squeezing past.

Henry watched them go.

Or perhaps such close accommodations did have *some* advantages, after all.

And yet the *Coelacanth* was definitely not a craft he could spend more than a day bottled up in. Wolves did not do well beneath the waves. He preferred the open sea and fresh air. No matter how much opulence one cocooned oneself in, all submersibles were susceptible to a loss of buoyancy and gravity, and could become more coffin than vessel.

He ran a hand over the brass pipes that curved along the walls. Every square millimeter was polished and etched with tiny porpoises and sardines and scallops. Still, it was a lovely sinking tin can. Gilbert ran a tight ship.

It was technology millennia ahead of anything else when it had been forged. There was nothing like it in all the seas. In thirty years, however, American or NATO or Russian naval engineers would have the technology to detect her subtle, silent movements through the waters.

Men glimpsing legends.

Which was one of the reasons Henry knew change was coming. "A matter of time" as Cornelius might have said, although he and the other Council members seem determined to ignore that fact as long as they could.

Henry moved through three pressure doors, down a spiral stairs and entered the launch bay. The walls of the cavernous chamber were ribbed for strength, and from the ceiling a variety of small submersibles hung like mechanized insects caught in a web.

The *Tinker,* however, was the one Gilbert had selected for their journey today.

Unlike the other modern titanium-and-polycarbonate-composite minisubs here, this diving bell had been part of this vessel's original complement, crafted by the same master of the seas who had forged the *Coelacanth*.

The *Tinker* was a treasured relic—a gleaming geodesic bubble of foamed gold alloy encrusted with half-meter circles of diamond windows coaxed from the earth and polished to perfection—constructed to withstand pressures that would crush her modern counterparts like Styrofoam coffee cups. The mermaids along her curves still gleamed and beckoned as if they had been carved yesterday.

The diving bell was lowered into the moon pool, and a soft blue light glowed to life as she touched the ocean.

Gilbert and Aaron waited for Henry, and from the crossed arms and look on Aaron's face, he could tell they had been waiting some time.

"Am I late?"

"Is that a question?" Gilbert muttered, and straightened the cuffs of his black captain's uniform. "By the way, have you seen my hat?"

ERIC NYLUND

"Not recently . . . ," Henry replied.

Henry could see why Gilbert, with beard trimmed in precise stylish angles, and the *Coelacanth* had inspired Mr. Wells to write an entire novel about them.

Aaron donned a leather bomber jacket and offered one to Henry.

"No thank you," Henry said. "I shall be quite comfortable."

Gilbert boarded the craft. Henry crossed the gangplank and ducked through the tiny doorway. Aaron was right behind him (cowboys boots clonking over the metal), and once aboard, he irised the outer hatch, and then wheeled tight the inner hatch.

Portals offered views all the way around, as well as up and down. Control panels, levers, and valves made a ring of controls along the outer surface of the *Tinker*—which Aaron and Gilbert busied themselves pulling and prodding and checking. One panel was dotted with empty vacuum tube receptacles, and a laptop computer had been soldered upon it.

Henry gravitated to the center of the craft, where shrimp cocktails lounged on a bed of chipped ice, along with caviar and fresh sushi. A dozen thermoses of heated sake were labeled: KAKUNKO JUNMAI DAI GINJYO.

Dire circumstances and the possible end of the world notwithstanding, Cousin Gilbert could always be counted on to be an impeccable host.

"Care to lend a hand?" Aaron growled.

"Not really," Henry replied as he munched on a shrimp.

Gilbert spoke into a tiny gramophone-like device: "Ready to launch, Mr. Harper. Steady as she goes."

"Aye aye, Captain," a voice from the gramophone replied.

"Mark gyrocompasses," Gilbert told Aaron.

Aaron flipped switches. "Online and checked."

The *Tinker* eased below the waterline. Her glow lines intensified to a brilliant blue as they descended into the darkness.

Gilbert then spoke to gramophone again: "Sever connections, Mr. Harper. *Coelacanth* to station keeping."

"Station keeping, aye, sir. *Tinker* away."

There was a *clack*, and then the diving bell floated free . . . and proceeded to sink to the bottom of the ocean.

The exterior lights were bright enough that Henry saw the seafloor beneath his feet. It grew as they approached a crack in the earth a hundred meters wide. This particular abyss had remained undiscovered by man, and Henry hoped it would remain that way for a long, long time.

They entered the chasm, and Henry spied the columns and stairs that zigzagged at angles that should not (in any strict Euclidian sense) exist. He averted his eyes and tried not to look at the tentacled idols and cavernous temples that clung to the walls like ancient crustaceans. The shadows of shadows moved within those places. These were the remains of a civilization that predated the Titans: the Old Ones who had vanished from this world . . . or as some feared, were still dreaming in a nonstate in the In-Between Places.

Henry just hoped that, as League experts predicted, this trench would in a century subduct under the mantle. Only then would he be able to safely forget about it.

Until then, everyone avoided the place . . . which was *precisely* why they were here. Eyes and ears had followed them everywhere else.

"Ablate the portals," Gilbert ordered.

Aaron twisted a dial and the windows darkened.

"Counter aetherics," Gilbert said.

Aaron tapped on the laptop computer. "Circuits warming; channels alpha through gamma all in the green."

"Initiate sound cancellation."

Aaron nodded.

"That's it, then," Gilbert said, and both men exhaled and seemed to finally relax.

Aaron grabbed one the silver bottles of sake, popped the lid, inhaled its steaming contents, and downed the thing in a single draft.

"We sulk about like children hiding from their elders," Aaron muttered with great sarcasm. He opened another sake. Although from this bottle, he took only a sip, and then set it aside because he knew—despite his bristling—these drastic precautions were indeed warranted.

"Tell us about Costa Esmeralda, Henry," Gilbert said.

His coconspirators leaned forward and listened.

So Henry told them what had occurred yesterday in Central America—everything that he and his spies had observed: Fiona's reaction during her Force of Arms class, and Eliot's and Robert's charge to her rescue.

Aaron's fists clenched harder as Henry related how Fiona had stood up to a Soviet T55 main battle tank, cut it down, and survived the resulting explosion.

Both men shared worried glances as Henry related the raw destructive force that Eliot had unleashed with his guitar.

Aaron let out a long whistle. "They've progressed further and faster than I would've predicted," he said, and tugged on his long mustache.

"Than anyone," Henry agreed.

"But how do they *feel*?" Gilbert asked. "Is the League's plan to make them sympathetic to their cause working?"

"Eliot doubts the League and their intentions," Henry told him. "A wise thing for any teenage boy to question authority. So, unless I have completely misread the situation, he is where *we* want him."

"I have a concern," Gilbert whispered. "There had been a hundred witnesses. . . ."

"In fact, an entire church full of them," Henry replied.

"And you took care of it?" Aaron asked. His eyes narrowed.

"Oh, relax." Henry patted his hands together. "Even I would not do such a thing to protect our secrets."

Aaron looked unconvinced.

"Besides, there was no need," Henry said.

Gilbert quirked an eyebrow. "A hundred 'God-fearing' people saw our nephew destroy several city blocks—and there's no need?"

"Well, 'god-fearing' is exactly the point." Henry reached into his pocket for a pack of cigarettes.

Aaron clamped a hand on his arm. "Must you always play the Fool? We're breathing almost pure oxygen."

"Oh . . ." Henry smiled. He had, of course, *not* forgotten; he just enjoyed rattling Aaron. "Where was I—oh yes, those hundred people did indeed see Fiona and Eliot. They believed them two angels sent to deliver them from evil."

Gilbert and Aaron sat perfectly still.

"The implications are chilling," Gilbert whispered.

Aaron scoffed. "A coincidence," he said, "that this happened on the footsteps of some Catholic church. Nothing more."

Gilbert raised both hands in a gesture of surrender. "Let us not waste our time with such superstitions, gentlemen. What of Fiona? Where is her heart on these matters?"

"That's the rub," Henry said. "Fiona has strong convictions and is not easily swayed. She is balanced among numerous forces . . . and suitors. Even I would not dare predict the mind of a lady in such a situation."

"Then we still have time to take action." Aaron stood halfway, remembered where he was, and stopped before he bumped his head. He looked like a caged animal. "We must convince her."

"In point of fact," Henry replied, "we are out of time."

"The Infernals?" Gilbert asked.

"Indeed," Henry said. "My contact at Paxington has informed me that a letter has been sent. The Fallen Ones make their move for the children . . . today."

"You tell us this now?" Aaron said, his eyes widening. "We must do something!"

Henry could practically feel his cousin's pounding pulse within the tiny bubble. "No—it is precisely why we *cannot* take action," he said. "We are bound by the *Pax Pactum Immortalus*."

Aaron loosed an explosive sigh. He grabbed the sake he had set aside and drank it.

They were silent a long moment. Henry sensed the crush of the endless sea around them and found it oddly comforting.

How he missed his uncle. Were Poseidon's ashes scattered in these very waters? What would he say to all this? *Madness? Folly?* Or perhaps *The game is on?*

"Your Paxington contact," Gilbert finally whispered. "Did they give you any specifics on the Infernals' plans?"

"The school is neutral, which makes them the most elusive, and perhaps the most dangerous, players upon the board." Henry's hand felt his throat (a silly instinctive reaction). "And the cost to extract even this morsel of data," he murmured, ". . . I must not push."

Gilbert nodded. His lips pressed together into a single grim line. "And Dallas," he asked, "can she be made to see our side of things? Help us?"

Henry flipped his hand dramatically. "Her loyalty flits and dances hither and yon." He cocked his head. "I don't know where she will land, but we dare not underestimate her. When she awakens, she may be our greatest asset to play . . . or our fiercest opponent."

Aaron shook his head. "I will not stand against Dallas, I—I cannot, if it comes to that."

"Well," Henry said, and eyed the sushi. "We need not decide such things today. Try the soft-shell crab. It looks divine." He plucked up chopsticks and mixed soy sauce and wasabi on a plate shaped like a flounder.

"How can you eat?" Aaron asked, sneering at the fish.

"Really, Henry. Don't you ever take anything seriously?" Gilbert demanded. "It's not just our necks on the chopping block if this goes badly. And not just Eliot's or Fiona's either. It's everyone. Everywhere."

Henry picked up a piece of sushi and toasted Gilbert. "Oh yes, yes, I completely understand the stakes, Cousin. That's precisely what makes it so much fun!"

64

FIRST TIME IN THE HEADMISTRESS'S OFFICE

Fiona crossed her arms tight over her chest and watched the others pace. Nervous didn't begin to cover it. When the Headmistress of Paxington called you up to her office . . . it wasn't going to end well.

She and Eliot and Robert were probably here to get expelled for what they did in Costa Esmeralda. That was fine. Fiona had done the right thing saving those people. Miss Westin could kick her out of school if that's what she wanted.

If that were the case, though, why had *everyone* on Team Scarab been called here?

"Here" was the waiting room outside Miss Westin's office. It was on the thirteenth floor of the Clock Tower attached to the Southern Wing of the House of Wisdom. The tower was a twin to London's Big Ben (except the roof of Paxington's tower was polished copper and gold filigree).[58]

This tower looked all the more startling because Fiona hadn't even seen

---

58. Much of the Paxington Institute in San Francisco was designed by Augustus Pugin (1812–1852). Pugin was an advocate for Gothic architecture (and attacked "Pagan" classical architecture). He is widely known for his work on the British Houses of Parliament and the clock tower Big Ben. After being recruited by the Paxington Architectural Trust, his views on classical design softened, and he blended Gothic and classical elements in what is now known as Mytho-Gothic. In his journal, he wrote, "My previous works are as pale imitations compared to Paxington. My dreams have taken on a life of their own." Pugin never saw his work finished, as he died after a mental collapse in 1851. *Your Guide to the Paxington Institute (Freshman Edition)*. Paxington Institute Press LLC, San Francisco.

it until this morning—not to mention the *entire* Southern Wing of the library. Where had *that* come from?

Like the smaller coliseum where she had her Force of Arms class and the helipad north of that . . . this was more of the Paxington campus that had just appeared as if it was kept hidden from freshmen. How much more of this place was there?

She gazed out the wall of windows. The school was laid out for her in miniature. The quartz paving stones in the main quad glittered like a jewel box. The Poseidon fountain was a blur of white spray, and a spiderweb of paths wound through the Grove Primeval toward Bristlecone Hall and other places that vanished deeper in the forest, and then there was the Main Gate.

Fiona squinted and swore she saw Mr. Dells standing there, looking back at her.

Blanketing the rest of the campus was thick, roiling fog.

As much as Fiona loved a good puzzle, she'd have to figure this one out later. There were more pressing problems today. She turned back to her teammates.

Apart from the large window, the other three walls of the waiting room were covered in cream-colored wallpaper with red pinstripes—perfectly aligned with the black-and-white checkerboard floor. The effect of pattern and reflection and geometry made her dizzy.

Jeremy and Sarah Covington stood together in the far corner, whispering, looking at her and then Eliot—probably, as usual, blaming her for this.

Amanda was by herself in the other corner, hovering near a standing bronze ashtray that smoldered with old cigars. She just stared off into the distance like she'd been hit over the head. Fiona was torn between going over there and asking what was wrong, and shaking her to snap her out of it.

Along the opposite wall were three red couches. Eliot and Robert sat there, far apart.

Eliot had his guitar in his lap. He looked at Fiona and shrugged apologetically . . . as if he had anything to be sorry for. It irked her that she'd needed saving in Costa Esmeralda, but she *was* grateful.

Fiona shrugged back. The Covingtons were probably right: If this trouble today was anyone's fault, it probably was hers.

Robert reclined and looked obnoxiously comfortable. She bet he'd love to get kicked out of Paxington.

Jezebel, of course, was still missing.

And Mitch hadn't shown up all week, either.

She sighed. This day had started out as normal as it could after yesterday.

She'd gotten stitched up last night and had her punctured lung fixed by Paxington medics. They'd told her that she healed at miraculous rate, owing to her genetics, and she'd be as good as new by morning.

A lot they knew: It hurt even to breathe, and every bone ached.

Of course, Audrey had insisted that if Fiona could stand, she walk to school. She wasn't even allowed to take the bus.

Their mother seemed impossibly distant. As if now that Eliot and she knew about their heritage, they were supposed to take care of themselves like they'd been part of the League all their lives.

Or maybe the distance Fiona felt from her mother was her own fault. She didn't bother to tell her about Costa Esmeralda. Uncle Henry and the others let her know. And why even *try* to win Audrey's approval? Might as well try to catch a breeze with her bare hand.

At least Eliot was his usual mopey self this morning. She tried to thank him for yesterday, but he'd told her that it "hurt too much to talk." She hadn't seen any cuts or bruises on him. It had to be Jezebel still depressing him. When was he going to get over her?

She didn't try to cheer him up with some vocabulary insult, either. Why waste calling someone a "monoicious Marchantiophyta" when they wouldn't even hear you?[59]

Fiona's gaze drifted to the fiery wood and bold brass fittings of Eliot's new guitar. It creeped her out. That thing had more power than his violin (it was more like artillery than a musical instrument, as far as she was concerned).

Eliot had told her when she woke up on the helicopter that it was Lady Dawn transformed. The change in shape wasn't what bothered her . . . it was that it was a magical thing . . . a thing that had been her father's . . . an Infernal instrument.

Like her bracelet—useful, but not to be entirely trusted.

But the thing that'd really thrown a wrench into their morning had been

---

59. *Marchantiophyta* is a division of plants commonly known as "liverworts" which are typically small and low to the ground with flattened leaves. *Monoicious* is a term indicating both male and female reproductive structures are located on different branches of the same plant. Therefore this insult makes reference to a person's small size and relatively primitive and isolated sexual characteristics. —Editor.

at Paxington's Front Gate. Mr. Dells gave them a note. On Paxington letterhead, in a typewritten script was the following:

The presence of Team Scarab is hereby requested in the Office of
Miss L. Westin, Hall of Wisdom, Clock Tower, thirteenth floor.
PROMPTLY at 9:45 A.M.

And so here they were.

Fiona checked her phone to see if Mitch had texted or called, but then the door to Miss Westin's office creaked open and a boy emerged.

He was maybe twelve years old, pale, and his dark hair was cropped short. He met none of their eyes. "You may go in now, good ladies and masters," he whispered, and held the door for them.

Fiona went first, and the rest of her team followed.

Miss Westin's office was long. There were no windows. The only light was from dozens of Tiffany lamps and light sconces. The walls were polished walnut, rubbed to a mirror sheen, and every five paces there were doors: double doors, tiny doors that looked like they belonged in dollhouses, even a round door. Between the doors were oil paintings, sketches, daguerreotypes, and modern photos of students in Paxington uniforms—some in powdered wigs, others in cloaks, some with peace symbol medallions. A few of the paintings were Rembrandts, Cézannes, and there was even a Picasso sketch.

There were no books, though. Not one volume.

That made Fiona even more nervous.

Miss Westin's desk was large and black, with thick claw-footed legs. The entire surface was a touch-screen computer. There were layers of icons and text files and windows.

Miss Westin looked up as they approached. With a single sweep of her hand, the screen blanked.

There were no chairs for them.

Fiona guessed Miss Westin didn't often have guests in her office . . . and when she did, they weren't supposed to feel comfortable.

Miss Westin assessed them from behind her octagonal wire-rim glasses and then said, "I have two announcements. I shall be brief, as we have class in ten minutes."

She opened a filing cabinet and withdrew two letters. The first was neatly typed on white paper and signed at the bottom. The other was ancient vellum and curled as if it had been rolled. Its letterhead was fes-

tooned with poppies and vines. It smelled of vanilla and sulfur, and it repelled Fiona.

Miss Westin tapped the ordinary letter. "Mr. Stephenson has requested
a two-week leave of absence, and I have granted it. His homework assignments shall be forwarded. His gym rank remains attached to Team
Scarab's, but obviously he cannot participate in any matches that may occur during his absence."

"Is he okay?" Fiona blurted out.

Jeremy Covington cleared his throat. "How are we expected to perform
without one of our best teammates?"

Miss Westin frowned at them. "I'm not at liberty to discuss Mr. Stephenson's personal matters," she told Fiona icily. To Jeremy, she said, "And I am
coming to the matter of your so-called team, Mr. Covington, if you'd be
kind enough to remain silent for thirty seconds."

Jeremy flushed. He shut his mouth, though, and looked at his loafers.

Fiona suddenly didn't care about her team or their ranking or anything
other than what might be wrong with Mitch. She strained to read his letter
upside down, but before she could make out a single word, Miss Westin
set the other letter on top.

"My second announcement regards Miss Jezebel," she told them. "Her
guardian has petitioned me to withdraw her from this semester at Paxington, citing internal Infernal matters that cannot be avoided. I'm inclined to
grant this request as well."

Eliot stepped forward. "Beg your pardon, ma'am," he whispered. All the
color drained from him. "So she's not coming back?"

Under normal circumstances, Fiona would've been happy to hear Jezebel
was gone for good . . . but the expression on her brother's face was almost
more than she could bear. It looked like he was going to die.

Miss Westin sighed and her impassive features thawed—for a
microsecond—as she told him, "She shall receive an incomplete for her
work this semester. If, however, she enrolls in summer school, she will be
able to make up her courses."

Eliot nodded and stepped back.

"This leaves Team Scarab with but six members," Miss Westin said. "If
you choose to play in such a state, there is little chance you would win
your next match, let alone survive the final. This leaves you two options."

Miss Westin stood and straightened her shirt, donned her black wool
jacket, and did up its pearl buttons all the way to her throat. She then

picked up a slender leather folder that held her class notes and marched toward the door they had entered.

"Follow," she ordered.

They did, and Miss Westin talked as they all walked. "According to school traditions, your first option would be to recruit two new members from disbanded teams. There are several excellent surviving players who now need a home."

She paused at the door. "Or Team Scarab may disband . . . and you each would have to find new teams."

Fiona felt as if she were sinking in quicksand. Disband the team? *Her* team? Had she been that much of a failure as Captain?

Miss Westin ushered them into the waiting room and locked her office door. "I leave the choice between those two options up to you." Her gaze fell on Jeremy and then Fiona, lingered a bit on Eliot, and then she blinked. "I must, however, impress the seriousness of this. Your team is below the grade cutoff. Fail Mr. Ma's class, and I will have no choice but to flunk all of you."

And with that, she turned and left them there. Stunned.

Fiona recovered from the shock, and started thinking . . . and getting mad. "This is completely unfair," she said.

"'Tis not like we haven't seen it coming," Jeremy told her. "Though 'tis a shame about Mitch. I thought him made of sterner stuff."

"Shut up," Robert said. "You don't know what's going on with Mitch. He said he'll be back in two weeks—maybe in time for our next match."

Sarah said to Robert, "I sympathize for whatever Mitch is going though, but I'm not going to risk graduating on 'maybe.'"

Amanda skulked to a couch and sat, head between her hands. "Maybe we should just disband," she muttered.

Fiona had to rally her team—while she still had a team. She went to Amanda and set a hand on her shoulder. The girl's skin was blazing hot. "I'm not giving up. Scarab is a good team. We stick together, and we can get through this. We'll win our next match, and who knows what the rankings will look like after that? Let's not panic."

Jeremy nodded. "No one be panicking, my dear Fiona. But we should consider the hard facts of playing without two key members. And what if we break apart as Miss Westin suggested? Would it be so bad to find open slots on a team that needs us?" He stared pointedly at Amanda as he said this.

"No way," Fiona told him. "Like I said, Scarab is a good team—maybe the best team, regardless of Mr. Ma's rankings. We beat *both* Dragon and Wolf teams during the midterm. And we would've won that last match against Falcon if Mr. Ma hadn't cheated. It's like they don't want us to graduate."

Jeremy considered this, then said, "A wee bit suspicious, I grant you. So let's consider Miss Westin's other alternative: get replacements for Mitch and our dearly departed Jezebel. If Mitch comes back—lovely—according to the rules, we then have an alternate attached to the team."

Robert flopped onto the couch. "I don't know. It makes sense . . . but it feels like we're giving up on them or something."

Sarah sat next to him, close, so her knees touched his. "They are the ones who left us," she said. "And it's not like we have much of a choice."

"But we do," Eliot whispered.

Fiona turned and saw Eliot standing by the door to the Headmistress's office in the only shadow in the room. He gripped Lady Dawn tight in his hands, and his eyes were hard and cold. "There's a third option Miss Westin didn't mention."

"Oh, come now, Post," Jeremy said with a little laugh. "What other option could there be?"

"Jezebel," Eliot said. "She's not here because she's trapped in Hell fighting a war. So . . ." He straightened and looked them all in the eye. "We go and rescue her."

65

A VERY LONG DISTANCE CALL

udrey shut and locked the door to her new office. Her space occupied the topmost floor of the house's Victorian turret.

It was a tiny space, clean, and lit by skylights.

Behind the plaster of walls and ceiling and under the oak floors were sheets of lead burned with mathematics and arcane symbols to keep outsiders out . . . and her thoughts in.

Her favorite books sat on the encircling shelves: The works of Aristotle and Thoreau, Norse proto-runesongs, and the secret whisper hymns of the Saints of Glossimere. These comforted her.

There was a chair with ample padding and a desk. What more did one require?

Privacy.

She strained to hear Cecilia prattling about the house. Not a sound. The old hag slept more each day, saving her strength, she claimed.

Audrey held her breath.

All this waiting drove her mad. Once she thought her patience limitless— before the twins had come.

She ran a hand over the desk and settled into her chair.

But was not waiting an action, as well? No. Waiting was waiting. All the philosophizing in the world did not change that.

Her desktop was a slab of partially marbleized limestone, streaked with color and crystal, and tiny snail and trilobite fossils. She traced their curls. So old. And like her, frozen.

She had to start, a tiny step forward, her journey toward action . . . by seeing what she could.

From a drawer, she with took out a corkboard, a box of plastic pushpins, and a ball of yarn. She picked pins at random and—without looking— stabbed them into the board. Her other hand wound the yarn about the pins.

She stared at the leaded crystal skylights; refracted rainbows streamed through the air and onto the blank walls. Audrey didn't think . . . she drifted . . . let her subconscious surface.

Her hands continued to move, sticking the pins, wrapping the yarn.

Some pinpoints turned in the box, and stabbed her. She let them taste her blood. This was part of the ritual as well.

At last, she exhaled and stopped.

Her pins had been arranged on the cork, and tracing a web of connections among them was the yarn, dotted with her blood.

In the center were two pins—one red, one blue—together (although they leaned away from one another). This represented Eliot and Fiona.

Surrounding them were random constellations of the other pushpins. The yarn twined about them, this way and that. Audrey discerned three linked groups: The League, the Infernals, and scattered hither and yon, the so-called neutrals of Paxington.

Two pins were near the twins: one green (this had to be Dallas) and one silver, leaning at a rakish angle (which was Henry).

One frayed line, however, connected Henry to a Paxington neutral. Curious.

She'd suspected, even *expected* him to be engineering some trickery with Aaron and Gilbert. But to align with the neutrals? That was trouble of an entirely other magnitude.

For now, she would keep this a secret . . . until it could be wisely spent.

Her hand drifted to the pin box. Only two were left: one black and one white. The white was bone white, death white—that was her. The black had to be Louis.

Where did he fit?

And more interesting, why hadn't she placed either of them among the others?

She focused all her attention back on the board, and only now saw there were dozens of pins along the very edges—as if repelled from the center . . . far away from the main players and events.

She touched them. Felt nothing.

They were not League members, nor were they Infernals, and all the Paxington neutrals were accounted for.

That left whom . . . the mortal magical families? She scoffed. All too feeble to be involved in any significant way.

This mystery drifted through her mind like mist, filling it with silence and dread. After all these years, who else was out there?

She jumped. Blinked.

There was no reason to start . . . but her gaze riveted upon the black 1970s-era phone on her desk. It had not rung, but it *felt* like it had. The ghost of its trilling hung in the air.

She waited for it to actually ring.

It seemed like it wanted to sound, as if there was someone trying to contact her, and yet so far off, it had not the strength to quite make the connection.

Audrey tentatively picked up the receiver and listened.

There was a hiss and a crackle, and a voice broke though the white noise.

It was Louis. He was singing off-key: *"Six little children to market went: Orpheus and Faustus, the Empress of Kansas, the Spirit of Christmas, Bacchus, and the Governor of Texas—"*

"Louis?"

He stopped singing.

"Audrey!" he cried. "Beloved, it is your Louis!" His enthusiasm deflated. "How long have you been listening? No, never mind. There is little time. I'm using Eliot's phone and a child's trick with a Klein sphere to make this connection."[60]

Audrey's first impulse was to hang up on Louis, the greatest of all liars. But he was also the Louis she loved.

She held those thoughts balanced in her mind. Tip one way and she would hang up and forever sever their connection on more than one level.

Or listen, and tip the other way: embrace this madness she felt for him still.

---

60. A Klein sphere is a contradiction in terms. In mathematics, a Klein bottle has a single continuous surface in a tube or bottle shape; i.e., there are neither distinct inner or outer surfaces (cf. the Möbius strip). A sphere, however, has distinct inner and outer surfaces. Modern mathematicians continue to puzzle over if this reference is a misnomer or if Infernals have a hitherto unknown understanding of topology. *An Introduction to the Mathematics of Myth*, Paxington Press LLC, San Francisco.

Cutting the tie would be easiest. She had done that before with Eliot and Fiona, leaving her maternal duty but severing the irrational love.

But what was *easiest* often was not *best* . . . and not without regrets.

"Please," Louis whispered. There was desperation in his voice.

"I'm listening," she said.

"This is not about us—well it is in a way, and I know I have made an ultimate mess of things between us, all my fault . . . again, not the point. What I'm trying to say is it's about the children."

Audrey glanced at the red and blue pins in its center of the corkboard. So many other pins surrounded her children, so many who would use them or remove them.

"I must be quick," Louis whispered. "I am down to one pixel on this phone's battery, and it's winking red."

There was a burst of static. Audrey pulled the receiver away until the noise died.

"Louis?"

"Yes . . . still here." His voice was barely audible. "My relations make their move *today*. You must save Eliot and Fiona before they make decisions that cannot be undone. Before they are lured—"

A whoosh of screams and crying and the laughter of the mad flooded the connection.

There was a click. Then nothing.

"Louis?" Audrey whispered.

Her heart pounded and she rose. She believed him.

She had to go to battle, fight, protect her children from the others, and somewhere in those feelings was the foolish urge to protect Louis as well.

Audrey looked back to the corkboard and yarn and pins.

She then understood why her subconscious had left those last two pins. She had to make up her mind—deliberately, and accepting all the consequences—where they belonged.

And so she did.

She set both black and white pins together . . . nestled next to the red and blue pins of Eliot and Fiona.

She slammed the receiver to the cradle and then picked it up and dialed the direct line to Lucille Westin's private and personal office. She'd have Fiona and Eliot pulled from class and kept with Miss Westin until she could get there.

If there was still time.

66

ONE THING ALMOST EVERYONE HAD FORGOTTEN

Cecilia watched Audrey storm out of the house, not even bothering to close the front door.

She followed and eased it shut, spotting Audrey's Jaguar XKSS through the door's stained glass windows as the roadster roared out of the driveway. The car smeared into a midnight blue streak of chrome and taillights.

Audrey was gone. Finally.

Cecilia locked the door and meandered upstairs to the dining room. The long-abandoned game of Towers she and Eliot had been playing had been moved to the end table. The circular mat and cubes were covered in dust. Smudges dotted some cubes where Eliot had touched them recently, perhaps thinking of his next move.

On the surface, this was just a game . . . but deeper, it was a magical metaphor for all their lives . . . and deeper still, it represented a game of dire consequences played by those with millennia more experience than she or Eliot possessed.

With that in mind, Cecilia had no qualms about cheating.

Her eyes filmed over milky white, and she fumbled over the playing field, feeling the threads of fate that wove about the pieces, pulling and tugging, and with tiny clockwork flicks advanced them forward to their next moves.

To the future.

Audrey would have Cecilia's head if she knew. But the great Cutter of All Things was not here to stop Cecilia this time.

Still, she took great care not to let a single quantum vibration escape her fingertips. There were others than Audrey who would not approve of her prying into their affairs, others who were *far* crueler.

In her mind, she saw the Towers field—lines and circles radiating from the center like a spiderweb. Many of the stone cubes were easy to identify: Audrey, Eliot, Fiona, that boy called Robert, and a smattering of Infernals, humans, and Immortals.

Fiona's piece was near the center, but tiny cracks crisscrossed the white marble. Eliot's cube was by hers. They both stood before a stack of five black, a tower whose might was unassailable.

Eliot's cube had one face smeared with soot (or possibly blackberry jelly), a black spot upon the white. Audrey would've denied it, but Cecilia knew this was an omen most ill.

Poor Eliot. It was too late for him.

But it was not too late to adjust *her* plans. She had always been good at turning lemons into lemonade—why, look at her now! How far had she come in this so-called body and her half-cheated immortality?

She blinked and her eyes cleared.

Yes . . . Cecilia knew what to do. She always knew. If others had not the conviction to protect her lambs, then she would.

She rolled up the Towers mat—pieces and all—so they scattered into chaos, and put it all in the cupboard. She then ambled back to the children's bedrooms.

Fiona's door was locked, but a simple word of unbinding did the trick, and she entered.

The room was as neat as a pin. Cecilia was so proud of Fiona. All that schoolwork and responsibility, and she still had time to make up her bed. There were precise stacks of papers on her desk, neat piles of books, flash cards, and a sketch of the Immortal family tree.

Fiona was a good, hardworking girl, and it pained Cecilia to do this. She took careful note of the location of every object—and then ransacked the room, turning over pillows, pulling out books, tossing clothes from the hamper, pulling out drawers and shaking their contents onto the floor.

When she got the lowest bookshelf, she tossed aside *Rare Incurable Parasites, Volume 3,* and found a hidden shoe box.

She cradled it with trembling arms and sat on the rumpled bed.

Inside, carefully placed was a scandalous bikini. Cecilia held it before her. She could not imagine her Fiona ever wearing such a tarty thing. She set it aside.

Next was a stack of old-fashioned Polaroids showing Fiona and that boy, Robert, splashing in the water, palm trees in the background. Those were from last summer, when Henry had flown them out to his island before school (chaperoned by Aaron, so she knew Robert had made no ungentlemanly advances upon poor, innocent Fiona).

There was one last item in the shoe box: a rolled-up sock.

Inside was something heavy and hard.

Cecilia took the sock out, unrolled it on the bed, and then gingerly coaxed out the object within.

She gasped as a sapphire the size of an egg tumbled upon Fiona's gray wool bedspread—gleaming with blue brilliance and crisp facets.

The stone's name was Charipirar. It was the mark of power of that Hell-creature Beelzebub, Lord of All the Flies, once Chairman of the Infernals, and the beast whom Fiona had killed—by pulling this, his own talisman, through his neck.

She'd kept the trinket as a souvenir.

And everyone had forgotten about it. Almost.

She found herself gazing into the depths of the stone, and quickly averted her eyes before it pulled her too deep. Using two pencils, Cecilia pushed and prodded the stone back into the sock and rolled it up.

This could change everything, even save Eliot . . . and perhaps damn millions of souls.

What did that matter? As long as Cecilia saved the ones she loved.

67

THE BIGGEST LIE OF HIS LIFE

Eliot stared at his teammates.

They stared back at him like he was crazy. Even Amanda—always on Eliot's side—looked shocked.

"Rescue Jezebel?" Jeremy asked with a smirk. "*The* Jezebel who is an Infernal duchess? The one who could pummel you if she had half a mind to do? *You* want to rescue *her*?"

Eliot took a step toward Jeremy. His classmate didn't know how far Eliot had come in the last few months. How Jezebel had smashed a rock against his head that should've crushed it and he'd barely felt it. How he'd leveled a few city blocks with his music in Costa Esmeralda.

And how . . . right now, he was more than willing to prove himself to the ever-irritating Jeremy Covington.

Sarah jumped up and stood between them.

Eliot's temper cooled a bit as he remembered how she'd been nice to him recently.

Jeremy, however, continued his mocking glare.

Sarah said, "It's a noble thing you're proposing, Eliot, but Jezebel has withdrawn from Paxington. There's nothing to be done."

"Jezebel withdrew because she *had* to," Eliot said. "Because she's trapped behind enemy lines. We get her out, and that all changes. Miss Westin said she was 'inclined to grant the request'—she hasn't actually done it yet. There's still time."

Fiona shook her head and wouldn't even look at him.

"She needs our help." But Eliot's plea was weak and pathetic—everything he was trying *not* to sound like.

How could he be so powerful and heroic one moment, and the next be such an ineffectual dork?

They were all silent. Eliot's gaze dropped to the black-and-white checkerboard floor of Miss Westin's waiting room.

"Just to be clear," Amanda finally whispered, "you are talking about going to *Hell*? The real burn-forever-in-eternal-torment Hades?"

"I've been there," Eliot told her, unfazed. He looked up. "It's not that bad . . . well, parts of it aren't that bad."

Fiona scoffed. "We were at the Gates of Perdition. Once. We never went inside."

"I'm not talking about that," Eliot said. "I took the Night Train into Hell. It runs from the Market Street BART station into the Blasted Lands, and then to the Poppy Lands where Jezebel lives. It's no big deal."

Fiona's eyes widened. "You did *what*?"

A few months ago, he would have told her everything he'd done. Now he was able to keep secrets.

He wasn't sure if that was a good thing or not.

Eliot explained it all to them: the Night Train, the conductor, and how there were even private trains in Hell to take them back.

"What about the war?" Amanda asked, twirling strands of hair about her pinkie. "That sounds dangerous."

"There are a few shadows loose," Eliot said. "But Fiona and I have fought them before. Heck, the six of us together? Nothing could stop us. It'd be easier than a gym match, I bet."

Jeremy laughed, sat, and reclined on one of the waiting room's chaises longues. "Oh, to be sure—minus the medics on standby and the ten-minute time limit, and being in the middle of one of the most treacherous-to-mortals places in the outer realms."

His cousin Sarah shot Jeremy a withering look, which he ignored.

Eliot continued, "But we're not going to *fight* their war. We get in, get to Jezebel's twelve castles, and get her out."

Sarah bit her lower lip. She looked . . . Eliot wasn't sure what the look on her face meant. It was the look she'd given him after he played at the Monterey Jazz Festival. Part impressed at his bravura, but something misty in her gaze that might have been disbelief at his stupidity. It was so hard for him to tell with girls.

"*No* way," Fiona said, folding her arms over her chest. "If you go, you're on your own."

"Then I'll go by myself," he said, "if I have to."

There was no challenge in that statement. It was simply a fact.

Fiona narrowed her eyes to gray slits and looked at him like she thought he was the biggest moron in the universe.

And maybe he was, because there was one small fact he hadn't told anyone: Jezebel didn't exactly *want* to be rescued. She was loyal to her Queen and the Poppy Lands. Her strength and life were literally tied to those lands.

So Eliot would stay there this time and fight with her—win this stupid war. How hard could it be? A few more Droogan-dors? What was that after he'd blown up a jet? And if he could get Robert or Fiona to come with him, it'd be that much easier.

Eliot decided not to mention this detail just yet. He figured it was already implied by him saying they had to "rescue" Jezebel.

No. He couldn't fool himself. That was a lie.

It was only a lie by virtue of leaving out selected truths . . . but that was worse. It was more calculating.

He knew what he felt, though. He'd gamble everything, his life and the lives of the others, lie, cheat, and steal to save Jezebel—or lose it all.

"I'll go with you," Amanda meekly offered. She stared at the checkerboard floor, unable to look up.

Eliot blinked, surprised. She was the last person he'd expect to go willingly to Hell.

"I'm part of the team, too, aren't I?" Amanda said. "I like Jezebel, though I don't think she likes me. That's kind of beside the point. I just want to help." She swallowed and continued, "Guess if our positions were reversed, I just wish someone would come and rescue me like that. That's what friends do for one another, right?"

Amanda pulled back her long brown hair and tied it into a knot. She finally looked up. Her dark eyes smoldered with determination.

"Hey, if Amanda's going," Robert said, "I'm in, too." He cracked his knuckles and then shrugged. "How hard could it be? Plenty of guys have gone to Hell and come back—Dante, Ulysses, Orpheus, Bill, Ted. Besides, you know I'm a sucker for that damsel-in-distress stuff."

"Thanks," Eliot told them . . . although a rotten feeling started to gnaw at his stomach.

No. He wouldn't chicken out now. He was going. And he'd take any help he could get.

And he'd accept all the consequences.

Sarah worked her mouth. Nothing came as she struggled with her words.

"It's okay," Eliot told her. You don't have to—"

"We be coming," Jeremy said, getting up from the chaise longue. "Was there ever any doubt? A bonny adventure in the outer realms? Perhaps even a wee bit o' treasure in it for us, eh?" He winked.

Sarah looked shocked.

Jeremy gave her a subtle look, and there passed between them some kind of speed-of-light nonverbal communication—just as Eliot and Fiona sometimes managed, but on a frequency Eliot couldn't decipher.

Sarah twisted back around, uncertainty and fear in her eyes, but she nodded. "Of course we'll be going."

"Uh . . . thanks," Eliot said.

Something nagged Eliot about Sarah's reaction and Jeremy's never-fading mischievous grin, and how easily he'd agreed to risk his own neck. But who was he to understand the motivations of a nineteenth-century Scottish conjurer, one who'd been stuck in the Valley of the New Year for hundreds of years and then thrown into the present?

Eliot turned to Fiona.

Fiona hadn't unfolded her arms. She hadn't dropped her narrowed slit of a stare, either. If anything, her arms were more tightly crossed and her gaze sharper as she turned and assessed them all.

"Don't encourage his suicidal delusions of grandeur," Fiona told them.

Eliot wanted to admit to her that above all others, he needed her help on this—that they were stronger together. But he couldn't say any of those things. It'd just give her a reason to stay—be the anchor that kept him here . . . because she *was* that stubborn.

He took a step closer to his sister and whispered, "In Costa Esmeralda, when you were about to get cut down by that strafing MiG—I didn't tell you what you were doing was suicidal or a delusion of grandeur."

"That was completely different," she whispered back, her face scrunching into angry lines. "People's lives were at stake."

"Yeah, it *was* different," Eliot told her. "I didn't ask any questions when I stepped between you and certain death. I just saved your life because I'm your brother, and that's what I'm supposed to do."

Fiona's eyes went wide and her gaze bored into his.

"You owe me," he said.

It was a rotten card to play on his sister, but Eliot had to. He needed her . . . even if it meant she'd be mad at him for the rest of his life.

Fiona hissed through clenched teeth, and it sounded like exploding steam. "You're going to get yourself and the rest of the team killed." Shaking her head, she continued. "So, I *cannot* believe I am saying this—but all right, I'll go. If for no other reason to make sure you all come back in one stupid piece."

Eliot wished he could tell her how much her coming meant to him, but he only managed a nod.

"But we make a beeline straight for Jezebel," Fiona told him. "Get her if we can and get out. And if things get too dangerous, we stop and turn back."

"Sure," Eliot said.

He looked over his teammates and considered telling them everything. They deserved to know all the details of Jezebel and her ties to the land.

He exhaled and shut his mouth.

He wished Mitch were here. His white magic had kept them safe before from the shadows. That would have come in handy. And having him there would have been a great boost to Fiona's morale.

Robert glanced at his wristwatch. "You said there was a train to catch?"

Eliot stuffed his moral misgivings into a dark corner of his mind to sort through later. "Yeah," he replied, "there's a secret entrance to the Night Train under the Market Street BART station."

Sarah pulled out her cell phone. "I'll have a cab meet us outside the Front Gate."

Before Sarah punched a single button, however, another phone jangled: an old-fashioned trilling bell inside Miss Westin's office.

The sound went straight through Eliot's skull and down his spine like a shock.

He jumped. And so did Fiona.

They looked at each other. Fiona's eyes were wide and her pulse pounded along her neck. Both of them went still.

The phone jangled again (he swore this time louder and sounding impatient).

Eliot and Fiona together whispered, "Audrey."

"She knows," Fiona said.

Eliot wasn't sure how they knew it was Audrey, or how they knew she knew what they were about to attempt . . . but he knew that feeling was right. Why else would she be calling Miss Westin at this *exact* moment?

There was a third ring—although this one terminated mid-jangle.

Eliot breathed a sigh of relief.

But an instant later, from inside Fiona's book bag came the stirring notes of Wagner's "Ride of the Valkyries." Her cell phone's ring tone.

"Don't answer it," Eliot said.

Fiona pursed her lips, and he could see her mentally teetering back and forth, deciding . . . but then she nodded.

"Come on," he told them all, "we don't have much time." He sprinted for the stairs.

They followed, running as if the building were on fire.

———

Eliot stared at the sign hung on the ticket booth window. He couldn't believe it. All that convincing and cajoling, all the struggling to overcome the moral ambiguity of the situation . . . for nothing.

They'd ditched class, run out of Paxington, and caught one of the eco-friendly SF Green Cabs. (A wad of cash from Robert persuaded the driver to let them all squeeze in.)

They'd gotten to the Market Street BART station, tromped down the out-of-order escalator, and found the hole in the wall. After carefully crossing the tracks, they'd entered the breach and clambered down the steep staircase into the hidden Infernal train station.

Only to find the ticket booth abandoned, and a sign that read

> *All trains, including but not limited to: the* Marshall Pass Express; *the* Six Pence; *and* Der Nachtzug *(aka the "Night Train") are hereby suspended due to civil conflicts in the realms they service. The management apologizes for any inconvenience this may cause, and full service shall resume as soon as possible (as demanded and required by the Infernal Transportation Code, Section IX).*

"Rotten luck," Jeremy said, reading over Eliot's shoulder. "I suppose our dear Jezebel will have to fend for herself." There was genuine disappointment in his voice.

"But there's another way," Fiona said. She stared at Eliot. "And you're going to try it, aren't you? No matter how dangerous it is."

"I am," he said. "Even if it is the long way around."

"What do you mean 'dangerous' and 'long way'?" Amanda asked, her fingers worrying together.

Fiona held up a hand to forestall questions, got her cell phone, and dialed. She handed it to Eliot.

"She said she'd give us a ride if we ever needed one," Fiona told him. "But *you're* going to have to ask her."

Eliot scanned the number and name just before the phone connected.

"Hi? Aunt Dallas? It's Eliot and Fiona. We kind of need a lift."

Fiona rolled her eyes at this colossal understatement.

"Really? Thanks. Where? I can explain on the way. Oh, uh, okay . . . well, Uncle Kino's graveyard. The Little Chicken Gate."

There was a long silence on the other end of the phone, so Eliot continued, "I need you to keep quiet about it. Yes—I'll explain everything. Outside the BART station on Market Street. Okay. Thanks again. Bye."

He handed the phone back to Fiona.

"She's picking us up in five minutes," Eliot said.

"And taking us where?" Robert asked, looking concerned for the first time since agreeing to go.

Eliot swallowed, and then replied, "The Lands of the Dead."

NOT A TIME TO BE COY

Fiona tried to scrunch down low so no one would see her as Aunt Dallas turned her 1968 VW van into Presidio Park.

Talk about embarrassing. Even in San Francisco, the van got looks. It was painted in tie-dye swirls, and over that were plastered decals of cherry and peach blossoms. It looked like the van had tumbled through an orchard and then thrown up rainbows. It also left a litter of real flowers in its wake.

Dallas kept well below the posted speed limit as they wound along the streets, creeping past a funeral in progress.

Fiona didn't see any of the roads Uncle Kino had used . . . and wondered if she'd ever have found her way back to the entrance of the Lands of the Dead by herself.

She glanced to the front passenger's seat, where Dallas had insisted Eliot sit (much to Jeremy's disappointment). Eliot scrutinized every tree and tombstone, leaning forward and searching.

Fiona hoped Eliot survived this attempt at heroics, *and* that he survived Jezebel. All by herself, that girl was more treacherous to her brother's well-being than any gym class or duel.

Fiona shifted in her seat.

By some unfortunate quirk, she sat next to Jeremy and Sarah on the middle bench of the van. Jeremy slid into her at every turn, no matter how slight.

Behind them, Robert stretched out, and Amanda had wedged herself in a corner of the backseat.

When Aunt Dallas had picked them up, both Covingtons had greeted her with great formality—even though Dallas looked like a college drop-out in her cut-off shorts, flip-flops, and a top that was little more than a handkerchief and spaghetti straps. Of course, thanks to Miss Westin's Mythology 101 class, they knew she was the goddess Clothos, sometimes called Mother Nature, and a dozen other equally impressive names through-out history.

Aunt Dallas had smiled at Sarah . . . not so much at Jeremy (who couldn't take his eyes off her tanned skin).

When she saw Amanda, however, Dallas made much over her, running her fingers through her tangled hair as if she were a beloved pet, and some-how smoothing out the mess and restoring its fiery luster. Amanda had hugged her, briefly but fiercely.

Robert bowed and muttered a greeting. Dallas had ordered him to sit in the very back. This chilly exchange had to be due to the fallout from when Robert quit working for Uncle Henry. Apparently, employees of the League were only rarely terminated (in the nonlethal sense of the word).

And Dallas's greeting of Fiona . . . well, there were no embraces or smiles. Dallas hadn't been able to get past her disappointment that Fiona wore her old, ill-fitting Paxington uniform.

Fiona tried to explain that Madame Cobweb's custom creation was dirty (as in blasted to tatters by an exploding tank) but Dallas hadn't listened.

Once the greetings were over, though, Dallas turned to Eliot and said, "Tell me what this is all about. And don't skip any details—especially about this girl."

No one had mentioned anything about a girl. Somehow Dallas just knew.

Eliot took a deep breath and told his story: who exactly Jezebel was— even how she'd been Julie Marks, died, went to Hell, and then got re-cruited by the Infernals to tempt him.

All light and happiness drained from Dallas's features as she listened.

Eliot explained that back in Del Sombra, Julie could have brought him over—but she didn't. Then she got punished and changed by the Infernals into one of them . . . although this last bit, Eliot admitted, was a guess on his part.

He went on telling Dallas that Team Scarab needed Jezebel to win the next match and their finals.

Dallas then turned her attention back to the road as it turned deeper into forested graveyards. The asphalt became covered in eucalyptus leaves, shadows crisscrossed their way, and the breeze stilled. It looked like no one had traveled down here in months.

The van whooshed through the leaves and the way became a dirt path that wound through trees and crowded headstones that leaned at odd angles.

The road branched, one way back to Presidio Park, and one way blocked by two posts with a chicken wire gate hung between them. A rooster perched upon a faded sun had been carved on one of the posts.

"Wait inside," Dallas ordered them.

She got out and examined the posts, and then got on her knees and looked up at the gate.

Jeremy leaned forward to get a better look (and *not* at the gate).

Fiona elbowed him.

Jeremy slammed back into the seat. "No harm done, dearest Fiona," he said, gasping. "Just observing the local scenery."

Behind them, Amanda gagged with disgust.

Dallas stood, hands on her hip, and touched the gate. With a squeak, the chicken wire door swung open.

A breeze swirled eucalyptus leaves into the air—blinding them to the outside world.

Dallas opened the driver's door and climbed in.

The leaves ceased their motion and dropped immediately to the ground.

Fiona got that "elevator sinking" feeling she was beginning to associate with shifts in space, although it looked as if nothing had changed.

Dallas swung her knees around to face Eliot. "Before we go any further," she said, "there are things I must tell you, and one thing I've got to get straight from you, nephew of mine."

Eliot swallowed. "Sure."

Fog covered the sky and the sun dimmed.

"Heroes are always tromping off to Hell," Dallas whispered, "but only the ones with a good reason *return* to tell the tale."

Eliot squirmed in his seat.

He was hiding something. Eliot was lousy at keeping secrets. They both were. Why bother to develop such a talent when Audrey had seen through every fib they'd ever told in their adolescent lives?

"For every Orpheus or Ulysses or Dante who came back," Dallas continued, "there were hundreds looking for knowledge, or eternal youth, or just very uncool treasure seekers"—she cast a sidelong glance at Jeremy—"and those guys never get out."

It was Jeremy's turn to squirm now.

Fiona pressed her lips into a straight line. This was ridiculous. She and Eliot had faced monster crocodiles and Infernal lords. Sure, a trip to Hell wasn't going to be easy—but they could handle it.

"We're not little kids," Fiona said.

Dallas held up a finger to silence Fiona.

Fiona (quite involuntarily) shut her mouth.

"So, clue me in, Eliot," Dallas said. "Tell me there's more to this than passing a gym class."

"Well," Eliot replied, his voice dry, "if we don't pass gym, we don't graduate our freshman year at Paxington." His gaze dropped to his lap.

Dallas lifted his chin so he couldn't look away. "There's a time when it's cool to be coy," she whispered. "This ain't one of them."

"Okay," Eliot said. ". . . I care for her."

"Care?" Dallas asked. "I *care* about puppies and daffodils, but I wouldn't risk my life for them. I wouldn't risk the souls of my friends and family, either."

Dallas scooted closer to Eliot. "Give me the truth and nothin' but, or I turn around."

Eliot flushed.

Fiona felt the heat from Eliot where she sat, but he wasn't embarrassed; his eyes gazed straight into Dallas's.

"I love her."

Dallas was quiet and stared back, nodding.

"When I think of Jezebel," Eliot whispered, "I burn. I can't think of anyone or anything else. I'd risk everything I had, or ever will have, for her."

Fiona's mouth opened to protest. Or maybe it'd just dropped open from the shock of hearing *those* words come out of *her* brother . . . the only occasionally heroic, and *always* nerd—now so determined, and against all odds . . . so romantic.

It was a side of him she'd never seen. A side, quite frankly, so devoid of reason, she could have done without.

And yet, it might be a sign that her immature brother was finally growing up. He was making the *wrong* choices, sure . . . but at least making *his own* wrong choices for once.

Jeremy rolled his eyes. Wisely, though, he said nothing.

Sarah and Amanda sat on the edge of their seats. They hung on Eliot's words.

Robert looked outside, pretending not to hear. (This had to be a macho guy thing; they'd die before they'd ever admit to having a romantic bone in their body.)

Dallas sighed and fanned her face and chest. "I believe you, and I'll do everything I can to help."

She put the van in neutral and rolled through the gate.

Then Dallas floored it.

The van raced down a stone-paved path and through a city of mausoleums. Rows of gravestones stretched to the horizon.

They went over a hill, and there were lawns and fields and a clear river running alongside them. Many mausoleums here had their walls torn down, and the stones used for barbecues and playgrounds and handball courts. People tossed Frisbees and ran and laughed and ate and drank and looked like they were having the time of their lives.

Fiona shuddered. But that wasn't right: no one here was having the "time of their lives" . . . because they were all dead.

The honored dead, Uncle Kino had called them, resting here before they went somewhere else. *"The dead are restless,"* he'd said. *"No one living, not even I, understands what moves them."*

The van's rear wheels slipped on a patch of grass. Dallas leaned over the steering wheel, concentrating.

Fiona checked her seat belt. "What's the rush? We want to get there in one piece, right?"

"Exactly why we need speed," Dallas said.

They slid around a curve. The van bounced, rocked, almost tipping.

"Kino has alarms that go off when anything alive enters his domain," Dallas said. "His guards will investigate, and then they'll fink us out."

She swerved around a tree growing in the middle of the road. The side mirror hit and shattered.

"Why should Kino care who comes here?" Eliot asked, hanging on with both hands to a ceiling strap.

"He protects Elysium Fields," Dallas replied. "Infernals, Outsiders, and Older Things always try and muck up the natural order. They collect souls."

Eliot looked at Fiona and shrugged.

Jeremy, though, nodded. He apparently had more experience with the dead, having spent centuries in the Valley of the New Year in Purgatory.

"I can get you to the edge of the Borderlands," Dallas said. "If *I* cross that, then Kino himself will notice and personally come. *That* would put an end to everyone's trip."

Fiona remembered how mean her Uncle Kino was. Worse even than Mr. Ma.

"So how are we supposed to find the gate?" Fiona asked. "You said you'd take us there."

"I said 'I'd get you there.' There's a big difference."

The road's paving stones became a broken jumble. The trees looked dry and sickly and the grass was dead. Wind buffeted the unaerodynamic van. Iron gray clouds covered the sky.

"We're almost there." Dallas looked right and left, squinting.

"What are we looking for?" Eliot asked.

"Your guide. Someone dead always shows up for a true hero. They never get top billing in the stories, but Dante had Virgil, and Ulysses had Old One-Eye Farius who figured *everything* out for him."

"But we don't know anyone like that who'd help us," Fiona told her. "I mean, no one that's dead."

Dallas perked up in her seat. "Then who's that?"

She pointed to a clump of twisted trees and the person-shaped shadow standing there. It stepped out and waved at Dallas's van.

69

BETRAYAL AT THE GATES OF PERDITION

Fiona squinted. She couldn't see who this "spirit guide" was supposed to be.

Aunt Dallas eased the van to a halt and flicked on the headlights.

The person waiting outside was a man.

Robert jumped up, banging his head on the roof, but that didn't slow him as he opened the side door, jumped out, and ran to the man.

It was Marcus Welmann—the middle-aged man who'd come to their old Del Sombra apartment on their fifteenth birthdays—the man who had taught Robert to be a League Driver—and the person who'd been killed by their mother. He'd also been nice enough to help them escape the Borderlands the first time they came here.

Mr. Welmann opened his arms and embraced Robert.

The two stayed like that as Fiona and the others climbed out of the van, and then Mr. Welmann released Robert and looked into his eyes.

Tears streaked Robert's cheeks, something Fiona thought she'd *never* see. She wanted to look away; it was such an intensely personal moment, but Robert then turned to face them, smiling (and quickly wiping away any traces of those tears).

Mr. Welmann wore the same AC/DC T-shirt, camouflage pants, and sneakers they'd last seen him in. Did the dead ever change clothes?

"Marcus says he can get us to the Gates of Perdition," Robert told them. "Open the thing, even, if we want."

"Mr. Welmann," Fiona said with a nod of greeting. "How'd you know we were coming?"

"Hi, kids." Mr. Welmann bowed toward Dallas, and he added, "M'Lady." He cleared his throat and straightened his shirt. "Remember how I said last time the dead are restless and get an itch to move on? Well, I got that feeling right after we parted ways."

Robert shot Fiona an accusatory glance that could have melted cast iron.

She'd never told Robert about Uncle Kino's kidnapping them and bringing them here, or about Mr. Welmann. But what was she supposed to say? *Oh, Robert—by the way, Eliot and I were in the Land of the Dead yesterday and we bumped into your old teacher, the one our mother killed.* That would've gone over well.

But Mr. Welmann had also asked her to pass along a warning to Robert: that whatever he was doing at Paxington, he was in over his head. That he should just ride away.

Between the relief at surviving that trip to the Borderlands, homework, and the dramas of gym class, though, it'd slipped her mind (Eliot's too apparently).

That, and she and Robert hadn't exactly been speaking to each other all year.

How had they ended up so far apart? What had started as her trying to protect him from the League by putting a little distance between them . . . had become a huge rift. She wasn't sure if they were even *friends* at this point.

"I felt pulled here." Mr. Welmann looked toward the darkening skies farther into the Borderlands. "It's not exactly the direction I had thought I'd be going." He shrugged. "But I figured it couldn't hurt too much to take a look-see."

He clapped Robert on the shoulder. "When you guys showed up, I knew it was right. Like fate or something?" His gaze drifted to Dallas, and he raised an eyebrow.

Dallas shook her head. "I wouldn't say that exactly. Hang on a sec." She rummaged under the driver's seat and got a purple day pack with a stenciled peace sign. She tossed it to Mr. Welmann. "A few things I'd packed for emergencies: granola bars, water, first aid kit—stuff like that."

Mr. Welmann hefted the tiny pack (which seemed heavy). "Thanks."

It was odd that Mr. Welmann got a "feeling" and came here just when they needed him. Coincidence? Aunt Dallas trusted him . . . but Fiona didn't know.

Dallas looked back to Elysium Fields and cocked her head. "If you're going to do this, you better move. I hear him coming."

"Kino," Mr. Welmann muttered. "Not someone to tangle with."

Fiona strained to hear, but heard only the wind.

"Go—" Dallas made little shooing motions. "I'll drive around and leave false tracks for that old sourpuss."

"Oh, Eliot, wait." Dallas leaned close to him and whispered. Eliot nodded, and then she kissed him on the forehead.

"This way," Mr. Welmann said, hefting the pack over his shoulder. "I know a shortcut." He bowed once more to Dallas (she curtsied back this time) and then he marched toward a forest of dead trees.

Robert followed, and so did Eliot.

Fiona looked back to Dallas for some encouragement or parting words of wisdom, but her aunt's attention was firmly fixed on the Borderlands. Without another word, Dallas climbed in the van and drove off.

The scant sunlight (and a fair amount of Fiona's courage) faded with her aunt's departure.

"Let's go," Fiona muttered to Jeremy and Sarah and Amanda—all three of them suddenly looking less thrilled by Eliot's quest.

Nonetheless, they followed Mr. Welmann into the forest.

"What'd she tell you?" Fiona asked Eliot.

He looked away. "It was personal."

Probably some advice on how to get a girl *not* to hate you—Eliot desperately needed that.

Fiona itched all over. She didn't want to be here, either. This was beyond stupidity; Eliot was going to get them killed . . . which was precisely why she *had to* go along: to make sure that didn't happen, dragging him back unconscious and bleeding if that's what it took.

But Fiona swore it was the last time she'd get him out of trouble of his own making.

They trod upon a crooked path through the forest. Overhead a few stars appeared through the tangle of skeletal branches. Fiona didn't recognize any constellations; the points of light seemed smaller and colder than they should have been.

The dead forest ended at the edge of a dry lake bed. The earth was cracked and blasted, and volcanic ash spiraled into whirlwinds. A hundred yards from here, the land fell away—plunged miles down to the lava fields of Hell. The sky was coal black, but beyond the cliff's edge, the horizon glowed like a furnace.

Amanda stood transfixed, staring at the roiling thermals and flashes of fire.

There was, thankfully, a fence between them and Hell. It looked as if a monolithic dinosaur had crawled onto the edge of the cliff, clung there, and then perished, leaving curved femurs and rib bones and talons that made a gigantic tumble of a barrier. For good measure, someone had added rolls of concertina wire (bits of cloth and flesh clinging to its spurs) along the top.

Set in the center of this fence stood the Gates of Perdition. They were bronze and rusted steel, gears and cogs and worn filigreed hinges oxidized blue-green. Spikes bristled from every surface. There were six combination locks . . . some thimble tiny, others that you'd need both hands to turn.

Only a certified crazy person would try to open this thing.

"So how do we open it?" Eliot whispered to Mr. Welmann.

"I can do it." Mr. Welmann ran a hand over his beard-stubbled face. "Then I'll jam the lock so it doesn't shut. It'd be a heck of a mess if we got stuck on the other side."

"How exactly are you going to open it?" she asked.

"I don't know." Mr. Welmann's bushy eyebrows bunched. "But I know I can. Like I knew to wait for you and your brother. I think dead heroes are *supposed* to be able to get into Hell"—he swallowed—"unfortunately."

Fiona heard the rumble of approaching thunder.

She turned.

Headlights pierced the haze of volcanic ash—far away, but they turned and vanished.

Robert closed his eyes and concentrated. "V-8," he said.

Mr. Welmann nodded. "That's a three hundred ten horsepower V-8," he corrected. "Specifically from a black 1957 Cadillac Eldorado Brougham."

"Kino's car?" Fiona asked.

Robert slipped on his brass knuckles.

"Don't even think about it," Mr. Welmann warned Robert. "Your aunt might be crazy enough to play chicken with Kino in that van of hers . . . but even she wouldn't dare tangle with the Lord of the Dead on his home turf."

Amanda trembled. "I don't know about this anymore," she whispered.

Jeremy and Sarah shared a worried glance, and then Jeremy gave his cousin a slight shake of his head.

"Get to the Gate and you're safe," Mr. Welmann told them. "It's Infernal property. Kino's not allowed to cross or even touch it. Just step across, and you'll have all the time you'll need to figure this out."

Amanda paled and looked sick—caught between the gates of Hell and the Lord of the Dead.

Eliot glowered at them, maybe understanding that everyone was coming to their senses and support for his crazy plan was faltering.

"Okay, listen up," Fiona said. "We run for the gate. Eliot and Marcus—take point. Amanda you keep up with me. After us, Jeremy, Sarah, and Robert bring up the rear and yell if you see those headlights."

This felt like a gym match: Fiona providing the strategy and Team Scarab pulling together to overcome a series of insane obstacles. It was as if they'd trained for this all year. Maybe there was something, after all, to Mr. Ma's methods.

She glanced over her shoulder. If this didn't work, if Kino got to them, it'd be best to scatter. She would make a stand and face him while the others got back to the forest.

"Go," Fiona ordered.

They sprinted for the gate (probably the first people in all history to actually run *toward* the entrance to Hell!), and then skidded to a halt before its closed doors. Six dial combination locks (the largest the size of a hubcap, descending to one the size of a dime) were set into a precise dotted line next to the Gate's massive bronze handle.

Far away headlights reappeared in the haze . . . turned to the right and then the left, and then crept forward.

"Hurry," Fiona whispered.

Mr. Welmann spun the combination lock dials—one by one, using both hands, not even pausing—then he stopped them and spun them the other way. "My birthday," he muttered. "Those lucky lotto numbers . . . license plate of my first car . . ."

He finished with the first, largest combination.

There was a click and a series of pings that resonated throughout the metal.

Fiona looked for the headlights. They were gone. A bit of luck, maybe.

Mr. Welmann stopped four more dials in quick succession and they clicked into place.

Fiona heard the ratcheting of large wheels, squealing and groaning as if they hadn't been oiled for centuries.

An engine's roar made the air tremble.

Fiona jumped as high beams flicked on and illuminated the Gate.

The Cadillac had crept up to them, lights off. It was a hundred yards away, now peeling out straight toward them.

Amanda clung to Eliot.

Eliot tried to shrug Lady Dawn off his shoulder and maneuver it around, but Amanda was in the way.

Jeremy and Sarah stepped forward, though, faces rigid with concentration. They held up their hands—waved them as if performing some sleight of hand stage magic.

Dust and ash filled the air, and the grit congealed into a pane of mirrored glass between them and Kino's car.

The Cadillac fishtailed to a stop, momentarily confused by the appearance of another pair of headlights racing toward it on a headlong crash trajectory.

"Nice work," Fiona said. For once, she was glad the two pain-in-the-rear conjurors were on her team.

But that trick wouldn't fool Kino long.

Mr. Welmann clicked the last dial in place.

The Gate's internal mechanisms hissed steam and sparked. A seam appeared and one side opened wide enough for a single person to squeeze through.

On the other side a rocky path zigged and zagged toward and over the cliff. Far below, lava geysered, rivers of molten rock snaked, and volcanoes belched smoke.

All they had to do was cross over—shut the door (but not completely)—and they'd be safe from Uncle Kino. But Fiona decided this was crazy dangerous . . . and they hadn't even gotten to Hell yet! So, she'd wait until Kino left, and then she'd abort Eliot's rescue mission, and get them out of here (dragging her brother out by his ears if necessary).

But Fiona couldn't move.

Her feet rooted to the earth, and fear chilled her despite the furnace heat that billowed through from Hell.

No—she was a goddess, the daughter of Death. She *was* scared . . . but fear would have to wait.

"Move," she whispered, and ushered Amanda to the opening.

But Amanda dug in her heals and stopped.

Robert stepped up and slipped one arm around her. "It's okay. We'll get through this," he told Amanda.

She nodded. Together they crossed over.

"Mr. Welmann," Fiona whispered. "Jam the lock. Eliot, get your guitar ready. We might need cover."

Eliot and Mr. Welmann passed through.

She glanced back. Kino's Cadillac sat there idling, not getting any closer.

Fiona inched toward the gate. Her shoes crunched over desiccated soil. She held her breath, closed her eyes, and stepped to the other side.

She exhaled and blinked.

It was hot, as if someone had opened the oven door and she stood in front of it. Not hot enough to blister, not quite. Hot enough, though, to make her instantly thirsty and sticky with sweat.

Mr. Welmann reached into the exposed lock mechanism. "I think I see it," he said. "Give me a second."

Jeremy and Sarah lingered on the Borderland side. Sarah frantically whispered to her cousin—not frightened. She looked agitated.

"Come on, hurry!" Fiona called to them.

Jeremy stepped up to the slight opening. His blond hair was plastered with perspiration. He grinned—and pulled Sarah behind him. She cried out in pain as he wrenched her arm.

Jeremy threw himself against the Gates of Perdition—

—and slammed it shut.

Mr. Welmann jerked his hand out of the gate's mechanism just before there was a series of clacks . . . as its locks clicked into place.

They were trapped in Hell.

WAR IS HELL

70

MISSTEPS IN THE BLASTED LANDS

Eliot banged on the gate. The gears of locking mechanism, the web of filigree, and the impenetrable mass of bronze—none of it budged.

And why should it? It had withstood the frenzied pounding of damned souls on this side for countless millennia.

He had a feeling it would stand until the end of time.

"Tell me you jammed the lock," he whispered to Mr. Welmann.

"Sorry, kid." Mr. Welmann wiggled his fat fingers. "I was lucky to get my arm out in time."

Why had Jeremy slammed the gate on them? It didn't make sense. Eliot turned. Still, they had gotten here . . . and this is where he wanted to be, wasn't it?

Not quite. This place was as different from Jezebel's Poppy Lands as you could get. The horizon wavered in the raw heat. There was no sun. Dull red light shone from *below* the edge of the cliff a dozen paces from the gate.

Eliot shucked off his Paxington jacket, already drenched in sweat.

Robert had his off, too. Amanda had her arms crossed protectively over her chest, jacket and all, as if she were cold . . . or maybe in shock.

The air had an iron taste and it made his lungs burn. The ground was ash and dust and pumice. There were footprints . . . lots of them, and Eliot swallowed, remembering the dozens on this side that had stormed the gate the first time he and Fiona had been here.

Where were all those dead now?

"W—what do we do now?" Amanda whimpered. She stood next to

Fiona, her back to the gate, trying to stay close to the edge of Hell, as if she stood right on the line, maybe no one would notice she was on the *wrong* side.

Fiona pounded on the gate. Her jaw clenched. "I'll tell you what we're going to do," she said. "We're going to kill them when we get back to school."

"We don't know why Jeremy shut the gate," Eliot said. It felt wrong to defend Jeremy, but Fiona's reaction was so violent. "Maybe he saw Kino coming and closed it to protect us."

"Sarah looked so"—Amanda search for the right words—"surprised. I don't think she knew why, either."

"Doesn't matter why," Robert said. "The Covingtons will either get caught by Kino, get away clean, or . . . if I know Jeremy, he'll talk his way out of trouble. But they're on the other side. We're here." He hucked a rock over the edge of the cliff. "On our own."

"Better scout around," Mr. Welmann told him.

Robert nodded. He pulled out his Glock 29 and inched toward the cliff.

"I know why he did it," Fiona said. "He'd wanted to reorganize Team Scarab. Now he can go back and say there is no more Team Scarab. He and Sarah can transfer to a team with a better ranking. Smart—in a cold-blooded killer sort of way."

"Jeremy is crazy competitive," Eliot replied, "but he wouldn't . . ."

He couldn't finish that thought, because it felt like a lie. What *wouldn't* Jeremy do to make sure he graduated? Suddenly Eliot wasn't so sure he was beyond murdering them.

Fiona turned, the color rising in her cheeks. "We're done," she said to Eliot. "This mission to get Jezebel, I'm calling it. We're down two people. I don't care if Uncle Kino pounds us flat"—she nodded at the cliff and the lava fields beyond—"there's no way we're crossing that."

"But we haven't even tried."

Eliot hated this: him pleading like he was her "little" brother. Like she was in charge of everything all the time. Why couldn't she just believe in him?

Fiona pulled the rubber band off her wrist. She stretched it into a line, staring at it until it was so slender that it flickered, half invisible. She let go. The stretched band stayed elongated and she held it like a rapier.

She plunged it into the gate.

Bronze sparked and squealed, protesting. Fiona pushed all the way in, grunting from the effort. With both hands, she dragged her edge in a large circle, slicing the metal.

The bronze heated, became molten . . . and sealed behind her cut.

Fiona withdrew and stared as the last bit repaired itself. "Huh," she said.

"You can't force the Gates of Perdition open," Mr. Welmann told her. "No one ever has, not even the Titans."

"We'll just see about that." Fiona rummaged in her book bag and took out the silver bracelet Louis had given her. It lengthened and its links swelled to the size of her fist. She narrowed her gaze, focusing. The edges of the rusty metal tapered and sharpened to glistening razors.

She swung it at the gate.

The bronze shrieked and sparks fountained like fireworks. Fiona became a blurry outline against the light.

Eliot had to look away and blink furiously.

The light faded and he looked back.

Fiona stood there, chain in hand . . . a slender bracelet once more.

She sighed at this failure and scrutinized the fence on either side of the gate. The bones and concertina wire curved along the edge of the land—and then over—spines and rib bones sticking out from the cliff.

"Wouldn't try that either," Mr. Welmann remarked. "Those bones are some of the exposed bits of the World Serpent. Start messing with that . . . it might wake up."[61]

They'd learned about the world serpent in Miss Westin's Mythology 101 class. That thing was supposedly strong and venomous enough to kill even gods.

Fiona chewed her lower lip. She turned to Eliot. "I know you think you need to do this," she whispered, "but it's crazy. I'm not helping anymore."

---

61. An intriguing Chimera Heresy penned by Sildas Pious in the thirteen century pertains to Jörmungandr (aka the World Serpent). In Norse mythology, the giant snake is prophesied to emerge from the ocean, poison the sky, and then battle Thor (the god and the monster slay each other). This event supposedly occurs at end of the world, Ragnarök. In the Pious's legend, however, valkyries with flaming swords and Christian angels fight the beast, chain it, and bury it under the earth. One of the chain links was forged into the Gates of Perdition. Centuries later, when Jesus Christ is said to have arisen and opened the gates of Hell, Pious explains these were the Dolorous Gates, not the Gates of Perdition. He claims that on the day the Gates of Perdition are destroyed, the Beast will rise, and it will signal *both* Ragnarök and the Christian Judgment Day, when the dead will be released from Hell. *Gods of the First and Twenty-first Century, Volume 5, Core Myths (Part 2)*. Zypheron Press Ltd., Eighth Edition.

She glanced at Amanda. "I'm hoping you're not going to force us to come along."

Eliot couldn't look her in the eye.

How could she even think that? Sure, he may have not told them the entire truth to get them to come . . . but he wasn't going to *make* any of them risk their lives.

"You know what I'm asking you to do," she murmured.

"Yeah," Eliot said. "I know. I'll do it."

He wasn't sure what hurt more: Fiona's accusation . . . or the fact that she was abandoning him when he needed her the most.

He unslung Lady Dawn and stepped toward the gate.

How to charm open something that looked like it could withstand a nuclear blast? Not with head-on force. The gate had shrugged off Fiona's attempt.

This required subtlety.

Eliot strummed Lady Dawn and picked out the notes of the "Mortal's Coil" nursery rhyme. He let the notes wander as he found his way to a new tune: a precise clockwork song with a metronome steady heartbeat. This was the song of the gate. Eliot heard the echo of the song in the gears and cogs, the wound springs, in every rivet and bolt. He picked his way over the notes, and felt blocks and tumblers—and with the tiniest of flourishes, he tickled one of those tumblers into place.

He smiled. This would be easier than he thought.

The gate, however, vibrated of its own accord—the barest rumble that flipped the tumbler back into place.

"It's fighting me," he whispered to Fiona.

"Then play harder—or faster—or louder," she said. "Whatever it takes."

Robert walked back from the edge of the cliff, his face drawn tight with worry. "Eliot, I wouldn't play any louder, if I were you. Look."

Eliot stopped playing. He put on his glasses and then he, Fiona, Mr. Welmann, and Amanda followed Robert back the edge.

The cliff dropped a mile straight down. Switchbacks started from the top and descended into smog. Rivers of lava snaked around mesas of black basalt—their bases eroded by the molten stone. Meteors streaked across the sky, so did the occasional on-fire, out-of-control airline jet.

Eliot winced as one plane crashed and burst into a fireball.

He'd gotten a glimpse of the Blasted Lands at the beginning of the school year. It'd scared him then . . . still did. But something was different.

Fiona said, "It's quieter."

Eliot knew there were damned souls here—dozens had rushed the gate and tried to escape last time—but Eliot hadn't expected to see *thousands* of them down there . . . and all of them quiet.

They formed lines that stretched to the horizon. Each person carried a large stone that, when they got to the end of the line, they dropped into the lava below . . . and then went back for more. The stones disappeared in flame, but elsewhere, they'd actually started to pile up, making jumbled shorelines, and in some places damming the lava altogether.

"What are they doing?" Eliot whispered.

Mr. Welmann wiped the sweat off his face with a red handkerchief. "Something, that's for sure. Since Beelzebub died, the Blasted Lands were taken over by a new Infernal boss. Looks like he's put everyone to work."

Eliot remembered with Louis had told him: *"We are monarchs of the domains of Hell, the benevolent kings and queens over the countless souls who are drawn there to worship us."*

But not everything was different under the new management. In some areas, people fought one another, full-scale wars waged atop a few mesas, the losers tossed over the side into the fire.

"You see them now?" Robert asked Eliot. "The crazy ones? I don't think we want *them* hearing you playing and coming up here."

Eliot imagined tens of thousands rushing the gates . . . and him and the others fighting, trapped with their backs against the wall.

He turned to Amanda, worried she might freak out.

But she wasn't; instead, she stared with open fascination at the lakes of lava and burning mountains. She took a step closer—and Eliot set a hand on her arm, pulling her back from the edge.

"Hey," he told her.

She blinked, breaking whatever weird trance she'd fallen into, and nodded at him. Amanda's eyes, though, still glimmered as if they'd absorbed the heat of this place.

Mr. Welmann dug into the pack that Aunt Dallas had given them. He took out a pair of binoculars and gazed through them. "Hmm." He handed them to Eliot and pointed between two mesas.

Eliot squinted into the binoculars, his gaze traveling over jagged obsidian, and smoldering fissures, and then saw what Mr. Welmann had: A simple suspension bridge swayed across the chasm. It was made of rusted cables and black metal . . . an arc a half-mile long that swung in the heat.

It looked amazingly untrustworthy.

He moved his view left and right, and spotted more of these bridges. They linked one mesa to another, and then to fields beyond the lava. The Blasted Lands leveled out there into plains of ash.

Eliot then spotted a fine straight black line—no, *two* parallel lines—that ran over the plain and vanished in the distance.

"The Night Train's railroad tracks." Eliot handed the binoculars to Fiona. "That's how we'll get out. We can use those bridges to cross, and then follow the tracks right into the Poppy Lands."

She looked and snorted and said, "The Poppy Lands are *not* the way out."

"They're our *only* way now," Eliot said. "I've been on those tracks. Nothing touches them—not people, flaming meteors, falling planes—even the ash stays off them. They're protected somehow."

Mr. Welmann nodded, believing him. The others, though, looked un-convinced.

"And they run straight to the Poppy Lands," he said. "Even if you don't want to help me with Jezebel, there's a station house there with a private train. I'm sure it'll take you guys back."

"You're sure, huh?" Fiona crossed her arms. "More likely we'll have to steal it."

"You have a better idea?"

She looked back at the shut Gates of Perdition and pursed her lips. "No . . . I don't." She thought for a moment, and then asked, "Can you play a few notes and clean up the air like you did in the gym match? We don't want to choke along the way."

Eliot nodded. He took a deep breath and plucked a few Spanish fla-menco notes on Lady Dawn, imagining a coastal breeze. The temperature dropped twenty degrees, and the air sweetened.

"Then okay," Fiona told him. "We'll give it a try. Robert, take point. Eliot after him—Amanda and me. Mr. Welmann, bring up the rear, please."

She was using her "team leader" commanding voice that was really get-ting on Eliot's nerves.

Robert must have felt the same way, because he hesitated and looked like he wanted to give Fiona his own version of vocabulary insult. Eliot gave him a slight nod. Robert nodded back and headed down the switch-backs.

Fiona pulled Eliot aside. "We'll catch up in a second," she told Mr. Wel-mann and Amanda.

She whispered to Eliot, "Are you sure about this? I mean, I'm your sister. . . . I've *got* to help you, no matter what." She looked extremely awkward saying this. "I think I know what Jezebel means you . . . but it's not just you and me at risk. Robert, he can take care of himself. And Mr. Welmann, well, he's already dead, but if his soul gets trapped in Hell . . ." She hesitated and swallowed. "But Amanda . . . I wish I could leave her somewhere safe. She has no idea what she's gotten into."

Eliot understood her frustration. Fiona was taking all the responsibility for this onto *her* shoulders—like she really was captain and this was another match. The responsibility must be driving her crazy.

"This isn't turning out like I thought," Eliot told her. "But it's still *my* plan—not yours. Whatever happens out there, I know you're doing your best to protect everyone, but it's my responsibility, and my fault, if anything goes wrong."

She stared at him, confused, as if it were an alien concept that Eliot could take leadership and responsibility for something, but then she nodded.

They tromped down the switchbacks, catching up with the others.

"Hey, cool air is back." Mr. Welmann turned as Eliot got close. "That's nice." He sweated profusely, which was weird, considering he was dead.

Eliot kept playing quietly as they walked. He didn't look back.

It took a while to get to the bottom of the switchbacks. How long, Eliot wasn't sure. Time felt "slippery," as if no time had passed, but simultaneously, it felt like it took forever, too.

No one spoke, heeding Robert's warning not to attract any undue attention.

That was a good thing, too. On a nearby mesa, a battle raged as hundreds of people screamed and hurled rocks at one another, clawing, biting, and punching. There weren't two sides; it was everyone against everyone else. It was like they had all lost their minds.

The trail ended. Here the first simple suspension bridge arced to an adjacent plateau (one with no obvious war waging upon it). The bridge dangled a half mile above a raging river of molten stone.

Eliot felt his resolve evaporate.

Robert leaned over the cliff's edge and spit. It sizzled into vapor the instant it was outside Eliot's protective musical bubble. "Whoa," he said, impressed.

But Robert, being Robert, stepped onto the bridge without another thought . . . and Eliot had to keep up with him or his friend would fry. The really strange thing was that Amanda, who had always been scared, walked right onto the bridge after Eliot.

The heat was terrific and the smell of sulfur and copper overwhelming. Eliot held his breath and played faster and louder so they wouldn't die from the fumes.

He didn't want to look down, but he had to see where he set his feet.

Far below, orange and red liquid boiled and churned and popped. Drifting by were tiny dots of smoldering solid stone crust.

They passed the low midpoint of the bridge and started climbing back up. Eliot spied the top of the plateau again. There were people there—not the crazy fighting ones, but the working ones.

The damned formed a line, shuffled along with rocks, dragging, rolling, and shoving them along until they got to the edge . . . where they pushed the stones into the river.

Then they turned back, presumably to get another rock.

And much to his relief, not one of them gave Eliot or the others a second glance; in fact, they seemed to be going out of their way *not* to look at them.

Some wore rags, but most wore nothing. Their nude bodies were gaunt and reddened from the heat. They were bruised and scraped, and they all had burns—mostly on their hands and bare feet, but a few of them were completely covered in burn scars.

It reminded Eliot of Perry Millhouse, whom he and Fiona had killed in their second heroic trial. Perry Millhouse, who Eliot knew had actually been the Titan Prometheus, long fallen from power.

That's where they'd met Amanda. Perry had kidnapped her and used her as bait.

He glanced back at Amanda. Her hair was plastered to her forehead and her cheeks flushed.

Funny, you'd think that someone who'd been the prisoner of a homicidal maniac whose preferred method of killing enemies was burning them alive would look a little *less* fascinated with fire.

They trod up the rest of bridge and stepped onto the plateau. From here, two bridges led to other mesa tops—both, more or less, getting them closer to the plains of the Blasted Lands.

"Which way?" Fiona asked.

Eliot stood on his tiptoes for a better look, which was when he saw the top of the adjacent plateau.

A thousand people crowded its edge—pushing and shoving to get onto the suspension bridge—running across, screaming and snarling . . . straight toward them.

71

THE HEROIC STAND OF AMANDA LANE

Eliot didn't understand why there were so many people—all angry at him.

What had he done?

Thousands crowded along the edge of the distant plateau. They raised fists, threw rocks, and hurled insults in a dozen languages.

Was it because he was alive? Or because he'd *willingly* entered Hell, and they'd all probably wanted out? Or maybe like Robert said: they were crazy.

Eliot faced the bridge connecting the two plateaus and turned up the gain on Lady Dawn to the halfway point.

Mr. Welmann's eyes widened, and he reached to stop him.

Eliot couldn't waste time talking. Mr. Welmann didn't know what he was capable of. In fact, it'd be simple to stop them. If anything, *that* was the scary thing: how easy it'd be . . . and how much Eliot had enjoyed the destruction before in Costa Esmeralda.

He blasted out a power chord.

The other bridge wobbled and the slack stretched taut from the on-slaught of sound. The damned on the bridge held up their hands to protect themselves—but were flung off like rag dolls.

Eliot belted out three more chords, and that felt good.

The rusty iron of the bridge heated and twisted like taffy . . . stretched apart and fell into the chasm.

Mr. Welmann clamped a hand on Eliot's arm over and pulled it away from the guitar.

"Let go," Eliot told him, annoyed. "I got rid—"

But Mr. Welmann wasn't even looking at Eliot; instead, he scanned the horizons. He lifted a finger indicating silence, and cocked his head, straining to hear.

"No," Mr. Welmann whispered. "Listen."

The sound was, at first, barely audible over the rumble of the distant volcanoes. Eliot heard one cry, then a shout of discovery, and then a combined wail of rage that spread over the land.

From the cliffs they'd traversed, the damned poured out of caves and crannies. Thousands and thousands of torches flared to life upon the slopes. And from every plateau and mesa, the shouts of not thousands—but tens, if not hundreds, of thousands of angry souls combined into a thunderous roar.

Eliot let the magnitude of his mistake sink in. He'd messed up in a big, big way.

"Nice," Fiona muttered, shaking her head.

"What'd you want me to do?" he asked. "Let them get to us? Fight them all? Don't you think that would've made a little noise, too?"

He started coughing, the air once again hot and reeking of metal. His hand drifted back to Lady Dawn's strings, instinctively plunking the notes that cleared the atmosphere.

Fiona started to say something, but her mouth stayed open, gaping, as she stared past Eliot.

He turned and saw what had shut his sister up.

Where the bridge he'd just destroyed had been, a thin line appeared in the chasm. It was spiderweb fine, but it thickened and buds appeared that turned into chain links—then another line stretched next to it, and strands of metal wove between them.

Like the Gates of Perdition that had sealed after Fiona had cut into them, this bridge was growing back.

The damned across the chasm cheered and jeered.

"We can't fight," Mr. Welmann said. "No matter how strong you kids think you are, they'll always be more of them to fight." He nodded toward the other suspension bridge that led to the Blasted Lands. "We go that way. Fast."

Without any argument, they raced for that bridge, their only escape.

A cluster of the working damned gathered at the bridge, all crowding to get on the thing and get away, too.

Robert sprinted ahead. He plowed into them, knocking six over with one blow, and clearing a path for him and the others to run ahead.

Eliot and Mr. Welmann jogged onto the bridge after him. Amanda was right after them. Fiona lingered, and came last.

And Eliot knew why.

As they tromped off the bridge and onto the next mesa, Fiona turned and severed the chains.

It fell into the lava.

If it was like the other bridge, though, it'd grow back. Destroying it would buy them only a minute or so.

The working damned here scattered, abandoning their rocks. Eliot jumped onto a boulder and looked around. Five bridges radiated off this plateau, connecting to others . . . only now, from every direction, the angry damned came. So many, he couldn't count them. They flowed across the land. The only thing preventing the damned from quickly overwhelming them were the bridges—they let them across only a few at a time.

If Eliot and the others didn't get out of here, they'd have no choice: they'd have to fight and fight—and against a few hundred . . . maybe even against the first thousand, they'd win.

But after an hour of battling, he and Fiona, Robert and Amanda would falter. They'd need food and water and sleep.

There was *one* way, though. One bridge clear for now. It led to another plateau, which in turn had a single bridge to the Plains of Ash.

"There's a way out of lava fields," Eliot told them, jumping down. "I can get us onto solid ground."

Robert had his brass knuckles on one hand, held his Glock in the other. "How many are coming?" he asked.

"All of them," Eliot replied.

"Just run," Fiona told everyone. "There's no time left to think this through."

So Eliot ran. He ran before the fear could catch him and stop him cold.

But as he and the others got onto the bridge, he couldn't stop thinking that this plan didn't make any sense.

So what if they got onto the plains? That eliminated the danger of them falling into lava, but if they wouldn't stop the bridges from reforming, and it wouldn't stop the damned from pursing them. How long could they all run?

At the midpoint of the bridge, Amanda halted.

Eliot turned and grabbed her hand. "It's okay," he said, not at all con-vinced of this. "Don't be afraid."

But as he saw the look on Amanda's face, he knew the word *afraid* didn't apply.

At least to her.

Amanda's lips pursed together and trembled with emotion. Her eyes still smoldered with fascination—*for real*. They glowed and flickered with mirage heat.

Amanda dropped his hand.

"I can stop them," she said. "You go on."

"What? . . ." Fiona almost ran into her—and halted, seeing her burning eyes, too. She stepped around her next to Eliot.

"You have to go." Amanda's hands gripped either side of the chain rail-ing. Where they touched the iron it heated . . . dull red . . . orange . . . and then yellow and smoldering.

"I can't hold it in much longer," Amanda said, struggling to get her words out. "It's this place. It's so hot. And their anger. I can feel it all burning."

Eliot reached out to touch her, but the heat was too great.

The heat. The fire. Eliot had seen one person with this power before. And so had Amanda.

"Perry Millhouse?" Eliot asked. "He did this to you?"

Tears welled in the corners of Amanda's blazing eyes, but they didn't get the chance to spill upon her cheeks; instead, they sizzled and steamed away.

Robert and Mr. Welmann came back to see what the trouble was, stop-ping, astonished at the sight of her.

"I can't even tell you," Amanda whimpered. "It hurts to even think about him. But after you saved me, everything changed. That night I had to get the heat out. I let it go. I had to . . . and I burned everything—my house—my dog—my parents . . . none of them survived."

She looked away, unable to meet their horrified gazes.

Eliot felt sick, but everything made sense about Amanda now. Perry Millhouse had had something planned for her all along. Maybe he'd wanted to pass his power on to another generation, or maybe it was some revenge thing aimed at the League—but whatever his reason, the Immor-tal fire of Prometheus pulsed through Amanda Lane.

And when Eliot and Fiona had rescued her, taken her home, no one un-derstood the power inside her. Uncle Henry and the others in the League of Immortals must've felt sorry for her and sent her to Paxington.

All those little fires on the obstacle course and when the dorms had burned over semester break: that had been Amanda.

She looked back at them, her eyes slits into a blazing furnace.

"I can't hold it much longer," she whispered. "And that's okay. Whatever's inside me, it's never done me any good, but now, I can at least save my friends."

Amanda inhaled sharply and winced.

"Don't," Robert told her. "Even if you melt the bridge, it'll just come back."

"You're so noble, Robert," she said, her voice stronger than Eliot had ever heard. "How I wish you were *my* hero." She didn't look at Robert, though, as she said this, rather her gaze firmly fixed on Eliot. "Don't worry. I *will* stop them."

The metal bars under Eliot's feet got too hot to stand on. He took two steps back.

"There has to be another way," Eliot told her. "Just give us some time to think."

Her hair lifted, charged with static electricity, turning to dull red and then orange. The metal she touched heated to white and sagged. "There's no time for me," she said.

Amanda Lane turned and walked back they way they'd come.

Flames licked her legs and arms and spiraled about her in jets of gold and green plasma. The heat from her body was tremendous.

Eliot and the others jumped back.

The army of the damned reached the edge of the plateau and streamed onto the bridge . . . pausing at the sight of her.

"Amanda!" Eliot called.

She kept walking, the air about her wavering, her footprints melting metal.

"We've got to move." Mr. Welmann pointed down.

The lava in the chasm boiled and churned. Geysers showered molten rock into the air. Waves rebounded and crashed against the plateaus, crumbling their bases.

A whirlpool formed beneath Amanda, following her as she moved along the bridge; the swirling lava glowed hotter until it hissed silver vapor and blazed a blue-white too painful to look at.

Eliot had to play her something, a song to cool her spirit.

How had she managed to keep all that heat inside for an entire year? She should've told them.

Or had been his fault? Eliot had been so wrapped up in his own problems, that he'd never really been a friend for her.

He focused, thought about her, and started to strum his guitar.

"No way, man." Robert grabbed him and pulled him back.

"Don't," Eliot growled. "I can do this."

Fiona shook her head. "Not this time," she told him. "Go! Before you get us all killed, you idiot."

So he ran, half pushed along by Robert and Fiona, and he didn't look back until he got to the other side of the bridge.

When he finally turned, he saw the damned running along the bridge toward Amanda.

They couldn't get close. The ones in front screamed and burst into flame, floundered, and blasted back into dust. The ones in back kept pushing forward, though . . . dooming those ahead of them.

Amanda blazed like a sun fallen to the earth.

The bridge melted and fell apart. She hovered in midair.

The lava under her erupted—plumes and gouts of molten rock and metal exploded. A tidal wave of lava surged in all directions, consuming the mesas and plateaus in its path.

Eliot turned and ran.

He no longer wondered how, or if, there was a way to save Amanda. He just ran. The encyclopedia part of his mind had nothing to say. Faced with a towering wall of pure fire, the only thing left was animal instinct.

They ran over the broken land, scrambled up dunes of ash, and crunched over a dry lakebed . . . until he and the others were out of breath and his legs felt like lead. (Even dead Mr. Welmann was panting and exhausted.)

They stopped and looked.

A volcano pushed upward where Amanda had made her stand. It spewed fire and rock upon the land and hissed clouds that blackened the sky.

Nothing would get through that—dead or alive.

As Amanda had promised.

Eliot watched for a moment. Lightning flashed among the clouds, but there was no rain.

He wished he'd been there for her at school. But he'd just complained about her and treated her like a weakling . . . when in fact, she had been just struggling to contain a power that, if she'd unleashed it, could have killed them all.

The words Eliot spoke not an hour ago echoed in his head: *"It's my responsibility. And my fault, if anything goes wrong."*

He'd gotten her killed.

Coming here and bringing her along had been his idea. But worse, even if he had known about her unstable power, if he'd had a choice to make between Amanda and Jezebel . . . he still might have made a choice, and it would've been Jezebel, not her.

That made him, what?

Was he like his father? Evil?

Eliot sank to one knee. He was dizzy . . . and unsure of everything.

He threw up.

Fiona came to him and set her hand on his shoulder. "It wasn't your fault," she whispered.

She didn't understand. Yes, he felt guilty over Amanda's death, but what he really felt terrible about was that along with Amanda dying, something had been burned out inside him, too.

Eliot hunched over and threw up again.

Coughing, he stood up straight. "I'm okay now," he told them, and then pointed. "That's the direction I saw the train tracks."

And then, one foot in front of the other, he started moving again.

72

THE TOWER GRAVE

Eliot walked down the center of the Night Train tracks.

He had Lady Dawn slung over his shoulder, and the instrument banged along his back. For the first time since Louis had given him the instrument, he didn't feel like lugging it around.

It was quiet here and merely hot (compared with the furnace temperatures elsewhere on the plains). Occasionally a meteor would slam into the dust and leave a crater, but they never hit the train tracks. Even whirlwinds that sprang up vanished before they crossed the tracks.

But quiet was the last thing he wanted because he kept thinking about Amanda, and how she'd died to save them, so Eliot could get the girl he *really* cared for.

Would he have done the same for Amanda? Or was Paxington making him selfish? Or was it his Infernal blood?

How had this all gotten so out of control?

Fiona walked next to him, and for once in her life, she had nothing to say.

That was driving him nuts, too. If she'd just yell at him—tell him how stupid his plan had been . . . something . . . then he could've defended himself.

The silence was like a knife slowly twisting in his brain.

Mr. Welmann took point, on the lookout for mobs of angry damned or onrushing trains. Robert walked on Eliot's right side, balancing on the railroad track. He'd unbuttoned his shirt all the way, and dirty shirttails flapped about him.

They were quiet, too.

More condemnation by the lack of conversation.

It was hard to tell how long they walked. The light from the furnace-orange sun was always behind clouds, and never changed. Robert's watch was busted. Fiona's phone displayed jumbled characters when she'd tried calling Mitch, and she got a "caller unavailable" message.

Mr. Welmann scanned the horizon. "Uphill grade," he told them.

Eliot nodded, not caring. It was as if this place evaporated his ability to think straight and all he could do was walk on these tracks.

There were channels and riverbeds alongside the rails now, bone dry as if there had been running water in them a million years ago. As the plains sloped up, black rocks jutted from the ash and seared red clay. There were even a few spots of lichen.

Eliot's mind cleared a bit when he spotted stunted sagebrush. There were scrub pines, too, twisted and tortured, but alive.

As they neared the summit of this hill, a breeze carried a hint of moisture.

He got to the top, and it was as if someone had drawn a line along the ridge—splotches of moss appeared on the other side, the earth was black loam, pine forests sprouted and thickened into a jungle that blanketed the valley beyond, and a ribbon of muddy river snaked down its center. The sunlight turned from blazing orange to a cool silver overcast.

Eliot took a deep breath, and smelled a "compost" scent mixed with honey and the perfume of a million flowers.

"The Poppy Lands," he said.

"Duh," Fiona muttered.

Despite her sarcasm, despite the fact they'd just lost one of their team, Fiona's eyes were wide, taking it all in and gleaming with curiosity. She'd always wanted to travel and see exotic places. This was about as exotic as you could get.

Flowers grew everywhere: fleshy orchids with inviting petals, drooping wisteria cones that dangled nectar-sticky stems, and carpets of pinhead-sized blossoms the color of cotton candy.

The train tracks continued down the slope—cutting through forest and jungle.

They followed them.

Whatever chemicals or magic protected the train tracks, it also kept the vegetation off. Still, as they entered the jungle, the trees crossed overhead and formed a tunnel.

The bugs left them alone, too. That was a good thing. There were clouds of metal wasps, giant beetles that bored into hardwood like it was Styrofoam, and butterflies that fumed acid vapor trails in the air.

"Doesn't look like there's a war going on here," Robert said.

Fiona took a few pictures with her cell phone camera.

Mr. Welmann held a hand, indicating they halt. "Don't be too sure," he said, and pointed ahead.

The train tracks ended. Jungle blocked their way.

"Line's been cut," Mr. Welmann said. "That's one of the first things you do in the war. Sever your enemy's supply routes and communication. Get them alone. Wear them down." He frowned.

Fiona stepped up to the jungle. "Everyone back." She pulled out her chain and spun it over her head. She turned the whirling mass flat, and walked into the jungle where the tracks used to run.

Branches, vines, and roots sheared about her in a circular path.

Eliot and the others followed—at a respectable distance, but not too far back, because as soon as Fiona passed, tendrils wormed back and new braches extruded.

Thirty more paces like that and they emerged back onto clear tracks.

Ahead was a train station that looked like a gigantic hothouse, one that someone had taken a baseball bat to and busted every pane of glass.

Standing outside the station were six knights in mirror-polished steel plate mail embellished with gold and emerald inlay. Foot-long thorns bristled from their armor. They held weapons that looked part hunting rifle, part medieval execution ax.

Robert drew his gun. Fiona touched the chain on her wrist, but then instead pulled off a rubber band and stretched it.

The knights saw them, and they sank to one knee.

"Well," Fiona whispered, "that's . . . different."

"Huh," Robert said. He lowered his gun, but didn't holster it.

"It will be okay," Eliot told them, and plodded ahead.

Like the Ticket Master who had bowed before Eliot on the Night Train, these guys had to have mistaken him for an Infernal Lord.

As Eliot and the others approached, the knight in front stood, and with his head still bowed, he said, "Most noble Master Post, and Miss Post, son and daughter of the Prince of Darkness, we are your honor escorts, the Knights of the Thorned Rose, Queen Sealiah's personal guards."[62]

These guys knew exactly who they were.

"Honor guard, right," Robert said with a snort. "Why should we believe you guys?"

Fiona shot him a look for being so rude.

The knight standing turned his stilted visor to Robert, and stared at him a long moment.

"Because, sir," that knight said, "the dismembered bodies of three hundred of the finest soldiers and knights litter the road from here to the Twelve Towers—proof enough that we have fought and bled and suffered long to clear a way so you may proceed unmolested to our Queen."

"Do we even really need to go any farther?" Fiona asked Eliot. She turned to the knight and inquired, "Is Jezebel with you? Or close? She's the one we want to talk with."

"No, great Lady," the knight said, and ducked his head apologetically. "The Duchess of the Burning Orchards is at the side of our Queen."

Fiona sighed. "Figures."

"A second, please?" Eliot said the knight in charge.

Eliot stepped back with the others and they huddled. "We have three options," he whispered. "Steal a train and get out of here."

"I'm betting the tracks are cut in *both* directions," Mr. Welmann told him.

Eliot nodded in agreement. "We go ahead, but on our own."

He gazed down the road and saw the burning remains of soldiers, twisted armor and broken lances, smoldering napalm, and torn bits of shadow slithering . . . a swath of ruin and battle for miles. Here and there, however, body parts twitched and moved.

What happened to the dead in Hell when they—what was the right

---

62. A universal symbol of beauty and romance, the rose has also been associated with power and secret societies formed to wield that power. Ancient Romans placed a rose on the door where secret societies would meet (the phrase *sub rosa*, or "under the rose," means to keep a secret). Examples of such societies are the Order of the Celestial Rose (League of Immortals), the Knights of the Thorned Rose (Infernals), and the Holy Rose Hunters (vampire killers among the Mortal Magical Families ca. sixteenth century). Mythohistorians claim to trace these groups to prehistoric pagan cults, worshippers of fertility and warrior spirits, which may suggest a common root origin. *Secret Societies in a Secret World.* Lucy Westin, Paxington Institute Press LLC, San Francisco.

word for it—died? Did they slowly come back together? Or did they just lie there in pieces forever?

Eliot swallowed, trying not to get sick again.

"Or," Eliot said, "we let these guys take us to their Queen."

"Into what might be a trap," Fiona reminded them.

"I think they're telling the truth about them fighting and dying just to help us," Eliot said.

Fiona chewed on her lower lip. "Well, they don't seem like they want to immediately kill us. That's progress."

"I don't want to go back through those Blasted Lands," Robert murmured.

"Or hoof it through the rest of Hell," Mr. Welmann added.

Fiona sighed and shook her head. "I guess we go with the welcoming committee . . . for now."

Eliot returned to the knights. "Please," he told them, "show us the way, sir."

The head knight motioned to his men. They rose and formed a loose circle around them. Eliot didn't particularly like being surrounded by armed warriors, but they *seemed* okay; none of them looked directly at them, and their weapons pointed away.

Still, instinct told Eliot not to trust anyone in Hell.

The Poppy Lands were worse than Eliot remembered from his previous trip on the Night Train. The earth was scorched in spots, frozen in others, and heaps of salt scattered everywhere so nothing could grow—some regions so blasted and broken that it didn't look like *either* Queen Sealiah or the attacking shadows controlled it.

These lands felt abandoned and wrong.

They hurried over terrain that looked like the surface of the moon—and over a half-burned bridge that spanned a river choked with vegetation and oil slicks and bodies and chunks of ice.

On the horizon glowed the Twelve Towers of Queen Sealiah. They perched upon the edge of a cliff. Each tower was different: one was an ancient tree with only a crown of a few spare branches; one was ghostly white and taller than all others; one flickered with lines of phosphorescing fungus. Searchlights played through the air. Cannon and cauldrons smoldered atop the outer walls. Industrial cranes stood among the towers, casting their long steel arms back and forth.

As they neared, one crane lowered a platform.

With a wave of his gauntlet, the head knight indicated that they get on.

Eliot hesitated. Once they got on this thing and were inside those walls, it would be harder to turn around and leave if they wanted to.

Queen Sealiah was more than just the monarch of this domain of Hell. She was also part of his family. And Eliot had met only one of his father's relations, Beelzebub. He'd tried to kill him and Fiona. Eliot didn't think that's what Sealiah had in mind, though.

He looked around, took a deep breath, and stepped onto the platform.

His sister, Robert, and Mr. Welmann got on, too, and it rose into the air.

He saw the land for miles around—desolate, burning, and shattered. Oddly, there was no fighting. If this was a war . . . where was everyone?

The platform lifted up and over the outer wall, where there were hundreds of artillery pieces poised ready to fire, archers, and knights peering through telescopes. Clouds of insects and bats swarmed around them in formations.

Within the great courtyard were tens of thousands of armored knights and soldiers. They hurried to reinforce the walls, sharpen weapons, and load rifles.

Before Eliot and the others they parted like a retreating tide, all falling to one knee in supplication.

This was completely weird.

One day, Eliot was a social zero at school, practically invisible. And here? He was treated like royalty.

He tried to smooth out his scorched and ripped school jacket, but it didn't work.

Their escorts led them to the tallest tower on the plateau. It was as large as a skyscraper and bone white, which Eliot saw was actually made from bones: dinosaur; elephant; whale; and countless grinning human skulls. Upon the top of the tower sat the three largest skulls, something Eliot had only seen in books, the teeth-filled fossilized remains of *Tyrannosaurus rex*.[63]

---

63. The Tower Grave is said to be built from the bones of those who offended the Queen of the Poppies. Even for an Infernal, this seems unlikely, due to the sheer volume of materials required and the prehistoric, fossilized nature of the larger specimens. Rough calculations indicate construction began prior to the War in Heaven, and may have been started by entities older than the fallen angels. It must also be noted that the size of Sealiah's Twelve Towers varies by account, seeming to swell and strengthen in times of conflict and constricting to modest dimensions in peaceful times (see also the mutable nature of the Infernal Realms, section 6). *Gods of the First and Twenty-first Century, Volume 13, Infernal Forces.* Zypheron Press Ltd., Eighth Edition.

As they mounted the hundreds of steps, a lone figure appeared at the top to greet them. Jezebel.

Eliot halted in his tracks.

It felt like he'd been struck in the head.

Part of him had thought he'd never see her again . . . thinking her dead, or captured . . . or a million other things that could have happened to her that would have kept them apart. They seemed fated never to be together.

Seeing her now. Here. Finally. He didn't know what to do but stare.

Her face was unblemished and luminescent, and her lips parted as she saw him. She was different from when he'd last seen her on the Night Train. Her features were too smooth and perfect . . . almost otherworldly. It was as if her face had been recast and fired and ground to a mirror fin- ish, like that of a porcelain doll.

While her face was enchanting, the way she was dressed was anything but inviting. She wore a platinum breastplate the same color as her hair, and it was enameled with roses and orchids, and covered in black metal thorns. A chain mail skirt the color of dried blood hung about her hips and covered high studded combat boots.

She took a step toward him.

Eliot couldn't resist; he started toward her again. His heart beat so hard, he thought it would explode in his chest. All he wanted to do was take her by the hand, turn around, and get out of here.

With every step, his blood warmed, heated . . . burned.

He felt intoxicated. Yes. He wanted to taste her again—even if her kisses were poisoned. He was addicted to how he felt when she was around.

Their escort knights halted on the steps ahead of Eliot. They bowed be- fore Jezebel, and she, in turn, inclined her head to recognize them.

"You are dismissed, Captain," Jezebel said, her tone icy.

The knights retreated down the steps.

Eliot jogged up to Jezebel. He would have thrown his arms about her or taken her hand at least, but with her in that thorned armor, he'd get im- paled if he tried.

Jezebel hovered near him; her gauntleted hand reached out for him, and then pulled back.

Her gaze darted past Eliot to take in Fiona, Robert, and Mr. Welmann as they walked up. Her eyes narrowed a bit—and then softened again as she looked back to Eliot.

"You came," she whispered to him, voice trembling. "After I tried so hard to push you away. Eliot, you will never know what that means to me." In an even lower voice, she said, "But there is more danger here than you can imagine."

Fiona was close enough to hear to this. "We're not getting involved in any Infernal thing, if that's what you mean. We just came to get you out of here."

Jezebel snorted and dismissed Fiona with a single glance.

"I'd show a little gratitude," Robert muttered, moving alongside Fiona. "We lost Amanda getting here."

That got her attention.

Jezebel blinked. "The little girl? Lost? You mean—?"

"She died," Fiona told her flatly. "Burned."

"A human sacrificed in Hell. . . . I am sorry for her." Jezebel looked away and took a deep breath, appearing for a split second like normal, flawed Julie Marks—then her features hardened. "But there is nothing to be done. We must see to our own lives now."

"You want to save lives?" Fiona stepped forward, clenching her fists. "Then get back to the train station and help us find a way back to school."

Eliot held up a hand to calm her.

"We came to get you," Eliot told Jezebel. "We need you back at school . . . gym class and finals." He faltered. "No . . . it's not that . . . well, only a small part. *I* need you, too."

Jezebel took a tiny step closer so they were almost touching.

He felt her heat and their mutual magnetic attraction. He wanted to take her in his arms—even if it cut him to ribbons.

"My hero," Jezebel whispered, a slight edge of sarcasm to her honeyed voice. "If only things were so simple."

Fiona set a hand on Eliot's shoulder and pulled him back. "Okay, you tried. She said no. We're out of here. We had a deal, remember?"

Eliot shrugged her off. He couldn't leave. How could he after Amanda had died so he could get here? And how could he now that he stood before Jezebel?

But he *had* made a deal with his sister, and he knew how crazy it'd be to stay.

He couldn't have it both ways. He had to decide.

Eliot had had to make this choice before. Back in Del Sombra, he had impulsively decided to go with the then Julie Marks—run away to Hollywood (which had been part of an Infernal trap).

And he'd made the wrong choice then, saved only because Julie hadn't followed through with the plan.

As he looked at Jezebel, Eliot knew he *had* to make the right choice now, because no one was going to save him this time.

Jezebel stepped back three paces, before he could tell her anything, though. "I cannot help you . . . and none of you can leave."

A hundred knights in the courtyard moved to encircle the steps. A dozen more knights appeared behind Jezebel, their rifle-lances at the ready.

Robert reached for his gun.

Mr. Welmann set a restraining hand on Robert's arm and stepped between them. "I believe, young lady, you were going to take us to your Queen?" He glanced back at Fiona, giving her a warning shake of his head. "Might as well hear what she had to say, after coming all this way, right?"

"That's just wonderful," Fiona said through gritted teeth.

"Don't do this," Eliot told Jezebel.

With a gesture, she indicated that they come with her. The guards aimed their lances at them.

Eliot marched forward and Jezebel walked by his side.

"There is no choice," she whispered to him, "for any of us. Be careful. Your next words may kill us all."

73

DUX BELLORUM

Fiona wondered if her brother had another supernatural talent beside his music, one where no matter how hard she tried, he got them both *deeper* into trouble.

And now it wasn't just him and her anymore. It was Robert and Mr. Welmann. And it *had* been Amanda, too.

Fiona was going to have a long talk with Eliot about responsibility when they got out of here.

If they got out of here.

They walked down a gigantic hallway you could've taxied a jumbo jet through—the arching walls made from skulls, all of them staring. Luminescent mushrooms sprouted from grinning mouths and eye sockets. It was super creepy.

Eliot strolled alongside Jezebel as if they were going to get some coffee at Café Eridanus.

His crush and the resulting lack of intelligence reminded her of the way she'd felt last summer for Robert.

Fiona cast a sideways glance at Robert. He pulled on his Paxington jacket, tucked in his shirttails, and smoothed his wild hair. He caught her gaze and smiled like everything was going to be all right.

She quickly looked away.

There was no sense mooning over *that* lost cause now.

She wished Mitch were here. What wouldn't she give to hold his hand— and jump back home or some exotic location (anywhere not in the middle of a war zone).

She turned back to Eliot. He looked like a dope walking next to his girl-friend. Fiona felt a flash of jealousy, but decided to let him be. Wherever Jezebel was taking them, it wasn't going to be the happy ending Eliot was hoping for.

The hallway opened into a room as large as a stadium filled with hun-dreds of guards (all with those deadly looking rifle lances). In the center on a raised dais was a throne of bones, held together with vines and sprouting blossoms.

Queen Sealiah sat there. She wore armor with scales beaten into the shapes of *phalaenopsis* orchid petals. On her hips were curved daggers, and a sheathed sword with a cracked hilt and ragged leather handle that looked oddly familiar.

But all this was secondary to Sealiah herself. Her hair was copper red and her skin the color of molten bronze. Her eyes flashed as if they were faceted emerald as her gaze swept over them.

And beautiful? She was way beyond beauty.

Fiona couldn't compare her to any other person or even goddess she'd seen. Not even Dallas came close.

This was an Infernal queen in her lair. And like some big fat spider, Fiona sensed countless threads of power radiating to her from the land around them.

Despite the contempt she felt for this side of her family, Fiona knew she had to show respect, and keep her fear and ever-shortening temper in check, or this could be a very brief audience.

"Greetings to you, son and daughter of the Prince of Darkness," Sealiah said. Her voice was liquid velvet. "Destroy everything you touch."

Fiona didn't understand the reference, but nonetheless she bowed her head. Eliot had the good sense to do the same.

But Fiona didn't bow too low. She sensed that showing *too much* re-spect would be just as bad as not showing any (and she wasn't about to take her eyes off the Infernal even for a second).

Jezebel fell to her knees and lay prostrated before her Queen. Jezebel, of all creatures—always proud and strong and never bending an inch—acting like a slave girl?

Eliot fidgeted and looked torn between wanting to pull her up and knowing this would be a breach of protocol.

It was so degrading.

Sealiah nodded at them, which Fiona guessed was a huge concession of respect, given the circumstances. The Queen rose and strode down to their level. She was a lot shorter up close—not even as tall as Fiona.

There was a smell from her, too: the perfume of every flower . . . with something toxic mixed in. Fiona tried not to gag.

Sealiah halted, scrutinizing them.

Fiona tried to meet the Queen's gaze, but she had to look away. The depth of the Infernal's stare was like her mother's—but worse because there didn't seem to be any soul reflected behind her eyes.

Could she be related by blood to something this evil? Miss Westin had lectured on the Infernals and told them the relationships between the fallen angels were not well understood by mortals. So Sealiah could be Louis's cousin, aunt, or even his daughter. She and Sealiah could be sisters for all Fiona knew. Ick.

She didn't imagine, however, that they'd have sleepovers or talk about boys anytime soon.

Eyes downcast, Fiona once more noticed the Queen's sword. She *had* seen it before somewhere. Part of her wanted to reach out and touch it—but she squelched that wild impulse, knowing it would be suicidal.

Sealiah moved to stand before Eliot, and her gaze lingered long, a look Fiona had seen before on hungry dogs.

"So wonderful to finally meet you in the flesh, Eliot."

He nodded, face flushing.

The Queen passed Mr. Welmann like he wasn't there.

She stopped before Robert and stroked his cheek with a long fingernail. He inhaled deeply, shocked at her touch. "And Mr. Farmington," Sealiah murmured. "An honor to have a true hero in our midst."

Hero? Robert? Fiona had no idea what Sealiah was thinking, but she definitely didn't like her lascivious smile as she looked Robert over—or her touching him.

Fiona cleared her throat.

Sealiah cocked an eyebrow at her. "Speak."

Fiona managed to sound as respectful as if she were addressing the League Council: "I beg pardon, Your Majesty, but we're not looking for trouble. We just came to get Jezebel and get her back to school."

"Oh?" Sealiah strode back to her throne, sinking upon it with a great flourish. "You're not looking for trouble? Then why do you look ready to do battle?"

Sealiah beckoned to Jezebel before Fiona replied, however, and said, "Rise, my protégée, and speak. What do you say to this request?"

Jezebel got to her feet. Even after degrading herself, she still looked regal and proud, without a speck of dust on her.

How did she do that? When Fiona couldn't keep one lousy school uniform clean to save her life.

"Nothing would please me more, my Queen," Jezebel said.

Eliot straightened and practically floated next to her at this.

"But," she said, "I cannot. My place is fighting by your side."

Eliot deflated.

"And even if you sent me," Jezebel continued, glancing at Eliot, "I could not live. The Poppy Lands are torn asunder. My power ebbs. If I were to leave, I would perish before I could cross the train tracks."

Every hint of an expression drained from Eliot's features and he stared straight ahead, thinking.

Fiona *psst*'d at him and he looked back at her.

She shot him a glance that said: *Okay—we tried again—let's go.*

The Queen's previous amusement cooled and her features hardened. "We fight for our lives against an ancient enemy. If we lose, Jezebel will, if lucky, die. If not, she will be captured by Mephistopheles and tortured for all eternity."

Eliot paled, but in a level voice, he asked, "What can we do to help?"

"Fight with us," Sealiah told him, leaning forward. "If you battle at Jezebel's side, our chances greatly improve. With your sister's strength and that of your hero companion added to that, victory would be assured." Her eyes gleamed, and Fiona saw a spark behind them now: the flickering green fires of bloodlust.

Whose blood, and whose lust, however, Fiona wasn't sure of.

"Excuse me a second, Your Majesty." Fiona held up a finger. "Eliot and I need to talk."

She pulled him six steps back. Robert and Mr. Welmann joined them.

"I'm staying," Eliot whispered to her.

Like she couldn't have guessed *that,* and yet, that didn't stop her from hissing back, "Are you crazy!"

Eliot shrugged.

"She's right," Robert said, looking physically pained to admit this. "I'm all for helping, but this side has its back against the wall. They're going to lose."

Eliot frowned and shook his head . . . but nonetheless looked uncertain.

Fiona had seen this before. Eliot knew he was wrong, but he was about to dig in his heels anyway and never give up.

She felt like slugging him, which actually had some appeal. She bet she could knock Eliot out, and then, as she'd promised herself, drag him back to San Francisco for his own good.

She glanced at the Queen and the hundreds of soldiers surrounding them. She wasn't sure how well walking out of here was going to go over with the Flower Queen, though.

She had to take charge before Eliot redoubled his resolve and went beyond being a mere idiot—and became a *suicidal* idiot.

"We can't help you," Fiona told Sealiah. She nodded at Jezebel, and said, "I'm sorry."

Jezebel gave her a curt nod. Not even a flicker of hate . . . as if she wanted them (okay, probably just Eliot) safe and far from here, no matter what it'd cost her.

Sealiah appeared unruffled.

Fiona didn't like that one bit.

"Perhaps," the Queen said as her predator smile reappeared, "I may offer some other incentive?"

"I *really* doubt it," Fiona said.

Sealiah arched one brow and gestured. Two guards dragged a man forward. He was bound in silver chains and a metal band covered his mouth.

It was Louis.

Fiona blinked and looked again. It *was* her father.

"Let him go," she and Eliot said together.

"Louis is my prisoner." Sealiah walked behind their father and yanked on his chain, pulling him to his knees. "We will do as we please with him."

Eliot unslung his guitar.

Fiona found that her bracelet was loose in her hand.

Around them, hundreds of knights leveled their rifles.

"Cool it, kids," Mr. Welmann whispered. "There are other ways to make deals—especially with them."

Fiona didn't get what he meant, but Eliot seemed to because he nodded, stepped forward, and asked, "So, you're saying if we fight for you, you'll let our father go?"

"I do not know about 'letting him go,'" Sealiah said with a theatrical wave of her hand, "but I will let him live, which is better than the fate that awaits him if Mephistopheles wins."

Fiona locked gazes with her father—he couldn't speak because of the gag—but something in his eyes said that there was a lot more going on here, and a lot more at stake than just his life.

"No deal," Eliot said.

The guards around them crowded closer.

Sealiah smile deepened and fang tips protruded. Bloodred claws appeared from her fingertips.

"Then," she purred, "we are at an impasse. Unless you wish to roll for terms?"

Louis gave Fiona and Eliot an almost invisible nod of his head yes.

Understanding dawned on Eliot's face. "You mean dice?"

"Yes," Sealiah said. "Just name the terms you wish."

"My terms . . . ?" Eliot pondered. "I'll fight for you—for Jezebel's sake," he said, "but I want you to let my father go immediately."

Sealiah tapped her full lips, thinking, and her claws retracted. "Agreed, as long as he is willing to fight for my side as well."

Louis gave a lamentable sigh.

"And," Eliot said. "You let my sister and my friends go back." He looked at them. "If, that's what they want."

"If you win the roll," Sealiah said. "Of course."

"Wait, I'm not agreeing to any of this," Fiona protested.

Sealiah held up her hand indicating silence, and Fiona thought she better shut her mouth.

Eliot had a plan—what precisely she wasn't sure—but if she lost her temper now, things would get bloody fast.

"And if I win," Sealiah told Eliot, "you fight for me and also pledge your life and soul with an unbreakable oath."

"No way!" Fiona shouted.

The thought of her brother bowing and scraping before this creature was too much. She started forward, her bracelet chain in her hand, growing and lengthening, links sharpening to circles of razor.

Could she even fight Sealiah and her knights? Would the *Pactum Pax Immortalus* neutrality treaty between the fallen angels and the League prevent her from interfering? Or was she enough her father's daughter . . . enough Infernal, to cut the Queen's head off as she had Beelzebub's?

Maybe it was time to put that to the test once more.

Eliot turned to her—and the look on his face stopped her dead in her tracks.

His eyes were cold and dark and resolute. Despite everything they'd been through, he looked like, for once in his life, he knew *exactly* what he was doing.

On the other hand, Eliot always—and she meant always, without fail—got them into *more* trouble.

But that look . . .

She finally blinked. "Okay," she murmured. "Just don't screw this up."

"You'll be the first to know," he told her.

Fiona figured it couldn't hurt to let Eliot try whatever it was he had up his sleeve—because if it didn't work, she planned on getting out of here anyway, Eliot in tow, even if that meant cutting down everything in her way.

"I offer you one in six odds," Sealiah told Eliot.

"Even odds." Eliot said. "Or no deal. Take or leave it."

Sealiah shrugged as if this were a trivial matter. She passed one hand over another, and as if by sleight of hand, a small white cube appeared. It was a six-sided die, with tiny symbols on its faces.

She descended the stairs to meet Eliot and offered it to him.

He accepted the die and examined the sides. Etched onto the faces was a scrimshaw head-eating-tail snake, two prancing dogs, three crossed scimitars, four stars, five hands (each making a different rude gesture), and six ravens on the wing.

"Odd or even?" Sealiah asked.

"Even, if your Majesty pleases." Eliot turned the die so six scrimshawed black birds faced up.

Eliot closed his hand and shook the die. He concentrated, blew on his fist, and cast the die onto the steps.

It rolled and bounced and spun up on one corner like a top.

Eliot leaned forward, his gazed fixed upon the die.

Sealiah, too, stared at it.

The spinning cube gyrated back and froth.

Dots of sweat appeared on the Queen's brow. Eliot's hands clenched and whitened.

The die tumbled, popped, and skittered to a halt. . . .

. . . Six crows.

Even.

Eliot exhaled. He'd won.

Louis shrugged off the chains and gag and stretched. "Well rolled, my boy. A pleasure to see you." He smiled at Fiona. "Thank you, too, my dear."

Sealiah seemed pleased. And why shouldn't she? Even losing she had Fiona's brother and father to fight in her war.

"You can go," Eliot whispered to Fiona. "This doesn't have to be your fight anymore."

"Don't tell me what to do," she told him.

Eliot was being so magnanimous and noble (and that positively irked her). There was no way she could just walk out on him. But there was no way she was fighting for the Queen of Poppies, either.

Louis rubbed his hands. "Before we go any further," he said. "I insist that if my son and I are to fight, it be as your *Dux Bellorum* with full honors and rights."

"Ducks Bell—what?" Eliot asked Fiona.

"Latin maybe?" she whispered. "Duke of war?"

She was pretty good with foreign languages, but this was a new one on her.[64]

Sealiah looked at Louis. "If you have something to fight *for,* I suppose you might actually risk your pretty skin. And since there will be much of the Hysterical Kingdom to divide should we win . . . I would throw you a scrap."

He bowed as deep as possible without taking his eyes off of her. "Your wisdom is exceeded only by your beauty."

Sealiah scoffed, drew one of her curved daggers, and pricked her thumb. She went to Louis and smeared his forehead with the shape of a little star. "By the bond of blood and war so joined," she murmured, and lingered close to his face a moment.

She withdrew.

Louis beckoned to Eliot and he came and got the same treatment.

Louis then turned to Fiona. "Come my daughter, join us, and fight by our side." He opened his arms as if he wanted to embrace her.

Fiona had often dreamed of a moment of reconciliation with her father. Her forgiving him. Him accepting her. It was something she'd *never* get from Audrey.

---

64. *Dux* is Latin for "leader." The earliest usage of *Dux Bellorum* appears in the literatures of King Arthur, where he is described as the "dux of battles" among the kings of the Romano-Britons in their wars against the Anglo-Saxons. The military title survived until the Fall of Constantinople in 1453 (although, the Italian Fascist dictator, Benito Mussolini, used the title of *Dux* [Duce in Italian]). The term also rarely appears among the Infernals and Fairies, most notable was the Green Knight, the *Dux Bellorum* of the Fey. *War Immortalus*, Benjamin Ma, Paxington Institute Press LLC, San Francisco.

But it couldn't happen like this . . . in Hell. Right in the middle of a war.

Fiona had to decide, though. Leave or stay. Fight or not. Get drawn into a war that was none of her business, or just walk away and go back to school where she belonged.

She took a step toward them.

There was a crack. The earth rumbled. The tower shook and skulls rained down.

The floor split, caved in, and from tunnels below—the shades of damnation poured forth.

74

UNDERLYING DARKNESS

Fiona fell back, knocked over by an emerging serpent the size of a bus.

Her adrenaline surged. Worries and thoughts of Infernal politics and family vanished as the snake's scales flashed before her eyes: jet black, mirror smooth, rippling muscle.

The snake circled, its body uncoiling from the tunnel below.

Fiona jumped to her feet, her blood pounding and her chain once more in her hands. There was no time to be afraid.

The snake hissed and struck.

Fiona held her chain before her—severed fang and sinew and flesh.

The serpent's head tumbled from its body. Venom and black blood pooled at her feet.

Shadow creatures wormed from the earth and fought Sealiah's knights everywhere in the enormous chamber. There were snakes, lizards, and crabs—part flesh and part shade. They tore and bit, and in turn, were shot and hacked by the knights.

Like the shadows Fiona and Eliot had fought in the alley by Paxington.

Not quite. These weren't changing shape . . . and they felt solid. Real. More dangerous.

Eliot held Lady Dawn and blasted a giant scorpion that squeezed out from between the rocks (although he just blasted it into a bazillion *tiny* black scorpions).

Soldiers crawled from the cracks in the tower's foundation as well. These damned souls had been stitched together with parts missing, or extra parts added, or blades riveted in place of hands. Robert pummeled two headless patchwork soldiers wielding obsidian knives.

Part of Fiona's mind rebelled. This was every nightmare she'd had come to life.

An overgrown black mantis that could've eaten a horse lunged at her—she whirled her chain—and it splattered into a mass of chitin and ichor.

So gross.

And so much for *deciding* if she was going to fight this fight.

The still-thinking part of her mind, though, thought this was like gym class: the tension . . . the ever-present danger . . . the urge to fight or run and not even think.

She knew what to do. She *had to* cool down and assess the tactical situation.

A thrall of Sealiah's knights encircled their Queen and leveled rifle lances at a horde of onrushing men. There were thunder and flashes and smoke—and the shadow soldiers were blasted into bits . . . but still they crawled forward.

Robert struggled and grappled with a black tiger.

Eliot strummed Lady Dawn and the air rippled; the light from the nearby glowing mushrooms on the walls dazzled to magnesium brilliance.

The cat withered in the light—and Robert snapped its neck.

Fiona moved toward them to help.

But the cracks in the floor between her and them widened.

A reptile hand pushed aside massive stones . . . with claws as big as scythe blades.

A limb thrust through, and then a smooth lizard head emerged from the earth—hissing and snapping; it devoured five knights with one bite.

This dragon pulled its hindquarters free and its tail whipped about, crushing everything in its wake, impacting the tower wall, and blasting skulls and stones and metal supports—making a hole to the outside.

Through it Fiona glimpsed flashes and motion. The battle wasn't just in here.

Queen Sealiah advanced on the great beast, and as she did, she grew talons and fangs, and flowers sprouted in her footsteps. She was as pale as the dragon was ebon. She drew her sword, its tip broken and jagged and dripping poison.

Fiona *had* seen that sword. Her father had skewered Beelzebub with it.

The dragon slashed at Sealiah; she stabbed its claw.

The beast cried out and the limb went lame. It hobbled and snapped at her.

Sealiah punched it in the snout.

The dragon had scraped her arm, however, and came away with her blood on its teeth. It reared back and roared. The veins in its neck bulged, turning a nacreous green with poison.

Sealiah laughed as the creature thrashed and fell . . . shivered, and became still.

But her laughter died as she saw three *more* dragons push forth from the fissures.

How many more of these things were there? Fiona had seen hundreds of these shadows in the alley near Paxington. If that many of these now more-solid shadows caught them in here . . . she and Eliot and Robert would get slaughtered.

Skulls and stones fell from the top of the tower and shattered on the floor.

Or they'd be buried alive.

"Outside!" Fiona shouted to Eliot, and pointed at the breach in the wall.

Eliot and Robert and Mr. Welmann moved toward the hole. Eliot hesitated, looking back at her, but Mr. Welmann hustled him through.

Sealiah and Jezebel lingered, though, fighting on.

And Louis? Her father was nowhere to be seen among the knights battling hand to hand, slashing with swords, or hacking with lances . . . and in turn, being bitten, crushed, and stung to death by the things boiling from the earth.

This was a losing battle.

They had to regroup and get some maneuvering room.

Fiona felt cold and her feet went numb. Should she stay and look for Louis? He wasn't even armed. Could he survive this carnage?

Eliot, Robert, and Mr. Welmann, however, were already outside—and that decided it. She'd stick with her brother.

She pushed soldiers out of her way, swung her chain, cleared a path, and jumped through the hole in the tower wall.

It was *worse* out here.

Fissures radiated from the tower of bone across the mesa. From them it looked like every shadow creature in Mephistopheles' army pushed through into the melee. The ten thousand knights and soldiers camped in the castles' inner courtyard had expected an attack from the outside, not from within their own walls . . . and they'd been caught unawares.

Thousands of men lay torn to pieces on the flagstones. Officers shouted orders—but few soldiers had the wits to listen as giant centipedes, and oily protozoa, and legions of patchwork men slithered from the earth and swept through their ranks.

Sealiah and Jezebel emerged behind Fiona.

"We must hurry," Sealiah said. "My knights in the Tower Grave pay for our escape. They will not last long."

The Queen of Poppies sounded irritated, as if those men dying for her were letting her down by *merely* getting eaten alive while she made small talk.

Fiona was about to tell the queen that there was no "we" to hurry, and to also ask her what the heck she was going to "hurry" up and do against a force of this size—when she heard Eliot.

"Fiona!" Eliot shouted, and waved to her to join him.

Eliot and Robert and Mr. Welmann had cleared a patch of solid ground by the far wall.

Louis was there, too. He leaned against the wall, brooding as he watched the slaughter . . . or maybe he was bored; it was hard to tell.

Fiona ran to them. Sealiah and Jezebel trailed behind her.

"This is where we shall make our stand against the Droogan-dors," Sealiah declared. She looked absolutely majestic, a queen defending the last of her land.

"Dad," Fiona said. "Grab a sword—some weapon. Do *something*!"

Louis smiled. "I am using my deadliest weapon, daughter." He tapped the side if his head. "*I* am thinking. As you should be if you care at all about your pretty head."

"Form a circle about me," Sealiah ordered. "I shall summon my power."

"I don't think so," Fiona told Her Regalness. "We're not going to be your body shields. Your strategy of brute force verse brute force hasn't worked so great against Mephistopheles thus far. It's probably not going to work now."

The Queen gave Fiona a look that could have melted tungsten.

Fiona shrugged it off. If dirty looks, divine or diabolical, could have killed her, she would have been stone dead years ago from Audrey's withering gazes.

One canon on the wall had been turned—it blasted down in the courtyard—and destroyed as many knights as shadow creatures.

Fiona cringed. "It's like the battle of Ultima Thule," she explained to the Queen. "Lots of inferior forces fighting a handful of superior ones—that's you." That last comment seemed to mollify Sealiah. "Only this time, there are too many opponents, and more coming every second."

The answer of what to do came to Fiona. Not the *how* of it, but *what* had to be done.

"We've got to seal their tunnels."

"They must have been digging through solid rock for days," Jezebel said. "Started beyond our outer defenses at the river."

"The entire plateau is riddled then," Sealiah replied. "With our power diminished, they cannot be sealed in time."

Eliot stepped forward. "I can do it, I think." He touched Lady Dawn and the ground trembled.

Sealiah looked at her brother and ate him up with her savage eyes. "My Dux Bellorum."

"An excellent idea." Louis set a hand on Eliot's shoulder. The smile on his face, however, dried up as he took a long look at the Lady Dawn guitar. "What have you done to my violin?" he said, horrified.

"Later—" Eliot shrugged off Louis's touch. "And she's *mine* now. You gave her to me, remember?"

Louis narrowed his eyes and continued to stare at the instrument, looking as if he'd been betrayed by it.

"Sure, you can collapse those tunnels," Fiona whispered to Eliot, "but can you do it *without* bringing down the entire mesa and killing us, too?" Fiona had seen Eliot's power unleashed firsthand: He'd leveled downtown Costa Esmeralda.

Eliot pursed his lips, thinking. "I just need to concentrate."

She gave his arm a squeeze. This was prohibited by their mutually agreed on "never touch each other" rule, but surrounded, about to be overwhelmed by bloodthirsty shadows, in the middle of Hell—it seemed like the right thing.

Eliot gave her an awkward smile.

"Give him some room," Sealiah commanded. "Let nothing distract him."

They spread out to defend Eliot.

And he played.

At first, even though Eliot's fingers strummed and the strings blurred, Fiona didn't hear a thing over the clash of steel and shouts and roars in the courtyard . . . but she did *feel* something. It started in her toes, a tingle that traveled through the bones in her legs and into her stomach, and grew into a rumble that made her teeth buzz.

Dust rose into the air.

Three oversized wolves howled at the subsonic noise, whirled, and charged. Fiona braced and swung her chain. Robert picked up a lance. He moved closer, but not too close to her, and held the lance high.

Robert threw the lance; it struck and impaled one wolf.

Fiona cut another down—but the third bit into her arm.

Robert punched the wolf and broke its skull.

Fiona shook the animal off, wincing as teeth pulled out of her flesh with sucking sounds. She winced again at the sight of her blood trickling down her arm.

She looked up at Robert and tried to communicate her thanks.

He met her eyes with a steady gaze.

Eliot's music ascended into an audible range: it was heavy and ponderous and classical, but older than anything truly "classical." It spoke of layers of stone and how they rumbled over one another, rising into hills and ridges and mountains, others plunging deeper, under the ocean floor, and into an endless molten sea.

The thick wall behind them cracked.

Eliot's song layered chords of bass notes over one another.

The earth beneath Fiona's feet shifted and plumes of dust shot up from the fissures.

"He's doing it," Jezebel whispered, her eyes wide with wonder.

Sealiah did not look so enthusiastic, frowning as she nodded at her Tower Grave. "My personal guards have failed us," she said.

A dragon within the tower poked its snout though the hole, and then pushed through the tower's wall, demolishing that section. The tower shuddered—base to steeple—and a thousand skulls rained down, clattering and shattering.

Another dragon pushed out after the first, casting its head about, and then fixed its dark stare at them.

Fiona braced, and drew her chain between her hands, ready to fight that thing . . . although not quite sure how she was going to fight something *that* big . . . let alone *two* such monsters at once.

"I will go," Jezebel said. She drew in a breath, trembled, and then she whispered to her Queen, "It is time."

Sealiah gazed at her protégée with what might have been called "pity" on a normal person, but on the Infernal's perfect features it looked alien.

Fiona was about to interrupt this little moment between them—those dragons were slinking closer, moving faster, sniffing and snorting, growing excited.

The Queen, however, stroked Jezebel's face and kissed her on the cheek. Whatever trace of pity that had been on Sealiah's features vanished. "Do what you must."

Jezebel looked over at Eliot once—then whirled about and strode toward the dragons.

Despite the eminent danger, Fiona paused. The skin at the base of her spine crawled. Something just occurred between Jezebel and Sealiah that had zero to do with this fight—something wrong.

"Hey!" Fiona said, and started after Jezebel.

Sealiah held out a slender arm to block her. "You belong by your brother's side. He is the only thing that matters now."

Jezebel crossed the courtyard toward the Tower Grave. She called to a dozen knights finishing off a squad of patchwork men. They came to her, lances at the ready, and together approached the shadow dragons.

Jezebel shifted form, tiny curled horns pushed out of her head, wings sprouted though slits on her armor, and claws grew out holes in the tips of her gauntlets, but it wasn't like gym class. She remained human size.

Eliot's fingers danced up in scale, the notes came faster, and he transitioned from a major key and an orderly Baroque cadence to a minor, insistent beat.

The ground splintered. Deep within the mesa came a grinding as stone stressed and then shattered with an agonizing noise that was oddly in harmony with Eliot's song.

Meanwhile, the dragons decimated Jezebel's knights—but even as they were ripped to pieces, Jezebel took a lance and stabbed one in its throat.

Fiona moved to join her. She had to help her. Sealiah couldn't stop her this time.

Eliot, however, did.

The mesa shifted . . . the *whole* mesa.

The ground under her dropped six feet. Fiona tumbled, and Robert caught her.

Dust exploded from the cracks about them.

The mesa tilted. The outer wall on the other side of the courtyard crumbled.

Then all motion stopped.

And so did Eliot. His hand rested on his guitar strings to still them. He sank to one knee and hung his head.

Fiona, Robert, and Mr. Welmann went to his side. Louis looked at the destruction and nodded appreciatively.

The knights fighting rallied, reorganized, and drove many of the shadows off the edge of the plateau.

"Should . . . do . . . it," Eliot said, exhausted. "All the tunnels are sealed."

But after he said this—an acre of ground of the far side of the courtyard fell away, taking tents and knights and shadows along with it.

"Okay . . ." Fiona held her breath waiting for more of the mesa to disintegrate . . . there were cracklings under her feet . . . but they slowed . . . and settled . . . and stopped. "Okay," she told Eliot. "That was pretty good."

There was a whoop of triumph, and Fiona looked up and found the source: Jezebel.

The Protector of the Burning Orchards and Handmaiden to the Mistress of Pain lifted the severed head of the last dragon over her head with both hands. She was drenched in black blood, her torso crisscrossed with claw marks, and a wild grin split her face. She let loose with another cry— part cheerleader whoop and part Viking war cry.

Behind her, the Tower Grave collapsed.

There were so many femurs and hips and ribs, so many skulls, it looked like the millions of bones fell in slow motion . . . even the large, fossilized, horned, several-ton dinosaur skulls from the apex tumbled through the air with a semblance of grace.

Eliot lunged forward.

Jezebel was so close. Any one of them could have crossed the distance between them in a few seconds.

But there wasn't a few seconds.

Fiona and Robert grabbed Eliot and held him back.

"No!" He struggled in their grasps.

Bones impacted and shattered about Jezebel. She looked surprised— whirled this way and that . . . and then realized what was happening. Too late.

One massive fossilized stone skull crushed Jezebel.

"No . . . ," Eliot whispered, and gripped Fiona tighter.

Fiona hadn't known how she felt about Jezebel. Was she a pawn of the Infernals? Or had she participated in their schemes to get Eliot with willful glee?

Fiona knew how Eliot had felt about her, though.

And seeing Jezebel killed in front of him while he could do nothing—that was the worst thing she could imagine happening to one person who loved another.

"Eliot," she said. "I—I'm sorry. So sorry."

She held him.

Louis came to them. "Alas," he murmured, "such is the agony of love and—"

Fiona glared at her father for his callousness. The look on his face, however, halted her from giving him the chewing out he deserved.

Louis's eyes were wide now. He was scared.

Not even when Fiona's mother had confronted him in that Del Sombra alley (and had been ready to kill him) had she seen her father scared.

What could possibly scare Lucifer, the Prince of Darkness?

She followed his gaze across the courtyard to where the wall had tumbled away.

Fiona saw the river valley beyond . . .

. . . and she instantly understood that the nightmare creatures that had crawled up through those tunnels and attacked them had been a diversion.

Covering the valley was a seething mass of shadow at least a hundred thousand strong, the full force of the enemy's army. Fiona's mind reeled at what she saw in the center of this: standing a hundred feet tall, a tower of blackness and blazing red eyes, was the shadows' lord and master— Mephistopheles.

75

BROKEN HEARTS OF HELL

The entirety of Hell and everyone in it—Fiona, Robert, Sealiah, Louis, and Mr. Welmann . . . along with the thousands of surviving knights upon the plateau—all of them blurred. Eliot's vision narrowed to a pinpoint on the girl he'd risked everything for.

He watched as the giant fossilized skull of the *Tyrannosaurus rex* plummeted toward where Jezebel stood unaware, smiling, her arms uplifted in her moment of triumph.

Eliot smiled. She looked so happy.

And then she was gone.

The skull had hit her and she vanished.

No. That was a lie his brain told him to keep him from going insane—but Eliot had learned to detect lies (even when lying to himself).

He *had* seen every moment: her arms and body crumpled and compacted, armor straps exploded, and bones snapped as the stone skull crushed her into the ground.

Eliot faltered and slumped into Fiona and Robert's grasp.

Where his heart had been, there was a hole now, gaping in his chest, crushed, cold, and empty, too. More agony than he thought he could feel poured forth from it, acrid and burning.

Jezebel was Infernal, though. She was in that impervious-looking armor. Maybe she was still alive.

Eliot's heart pounded with new hope. He had to get to her. He struggled free from Fiona and Robert and ran toward the ruins of the Grave Tower.

He kicked through the piles of femurs and ribs and stones and rusted

metal supports and halted before the giant skull. It wasn't like any *T. rex*
he'd ever read about. This one had horns. Its teeth curved up past the eye
sockets. It was solid fossilized agate and the size of a small house.

It had impacted the paving stones with force enough to embed two feet.
Completely unmovable.

Eliot saw a hand, too. At first he thought it was just another bone . . .
but with horror he realized it was actually the articulations and the joints of
an armored gauntlet.

Jezebel's hand. The only part of her not crushed under the stone.

He threw his body against the skull. It didn't budge.

He hammered on it with his fists. Useless.

Eliot fell to his knees by her hand and tried to remove the gauntlet, but
all did was cut his hands on the serrated metal. Her blood oozed through
the armored scales and mingled with his. It was still warm.

He had to get this thing off her. Maybe blast it off with Lady Dawn.

He didn't have the control for that, though. He could shatter the rock,
sure, but the force would kill her if she was still alive.

His hands clenched and unclenched, his frustration building. He'd
wanted that power. He had enjoyed destroying things in Costa Esmeralda.
But at this moment, he would've dashed the Lady Dawn guitar to a million
splinters to get back his old violin.

He didn't know what to do. A genius IQ and he couldn't think of a single thing.

Robert came to his side. "Whoa . . . ," he murmured, seeing the pro-
truding limb.

He pulled Eliot away. "Let me try," Robert told him, and then he drew
back his brass-knuckled fist.

Robert punched the skull three times, and when the dust cleared, he'd
broken the upper jaw and wrenched it away. He paused, seeing what was
there underneath . . . and the color drained from his features.

Eliot stepped closer, unsure of what he was seeing. There was so much
dust and dirt. The smell of vanilla and cinnamon and blood was thick in
the air.

Jezebel lay in the crater, unearthed from the waist up. Her armor had
protected her from the initial impact, but it hadn't been strong enough to
withstand the full weight of the stone; the metal had been squished to half
its former width . . . and bones and softer tissues poked out.

Eliot wanted to scream—but there was no air in his lungs.

ERIC NYLUND

Her arms and neck were at the wrong angles. Her skull was cracked. Like a doll that had been dashed to the ground, all the pieces were there, jumbled and wrong, and yet she was still somehow lovely to him.

Her hand twitched.

Eliot's shock vanished. He found he could breathe again. "Help me! She's alive!"

He knelt by her and, this time starting further up her arm, worked off her gauntlet.

Eliot took her hand in his.

There was a pulse. Faint and weak. But there. She *had* survived.

Her hand tightened about this. Her eyes fluttered open. Her mouth parted and blood spilled from her lips.

"Eliot . . ." The sound was so faint that he had to move so their faces almost touched to hear.

"I'm not going anywhere," he said. It took all his resolve to keep his voice from cracking. "Don't worry."

"You came back for me? I can't believe how stubborn . . . You are a fool. My fool."

She tried to laugh, but it came out as a ragged breath.

"Listen to me," she said. "They all want you. And if they can't get you, they will destroy you."

Eliot nodded. She was talking about the Infernals. Maybe the League, too. He knew all that. It didn't matter. Nothing did but her.

"We'll worry about that after we get you out."

Her split lips formed a smile. Her grip weakened.

"Nothing can save me, Eliot. My soul is rotten and belongs here in this darkness. I am part of this place—dead when I met you. Twice damned now."

"I don't care." He grasped her hand tighter. "Just stay with me."

"No . . . ," she mouthed. "No soul deserves a *third* chance. I'd just mess it up. I always have."

"But *I* need that chance with you," Eliot protested. "Us together, we can be stronger than all the others."

"No. Let me do this one thing for you. Let me go to my oblivion."

"I can't."

But even as Eliot held on tighter, her hand went limp. Her green eyes stared upward and reverted to their mortal blue as the animation faded from them . . . and she was dead.

Eliot shook her hand gently. "I'd do anything," he told her. "Please?" His vision blurred with tears. "Jezebel? Julie?"

He felt nothing . . . except the desire to lie next to her and die—so he wouldn't have to feel the pain he knew was coming . . . pain, heavy and cold, already filling the hollow spaces inside him . . . pain that would consume him.

How had this happened? They'd come so far—lost Amanda—risked everything to save Jezebel . . . and now she was gone?

Eliot refused to accept it.

But *was* she gone? What happened to the damned in Hell? They didn't die.

He blinked away the tears that threatened to spill down his face. There had to be a way to make her whole. Like jigsaw puzzle pieces jumbled in his mind—he knew there was an answer, he just had to look hard enough to find it. He couldn't give up.

The pain in his chest lightened. Hope. There was always hope, wasn't there?

He'd had seen Sealiah's soldiers blasted to bits, still moving. And those pieces tried to gather themselves back together. Why couldn't Jezebel come back?

Eliot reluctantly extracted his hand from hers, and with the greatest care folded it upon her chest.

Robert covered Jezebel with a knight's cloak. It was red with roses embroidered about the edges.

The others gathered about him. Fiona looked like she wanted to hug Eliot again—and as comforting as that might have been, Eliot needed answers more than anything else.

"What happens to the damned and Infernals when they get hurt?" he demanded of Sealiah.

Sealiah glanced at Jezebel with no expression, as if she looked at a piece of trash that needed sweeping up, beneath her consideration.

Eliot kept his anger in check, though, and asked, "They heal, don't they? No matter how bad their injuries?"

"Of course the damned come back," she told him. "Their torment *must* be eternal. But Jezebel is neither one of the damned dead nor a true Infernal. She is an elevated creature, born of my power, and as there is so little land and power left to me, her existence has been . . . snuffed."

Eliot took a step closer to the Poppy Queen. "There has to be a way."

Sealiah smiled at the challenge in his tone.

His blood burned and he struggled to keep his anger from rising. He took a deep breath, held it, and slowly exhaled.

He realized Sealiah hadn't answered his question about what happened to dead Infernals—but he had to keep his focus on Jezebel. She was the only thing that mattered.

"She's gone," Eliot whispered to her, "but there *is* a way to get her back, isn't there?"

Sealiah's smile vanished. "As I said, she is tied to my power and lands. Help me recover them."

Eliot pursed his lips. "I've already agreed to help you fight."

"You must do more than that, Eliot. You must fight *and* win. Do that and only then can I restore her."

He nodded. As if he had any choice now.

Sealiah moved off and shouted orders for her knights to gather weapons, ready artillery, and prepare for battle.

Eliot looked at Fiona. He needed his sister more than ever.

Fiona still looked uncertain. He didn't blame her. This was all part of a complicated Infernal plot—and they both knew it. For his part, however, it was a plot he'd walked into with open eyes to save Jezebel. For him there was no turning back.

He glanced at his father, who looked like he had something to say, but remained silent. He'd probably tell Eliot that there is no difference from someone in love and someone damned in Hell—eternal torment for both. Maybe he'd be right.

Fiona stood straighter and finally nodded.

She didn't have to say a thing. He knew she'd made up her mind to stay and help. Fiona would always be there for him.

He'd never take her for granted again. He'd never forget what he owed her.

Mr. Welmann ran his hand over his unshaven chin. A dozen expressions passed over his face and his forehead crinkled in deep thought. He caught Eliot's gaze, however, and nodded, too.

Robert wiped dirt and blood off his face and then spit. "This sucks," he told Eliot. "Let's just do it and get out of here." He glanced at the covered form of Jezebel. "Get you both out of here."

Eliot marveled at Robert's bravado as his friend assumed that they even had a chance outnumbered ten to one, and facing a fully powered Infernal Lord on the battlefield.

He gazed at where Jezebel lay. He wanted to sit next to her. But that wasn't going to get her back. Fighting—with as much power and ruthlessness as he could muster—smashing Sealiah's enemy and recapturing her lands—that brutal act was ironically the only way he'd be healed and whole once more.

Louis stepped forward. He smiled sympathetically as if it were an afterthought. He set his hands on Eliot's shoulders. "May we speak? Alone? Father to son?"

Eliot glanced over the edge of the plateau. Mephistopheles' armies moved closer. Eliot swallowed, trying to be brave as he listened to the enemy's thunderous approach.

"Make it quick," he said Louis.

Eliot braced himself for what he expected to be a speech from Louis about love, and lost love, and how all these things were parts of life, and he was really better off without women—like he needed a lecture in *that,* right now.

Instead Louis removed an envelope from the folds of his shirt. It was so worn, the paper was fuzzy. He handed it to Eliot.

Eliot accepted it. "What's this?"

"It is for your mother, should I not survive." Louis glanced about. "It was something that she ought to have taken from me in the first place."

The envelope was unsealed, and Louis hadn't said he couldn't look, so Eliot did.

Within were shreds of paper: newsprint and cereal-box cardboard and old phone bills.

Eliot cocked his head, uncertain what they were.

"My heart," Louis explained. "At least all that's left after your mother ripped it out and tore it to bits." He closed the envelope and set his hand over Eliot's. "I have a feeling you'll be seeing her after this . . . and I will not. Please."

Eliot didn't get it. Was this a metaphor? Or Louis playing another cruel joke on his mother?

He looked serious. Eliot detected no outright lie, either.

Eliot tucked the envelope into his pocket.

He had a million things to tell his father. He didn't know how to say them with any eloquence. But there was no time left.

"Look," Eliot whispered, "I just wanted to say you haven't been the world's greatest father. I wish you'd been there when we were growing up.

I guess I wish a lot things that will never happen now. Just be careful so there a chance we can get to know each other . . . after."

"I am always careful, Eliot," Louis whispered. "Especially in the matters of my own skin." He leaned closer. "Now, allow me to instruct you in the thirteen ways to avoid getting hit in battle. First there is the classic *Secret Principle of Cowardly Misdirection. . . .*"

Louis's voice faded as Sealiah approached them. Five people trailed behind her.

Louis cleared his throat, and continued, "As I was saying, be brave and give the enemy no quarter."

The people with Sealiah wore no armor and carried no weapons. There was a man with a guitar, a man holding a bass guitar, and one carrying bagpipes. (Eliot had only ever seen pictures of that instrument.) The last two, a man and a woman, had long wild hair and carried no instruments.

Sealiah halted before Eliot and gestured to these people with a wave of her hand. "Eliot, allow me to introduce Kurt, Sid, Bon, James, and Janis."

They bowed low before him.

"Uh, hi," Eliot said, and waved. "Who are they?" he asked.

The Queen of Poppies arched a long delicate eyebrow as if this were the stupidest question ever asked in all of Hell. "I would not send you into battle ill-prepared, my young Dux Bellorum. They are your band."[65]

---

65. Fans have speculated for decades who precisely composed Eliot's original band. While the surnames commonly mentioned match famous personas, one must not forget that Sealiah, the Queen of the Poppy Lands, was at that time responsible for the souls of those who had died from overdoses—a very large number of musicians, indeed. Eliot remained tight-lipped about the identities of his band members, not wanting their fans or families to unduly suffer, knowing they were in Hell. Still, fans wonder, and most would have "sold their souls" to hear them perform together. Having heard the band play firsthand, I can tell you that price would've been a bargain. *The Secret Red Diaries of Sarah Covington, Third Edition*, Sarah Covington, Mariposa Printers, Dublin.

76

LAST MOMENTS TOGETHER

Eliot felt broken inside and that broken part didn't care about anything anymore. But part of him wanted to scream and toss caution to the winds and play the heck out of Lady Dawn and smash Mephistopheles' armies to atoms.

. . . And maybe then Jezebel would be by his side.

Or was it being in Hell that made him feel that way? Maybe after this was over, he and Fiona and Robert should just go back to Paxington, hit the books, and figure out how to get through the rest of the school year without being killed, maimed, or flunking.

Eliot shook his head clear of those thoughts. He stood on a stage that had been set up near the edge of the mesa.

To the left, the land sheared away where he'd collapsed the tunnels. That now provided a way to the top of the plateau, a treacherously steep slope, but one soldiers and shadow creatures could rush up. He flushed with embarrassment that he'd caused this, but better that than letting the enemy crawl up through the middle of their defenses.

This was where Mephistopheles' armies would try to overwhelm Sealiah's forces—and it was where the Queen had concentrated her armies and artillery.

Archers and cannon had been positioned along the walls on either side of the slope. Industrial cranes dangled platforms piled with rubble—ready to release those loads and start an avalanche. Five hundred soldiers with rifle lances and tower shields formed a phalanx in the center of a breach. To either side, two thousand foot soldiers waited with ax and crossbow, net and pike. Mr. Welmann was there, too, with saber in hand and flintlock pistols tucked into his camo sweatpants. Behind them were the Poppy Queen's Calvary—three hundred mounted knights who could rush through the line and knock the enemy back . . . although Eliot thought this a measure of last defense, because once they charged down that steep hill, getting back up wouldn't be an easy option.

Eliot had read about every important battle, thanks to Audrey and Cee's homeschooling: Thermopylae, Waterloo, and Gettysburg. He remembered how high the casualties had been even for so-called victories.

Sealiah's defensive line looked solid, though.

But enough to win?

At the base of the Twelve Towers Mesa, shadows flitted, crisscrossed, and grew longer and darker until they reached the river in the valley. Beyond those riverbanks was a solid mass of black. Clouds the color of coal covered the sky and plunged this world into night.

Eliot put on his glasses, squinted, and caught glimpses of what moved in that darkness: large forms with haunches and pointed insect legs and blinking eyes that crawled over one another like it was all part of the same thing. The dark stretched to the horizon, endless and impenetrable.

Mephistopheles stood at the head of his ranks. The Infernal Lord rummbled within a swirling thunderhead that rose a hundred feet into the air. He was a giant flickering in and out of sight: an armored leg, a muscular arm, a barbed pitchfork the size of a telephone pole.

A pair of eyes, red and unblinking, stared back at Eliot from those clouds, two concentrated points of fury that meant to destroy them all.

Yeah . . . whatever.

As if Eliot hadn't seen *that* look a million times before from almost every relative he'd met since his fifteen birthday.

But this bravado was another lie. The truth was, he *was* scared.

It wasn't like when he had Fiona had fought Beelzebub. The Lord of All That Flies had been holding back because he'd wanted to take them alive. And he'd trounced them . . . up until Fiona had decapitated him with his own necklace.

This was entirely different: an Infernal Lord ready to battle, not holding anything back, with the full strength of an army at his back and drawing upon all the power of his lands in Hell.

Something inside Eliot wanted to curl up and hide.

He glanced at Fiona and Robert. They stood nearby onstage. Maybe

they all wanted to be close before the battle started. Of maybe it was because the stage had the best view. Or maybe it was because Fiona wanted
to be far from the Queen. (He had a feeling that if his sister wasn't about
to fight Mephistopheles, she'd be going at it with Sealiah.)

Fiona talked strategy with Robert—well, actually, they argued about the
hows and whys of the upcoming war like it was another gym match.

Eliot stroked Lady Dawn, his fingers magnetically drawn to her strings . . .
feather touches that make the lightest of notes. That steadied his nerves,
and he got a weird feeling it calmed Lady Dawn as well.

He took off his glasses and carefully put them away.

"Hey, man . . ."

Eliot turned. The guitarist Sealiah had called Kurt nodded through his
long hair at Lady Dawn. "That was cool, but you better plug in." He
hitched his thumb at the wall of amplifiers behind him.

Eliot shook his head.

Kurt looked confused; then he glanced at Lady Dawn and this gaze
wandered over her polished wood and brass fittings. "Got it," he whispered.
"You're the man. We'll jump in as soon as you go."

"Thanks," Eliot replied.

Kurt went back to the guy on bass, Sid, and the one with the bagpipe,
Bon. They murmured to one another, Sid looked at Eliot and then Lady
Dawn, and his upper lip curled in a half snarl and he nodded appreciatively.

Meanwhile, the singers, James and Janis, sauntered up to the microphones on either side of Eliot. James took off his shirt, tapped the mic, and
said, "Do your thing with the Lizard King." Janis smiled at Eliot and
mouthed, *It's cool, baby.*

He smiled back at him, but inside his stomach churned.

How was he supposed to play *with* these people when he had a hard
enough time just controlling his own music?

Fiona came to him, sparing a few uncertain glances at Eliot's band.

"Here's the plan," she whispered, all business. "Robert and I are going to
try a blitz to get to the rear of their lines after the initial clash. There
should be enough confusion for us to move quickly."

Eliot imagined his sister and Robert strolling casually past the thousands that would be trying to hack one another to bits.

"That's crazy," he told her.

"Sure it is," she replied, and frowned. "But I'm betting this is like any
other gym match."

Eliot gave her that special *you've hit your head* look that he saved for occasions like this. (Okay, there had never been an occasion like this before . . . but he gave her that look anyway.)

"I mean, there's a goal," Fiona said, exasperated that she had to spell it out for him. She nodded at the towering clouds that shrouded Mephistopheles.

"You've got to be kidding," Eliot said.

"We take him out and we're betting his army falls apart. It's simple."

"Okay, that makes a microscopic amount of sense," he told his sister. "If you *don't* consider that Mephistopheles is probably a bazillion times as powerful as Beelzebub was, has an army . . . and that we almost *lost* to Beelzebub back in Del Sombra."

Fiona crossed her arms and frowned. "Got a better plan? I'm listening."

Eliot thought about it. Yeah, sure, if Robert or Fiona could stop Mephistopheles, his army would scatter, scared by anything that could kill their Lord and Master. So it was a fine plan . . . provided they had a small tactical nuclear weapon with which to take out the Infernal.

But Eliot finally said, "I guess we go with your plan."

He resisted the urge to say *stupid plan*.

"I'll need your help," Fiona said. She bit her lip and glanced at his guitar. She always got weird when she talked about his music, as if it was something she didn't like or understand but nonetheless had to tolerate it. Like Cee's cooking.

Eliot guessed he felt the same way about her cutting. He suppressed a shiver.

"You're going to have to do something to help us get close to Mephistopheles," she said. "And when we get there, you'll have to weaken him . . . but in a way that doesn't blow us up or anything."

Eliot wasn't sure how it was to accomplish any of that; he was making this up as he went along. He just hoped he didn't get her or Robert killed.

"I'll do my best," he said.

They stood there. There was a long moment, awkward silence.

Eliot then looked Fiona square in the eyes. "I'm really sorry."

How to explain it? He wasn't sorry he'd come to save Jezebel. But he was sorry he had risked their lives. And he was sorry he'd gotten them into a jam with no way out except a bloody fight that might end get them tortured for all eternity if they lost.

She punched him in the shoulder. "What else was I going to do on Wednesday night except study for finals?"

Eliot tried to smile, failed, and shrugged. *"Trogium pulsatorium?"* he muttered.

That was the soft-bodied, wingless insect commonly called a "book-worm" (although technically it was a louse). This was a poor attempt at vocabulary insult, but it was all he had at the moment.

It was nice to have a moment of something normal between them. Maybe the last time that'd happen.

"Good one," she replied, and uncharacteristically offered no counter-insult. Instead she looked around and sobered. "Have you seen Louis?"

"Just a second ago. He was at the back of the lines."

Louis was no longer there, though, and Eliot wondered if his father would be fighting . . . or hiding?

Sealiah mounted the stairs to his stage and joined them. Tiny star-shaped orchids sprouted from the links in her armor and drizzled pollen, a cloak of wisteria-laden vines flowed behind her, and clouds of wasps circled high over her head.

Her perfume was intoxicating. Eliot felt dizzy and drowning, but he didn't mind.

She looked more beautiful than before, like a carving by Michelangelo, as if the impending battle and bloodshed brought out the best in the Infernal queen.

Eliot's band fell to their knees, and even Eliot felt obliged to give her a short bow.

Fiona stood with her hands on her hips.

"Soon it starts," Sealiah said to them. "There is a final detail to attend to. Mr. Farmington?"

Robert shucked on his Paxington jacket, came over, and gave her a short bow as well.

"While Eliot and Fiona have more formidable weapons than I could ever provide," Sealiah said as her gaze slid over the length of Robert. "You, my young hero, have only that toy." She nodded at the brass knuckles on his hands (the ones that could punch through solid stone).

Robert cupped his fist. "Yes ma'am." He flushed, but then recovered. "But I know how to use them."

"No doubt." She drew her broken sword and held it at an angle so Robert could see its jagged tip, the length of its patterned Damascus steel, and the poison that flowed and dripped onto the stage. "But would you accept the sword Saliceran and wield it in my name?"

Robert's eyes drank in the weapon, and his hand drifted toward the handle.

It was terrible. And powerful. Eliot didn't meet any special sense of magic to understand that. It was also something old. Something never meant to be touched by human hands.

"Don't," Fiona whispered.

Robert pursed his lips, and purposely *didn't* look at Fiona. "Thank you, ma'am. I'll take you up on that."

"Then kneel, hero," Sealiah commanded. Robert did. The Queen passed the sword down his left side, over his head (without touching the poisoned blade to his shoulders as was traditional) and then down his right side. "I declare you my champion on this battlefield. Rise, Sir Robert Farmington, Captain of the Legion of Lotus, and wielder of Saliceran, the God-Broken."

She gingerly turned the sword and Robert took it. He stared into the pattern of light and dark metal, fascinated.

Sealiah unbuckled the sword's sheath and handed it over. She then stood on her tiptoes and kissed Robert on both cheeks . . . and as she did so, looked at Fiona.

Fiona glowered and her hands clenched.

Sealiah then stiffened and looked across the Valley. "Ready yourselves," she told them. "Destroy everything you touch."

And with that, she strode back to her army.

"Why'd you take that thing?" Fiona rasped at Robert.

Robert turned from her. "Why not?"

Fiona's mouth opened and she stared at him. "Why? Let try: *it's evil?* A gift from an Infernal? Come on, Robert! It's a trick."

"Is it a trick," Robert said, "that the Queen gave me something that might save my life out there?" He turned back and met Fiona's eyes. "Maybe it bugs you because it levels the playing field between you and me, huh?"

"What's *that* supposed to mean?"

"It means you've enjoyed bossing everyone around all year. That now that I have some power of my own"—he shook the sword—"you don't like it."

"You don't know what you're talking about," she said through clenched teeth.

Eliot wanted to step between them, say something, and fix this. He knew better, though. They'd just focus all their unresolved issues on him— and that wouldn't do *anyone* any good.

It was *so* obvious they cared for each other. Equally obvious that they didn't understand each other.

Fiona had all this power, but more than that, she had all the responsibility that went with that power and being Team Captain and a goddess in the League of Immortals. She felt like she had to protect everyone and win every fight. She'd forgotten that she wasn't alone.

And Robert? He just wanted to be near Fiona. Surrounded by Immortals and magical families, Eliot could only guess how inadequate he must feel—especially after he'd been fired by the League.

Eliot felt sorry for them.

Robert loved his sister. Fiona probably loved Robert, too, despite her recent dates with Mitch Stephenson. Mitch was nice, had magic, prestige, and was the most well-mannered guy Eliot had ever met . . . but he wasn't Robert. He'd never be the first person Fiona had fallen for.

Robert ducked his head as if he was about to apologize—but the poison dripping off Saliceran smoldered and bust into crackling blue flames.[66]

Fiona backed off three steps. Robert, too, as he held out the sword at arm's length.

"That's different," he whispered.

He sheathed the broken, flaming blade. It extinguished with a sizzle.

Robert and Fiona looked at one another, their anger suddenly quenched as well.

Fiona reached out for Robert. Her brow scrunched together, as she tried to say something.

Which was when Eliot heard the roar of the Mephistopheles' army—a hundred thousand strong—as they charged across the valley.

---

66. The magical nature of the God-broken sword, Saliceran, mirrors the heart of its wielder. When held by Infernals, it drips poisons with a wide variety of effects (most involve a painful, lingering death). In the hands a true hero with a noble purpose, it glows or flames. Other accounts have the weapon singing, and even fighting on its own. Of course, it's most unspeakable incarnation manifested at the end of the Fifth Celestial Age when wielded by one of the Immortal–angel hybrid Post progeny. *Gods of the First and Twenty-first Century, Volume 13, Infernal Forces.* Zypheron Press Ltd., Eighth Edition.

77

TIDE OF BATTLE

Eliot almost dropped Lady Dawn. Nothing had prepared him for tens of thousands of screaming patchwork men, roaring beasts, and buzzing insects that filled the valley and echoed off the mesa.

Robert and Fiona took a step toward that battle cry. How could they be so brave? Was that courage or crazy?

This was Eliot's fight, if anyone's, and he felt shaken to the core by that sound . . . not drawn to the battle. His cheeks heated with shame.

Fiona turned to him. "We have to go. Do what you can."

Her face was lined with worry, but then it hardened as her thoughts focused to what Eliot's had come to know as her "cutting" mind-set.

Robert clasped Eliot's forearm, said nothing—just gave him a nod.

Fiona and Robert raced toward Sealiah's defensive lines and vanished in the crowds.

Eliot took a deep breath to steady himself. They were counting on him. He faced his band. "Just follow me," he said.

Kurt, Sid, and Bon nodded. James and Janis cleared their throats and grabbed their microphones.

Eliot would try something soft to start with, try to quell the violent noise from the opposing army and drain their fury. He wasn't sure how to do that, though; so he tried a few simple notes to feel his way forward.

Sid jumped in right after him on his bass, the beat too fast.

Kurt followed, then stopped as their notes clashed and he realized that wasn't where Eliot was headed.

Bon released his bagpipe's mouthpiece, looking disgusted.

"Hang on," Eliot said. "This isn't working."

And why should it? They'd never played together before. Eliot had never played with *anyone* before.

He looked over the edge of the mesa. In the vanguard of Mephistopheles' charging army were black-and-blue splotched dinosaurs—velociraptors, an *Allosaurus,* and a *Tyrannosaurus* that sprinted ahead. A good (if not terrifying) choice. If Eliot could have formed anything from the shadows, a few hundred tons of razor-clawed killing machines would have been his pick as well. They'd tear though Sealiah's phalanx.

Behind the extinct reptiles ran centaurs (patchwork men stitched together with their own horses), legions of axmen, sinuous panthers, and truck-sized ants with huge mandibles.

The giant Mephistopheles extended his hand from the thunderheads swirling about him. He stabbed with his massive pitchfork into the river, and the water froze about it—the river crackling and turning to ice along its entire length.

The Infernal Lord left his weapon there. Smoke in the air materialized into a *new* pitchfork, and he led his reserve forces across the now-solid river.

Eliot blinked and forced himself to look from the monster. He ran his hand over Lady Dawn's smooth wood grain. He had to focus on what he was good at: Making things happen with his music.

His band looked worried, but also eager to try.

"Follow this," he told them. "Sid, you first."

Sid's lip curled back, half smile, half grimace.

Eliot started with the first music he'd learned: the simple "Mortal's Coil."

Five notes in and Sid jumped in with the beat. He got it perfect and bobbed his head to the rhythm.

Eliot imagined six kids running around a Maypole, laughing and singing. He took it as a good sign.

He nodded at Kurt, who joined him, perfectly matching Eliot's notes.

Then Bon added to the song with a low moan from his bagpipes.

Janis and James start to sing, both a little dissonant, but together harmonizing:

> Girls and boys run too fast
> wheel o' life never lasts

grown up and knowing sin
that's when fun really begins!

Eliot picked up the pace, changed the tone from light to dark—and his band followed as neatly as if they were linked and he'd yanked them along.

The image of a Maypole danced in his mind, and all of them pranced around it, the colored ribbons tangled about the pole and their hands.

Eliot felt like they had been bound to his music and his will.

That was creepy. But okay, for now, because it was also extraordinarily useful.

He glanced at Sealiah's defenders bracing on the edge of the mesa. The phalanx tightened their formation. Archers clustered about lit braziers and readied bows.

At the very edges of her army, Eliot spied his father, dressed in black leather and holding two curved swords. He grinned, stepped to the shadows, and could no longer be seen.

So Louis wasn't a complete cheater and coward. He *was* going to fight. There was more to his father that Eliot had realized.

The Queen's personal knights made a ring about her as she knelt and touched the earth. The ground moved; roots appeared from her fingertips. A shudder ran through the mesa.

Several men on the walls shouted and pointed below.

Along the steep slope and about the base of the mesa, vines wormed to the surface, coiled and uncoiled and sprouted fleshy leaves that split into Venus flytraps large enough to snap up a cow. Along every branch extruded spikes that oozed sap. The vegetation grew and piled up on itself until it was high as a man and wider than a two-lane highway.

Sealiah collapsed, one hand forestalling her fall. Her knights came to help her, but she waved them off and shakily got to her feet.

The shadow dinosaurs hit this wall of thorns—impaled on the living spikes, they died there. But more came, and leaped upon the backs of their fallen numbers—and hurtled over the barrier.

Behind them, the centaurs and axmen hacked at the vegetation, some throwing themselves on the tangles to become bridges.

"Light arrows!" Sealiah cried.

Her archers lit arrows, notched them, and pulled back their long bows.

"Fire!" she commanded.

A cloud of spiraling flame rose into the air, over the defenders, and down the slopes—hitting the charging dinosaurs, felling them by the dozens—and more arrows plunking farther down the steep banks—lighting the wall of vines.

The sap ignited and flared like napalm, sputtering from the plants. The coils of vegetation blazed.

A thousand of Mephistopheles' warriors writhed and cooked in the tangles. Their screams mingled with the smoke filling the air.

There were, however, thousands more behind them, all pushing forward. They threw themselves on fire by the hundreds to smother the flames; others slashed at the vines while hands and arms blistered and burned.

The enemy breached the wall of flaming thorns, streamed though, pushing and cutting, and made the way larger.

Eliot cranked the gain on Lady Dawn to the sixth notch. He nodded with grim determination at his band. They nodded back, understanding they had to do more.

He belted out the opening chord of "The March of the Suicide Queen," curdling the notes with a heavy metal edge.

After a beat, his band joined him. A wall of sound erupted from the amplifiers.

James and Janis sang:

> Show no mercy
> Ask no quarter.
> Rivers of blood
> blade and mortar.

Eliot pumped his arm, feeling the hoofbeats of his summoned cavalry; the bass punctuated the air with the echoes of cannon shot, sustained by a long wail from Bon's bagpipes and James and Janis . . . that became the battle cry of the dead Napoleonic soldiers—

—as they materialized, marching forth upon the steep slopes between Sealiah and Mephistopheles' forces.

French horsemen lowered their visors and set their lances; riflemen stopped in an orderly line and leveled their muskets, men wheeled cannons into place, aimed high, and lit fuses. Musket shot and cannonball and flashing hooves and sabers cut down the onrushing hordes of darkness.

They clashed and fought and died—on both sides—by the hundreds. The slope grew muddy and slick with blood.

Eliot and his band played on.

More soldiers appeared and fought, and screamed, and died for him.

Not enough, though.

Mephistopheles and the vast bulk of his remaining army reached the base of the mesa. The clouds darkened.

Patchwork soldiers and giant ants tore through Eliot's exhausted army.

Eliot stopped playing. His arm was numb, and he felt as if he'd run out of notes in the song. There had to be some limit on how many ghosts he could raise.

A hundred centaurs broke though and charged Sealiah's phalanx.

The Queen's warriors set their rifle lances.

The centaurs fell upon them, hacked and clawed—but their assault was thrown back and they tumbled down the slope.

Archers rained death on the enemy as their ranks slipped and struggled in the mud.

The glowing red eyes of the Infernal Lord surveyed the terrain, and his terrible tactical situation. Mephistopheles thrust his pitchfork into the ground and it crackled and frosted, spreading up the hillside, freezing bodies and streams of blood in place, turning the landscape into a gruesome collection of solid shadow, contorted anatomy, and broken weapons.

The Infernal shouted, and it sounded like thunder.

His army roared in response—and charged up the hill with renewed strength.

Sealiah ordered the howitzers that squatted upon her walls to fire, and commanded the industrial cranes to tip their loads.

Eliot gaped as Mephistopheles' armies stumbled and faltered. Shells exploded about them; tumbling rocks and debris crushed them; clouds of arrows pierced them.

Ten thousand lay destroyed before Sealiah's final defenses.

Mephistopheles raised his pitchfork, and with a low growl, motioned them away from the Twelve Towers Mesa.

His scattered forces, stopped, turned, and retreated.

Had Sealiah won?

Eliot had never imagined the tide of battle could have turned so fast.

The Queen of the Poppies moved to the front of her line. She called for a horse and an Andalusian mare was brought to her. She hoisted herself into the saddle and took up a rose-twinned lance.

"Trample their bones!" she shouted.

A cheer rose from her army. Sealiah's cavalry, the Knights of the Thorned Rose, joined her, and they charged at breakneck speed down the hillside. Soldiers and archers followed.

Eliot spied Mr. Welmann on horseback, too, a gun in one hand, a cutlass in the other.

He also spotted Robert and Fiona moving more cautiously down the treacherous slope, straight for Mephistopheles.

This was wrong. How had Mephistopheles, who had steadily won battle after battle and gained so much land, power, and troops . . . so badly miscalculated?

Sealiah should have stayed put, reloaded her artillery, and shored up her defenses.

But she'd sensed victory. She'd smelled blood.

Eliot smelled it as well and his pulse pounded. Bloodlust. It was intoxicating. It clouded his thinking.

And he bet Mephistopheles knew that, too.

Sealiah and her knights rode down and trampled everything in their path.

Mephistopheles and his armies retreated to the river's edge. The Infernal Lord grasped the pitchfork embedded in the ice, the one he had used earlier to freeze the river. With a crack, he pulled it free, shattering the frozen layer, sending a massive ripple up and down the length of the waterway.

Eliot didn't get it. He'd just *blocked* his own retreat.

Unless . . .

. . . this had been a lure to draw Sealiah out.

From the depths of the river for miles in both directions, shadow creatures and dripping patchwork men emerged onto the bank. Thousands of them appeared from their murky underwater hiding place—and they kept coming, drenched and nearly frozen . . . but ready to fight as they swelled the enemy's ranks.

Mephistopheles laughed. It was the sound of bones shattering and metal wrenching.

It made Eliot want to hide and close his eyes. It was as if everything he'd been through in the last year vanished; he was a little kid again hiding under the covers, afraid of the dark.

The two armies met on the slopes.

Sealiah's forces had momentum, but they were now vastly outnumbered.

They fought valiantly, slashing and shooting. The Poppy Queen's warriors pulled back into defensive circles—but they were no match for Mephistopheles as he laid waste to scores of knights with a single swipe of his pitchfork.

Queen Sealiah touched the earth and screamed her frustration.

It was frozen. Nothing could grow here.

Eliot snapped out of the terror that gripped him.

He shifted his mental gears and prepared to play his most powerful piece of music, "The Symphony of Existence." He'd jump to the last movement about the end of the world; he'd bring earthquake and floods.

And while he was sure that would work . . . wouldn't that destroy *both* sides down there? He had nowhere near the control he'd need to keep from killing Robert and Fiona, too.

Fiona, chain in hand, sliced her way through the shadow legions, moving toward the Infernal Lord.

All about her Eliot glimpsed flashes of silver—the lighting fast motions of two curved blades. It was Louis. He was there. Then not. Then back—stepping from shadow to shadow and never appearing in the between spaces. His father cut down patchwork soldier, panther, and the countless nameless things that rose from the dark to strike from behind at Fiona.

Without Fiona ever noticing.

She fought her way forward—to within a hundred yards of Mephistopheles.

Robert, however, got to him first. Saliceran blazed in his hand, and he didn't even have to touch the shadows to make them wither and die. Robert looked strong and courageous. He was the real hero here—not Eliot—no matter what pronouncements the League had made.

With that flaming sword, Robert might have a chance against a creature that was part shadow.

Eliot knew then how he could help.

He turned to his band. "I've got to play something . . . personal," he whispered.

"You play it, baby," Janis murmured and set her hands over her chest. "Go ahead and I'll sing my heart out for you."

The others in his banded nodded.

Eliot played "Julie's Song."

More than anything now he wanted to hear the hope in that song . . . and with luck, see the light that'd come with that hope. Light enough maybe to weaken the shadowy Mephistopheles.

He plunked out the notes slow and smooth, thinking about Julie's life and her pain and how it all ended.

Sid and Kurt joined him, adding a bittersweet rhythm. Bon let the bag-pipe sigh with remorse, and James and Janis let loose a lamentable wail.

Eliot wanted to cry. They'd gotten it. It was so sad.

Would it work, though? Julie was long gone. And even Jezebel existed no more—she'd been "snuffed." But that didn't mean Eliot's hope for her and him together had to die as well, did it? Could hope survive in Hell? Or was it supposed to be annihilated here the instant it was created?

No. He felt it—warmth and pain and longing that churned in his heart

In fact, he'd never felt more than he had now—maybe because it *was* impossible and doomed. Those things just made his hope stronger.

He turned her song around, struggled to move the notes upscale, bring-ing the story of Julie and her life back to the light.

The sky brightened.

Eliot played louder, building in complexity, building until he thought his heart would fill and burst.

Sid and Kurt belted out this new tune; Bon trilled triumph on his bag-pipes; Janis and James cried tears of joy.

Over the battlefield, clouds dissolved, and a beam with sunlight cut through the air. Where it struck the ground, the ice thawed. Where the light touched the shadow creatures—it obliterated them.

Mephistopheles paused from his slaughter.

He turned his red gaze at the sky, blinked, and nodded as if in appreci-ation.

He then stretched one hand toward the horizon.

A cracked moon rose over the distant hills, smoothly and silently crossed the cloud-covered sky . . . and interposed itself between the sun and the land. The sun's brilliance danced about the moon's circumference in a coronal display—and then dimmed.

Eliot stared, stunned.

An eclipse? He had to be kidding.

The Infernal Lord had the power to move planets in this world? How could *any* of them stand against that?

Fiona stopped her charge and gaped up in awe.

Robert, though, kept running. He screamed and closed in on Mephistopheles, Saliceran raised to strike him down.

The Infernal Lord of the House of Umbra narrowed his eyes with disdain. He tossed his pitchfork. The lance struck Robert—impaled him, and pinned him to the ground.

Robert lay there limp . . . and dead.

78

JUST THE TWO OF THEM

Fiona involuntarily clutched her stomach as if she'd been stuck. "No," she whimpered. Something that size impaling a human body—it would've shattered internal organs, broken the spine.

Robert was still. His blood pulsed out onto the ice.

Mephistopheles had killed him.

Robert had been her friend (although she hadn't let him be much of one) . . . and he'd so much more than a friend last summer. She'd only wanted to protect him and had pushed him away, replaced him with Mitch.

He'd been the one. The first boy she'd kissed and the first one she had had feelings for. The only one for her, hadn't he been? Now there'd never be a chance to explain any of this to him.

The hate and heat came, spreading through her—blood on fire, boiling into her extremities.

She'd see Mephistopheles dead at her feet.

Fiona pulled her chain taut. The air between its links crackled and screamed.

Mephistopheles turned back to her. His army moved toward Fiona, but he growled at them, and instead of charging her they spread out in a wide circle around them.

His meaning was clear: they'd fight, just the two of them.

Fiona barred her teeth. Perfect.

From the swirling smoke, a new pitchfork materialized in Mephistopheles' hands and he swiped at Fiona. It was huge. He couldn't miss.

She braced and held her cutting edge before her like a shield. It sliced though the first and second tine—but the last tine twisted under her edge and swept out her legs.

Fiona tumbled, bounced, but rolled to her feet. That blow should have snapped her shins like matchsticks, but her Infernal hate made her invulnerable.

Her vision tinged red with pulsing blood and rage. One thought throbbed in her mind with each heartbeat: *Kill.*

She swung her chain. It grew a dozen feet longer, links now the size of hubcaps and sharpening to twists of razor. She scrambled toward Mephistopheles.

He had a formed a new pitchfork and thrust it at her.

Fiona grasped her chain in the center and whirled both ends back and forth and cut his weapon to bits.

She gloated over that maneuver—for a split second.

Mephistopheles spun the shaft around and hammered her with the blunt end.

Fiona barely blocked with her forearm. The force sent her skittering back.

But it didn't even hurt.

She ran toward him, got close, and whipped her chain, letting it out to this full length. It wrapped about his leg. She pulled.

It cut and came free.

The appendage fell away.

But Mephistopheles stepped onto a *new* leg that formed from the amputated stump; smoke and shadows becoming solid as Fiona watched. He seemed to shrink a tiny bit—not that that mattered: he was still ten times her size.

She stared, not believing it. Her rage cooled to confusion . . . and then fear.

He clubbed her with a gauntleted fist.

Fiona slammed into the ground, face first. Ice cracked and she struggled to rise from a spreading pool of her own spit and blood.

That she felt.

She shook her head and stood—

—in time for Mephistopheles to hit her again.

She'd done this before, though, fighting Mr. Ma, and her hands remembered, even if she didn't: they raised her chain—cut metal and flesh and the bones of Mephistopheles' armored hand.

Fiona grinned and felt satisfaction pulse though her. Ha! Let's see him hit her now without a weapon or a hand to wield it.

But in a heartbeat a fresh pitchfork appeared in Mephistopheles' other hand—and he jabbed—caught her square in her gut.

Ribs shattered. Fiona fell.

Pain blotted out everything: her rage . . . her grief . . . and her consciousness wavered.

He stood over her and set the butt end of his pitchfork on her body, immobilizing her against the ground.

"GO HOME," the Infernal Lord rumbled down at her.

He snagged her chain and flicked it far away.

Mephistopheles shrank to the size of a man.

"Whh-what?" she managed, although this brilliant reply took the last of her breath. Did she hear right? Was he telling her to leave and *not* killing her?

"This is not your fight, noble born," Mephistopheles said. "You are used and know it not."

Fiona didn't have her chain anymore—but her rubber band was still on her wrist.

She pull it out into a line, squirmed, turned and—

Mephistopheles slapped her square in the face.

Sensation left her body in a flash of black stars . . . until throbbing pain returned her to the shadowy world.

"Do not try my patience," Mephistopheles whispered. "Take your brother and withdraw."

Fiona's vision cleared.

The shadows and clouds and smoke about Mephistopheles were now wisps. He wore Maximilian armor of thick cast iron, encrusted with spikes and scratched by countless claws. His helmet had horns and a stylized hawk's beak.

"Why would you let us go?"

"Question not the quality of my mercy," he told her.

Fiona should have marched off the battlefield, grateful for *any* mercy, but she felt a flicker of her old anger. "You killed Robert. And Jezebel."

"I tried not to," he said. "I know what they meant to you and Eliot. It was never my intention for you to suffer."

Wait. . . . He knew who they were? That Eliot had a thing for Jezebel?

His voice was different, too. It no longer rumbled with thunder. It was kind of . . . ordinary.

Mephistopheles removed his horned helmet.

Fiona felt as if she'd been struck again—this time right between her eyes—because she found herself unable to understand what she saw. Standing before her, looking sad and tired, but just as she'd seen him last a few weeks ago with his tousled brown hair and perpetual smile . . . was Mitch Stephenson.

79

ONE IN A MILLION

Robert! Wake up!"

"Five more minutes," Robert muttered. He'd gotten twisted in the bedsheets; they'd wrapped around him like a python. He'd deal with that when he got up for work.

"Robert! *Now*—unless you want to die in Hell!"

Robert remembered. Hell. The kind with lava and armies of damned souls.

His eyes snapped open, and he was wide awake.

Marcus stood over him. He held a saber in one hand, and flintlock pistol in the other—slashing one of Mephistopheles' sewn-together soldiers—blasting another guy in the face.

Shouts and screams and explosions rang out around him.

"Rise and shine," Marcus yelled.

Robert blinked and straightened the facts out in his buzzing brain. Not in bed. Not in sixth grade, as he was dreaming. He was in Hell fighting a war . . . which he'd thought they were winning when the tables suddenly turned. Got it.

He tried to stand, but a giant fork pinned him to the frozen ground. The haft was the size of a telephone pole. It was cast iron and must have weighed a ton.

And Mephistopheles had tossed that thing like it was a cardboard tube.

Robert wriggled; that hurt, and the pitchfork didn't budge. The outer and middle tines had torn into his sides, a tight fit—right up to the rib cage.

Only then did Robert see how close a fit it'd been. A smidge to the right or left and those pitchfork tines would have skewered his liver, heart, and spine.

Had it been a one-in-a-million lucky shot? Or had the Infernal missed on purpose?

Luck, he decided.

He grimaced at his wounds. They were two deep slices on his sides, but no arteries or organs had been punctured. He brought his blooded fingers to his nose.

The stuff smelled of brimstone and spice. It reeked of Mr. Mime's Soma.

He looked back at the cuts. They'd sealed. The skin had scarred over . . . and those scars already fading.

What had Henry done to him? And how did Robert get *more* of that Soma stuff?

His gaze lit on the broken sword on ground. Saliceran. The Sword of Sealiah's champion.

He tried to grab it—just out of his reach.

He stretched . . . ripped open his wounds . . . and touched it.

The blade flared with light and dripped fire.

He set the sword on the cast iron and the pitchfork turned to ash as if it were paper under a blowtorch.

"A hand here?" Marcus said as he tried to pull his saber from the chest of a patchwork soldier. The soldier, however, held on to blade with both hands.

Marcus's AD/DC T-shirt was ripped down to his love handles, and he had cuts on his arm, but he laughed as he twisted the saber free, and kicked the soldier down.

He was enjoying this, but he wasn't watching: three more guys and a pair of gorillas charged him from behind.

Robert jumped to his feet.

He slashed in a wide circle. The flames of Saliceran were so hot, the patchwork soldiers burst into flames without being touched. Shadow creatures winked out of existence with hissing screams.

"Looks like you got it all under control," Robert told his former mentor.

Around them, knights fought from horseback and on foot against soldiers and black elephants, velociraptors, giant crabs, and armored centipedes.

"No sweat," Marcus muttered.

Robert figured he was going to die here. It was one of those things that just came to you with complete certainty—like knowing who was calling on the phone or betting the bank on that inside straight. That was okay . . . as long as his death meant getting Fiona and Eliot getting out of here in one piece.

Saliceran burned brighter than ever, magnesium–white hot in his gasp, but it didn't singe a hair on his body.

He turned to Marcus. "Where is she?"

Marcus understood exactly who he meant. He nodded across the field.

Past a hundred soldiers and a dozen of Sealiah's knights fighting to stay on their horses, there was a ring of those shadow gorillas—and past them stood Mephistopheles in a clearing. He had his back to Robert. He wasn't so tall as Robert remembered, but still three time the size of a professional wrestler.

And through the fighting and bodies and bloodshed, Robert caught a glimpse of Fiona on the ground, struggling to get to her knees . . . as Mephistopheles strode toward her.

He couldn't believe she'd been stupid enough to fight that thing without his help. She always thought she was better than him—than everyone.

Robert would show her, though; he'd save her . . . and what?

Nothing. He wouldn't say a word. He had nothing to prove to Fiona.

He just wanted her safe.

Marcus grabbed Robert's shoulder. "You can't," he said, guessing his intention. "That's an Infernal Lord on his own land. Fiona *might* have a chance. Maybe Lucifer or Sealiah or even Eliot. But you? No way."

Robert shrugged off Marcus's hand.

He was about to tell him what he could do with his warning when he heard Eliot's music . . . close . . . swelling through the air and up to the sun.

Robert looked—blinked as he saw the sun in eclipse, blinked again as solar flares lanced from the edge of the dark disk, and the star swelled along with Eliot's song, growing larger and orange, then became a red giant star, flooding the battlefield with its blood-colored light.

Eliot did that.

Robert stared dumbstruck, trying to figure what kind of power that took.

Across the battlefield Mephistopheles' soldiers panicked and the shadows cringed.

And Robert knew he had his chance.

He charged; slashing and burning through the soldiers and blasting any shadow that stood between him and Fiona. A spear grazed his back, but he ignored it, ran forward—and broke into the clearing.

Twenty paces away, Mephistopheles stood over Fiona, his back to Robert.

The Infernal reached for Fiona.

She was on her knees, one had outstretched before her to ward him off. She wasn't fighting. She looked frail and beaten.

One quick grab, and Mephistopheles would snap Fiona's neck.

Robert couldn't cross the distance between them in time. He hefted Saliceran and hoped it was his day for one-in-a-million shots.

With both hands, he raised the jagged, broken blade over his head.

As hard as he could, he threw it.

THE LAST MOMENT WHEN EVERYTHING WAS STILL POSSIBLE

Knights and shadow creatures hacked one another to pieces, but Mephistopheles' army had encircled and guarded him and Fiona (a relatively easy thing . . . because they were trouncing Sealiah's soldiers).

Fiona sat with in a clearing twenty paces across: a spot of peace among the chaos and bloodshed—not that *that* made figuring out what she was seeing any easier.

"This is a trick," she whispered to the thing that looked like Mitch.

Mitch was from the Stephenson family, wielders of white magic, and *enemies* of the Infernals. How could he be in Hell? He'd told her that he had to deal with "family matters . . ." that was back in Germany, wasn't it?

"It *was* a trick," Mitch—or Mephistopheles—or whatever he was said. "At least in the beginning." He held up a hand and indicated the war. "All this, a plan concocted by the Infernal Board of Directors to draw the offspring of Atropos and Lucifer into our influence."

Fiona heard the words but they didn't make any sense. Her face contorted with confusion.

"It was actually your father's suggestion."

"Louis!"

Of course *that* made sense: him being the cause of their trouble. With all the restraint she could muster, however, she focused back on Infernal Lord standing in front of her. Fiona was going to ask how a war—of all stupid things—was supposed to get her and Eliot to *like* the Infernals.

Her mouth hung open, however, as the answer slammed into her brain.

She'd seen it happen: Eliot enraptured with Jezebel from day one at

Paxington—her injuries during the school year calculated to yield the maximum sympathy—his rushing to her rescue like an idiot—Eliot almost gambling his life and soul away for her—and her "tragic" loss an hour ago at the tower.

The heroic drama would be irresistible to Eliot; that, and the honey-dipped, platinum-bleached bait.

Mephistopheles nodded as he saw her get it.

"What about me?" she asked.

If Jezebel had pulled Eliot into this, how was Mitch supposed to have gotten her involved? They'd been friends . . . he'd taken her on those wondrous walks . . . and there'd been that kiss. There could have been a lot more, too. Fiona had been willing and ready, but it'd been Mitch who'd stopped.

"I was supposed to bring you in," he told her with a sigh. "Everything fell into place. The Stephenson boy was going to Paxington. I have a connection with their clan from the time of Dr. Faustus, so I approached him."[67]

"You killed him?"

"No . . . and yes," Mephistopheles said slowly as if he were explaining this to a child. "Young Master Stephenson saw the wisdom of an alliance. I could help him in school and he would succeed beyond his wildest expectations."

Fiona shook her head. Mitch would have never done that.

But what Paxington student *wouldn't* have jumped at the chance at passing their classes—guaranteed? Mitch had been the only boy at school not obsessed with winning . . . but maybe that's because he knew he already would.

---

67. The first printed Faust legend is *Historia von D. Johann Fausten* (1587) written by an anonymous German author. The publisher Johann Spies (1540–1623), however, claimed the chapbook was culled from the journal of the original Dr. Faustus. He explains that Faustus ritualistically invited the Devil to reside within him, so that the Devil could share mortal experiences (such as love), while he would gain Infernal knowledge. In a note scribbled on his first draft—Christopher Marlowe (1564–1593), author of the English *The Tragical History of Doctor Faustus*, claimed to have used the same ritual. Marlowe was reputedly an atheist, and while awaiting trial for heresy, Marlowe died. Numerous accounts say that he was killed in a drunken brawl, assassinated, while some claim that he stepped into a shadow and was never seen again. Marlowe was buried in an unmarked grave at St. Nicholas, Deptford, so this later assertion cannot be disproved. The Journal of Dr. Faustus resides in the Beezle Collection, part of the Taylor Institution Library Rare Book collection, Oxford University, and may be viewed only by special permission from the Stephenson Family Trust. *Golden's Guide to Extraordinary Books*, Victor Golden, 1958, Oxford.

"All he had to do was let me possess him—but as deep a possession as our kind can commit to with mortals to avoid detection of the other Immortals. It is a melding of personality and souls."

"So you're Mephistopheles *and* Mitch?"

"Yes." Mephistopheles examined his bare hand. "But in truth, very much more of one . . . and very little of the other."

Her stomach twisted. She had kissed him! The thing that had fangs and claws and had been a hundred-foot tall monster. She struggled to push down her rising bile.

Months ago Mitch had used white magic in that alley by Paxington to repel shadows creatures. He'd looked pained, and she'd thought then it had been the strain of producing such a powerful magic. But that hadn't been it at all. The white magic had burned him because he was part, or mostly, Infernal.

Fiona wasn't strong enough to stand . . . so she scooched back from him. "Was *everything* you said to me this past year a lie?"

She bet normal girls didn't have to go through this when they broke up with their boyfriends. A little shouting, some hurt feelings, and it was over. Not a full-scale war; fighting with your about-to-be-ex until he almost kills you; and having thousands of broken, damned souls lament along with you.

Lucky her.

Mephistopheles looked as if she'd struck him. "I have *never* lied to you, Fiona."

Fiona looked into his smoky brown eyes. She didn't believe that. . . .

He took a step closer. "Everything changed once I knew you. I could not use you and I would never endanger you." He glanced away. "So I left school to finish this war *without* your involvement, even if that meant losing my lands . . . and my life."

Fiona snorted. "Looks like you did okay to me."

Mitch smiled. It was the same smile that made her feel warm and loved, but there was an edge to it, something that reminded Fiona of a wolf.

Mitch's voice became deeper. "Sealiah lost focus on the war, obsessed with wooing Eliot to her side. She succeeded, but his help was too little, too late."

Eliot. And Robert.

Fiona had almost forgotten them, she was so engrossed in her own drama.

"Then why kill Robert?" she said, struggling to keep her voice from breaking with sorrow. "And why fight me if you cared so much?"

"I didn't realize it was you and Robert until too late. I mean, I knew . . . but the blood . . . when it burns . . ." Mephistopheles looked exasperated as he tried to explain. "I would have never consciously harmed you."

Fiona had felt that way before. When her blood ran hot—she could have killed without thinking.

But what about Robert? Dead on the field somewhere. How could she ever forgive that?

She couldn't. But she couldn't think about Robert anymore. Her blood would demand revenge . . . and that mustn't happen now—not when she was on the verge of being able to accept Mitch's mercy and get Eliot and herself out of here in one piece.

Oh, but Eliot! He'd never leave without his stupid Jezebel.

"Okay," she said, lost for a moment as she struggled to hold her anger in check. "You were attacked. You got hot. You defended yourself. I get that. But winning isn't everything."

Mephistopheles gazed down at her, suddenly wary. "What do you mean?"

"Can't you stop? Leave Sealiah one scrap of land so she can fix Jezebel?"

Mephistopheles looked like this was a bad joke—then his face fell. "For Eliot. Yes, as he goes, so do you."

Was that true? Would she stay and fight even now for Eliot? After she had been so badly beaten? Amanda and Robert were gone, and she was tired of always fighting. There'd been so much bloodshed. She was sometimes even tired of being Eliot's sister.

But that was the right thing to do. Family stuck together. No matter what.

Fiona looked up into Mitch's face. Even if it was Mephistopheles . . . it was Mitch Stephenson, too. She couldn't stop thinking of him as the boy she knew.

Eliot was playing his music again, that same song, the one full of hope. The sky brightened.

Mephistopheles winced, but he didn't notice the strange orange half light as he continued to stare into her eyes.

"Yes," Mephistopheles told her. "For *you* I would leave on the brink of my victory." He blinked, surprised by his own words. "What an impossible thing you have made possible."

An impossible thing: hope in Hell, and mercy in the depths of darkness.

."Thanks," she whispered.

The battle continued about them—shouts and gunfire and screams.

"I will leave," Mephistopheles said, "*if* you let me take you back to school. And if we can go back to being friends . . . perhaps growing into something more in time."

Him and her? Friends? More than that? After he had revealed what he was? After she'd seen him murder Robert? Taking his mercy and escaping Hell was one thing. Going back to the way things were? No way.

But would she have done any different in his place? Her Infernal blood on fire? She didn't know.

Fiona's head swam. This was so confusing. There were too many feelings to sort through . . . and since she'd cut herself, she didn't trust her feelings anymore. She actually felt as if she were balancing on her tiptoes—one tiny push either way and she'd land . . . but which way? Give in to her burning hate and avenge Robert? Or stay collected, make peace, and live to fight another day?

This was the same decision she'd been struggling with all year: choosing between Robert and Mitch (although right now *neither* seemed like the correct choice, because one was *dead,* and the other was *evil*).

But while she was trying to figure this out, Eliot and others were dying around her.

She could stop the fighting. She *had to* stop it. For all their sakes.

So she decided. She and Eliot would get out of here alive.

It was funny—she was about to make peace with an Infernal Lord, one who'd been part of a plot to get her on their side, one who'd walked away from those schemes to save her . . . and they'd both ended up *exactly* where the Infernals had originally wanted them to be.

"Delicious irony is ripe in the air," Mephistopheles whispered. "Let us not waste the moment." He offered her his hand. It was the hand without the gauntlet, the one she'd cut off, the one that had grown back—flesh and shadow: white smooth skin and long articulated fingers, reaching for hers.

"Come with me, Fiona. Come and we will walk and talk and be together."

The last thing in the world she wanted was to touch him . . . but something in her blood called to his blood. Like the bloodlust she'd felt before in battle . . . only this was far more passion than rage.

Fiona couldn't help herself.

Her hand was drawn to his. She dared to reach for him, fingers outstretched.

They touched and he pulled her up to stand with him.

There was heat and life and the world around them stilled.

All other thoughts of the battle and her exhaustion and grief stilled.

This was everything she'd wanted: a way to survive this war she'd been dragged into, and a way for Eliot to get his rotten girlfriend back so he wouldn't make *everyone* miserable for the rest of his life.

And Fiona would be with Mitch.

Her suspicions slipped away. Her pulse hammered in his chest and throat.

In her haze she saw them together—not because of any tricks, but because he'd been noble and protected her when everyone else in her life only wanted to use her. With their powers combined they could leave—go anywhere—do anything . . . even if that was simply go back to school and figure things out, one slow step at a time.

Fiona felt hope and happiness and knew everything was possible for them. It would be a moment she'd treasure and reflect upon every day for the rest of her life.

A sound intruded on their moment: a helicopter *whoop-whoop* of blades slicing the air—then metal screeching against metal.

Mitch stiffened. His face contorted with agony. A dent popped in the center of his chest plate—pushed out from the inside.

His hand jerked from hers. He turned.

A sword stuck out from his back.

Fiona stared, shocked, dumbfounded . . . as she recognized the weapon. It was the broken sword her father had tried to kill Beelzebub with, the same one Sealiah had given Robert. It penetrated Mitch's spine between his shoulder blades, and the Damascus steel dripped fire that transformed his black plate mail to ash.

He fell.

She caught him.

Robert stood at the edge of the clearing, staring at her and Mitch . . . looking triumphant . . . perplexed . . . and then shocked.

Robert was alive? But she'd seen him impaled.

Every shadow creature on the battlefield fell and dissolved under the brightening red sunlight.

Mitch coughed out smoke and embers. He and Fiona together sank to the ground. She turned him so he lay on his side in her lap.

Flames crackled and spread around the blade.

Fiona, horrified, reached for the handle to pull it out.

"No," Mitch rasped. "That blade destroys whatever it touches—using the power of its wielder, whatever that may be. Touch it and you will *cut* me to my core and kill me. I would not have that weight upon your soul."

"But you're going to die with that thing in you," she whispered.

The flames spread across his back. He shuddered with pain. He clutched her tighter. "Assassination," he said. "Backstabbing. It is our way. Even you, Fiona, played your unwitting part."

"Me?" She never wanted *this*. Fire licked Fiona's arm and she didn't feel it.

How had this happened? They had made their peace. It was all fixed. They'd be together and happy. But that one moment when nothing else mattered, when everything was still possible . . . now burned before her eyes.

"Sealiah found a hero and his lady in need of protecting," Mephistopheles whispered. "With the sun coaxed by hope, and with the God-broken Blade, she concocted a brilliant last-minute gambit." He chuckled. "Or perhaps she had it planned all along—the intricate, devious machinations of an Infernal. I have lost to a superior opponent."

"No!" Fiona cried. "Don't give up! Someone else can take the blade out."

The last shadow on the field dissolved under the sun as it fully emerged from the moon. The ice on the ground steamed.

"Too late," he told her. "The light has won this day. My time is over. Yours is just beginning, fair goddess. And our time, alas, was never to be." He reached up and touched the tears that streamed onto her cheeks. "Still . . . a fine death if it be in your arms."

"Fiona!" Robert cried.

She ignored him and held Mitch close. The flames rose higher and engulfed them both. Mitch held her. They burned together.

This wasn't happening. She wouldn't let go. Not ever.

The flames crackled with renewed intensity, they flared and sputtered and sparked. Fiona felt his strength fade . . . and his very touch dissolve to dust.

The fire guttered and died.

Mephistopheles' shadows were gone. His patchwork soldiers stumbled and fell apart. A mighty cheer rose from Sealiah's knights.

Fiona had nothing but an armful of ashes. She tried to hold them; they blew away. When she looked up, her vision blurry with tears, she saw Robert standing near.

Louis sauntered up, and his smile faded as he beheld Fiona and her blackened hands.

Eliot ran up to her as well—stopped short, seeing the sword and the ashes—having no clue what had happened, but able to read Fiona's pain.

And finally Sealiah and a retinue of knights approached. Where she stepped the soil churned with worms and roots and covered with flowering moss. She nodded at each of them, practically glowing with pleasure, and looking more regal and lovely than ever.

"The war is over," the Queen of Poppies announced. "The House of Umbra has fallen. We are victorious."

Fiona glared at them all—hating them more than she had anything, most of all Robert. She wanted to get up and cut them to pieces. The rage built within her until all she saw were red pulses.

But she held back.

Fighting without thinking—what had it cost her in blood and pain and the people she'd loved? That's how she'd gotten here in the first place. She vowed she wouldn't repeat that mistake.

It'd take time, but she had to consider what this meant to her. She wasn't sure what exactly she had to do first . . . but Fiona knew with all her heart and soul that *her* war with the Infernals had just begun.

INFERNAL LORD

By the time Eliot pushed and shoved his way past Sealiah's knights, all he saw was Fiona. Mephistopheles was gone.

Sealiah, Robert, Mr. Welmann, and even Louis were all there, staring at his sister.

Fire burned in Fiona's lap. The coals disintegrated to ash even has Eliot watched. The heat didn't seem to hurt Fiona or even scorch the shreds of her school skirt.

Eliot was about to ask her what had happened—but shut his mouth as his eyes met hers. They were red from crying and full of pain . . . and utter contempt for all of them.

Across the battlefield shadows dissolved and vanished; patchwork soldiers either fell apart, or they came to their senses and rejoined Sealiah's army.

The war was over.

Eliot wanted to shout in triumph, but his elation died as he glanced at Robert, who looked like he'd been hurt, covered in blood . . . but more than that, hurt on the inside. Mr. Welmann held him back from Fiona.

Eliot couldn't stand it. "Fiona," he whispered. "What happened?"

The fire in her lap guttered and went out. Fiona examined her ash-covered hands. She finally looked up at Eliot. He'd never seen her in such agony.

"It was Mitch," she said.

She had to be dazed. Eliot shook his head. "That's not possible. It was Mephistopheles."

In hushed tones, she explained exactly how it *was* possible. How Mephistopheles approached Mitch, the distant progeny of Dr. Faustus—how Mitch had let him in—how Mephistopheles purposely had *not* dragged them into this war . . . as it had been planned by Sealiah and Louis and the rest of the Infernal Board.

As she related this last bit, she glared at their father.

Louis rolled his eyes and made a gesture with his hands as if to say, *What exactly did you expect?*

Eliot had never suspected Mitch. He'd studied and fought by an Infernal all year and hadn't even sensed it? Eliot *had* known about Sealiah's part in this, though. Jezebel had admitted as much. That little truth and trust between them had made it all the more difficult to abandon her.

But the thing that really got to Eliot was how connected it at all been. The Infernal Board had been involved? His father?

"Mephistopheles had just agreed to leave Sealiah a bit of land," Fiona continued in a whisper. "He would have withdrawn. There could have been peace between everyone."

There was more to this she wasn't telling. Eliot picked up on it: how Fiona had liked Mitch . . . and how she'd been reaching out to him before Robert had struck him down. Things had been strained and awkward between Fiona and Robert before this. Now? There'd be a rift between them that'd never heal . . . because it wasn't just Mephistopheles who had been ready to leave the battle—Fiona had been ready to go *with* him.

"There would have been peace?" Sealiah said with a toss of her coppery hair. "Then disaster has been averted. An ignoble death for our opponent, and all's well that ends well."

Eliot felt Sealiah's power return in a tidal rush. Her connection reestablished to her lost domains . . . as well as Mephistopheles' now-conquered lands. A crown of woven thorns snaked through her hair and blossomed.

Fiona glared daggers at the Queen, which Sealiah ignored as she turned Robert. "And our thanks to you, my Champion. You have Our favor."

Robert nodded, accepting this "honor," and handed Sealiah back her sword's scabbard. All the color, however, drained from him as he took in Fiona's pained expression.

Sealiah retrieved Saliceran from where it lay in the dirt. She flicked the blade and char sloughed off. The Damascus steel once more wept poison, and fumed where this dripped upon the earth.

Sealiah put the sword away. Eliot shuddered at the wet scraping sound as it slid back into its sheath.

"There is still much to do," Sealiah told them, a smile spreading across her face. "There are the spoils of war. Celebrations. Honors and treasures to take!"

Fiona stood with great deliberation. She looked at them. Behind her gaze was unstoppable death. Hate rolled off her in waves.

She blinked, however, and looked away.

"*You* celebrate." She turned and walked off. "I've lost . . . everything."

No one followed her. No one said a thing.

Eliot knew that he should let her be. In her current emotional state, one wrong word could set her off. Better to let her cool and then they would talk.

But as much as he knew that was the logical thing to do, he couldn't let her suffer alone. He had to stand by her side as he always had for him. Cee had always said: they were stronger together.

"Fiona," he whispered, catching up to her. "Talk to me. Please."

She turned and examined him. There was no hate or pain in her eyes anymore, just a long thoughtful glance. She shook her head.

Had this been his fault? Certainly part of it had. If they hadn't come to Hell, Amanda would be alive, that's for sure. Sealiah would've lost the war, though, which meant Jezebel would've been dead—or worse. And Mitch . . . wasn't it better that they found out about him?

Either way, no matter what he would have done, *someone* lost.

And either way, one of the Infernals gained something: either Eliot helping Sealiah, or Fiona unknowingly falling in love with Mephistopheles.

"It's not your fault," Fiona whispered, guessing what he was thinking. "It's theirs." She nodded at the Queen and Louis. "The Infernals have used us from the start."

"Yeah," Eliot whispered back. "Maybe."

"They are evil," Fiona said. "We have to stop them."

He nodded.

And yet, Eliot wondered how different the Infernals were from the League. The Immortals manipulated them; they manipulated the entire world. What had happened in Costa Esmeralda had to be the tip of the iceberg.

"Eliot," Louis called. He made a come-hither gesture and pursed his lips tight to indicate some urgency.

"I better go see what he wants. Are you going to be okay?"

Fiona considered a moment. "No," she said. "But I'm not going to do anything rash. This is going to take a lot of thinking to figure out."

Eliot reached out and gave her elbow a squeeze. The corner of Fiona's mouth worked into a microscopic smile, then faltered and collapsed.

Something inside Eliot wanted to take his sister's hand and run as far and fast away from this place as he could. Everything was changing around them. Literally. The land thawed and grass pushed up from the earth. The sun shrank to a golden orb. Iron gray thunderheads lightened and spread across the sky in a silver layer of overcast.

There was more. He felt it. But he couldn't *understand* any of it yet.

"Eliot," Louis called.

Against his better instincts, Eliot jogged to his father.

Robert met him halfway. "How is she?" he asked. "I didn't know it was him."

He meant Mitch, or rather, Mephistopheles. Every trace of Robert's cool was gone. He looked worried and guilty and more than a little angry that he had supposedly delivered the winning blow in this war . . . and lost Fiona in the process.

"It looked like he was going to . . ." Robert's forehead creased. "I didn't know what he was going to do. I just knew that I had to stop him."

Eliot wondered for a split second—if Robert *had* known it was Mitch, would he have stopped and let him take Fiona? Or would he have still thrown the sword and killed him? No—he dismissed that idea. Robert didn't work like that.

"Fiona will be okay," Eliot told him. "She just has a lot to think about."

Robert took a step toward her.

"I wouldn't talk to her yet, though. Seriously."

Robert considered that, nodded, and wandered off.

Eliot finally got to Louis, who arched an eyebrow at how long it had taken him. He motioned for Eliot to stand before him, and Louis set his hands on Eliot's shoulders and angled him at Sealiah.

The Queen gave rapid orders to her knights: "Release any souls in thrall—those loyal to Mephistopheles grind up to replenish the land—send runners for engineers and gardeners—strengthen our borders or we may lose the edges."

Louis cleared his throat.

Sealiah turned and regarded Louis with distain.

"You," she murmured, ". . . are still here. Why?" Her gaze softened as she took in Eliot. "And my young Dux Bellorum who coaxed out the sun out and won the day. Worry not. Our Jezebel shall be reconstructed, lovelier than ever."

"I believe you said something about the 'spoils of war'?" Louis said.

Her face grew cold. "Did I?"

"As one of your generals," Louis said, "I claim my share in land."

Sealiah laughed. "Why not wish for the moon, Louis? You barely fought. It was Eliot, Fiona, and Robert who deserve the glory."

Louis shrugged. "Nonetheless, I played my part as your Dux Bellorum. It matters not the state of my cowardice or the quantity of blood spilled. I was here. I participated. I claim my right." His sly smile returned. "Unless you wish to renege? I could take my dispute to the Board."

Sealiah's red lips turned white. "Name the domain from our conquered enemy," she said. "But try not my patience, Deceiver."

"I would never dare such a thing," Louis replied with a nod. "I claim . . ." He cupped his crooked chin, thinking. "Just an acre or two from the Hysterical Kingdom—far from here, I assure you. The Mirrored City?"

Louis's gaze traveled to the ground and he licked his lips. He bent over and found a mass of twisted, charred cloth at their feet. "The small bit as well," he said to her. "After all, it was mine to begin with." He shook the tangle out and ashes filled the air. Eliot thought it might have been the remains of a black velvet cloak. Mephistopheles'? It was hard to tell.

"Done," Sealiah declared. "But take great care, Louis, not to push your city limits farther into the Hysterical Kingdom . . . which is now mine."[68]

Louis bowed low—but not so low that he took his eyes off her.

Sealiah blinked and turned back to her knights.

Louis cleared his throat again and gestured to Eliot, as if presenting him to the Queen for the first time.

---

68. Tectonic Theory of Infernal Dominions. The word *tectonic* normally pertains to either (1) construction or building or (2) relation to, causing, or resulting from structural deformation of the earth's crust. Infernal tectonics incorporates *both* definitions. The mythohistorical record provides evidence that the borders of Infernal Lords' domains expand and contract with their masters' power. The nature and reality of those realms are plastic, subject to the personal tastes (some would argue the psychosis) of their rulers; their borders, however, are not. These boundaries are subject to the *counter*pressure exerted by surrounding Infernal lands. Additionally, which realm borders which is not fixed, but dependent on political treaties, alliances, and vendettas. See additional entries on the higher-dimensional nature of the Infernal spaces for details. *Gods of the First and Twenty-first Century, Volume 13, Infernal Forces*. Zypheron Press Ltd., Eighth Edition.

Sealiah seemed to understand this and smiled.

Eliot shifted, uncomfortable under her smoldering gaze.

Sealiah said, "And what treasure do you wish, my young noble born?"

"What do I want? I don't—"

Louis poked a sharp fingernail into Eliot's back.

Eliot stood straighter. That hurt, but it'd been a clear warning. Something was going on here that he did not understand . . . something Infernal.

What *did* Eliot want? Sealiah had already told him she would heal Jezebel. That's what this had all been about: him and her. Right?

But it *wouldn't* just be him and Jezebel; she would always be Sealiah's protégée—her slave, actually.

Eliot felt sorry for Jezebel. He loved her, too. But the magnitude of political intrigue and her Infernal ties meant that they could never have a normal boyfriend-girlfriend relationship. If Sealiah ordered her later to stab Eliot in the back, he wasn't sure Jezebel could refuse.

Why was it so complicated?

He was missing something, though, right in front of him. He could feel it just out of his mental reach . . . at his fingertips . . . in the air around him . . . in the dirt under his sneakers.

Yes, the land.

He cocked his head back to his father. "Why did you want land?"

Louis smile seemed to melt from its usual mocking crookedness to something genuine. "Land is *everything.*" He gave a theatrical wave of his hand. "If I were you, I would pick a Dolorous Archipelago on the Mirrored Sea, next to my city."

"Quiet your wagging tongue, Louis." Sealiah's hand rested on the pommel of Saliceran. "Or I shall cut it out and feed it to my dogs."

Louis shut his mouth with an audible clack of teeth.

"You do not want land, Eliot," Sealiah told him as if he were a child about to stick his finger into a light socket. "It's a tremendous responsibility, one that would be impossible to manage while you were at school." She tapped her lower lip, considering. "Why not let me give you a mansion in San Francisco? One with swimming pools, game rooms, a kitchen, and a full staff?"

She sounded worried. Eliot had definitely stumbled onto something.

"Or a yacht," Sealiah continued. "Or a real, living band and a recording deal. You would be the next big thing. The whole world would flock to your concerts."

While Eliot had grown to appreciate having a band to play with, the thought of tens of thousands of people in an audience made his stomach churn.

What *was* he missing? Was what it about land that had everyone so worked up?

He knew it'd look strange, but was drawn to the earth, so he knelt and touched the dirt. There were worms and beetles and tiny bell-shaped flowers with blue veins that uncurled in the soil.

He remembered when he had touched the dirt through the Gates of Perdition—when Uncle Kino had ditched him and Fiona there. That earth had been dead, lifeless for a billion years . . . but there had been a "malleable" quality to it. It was hard to explain, just a feeling that he *could* make something out of it if he put his mind to it.

What Louis had said about land came rushing back to him: *"We are monarchs of the domains of Hell, the benevolent kings and queens over the countless souls who are drawn there to worship us. Without land, we would be the lowest of the low."*

"So," Eliot said, "if you own land in Hell, you're the king or queen of it? You control the souls there?"

"Land," Sealiah replied, "is what defines an Infernal Lord. And yes, the souls belong to you . . . but the damned are far more trouble and time than they are worth."

Fiona wandered back to where they stood.

"What's going on?" Fiona asked, concerned. She must have sensed the same "something" about to happen as Eliot had. The change in the land, and more than that, the change about to happen in Eliot.

He almost had all the pieces put together. What he wanted. How to save Jezebel. And, unfortunately, a string of consequences that he was sure he would have to pay for later.

"I can claim *any* piece of land?" he asked the Queen.

"Eliot," Fiona said, a warning edge to her voice. "If you're doing what I think you're doing—"

Sealiah held up one hand indicating that Fiona be quiet.

Louis's grip on his shoulders tightened, and Eliot was glad for the extra support as he felt his knees tremor. He was about to do the smartest and bravest thing—and possibly also the stupidest thing—he'd ever done.

"You may claim any land that *belonged to the enemy*," Sealiah corrected. Her tone was deadly serious.

"But," Eliot countered, "Mephistopheles conquered all these lands—right up to your Twelve Towers. So every piece of land here belonged to him."

"That is *technically* accurate," Sealiah said.

Eliot inhaled and then let out all the air, trying to steel himself.

The land. The power. The souls attached to the land. All dominoes set up and directed toward one inevitable conclusion—one that if he set in motion could not be undone.

But what else could he do? *Not* take the chance?

Not be the hero he'd always dreamed of?

No. He *had* to do this.

"Then," Eliot said, "I claim for my part in this war as your Dux Bellorum the realm of the Burning Orchards."

Sealiah's gaze held steady, but the slightest flicker of irritation crossed her eyes. "You have that right."

If Eliot had that land, he'd control all the souls therein . . . including Jezebel's, the Duchess of the Burning Orchards. He could set her free.

"No," Fiona whispered, horrified. "Eliot, you can't. That'd make you one of them."

"There's no other way," he said.

Fiona's features hardened. She looked at him as she had looked at their father, like Sealiah—like *he* was the enemy.

Sealiah crooked a half smile. "You have all that you could ever wish for now," she said. "Well played, Eliot Post . . . our newest Infernal Lord."

SECTION

VIII

GRADUATION

82

SECOND TIME IN THE HEADMISTRESS'S OFFICE

Light streamed through the wall of windows and lit the black-and-white checkerboard floor of Miss Westin's waiting room. It was ordinary sunlight, but Fiona winced at it. She wasn't used to real light yet.

Eliot sat on the padded lounge next to her. He squirmed in his school uniform, but then smoothed out the wrinkles and look halfway comfortable.

Fiona shifted uneasily in her uniform, too. Even one of Madame Cobweb's custom-fit creations felt wrong on her today.

Then again, *everything* felt wrong this morning.

She scooted away from Eliot and got out her phone. She checked the time: five minutes before their appointment. They were early for once.

Although this one time, she wouldn't have minded being late. Very late.

She checked the time again, though, just to be sure, because she didn't trust any clock since they'd been in the Poppy Lands. Fiona thought they had been there a day—two days, tops—while they got the railroad tracks fixed and then rode that creepy Night Train back to the Market Street BART Station.

But the time on Earth?

They'd been gone fifty-eight days. More than eight weeks.

Mr. Welmann told her before they left that time worked differently for the dead, and it worked very differently for the damned dead.

Great for them.

For the living, though—namely her, Eliot, and Robert—they'd missed most of spring semester, the last two matches in gym class, and finals . . . which was why Miss Westin had called them up to her clock-tower office.

Fiona had no doubt the Headmistress was going to fail them. She could see her chewing them out and then having Mr. Dells march them off campus and slam the gates shut on them.

She checked the time, scared that it'd somehow slip away from her again.

Four minutes to go.

She looked at her text messages. Nothing new . . . just that last message from Mitch—how he told her he had some family business to take care of (technically, not a lie).

She felt a twinge and something hollow where her stomach used to be as she remembered how he had taken her on magical walks . . . how she'd loved his company then . . . and that last moment together in Hell . . . and everything that *could've been* between them.

Before her ex-boyfriend had planted a sword in his back.

She pushed that thought aside. She had to focus on the disaster that was about to happen.

What was Audrey going to say when they got kicked out? And the League of Immortals? Their two new star members were going to flunk their first year.

Of course, Audrey hadn't even been home when they'd come back. Cee had been all over them, tried to feed them, coddle them, and then she'd told them that Audrey had heard what had happened. She'd gone to the League Council to decide what they were going to do.

Decide what they were going to do, that is, *without* her or Eliot's input. As usual.

She cast a sidelong glance at her brother. Time, however, hadn't been the only thing that had gotten away from her in Hell.

She'd lost a part of Eliot down there.

Okay—first off, she acknowledged that them missing school wasn't *entirely* his fault. There was no way he could have known about that time-in-Hell thing.

And it wasn't his fault that Amanda had exploded. No one could have seen that coming, either.

She swallowed, feeling as if she were still drowning in guilt about that, though.

But Eliot *had* made the choice to take a piece of the Infernals' lands and become the lord of that domain. No matter how small his land was . . . that still made him an Infernal Lord.

He'd gotten exactly what he set out to get: his evil, backstabbing, sort-of girlfriend was now free of Sealiah. Eliot would be able to handle *her* as well as he could control a runaway nuclear chain reaction with a pair of pliers and a screwdriver.

He was in way over his head.

And what was he going to tell Audrey? *Hi, Mom. Guess what happened while we ditched school? I joined your enemies, the fallen angels.*

And there he sat, looking as smug as if he'd just won seven rounds of vocabulary insult. His hair, uncut all year, was all curls and cowlicks, but he was finally able to pull back. Despite the astonishing and astronomical odds against it, Eliot almost looked cool.

Crazy. This entire situation.

Maybe Uncle Henry could help her slip Eliot some quick electroshock therapy to bring him back to his senses.

But really, what did it mean to own land in Hell and be *called* an Infernal Lord? It was just a title, right? He couldn't really be one of them.

The door to Miss Westin's office opened and the pale boy who had ushered them before emerged. He bowed. "Good Lady and Master," he said. "Please, the Headmistress will see you now."

Fiona's heart pounded in her throat. She was like a little kid again about to be punished for leaving her clothes on the floor. How did the adults in her life always do that to her?

Eliot got to his feet.

There was no way she was going to let him be the brave one, so she stood, got ahead of him, and led the way.

Fiona remembered Miss Westin's office as being long—but today it seemed like it had stretched to the length of a football field as they walked past dozens of Tiffany lamps, acres of walnut paneling, a hundred different doors (which Fiona was sorely tempted to bolt through). There were all those oil painting and class photographs, too.

She spotted one picture that made her stop in her tracks. Eliot did the same, and they stared at a group of freshmen.

Among the hundred or so students were Tamara Pritchard, David Kaleb, and even, much to Fiona's chagrin, Jeremy and Sarah Covington.

It was *their* freshman class portrait . . . one they weren't in because they'd obviously missed picture day at school.

Her hands twisted together, and for a moment she wanted to cut that thing in half—right through Jeremy Covington's face.

"Nice," she muttered, and kept walking.

Miss Westin's desk was a few paces ahead. Last time there had been no place to sit. Today, four high-backed chairs sat opposite the Headmistress. Not a good sign. Miss Westin obviously wanted them off their feet when she delivered the bad news.

Miss Westin sat there, nodded, and murmured something, but didn't spare either of them a glance. Her attention was focused solely on those chairs.

There was another person. A pair of skinny legs and the edge of a skirt dangled over the seat, but the chair's high back obscured the rest.

Miss Westin finally finished and then gestured for that person to leave. Only then did the Headmistress glance at Fiona and Eliot, and all traces of civility left her face.

The other person got out of their chair.

Fiona stared, not believing what she saw.

"You're . . . dead," Eliot whispered.

Amanda Lane looked them over. Her lips pressed into a frown, and her gaze narrowed.

For someone whom Fiona had seen blown to smithereens, Amanda looked great. Her school uniform was neatly pressed. A tiny daisy was pinned to her lapel. Her hair had been cut and feathered back from her face—hair that now had a lot more auburn in it that Fiona recalled.

She wanted to run over and give her a hug, but Fiona still couldn't believe she was real.

Amanda stood tall and proud, though. Her skin flushed and Fiona felt the unnatural heat from where she stood.

"I'm not dead," she told them. "Obviously. But no thanks to either of you."

"The bridge . . . ," Eliot started.

"And that volcano . . . ," Fiona added.

"*I* did those things," Amanda said, her voice rising. "And what'd I get for my trouble? For risking my life? No one came back to even look for me. Do you know how hard it is to climb out of a river of *lava*? While it's *solidifying*?"

Fiona blinked and tried to process this. Shy, helpless Amanda was telling them she had caused all that massive geological-scale upheaval—and then had survived it, apparently immune to the tremendous heat.

"Do you know how long I had to look until I found those stupid train tracks?" Amanda set her hands on her hips. "And how long I walked until I found the tunnel back to the Market Street station?"

"I'm so sorry," Fiona said. "We just assumed . . ."

"I was ready to *die* for you guys," Amanda told her. Despite the heat coming from her, her voice was icy. "And you just marched off looking for Jezebel. What kind of friends are you?"

Fiona crossed her arms over her chest. She wanted to tell her they got a *little* occupied trying to outrun a tidal wave of magma—worried about the millions of damned souls that might've chased after them—oh, and not to mention their complete astonishment at seeing her turn into a miniature sun and then going supernova on them.

Eliot, however, spoke first. "You're absolutely right," he said. "We shouldn't have left you there. No matter what. I'm sorry."

Amanda's lip trembled, and Fiona thought she might cry.

She stuck out her chin, though, and recovered. "At least I know where I stand with my so-called friends now." She moved past them, adding in a whisper, "At least the people I *thought* were my friends."

Amanda crossed Miss Westin's office and slammed the door shut.

Fiona was thrilled to see her alive, but she wasn't sure what was more shocking: seeing her alive, or seeing her so strong . . . and so angry. Fiona felt like Amanda had just kicked her in the stomach.

Miss Westin tapped a pen on her desk to get their attention.

Fiona and Eliot hurriedly took their seats.

The high-backed chair was hard, squeaky, and uncomfortable. Eliot sat two spots away from her.

Miss Westin examined them and steepled her hands on her desk. "Miss Lane has embraced the Fire of Humanity. It is a great responsibility. A great burden as well. She needs good friends at a time like this."

That's all Fiona needed was another "friend" who hated her (although that wasn't completely accurate, because right now, she didn't have *any* friends).

"And where is Mr. Farmington?" the Headmistress inquired.

Eliot and Fiona looked at each other.

"Was he supposed to be with us?" Fiona asked.

Miss Westin made a note in her little black book and didn't answer.

Funny how she asked after Robert, but not Mitch. How much did she know?

"Down to business, then," Miss Westin said. She tapped the large computer touch screen that doubled as the surface of her desk, and their official Paxington school records popped open. "I have here a list of regulations you have broken, and a few new rules that have been created to cover your uniquely reckless behavior."

With her long bony index finger, she traced down this list. "Unauthorized departure from campus during school hours . . . missing weeks of class and gym practice without prior written approval . . . destruction of school property—"

"We didn't break anything," Eliot said, annoyed.

"Your uniforms," Miss Westin told him. "You have paid for them, but technically that is only a lease. All things bearing the Paxington insignia are school property in perpetuity."

She glared at him. Eliot met her eyes without flinching.

"And," she continued, "there is still a matter of you missing your final exams in Mythology 101, Force of Arms, and the Power of Music class— not to mention the final match in gym."

She looked at Fiona as if expecting her to say something in her defense.

What *could* she say? They *had* missed everything.

Fiona had heard about the final in gym: all the teams at once on the obstacle course—and for once, no time limit. Mr. Ma had only eliminated the slowest two people from the roster. There'd been a broken finger and one dislocated arm.

Some final. What a joke.

Meanwhile she, Eliot, and Robert had been in a *real* war.

She wanted to tell Miss Westin what she could do with her list of infractions, but she kept her mouth shut. Nothing was going to save them now. And being rude to an adult who is technically correct? Fiona had been brought up better than that.

Miss Westin continued to stare at her . . . the silence stretching on and on.

Eliot cleared his throat. "Was there something else, ma'am?"

"There most certainly is," Miss Westin replied.

The Headmistress opened a drawer and pulled out two legal-sized parchments.

Fiona held her breath. This was it. They were going to officially flunk out—Miss Westin was going to sign some papers and they'd be told to leave.

Fiona stared at the documents. They smelled of brimstone and there were wax seals and gilt inscriptions and blood spatters. Fiona tried to read the upside-down lettering, but it was mostly little triangles and arcs and dots.

"I have here," Miss Westin explained, "signed and notarized affidavits from Sealiah, Infernal Queen of the Poppy Lands, and Lucifer, Prince of Darkness and Lord of the Mirrored City. They describe how you two were instrumental to their victory in the recent civil war in the Lower Realms against Mephistopheles."

Miss Westin paused and arched an eyebrow. "Quite impressive."

Fiona blinked, not entirely understanding.

"They have petitioned the School Board," Miss Westin continued, "that in lieu of your classes and final examinations that your actions be considered . . . 'off-campus work experience.'" She brushed the pages aside. "After consultation, the Board has ruled in your favor."

Fiona couldn't believe it. Was she hearing, right?

"So . . . ," Fiona whispered softly (because she thought if she said this too loud, it might pop her fragile hope). "We're still in school?"

"Provisionally," Miss Westin said, and gave that single word the weight of a falling executioner's ax. "Mr. Ma has accepted your participation in battle as proof that you would have passed his final examination in gym and Force of Arms class. Ms. DuPreé has likewise waived Eliot's participation in her final concert."

Fiona sighed.

"But," Miss Westin said, "*I* do not accept you missing *my* classes or final."

She produced two more papers and slid one each toward Fiona and Eliot.

In the fine print was a list of books—*Bulfinch's Mythology,* everything ever written by Cicero, *Languorous Lullabies, Golden's Guide to Extraordinary Books,* and on and on, dozens of texts, endless volumes, and ancient scrolls.

"Read these over the next few months," Miss Westin explained, "and you may then take my makeup final examination at the end of summer."

This was as much reading as they'd been assigned for the entire year. So much for getting a break.

Fiona had read some of these already, however, digging up background on Zeus and the rest of her Immortal family. Still, even for her it'd be a spend-every-free-moment-of-vacation-with-nose-in-book deal.

"Thank you," Eliot said, and tucked the paper into his pocket. "You didn't have to do this."

If Fiona had been sitting in the seat next to him, she would've elbowed him in the ribs. Why did he say that? Did he want her to change her mind?

Miss Westin's features softened a bit, and she set her hands flat on her desk. "You're quite welcome, Eliot. I recognize both your unique talents and your unusual circumstances." Her face hardened once more. "But let me make this *perfectly* clear: You get only this *one* chance."

Fiona swallowed. "Got it," she said. "We'll pass the final, no problem."

Miss Westin took out her pocket watch and glanced at it. "Now, if you children don't mind, I have another appointment." She nodded to the door at the far end of her office.

Fiona and Eliot got up. Fiona tried to walk with as much dignity as possible toward the exit. Once she was outside—then she could collapse. How was it that she was able to march into Hell, charge an army of the damned, but almost flunking a few classes turned her to jelly?

She stood straighter. She was a goddess in the League of Immortals, after all. She didn't *have to* feel this way.

Besides, there were lots of other more important things to consider than school. She still had to figure out her place in the world. How she fit in among the Immortals . . . and how to stop the Infernals from messing everything up again.

She nodded at the pale boy by the door and he opened it.

Fiona and Eliot walked into the waiting room. She blinked in the sudden sunlight. As her eyes adjusted, she saw two other students waiting for Miss Westin.

Sarah and Jeremy Covington.

Their uniforms were immaculate. Sarah had her hair up and coiffed. Jeremy's long hair was back and tied with a black ribbon so he looked like a Colonial revolutionary.

"Why, Fiona!" Jeremy beamed and opened his arms wide as if to embrace her.

Sarah stood there, mortified. She looked at the floor.

"'Tis a delight to see you back," Jeremy continued as if nothing were wrong—as if he hadn't slammed the Gates of Perdition on them.

Fiona finally found her voice, at least a low growl of a voice, and said, "Give me one reason why I shouldn't cut you in half—right here and now."

Eliot, who had been calm and collected all morning, didn't try to stop her; instead, he merely crossed his arms and glared at Jeremy.

"Ah . . ." Jeremy's smile faded a bit. "Well, you'd miss my good looks and charm, wouldn't ye?"

Fiona's hands twitched and she fingered the rubber band on her wrist. It took all her will to keep her blood from boiling, and from doing something she wasn't quite sure she'd regret.

The pale boy behind them said, "Pardon me, Masters and Ladies, but Miss Westin would like to see the Covingtons."

Jeremy tilted his head. "And I suppose because you'd be murdering me in front of the Headmistress?" His impish smile returned.

Fiona hissed out a sigh.

Jeremy's expression sobered. "Look dearie, what happened at the gate— 'twasn't what I had planned. But you and Eliot are all right. Perhaps we should let bygones be bygones?" He extended a hand.

Eliot snorted.

Fiona glared at his proffered gesture like it was a rattlesnake. "Once we are out of the picture, did you and Sarah get on a winning team like you wanted?"

Jeremy tilted his head, but said nothing.

"If I ever catch you off campus," Fiona said, "there won't be any rules or Headmistress to save you."

"Oh, Fiona." Jeremy retracted his hand. "I so love your hotheadedness. Completely endearing. You'll come around."

He squeezed past her and entered Miss Westin's office.

Sarah remained where she was. "I am so, so sorry," she squeaked. "He's always doing things like this. There's this archaic seniority system in the Clan Covington . . . and he's technically the eldest member. I *have to* go along."

"You don't have to go along with *murder*," Fiona said.

Sarah flinched. She looked deeply conflicted, and then finally said, "Aye. You're right. There's no excuse for what we did. I promise, I will make amends."

She nodded to Eliot and then Fiona, and hurried into Miss Westin's office.

"Maybe she wasn't to blame," Eliot said. "Jeremy did throw her back at the last moment before he locked the gate. She couldn't have been responsible. "

"Whatever," Fiona muttered. "I've got better things to do than worry about the Covingtons right now."

She glanced at her book list, picking out the ones she'd already read try-ing to track down what had happened to Zeus.

Zeus, the once-leader of the Immortals, the one who had united them

against the Titans, and had led them against all odds in battle with the Infernals.

A leader. That's precisely what the world and the Immortals needed—
now more than ever.

Fiona stood there . . . as a plan took shape in her mind.

LAST-MINUTE DETAILS FOR ARMAGEDDON

Sealiah, undisputed Queen of the Poppy Lands and the Hysterical Kingdoms, shivered with pleasure. No more armor. While the metal plates, layers of chain mail, and padding had been a necessity to survive, she required a new kind of protection for today's dangers.

She spun, and the layers of gold chiffon drifted about her and then settled against the coppery curves of her body. Much better.

She was alone in her map room. No guards. No Jezebel. The Post twins long departed—and the sounds of all their whining and pleading for their lost loves finally silenced.

She lingered a moment, thinking of Robert Farmington.

Him she would miss. She did so appreciate a hero of few words.

Overcast light filtered through the open windows and mingled with the shadows.

Sealiah slipped into a pair of gold sandals and checked the fit of her summer dress, making sure just enough was hidden and just enough showed through its sheer layers. It was infinitely impractical, and yet the most effective tack for those she was about to face: her cousins on the Board. Those malefactors would never dream of a simple frontal attack . . . when they had such expertise in the art of betrayal.

Her best defense was distraction.

She moved to the map table and examined the dire state of the battle when it had last been updated: her twelve towers surrounded and Mephistopheles marching upon her.

Tiny figurines lay on their sides, souls that had fought for her cause. She touched one, a Napoleonic dragoon, and righted it with her fingertip.

Tragic was their suffering . . . but why else had these souls come to her domain? That was their fate. It was what they deserved. It was what they wanted.

What would they do if she released them? Would the souls of the damned be lost without their torment? Would they even know where to go after all this time? Or would they crawl to her and beg her to take them back?

Well, she would never know. They were forever hers.

These philosophical musing aside, the important thing was that she had prevailed in the war by her superior cunning—or, at least, she had not been so distracted by noble sentiments as poor Mephistopheles had.

She touched the shattered obsidian figurine that represented her Infernal cousin.

And where was his soul now? Dust and ashes? Somewhere rich and strange and far beyond her? Or some place dark and deep—torment that not even she could imagine? That was always the question, was it not? The rhyme and reason for all that happened since they had left their brother and sister angels in the light.

She sighed. What silly sentimentality and dreams of things no longer possible.

She swept the obsidian shards off the table.

Mephistopheles has been a fool. He could have won; he *should* have won, had he but tempted Fiona to his side . . . the thing that almost happened at that last precarious moment.

Almost.

Pity. Love. Honor. Weaknesses all that had caused his downfall.

And yet, she wished, just for once, one of her kind would act thusly toward her. Even her departed Uri's ambition had tainted his loyalty. Where was her unrequited, self-sacrificing hero?

Sealiah laughed halfheartedly and drew a cover over the map table, desperately trying to ignore the lump in her throat . . . the longing for just one taste of love again.

She inhaled and banished these thoughts. They were dangerous at any time for their kind—doubly so before a Board meeting.

She turned her attention to the smaller table that held the circular mat and stones of her Towers game.

Sealiah touched the cubes and retraced her moves—the maneuvering of her Jezebel to Paxington—capturing Eliot in her orbit and with him drawing in his sister and Robert—all vital pieces used in her final ploy.

She shuddered with satisfaction. It had been a good opening round.

But far from over.

She moved the basalt cube that represented Jezebel to the opposite side, stacking it upon the two stones that were now Eliot's, nestled them together in the square that was his domain, The Burning Orchards. Precisely where she wanted them.

Wheels turning within wheels, as Louis was fond of saying.

She then stroked the stack of three white stones that now displayed hairline cracks. That was Fiona Post. Indeed, she had plans for her as well.

Sealiah dragged her fingernail along the curve of the game board until she rested upon another white cube, whose edges had been smudged with soot.

Would this be her hero? A minor piece, to be sure, but often it was useful to let some pawns believe they were knights . . . at least for a time.

A knock on the door distracted her. Sealiah's temper flared, and then cooled as she recalled the circumstances of today.

"Come," she commanded.

The door opened, and one of her personal maids entered and immediately fell to her knees.

"Are they ready?"

"Yes, Your Majesty," the maid said, groveling upon the floor. "They have assembled and await your glory."

With a flourish, Sealiah floated past the supplicant maid and up the spiral staircase. She emerged atop the tower called the Oaken Keeper of Secrets. Overhead the sky was luminous silver, the sun properly buried behind puffy layers of steaming altostratus clouds.

She strolled into the hedge maze of her tea garden, past the legion of gardeners who made sure the topiary was in tip-top shape, clip-clip-clipping the thorns and twisted branches of the agonized souls within, which had been meticulously shaped into rows of flamingos and prancing horses and elephants balanced upon turtles.[69]

---

69. Father Francis Limehouse, an associate of Charles Lutwidge Dodgson (aka Lewis Carroll) reported in his diary having related his "daft and endless" dreams to Mr. Dodgson of visiting a garden party with a less-than-mentally-stable hostess and company. In 1886, Limehouse was

Heirloom roses bloomed at her approach, and their colors popped along the perfumed pathway. She stepped in the center yard, where fountains sprayed champagne and a long table had been set with a hundred different teakettles, trays overflowing with pastries and sandwiches, and serving sets arranged with raw sugar and opium honey and lemons and cream and three dozen types of serving spoons and red current jam and orange marmalade and royal queen bee jelly.

All these preparations and delicacies, of course, were lost on her assembled cousins . . . save, perhaps, Ashmed, the Chairman of the Infernal Board and Master Architect of Evil.

He stood at her approach, brushed his lips with a napkin, and pulled out a chair next to his at the head of the table. Ashmed was as professional and handsome as ever, in a light gray suit and silver tie, tastefully accessorized with mirror-polished gold cuff links. His hair was groomed into a dark wave, and he smiled, genuinely pleased to see her.

And why not? Sealiah and delivered for him and the others the means of their salvation.

And Sealiah—now with lands and armies to rival Ashmed's—was his near equal in power.

It was a powerful aphrodisiac.

She bowed graciously and took her seat (first, however, looking about the table for any potential threats . . . of which there were many).

Abby, The Destroyer, Handmaiden of Armageddon, and Mistress of the Palace of Abomination sat on her immediate left—a little too close for comfort. Abby had wrapped herself with black velvet ribbon, skintight over her slender curves. She played with a mouse, letting it scurry across the table—then trapping it with an upturned bone china cup—letting it go—capturing it again . . . and laughing all the while at the creature squeaking its sufferings.

A giant wasp sat on Abby's shoulder, cleaning its antennae.

Across the table sat Leviathan, the Beast, Horror of the Abyssal Depths. About him was a disaster of broken plates and cups and saucers

---

defrocked for alleged sexual liaisons with various socialites of the era, and soon thereafter died from a morphine overdose. Mythohistorians speculate that Limehouse's dreams may have been an opiate-induced, near-death experience—and the Mad Hatter's tea party in Dodgson's subsequent "Alice" books might have been a secondhand account of the Poppy Queen's nightmarish realm in the nineteenth century. *Gods of the First and Twenty-first Century, Volume 13, Infernal Forces*. Zypheron Press Ltd., Eighth Edition.

and spilled teas—which he dabbed up with a fistful of sponge cake. With his other hand, he brushed crumbs from the ripples of his tent-sized Nike jumpsuit and smiled a mouthful of food at her.

Sitting by himself at the other end of the table was Louis.

Sealiah hide her surprise as well, but she feared she let slip a double take. Louis looked . . . delectable.

His hair had been trimmed short and neat on the sides, and the rest drawn back into a ponytail of silver and black and secured with a bloodred ribbon. His sideburns pointed to a stylish soul patch and pencil-thin mustache. He wore a black Armani tuxedo and a white shirt with diamond studs for buttons.

He smiled at her—all promises and remembrances of the passion that they had shared in the past.

This version of Louis had been copied by men throughout history: Don Juan, Clark Gable, Brad, and Johnny—all who were adored and made women's hearts pitter-pat. None, however, did it as well as Louis . . . the original seducer of them all.

Flowing off his shoulders was a cloak so rich and black, the material seemed to absorb the light. It had been stolen by Mephistopheles long ago, and recovered by Louis on the battlefield. It looked better on Louis. Truly, Lucifer was back among them, the real Prince of Darkness, now fully restored to his proper power and prowess and pride.

Gooseflesh crawled up Sealiah's arms and over her chest and caressed her neck. She shivered and regained her composure. "Lies and salutations, Cousins."

"That was some nice work," Lev muttered to Sealiah, spilling half-chewed contents from his mouth. "Never thought you'd get Meph to turn his back on *you*!" He made a fist and shoved it into the air for emphasis (jiggling his layers of fat as he did so). "Bang-O. A classic move."

Abby lost her concentration at Lev's motions and accidentally slammed her cup down too hard on her rodent plaything—smashing china and fur and splintering the table. She frowned at her broken toy, then shot the Beast a cross look.

She turned to Sealiah and raised both her eyebrows. "I suppose congratulations are in order," she grudgingly offered.

That was the first. Sealiah had never heard Abby utter a kind word before.

Indeed, things were changing.

Sealiah inclined her head, and with tremendous difficulty, she replied, "Thank you very much, Cousins."

Ashmed cleared his throat, uncomfortable with all these pleasantries. "Perhaps before we all lose our collective heads with Sealiah's success, we should take care of one procedural item first."

All of them glanced at Louis as he straightened in his chair, intensified his smile, and remained uncharacteristically silent.

"We have numerous petitions and pleas to be considered for the vacancy on the Board." Ashmed gestured to a stack of paperwork on the table, considered it, and brushed it onto the ground. He lit one of his Sancho Panza Belicoso cigars and flicked the still-flaming match onto the heap of papers. They burned and the flames reflected in his dark eyes. "I move that we instead vote for Louis. His expertise with his son and daughter has proved invaluable . . . and will continue to do so." Ashmed puffed and blew smoke rings. "Besides," he added with mock sincerity, "we have *so* missed him."

There was silence in the garden as the Board considered. Even the bees stopped their incessant buzzing, leaving only the sound of the foaming champagne fountain.

Sealiah had never recalled silence at any Board meeting. Perhaps after a scuffle when their personal retainers lay about bloody and dead, but this was something else.

Abby finally shrugged. "Fine," she said. "Whatever."

Lev nodded. "Yeah, sure, why not?"

Sealiah held her tongue as she considered all the possibilities swirling about her: war and peace, victory and obliteration, all deliciously tempting. But most curious to her was that her cousins seem to be agreeing and moving forward because of Eliot and Fiona. Those two were the catalysts.

Yes, it was the end of all they knew, and the beginning of something wonderfully horrid.

As Sealiah had predicted and wisely positioned herself to be in the center of . . . and benefit the most from all who would suffer.

The one thing she had not predicted, however, was Louis.

He looked proud of his new potential position on the Board, yet wary, his gaze flitting from person to person . . . and then lingering upon her.

Would he be her greatest adversary? An ally? Both?

Whichever outcome, she could ill afford *not* to keep him near, where he could be watched.

"Of course," she said without taking her eyes off Louis. "He would be a most welcome addition."

Louis smiled, part shield, part gloat—which faltered but for an instant.

But in that instant, Sealiah detected something else in the Great Deceiver's eyes: a flicker of indecision. And yes . . . vulnerability.

She had seen such a look on him when he had been at his son's side, proud and worried and so piteously feigning his indifference. She had also seen him protect Fiona on the battlefield (placing himself in danger for her sake). What else could it be but a father's protectiveness? Even love?

Such foolishness. She envied him this love, but she also knew it would destroy him.

Sealiah settled into her chair, knowing everything was going to be all right now, her plans would remain on track, and soon she would command all.

There was, of course, one minor detail left to arrange: Fiona. But she would see to that soon enough. She smiled, thinking how pleasurable it might be.

"Very well," Ashmed said, and stood. "By acclamation we welcome Louis Piper to the Infernal Board of Directors."

Louis stood as if to make a speech, but Ashmed cut him off. "Alas, all ceremony and pomp must be postponed. The League of Immortals will move quickly to block our progress."

Louis sank back into his seat, looking sullen.

Lev smashed his huge fist on the table—destroying that end of the table. "Let's crush them before they can see it coming."

"Precisely what I was thinking, Cousin," Ashmed said. "Let us then discuss how to best use Eliot Post to destroy them, and how he will lead us in a glorious war."

Sealiah's smile intensified, knowing that war was inevitable. As was their victory.

84

CYCLE OF VIOLENCE

Cornelius—once called Cronos, and later Chronos; the sole surviving Titan in the Middle Realms; Ph.D. from MIT with degrees in computer science, political engineering, and theoretical physics; and Professor Emeritus of Stanford University—sat in the lotus position staring into the depths of the program running on his tablet computer . . . traces of red and blue chaos that looked much like a butterfly in flight. He had missed the last Council meeting in order to implement the last lines of code. It had been worth the time and effort, though; it would give him a glimpse of their future.

Audrey would have called it "unscrambling a tangle in the weave of Fate."

He called it meticulous programming and multivariate transcendental calculus.

He looked up, resting his old eyes, and taking in where he was (for sometimes he became so absorbed in the mathematics of the thing . . . that he forgot what precisely that "thing" was).

Had he a map he could have pointed to the Aegean Sea, between modern-day Greece and Turkey. A place once called Ieiunium Aequora or "Hungry Water" by Byzantine sailors for all the ships that entered the region vanished.

Today no such thing occurred. It was just another stretch of water among a million other stretches of similar waters . . . with a tiny rock of an island.

Millennia ago, however, that rock had been the high point of an archipelago upon which sat the grand city-state of Altium, grandest city of Atlantis. It had perched upon its hills like a bejeweled crown.

Under dark water, and accessible only through a submerged cavern guarded by beasts of mechanical construct, the city lay buried and sleeping.

In grottoes and forever in shadows were palaces, streets, gold-paved plazas, statues of heroes and gods and Titans and the mighty things that came before them; libraries with mountains of moldering scrolls; paintings that showed earthly paradises, battles among races that no longer lived, and portraits of the most beautiful men and women who ever existed—now all so faded, one could barely see a glimmer of their glory. It made him sad to think of how all was lost to Time.

Among this decaying splendor was the temple where Cornelius now sat, whose central domed chamber was held aloft by ivory mammoth tusks and columns of cracked crystal, and whose floors was paved with turquoise and lapis and jade.

This was the Chamber of Whispers, where Zeus had hatched his plan to overthrow the Titans.

Cornelius shifted on the uncomfortable stone bench, and rearranged the Dodger Stadium seat cushion he'd brought along with him.

Much better.

Within this chamber, holding the Council's most precious secrets, was the Vault Eternal. The mad genius and master mechanic, Daedalus, had fashioned it to be impenetrable, with locks so intricate that even after a thousand years of study, Cornelius had only a hint of how it worked. To open it required three keys and three combinations simultaneously applied.

Proof against any thief.

One of the three keys was held by him.

Another key was held by Lucia, who had perched on the bench to his left.

She had toweled off from her recent swim through the entrance and had slipped into a set of ordinary sweats. Even in the gray cotton she looked elegant. Women had talents that eluded his scientific senses . . . and he appreciated that.

Lucia was wise, but always competing with the beauty of her younger sister, the ferocity of her older sister, and with herself (never quite perfect enough to live up to her impossible standards).

"Narro, Audio, Perceptum," Lucia said, and rang her tiny silver bell. The tinkling echoed off the dome and was swallowed by the silence of this place. "I call this meeting of the Council of Elders for the League of Immortals to order."

Gilbert sat opposite them. He glanced at his watch as if expecting someone to show (and indeed this was a possibility), but the deep worry on his face was something Cornelius had never seen on the Once King.

Kino sat on Cornelius's right and wore black slacks and white shirt. He and Cornelius had come here together in Gilbert's submersible. It had been a quiet, unpleasant journey.

Aaron stood apart from them, still dripping in his EVERLAST trunks, his chest hair plastered to his muscular chest.

Henry was missing.

In absentia also was Dallas—called before the Council by special summons. Her tardiness would no doubt be an excuse for Lucia to try to punish the girl.

No surprise, really, that neither had showed. It was not in their natures to respond to authority.

Audrey, however, had also failed to arrive . . . and she was never late or shirked her responsibilities once she accepted them. It was a dark omen.

"I suppose we have a quorum," Gilbert admitted, and glanced again at his watch.

"Have we all seen Fiona's e-mail?" Lucia asked.

They nodded. Cornelius opened the document on his computer.

Fiona's e-mail was a pledge to help the Immortals defend themselves from "the looming threat of Infernal machinations and incursions into our world" as well as a plea to help her find new leadership to stop this threat.

"I'm enormously pleased with this development," Lucia said. "Fiona has matured far beyond my expectations. We need to bring her onto the Council; perhaps some sort of internship?"

"She is a child still," Gilbert protested.

"Hardly," Aaron muttered. "She has fought and won a war in Hell! What more proof do you need for abilities?"

"Of her abilities?" Kino said. "None." He made a sideways slash with his hand. "But she is barely a woman and in desperate need of our guidance."

"Yes, guidance," Lucia said. "Which brings me to the other matter, one our spies in the Lower Realms have brought to our attention. Eliot."

Kino stood. "The boy is now a landed Infernal Lord who is also half Immortal. This is a disaster! His powers will grow beyond our measure, and his mind will warp until it is evil."

Aaron shook his head. "I don't believe that. Not Eliot."

Gilbert looked uncomfortable between the two men, and he stood as well. "I do not wish to discuss Audrey's children if she is not here."

"There is no discussion necessary," Lucia told them. She got to her feet, and her cheeks flushed. "This has already been decided, last year—for just such a contingency. You all put your mark to the document, even you, Gilbert! Do not evade responsibility when it becomes difficult."

They stood in silence (save Cornelius, who remained seated in silence). They knew exactly what she was talking about.

Last year when they had proclaimed Fiona a young goddess and Eliot a hero within the League, the Council had feared this very thing: one or both of the children's Infernal sides would call to them, and they would succumb to its temptations.

Each Council member had signed a Warrant of Death so action could be taken without delay. All that remained was for Lucia to fill in the date and the document became binding . . . and every one of the League's members would be compelled to find and destroy Eliot.

Cornelius rubbed his hands to ease the arthritic ache within his bones.

In truth, his loyalties were conflicted, for he liked Eliot and Fiona. There were grandchildren to him . . . at least, that was how he had begun to think of them.

His own children were lost. Zeus had met his fate. No one had seen him since Ultima Thule, and Cornelius knew in his heart he was dead. Poseidon had taken his own life in a flash of light, and his ashes were now scattered across the seas he so loved. And Kino? The Lord of Death was so far from the child Cornelius had reared, he might as well be dead to him.

He sighed.

Violence was no stranger to *this* family. Cornelius's children had plotted the genocide of Cornelius's own primordial brothers and sisters. Oceans of blood had flowed that day. It had to be done, and Cornelius had chosen then to save the young members of his family by murdering the elder Titans.

Had not the same thing happened to him? Had he not killed his own father at the urging of his mother?[70]

This time, however, something was different: it was not just his family—but the Infernals as well.

The fallen angels were insane and wielded far more power than the League. They were also alien and more evil than the primordial deities had ever been.

And where was the League's leader this time to stop the gods' petty disputes and rally them?

Cornelius's gaze fell upon his computer and Fiona's passionate e-mail.

Her, perhaps, *if* her great threat were removed.

Violence—why was that their solution to everything? Were not there other ways?

Yes . . . but none better to permanently solve problems. He had seen so much: He knew this was the unpleasant truth. Or was it *because* he had seen so much that he was blind to any alternatives?

"Open the vault," Cornelius whispered. "Retrieve the Death Warrant for Eliot."

The others looked at him.

"Why do you say this?" Gilbert demanded. "More coldhearted mathematics?"

"This is not based on calculation," Cornelius replied, "but rather that Fiona's brother among all the Immortals and Infernals has been her greatest ally . . . and is now her greatest vulnerability."

Aaron looked as if he wanted to challenge this assertion, but he instead cupped his hand over his chin, thinking.

"What if she follows him as she ever has?" Cornelius continued. "But this time to the other side? Or worse, what if Eliot becomes so twisted that he . . ."

Cornelius didn't need to finish that thought. They had all seen brothers and sisters among their ranks murder one another.

"Very well," Lucia said. "Kino? Cornelius?" She strode to the vault door, slender key already in her hand.

---

70. Cronos was offspring to the primordial entity and then self-proclaimed "ruler of the universe," Ouranos. At the urging of his mother, Gaia, Cronos and all his brothers gathered to ambush their father. Only Cronos had the courage to do so. Even as he wept over his father's body, the young Titan Cronos was proclaimed leader over the first generation of his kind. *Gods of the First and Twenty-first Century, Volume 4, Core Myths (Part 1)*. Zypheron Press Ltd., Eighth Edition.

Kino joined her, and Cornelius fumbled out a key ring from his pocket.

Amid the keys to his VW bug, the trailer he lived in, post office box, and pool room, was the one required: the worn metal cylinder with vein-like ridges (more circuitry than mechanical lock).

He walked to the hinge portion of the vault door and found a proper keyhole.

Lucia and Kino held their keys. "On three," Lucia said. "One, two—three."

They inserted their keys.

Cornelius then dialed in the combination, sliding tiles encrusted with ancient symbols into the proper alignment.

As he did this a series of clanks and clacks and mechanical ratchetings vibrated within the vault door . . . but there was also a grinding noise that he'd never before heard.

Lucia's brows scrunched together at the noise as well.

Kino pulled on the door, his muscles tensing as tons of metal swung on a perfectly balanced hinge. He entered the vault chamber.

Cornelius peered through. Within were rows of sealed, spirit-filled Ming vases; jars of blue fluid containing floating brains, a lockbox kept for The King's Men whose extra-dimensional spaces were best left forever sealed, Leonardo da Vinci's one true notebook . . . and similar, dangerous and fascinating objects.

Kino grabbed two alabaster scroll tubes and marched out.

Lucia hovered near Kino's side, looking childlike next to his great height. Kino unstoppered the containers and shook out their contents—one for him and one for Lucia.

As they unrolled them Kino's dark features turned pale, and Lucia's face flushed deeper and twisted in outrage.

She held up the document for all of them to see: it was not the vellum Warrant of Death they had put in there for safekeeping, but rather a rolled-up *New York Times* crossword section.

"Where are they?" she demanded.

"The vault is impervious to force," Kino said. "Proof against any thief."

Cornelius approached. He took the newspaper crossword and held at arm's length, squinting.

"Thirty seven across reads: fastest bird," he said. "That would be a peregrine falcon." Cornelius noted and recited the penned-in answer: *"P-E-A-R-A-G-R-I-N."*

Only one among them had the talent to enter the vault without the keys. And only one spelled so poorly . . . even when he was sober.

"Proof against any thief," Lucia screeched, "but not *fool*proof. I want Henry found. I want him dragged in front of this Council!"

Cornelius slowly shook his head and took his seat. One might as well try to bottle the four winds.

He saw that his computer simulation was almost done. Good. Objective analysis would be most welcome at this point.

"We must draw new warrants," Kino suggested.

"No," Aaron told him. "I will not debate this without Audrey present."

"You will do as this Council tells you," Lucia said.

This was a mistake. Push Aaron, and he pushed back. Push him a second time—and he was likely to push hard enough to end the matter.

Aaron's hands curled into fists, but then he relaxed and gazed at them all. He smiled—turned, and strode from the temple.

"If you leave in the middle of a session," Lucia told him, "I will remove you from this Council."

"Remove this." Without turning to face her, Aaron held up his hand and made a gesture most ancient.

"So be it," she murmured. "We shall vote in a new member to replace him."

"Maybe," Gilbert told her. "But we're done for today. We no longer have a quorum."

Lucia sighed with frustration.

A ping sounded from Cornelius's computer tablet. His simulation to predict which side would prevail in a conflict with the Infernals ended.

The result flashed at the bottom of the screen: zero divided by zero. That was an unbounded result, one in which there is never enough information to define a true value as it bobbled between all values between zero and infinite.

There had been no programmatic error.

So what did it mean?

Dread congealed within Cornelius as he feared this meant that *neither* side would prevail. That only ashes and the primordial chaos would remain when they were done.

CEREMONIES

There was tension in the air. It made the hair on the back of Eliot's neck stand. Something was about to happen—why else had Miss Westin canceled their last class and marched every freshman into the Grand Spring Ballroom? They all stood facing a podium . . . waiting.

From the grim silence that solidified around even the chattiest girls (Tamara Pritchard and her elite social circle)—Eliot knew this couldn't be good.

Fiona stood next to him, arms crossed over her chest, looking annoyed and nervous and bored all the same time.

Where was Jezebel? Sealiah had said she would be back for the last day at Paxington. She had to know about the weird time effects in Hell.

The floor-to-ceiling curtains in the ballroom had been opened, and sunlight streamed through, warming Eliot's face.

Why couldn't he relax?

Everything had turned out okay. They had even made it through the school year (provided they passed the exam at the end of the summer).

And okay, sure, Mitch was gone, but he had been an Infernal who was out to draw Fiona into his world. That didn't mean he deserved to die, though.

Amanda wasn't dead, at least. He turned and spotted her at the back of the room.

She saw him looking, and glared back.

Miss Westin entered the room. She wore a white linen summer dress—which shocked Eliot after seeing her in nothing but those high-necked things all year. Her skin was the palest he'd ever seen. A spiderweb of blue veins traced her bare shoulders and neck. She smiled at the assembled students. Another first.

Mr. Dells, Ms. DuPreé, Mr. Ma, and a dozen other teachers Eliot had never seen before trailed in behind her.

Miss Westin went to the podium and faced them. "Salutations and congratulations," she said. "I wish to extend my regards to those of you continuing at the Paxington Institute." She took a deep breath. "And to those who will not, you did your best, and know that even surviving a single year at Paxington is an achievement to be proud of."

She opened her little black book and gazed at it. "Will the following students come to the front of the room: Donald van Wyck, Lilly Orrins, Benito Harris . . ." She read off twenty-six names.

These were the students who had failed, been expelled, or were so injured they couldn't continue on at school. Add to that the six dead on Team Soaring Eagle and the total came to thirty-two.

The students so called then walked or limped to the front of the auditorium. (Lilly had to be pushed up in a wheelchair.)

How humiliating. It wasn't bad enough they weren't graduating, but Miss Westin had to parade them up in front of everyone?

It had to be especially hard for Donald van Wyck, who had been expelled earlier in the year. They must have brought him back just for this ceremony.

Mr. Dells moved to them. He looked apologetic . . . but that didn't stop the Gatekeeper from marching the more than two dozen ex-students to the door, ushering them through, and then escorting then across campus one last time.

Eliot wondered if Donald and the others were the lucky ones to be leaving. They could do whatever they wanted now—no more gym classes that could get you killed or maimed, and no more insane competition.

And yet, as Eliot looked back on this year he realized he'd learned so much about his music, his magic, his and the other magical families. Even Mr. Ma's sadistic class had helped. If Eliot hadn't been in shape, hadn't been exposed to the cruelties of mock battle in gym—would he have survived the real war in Hell?

"Class catalogs and other information will be sent within the week," Miss Westin continued. "Feel free to browse and prepare for next year's courses. Registration materials will also be sent for those of you joining us for the summer session." She removed her octagonal classes, and almost as an afterthought said, "And for the rest of you, enjoy your vacation."

The surviving freshman class let out a collective sigh, and there were whoops of joy—and then they all broke into smaller groups, excitedly chattering to one another.

"We made it," Fiona said with as much enthusiasm as if she'd just commented on the weather.

"Until next year," Eliot replied.

Parents entered the ballroom, hugging their sons and daughters, clasping hands, and enjoying the moment. Apparently the Paxington rule about only students and instructors allowed on campus had been lifted today. The Scalagaris were easy to spot in their tailored suits and chiseled Italian features. There were some of the Dreaming Families here as well—Pritchards and Rhodes and De Marcos, all sporting Rolexes and looking literally like a million bucks.

Eliot wished Audrey or Louis were here to share this. Okay, his mother and father would probably kill each other on sight—that was beside the point.

But even the Covington clan had a gathering here today—old men in kilts, and all of them laughing uproariously at Jeremy as he told a joke.

Fiona's jaw clenched as she saw him; her hands curled into fists . . . but she said nothing.

She'd been so withdrawn since they'd come back from Hell. In fact, since Sealiah had declared Eliot an Infernal Lord, Fiona had said the absolute minimum to him, like: *get out of the bathroom,* and *move* and *we're going to be late,* and other various grunts that had meant yes or no.

Dante Scalagari broke from his family and moved to them. He straightened his sports jacket. "Congratulations," he said, "both of you. I'm here for my cousin, Gina, but I couldn't help but intrude when I saw you. That first day of school, I thought you wouldn't make it. Now you're the talk of the entire school!" He smiled and actually looked impressed.

Eliot was about to explain that technically they hadn't graduated yet. They still had to pass Miss Westin's makeup final. Instead, he just said, "Thanks," wondering what would impress a Scalagari upperclassman.

"Going to Hell and back to rescue a team member?" Dante continued. "You two are legends now."

Eliot and Fiona shared a look of shock. That was all supposed to be secret.

Then Eliot spotted Jeremy laughing across the room.

Of course. Jeremy would've told everyone and probably claimed that *he* led them heroically to Hell himself—defending them at the Gates of Perdition at great risk to his life.

A group of girls came up to Fiona, surrounded her and gushed congratulations. They wanted to hear absolutely everything that happened in the Lands of the Dead.

Eliot silently stepped back and felt as if he'd melted into the shadows.

Dante and the girls maneuvered around Fiona as she protested, but then she relented, saying it was no big deal and then telling them all about Elysium Fields.

Eliot let her. It might cheer her up.

It didn't matter that Eliot was socially invisible once more. Apparently even though he was a school "legend" *he* had somehow nothing to do with their adventures.

Good. This time he was grateful for it. He would watch Fiona in the limelight and *not* have to answer a bunch of awkward questions.

It was as if nothing had changed.

He looked at his hands, and realized that nothing *had* changed. There were no claws. No scales. And he wasn't going to be growing bat wings anytime soon, either, or suddenly becoming a superstrong six-story tall monster. The title of Infernal Lord was just that, a title.

So there was no big deal about winning a piece of land in Hell . . . besides being able to free Jezebel.

He looked around. Where was Jezebel?

He saw Sarah Covington staring at him—the only person in the room who noticed he was there. She looked at her loudmouth cousin and then back to Eliot, and rolled her eyes in exasperation.

Eliot then realized that one other person was missing. Robert.

Robert was probably the only one who even had a clue how he felt. Fiona hadn't said a word to him after the battle. Robert hadn't said much to her, either. When they'd all returned, Robert had told Eliot he needed "to take a ride." He'd walked straight away from the BART station and they hadn't seen him since.

Eliot called him from home, but just got a recorded message saying that number was out of service.

The ballroom doors opened, spilling light into the room.

A girl entered.

The way the light hit her, and from where Eliot stood, he could just see her silhouette.

Heads turned . . . a few at first . . . and the people who saw her trailed off in their congratulations. More people looked . . . until everyone stared at her and the ballroom was silent.

She sashayed in and the crowds parted for her.

Miss Westin and the other teachers looked astonished, and then their expressions soured into serious disapproval.

Then Eliot got a good look.

Jezebel. It *was* her, but not like he'd ever seen her before.

She was in her Paxington uniform . . . sort of. Instead of loafers, though, she wore thigh-high, high-heel boots of coffee-colored leather. Bronze studs curved from her ankle and spiraled about her leg. Fishnet stockings highlighted the hint of flesh that showed between those boots and the hem of her pleated skirt. A wide belt cinched her waist and covered half her bare midriff. The gleam of an emerald swayed in her pierced navel. She *did* have on the standard Paxington jacket with its distinctive school crest on the lapel, but instead of the white dress shirt, she had on a black T-shirt with a poison green radiation symbol stenciled with the words ATOMIC PUNK.

Her hair was straight and platinum blond, but streaked with black. She wore heavy eyeliner that made her blue-green eyes seem large and luminous.

Her features were no longer that perfect porcelain, either; they were human. Not the Julie Marks he had known, but part Julie, part Jezebel, and something entirely new. A hairline scar traced down from her temple to the corner of her mouth.

Her lips slipped into an easy smile as she saw him. It was the same dazzling hundred-watt smile he had fallen in love with, full of joy in life and the promise of what Eliot hoped might be a happy ending to their drama.

Jezebel walked toward him—a crooked stride that was hypnotic. She then stopped before him, beaming.

"I . . . I don't know what to say," Eliot murmured to her.

"Then don't say anything," she told him, the faintest hint of her old Southern accent back in her voice. She drew close, wrapped her arms about him, and kissed him.

He held her and kissed her back, slow at first, but tasting her—feeling her poison spreading through him—not numbing like that last time on the Night Train; it tingled and burned and was a honeyed drug he couldn't get enough of.

But he pulled away, coming up for air . . . and she set a hand on his chest and pushed gently back.

"There is good news and bad news, my liege," she whispered. "Which would you like to hear first?"

Eliot hesitated, trying to wrap him mind around her calling him *my liege* after an entire year of her calling him a fool.

He supposed, technically, there was some sort of feudal relationship if he owned the land she lived on. It felt weird already, though, that she had kissed him and been so friendly, considering their new—what? Business relationship?

But that had been his plan, hadn't it? Claim the land that Jezebel had been tied to and then set her free?

He took a step back and collected himself. "Uh, good news, I guess," he said.

She licked her lips. "Miss Westin is giving me a chance to graduate. Even after missing the last semester."

Eliot then noticed that almost everyone stared at them—especially Miss Westin, whose gaze was heavy with displeasure.

"The bad news," Jezebel continued, and frowned, "is that to do so, I have to make up all my classes at summer school. *All* summer long."

"Then you're staying here?"

She nodded. "Sealiah has paid for everything: tuition, room and board, books, but . . ." Her gaze dropped to the floor. "It is now for *you* to decide if I stay at Paxington and continue on next year, or if I am to return with you now."

Eliot lifted her chin. Her eyes were the color of aquamarines, and there wasn't a trace of humor or falsehood in their depths. She wasn't joking.

How was it his decision what she did? And return with him where?

"I'd never tell you what to do," he said. "It's your life. What do *you* want to do?"

Jezebel twisted from his hand. "As I said, it is for you to tell me. You are now the Lord of the Burning Orchards. I'm a part of those lands." She added in a sad whisper so soft that he barely heard: "I belong to you."

Eliot shook his head. "Nobody 'belongs' to anyone. Okay—forget that. It's probably some weird Infernal custom. I'll just set you free."

She looked at him with a mixture of frustration and adoration on her face. "Oh, Eliot, it doesn't work that way. No one can be set free in Hell. Ever."

This was too much. There was no way Eliot was going to *own* another person. He was about to argue further, but sensed someone behind him.

"I hate to interrupt," Fiona said, sounding very much like that was precisely what she wanted.

He turned and saw Fiona locked in a hate-filled stare with Jezebel.

Jezebel met Fiona stare for stare, and flashed her a smile.

"If you're done embarrassing yourselves with that tacky liplock," Fiona told her, "I need my brother back."

Jezebel's hand snaked around Eliot's neck. "Oh, I don't think we'll be done for a long time. Why don't you occupy yourself in the meantime with your *own* boyfriend?" She feigned a concern expression. "Oh, I'm sorry. I forgot. You chased one of your boyfriends off . . . and the other one's dead."

Fiona turned white. She growled through clenched teeth, "Shut— your—mouth."

Eliot extracted himself from Jezebel and stepped between them. To Jezebel, he said, "Don't. We'll talk later." He turned Fiona. "You have my full attention. What's up?"

Fiona grabbed Eliot's hand and dragged him across the room. "We forgot someone—or rather, some*thing*."

"What are you talking about?" Eliot pulled away from her and halted.

Fiona glanced back at Jezebel. "One day your girlfriend is going to go too far." She then strode off without Eliot. "Come on. We have an appointment to keep."

"Hey, wait up. I still don't—"

Fiona marched straight to the Covingtons.

Eliot hurried after her.

"Ah, my dearest Miss Post," Jeremy said, bowing with a flourish and shaking his hair into a golden mane. He held a flask in one hand, and the smell of whiskey hung in the air. The others in the group (Eliot assumed they were Covingtons, too, from their similarly freckled sardonic features) backed up a pace at the sight of Fiona.

Sarah, however, moved to Jeremy's side. Her hair was pulled back into a tight bun and her uniform was freshly pressed. She looked wary and apologetic at the same time.

Fiona asked Sarah, "You said before you wanted to make amends?"
Jeremy looked at his cousin, and his stupid drunken grin faded.
"Aye, I did," Sarah whispered.
"You have a car?" Fiona asked. "We need you to drive us someplace."
"Of course," Sarah said. "Where?"
"Del Sombra."

ALL THAT LIVES MUST DIE

iona kicked through the sand and watched tumbleweeds roll by. She wasn't sure she could find the place again among this suburb that had never been. There were cinder block walls, ribbons of faded asphalt, and the fragments of house foundations.

"What are we looking for again?" Sarah asked. She put on sunglasses and a baseball cap to protect her freckled skin from the raw sun.

"Manhole cover," Fiona told her.

"Do I want to know why?" Sarah wrinkled her nose.

"Not really." Eliot grunted as he carried all their equipment: a backpack picked up at their Pacific Heights house on the way out here—filled with flashlights, Fiona's old shotgun, shells, and rubber waders. He also had his guitar slung on his back.

Fiona heard the resentment in her brother's voice.

Yeah—she knew he wanted to be with Jezebel (she practically gagged thinking of them kissing)—but he had been just as curious about this . . . once he remembered.

Fiona glanced up. To the east was the Del Oro Recycling Plant, shuttered and closed. To the west was Del Sombra, at least what was left of it.

She felt a pang of grief as she saw dust devils spinning down what had been Midway Avenue, where their apartment building had been . . . and Ringo's All-American Pizza Parlor . . . and the Pink Rabbit. A few skeletal building supports stood erect, but everything else had been burned down.

And while some agro-entrepreneur had planted fields of grapevine between here and there, the city had been left alone.

She asked Eliot, "A little help?"

Eliot sighed like she'd asked for six pints of blood, but relented and dropped the backpack and pulled his guitar around. He plunked the strings and the notes sounded like drops of water.

The sands shifted.

He plucked out more three chords that reminded her of running trickles and currents and something alive snaking through that water.

A line in the sand traced from Eliot, curved thirty paces straight ahead, until it spiraled to a stop.

Fiona strode toward the spot. She knelt, brushed aside the sand, and found the steel underneath. There was a tiny hole in the manhole cover, and she stuck her finger in it and tugged. No way. It weighed too much—and the thought of being stopped by such a trivial thing made her anger flare.

She ripped the thing out and tossed the solid metal disk like it was a Frisbee.

Eliot handed her a flashlight and a pair of rubber boots.

"What's down there?" Sarah asked.

"Sewer," Fiona replied, pulling on the too-tight boots.

"I can see that. But why are *we* going down there?"

"There's no 'we.' You're staying up here." Fiona regretted the commanding tone she used. Sarah was trying to do right by them. "Look," she added, "it's going to be dangerous. There's something . . . well, not evil, more . . ."

"Hungry," Eliot finished for her.

Sarah arched an eyebrow. "I can take care of myself."

She meant it. But why would anyone want to crawl into a sewer with them?

Then Fiona understood: Sarah wanted to prove she was their friend and would have followed them into danger . . . even into Hell, *if* she'd been given the chance.

But that was stupid. This could really be dangerous.

On the other hand, Fiona wanted her to come and prove her sincerity. She knew that was wrong: Friends didn't do that to each other.

But had Sarah truly ever been her friend?

"Suit yourself," Fiona told her. "But if you chicken out halfway there—you're finding your own way back. Eliot and I have business to take care of."

"Hey," Eliot said. "That's not right."

"It's okay," Sarah said, casting an uncertain glance down the hole. "I'll be fine."

Fiona clambered into the sewer hole and down the ladder. Last time she'd plunked into the water. This time, she found the ledge by the channel and stepped onto it.

She played her flashlight beam over the cinder blocks of the intersection. Mats of slick algae covered everything, hanging down from the ceiling like boogery stalactites. She imagined herself slipping on the stuff and going headfirst into the slimy water.

Sarah came down next and then Eliot.

Eliot plucked a note and it echoed down a single passage only. "That way."

Sarah tested her foot on the ledge. "Hang on." She knelt and touched the concrete ledge. The cinder blocks shifted; a ripple in the stone spread outward and raised into a waffle pattern. "A bit of traction, courtesy of Covington conjuration."

"Thanks," Fiona murmured, and plodded ahead.

No rats this time . . . although Fiona almost wished there were. She spotted a pile of algae-covered rodent bones. Ick.

They spiraled down, and the water gurgled faster in the channel next to them. Cinder block was replaced by ancient brick and rusted supports, and the air was thick with humidity and the scent of blood.

Ahead was the chamber they were looking for. It was bigger than Fiona recalled, half a block wide with three holes in the roof where sunlight filtered through from the surface. The room was flooded; in the center of this lake was an island of bones—all chewed and broken.

Sitting upon the island was Sobek, oracle crocodile, the once–Egyptian god of the passages to the Underworld.

It had been their first heroic trial to "vanquish" the forty-foot-long reptilian beast that lived in the Del Sombra sewers. It was all part of some weird urban legend about alligators flushed down toilets that Fiona had never understood.

A year ago, Sobek could have easily killed them. It had even pinned Fiona to the ground and opened its maw as if to devour her . . . and she'd gotten a look into the black oblivion inside the creature. It had been injured, however—a spike driven through its shoulder, and they had made friends with it by pulling the thing out.

She and Eliot had been weak and naïve then, and survived only because the crocodile had been convinced by his prophetic powers that *they* were going to kill *it*.

Maybe it hadn't been wrong. She and Eliot were young gods now, tested in battle.

Everything had changed.

But so had Sobek.

Its body was as big as an eighteen-wheel semitruck, and its thick tail sinewed about the island of bones. Its armored scales were glossy ebon black flecked with green and gold.

A pair of slitted eyes opened and stared.

Fiona's stomach sank. It was like something she might've seen in a science book on the Permian period, something that lived before even the dinosaurs . . . something primeval, instinctively cunning, and utterly savage.

There was a pull from the creature, and she felt her feet involuntarily shuffle forward through the water.

Eliot set his hand on Lady Dawn strings and the light vibration snapped her out of the reptile's hypnotic sway.

Sarah, who had put on a brave face all the way down here, now stood locked with terror.

"Stay here," Fiona whispered to her.

Sarah gave a nod, and remained frozen in place.[71]

Fiona and Eliot waded through the water to Sobek.

Its tail uncurled, slid into the murky pool, and swished with irritation. "You have returned too early," he told them with a voice so resonant that it shook Fiona's bones and made ripples dance on the water.

"Only—" Fiona's voice broke.

Sobek had told them to return in a year . . . when he'd answer questions for them. A year in which the crocodile had said it needed to eat and replenish his strength. Fiona had thought that exaggeration at the time, but looking at the jumble of bones and its increased mass . . . she wondered.

She cleared her throat and tried again. "Only twenty-six days until the year is up," she managed.

---

71. "I have stared into the eyes of Ancient Death. Was this our future? Our doom?" Thus begins Sarah Covington's first entry in what would later be known as her notorious *Secret Red Diaries*. Sarah Covington had kept journals before and concurrent with her "red" diaries, but those contained details of her pre-Paxington personal life, ongoing Covington political dramas, and her familial teachings. The *Secret Red Diaries*, on the other hand, detail her long and tortuous relationships with the Post twins. Given where those relationships ended, her writings provide a unique mortal's perceptive to their fantastic journeys, the wars to come, and the eventual fate of the Middle Realms. *Gods of the First and Twenty-first Century, Volume 11, The Post Family Mythology*. Zypheron Press Ltd., Eighth Edition.

"We need to know what's going to happen," Eliot added.

A snort exploded through the reptile's snout. "I have foreseen your early return. So I'm here. And ready. Come closer."

Fiona swallowed and moved toward the island of bones, careful not to slip on the slimy remains and impale herself. She touched her rubber band always on her wrist in case she needed it.

She and Eliot halted thirty paces from Sobek, close enough to speak, but, she hoped, out of the crocodile's lunging strike range. How easily could such a monster just snap them up? They might not even get a chance to fight back.

It smelled of blood and rotten meat, and a musky scent that her primitive brain defined as "reptilian."

"So much has happened," she whispered.

"I have watched the water and read your futures," it said. "Come and see with thine own eyes."

Was this a trick to lure them closer?

Fiona didn't think so. How could this thing *still* be hungry? And yet she hesitated because the animal part of her brain was rightfully afraid and suspected the creature had a supernatural hunger that was *never* sated.

Eliot, however, stupidly brave as always, walked forward.

So Fiona followed.

One foot in front of the other she moved until they felt Sobek's stinking, moist breath on their faces.

There was a rivulet between them and the crocodile—a stream through which water burbled along with strings of algae and floating bits of paper.

"Look," it commanded.

Fiona squinted into the water (one hand still on her rubber band). Her eyes defocused, and she saw the waves and currents blur into lines of light and shadow that crossed and fluttered and stretched from here and now . . . farther downstream and off in the future.

As Aunt Dallas had showed her how to do so long ago.

Her lifeline stretched on and on as far as she could see. It pulsed like quicksilver. There were many others in the surrounding weave: golden threads and silver lines and coarse flax fiber and taut leather cords. Some wound about her thread. Some snapped and fell away. Some new strands joined with hers farther on—ones that glimmered like emerald and ruby and sapphire and threw off sparks of light.

It seemed normal, she guessed. Was it possible everything was going to be okay?

Farther along, however, she saw new threads: concertina barbed wire and battered chains. Her line cut through those, leaving snapped and severed lives in the wake of her destiny.

She smelled brimstone and fire and blood.

There were smaller fibers, too: thousands of fine ordinary cotton threads that were broken or burned away by the larger lines pushing forward and distorting the pattern.

War. There was going to be a war, and Fiona would lead the charge.

How many would die because of her?

Or was the right question, How many would she *save*?

It was so obvious now—Immortal versus Infernal. Good versus evil.

And where was Eliot's thread? There was nothing there that felt like him.

Far off, though, waves and melodies rebounded through the fabric, ripples and blurs that had to be his music . . . but it was not bound to her thread.

She blinked and looked up.

Sobek had crept so close that Fiona could have reached up and touched its snout.

Eliot shook his head. "I don't see anything. It's all tangled ahead."

But Sobek's slitted eyes locked with Fiona's. "*You* saw."

"Yes," she breathed. "A war."

"Not *just* a war," Sobek rumbled. "*The* war. Among the gods and the angels . . . war among everyone . . . everywhere. Armageddon." The reptile looked at Eliot and then back to her. "And you will choose sides."

Deep down, Fiona had known this was coming. She had once hoped that both sides of her family could get along—that there'd even be some sort of corny reunion between her mother and father and all their relatives.

But now that they'd gone to Hell and come back?

It was clear how evil the Infernals were . . . that given a chance, they wouldn't stop at fighting for *just* their lands . . . they'd come to mortal realms. And the only thing that had been stopping them was the League of Immortals and the *Pactum Pax Immortalus* . . . until she and Eliot had come along.

"It'll be like Ultima Thule all over again," Fiona murmured. "We'll need someone to lead us in battle. Is he still alive?"

"He?" Sobek held her gaze a long time, and then said, "Ah, Zeus? Odin,

Ra, Titan Slayer, and Dux Bellorum of all Battles? I cannot see him. Not since long ago." ·

"But is he alive?" Fiona whispered.

"I cannot say."

That wasn't an answer—but it didn't matter. There were answers enough here for Fiona. She knew what she had to do.

"I'm going to find him," she said, stood tall, and took in a deep breath, despite the stench. "And if I can't find Zeus, or if he's really dead, then I'll find another to lead the Immortals."

And if she couldn't find a leader among them? She wasn't sure. She'd cross that bridge if she came to it.

"Don't," Eliot said. "Hasn't there been enough fighting? There's got to be another way. Let me try to talk to Dad and Sealiah."

Fiona laughed. "Talk? That's not what they do! All they do is lie and backstab and take whatever they are strong enough to take."

She heard the truth in her statement ring like a silver bell in the air.

"There *will* be war," Sobek declared. "That much is clear. Many will die . . . though you should not grieve. All that lives must die—the gods—the angels—all must move on."

Fiona felt a stab of sorrow as she thought about Mitch and all the other people she might know who could be killed. But how many more would die if she did nothing and let the Infernals have their way?

Eliot, however, went on as if he hadn't heard Sobek's prophecy. "Just give me a chance to fix things," he said. "I can do it."

"You can't fix Mom and Dad," she spat. "You can't fix any of them. They all *want* this. And they want you, too." She stared into his eyes, pleading. "Don't go over to their side. Come with me to the Council. They can help us. And give up Jezebel—she's nothing but poison."

"I know what she is," Eliot whispered. "But there's more to it now than just her." He stared at some distant point and his forehead crinkled in frustration. "I have to find out what being part of that family means. We're *both* half Infernal."

"No," Fiona said with absolute certainty. "It's my *choice* what I want to be."

"Then it's my choice, too," he told her.

"Don't be stupid," Fiona whispered. "Things can't end like this: us on different sides."

Eliot shook his head. "You just don't understand." He turned and walked away.

Sarah started after him, but stopped when she saw the look of contempt on Fiona's face. She hesitated, took a step toward Eliot, but then halted and stayed with Fiona.

Fiona could have gone after her brother—maybe even have stopped him, or at least, *made* him listen to her.

But she didn't.

He had gone too far. He was lost to her.

"And so," Sobek murmured, "as I have foreseen: the Heralds of the End of Days are split asunder."

PATCHED

This was a bad idea. Audrey felt it chill her to the bone, despite the cash-mere wrap about her shoulders. She set her hands over the votive candle on the table and let the light and shadows play over her fingers.

When she had heard what happened to Eliot and Fiona—after worrying for weeks and weeks when they'd disappeared—that they'd fought in a war in Hell . . . she had almost died.

She had sworn to kill Louis for his recklessness.

Then she calmed and understood that it had been a logical move for the Infernals . . . that her children were more powerful than ever . . . and that certain opportunities now might present themselves before the end of the world.

It was a childish dream that she could love again or that her family could ever be whole.

She sighed.

A pity she had not the courage to cut *Louis* from *her* heart. Had that been selfishness or foolishness?

She looked across the walkway and saw moonlight flicker like a thou-sand fish upon the waters of the Canal Grande of Venice. Lovers strolled arm in arm by the sidewalk café. A breeze ruffled the jasmine in their planter boxes and filled the air with their cloying scent.

She was surrounded by people in love in the most romantic city on Earth . . . ironic, because she was alone.

This was the spot where she and the then-masked Louis Piper had talked all night, waxed poetic about life and longings and how only simpletons fell in love. As the dawn had broken upon the canal and tinged the silver waters red, they had lifted one another's masks—and she had felt the piercing of her heart, and known that she was a simpleton, too.

Love.

Cornelius had told her even the Primordial Ones had loved after a fashion, although it had been a savage thing compared with the refined emotions of their Age.

The waiter came and refreshed her cup of minted Turkish coffee. "Still waiting, madam?"

She nodded.

Indeed, what a simpleton she was then *and* now. She rose from her seat and straightened her silver silk gown. She had dressed for the opera with matching arm-length gloves, pearls, and heels—all courtesy of Madame Cobweb. Her effort wasted.

She was about to turn and walk away, when she spotted him.

Louis, the Grand Deceiver, and the only man who could so irritate her, hurried through the crowds. When he saw her, his face lit with all the passion and intensity she remembered from their first morning together. He wore a tuxedo with tails and diamond studs—and turned every woman's head.

"Audrey, beloved," he said, and reached for her hands (which she pulled away). "I would have rather died than be late, but there was something of the utmost importance that required my personal attention."

He implored her to sit, and she reluctantly did so.

"Really?" She mustered as much icy sarcasm as she could, and yet Atropos, Cutter of all Things, and Death incarnate, felt her heart flutter and her pulse race with warmth she thought she would never feel again.

A black cat leaped onto the linen-covered table between them—its tail fluffing into Louis's face.

Louis stiffened and grabbed the animal by the scruff of the neck. In response, the cat's claws extended and dimpled into the tablecloth, dragging it with him.

"Don't, Louis." She gently took the animal and set in the seat next to her.

The waiter stared at the cat, frowning—but Audrey stopped any protest from him with a single glance.

She stroked Amberflaxus and the cat turned and turned and nuzzled her hand for more. "I'm surprised more people haven't noticed this poor creature by now, and drowned it in a well."

Louis shrugged. "That might be for the best."

"You don't mean that."

He thought about it a moment. "No." He narrowed his eyes at the cat, then his gaze roamed over her gown, and his mood brightened. "You look absolutely radiant tonight, my dear."

Audrey stopped petting Amberflaxus and held up her hand. "Let me make it clear that I came only because you said you wanted to talk about the children."

His smile flickered to life. "Do you think you can lie to me? About this? Your coquettishness flatters me."

Audrey closed her eyes. How could she forget? Louis, the Father of Lies, of course, would hear the false words spilling from her lips.

She exhaled. "Yes," she admitted, "I came for the children *and* to deal with you once and for all—but mainly for the children."

His smile turned mischievous, and he reached into his tuxedo and pulled out a folded manila envelope. He pushed it across the table.

Audrey opened the flap. Inside were two sheets of curling vellum that felt rough and cold even through her gloves. She unrolled them and read along the top:

WARRANT OF DEATH

Her breath caught as she scanned the bottom of the page, seeing the filled-in name: ELIOT POST.

She flipped to the other page and saw: FIONA POST.

Only Louis ever had the ability to render her speechless—but this, even for him, was going too far. Audrey, however, found her voice. "How did you get these? You shouldn't have even been able to enter Altium—"

Louis waved her concerns away. Yes, yes. Technicalities and details. That pesky *Pactum Pax Immortalis*. I shouldn't be able to touch anything that belongs to the League." He slapped his hand across the page in utter defiance of the centuries-old treaty.

"Unless one of us gave it to you," Audrey whispered. "Unless you had help."

"Before you ask how and who," Louis replied, "allow me my little secrets for a while yet. Without an air of mystery, I fear I would as bland as all those other dull Immortals in your life."

Audrey knew prying information out of Louis when he was being difficult would be harder than wrestling the ocean. But what Immortal in their right mind would have helped Louis? And the more important question: Why?

She returned her attention to the documents and pulled off her opera gloves. She had an opportunity. She slid her finger down the center of the pages—then across—and then made two diagonal marks with her fingernail.

The pages shuddered, sparked with magic, and flowered into a thousand shreds of confetti.

Audrey brushed the trash off the table.

"Well," Louis said, raising an eyebrow, "that should keep Fiona and Eliot safe from the League—at least until the Council can come to consensus again. Which should that take what? A month? All summer?"

"Perhaps," Audrey murmured.

Would Lucia wait that long? Had the League ever taken action without its bureaucratic processes?

"Does that then satisfy your need to tend to our children first?" he asked.

"No. It delays the danger; it does not eliminate it."

Louis sighed. "The world in which our children live will always be filled with danger. We cannot eliminate it, and it would be foolish to try."

Audrey considered this . . . but said nothing.

"There is one more thing we might do, however," Louis whispered and looked about. "We can gather support, in secret, for the coming war. Not for one side or the other, but for *them*."

Louis would not mention such a thing unless he had already taken action. "You will not be able to keep *that* secret for long."

"No," he admitted. "The best secrets are the ones least kept."

"When they find out—both families—we will have to take bold, bloody action. Will you be ready for that?"

"It gives me chills of pleasure when you speak thusly," Louis purred.

He reached for her hand again, but she moved away before he could distract her.

Audrey opened her clutch. "I have a gift for you as well," she said.

"Oh?" Louis said and looked surprised for once in his life.

She wasn't sure she should do this. It would be as dangerous as slipping Cerberus from his leash . . . or arming a nuclear device. But all her second-guessing couldn't stop her now; this already been decided—not with her head, but with her newly awakened emotions.

Audrey took out a battered enveloped, so worn the paper was fuzzy and it almost fell apart at her touch.

"Eliot left this with a note explaining how you gave it to him before the final battle in the Poppy Lands. I . . . I was moved."

She gingerly removed the contents: bits of bank statements and torn dollar bills and old restaurant receipts and post-it notes and tissues—all of it had been meticulously taped back together into a proper heart shape.

Audrey set the thing on the table between them, took Louis's hand, and set it upon the battered token.

His smile went slack with astonishment as he beheld it. "What have you done?" he whispered.

She patted his hand. "I give you your heart back, Louis, healed and whole."

He gazed at the paper heart, tracing its rough edges, speechless for the first time .

"I'm sorry," she said, uncomfortable with his silence. "I am so good at cutting things . . . not so good, though, at patching them together. It was the best I could do."

Louis met her eyes. "You realize, of course, you may have just sealed the both our dooms? I forgive you—and more. Much more."

Louis picked up the token in both hands, brought it to his chest, inhaled, and savored it for a moment . . . and then presented it back to Audrey.

"For you," he told her. "It was always yours to do with as you wished: to treasure and keep safe—or to tear into a million pieces again. I have no defenses against you."

She hesitated, actually reached out and touched it—then halted. "No," she whispered. "I am not ready. Perhaps one day, Louis, but not now."

Louis frowned and it made his nose and jaw seem more crooked. "Of course, my dear. What else do we have, if not all the time in the world?"

Amberflaxus batting at her hand, interested in the heart.

"No," she told the cat. "This is not a toy."

Louis snorted. "Watch that wretched animal," he warned her. "Of all the creatures in all the worlds, *that* one would most love to get a piece of me to devour."

He retrieved his paper heart and tucked it into his tuxedo.

Audrey stroked that cat's back to mollify it (and grateful for the distraction). "No one has noticed your pet, and your lack of . . . ?"

"I have been lucky," Louis told her.

Audrey scrutinized Louis and the space about him that flickered in candlelight. The deviation from normality was subtle at night, and yet, when one knew what to look for . . . it was glaringly obvious.

Louis cast no shadow.[72, 73]

That was Audrey's fault. When she had first learned that Louis was Infernal, she had flown into a blind rage—stabbed at him, meaning to sever his power from his physical form, and then cut his heart out so he could love no other.

All of which she managed, but her first strike had astonishingly missed, and instead cut off his shadow.

And like all parts of the Grand Deceiver, it was wily and evasive, and had run from her, finally taking the form of a cat.

A shadow cat that had grown to enjoy its freedom.

She scratched under Amberflaxus's chin. The cat purred. It was still a part of him, yet somehow, a creature all its own: an annoyance, his spy, a mischievous imp that was Louis incarnate.

Louis scattered a handful of euros on the table to pay for her coffee. "Come," he said, "and leave that creature or he will tear your gown."

"Are you taking me to the opera? I've heard Ferruccio Busoni's *Doktor Faust* is playing tonight."

Louis's face curled with disgust. "Surely you jest."

Her lips formed a rare half smile. "I do. No, I thought we would walk and talk. It has been so long, Louis. And there is so much to consider."

He smiled back. "Just talk?"

"Yes, for now. But it *is* a start between us."

---

72. On the Nature of Shadows in Identification: Unattended shadows are thought by some cultures to be ghosts unable to end their existence in the Middle Realms. The Zulu tribe holds that a dead body cannot cast a shadow. An alternative view is that shadows are a representation of God's presence around an object (cf. a halo). Early European beliefs claim that a man without a shadow was a witch or had sold his soul to the Devil. These legends remain hypothetical; however, it is a fact that vampires cast no shadow as do all similar limbic undead species. *A Modern Hunters Guide to the Unliving,* Valor Mitchellson & Nikola Telsa, Double Fork Lightning Press, 1890, London.

73. Wendy sews on Peter Pan's shadow after he has lost it in J. M. Barrie's *The Boy Who Wouldn't Grow Up.* —Editor.

Louis considered for a long time, his expression uncharacteristically solemn, and then finally nodded. "A start then." He offered her his hand.

Audrey didn't trust Louis, the Prince of All Lies; she never would, either. But they had a common interest: the welfare of their children. And, counter to all her common sense, part of her still adored Louis. Or was this merely the memory of a younger love that she still felt?

The old passion was gone; they could not go back to it . . . but she was willing to moving forward with Louis, as what? Friends, enemies, allies, or lovers once more?

She wasn't sure. But she was sure that she wanted to find out.

Audrey took Louis's hand, and together they strolled into the darkness.

"Tell me, then," she whispered to him, "everything."

THE STORM THAT NONE SURVIVE

Dallas looked from her penthouse suite across the winking lights of night-time Manhattan.

It was dazzling. Like herself.

She had dressed to the nines for the occasion in a slip of a black thing, sequined stockings, and five-inch stiletto heels. But she had had a lifetime of this glamour—several lifetimes, in fact . . . and was ready to leave it behind.

Grow up? Not a chance. She had grown up before, and it wasn't her.

But the time to change to *something* else had come.

She turned the card over and over in her hand . . . as if she flipped it enough times she would see the secret message on it, explaining it was just a bad joke.

It had arrived by special messenger this morning—a goshawk that had perched on her balcony, screeched once at her, left the card fluttering to the floor, and then had flown off to slaughter pigeons.

The card was engraved with curlicue calligraphy that was nearly impossible to read.

Lucia sent it—to annoy her—to worry her—to make her cry.

She understood why her older sister, Audrey, was so cruel. She had strategic reasons.

Lucia was cruel, not out of necessity, but because it made her feel powerful and others around her weak. Dallas supposed that was a strategy as well.

She sighed, wondering if all sisters tortured one another so, and then read the message again:

You are summoned before the Council of Elders, the Temple of Whispers, immediately and forthwith to receive instructions. We meet at
dawn. This is NOT a request.

Dallas had already heard what had happened to Eliot and Fiona. She
knew Lucia wasn't going to "instruct" her on anything. First she'd grill her
on how she'd escorted the twins through the Lands of the Dead. (Kino
would absolutely die.) They'd talk about her "lack of responsibility," assign
some punishment, but ultimately, they'd do what they always did and dis-
miss her as inconsequential . . . and then move on to what they really
wanted to talk about: how Eliot had gone over to the other "side."

It had all spun completely out of control.

And while Dallas could take care of herself and any League meddling,
Eliot and Fiona could not.

She had gotten a glimpse into the psyches of the twins. They were
young and yet they understood more about the truth of things than most
Immortals.

Fiona would take responsibility for the entire world if they let her. It
could crush her. But Fiona knew the League needed a real leader—not a
bureaucracy. If they didn't kill her first, she might one day be that leader.

Eliot, on the other hand, just wanted enough freedom to figure out who
he was. Poor kid. He believed that there was neither clear-cut good nor evil
when it came to Immortals and Infernals . . . just individuals with their
own agendas.

There might be some truth to that, too.

Certainly their father had helped—perhaps for his own selfish reasons,
but nonetheless he had helped them . . . while many in the League would
love to see both twins dead in the name of political stability.

Dallas wasn't sure of anyone or anything anymore.

She crossed the room, her high heels clipping over the marble.

She considered many in the League her family . . . but that didn't excuse their bad behavior and paranoia . . . the preservation of their power
at any cost . . . or that their next move might be to murder her youngest
nephew.

She tossed the Council summons into her fireplace and pressed a button on the wall.

Flames whooshed to life and consumed Lucia's note.

There would be complications and consequences for that little rebellion. No one simply defied the League . . . and no one quit the League of Immortals once a member.

Across her vast living room, clapping echoed off high walls covered with Picasso paintings.

"Bravo!" Henry cried.

Dallas didn't turn. It was no surprise that he had entered her sanctum without knocking (she had, after all, extended him an open invitation), but for some reason this time, the violation of her privacy made her irrationally angry.

"How long have you watched?"

"Not long." She heard his footstep approaching. "Just enough to see you finally come to your senses."

"Sense! What do *you* know of sense?"

She spun, ready to confront him—but stopped . . . and had to laugh.

Henry looked ridiculous. He was dressed as an eighteenth-century French nobleman in a silver-and-black waistcoat with embroidered peacocks chasing peahens up and down the sleeves, with silver buttons, black velvet pants that tied at his calves, silver stockings and buckled shoes. Topping it all off was a ridiculous powdered wig.

Henry the Fool. He would live as a fool—continue as a fool—and one day die playing the fool.

And she loved him for it.

"I'm off to the Governor's Ball," he told her, with a luxuriant wave over his outfit. "It's a costumed affair. Would you care to join me? You're a bit underdressed, but I doubt anyone will be looking at your clothes. . . ."

"No," she told him. "I need to think about everything you've told me of the twins and the Infernals and the League . . . and *your* plans."

He nodded. "Thinking is overrated, darling Dallas. That's the League's modus operandi, not mine. I require the Dallas who acts."

That Dallas.

He was talking about part of her she had long buried. There is no need for that creature in this world. And yet . . . if the world was ending—why not summon the demons of her past?

"Do you know what you're doing, Henry? Really?"

"The costume ball? Oh . . . no, I see you mean that *other* thing. No. I don't 'know' anything." Henry sobered. "But it is my best *guess*."

"It all comes down to a guess?"

Henry shrugged.

Dallas sighed, knowing her heart of hearts that she'd trust one of the Old Wolf's guesses over any of Cornelius's laser-precise calculations or a Council consensus engineered by Lucia.

She marched over to the wet bar.

Henry followed, helping himself to her sixty-year-old scotch.

Dallas set her hand on a black marble square. It warmed under her touch.

There was a hum and the wall parted, revealing racks of gleaming knives and swords, and the polished wooden and the blue steel of pistols and rifles.

These did not belong to the carefree hippie girl façade she had enjoyed as much as Henry had enjoyed his multitude of masks. These instruments of destruction belonged to her alter ego.

Her finger lit on of her twin gold swords—last wielded at Ultima Thule and still as sharp as the day when Audrey had given them their edges.

There were two matchlock pistols with barrels the size of her fist. Hand cannon, Aaron had called them.

It was a small collection, nothing like Aaron's armory, but there were all dear to her, and almost every weapon here had a matching mate. Lucia was always telling her that she didn't know her right from her left most of the time.

True enough. She was perfectly ambidextrous.

As Dallas gazed at these instruments, she grew afraid—not for herself, but for all those that she loved.

She turned back to Henry. "Are you sure? Once I start, I won't be able to take it back. Aaron and Gilbert—they will be devastated."

"I know they will be," Henry whispered. He swirled scotch and peered into its depths. "I also know your aim is unerring. I'm counting on both."

She stared at her beloved cousin, taking in every silly detail of his face. It would be the last time "Dallas" would look upon him.

She closer her eyes and turned.

When she opened them again she beheld one of the two weapons that had no mate: a bow of fused ram horns with a row of golden arrows next to it. It was deadly . . . but a relic from another Age.

She moved to its modern counterpart, forged in 1915, when she had believed the Great War might've been the last war on Earth. It had been centuries ahead of any other weapon constructed on this world, and even today, none was its equal. It was a matte gray bolt-action rifle with a thirty-inch barrel, a stock of fine-grained ebony (tiny snipes on the wing engraved upon it), retractable bipod, a mounted telescopic sight that could see through walls and in the dark and heat sources and aetherics and was self-focusing and had built-in microsecond "wink" flash suppression.

Arranged under the sniper rifle were rows of modified .338 Lapua Magnum ammunition, each round the length of her index finger, and each individually tailored to her exact specifications of powder load, overall weight, and metallurgical tip composition. Each was engraved with identifying mnemonic phrases like: "Double Down," "Flush," "Inside Straight," "Wildcard," "Stand Pat," and the ultimate, "Last Call."

She could obliterate a dime-sized target on a moonlit night in high winds from two kilometers.

She could kill any living creature from a *considerably* longer distance.

As she ran her fingers over the cold metal, she remembered the pleasure of its recoil.

Dallas submerged into memory and was no more. She was a child's toy that had to be lovingly packed away, perhaps to be taken out and played with another time . . . but not in this Age.

All believed that Audrey was the most dangerous of the Sisters of Fate—the Cutter of All Things, the Pale Rider, Kali, and Death incarnate; she was indeed terrible and impressive.

Some said that Lucia was the most powerful—the Weaver of the Threads of Fate, the Balance, Blind Justice, Lady Liberty, and She Who Topples Nations. She was certainly the most articulate and cunning of them.

But Dallas had also worn many names throughout history as well—happy-go-lucky avant-garde Dallas, Mother Nature, or simply Little Red . . . but before all these she had been dark and full of wrath, and cataclysms and destructions had followed in her wake.

And they had all forgotten.

She was the Waning Moon, Hecate, and the Storm Which None Survived.

She was once more Artemis the Huntress.

89

NO REST FOR THE WICKED

Robert kept his eyes closed and wished the world would go away.

Behind his lids the sun beat on him—a nice, natural sunshine. The surf churned thirty paces from where he lay in the sand. He smelled the open cerveza and limes wedges in a nearby ice bucket.

He should've been 100 percent chill.

But all he saw when he closed his eyes with that swollen red sun in Hell . . . the flash of swords and shadows . . . and Fiona's tear-streaked face as she cradled Mitch, watching him burn and die.

He felt his gut twist because the one girl he'd been hooked on now hated him.

He wasn't in Hell anymore, though; he was in his hidden fishing cove near Puedevas, Mexico—a six-pack and lobster enchiladas from the cantina, and him lounging in the sand.

So why feel lousy?

Maybe living people weren't supposed to come back from Hell. How had Dante Alighieri done it? (*Inferno* was one of the books Robert had read and actually enjoyed in Miss Westin's class.) Dante Alighieri had walked through Hell, into Purgatory, and then into Heaven. He'd been able to do that because he got a hand from the poet Virgil, and his one true love, Beatrice.

Robert's spirit guide, Marcus, hadn't *led* him anywhere—except smack into a war. And he sure wasn't no poet or Beatrice.

Robert also felt bad about Amanda. He should've gone back to look for her body. But how to get past all those angry dead in the Blasted Lands?

The thought of her soul suffering in the fires of Hell made him shudder, despite the warm sun.

And what about Eliot? Now that he had Jezebel and was an Infernal Lord, was he staying in Hell?

Robert grabbed a chunk of ice from the bucket and pressed it to his forehead.

Trouble hadn't miraculously stopped when Robert got back to San Francisco, either. There'd been a note on his apartment door: a summons to the Headmistress's office.

Like any of that mattered anymore. Robert wasn't going back to school.

There were also three voice mail messages from Henry. Robert had responded to these by ripping the answering machine out of the wall.

Sure, Henry could find him. He knew Robert's hiding spots. But Robert thought he might be strong enough now to refuse Henry's subtle suggestions and his not-so-subtle threats.

Robert curled his fist until bones cracked and sinews popped with tension. His new strength was from Henry's Soma. How long would that last? And he wasn't just physically stronger. Robert felt something hard in his mind now, too.

He grabbed a bottle of beer, but just held it, the cold glass sweating in his hand.

So now what? Robert was unemployed, maybe with no living friends on Earth, and certainly with no girl to worry about.

He laughed. This emo-feeling-sorry-for-himself thing just wasn't him.

Okay . . . he did feel a little sorry, but Robert knew he was going to be fine. He'd get over Fiona. Heck, he could stay right here and do a little fishing. With the cash that Henry had given him for school he might carve out a nice life on the Sea of Cortez. Maybe learn how to surf.

His fishing line tugged and the bell tied to it tinkled. His pole bent toward the water.

Robert got up. All this deep thinking stuff was fine—but not when it interfered with the barbecued sea bass he was counting on for dinner.

He blinked as his eyes adjusted to the sunlight . . . and saw something was wrong.

No, not *a* something—a *bunch* of somethings.

There were fish in the water, hundreds of them: perch and damselfish, and even a bluefin tuna or two thrashing in the surf. Behind them were sharks—white-tipped reef and nurse and even a flashing set of great white jaws—all frothing and fighting along the beach.

Tuna and great whites never got that close to shore.

There had to be a freak storm or a tsunami to get them all here at once.

A girl stepped from the blood-tinged surf as nonchalant as if she were stepping out of a chlorinated swimming pool.

She had all the right curves, and the sun glistened off her tanned skin. Her hair was red and gold and snaked down her neck, curling about her breasts . . . which was when Robert realized that she only wore a few strategically placed bits of clinging seaweed.

He took a step closer—but halted, realizing that besides the weird fish something was very wrong with this male fantasy come to life.

First: whenever he'd been attracted to any girl recently there'd been trouble. So that immediately set off alarm bells.

Second: the color of her skin wasn't anything he'd see before—bronze mixed with gold that glimmered like molten metal.

Third: she *was* wearing something, an obsidian knife strapped her shapely calf. A knife coated with blood.

And fourth: he got it, finally. He knew her. It'd just taken a moment because she wasn't in armor, and she wasn't supposed to be here—on Earth, that is.

This was Sealiah, Queen of the Poppy Lands.

She moved across the sand toward him, her steps crooked, and her body swaying and switching back and forth. Far shorter than Robert's six feet, she somehow managed to make it feel like she towered over him—naked and slight, but radiating enough regal confidence that he felt like dropping to his knees and kissing her feet.

He wasn't so stupefied, though, that he'd forgotten his manners.

He hitched his thumb at the bucket of beers. "Thirsty?" he asked. "Help yourself."

She smiled. Robert noted her blood-rimmed lips.

Sealiah took one of the beers and chugged, rivulets of foam dribbling down her chest and stomach. She finished and grabbed the lime and wiped her lips with it. "Ahhh . . . ," she purred. "Your hospitality is appreciated."

Robert stared unabashedly at this performance (what else was a guy supposed to do?) and he struggled to remember that this wasn't a woman standing before him. She wasn't even human. Not even close.

He could smell her now, though, and it was like every flower that had ever bloomed. Her perfume teased and pulled at him.

"So . . . ," he said, drawing on some supernatural cool from the center of his soul. "You just swimming by, or was there something you wanted?"

"Oh, there is very much something I wanted." She inched closer and her lips parted. "But I thought we would discuss business first, and then we could see to the pleasure part of the transaction."

Robert backed up an inch, although it took a great deal of effort.

He tried to see the monstrous creature with tendrils and horns and bat wings inside her, but instead, all he could see was a woman that would make every supermodel on the planet weep with jealousy, and he found himself staring at her—all the way to the tiny down blond hairs that covered her red-gold flesh.

"I've come to offer you a job," she said.

That snapped him out of it.

Yeah, she was gorgeous.

Yeah, she was close enough to grab.

And yeah, she smelled great.

But she just wanted what every other otherworldly creature had ever wanted from Robert: to stick him in a bind where he'd risk his life and limb and soul for some twisted scheme.

Something clicked inside Robert. His pulse slowed and he felt cold, and strong in a way that he'd never felt before: impervious on the inside.

"No thanks," he said. "I've had jobs before. None of 'em ever seemed to work out for me. Guess I'm what you'd call a lousy employee."

Sealiah's smile faltered.

Now Robert could see the monster inside—smoldering in her eyes.

He pushed his luck and added, "If that's all you wanted to say, no offense, I'd just like to be left alone . . . and left to forget, ma'am."

Robert went back to his towel and lay down, crossed his arms behind his head and gazed up at the infinite blue sky (but also watching the Infernal out of the corner of his eye).

Sealiah stayed where she was, staring at him, still smelling insanely good to Robert. Her lips pressed together, and the air around her heated and shimmered—but then she chuffed with amusement.

"You are stronger than I realized." She came over and sat on the blanket next to him.

This close, Robert felt her pulse thrum in the air between them. His blood wanted to race and catch up and run with hers. He took a deep breath, though, and kept his cool.

She scooched closer. A few drops of seawater dripped onto him. "You want to be left alone, Robert? Really? Are you hiding? Licking your wounds?" She looked him over as if he were a prime rib.

He shrugged.

"You can, you know," she said. "But in a few months, perhaps a year or two there will be no neutral parties left. There will be nowhere to hide. *All* will be involved in this. Or they will be dead."

Robert was suddenly thirsty. More than anything he wanted to grab one of those beers just within his reach and drink the whole thing. But to do that he'd have to reach past her, touch her, and that would be like falling . . . and he wouldn't be able to stop himself once that happened.

She leaned closer. "You will eventually have to choose a side." Her breath whispered over his chest, and gooseflesh pebbled there.

It felt great, and Robert became dizzy for a moment, but then found his mental footing again.

"Then," he told her, "I choose *my* side."

Sealiah threw back her head and laughed. It sounded like funeral bells. Birds in the nearby trees took wing, screeching in fear.

"I was correct to choose you as my champion against Mephistopheles," she said. "In a sense you possess the strength to do for me more than any other ever has. . . ." Her voice trailed off as if she'd just realized something and it had halted her super seductress act dead in its tracks.

She blinked and shook her head. "I can help you as well. I could make you stronger than you ever dreamed. All you need do is remain my champion, Robert Farmington of Arkansas."

Her fingertips brushed against his forearm, and shivers of pleasure arced from her to him.

"And all you need do is swear one tiny oath of loyalty."

"No way." Robert pulled away. "No oaths. No contracts. No blood ties. Like I told you: I'm done working for *anyone* else."

She looked him a long time. The ocean pounding sounded like a typhoon.

"No," she finally said, "I can see that now. You are *too* strong, perhaps."

Again, for a moment, she didn't look like any Infernal he'd ever seen before as the skin between her perfectly smooth brows crinkled with frustration.

Her gaze then dropped to the sand and she murmured, "Is it because . . .

I am what I am? You think me evil? Twisted? And you believe that is all that I am?"

Robert heard the hurt in her voice. Infernals were really good liars, though, so he couldn't be sure it wasn't just a game. Robert was always rushing to save damsels in distress. This time, though, something told him this was real vulnerability, something maybe none other had ever seen in the Queen of Poppies.

"Isn't that all you are?" he asked. "Maneuvering Eliot to your side, and getting me and Fiona to kill Mephistopheles? All those tortured damned souls you keep in Hell?" He licked his lips, afraid he'd said too much, but nonetheless he pressed on. "*You* tell *me* if there's more to being Infernal."

"You wound me with the truth." She looked up, the pain shining in her eyes. "We were once all so much more."

She pulled her legs into a kneeling position and stretched out her arms. "And perhaps for you, Robert Farmington, I can summon one brief glimpse of our past."

Sealiah arched her back and looked as if something red-hot had been shoved into her center—and then light burst forth and blazed pure white: she was a creature of divine beauty that shone *through* Robert's mind with wide white wings and angelic glory.

And then it was gone, and Robert was left blinking at splotchy purple afterimages.

Sealiah lay huddled before him, panting. "That is what we once were."

She sat up, her face pale and lined with exhaustion. "And I fear you are correct: we are no longer those creatures. My last chance to touch that part of me dies with your refusal, hero."

She slowly stood and stumbled back toward the ocean.

Robert got to his feet. "Wait."

She stopped but kept her back turned.

Sealiah was the ultimate damsel in distress. She wasn't human—Robert had to remind himself of that, but did she have to be human to need saving?

What if he could save her? Change her? That might change everything.

He'd never been able to say no to any woman who needed help. It wasn't in his DNA.

And what needed saving in all the worlds more than a fallen angel?

Still with her back to him, Sealiah whispered, "You also said you wanted to forget, Robert. I could . . . could help you with that as well. I would look forward to it."

Forget? Could he?

Fiona? Everyone at school? And the League?

Robert didn't think so, as much as he wanted that. But maybe—just maybe, he could grow out of his mistakes and regrets and become something *more* than just Robert the messenger boy, Robert the spy, and Robert the pawn.

He took her hand, whirled her around—pulled her into his embrace.

Sealiah curled against his chest, and tilted her head up.

They kissed and wrapped around each other.

The ocean surged about their feet and splashed up their legs.

Robert felt as if he were drowning.

He let the tide of her passion take him.

90

THE LONG WALK HOME

Eliot couldn't figure it out. This was just too much stuff.

He stepped back and looked over the items spread on his bed: jeans and sweaters and T-shirts, soap, toothbrush and toothpaste, first-aid kit, flashlights, a white-gas stove, tent, sleeping bag, rain jacket, sun hat, parka, waders, a box of extra guitar strings, and books—stacks and piles of ancient tomes and scrolls and moldering texts that were his required reading for the summer. The books by themselves weighed fifty pounds.

He *had* to take it all though, because where he was going he wasn't sure what to expect.

Could he really do this?

Yes. He'd already made up his mind. The rest was just details.

How he'd come to this particular life-altering decision was a combination of logic, guesswork . . . and a feeling that he was 100 percent absolutely correct. It was instinct: like a plant heliotropes toward the sun, or stone falls because of gravity.

He was going.

His gaze landed on his guitar case. Lady Dawn—he couldn't forget her. He'd need a wheelbarrow for all this stuff.

Eliot went to the window, opened it, and let the rare unfogged San Francisco sunset stream into his room. He took a deep breath. It smelled clean.

He *was* doing this, he told himself again. And yet, if he was so sure, why was he terrified?

There was a tiny tap at his door—followed by several raps, too loud, like the person on the other side was overcompensating for their initial timidity.

"Come in?"

Fiona opened his door. She wore one of those outfits Aunt Dallas had got her in Paris, a blue-silver jacket, silk blouse, and matching skirt. It made her seem ten years older. She also had that silver rose pin the League had given her. Fiona looked annoyed at Eliot—then her face went slack as she saw the stuff on his bed.

Had she come here to chew him out again for claiming the Infernal land and saving Jezebel? Was she going to play the "older" sister and give him advice and order him around?

Or was it something else?

There was a look on her face: one you might give some mentally ill person walking repeatedly into a corner, or the piteous glance you might give a homeless person huddled in a cardboard box.

Which, in Eliot's near future, might not be too far from the truth.

She asked, "What do you think you're doing, *Rheinardia ocellata*?"[74]

Eliot ran fingers through his unruly hair. He hadn't had time to get it cut all year and it was one long mess.

He had more important things, though, to occupy his thoughts than his hair or devising a return shot in for vocabulary insult like *fescennine absquatulative physagogue*.

"I'm packing," he told her.

"I can see that." Fiona set her hands on her hips. "Look, forget whatever you're doing. We need to talk about what Sobek said: that parting of the ways thing. It has to be a metaphor."

"No," Eliot replied. "It means that you and I are going in different directions."

"I know that," she said. "Like your music and my combat training." She shook her head, dismissing any other notion. "You need to get dressed, because we're scheduled to see the League Council this evening. They're going to help us figure it out."

The skin at the base of Eliot's spine crawled. The thought of him standing in front of all the Elder Immortals, explaining that he was an Infernal, was the last place in the world he wanted to be.

---

74. *Rheinardia ocellata,* also the crested argus pheasant, is best known for its wild tuft of feathers spiking up from its head and its long (up to six feet) tail feathers. —Editor.

"I don't think so," he said. "I've already got my part figured out."

It hurt him to say those words because he knew he couldn't take them back, that what he was doing now would be irrevocable.

Fiona scrutinized him, and then moved over to his bed, cataloging all the equipment. "You're going back, aren't you?" Her voice dripped with contempt. "To Hell—and those Burning Orchards?"

Eliot kept his voice level. "I have to."

"I bet you do," Fiona said with a sneer. "You and Jezebel together all summer long? I'm going to get sick just thinking about it."

"You've got it wrong. I'm going, but Jezebel is staying at the Paxington dormitory. She has to make up the classes she missed or she won't be coming back next year."

Fiona stared at him, her mouth open, not understanding.

Eliot wasn't sure he could explain it—but he tried. "She and I talked about it. She wants to learn more . . . and I'm not going to hold her back."

Eliot tactfully skipped the part of the phone conversation he'd just had with Jezebel twenty minutes ago where she had spelled it out for him: she was basically his slave—bonded to land he now owned, and that Eliot could've ordered her to come back with him . . . and be with him.

That had kind of soured the entire heroic fantasy he had had about him and her. After all he'd been through to save her—he didn't even know if she really liked him . . . for him.

Someone like Jeremy would have been okay with that, but Eliot needed someone by this side (raw animal sexual attraction, notwithstanding) because they *wanted* to be there—not because they were *forced* there by some magical bond.

Eliot would figure what to do with his sort-of girlfriend, but later, after he solved a much bigger problem.

"So, why *are* you going back?" Fiona asked. "Are you going to give that land to Dad?"

"You don't understand," Eliot told her, exasperation creeping into his voice. "I *can't* give it up." He forced what he'd been feeling since he'd taken possession of his domain in Hell into words: "That land is bound to me. It's *part* of me. If someone takes it, they take me . . . my soul, too."

Fiona's blinked, absorbing what he said, and then her hands clenched into fists. "Then we have to do something. There has to be a way to sever that tie."

Eliot held up both hands. "Don't!" He swallowed, his throat suddenly dry as he imagined Fiona cutting out a part of him. "I want this," he said. "I can feel the land calling to me, making me stronger, something more than just ordinary Eliot Post."

"Ordinary? You're a hero in the League of Immortals, for crying out loud! Think about it. If you go back there, they'll kill you. You saw how Sealiah and Mitch—Mephistopheles fought for their lands. What makes you think a bunch of Infernals won't gather their armies and just take your land?"

"I don't know," Eliot whispered. "There's no reason they wouldn't. Maybe Dad can help." This sounded unconvincing, even to himself. "But I have to be there, Fiona. I can't help it."

"Well, I can't—I won't accept that," she told him, standing taller. "I'm not going to stand by while you fight for your life. There has to be something we can do."

They locked stares. Eliot so wanted to communicate everything he felt—the pull of the land, and the need to prove himself. Why didn't she get that? They used to be able to explain encyclopedic volumes of information and feelings with a single glance, but Fiona wasn't listening to him anymore. She was trying to communicate something entirely different: her disappointment, her displeasure, her disapproval—that she knew what was right for him.

"Eliot? Fiona? My doves?" Cecilia poked her head through the open door, glancing over them both, and her eyes hardening as she took in the equipment on Eliot's bed. "Your mother would like to see you in the dining room." She smiled with trembling lips, but Eliot heard the iron authority of Audrey behind the polite request.

"Great," Fiona muttered, and strode past Eliot. "We're not done talking about this."

She had no idea how made up his mind was . . . although, what was he going to tell Audrey? And how could he stop *her* from stopping him?

Cee stood waiting for him, her smile brightening. She wore pants, nineteenth-century things with flared thighs and a white canvas belt—like she was going elephant hunting with Ernest Hemingway. (For all Eliot knew, that's precisely what she might've done last time she wore them.) She had on a khaki blazer and wore desert camouflage army boots.

"We better see what you mother wants," Cee told him.

"Yeah." Eliot had a feeling that someone in this family (other than him) was about to pull a fast one.

He marched into the dining room.

Audrey and Fiona stood side by side. It struck Eliot how much they looked alike: tall, thin, and serious, but Fiona was in gray and his mother in a neat black dress. He'd never seen his mother in black, though, and it made him stop and stare. She looked like she was going to a funeral . . . and somehow it looked good on her.

On the dining table sat three cloth sacks. They were full of bottled waters, beef jerky, boxes of cereal, vitamins, and protein bars.

Fiona crossed her arms over her chest. "You know what Eliot is doing?"

Eliot pressed his lips into a single white line, astonished that she would break their confidential trust. Technically, though, she hadn't really snitched on him . . . but it was darned close.

How could he be mad, though? Fiona was just worried. And he *was* going to have to tell Audrey something.

"I know everything," Audrey told them.

Eliot's and Fiona's eyes went wide.

"You do?" they asked at the same time.

"I know that Eliot has arranged for his vassal to stay at Paxington over the summer." One of her eyebrows arched. "Very wise to attend to business first, I might add. I also know that you intend to spend the summer in the Lower Realms. You have packed, but Cee and I have taken the liberty of buying a few snacks to tide you over on your journey."

Eliot stared at his mother, unable to read her face. How had she known all that? And more important, why wasn't she stopping him?

"You're just letting him go?" Fiona asked, her voice breaking.

"I must," Audrey told her. "As a member of the League, I am forbidden to interfere in Infernal affairs."

Fiona turned pale as this sank in.

So Eliot was free. Finally free.

But the elation of his new freedom faded because it also meant he was alone now, too.

"Besides," Audrey said to Fiona, and set one hand on her shoulder. "One must not separate an Infernal from his lands for too long. They do not fare well."

"But Eliot's really not an . . . ," Fiona's voice trailed off. She looked at Eliot like he had a terminal disease—or like he was already dead. She regained her composure and said, "Well, he *can't* go. How is he going to carry all this?" She gestured at the table. "That's not even taking into account all the books he's going to need to pass Miss Westin's final exam."

"I don't know," he admitted.

Cee then entered the dining room carrying a large bag in each hand, and with Lady Dawn's case bouncing along on top of one. The bags were made of a heavy tapestry-like tan-and-purple paisley material.

Eliot didn't know what she was doing, but he immediately went to his great-grandmother to help. "Let me get those." Eliot tried to lift one of her carpetbags. He couldn't budge one with both hands. It must have weighed two hundred pounds.

Cee handed him his guitar case.

"Cecilia has packed your things," Audrey explained. "She's going with you, Eliot."

Eliot blinked and looked between Audrey and Cee. They weren't kidding.

Relief coursed through him. He wouldn't be alone . . . even though he'd have to deal with Cee's cooking—it was a small price to have someone he knew, someone he could trust, by his side.

Cee patted his arm, seeming to understand everything.

Audrey beckoned to Eliot. He set his guitar aside and embraced his mother—clutching on to her because it might the last time he ever hugged her.

Audrey went through the motions, but there was no warmth. Her embrace was rigid and dry and without feeling.

He started to pull away, but she held him, turned, and whispered so softly into his ear that he barely heard: "Your father told me of your tie to land. You and Cecilia must hurry. There is good reason to do so, which she will explain on the way. Now go, and be safe, my Eliot."

Audrey squeezed him once, and then released him.

She'd been talking to his father? Since when were they on speaking terms?

He stared into Audrey's eyes. There was no love in them, but something new, a steely concern. Was that all she had to give him?

No. Something else glimmered in her gaze: something . . . . strategic.

He nodded, not entirely understanding, but at least acknowledging that he had heard.

There was an awkward moment when Eliot couldn't move. He felt a crushing impulse to stay where he was, to stay home and stick with what he knew.

But he had to leave because it would be his first step on his own, as an adult, and if he didn't move now, he never would.

So, without a sigh, he picked up Lady Dawn and marched down the stairs.

Cee, Audrey, and Fiona followed.

He stood in front of the door, pausing to trace over the patterns of color and light on its four stained glass panes. He must have passed those every day and until this moment he hadn't realized how much he was going to miss something as simple and stupid as the geometric lines that made the mosaic of a field of grapevines and harvesters.

He opened the door, stepped onto the threshold, and turned back to them.

Audrey nodded and held up one hand, then curled it and dropped it to her side—a motion that seemed to communicate both *good-bye* and *stay.*

Fiona stood by their mother, her arms folded in front of her. "Please don't do this, Eliot," she whispered.

Eliot wanted to move to his sister, but there was a barrier between them now that hadn't been there a moment ago. He looked into her eyes. They glistened with tears, but Fiona quickly blinked them away.

And for the first time in his life, he couldn't read her. There was no connection.

He turned his back to them. "Come on, Cee."

He marched down the stairs and onto the sidewalk. He heard Cecilia mutter her good-byes to Audrey and fuss over Fiona to take care of herself and to study hard—and then she trotted to catch up to Eliot.

"Your mother told you?" Cee whispered. "We must make all due haste?"

"Yeah."

But once again, Eliot found his legs immobile. What he wanted to do was turn around and try to explain everything to Fiona, make her see his point of view, to somehow get her back on his side.

They were supposed to be stronger together.

But he couldn't turn—if he did, he knew he'd chicken out and never have the strength to move forward.

He turned anyway and looked back.

Audrey was on the threshold, gazing longingly after him . . . seeming both sad and proud.

Fiona, however, had already gone back inside.

Audrey gave them both a tiny wave, and then hung her head and shut the door.

He somehow found the strength to turn and walk down the sidewalk.

After a block, he asked Cee, "So what's the big rush?"

Cee kept pace with him, even though she carried those too heavy carpetbags. She wasn't even panting. In fact, she looked a lot healthier than any 105-year-old woman had a right to look.

"The League of Immortals will soon know of the Night Train Station under Market Street," she said.

"Because of Fiona," Eliot finished for her.

Of course, Eliot's departure was going to come up at the Council meeting tonight, and they'd want to know all the details of how he was getting back to Hell. If Fiona didn't tell them outright . . . they'd find a way to get the information out of her.

"How long do you think the Immortals will tolerate an open path to Hell in the Middle Realms?" Cee asked.

"But the *Pactum Pax Immortalis*—," Eliot started, and then stopped in the middle of that thought.

He was about to say they couldn't do anything, because it was Infernal property.

But sure they could. They could fill the secret stairway to the Night Train Station with concrete—technically not touching any of the Infernal property, but nonetheless making it inaccessible. Or, if Eliot knew the thoroughness of the League, they might cause an earthquake and shift an entire tectonic plate over the site.

"I get it," he said to Cee. "So once there, how are we going to get back?"

Streetlamps flickered on Pacific Avenue as the sunset faded and the eastern horizon darkened. Two crows landed on top of lampposts and stared at him.

Cee took Eliot by the crook of his elbow, sped up, and surprisingly pulled him along with her.

"You are an Infernal Lord now, Eliot. It is time you started thinking like one. You will find a way back if desire it. You will *make* your own way if necessary!"

Eliot didn't know about that. Crossing dimensions was something only . . . only what? Only something fallen angels could do? Only the mighty Titans and gods had ever managed?

In his blood pulsed all those mingled lineages.

He was strong. He *would* find a way.

"And here's something that will help." Cee stopped, reached into one of the carpetbags, and pulled out an object wrapped in brown paper. She handed it to Eliot.

As he took it, Eliot felt that the thing possessed a gravity all its own. He felt a thrum of power within the paper and he heard a distant music, echoing and calling to him.

He unwrapped it.

A fist-sized gleaming sapphire nestled within the paper, and hundreds of water blue facets reflected his amazed face back at him. A tiny silver loop clutched the top of the stone, and a cord of leather snaked through it.

Eliot knew this thing. The last time he'd seen it, Fiona had pulled it through Beelzebub's neck—decapitating that monster and saving them both.

"Every Infernal lord has a talisman," Cee told him, as if that explained everything. "But hide it well. Even your mother does not know I took it. It is dangerous. But I believe it is absolutely necessary if you are to claim your rightful place."

Eliot touched the stone. It felt cold, but warmed quickly under his fingertips. The dazzling blue tinged to midnight dark and then a coal black.

He made a fist about the stone.

It was now his—the power within, along with responsibilities he had yet to fathom.

He was Eliot Post, Master of the Burning Orchards, and Infernal Lord and Prince of the Lower Realms.

He undid the leather cord, pulled it through, and tossed it. There is no way he'd ever wear this thing around *his* neck.

"Let's catch that train," Eliot said, "or it's going to be a long walk. We have a lot to do before school starts next year."

The Mortal Coils series continues soon with
Book III: ***What Fools These Mortals.***

READER'S GUIDE

In the second book of the Mortal Coils series, Eliot and Fiona enroll in the Paxington Institute, a most unusual high school for the children of the gods, Infernals, and the mortal magical families. Here more of the legendary world is revealed—filled with high-stakes politics, intrigue, and magic as well as the normal high school social dynamics that any teenager must survive.

[**Warning**: if you haven't read the book yet, there are definite spoilers in this section!]

1. One of the concepts drilled in at the Paxington Institute is to win at any cost. Is winning at any cost justified under *any* circumstances? Is there a difference between winning in gym class and winning on a real battlefield?

2. At Paxington there are definite social layers based on which family the students come from. Why do you think Jezebel, an Infernal, is set so high in the social order? Why do you think that when Fiona's origins are revealed Eliot's social standing doesn't change?

3. Name as many things as you can that seem unfair to you about the Paxington Institute. Is/was your high school in any way similar? Given the chance, would *you* want to go to such a school?

4. While some Paxington instructors have been explicitly identified, two have not: the Headmistress, Miss Lucille Westin, and the music

instructor, Ms. Erin DuPreé. Who do you think their mythical counterparts are?

5. When Fiona wounds Mr. Ma, Robert tells her that everyone is afraid that this is an omen of Armageddon. Is there any evidence that this might be true?

6. In *Mortal Coils*, Sealiah's Twelve Towers is a large but otherwise ordinary villa. In *All That Lives Must Die*, the villa has transformed into a formidable castle. How is this possible? What does it imply about the Infernal rulers and their domains in hell?

7. At the end of the war, Eliot is offered a reward for his assistance, while Fiona is not. Why? If she was offered a reward, would she have taken it?

8. Why does Fiona consider Mitch's offer to join him at the end . . . even after he had deceived her? What would you have done?

9. There seem to be three "sides" in the upcoming conflict: the League of Immortals, the Infernal clans . . . and a different third group of individuals. Who's on this side? What are their goals? How does the "win at any cost" lesson learned at Paxington apply here?

10. What would you have done about Jeremy and Sarah Covington after they betrayed you? Would you have believed Sarah?

11. Do you think Amanda's reaction to the twins at the end of the book is justified?

12. Who is more powerful, the League of Immortals or the Infernal clans? On a *modern* battlefield who do you think would win?

13. Eliot and Fiona end up on very different paths at the end of this book. Would you have made the same choices?

For more information on Eric Nylund and the Mortal Coils series, visit www.ericnylund.net, which includes a biography on the author and additional information about his novels.